Coronach

Kimberley Jordan Reeman

authorHOUSE®

AuthorHouse™ UK Ltd.
500 Avebury Boulevard
Central Milton Keynes, MK9 2BE
www.authorhouse.co.uk
Phone: 08001974150

First published by AuthorHouse 9/14/2007

ISBN: 978-1-4343-1298-3 (sc)
ISBN: 978-1-4343-1299-0 (hc)

Library of Congress Control Number: 2007903944

Printed in the United States of America
Bloomington, Indiana

For Douglas, my love, my star at sea, my life.

Every one knew before he engaged in the cause what he was to expect, and shou'd have staid at home if he cou'd not face death in any shape.

Charles Edward Stuart
January 1746

****

When I came into this Country, it was my only view to do all in my power for your good and safety. This I will allways do as long as life is in me. But alas! I see with grief, I can at present do little for you on this side the water, for the only thing that now can be done, is to defend your selves.

Charles Edward Stuart
April 1746, after Culloden

Table of Contents

I wish to thank the Lady Jean Fforde for her kind permission to quote from the Arran journals of John Burrel; my parents and my brother Stan; and my cherished friends, Dale Burnett, Winston Graham O.B.E., and Carol Spendlove, for their faith and encouragement.

Prologue

You ask me, how shall we overcome these shadows? How much truth is unbearable?

I have known the darkness, and the poignancy of the light. I shrink from neither, deny neither.

They are my truths; it was my life.

Here it began, and, for me, ended.

Glen Sian, the glen of the storm, is a narrow, torturous scar in the mountains between Loch Ness and Loch Cluanie. A minor military road twists up from Fort Augustus to mount a thousand feet over the heights before dropping to the glen itself. The road, no more than a path now, follows the course of the River Sian to the place where it meets Allt na Dour Oir, and a waterfall throws a bridal wreath of spray over the black rocks at the Bridge of Sian.

The military road drives further on through a pass to Kyle of Lochalsh some thirty miles to the west, bringing nothing, taking nothing away, although this was not always so.

The windows of the great house of Ardsian, far up in the sweet silence of the eastern glen, still look toward the heights: Carn Dubh, Carn Mhor, Creag na h' Iolaire, black peaks where the mist hangs and the eagles and the storms breed. They are laced with a thousand nameless streams, silver in the light of morning, soft and dark with peat, and the sound of water is sometimes the only sound in all that vast and empty silence.

There were crofts; they are ruins now. The gardens are overgrown, the old roads reclaimed by ling and bracken. No one goes there. No one is left to go.

On the morning of Thursday, the twenty-fourth of April 1746, George Keppel, Lord Bury, rode with his escort at a racking gallop down the Great North Road into London.

He was a king's son's messenger and he brought with him momentous news, but the word of victory had preceded him, carried in the middle of the night by a hireling of the Lord Justice Clerk of Scotland. The King's army under His Royal Highness the Duke of Cumberland had met the Jacobite forces of his cousin Charles Edward Stuart and defeated them on the field of Culloden, six miles outside of Inverness. The news was a week old when Bury brought it.

By noon, the great guns on Tower Hill were firing salutes. The ships in the river from London to Greenwich answered them. The Household Brigade, drawn up in Green Park, began to fire volley after volley, the sharp crack of musketry drowned out by the cheers of the watching crowd. The bells of every church were ringing. Broadsheets, hastily printed, spread lies and speculation about the battle.

By evening the town was blazing with fireworks. Drury Lane presented an old play resurrected from the War of the Spanish Succession called "The Honours of the Army". The New Wells, in Lemon Street, offered "an exact view of our Gallant Army under the command of their Glorious Hero passing the River Spey, giving the Rebels battle, and gaining a Complete Victory near Culloden House." The broadsheets gave out the King's message to that hero, his son William Augustus: "I desire you may give my hearty thanks to those brave officers and soldiers who fought so gloriously at the late battle, and assure them, no less of my real esteem than of my constant favour and protection."

The bells pealed all evening. The crowds in St. James's, Piccadilly, Pall Mall, swelled and with nightfall became a mob. Any stray soldier was cheered and fêted. A Court of Thanksgiving was planned for Sunday the twenty-seventh to celebrate the Royal Family's deliverance from the Jacobite threat. Overhead, the sky-rockets burst into a million shards, brighter than the brightest jewel in a lost crown, fading like the fading of a dream.

By Tuesday the mood of the mob had turned ugly, from celebration and gratitude to vengeance, and violence, and blood.

For Scots in London, for Catholics, for Jacobites and suspected Jacobites, the flower of safety faded quickly. In the mist-shrouded Highlands, uprooted by the sword, it was already dead.

1746: THE LOST CAUSE

I

It was nine o'clock. It had been raining all day in Glen Sian, and the rain stood in pools on the wet stones, throwing back the light. The grey service gaiters of the drummers beating Tattoo were spattered with mud.

They had been here two days, three officers and a hundred men of His Majesty's army from Inverness. It was July, high summer, and bitterly cold. A man woke chilled to the bone, under canvas unless he could find any better shelter— and then the houses were claimed by the officers first— the canvas sweating with rain or dew and the air inside fetid with the breath of five other men and the smell of clothing and boots too long worn, bodies too long unwashed, and the mould that could not be kept away.

Then, with the drums beating Reveille, that man, any man, any common soldier, sprang up shivering and went shivering to the latrine trenches and returned to hear the day's orders. It might rain, dampening his powder, rusting his bayonet and firelock and wetting him to the skin, shrinking his already ill-fitting coat so that it caught him under the arms and across the shoulders; or it might be so cold that his fingers ached; or it might be windy, with an edge to that wind as keen as a surgeon's knife, cutting through his damp clothing and setting his bad teeth chattering in his head. Of one thing he could be certain: he was almost as likely to sight the sun as he was to escape a flogging, or see his pay raised to something he could live on.

The miserable conditions served only to sharpen the army's resentment of Scotland. It was overwhelmingly lonely, foreign, and bleak: it seemed, even in defeat, indefinably hostile. It offered nothing, not the frailest compensation, not warmth, not colour, not comfort, not welcome, only a landscape of monotonous greys and browns, sullen mountain, fog, stretches of black water under lowering skies: no sound but water and crying birds and wind, nothing for the eye but a naked desolation. If it had revealed to them any of its beauty, and beautiful it was, although haunting and empty and immeasurably sad, not a man among them would have found it so.

The rain had stopped. It was ten past nine.

The second-highest ranking officer in Glen Sian was alone at that hour in his quarters, attempting, as adjutant to Lieutenant-Colonel the Honourable Aeneas Bancroft, to resume a semblance of correspondence to his generals at Fort Augustus. On the table lay the records of the regiment: the Orders of the Day in their mottled covers, his journal with assiduously kept accounts, the payroll, and several drafts of a difficult letter to the Quartermaster-General, requesting reimbursement for boots, stockings and ammunition loaf purchased by Bancroft for the regiment out of his own pocket. They constituted his third such submission within the past six months; the others had met with resounding failure. He wrote, in an austere and disciplined hand, supporting his wrist.

> Lieut Col the Hon Aeneas Bancroft begs Leave to Acquaint the General, that he has not yet been repaid monies owing him for the outfitting of two Companies of ye 4th Regt of Foot, at Newcastle in the month of January of this year, and asks once more that this be done, also that ye Regt be supplied w/ twelve new Tents....

He was twenty-nine years old, half English, half Irish, a gaunt, raw-boned, enigmatic man who had held his first commission at the age of barely sixteen: he had been ordered into the army by his father, one of Marlborough's generals, who had thought effeminate his youthful preoccupation with music and been determined to put an unequivocal end to it. He had served dispassionately, a dedicated if not inspired soldier, a career officer. There was very little choice for a younger son, without fortune or the expectation of a brilliant marriage.

The writing hand paused. The skin was cracked with eczema, the nails broken and unkempt. The broad, soiled cuff of the scarlet coat was the dark blue of a Royal regiment, ornamented with two tarnished bands of gilt lace in the regiment's distinctive zigzag pattern, and three coinlike buttons. The fourth had been torn off, and it was symptomatic of his own state and of the army's endemic squalor that he who had once been fastidious had made no attempt to replace it.

His wrist was aching. It was massively scarred, the result of an injury suffered at Dettingen in the second year of the Austrian war. It had been thought that he would lose the hand, and his frenzied insistence that it be saved had not been welcomed by a surgeon intent only on closing the other wounds in his body and transferring his attention to the next casualty. The suturing had been perfunctory, and later he realized that it had done more to cripple him than any effort of the enemy.

He was a man profoundly disillusioned by life, a cynic and an atheist whom circumstance, and physical pain, and a growing mental disquiet had rendered irritable and intolerant: younger officers found him a pitiless superior, and he felt the depth of his estrangement from them as from another generation. He had cherished ideals, and conceptions of honour which he now considered absurd, and they had been destroyed in a bloody sewer of war which had also claimed his politics and his ambitions. He had no friends— they had been slaughtered while, incomprehensibly, he had lived— and no fears, only an insensate courage born of prolonged exposure to death. And he had expected to die in Flanders: when death had overlooked him, he had submitted to the next twist in the game he perceived fate to be playing with him, and at the end of 1745 joined the Fourth, an old line-regiment bound for British soil after four years of foreign service. Seven months later in Scotland he remained with it, held by a curious paralysis, inertia, or the remnants of a troubled loyalty, although he knew himself balanced on the edge of some crisis, and recognized in this his last commission, and these as the final months of his career.

The rain had begun again; the drums had fallen silent. It was dark in the room, and penetratingly cold: he groped for flint and steel and struck a spark to light the cruisie lamp on the table, a cast-iron Highland affair with a rush wick held by a clamp. As it caught, the rush smoked foully in its pool of rancid oil. Some one, Bancroft's sentry he surmised, coughed outside, and the sound carried clearly. The wind moaned a little in its dismal, sobbing undertone.

He closed his eyes and let his thoughts carry him, the old regret, a certain passive resentment and surprise at the docility with which he had come to a life he had never chosen, until a staccato rapping at the door drew him back, unwillingly, to the present.

He called, "Come," and glanced up: his eyes, a keen greyish blue, rested inscrutably on the dark blue lapels and filthy knotted sash looming out of the shadows, and resumed their study of the Quartermaster's letter without rising to the sergeant's face.

"Lieutenant Brevet's compliments and he returns the muster book, sir."

The clutter on the table was hesitantly disturbed. An unmistakable smell began to pervade the still, cold air.

"How many men were absent without leave?"

"None, sir."

"Was the colonel present?"

"No, sir."

"It was fortunate for you that he was not." There was an uncomfortable silence. "Do you mean to tell me that you have not been drinking geneva? Where is the punishment book?"

He opened it and entered a terse statement. Although he was known to drink heavily himself he had no pity for non-commissioned or enlisted men who did likewise, only a clearer perception than most officers of his own hypocrisy.

3

"Your pay will be docked two shillings sixpence. You may be relieved it was not more, and that I am not Colonel Bancroft."

There was no sign of anger or embarrassment and he had expected none; the sergeant's expression remained stolidly blank.

"Lieutenant Brevet begs leave to ask will there be anything else tonight, sir."

"No. That will be all."

"Very good, sir." He saluted and turned on his heel, the greased queue swinging to the small of his back with the movement.

The muster book lay closed, its cover misted with rain. When he was alone again the adjutant opened it: in the faulty light the names stood out like the dramatis personae of some remorseless Greek tragedy, headed by Aeneas Alexander George Robert Bancroft, Lieutenant-Colonel; and then, of the two majors, his own name, Thomas Achill Mordaunt-Collins; among the lieutenants Henry Francis David Brevet; and the others, their existence documented in a clear, elegant hand on pages softened with use. Here and there a stark phrase recalled the losses of a regiment mauled by the Jacobite charges at both Falkirk and Culloden.

"Discharged dead... discharged dead, of wounds...." "Private soldier aged 20 years, at Inverness...." "Private soldier aged 18 years... drummer aged 15 years... ensign aged 16 years... serjeant... corporal... grenadier... grenadier...."

Culloden. He took his thoughts from it and from Inverness and signed the letter to the Quartermaster-General.

The evening progressed. His fingers cramped on the quill, his eyes tired in the unsteady light, the rain drummed endlessly. From time to time he coughed, dryly, and with pain: he had had pleurisy at the age of twenty-two, which had almost taken his life, and it had begun with similar symptoms under similar conditions of exhaustion and neglect. He had had five months' convalescence in Naples, secured by his father's influence, and he had spent it in an idyll of uncharacteristic sensuality, under the tutelage of a pupil of Domenico Scarlatti and, under the auspices of Neopolitan friends, in less aesthetic pleasures. He had been upon the point of resigning his commission: his father's death had forestalled that decision, summoning him back to England too late to do more than regret they had not been closer, and that he had lied in his letters when he had promised Marlborough's general that he was not consorting with whores and musicians. On his return he had met his brother's wife, and, already weighted by guilt and grief, he had not resisted the circumstances impelling them toward a liaison.

He tried to hold his memories of her, but they were scattered and indistinct: time and absence had begun to blur the details of her face. He had not seen her for three years, and her image, like others of a civilized world, was becoming remote.

4

He read through the remainder of the waiting correspondence, drinking purposefully. At this hour the likelihood of interruption was slight, and without it he would not sleep. His watch had stopped, but he sensed it was well after midnight: time in any case except as lived by the drums had ceased to be relevant here. When he woke it was to pain, and the terrified uncertainty of not knowing where he was: the lamp had burned down, his clothing was damp, the sweat stood on his face and he was shivering. He had no idea what had disturbed him.

He remembered nothing of opening the door, only the sensation of the rain, and the gradual emergence from grey obscurity of a sordid little tableau of rape. The assailants, private soldiers, must have seen him silhouetted against the light from the doorway, and he knew a word from him would have stopped them, if only for a time. But he did not give the word. He turned his back, and closed the door on them, and sank again into fitful sleep. Outside the sounds went on, and the unheard cries, and the rain.

He dreamed of Catherine. The familiar dreams, brutal and erotic: toward the end they changed. He saw her, standing on the lawn that sloped to the river at Evesham, the Jacobean house in the north of England where he had been born. It was spring and the daffodils were blowing at her feet, and he saw her there as clearly as if it had been yesterday, all except her face. He was calling to her, but he could not seem to say her name, and she remained indifferent or unaware of him, standing among the golden heads while the river ran like an unbroken mirror, twisting and turning and giving no reflection either of her or himself.

He oversaw a burial party the following afternoon. Four deep trenches filling with rain; macabre play among the men such as he had witnessed after Culloden, one striking another with a severed arm; the corpses, under canvas, lying in precise lines on the ground. The air was heavy with a stench of decay which had begun to cling to their very clothing. The men of the burial party, volunteers all, were a notorious group of companions: as they dug and splashed they conversed freely in a dialect familiar to him. Their speculations ranged over every aspect of their own and their officers' private lives, then shifted to less inflammatory matter: the usual brothel boasts, a proposed session with the dice, itself an offense punishable by the lash. It was dismissed without so much as a glance in his direction. "Ee naw, aa canna, aam skint— yon's the bluidy basted wi ma brass." The splashes continued, and then a silence fell, punctuated by mutters. They were in the pit gazing at the uncovered face of a dead woman. "Naw they's a reet coostie sluice— worraad na mahn ter dee wi a bitta that." "Och, ye hacky basted, haddawa." There followed an

5

unseemly grunt and a snort of muffled, indefinably disgusting laughter. He walked to the edge: they were standing in water to their knees, and froze in their attitudes like caught, perverted schoolboys. Each man but one had an arm or a leg and the corpse, naked and discoloured with putrefaction, reclined submissively. The one held his erect penis in his hand.

Mordaunt said nothing; whatever they read in his face was enough. The offender shrugged and fumbled with his clothes; the others remained as they were, filthy, sodden and unregenerate.

He said, "Follow your orders. The first man to disobey will be hanged."

He stood watching, immobile, until they had climbed out and were shovelling dirt into the trenches, then he returned to his quarters.

He made his evening rounds shortly after six o'clock, a slow perambulation past the tents of all enlisted men to remind them of a senior officer's presence, something Bancroft in his unhappy solitude seldom deigned to do; and then, with the men sufficiently disconcerted, the spirits hidden, the dice boxes vanishing with a rattle and a guilty start, he left them, picking his way toward the outskirts of the village. It was an evening like the preceding: grey air, grey light, the eerie silence, the smoking, miserable fires.

He walked with effort, the pain of a leg wounded at Dettingen aggravated by the dampness, leaving behind the stained and rippling canvas, the burnt, reeking dwellings in the street, the smell of tethered horses and latrines. The mud gave way to cultivated ground, alternating grain and fallow; when he paused at the end of the rutted track he saw the village beneath him like a crumpled map, unclean and discarded. There was no sound but the rain beating on his hat brim and his laboured breathing. He walked on.

Within a few minutes he was no longer alone; he had reached Bancroft's outlying picquets, bored, soaked, shivering, and shouting to one another to pass the time, a habit from which they could not be discouraged. His appearance provoked a flurry of soldierly activity: the obscenities ceased, the muskets snapped up, and every streaming hat was doffed in salute.

He did not acknowledge it. To ignore them gratified some obscure desire to be dissociated from them: they were not the men of the afternoon's incident, nor of the previous night's, but their record on other occasions was sufficient to reduce them to a common level of depravity, from which he knew he could not be excepted. If they sensed his hostility it excited no interest. They stood rigidly, the rain beating on their bared heads, accustomed, like much-abused dogs, to the irrational contempts of officers.

He left them, and dismissed the army from his mind. Here it was quiet: the rain was clean and pitiless, and nothing flawed the vast emptiness of the moor. It did not intimidate him: he had been born to land like this, and these might have been the rough fells west of Teesdale, and this country not alien but loved.

It was a dangerous illusion and he paid for the peace it gave him. A weight struck his spine and he fell, and a knife hit his gorget; the impact of the point on the gilded metal knocked the breath from his lungs. The blade slashed for his face; he deflected it, disarming the filthy hand; the body stank of wet wool, smoke and acrid sweat. They rolled in obscene struggle, the bracken showering them with rain, and came to rest in a shallow depression, the wet hands strangling him with the gorget. He tore at them and his attacker spat in his face; he felt the spittle drip from his cheek.

It enraged him. With enormous effort he thrust his shoulder up and drove his fist into the jaw: the head fell to one side, the eyelids closed, the profile delicate. It gave a fleeting impression of femininity at which his exhausted mind recoiled. Then the right hand, the killing hand, thrust up again, and he forced it to the limit of the bone and broke the wrist.

The boy thrashed beneath him in an ecstasy of silent pain, and lay still, washed with a sweating pallor, his head resting on granite. Then there was no sound; the breathing ceased. Mordaunt raised himself cautiously, and the boy convulsed, driving a bare knee toward his groin and raking for his eyes.

He seized the head and smashed it on the rock, raised it by the hair and smashed it again; there was no resistance, and eventually he knew the boy had died, although he could not stop his frenzied assault until he felt blood gushing over his hands. He raised the head and saw that the eyes were glazed. The stone was clotted with viscous brains.

He staggered to his feet. The picquets were running toward him, muskets held high, gaitered knees flashing above the heather.

He stood aside, dashing the rain from his hat against his leg as they prodded at the corpse. Some one pulled up the head: the face was young in death, younger even than he had imagined. The eyes and the mouth were open.

They were waiting. The more experienced had unclipped from the frogs suspended at their waistbelts the sixteen-inch bayonets, and were affixing them with enough deliberation for him to see their intention and thwart it if he wished. When they saw that he could not or would not give the order, first one and then the others plunged their weapons into the body, ripping the stomach, bowels and chest, ostensibly to ensure that it was dead or merely to demonstrate their contempt. He watched the increasing violence of their orgy until a blackish fluid spilled from the mouth, and revulsion stirred in him.

"Stand off." They turned, as if surprised by some quality in his voice. "Fall back, all of you, and leave me enough to look at."

They shuffled aside reluctantly, with their gory, fluted steel: their efforts had disembowelled the corpse and the stench was indescribable. He knelt, searching for letters, documents, louis d'or, anything that might identify the bearer as a Jacobite courier. A louse crawled on his hand and he killed it between the bloodied nails of thumb and forefinger.

He found nothing. The awed, brutish silence over his head continued.

"You and you, take him away. The rest return to your posts."

They dragged the corpse off by the heels. As it was moved the heavy folds of the féileadh mór, the great kilt, slid over the buttocks, revealing a stain of reddish pubic hair and a disproportionately swollen penis. Comments ensued, and a little play with a bayonet: they would emasculate it once they were out of the repressive presence of an officer, venting upon it their hatred of the country and the army and possibly mankind in general before leaving it to the ravages of the crows.

The others were loitering, examining the scene. He said coldly, "When you are quite finished," and they removed themselves with every evidence of regret.

He walked down to the river and the dripping privacy beneath the trees and attempted to vomit. The retching worsened the pain in his throat and relieved nothing. After a time he made his way to a rock and sat, watching the river and the slow death of the light with an immense detachment; the events of the evening and afternoon withdrew, and had no more significance than those of past months or years.

He returned from it, from an absence of mind more peaceful than any sleep: it was imperceptibly darker and the rain still fell. He was aware that he had killed, but not of the circumstances, and he groped for memory, haunted by the fear that rape had preceded it, that he had killed a woman whose face he could not now recall.

Eventually recollection came, and he thought, oh, my God— no— no, and for a moment it slid back into the twisted, violent skein of his dreams. But the sound of the river continued, and the shivering rustle of the leaves, and the rain stung the wounds on his face, and pain began to make small claims upon him, insisting on its own reality.

He stepped into the water and washed the clotted blood from his hands. The blood and matter spattered on the coatskirts was stiffening to black.

He left the place, walking back the way he had come.

He met Bancroft before he had gone very far inside the picquet. He did not want this meeting, and his first, desperate impulse was to turn away from it, then he thought, no, by Christ, you deserve this.

Bancroft had not yet acknowledged him. A slim, upright figure shrouded in a military cloak, he seemed preoccupied and curiously at peace, as though in this vigil he had found both rest and satisfaction, and was prepared to continue it indefinitely. By the state of his clothing he had been waiting some time.

When he turned it was to show a face of great austerity and elegance, refined by recent suffering. He had never been strong, but he had always contrived to appear so; he admitted no frailty in himself and tolerated none in others. Before his disfigurement he had been vain, and that vanity had not left him, and now there was an angry defiance in it that was both moving and gallant. His dress was as fastidious, his carriage as strikingly erect; neither pain nor illness would release him from a lifetime's habits.

Their acknowledgment of one another was formal. This too, was habit, and was defense.

The hooded eyes rested on him, a remarkably clear, piercing grey.

"There is blood on your face." He wiped the bloody furrows with his cuff. "Shall we go back?"

"No."

"As you wish." When nothing else was forthcoming he spoke again, and it was not a question. "You do not anticipate any further disturbance."

"I am convinced he was alone, if that is what you mean."

"Had you gone very far?"

"I was no more than a hundred yards out. Although in this country that is generally enough."

Bancroft moved away, his eyes now on the landscape. Eventually he said, "This is not Flanders," and Mordaunt redirected his aching mind to follow this new tangent.

"No, by God, it is not."

"I think of all the men we knew, only you and I are left." There was a pause. "I am not unaware of your difficulties of late, although you may think I care nothing for them." Another pause. "We have not... been close. I know we are not close now. But if I may help—"

The silence was absolute: some quality in it seemed to embarrass him. He said, "No, no, do you take me so?" and then with great care and earnestness, "Achill, believe me, I meant nothing by this. Only to reassure myself that you was safe."

Voices drifted up from the tents. As though glad of the distraction, he glanced that way. "Have you heard from your wife?"

"No."

"That's a pity."

"I never took you for such a damned lying hypocrite."

The rain fell faster. The wounds stung his face: his mouth tasted of salt and iron. And the pain was more intense, all the smaller pains, the lesser injuries of the assault, coming together until his body ached as one vast wound.

There was no warning and no sensation, only nausea; he was aware of Bancroft's arm supporting him. "Don't try to stand. If you fall I cannot lift you. It will pass."

He said, with more violence than was necessary, "Don't touch me," and the arm was withdrawn.

He stood. Bancroft's eyes met his, stark with some emotion, although he could not determine what it was.

"I take your meaning— God's blood, you make it plain. There is no need to be vulgar."

There was silence.

"Are you able to walk? Then walk with me. The men will think it strange if we go separately."

It gave an appearance of normality, and gradually the semblance became fact; when Bancroft's subtle probing began it was tempered with sympathy.

"What possessed you to go beyond the picquet? You knew my orders."

"I thought I would go mad if I saw much more of the army, if you must know."

"We all think that at times."

"I daresay my little transgression will be noted, nonetheless."

"I may contrive to overlook it."

"I can offer you only indifference, if you were expecting my gratitude."

The tents huddled in their long, pale lines ahead, the streets of the regiment laid out in perfect order. Bancroft wiped the rain from his eyes.

"At least walk with me to my house. I've been so damned lonely... your company that far would be something."

The sentry had already been posted near the slate doorstone.

"Ah, my little home from home, and my porter guarding the door. Come in, will you," and when Mordaunt did not move, "Shall I take this as a personal affront, or will you spare me by speaking of your duty?"

In the silence some unknown bird cried plaintively, winging toward the moors in the loneliness of evening. The sheer, bitter loneliness of it all: the rain and the cry and the coming night. Whatever else would lie in solitude for him tonight, it would not be comfort.

The single room was much like his own quarters, dank and airless, and lit only by another of the foul little lamps, but something in it was indefinably alarming. Not so much Bancroft's essence, although his unmistakable stamp was on the room, in his possessions scattered throughout: the folding cot, the clutter of baggage, the gemlike Murano glassware he had brought from Venice and carried on every campaign.

What he felt in this room was London itself, and the shadow of another night like this, a spring night, and raining, the many bells of the city striking the hours throughout the darkness. It was not so much sensed as intangible: the faint smell of pomade and powder, the very stillness, the introspection and composure of Bancroft's face... even the words he spoke were hauntingly familiar.

"Welcome to my poor place." Out of habit he let the wet cloak slide to the floor, then, recalling the absence of any servant, he retrieved it and threw it across a bench: his batman, like Mordaunt's, had died at Culloden. "Will you have brandy?"

First the brandy. Everett: offered before, and drunk before, on a night like and unlike this.

"My cards are on the table. Will you play me a hand of piquet?"

He looked up, disquieted, saw only the familiar figure, half turned, shaking the folds of linen down to conceal the wound in its dressing. Bancroft said over his shoulder, "Are you thinking how pathetic I am? Don't you find me pathetic— contemptible?"

"When a man has suffered as you have, I think he is entitled to his bitterness."

"But he shouldn't make a crown of thorns out of it, eh?" He brought the Murano glass to the table, returned for the second, each act deliberate. "Well. What shall we drink to? Going back to Flanders? Going straight to hell?"

"To the past."

"The past, then. When we were so much happier."

"Were we? Were you?"

"I doubt it. The past always remembers better than it lived. Love was kinder, pain was not so cruel... even this will look better to you in time, although you won't credit it now." A slight, quizzical smile. "My dear Achill, you do not drink, and neither do you deal."

They wagered; Bancroft took the elder hand and led. The smoke from the lamp was suffocating.

"I see you study me. Do I look old to you?"

"You look the same, Aeneas."

"You're a damned liar, but I thank you for your kindness.... You was always kind to me. You do me good. Can you wonder that I should care so much for you?"

The cards... the brandy... the prelude.

"I didn't mean to say it— I won't say it again." He laid the cards down and rested his head on his hand. "God, I never thought I'd come to this. I used to say I would rather be dead. I daresay I should be grateful... I might have lost an eye or a leg or had half my face blown away. I would be truly hideous then. As it is— Christ."

He refilled the glasses, seeming not to notice the absence of comment.

"I've decided to quit White's. I don't know if I could bear it. The scrutiny of a dozen levelled glasses... a murmur, sotto voce, of, 'egad, there's Bancroft. Twenty years a soldier and look at him now, not a hand to wipe his arse with.'" Then, "Have you ever wanted to take your life?"

"Have you come to that?"

"Sometimes I think I have. I find I don't want to live like this. Looking like this."

"Other men do."

"I am not other men." He turned the glass idly. "Why should I live? The army don't want me, and you know it was all I had. You... well, I've only to look at you to see how monstrous you find me."

Mordaunt drank and said nothing.

"But then, you always have, haven't you? Found me monstrous, one way or another."

He said dully, "I had hoped this was over with, Aeneas."

"Did you? I wish the hell it were. Repic, and be damned to it."

He won the trick and the game and slid the coins across the table. Mordaunt shuffled and cut for cards and seats.

"Double the stake."

The cards rustled.

"Carte blanche."

Mordaunt noted the score.

They discarded, Bancroft with his teeth, and drew.

"Tierce."

"Good."

"Tierce again."

"Good."

"And a sequence of five to the jack."

"Not good."

Mordaunt noted the score and led.

"Do you believe in hell, Achill?"

"No."

"I do. I think one pays for one's sins eventually, one is called to account. Not in hell, not in hell *fire*. I think hell is here on earth and each man makes his own. I know what mine is. Sometimes I wonder how largely I figure in yours."

Their eyes met.

"Don't do this, Aeneas."

"I can't help it. You can't imagine the sick fancies I have when I am so much alone."

The nine of diamonds lay on the table in the flickering light.

"Do you know what they call this card? The curse of Scotland." A sound of boots in the street, then it died away. The lamp was guttering. "I have had such strange thoughts. May I share them with you?" He studied the cards. "For example, one night, I thought I might want a son." There was silence;

he drew from it what he imagined. "I may be unnatural in most things, but I still have one or two instincts which may properly be called a man's."

"You could marry."

"I have never granted you my private life as matter for your wit."

"Nor is it. I really do not see the insurmountable obstacle."

"Is it so damned satisfying to prick and pun? Is it the little taste of blood that excites you?"

Mordaunt discarded his cards and stood.

"Mordaunt." He walked to the door, reached it. "Will you make me abase myself still further by asking you to stay? Stay, then. I ask you to stay. I... implore you."

"These attitudes are not necessary. Please spare yourself and me."

"Christ, is that all they are to you? Well, I am sorry to trouble you with my affectations. My pain is an affectation, my loneliness is an affectation— I am ludicrous to you and so you give me your mockery and your contempt. Or your indifference. This is the first time in months you have spoken to me privately. Do you mean not to know me? Are you ashamed of me? Do you fear what I might say?"

The lamp flickered over the pattern of the lace, the discarded cards on the table. The stump was hidden. The left hand was trembling.

"I have not pressed you. I have not singled you out. I have not favoured you. I have never shown my feelings— I have not spoken of them to you until now, because you said—"

"I know what I said, and it holds true still. Do you understand me?"

"Then why did you come here tonight?" He seemed to recall the sentry's presence outside; when he spoke again his voice was quiet, dry. "Was it pity?"

"It may have been. More for myself than for you."

"Well, I shall take heart from that, your modicum of pity, because you're a cold, bloody, impotent bastard, and pity is all you can give."

Mordaunt opened the door, closed it. The sentry did not move.

In the silence of his own quarters he swept the regimental papers to the floor and wrote in one scrawling, savage draft the resignation of his commission.

He sat listening to the rain and the drums of Tattoo beating, closing his eyes against the twilight, the indefinite shadow between day and night. Eventually he signed the letter, and pushed it away with inexpressible relief.

The past came. But it could not touch him, nor harm him. Nothing could harm him now.

***

13

He had been twenty-five when they met, four years a captain, newly come to the Twelfth regiment of foot and a stranger to most of his fellow officers. The first time he saw them en masse was that morning on Blackheath Common, with the drums thundering and the fifes trilling "Lilliburlero" and the air blazing with regimental colours unhoused from oiled-silk casings. It was the twenty-seventh of April, 1742: there were transports moored in the Thames, and the army under the Earl of Stair was preparing to embark for Flanders.

The officer had been watching him for some time: as a newcomer, Mordaunt thought it natural that he should be observed. Eventually the other man kneed his horse closer and said in a harsh, distinctive voice, "Give you joy of your new company, Captain. I hope they fight as prettily as they parade."

They met formally aboard the transport: he was Major the Honourable Aeneas Bancroft, younger son of the Earl of Lynton, and Mordaunt found in him a witty, generous companion of great charm. He was thirty-four, unmarried and, although physically frail, a fearless and resolute commander held in high esteem by his men.

Despite the closeness of their friendship, Bancroft's private life remained an enigma: he had no intimates, and it was said that his family did not receive him. But Mordaunt, in love with his own brother's wife, adamantly private in all matters concerning their affair, and increasingly fond of the elegant man who had befriended him, sensed some similar need for secrecy in Bancroft and never questioned him.

Other, more important matters began to oppress him: it was winter of '42, then the new year came in; the army was quartered in Ghent, and Catherine's letters arrived with a terrible regularity. He could not go to her; he could only read of her suffering as his brother turned from the first, exquisite harassment of his adulterous wife to physical and sexual abuse. And then the letter came, not from her but from an unknown solicitor: Arthur was dead, of a cerebral haemorrhage following a duel in St. James's. There was no other legitimate heir.

He was granted leave, and went to London at once.

He was still in town on March twenty-third when Handel's "Messiah" opened at the Theatre Royal, Covent Garden. Catherine was ostensibly in mourning, and he knew he should not attend, but as a passionate admirer of Handel he went alone to the premiere engagement. To his surprise he met Bancroft in the foyer, and was touched by the warmth of his greeting. Bancroft had taken a box for the performance, and would not hear of his going to the pit.

He hesitated only when he saw the bottle of claret and the glasses waiting.

"Surely you were expecting some one else?"

Bancroft smiled, but there was some curious reserve in it.

"Not at all. I merely hoped to share my pleasure with an appreciative companion." The flash of an enamelled snuffbox. "I knew you was in town, of course. That was no secret to me."

"You had the advantage of me, then. When did you leave Ghent?"

"Shortly after you. I flung the Earl's name about rather contemptibly... sometimes I find it advantageous to be Lynton's son, although Lynton, I have no doubt, is sorry that I am." Again the faint smile. "Enough of me. You look so drawn I hardly knew you. Has it been so very difficult?"

"One of the outer rings of hell, although I could hardly have expected otherwise."

"Were his affairs in very great disorder?"

"I am grateful for the entail. It preserved what he would otherwise have lost."

Perhaps Bancroft sensed his bitterness; perhaps the talk of money seemed vulgar to him.

"No matter. We shall enjoy ourselves tonight. There'll be little enough time for it once we leave Ghent."

"You foresee a long campaign, then."

Bancroft had offered the snuffbox, then closed it with a snap. "No, you don't take it, do you?" and leaned back. "Oh, I know one suffers all the blood and misery as a matter of course, but the older I grow... I have such a fear of dying sometimes, far away from home." He was silent for a moment, meditative. "A pox on that. We're here together, and Flanders is far away."

"Not far enough."

"Put it from your mind." The other boxes were occupied; the dark theatre blazed with jewels. "What a glorious night!"

"You enjoy society, Aeneas."

"I like a particular kind of life, and while I am here I indulge myself in it. It is not usually possible upon service."

"Is Ghent so bereft of opportunity?"

The grey eyes measured him for a second.

"Ghent is the loneliest of cities for me. No one there gives a damn if I live or die." The glass caught the candlelight as it was filled. "Achill, I must say something, out of friendship. I think it might have been politic on your part to have avoided this occasion."

"There was no love lost between my brother and me. Why should I play the hypocrite?"

"The town sometimes requires hypocrisy."

"The town can go to hell."

15

"I said that once. In fact, I said it to my father. But I'll tell you now, I learned a brutal hard lesson from it. So have a care." He leaned forward, touching Mordaunt's hand. "Dear boy, don't mistake me. You have come into a great estate, and I wish you joy of it with all my heart. You take no offense?"

"From you, never."

"Good. Where are you stopping in town?"

"Albemarle Street, with my sister-in-law." Then, "Do you find that indiscreet too, that I presently share a house with my brother's widow?"

"Don't mock me, Achill. I don't like it."

"I don't mock you. I appreciate your concern, and it hardly matters in any case. I shall sell out soon."

Bancroft said nothing more, but his mood was visibly altered. There was a stir in the audience, and his words were almost inaudible when he spoke again.

"I shall be so sorry to see you go. Ah... the King."

They stood; around them the house rose as one. The royal box was seated, the house lights snuffed, and the first notes of the oratorio rang out into the smoky darkness.

At the interlude they finished the bottle, and a second was sent for.

"Why do you speak of selling out? Do you have some fear for yourself?"

"I have an odd premonition. One way or the other, I don't believe myself long for the army."

Bancroft said abruptly, "Don't be morbid, Achill," and looked away across the pit.

"I am half Irish, after all. Morbidity runs in my veins." He traced the twisted stem of the glass, staring at the wine, wanting to speak of Catherine now, finding it necessary to speak of her. "Morbidity, and a strange consciousness of sin...."

Bancroft had turned back, and was observing him with a quality of something he could only think of as stillness, a waiting, measuring stillness.

"What did you say?"

But he did not answer, thinking of her and the desperate tenderness of their intercourse in darkened rooms, and the black, malignant fear that he would pay for their adultery, perhaps with his life in Flanders. The sense of having been granted too much time, too much grace: that some retribution, some reckoning was at hand.

Bancroft was repeating, with an odd, persistent gentleness, "What did you say?"

"Did you ever meet my brother? He looked like an angel. The brightest. Lucifer."

16

"He is dead, Achill. Let him rest."

"He *knew*," he said, knowing he had already said too much, not knowing how to prevent himself from saying more. "The guilt is poisoning me—"

He was aware of the compassionate silence, the utter privacy of the box, the sudden devouring need for male companionship. Forgetting her, not forgetting her perhaps but simply putting her aside, Catherine and the cold house in Albemarle Street and the malevolent presence he would always feel there, and the unknown future in Flanders, wracked with intangible fears.

"Thank God you found me tonight."

Bancroft murmured something and he continued to talk, a heedless flood of words so unlike himself that he listened as if to a stranger, wondering if it were alcohol or some twisted, bitter grief that made him speak. Eventually he paused. The bottle was empty.

"My dear Achill, I fear you have lost me. What was it your brother knew?"

"He knew that I— you *know*, don't you? And, my God, what a weapon he made of it. Even my annuity...."

"Lynton did the same to me. He gives me a pittance, nothing more."

"Why? Had you... loved unwisely?"

"By some lights. I loved where I should not have."

"And, deeply?"

"I thought my life would end when it was over. It very nearly did."

"And love with guilt? You know of that?"

Bancroft said, "Yes," staring into the dimness. "Oh God, yes, like my own name."

He sat in silence for a moment, and then said, "Desire transcends the laws of men. There is no shame in this."

"Then you understand. And I thought you were... cold. In Ghent."

"They know nothing of me in Ghent, I assure you. And nothing of you." He smiled again, a little. "You are very drunk, ain't you, Achill? I wonder if you know what you are saying."

Mordaunt began to speak and was silenced with a patient, "Hush, the interlude is ended." The house lights were being snuffed; the smoke drifted acridly from the pit. The performance recommenced.

He sobered somewhat during the course of it, and apologized. Bancroft shook his head dismissively, seeming intent on the splendour of the oratorio.

"Messiah" ended. It would be attacked by the clergy and the London critics and withdrawn after three performances, but it had brought the King to his feet in the glorious Hallelujah chorus where he had remained until the finale, and it left Mordaunt exultant and unwilling to conclude the evening. They went on to White's, drinking and gambling heavily. It was three o'clock

17

before they left; Bancroft had two shillings in his pocket. St. James's was still thronged with people.

They returned to Bancroft's townhouse, part of the pittance granted his younger son by the Earl of Lynton; Mordaunt could not recall having accepted the invitation; it must have been spoken carelessly over cards. He found his lost reason for a moment, protesting the lateness of the hour, and allowed himself to be overruled. The spectre of war, of retribution, of his own mortality, was haunting him; he had felt it at his shoulder even in the crush and glitter of White's and knew it must be confronted before long; it would soon overwhelm them both. For all he knew, they would both die in Flanders: there might never be another night like this.

The house was new, one of eight in Great Cumberland Place. He was very drunk but he retained scattered impressions of its beauty and of the time he spent there, in a richly furnished room with a Turkish carpet on the floor, and of the footman in black livery who brought a bottle and waited while it was approved, and withdrew. They were not disturbed again.

There was cognac, the silken Everett, and deep conversation, and then not enough of either. His golden mood had deserted him; his head was aching, and with fatigue came depression. He wanted only to be gone from this austerely beautiful house, where something he did not wish to acknowledge was making tentative efforts to be known.

He could not later recall what had begun it, a half-spoken phrase, a gesture whose meaning was no longer in doubt, but suddenly he was confronted by all the rumours he had heard in Flanders and knew their indisputable truth. He lost his head; things happened too quickly, things done and words spoken born of drink and despair that were regretted on both sides, then there was a ghastly silence. He groped for the door, sickened and repulsed. Bancroft remained where he had been kneeling, his face averted, filled with a pain beyond imagining.

He told Catherine: there were no secrets between them. In the second week of April he married her by special license, an act of passion and of desperate fear. At the end of the week he took ship for Ostend.

The afternoon he arrived in Ghent Bancroft met him in the mess and congratulated him on his marriage, news of which had preceded him from some unknown source. Four other officers who were playing faro overheard and proposed a toast, in which Bancroft joined, and then, unobtrusively, he took his leave. It was his gesture of abdication: they did not speak again.

The campaign, the dreaded spring, ground on relentlessly, defeat after defeat, marked by illness, hunger and brutal weather. Mordaunt might have resigned his commission at any time, but he was held by a peculiar sense of responsibility to his men and to the regiment, and the chimera of his withdrawal obsessed him: the army was a monster both loved and hated, which fed upon his life, and his loyalty was the chain that held him to it. Catherine's letters, when they reached him, ceased to speak of his homecoming.

Time became a bloody river bearing him from day to day. He wept for dead friends, then they became part of the river, were lost, forgotten, left behind. The faro players at Ghent were shot, mutilated, decapitated, eyeless: they died one by one until it seemed the bloody ground must have them all, until only Bancroft's face was familiar. Dettingen was a victory, Fontenoy two years later in May of 1745 a defeat: to one who suffered in both actions, it was difficult to know the difference. Mordaunt bore the scars of Dettingen on his right wrist and his thigh, gaping wounds stained with powder, sewn up by a drunken stranger in the smoke behind the lines; at Fontenoy a brigade of Irish Jacobites cut his company to pieces as he watched, deafened by mortar fire and half-blind with his own blood. He could not hear the men scream as they fell; he could only watch the soundless nightmare of their deaths, and call to the living to retreat in good order in a voice he could no more hear than the dead who lay mangled at his feet.

Bancroft saw no action at Fontenoy. He had taken the lieutenant-colonelcy of a regiment which was never ordered out of Ghent, and when that regiment, the Fourth, was one of the first to be dispatched to England in November to put down the Jacobite rebellion, he was more than willing to go. A majority fell vacant in the Fourth just before they were due to embark. He himself wrote to Mordaunt, urging him to bid for it.

The Highland army had reached England by that time. Driven only by his desire to see Catherine, Mordaunt purchased it.

He went home from Newcastle for the first time in four years. He found Evesham deserted except for his steward and the staff; frightened by the rebels' advance, Catherine had fled to London. He drank himself insensible, and left Durham with nothing more of her than a handkerchief to carry into the coming action, and a memory of her face which had long since ceased to be clear.

He rode north. The countryside was uneasy but quiet. The Highland army, failed by its French ally, met with apathy by English Jacobites and wracked with dissension, desertion and fear in its own ranks, had turned back at Derby. By Christmas Day it had retreated as far as Glasgow. During the last days of December, the royal troops under Lieutenant-General Henry Hawley began moving north from Newcastle. Mordaunt, riding with a baggage train for the Fourth, joined Bancroft's officers in Edinburgh on the tenth of January in the new year of 1746.

It was a strange meeting, passionless, drained. They spoke only of the regiment. They had not seen one another since Bancroft's transfer nearly a year before; he had been ill, and he despised the cold and the bleak Scottish capital. He did not have to endure it long: on the fifteenth of the month the army left it, marching in force to the relief of Stirling, besieged by the rebels. The evening of the sixteenth saw them encamped west of Falkirk where it was thought they might engage, near the slopes of a wooded hill skeletal with winter.

The Highlanders were sighted, but no alarm was given. The army under Hawley was oddly purposeless and disorganized, and Hawley himself was unconcerned. No commands were given that night, nor the next, raw morning when the enemy was seen to be moving south of the Torwood, the old forest near Falkirk hill, and forming into some order of battle. Hawley remained supremely confident that he would not be attacked. The army stood to arms at about eleven o'clock when the enemy was seen moving with the Pretender's standards and colours flying, but stood down after a quarter of an hour. Hawley returned to Callander House, where he had billeted himself upon the Jacobite Lady Kilmarnock, and demanded his dinner; the rest of the army foraged for a midday meal that would not be found. Shortly before one o'clock a local man hurried into the camp, shouting, "Gentlemen, what are you about? The Highlanders will soon be upon you!"

Two officers of Howard's Old Buffs, climbing a tree with telescopes, verified this. Their lieutenant-colonel rode to Callander House with the news. Hawley dismissed it, and gave no order to stand to arms.

Between one and two o'clock a party of volunteers spurred into the camp with even graver information: the Highland army was fording the River Carron, with the apparent intention of choosing its own ground on the high plateau of Falkirk moor. A messenger was sent to Hawley. Attack was imminent.

He arrived hatless, at the gallop, cursing like the old cavalryman he was. The ground and the light were bad and would be worse, the wind and rain already biting from the southwest. The sky was dark with storm. The drums beat to arms at two.

Bancroft's regiment, the Fourth, found itself part of the second line of battle, facing a steep ascent. The wind cut keenly into the faces of the men. By four o'clock the light was failing, and the shouts and challenges coming more clearly on the gusts, with the high, terrible skirling of the pipes. Mordaunt, armoured in the cold composure that always came to him before battle, watched the men in his battalion. The enemy before them was unknown and nightmare, unlike any civilized force they had encountered in Flanders, and the regiments it had broken at Prestonpans in September had given frightful warnings of the Highland charge. They were waiting uneasily, fearing the moment when it would come, and he, with a strange perception, knew that they would never stand.

With his infantry only half formed, still wheeling and dressing into line of battle, Hawley sent forward Ligonier's dragoons. He was contemptuous of the Highland ability to withstand a cavalry charge. The dragoons rode straight into a well-directed volley of musketry at a range of ten yards, and eighty fell dead from their saddles. The rest, with a few honourable exceptions, turned and fled.

Shouts of "Claidheamh mor!" went up along the ragged Highland ranks, and, unable to reload in the driving rain, the first clansmen threw away their muskets and ran forward with sword in hand. Confronted by the dreaded charge, the royal infantry returned a scattered, irregular fire and then, blinded by the rain, confused and shaken by the blundering rout of the dragoons, they turned their scarlet backs to the shrieking enemy and their powder-blackened faces to the second line, and they, too, ran. The contagion of their panic spread. Amid the shouts and curses of officers, almost the entire second line broke rank and fled with them.

The Fourth stood fast. Bancroft, on horseback, dimly seen through the rain and the coming darkness, galloped up and down the line, pouring a torrent of abuse and invective on his men, and out of either fear or loyalty they heard him and stood. An aide-de-camp thundered up bearing orders for the shattered regiment.

An eyeless, senseless body on creeping, gaitered legs, the Fourth advanced, moving forward in the blinding rain to join the only two front-line regiments which had held, Ligonier's and Price's. Under the orders of Hawley's generals in the field, Major-General John Huske and Brigadier Chomondeley, they loaded, fired and fell back to reload, biting their cartridges until their lips were black with powder, firing at the command, pouring a surprisingly well-ordered fire into the rebels' flank.

They remained engaged in the faint light and the slashing rain until Irish Jacobite picquets were ordered up from the Pretender's reserve to face them, and aware that they could not stand alone against fresh attack Huske gave the order to fall back. The three regiments retreated in good order, followed by the regrouped dragoons.

Near Falkirk, retreat balanced precariously on the brink of full-fledged rout. The royal camp was in disorder: guns had been deserted in the mire, gun captains and horses fled; tents, baggage, clothing and small arms were being burned, abandoned or destroyed. Mordaunt took only the writing case with Catherine's letters and mementoes, his Barbar pistols, and a sword that had belonged to his father. Three private soldiers were waiting impatiently to pull the tent down and fire it; he waited a moment, then when he saw that it would not burn and must be left trodden into the mud for the rebels he tied the baggage to his saddle and rode away without looking back.

The army withdrew that night to Linlithgow; it was said that Hawley broke his sword in fury against the market cross in Falkirk as he left it. They reached the royal burgh late in the evening; it was raining heavily. At some point in the journey Mordaunt found himself riding stirrup to stirrup with Bancroft— the defeat seemed to have crushed him utterly, although he had no reason for shame: out of six line-regiments engaged in the rear, his alone had stood. Yet still he was silent, and when the lights of Linlithgow fell across his face it was to be seen that he had wept.

The dead of Falkirk lay where they had fallen, some four hundred men, left naked on the hillside in the rain, stripped and plundered by the jubilant Highlanders. The royal army returned to Edinburgh, to the shouts and jeers of Jacobite sympathizers there, and the recriminations for Falkirk began at once. Thirty-one dragoons were hanged for desertion, thirty-two of foot shot for cowardice. Casualties among the senior officers had been unusually heavy: among the dead were three lieutenant-colonels, and a fourth died shortly afterwards of pleurisy. Five officers were arrested and court-martialled; one, a man known personally to Mordaunt, attempted to commit suicide by slashing his wrists. He was cashiered with infamy when he recovered.

Early in the morning of January thirtieth, His Royal Highness the Duke of Cumberland arrived in Edinburgh to take command from Hawley. A king's son the same age as the Pretender, his cousin Charles Edward Stuart, he brought with him an artillery train from Newcastle as well as cavalry and infantry reinforcements. With his coming, the tide of defeat had turned.

On the last day of January the royal army marched out of Edinburgh to Linlithgow once more.

Perth, Aberdeen, Elgin, Forres. They reached Nairn on the fourteenth of April, close behind the fleeing Jacobite army. Charles camped on the evening of the fourteenth upon the edge of the moor at Culloden, and at dawn he marshalled his dwindling forces in order of battle. They made no move throughout the day. The fifteenth was Cumberland's birthday, and the men were issued rations of brandy. When they had drunk their loyal toast to him they slept in their clothes with their arms beside them, at Balblair, a mile southwest of Nairn.

It was a heady celebration for a young man just turned twenty-five, with nine thousand men to drink his health and his cousin's army awaiting defeat on the morrow. Cumberland was confident of victory.

Mordaunt woke to the long roll of the drums at four: the General Call to Arms. Sleet was drumming a bitter tattoo on the stained canvas over his head. The tents were struck at five; there was no breakfast to be had. It was a black, miserable morning. The rain fell, and the raw wind scythed up from the Moray, bringing the smell of the sea. It was wretchedly cold.

And for the rest: only defeat. It was simply said. It was almost as simply done. The lessons had been well and hardly learned and the mistakes of Falkirk were not repeated: folly dwelt instead on the other side of the moor where the Pretender sat astride his grey gelding and watched the royal artillery tear his Highlanders into thrashing, limbless abortions. It was over very soon. The victory was complete.

Seven months ago, only seven. Two battlefields, Falkirk and Culloden, and some two hundred days.

He looked up, from his hands, from the table, from the past and the sickness of his thoughts. The commission lay forgotten at his elbow, the ink on the fallen quill soaking into the damp page, obscuring his signature.

He looked at the watch she had given him, with its passionate inscription. It had stopped at twenty minutes past ten. He thought it might be midnight now, or later.

He walked, shivering, listening to the rain. It might be raining at Evesham now, two hundred miles to the south; it had smelled not unlike this on many summer nights, with the rain beating in on an easterly wind. If he were there, he would be playing for her, Bach, Handel, and the difficult, scintillating Scarlatti. She seldom listened, preferring to tease and interrupt, ignorant in the presence of a genius neither recognized, sometimes a child, sometimes a whore.

He tried to find her face among his memories. It eluded him.

He sat again, opening the watch. The inscription had no power to move him; it signified no more than a line in a long-dead language, once loved and spoken fluently, now irrelevant and forgotten.

He held it, the gold warming to his hand. There had been no letters from her, and he had ceased to write. What should he say? That he had seen crimes committed here by men he thought he knew, and wondered if he was capable of committing them himself, and then found when the time came that he was capable of anything? That he had fought savagely, and was fighting still, although daily he knew he was losing, to the older enemy, the most insidious, because it wished not to destroy but to embrace him? That sometimes he doubted his sanity, as he had come to doubt his humanity, and that more and more he thought any hope of preserving either lay with another man?

The night gave up its memories again, like the dead from a chaotic sea on the day of judgment. She had miscarried after his return to Flanders. The knowledge had hurt him bitterly then; now it brought no more than indeterminate pain, easily ignored.

He knew why the child had not survived. He had committed murder, he had committed adultery, he had married within the bounds of consanguinity and he was damned; they were both damned, and their marriage was and

23

always would be a hell of barrenness, founded upon and hedged with pretense and lies and recriminations, because whatever was in him was not capable of giving love, or giving it to a woman.

He stared at himself in the fragment of shaving glass, into the eyes, callous and unmoved.

You bloody monster, he thought. You bloody, bloody monster. What are you?

What had been offered had been unthinkable in London. Sometimes, to the man he was now, with his fears and his memories and his overwhelming sense of damnation, it was not so unthinkable here.

Bancroft was thinking of Culloden.

His thoughts came as shattered vignettes, without sense or sequence: the ranting clans, the sleet, the standard rippling in the wind. His place was behind the colours, and he remembered waiting there with the orderly drummer beside him and the lion standard of blue silk, gold-fringed, teasing the corner of his eye as he listened for the opening fire. The ensign holding the colours was a boy of fifteen with a sweet face, now white and rigid as if aghast at the nearness of death, or such a splendidly-arrayed superior, or both.

It was well past noon; they had marched from Nairn at five that morning and he was hungry; the sleet was beating on his back and in the enemy's face. The first shot came from the rebel lines; he remembered flicking open his watch. Two minutes later the shattering roar of the royal artillery set his mare Peggy rearing with fright, and he brought her down with an iron hand and a sharp, insistent knee. It was a little after one o'clock. He felt for the watch again, wondering what would become of it if he fell. It had been a gift to him and he wished Mordaunt to have it, but no one would know.

Mordaunt himself was off to the left at the flank of his battalion; through the sleet and with the smoke rolling it was hard to see him, and would be harder yet. He watched him, trying by the force of his gaze to draw his eyes, but Mordaunt, motionless but for the hand calming his horse, did not look toward him. The sleet stopped. Five hundred yards away Clan Cameron broke into the charge.

The whole right wing of the rebel army followed, throwing itself on his men. The shock of the charge shattered through the regiment, and over the screams when it broke on the bayonets of the front line the sergeants were shouting as if insane, "Close up! Close up! Close there, damn you, by your right man, close!" The ranks thinned, holding the charge, throwing it back, then it surged again and broke them. The line swayed, the colours dipped and faltered; he felt blood on his face but no wound, no pain, and looked beside him. The ensign was dead, the staff of the colours holding him upright.

Sharp musketry from the left, Wolfe's regiment supporting his own, sending volley after volley into the rebels' flank. Covered by their fire, he spurred down toward the front, knowing the sight of their commander would hearten his men more than curses, and in the interlude between one rush and another they saw him and found the breath to give him a short, barking cheer. Then the clans came on again and the second wave caught him where he was; he had seen his danger, but whatever else he was in other men's eyes he was no coward, and he sawed the mare's head round savagely to meet it with his sabre in his hand.

It engulfed him: screams and splitting metal and the hollow clang of steel blade on musket stock and barrel. The mare foundering over the bodies of men, some of whom were not yet dead. Screams, and smoking blades and the aching heaviness of his sword arm, the cramp in his fingers, and everywhere the smell of death, not blood and not the tearing pungency of gunpowder but the smell of shit, of ripped bowels. And then he thought he saw Mordaunt's body lying on the ground.

A jarring shock brought him back to himself, a rush of heat and blood and a dripping wetness on his thigh. The sabre was gone; he held his arm up to his eyes in disbelief and a geyser of blood sprayed his face. Both blade and hand had been hewn from his wrist.

He remembered nothing more, only the iron cauterizing the stump and the charred stench of his flesh, and the screams tearing out of his throat. They had held him down, and, spilling his urine, he had fainted.

He opened his eyes and found the vial of laudanum and tilted the dose into his brandy. He had begun to take opium for the pain; he was well aware that it had become something else for him. He had known many drugs in his time, promiscuity among them, and at one point a brief and anguished bout with religion: the effect was the same, soporific, deadening, a taste, momentarily, of Lethe.

He drank it off and waited, feeling the first excitement of the drug, the flush of pleasure, the sense of elation. It would soon leave him.

He would have no other companion tonight, or none that he wanted.

He was not a happy man: he could recall very little happiness in his life. In Venice, briefly, with a young inamorato who was soon taken from him, and the early months of his acquaintance with Mordaunt. He had preferred their friendship. His love, when it came, brought him nothing, only fear: of discovery, death or hideous disfigurement, fear of his only rival, a woman and her beauty. He remained what he had always been, a desperately lonely man, wracked between jealousy and tenderness.

25

He tried to recall his conversation with Mordaunt earlier in the evening but the laudanum was mounting to his head. He could not remember what he had said, if he had pleaded, if he had been arrogant or pitiful. He never knew if he were speaking as a lover or an officer. He had once been able to keep them separate. Now he no longer could.

The pain had dulled to a heavy throbbing; the stump remained hidden by the deep fall of lace at his wrist. Its grotesqueness haunted him, as everything did of late: his loneliness, his own appearance, the sharply drawn face in his shaving glass that told him he was aging and mocked him with his fears and his pain and the past, and his passion for a man who would not love him.

He sat listening to the rain, drumming the fingers of his left hand until the hand tired; there was no strength in it. The smoky lamp he despised guttered on the table beside him and the light threw strange shadows across his face, turning it into a mask with empty eyes.

It was nearly midnight when Brevet's patrol came in, and Brevet presented himself, out of breath, some twenty minutes later. He was a haughty, pretty young man with a look of self-indulgent wealth, and he had held his commission as lieutenant for less than a year. The Highlands had offered him his first taste of military life and he hated it; other officers, Mordaunt among them, had often wondered what he would have done had he been thrown unblooded into the field in Flanders, where the butchery was not so one-sided.

He had been sent to the army as a punishment, and only parental goodwill or favour from some other quarter would release him from it. He was in no mood to curry favour where it might be necessary tonight.

He had had a bad day of it, and his language was as foul as his temper when he received his summons to Bancroft. He had the day's conduct to explain, and he was acutely aware that he had not succeeded in this, his first mission without the direct supervision of a superior officer.

It had begun auspiciously enough, with three clansmen wading into the River Sian toward him, shouting and waving weapons over their heads. Because he had not understood what they were saying, he had ordered them shot. Afterwards he had discovered that two of them had warrants of immunity proving they had taken no part in the rebellion, and the third was a boy no more than ten. Leaving the bodies in the shallows, he called his men to order and marched them deeper into the glen, muskets slung and a drum beating out the step. They found several hovels not yet burned and remedied the oversight, and this afternoon he had taken part in a rape. He had been feeling slightly soiled ever since.

They had spent the remainder of the day wandering on the moors, ignominiously lost. The blame for that lay squarely on his shoulders, and he was prepared to malign his men in his anxiety to shift it elsewhere.

Bancroft was playing patience when he arrived. His shirt was open, his wig tossed aside to reveal dishevelled chestnut hair, which Brevet noted with dispassion was beginning to grey at the temples. He had been drinking to prolong the effect of the laudanum, but it was leaving him. The pain had not ceased.

He looked up to find Brevet watching him in an attitude of poised disinterest.

"I didn't hear you come in, sir. Was you never taught to announce yourself?"

"I knocked, sir, and then saluted you. I believe I made some noise coming in. I beg your pardon if you did not hear me."

"Ah. And now you think me deaf as well as crippled."

Brevet said nothing; it was too dangerous a remark even to be acknowledged. Bancroft said harshly, "Sit down," and when he hesitated, "I said sit down, damn you! What do you think I am that I should stare up at you?"

Brevet sat gingerly. His mind was trying, like a rabbit in a snare, to test all the perimeters of this strange situation and find a way out of it unscathed. He had not known Bancroft long and they had never cared for one another, but their relationship had undergone a subtle change since they had left Inverness and Brevet was not yet certain why.

He said in a tentative voice, "I was given to understand, sir—"

Bancroft looked up.

"—that it was a matter of some importance...."

"You may entertain me with your account of how you passed your day, Lieutenant, if you think that sufficiently important. You may tell me how you detained so many of my men for so long, with so little to show for it, and you may begin directly."

He returned his attention to his cards.

The blood came and went in Brevet's face and he persevered in a cold, restrained voice for a time, then, aware that he was being ignored, he fell silent. Bancroft's hand hesitated over the tableau, dropped a card into place. Brevet sat looking at his own; the nails were not clean. He closed the fingers on themselves in distaste.

Bancroft had been speaking.

"I beg your pardon, Colonel. I did not attend."

"I said you made a sad botch of this, and I am being very patient with you as you damned well know."

"I am very sensible of that, sir."

"So you should be. But, by God, my patience has its limits, and you try me sorely. I will expect improvement from you, otherwise I shall not find it easy to speak well of you when I am asked. Do you understand me?"

"Perfectly, sir."

Those other, impeccable nails drummed lightly for a moment.

"God's blood, what am I to do with you? I suspect your sire of sending you to me because he was more than happy to see your back.... How old are you?"

"Twenty, sir."

"Twenty. God's blood, when I was your age I was a captain and an aide-de-camp. I cannot imagine you—" A harsh laugh. "Your face betrays you, sir. You should govern it better."

"I don't—"

"I can see what you're thinking. My God, you thought, was he ever twenty? You think me an old man, don't you?"

"No, sir."

" 'Yes, sir', rather."

"I do *not*, sir."

He smiled thinly. Brevet's pique amused him. He liked to bait his lovers, enjoyed their temper and sometimes their pain. He laid another card down, aware that Brevet was watching him with hatred.

"You wasn't at Oxford, by any chance?"

"Yes, sir." With sulky courtesy.

"So was I, once. Did they send you down or did you leave?"

"I left."

"You are a liar, sir." But he said it gently, as if it were nothing. "What college?"

"Magdalen."

"Ah. Mine was Trinity. There was a scandal and they threw me out.... Was you hazed?"

"Sir?"

"Was you hazed at Magdalen?"

"Yes, sir."

The fine profile flushed. He watched it with interest.

"Was it very bad or did you mind it much?"

"It was... bad... at the time."

"You needn't tell me." There was a short silence, during which Brevet picked at the lace on his cuff. "Let my cat in, will you? I hear her at the door."

It had been his pet since he had found it starving in a lane in Inverness. He gave it his full attention when it came, lifting it bedraggled to his knee, holding it there firmly with his right arm and rubbing it dry. The left hand was fumbling and uncertain now; his efforts with the cards had tired him more than he knew. He leaned back, holding the cat on his knee and stroking it; he found the feel of its damp fur exquisitely sensual.

"We was speaking of punishment. I don't care for it myself. I am a kind man, in my way... I think there must be kindness shown in any beginning. Don't you agree?"

The cat stirred luxuriously. He called it by the name he had given it, as if it were a secret between them, and stroked it, sighing a little. For a moment he had almost imagined himself somewhere other than in this draughty, dismal hovel with its ugly guttering light and the sound of the rain and the grotesque shadows on the walls.

"I am pleased to have company tonight, Lieutenant. I was lonely before you came. What was I saying? It don't matter. Do you like music, sir? Are you musical?" Brevet murmured something. "Are you acquainted with Vivaldi's concertos for violin and cello, Le Quattro Stagioni?"

Brevet coughed to marshal his wits.

"I believe I heard them at Bath once."

"The largo of the winter concerto— I find it exquisite. You are familiar with the piece? I have no voice, otherwise I would recall it to your mind." He was not aware of Brevet's silence. "I was in Venice when I heard it first... it seemed to say so much to me. It reminded me of everything I had lost, love, youth.... I wept when I heard it. I wanted them to play it over and over—"

He sat for a time, staring at the pattern of the cards, possessed by that sweet, haunting cadence, and he felt grief again more sharply than it had touched him for years, and a desperate yearning at the memory of Venice.

He drew himself out of it with difficulty.

"No matter. No matter. You did very well today after all. I am not so displeased with you as I make out."

A delicate game to be played now. He suppressed his doubts, knowing what it would mean if he were wrong, but he seldom was, and he was lonely, lonely....

"You may leave me now, Lieutenant. You look a trifle hipped. I am sorry to have kept you so long."

Brevet glanced up uncertainly.

"No, sir, I—"

"You are welcome to stay if you like. Perhaps a hand of piquet before you go?"

They played, and drank, and Brevet, with the elder hand, won. Bancroft said coolly, "You take advantage of me, sir."

Brevet flushed.

"Faith, sir, you let me win."

29

"Faith, sir," Bancroft said, "you flatter yourself. Your winnings."

The guineas changed hands.

"More brandy?"

"Thank you. Shall I?"

"I am quite capable, I assure you."

His hand was unsteady, from fatigue or weakness or the drug or the knowledge of what was so surely coming, and its nerveless fingers relaxed on the stem of the glass. It smashed, and the brandy ran to join the pattern of rain on the earthen floor. He swore, and Brevet looked down.

"Some one begrudged it me. You needn't pour another, sir. I'll just—"

"Your discretion is most endearing. Leave it—" Brevet had begun to pick up the shards.

"Your cat might do herself an injury."

"Yes, that's quite true. I'll see to it." A silence, then, "Your name is David, ain't it."

"Yes."

"Mine is Aeneas." Again a silence, fraught with meanings. "Call me by my name."

They looked for a moment into one another's eyes. His were reddened and dilated with the opium he had taken to nerve himself to this unwanted substitution, and he knew he looked older than his years, and desperate, but it did not matter now. Nothing mattered.

Their lips met briefly, tentatively, exploring the extent of one another's desire, then more deeply. The old hunger gave way to a new, certain of fulfilment.

After a time, Brevet spoke. His voice sounded very young.

"Shall I undress, Aeneas?"

An hour or two later when he was again alone, Bancroft rose, naked but for the shirt that concealed his wound, and took the night's second draught of brandy and laudanum. He lay down again, hoping for sleep.

It did not come. The encounter had left him strangely shaken, not for itself, for what it was; he had come to expect them to be like this, casual, even indifferent, and sometimes necessarily degrading. But it had been without love, without even affection, and as with all such loveless acts it left him more depressed than satisfied. The loneliness that followed was almost impossible to bear.

He dressed, and thought of Venice, and wept a little, then called his cat and stroked it while it slept in his lap, a long, gentle caress as it curled with its ears brushing the empty lace at his wrist. The laudanum took him deeper although it did not bring him sleep, and he drifted with it, his mind a river.

30

Venice, and his house in London, and that night and how it might have ended. He slept or thought he did, and when he woke it was to the sickness and heaviness of too much brandy and too much of the drug, and the inevitable emptiness of the room and the day and the bed.

Seven men were lying in the darkness of the caves above Glen Mor. The prices on their heads ranged from twenty-five guineas for their leaders to the few shillings for any man or boy who had borne arms against the King, and the inevitable reward for the few among them who still dared to call themselves MacGregors, although their name and all their rights as a clan had long since been outlawed.

The land of Glen Sian was held by Ewen Hilaire Gunn Stirling. He had not led his tenantry into rebellion; if he had fought anything in the past year, it was their involvement in that very rising. The leaders were two men whose backgrounds could not be more dissimilar, one a displaced MacGregor who had settled on the land after the Campbells had driven him out of Glen Lyon, and the other a minister of the Presbyterian kirk. MacNeil, the minister, was an impassioned fanatic, who had openly demanded that Ewen recruit for the Stuart cause. Born in exile for the previous generation's participation in the abortive rebellions of '15 and '19, Ewen had refused to commit himself, although he made no attempt to dissuade any of his tenants who wished to accompany MacNeil. In the summer of 1745 a hundred men had left Glen Sian, and Ewen had watched them go with a prescient dread, unreassured by MacNeil's prophesies of glory.

England had not risen, and some of the hundred had deserted early, reluctant to follow the Prince's army across the border. Others had persisted until Derby, although they had known they were betrayed; no winter could be more bitter than the welcome they received from English Jacobites. The affair went the way of all the Stuart risings, a sad history of failure and defeat, treachery and rivalry, ill management and misguided passions. Except that this time it was not forgiven so easily. When London turned its fury on the Highlands for this last in a troublesome series of attempts to overthrow the Hanoverian, it was on men of gentle birth and suspect politics that its vengeance fell first and hardest.

The seven had been together since a few days after Culloden. If taken now they would be shot or hanged, or sent chained to the prison hulks and transports moored at Inverness. If they remained at liberty until the winter, they would starve. It was only a matter of time.

They had been eight men yesterday: they would be six tomorrow. One of them was dying of gangrene, and the stench filled the crowded darkness like a noisome presence, an unseen phantom of death. The man, when reason returned to him, thought of his wife and son in Glen Mor, and wondered if the English had killed them.

Lachlan MacIain MacGregor, on whose head rested one of the twenty-five guinea rewards, was leaning against the wall, listening to the water singing in the depths of the cave, and thinking, too, of death. Two of his ghillies, all that remained of a chieftain's tail of a dozen, sat with his broadsword and pistols in case he should want them. He did not look at them. His hawk's face was matted with a tawny beard and his eyes were also tawny, empty and brilliant as a bird of prey's. His cousins were dead, his brother, his foster brother, whose cut wrist he had bound to his own to mingle the blood and whose mother had suckled him from the same pap. His piper was dead. His last blood relation had survived the battle to die in the bracken above Glen Sian. They had crept down and stolen back his desecrated body, and had buried it beneath a cairn to spare it the buzzards and the crows. And they had seen the English thrashing past like lost men in the heather. Melting away like shadows, they had crouched and watched, and it was only with difficulty that MacNeil had restrained them from falling on the red soldiers, outnumbered though they were, and making the ground run redder with their blood.

Lachlan thought, but did not move.

"MacIain," one of the ghillies said with great courtesy and gentleness, "will you not sit down and eat a little?"

He turned his face away.

He had not fought because he had any great love for the House of Stuart; he loved nothing and no one. He had fought only because any clash with the Hanoverians would bring their Campbell allies into the field, and an opportunity to avenge his people's lost lands of Roro on the Campbells of Glen Lyon was not to be missed. So he had raised a hundred men to match MacNeil's, and to do it he had burned and cursed and threatened his way across their holdings. In the end, a little more than two hundred men had followed MacNeil's flaming dream, and sixty had returned.

Few of those were MacGregors. Lachlan had driven them by the force of his will and the flat of his sword into England when they would have left him, back into Scotland when England became a bitter host, and into the charge at Culloden when they turned to flee. He sent them running across the moor with the sleet in their eyes to their deaths on the English bayonets, and when the clans broke at last he followed his men, weeping, swearing, calling them children of the race of kings, urging them to a final, desperate attempt. They died as they stood for him, dumbly, like dogs, and slashing at the heather with his broadsword he was himself dragged bodily from the field.

Now, chieftain of nothing, he sat huddled with his back to the stone and stared at darkness. He was twenty years old.

He was not alone in his guilt or his grief, if he felt either of those emotions, as a leader in a failed cause. Patrick Inglis MacNeil had not taken his god into battle with him, and he did not summon him now for any lugubrious spiritual comfort.

He limped from one end of the cave to the other, a tall, vain man of striking appearance, black-haired, with a pale scholar's face and hypnotic eyes. He knew this darkness as well as his own heart, and found as much to loathe in it; he knew every man in the place he had claimed and avoided them all, pacing, turning, caged by the cave's night as much as Lachlan and hating it with the same cold ferocity, but physically resisting it, while Lachlan sat mute and immobile like a falcon under the hood, unwilling to fight where he was blind.

Part of the fire that consumed him was sexual; he had been absent for a year and known no company but his fevered dreams of a wife much younger than himself. He had repressed love so effectively that he no longer knew how to acknowledge or express it, but his thoughts took him to her again and again, away from the fetid darkness and the men who shared it with him to the passion of their first nights together, and when the memories began to give him pleasure he thrust them aside, condemning himself for his indulgence.

He stooped once and spoke to the dying man, his voice beautiful and resonant. He had used his voice from the pulpit as the greatest of actors would, consciously and deliberately, to summon men to his side. Now he used it to comfort them as, one by one, they left him, slipping into a night deeper than this, and lit by no fitful dreams of his making.

He more than any one had led them, and he more than any was aware of the terrible consequences. He felt their eyes upon him, their attentive silence as he walked. They would not disturb him, but they were like children wanting to know of a father what they should do next.

It was not that they did not forgive him; they could and did. It was he who could not forgive himself.

The wound in his thigh, taken not at Culloden but in a skirmish and flight several weeks after, had filled again with suppuration, and he knew that if it was not lanced and treated he would die. He welcomed the pain now as he walked; it obliterated everything else, all the other agonies, the names and the faces, his wife, his sister, who would have fought beside him if she could, Ewen Gunn Stirling of Glen Sian, who would pay for all.

Iain Mhor Cameron, the dying man, moaned again, seeing what dreams or visions of hell or eternity none of them could imagine. One of Lachlan's ghillies leaned over him, nursing him as gently as a woman.

Lachlan had not moved; but for his eyes he might have been stone. His eyes and his hand, shredding the eagle's feather from his bonnet.

Some one spoke. MacNeil, alert for footfalls, snarled at him to keep quiet. The silence deepened and festered. Each man lay or stood or sat, fierce with pain and cold, hunger, distrust, old hatreds flaring at the slightest provocation. They had been hunted so long and hidden so long that they had begun to think and behave like animals, every man with lousy beard and filthy, broken nails, teeth bared, hands flickering for dirks or sgians, cursing more fluently than they spoke. The cave stank of their waste and their suffering.

Waiting, watching. Four hours' guard, four hours' sleep, scavenging for food, for fuel. MacNeil had kept them together. Now some of them thought even MacNeil was breaking.

The ghillie began to sing, slowly, mournfully, to comfort the dying man.

> O, the Boatman, na hóro eile,
> O, the Boatman, na hóro eile,
> My long farewell wherever you go to

Lachlan raised his head. The hard golden eyes fell upon the man for a moment, his gaze not seen but felt, and the effect was more savage than a curse. The ghillie was silent.

The song persisted in MacNeil's head, a love ballad long sung in the Highlands. His wife had sung it at her spinning wheel.

> My heart within is bruised and broken
> And from my eyes the tears are streaming
> Come you tonight, or come tomorrow
> And sad am I if you come never
>
> O, the Boatman.....

He leaned his head against the cold rock. He would never see her again.

Lachlan sat still, his back to the wall, thinking of strange, irrelevant, disconnected things. His childhood, harried from glen to glen, rootless and unwelcome, without name or home. Reiving black cattle from the summer pastures of the Campbells, in winter starving and shivering. Thinking, drifting with the sound of water, hearing voices in it, old legends.

His mind began a fantasy and his body responded. A woman came to him, brought him wine in a jewelled cup, a white-skinned woman of the Sitheachan, the fairy race older than man. She came naked to him, mantled in her black hair and the blackness between her legs, and her face might have been old or young. He saw the face and its fierce green eyes, and took the mouth with his, running his hand down into the blackness of the pubic hair.

Her name came to him, out of the past, and they began the making of hate together, fighting and tearing at one another until he was in her and of her and she lay still beneath him, ravished and subdued.

He closed his eyes, feeling himself harden, hating his lust and the woman who had caused it. The eagle feather broke in his hand and he drew his knees up, his back against the damp stone. He put his head down on his arms, withdrawing into darkness.

II

In the autumn of 1727, Robert Lyon Campbell of Glen Lyon burned the crofts and evicted the last MacGregor tenants on his lands of Roro. He brought his twins, his son Magnus and his daughter Margaret, down to see the burnings because the MacGregors were their hereditary enemies, and it was well they should remember it.

Margaret was wearing a man's bonnet and her brother's old riding coat with a heavy plaid pinned at her shoulder, and she rode astride the garron with brogans laced to the knee. She looked little more than a child: she was in fact fourteen, and she had come down to watch the evictions rather than endure the company of her second cousin at her father's house.

She was called Máiréad Dubh, Black Margaret, in Glen Lyon, not only to distinguish her from all the other Margarets in the Campbell connection but because in a clan known for its reddish hair she stood out like a raven. She had had few offers of marriage and her father had ordered her to accept this one, but she had no use either for her cousin or his suit, and he was no more in her thoughts now than if he were in another world.

Her hair blinded her as she sat her garron in the cold wind, watching rooftrees pulled down and stone taken from stone until nothing was left standing. There was fire in the fields, in the ricks, on the heath, and a pillar of smoke staining the sky the length of Glen Lyon. It seemed the whole township was burning.

The wind veered and blew the smoke south over Roro, toward Eilean Ran and Finlarig and Loch Tay.

Her brother leaned from the saddle and took her rein.

"Come home," he said. "There's nothing left to see."

She counted herself pure Campbell, despite the MacDonald blood that flowed in her veins, and she knew her genealogy and the history of her clan from the present generation through the men who had died for Argyll when the traitor Montrose led their enemies against them in a winter long before she was born. Her father had been a boy riding with the great Glen Lyon to smoke out the hornets' nest of robbers deep in their snowbound glen; she knew what he had done by the River Coe and had neither qualms nor pity, because there was no infamy in murder when it was MacDonald blood on the snow. She knew all the old legends and the songs of Cuchullain, and Fionn whose warriors slept in the green hills above her home, waiting for Fionn's horn to waken them; she knew of Deirdre and Naisi and the High King, Conchubar; her father had told her as his father had told him; and as she would tell her son. And, secretly, she kept the old feasts and the prayers to older gods, untainted by Robert Lyon's new Protestantisms. She had a step as light as a hunter's, and at the weddings she danced with grace and sensuality, and sometimes when she looked into the patterns of blood spilled at the autumn killings she thought she read her future.

She had an ordinary childhood, perhaps more unfettered than most, but her adolescence was marked by a growing unhappiness and alienation. Her MacDonald mother was a weak, spiritless, hag-ridden woman, married to keep peace and knowing little of it in her domestic life, and her lusty red-haired father had never known quite what to make of his coal-black daughter, or for that matter his strange and solitary son. They were as unlike him as ash from flame; privately he thought them changelings, sent on him in retribution for his many carnal sins. It was impossible to believe he had got them, or that they had come from the womb of that sick, frail creature whose bed he had not invaded for years.

So he went about his affairs, an impoverished but fiercely arrogant man, the poorest of poor cousins to Glen Lyon himself, keeping his tack and paying his rent only by abusing his MacGregor tenants, conscripting the men and bedding the women, sowing wild oats in others' fields and reaping a harvest of bastards whom he ignored. It was possible that one of these was the child born to a MacGriogháir in the winter of 1726, when Margaret was thirteen. The child was tiny and wizened and had hair like the red gold of Robert Lyon's avaricious dreams, and the woman who bore him named him Lachunn.

He might have been half-brother to Margaret herself but she never knew, any more than Robert Lyon could have told her, and in any case he was too small to be noticed when Robert Lyon, impatient with his miserable tenants and thinking of the money to be had from raising cattle on their lands in Roro, evicted the MacGregors and scattered them throughout the Highlands, as far as the eagles flew.

At fifteen Margaret was contracted to marry the cousin she despised. He had money, and she had no beauty and no dowry to speak of; she was lucky, her father told her, to have had so patient a suitor. The wedding was arranged, the betrothal feast given, and she suffered the attention of her mother's women while the gown of stiff white silk was fitted to her unresisting body; her breasts were already bruised from her prospective bridegroom's questing hands. On the morning of the wedding she ran away, leaving her father at the altar with a mouthful of obscenities and a face as red as his hair.

He knew her haunts; he ordered his son to find her, and when Magnus declined he went himself in his wedding finery and dragged her down by her hair. He beat her once to change her mind and once more when she refused, careful not to mar her face in case his cousin should still want her, then he left her to his silent wife and returned to the sweaty company of the men to drown his disappointment in a quart of claret. The silk gown was packed away to serve as his daughter's shroud.

At sixteen she was rumoured to have a lover; no one knew who it was. When she was seventeen, Magnus went suddenly to France; she was bedridden for some time, and it was autumn before she was seen abroad again. Then she passed her days riding and walking in the hills overlooking Rannoch. She had no suitors; men were frightened of her, women said she had the two sights. She laughed at them.

They said other things too, until fear of Robert Lyon shut their slanderous mouths. But Magnus Campbell was never seen in Glen Lyon again, and she was never what she had been before he left.

She turned twenty-two in another, later autumn, and another of her cousins was married that winter. At the wedding she met a stranger. Murdoch Scott had been riding through Glen Lyon that day, and with the generosity of the Highlander the bride's father invited him to partake of the celebrations. He was factor to the Stirling of Glen Sian, a little chieftain with land west of Loch Ness, although the title was more courtesy than fact; his sole duties consisted of rent collection and the conduct of cattle to the markets. He had no knowledge of estate management, and only the rudiments of an education; he was almost illiterate.

He was thirty-two; he looked fifty, a tall, weather-beaten man with grey eyes and a hard, handsome face, and a splendid body scarred from countless brawls and the abuse he offered it in the name of pleasure. The raw sexuality of his presence affected her like a drug.

He would never marry her, and he would never be faithful to her, and instinct told her this even as she allowed him to seduce her, but it did not signify. They made love throughout the night, and in the morning she went with him when he left Glen Lyon.

She rode pillion, bareheaded and barelegged like a tinker woman of the roads, wrapped in her old riding coat with the faded plaid on her shoulder, and she went without Robert Lyon's approval, and consequently penniless.

She slept under the sky rolled in her plaid beside the stranger to whom, after a single night, she had committed her life.

She had conceived of that first wild cleaving in Glen Lyon, or the nights on the hard ground which had followed it, and she pleaded for marriage now in earnest so the child would have a name, but neither marriage nor the rite of handfasting was offered.

She might have left him; she stayed because she was proud, or because whatever he had felt for her she still felt a bitch's faithfulness toward him, or so he contemptuously called it. His work took him away from her more often as her pregnancy progressed; he went to the far reaches of the estate and to women who lived there, or to the great house of Ardsian where Margaret dared not follow. Her labour began at first light on the last day of October, and she was alone until the darkness brought him home. It was midnight before she was delivered.

Her life was lonely, but she had always been solitary and days spent without the sound of a human voice were no trial to her. Her son gave her great joy; she had given him her brother's full name, Malcolm Magnus Alasdair, and in his face and the green eyes, her eyes and Magnus's, she saw Magnus restored to her, in the innocence of his childhood. She did not know the thoughts that possessed him, or any aspect of his secretive, introspective nature; although he was of her womb and her flesh, she never knew the child she had made.

She had paid for his love by losing Murdoch's, but she was happy for a time. She had not forgotten Glen Lyon or its dark beauty, but the need for it no longer troubled her so intensely. She was not of Glen Sian either; it held no welcome for her. She existed like a spirit, between two worlds, and yet, not unhappy.

She thought the past had forgotten her. Glen Sian was the last place she expected it to become manifest.

A party of MacGriogháirs had settled on the estate in the autumn of 1741, after another season's hopeless wandering. They were Glen Lyon people, whose names Margaret recognized, and among them was a youth who called himself Lachlan MacIain. They had never met, and he did not know her. The oversight was remedied by those who remembered Robert Lyon's black daughter and the forfeited lands of Roro.

She had no reason to fear the youth or any of his people, and yet she did fear them. Even now, on this cold morning in the summer of 1746, in the knowledge that he was absent, perhaps dead, his name was enough to bring that black shadow out of the corner of her mind.

She thrust the spider of fear aside and shrouded herself in her plaid, watching the trout strike at flies on the glassy surface of the lochan. She was not yet thirty-four, but the little promise of beauty youth had given her had been withdrawn; the mane of coarse black hair was streaked with silver, the delicate hands so envied by her Glen Lyon cousins callused and arthritic. She thought they would not know her now. She hardly knew herself.

She sat on the rock, her place of meditation, and stared over the water at the house. Sometimes when she sat in these idle dreams she saw Fionnaghal Scott, the old woman, bending her back in the garden, or leading the blind girl, Murdoch's sister, on a rein like a child. Stone steps came down to the water's edge, and here the blind girl beat the household linens clean, although she was easily distracted by sound, a flight of curlew, a nesting diver, or a sensation of Margaret's presence. She had never made herself known to either woman: she remained what she had been for a dozen bitter years, the silent observer of their lives.

The house drifted on its hillside in the mist, and the scent of the garden teased her with memories of Glen Lyon. And Magnus....

He would no more return to Glen Lyon than she. He was dead. Joined with him in birth and life, she had known the instant of his death.

She drifted in the lost sweetness of the past.

Mordaunt rose at four, aching with lack of sleep. Outside the dampness of the house the morning was grey and piercingly cold; the world lay washed with shadows like a monochromatic sketch. Nothing stirred, no bird sang in the windless stillness; the cloud or mist hung lower on the slopes than he had ever seen it. The black, stinking ruins filled him with a persistent horror.

He resumed his silent walk through the camp. It was still bitterly cold but the sky gave a little light now; it was less like walking through some ashen morning at the end of the world. Blue smoke rose thinly from the fires outside each tent, and there were signs and sounds of movement; at six o'clock the drums would beat Reveille, and start the affronted echoes from the hills once more.

He passed Bancroft's quarters on the way back to his own. There was no sign of life.

Assembly. Bancroft absent: it was a rare day when he was not. Brevet called the roll, something he did irregularly and with relished authority to discover who was absent without leave, then, having reported all present, he stood back with his hands beneath his coatskirts and the muster book tucked under one arm. His face was sphinx-like in its detachment.

Mordaunt spread the marbled covers of the order book. The orders themselves, in Brevet's innovative spelling, were almost illegible, and he had the impression that this small inconvenience to him was deliberate. He read in a strong, carrying voice, not that it mattered much; there was always some one in the ranks who would later claim that he had not heard.

The orders were very much Bancroft's, despite the fact that he was seldom seen, and again the hallmark of the army rang through.

"The sentries are forbid to sing or whistle or make any sort of noise upon their posts, by talking loudly to one another or otherwise, and particularly in the night; whoever disobeys this order will be immediately relieved and punished; a sergeant who suffers his men to disobey will be broke.

"Any sentry who is negligent on his post or disobeys any orders he shall have received shall be severely whipped.

"Any soldier who is found with plunder in his tent or returning to the army with plunder of any kind not taken by order shall be severely punished. No plundering on any account except by order and in the presence of an officer...." And something directed personally to him: "It is ordered once for all, that all are to keep close to the encampment and are not to pass through the outguard and wander through the country."

As he read, his mind ran upon a concurrent course. Glen Sian was a point from which to launch punitive expeditions, and also a rendezvous. Despatches and warrants for arrests in the neighbourhood might be forthcoming, the remainder of the baggage and another platoon were expected daily from Invermoriston, and two hundred Campbell militia, ostensibly searching for the Pretender, in reality savaging the lands of their enemies, had been given orders to appear at Glen Sian on or about the eighth of July. Some of those arriving would bring rumours of Fort Augustus, and the men were already restive; there would be no restraining them once they heard the news. There was much flogging at Fort Augustus, more than at Inverness, but there were fortunes to be made, cattle and plunder to be sold, horse racing and horse dealing, and sutlers' wagons full of brandy. Leavened only by the severity of the discipline, it was a soldier's dream.

"Those who are found in arms are ordered to be put immediately to death... those who abscond from their homes shall have their homes burnt, their cattle confiscated, their ploughs and other tackle put to the flames...."

He read on, and the concurrent flow of thought became a river of blood from Inverness to Glen Moriston. Women raped and slashed with bayonets and sabres, men hanged or shot or obscenely mutilated, their severed genitals placed in their hands, their penises protruding from dead mouths. Houses destroyed, stone taken from stone and scattered, trees and gardens cut, uprooted, despoiled.

"That wherever arms of any kind are found, that house and all houses belonging to the proprietor or his tenants shall be immediately burnt to ashes; and that as some arms have been found underground, that if any shall be discovered for the future the adjacent houses and fields shall be immediately laid waste and destroyed. This by general order of His Royal Highness the Duke of Cumberland...."

At some point Bancroft had emerged from his quarters. His appearance was ghastly, grey-faced and ill, and he retired after listening to the orders. He was not seen again.

There was one final scrawl on the page.

"Whereas, by mistake, some soldiers took away a greatcoat with gilt buttons belonging to Lieutenant Brevet in the march from Invermoriston, the person or persons who have it will return it to the owner and receive a guinea reward."

He closed the book. Brevet was studying him with cool dark eyes as if anticipating some sarcasm. His own dislike of Brevet was as strong as it was irrational, but until this morning he had never seen it returned with equal fervour.

It was a strange, shattered, haphazard day. The Campbell militia swaggered out of the dimness in the forenoon, laden with plunder from disaffected households and blithely unconcerned over their orders. He had an angry exchange with their cadet, who demanded to see the colonel, and was closeted with Bancroft for nearly an hour; he emerged in a pique and set up camp where he was told, but it was not far enough from the English for whom they felt such hatred and mistrust, and several fights broke out. The last regimental women, with the rest of the men and pack ponies bearing baggage and bread, arrived in the afternoon.

He had never liked women on campaign; if anything they became more inhuman than their men, and the brutal, toughened creatures who had followed the Fourth through the Low Countries were no exception. Thieves, whores, harridans, seldom loyal companions, they had lost every vestige of pity or compassion, and they looked with indifference on the activities of their husbands or lovers in the green glens from Inverness to Fort William. The army was their home, the army's business their livelihood. They could not afford to criticize its methods.

There was, however, no need to revel in them. Four of them were gossiping within earshot, elaborating on the experiences of their journey. He tolerated the singular perversion of their conversation for a time, then he flung open the door and shouted, "God damn you all for unholy bitches," and slammed it. Silence ensued.

The day wore on. His breakfast had been dry bread and brandy; he continued to drink throughout the afternoon, every sound and interruption an assault on his nerves; the obscenities of the women in particular offended him. His head was aching and he felt sick with alcohol, but he was not drunk; all he had achieved was an unendurable, sodden sobriety.

There had been some post, but it was for others waiting at Fort Augustus. There was nothing for him, and he could not write; there were now no innocent words, no reassurances to give her, no contemplation of a future beyond this present hell.

By mid-afternoon he was forced to light the cruisie lamp in order to read the reports from Inverness. They were neither urgent nor of great importance, but they were Bancroft's concern; Bancroft was seldom in the humour to deal with them and was not so disposed today. Brevet had brought them in, with his cool, God-damn-you deference and inscrutable smile. Except for that brief appearance, Bancroft himself had not been seen.

Then he was alone again, or so he thought.

He became conscious of a presence in the room and looked up, resenting the violation of his privacy. The girl was watching him with patient eyes.

"What the hell do you want?"

"I just wanted to ask you summat, sir."

"What is it that it cannot be answered by your sergeant? I am occupied."

"My sergeant won't keep his hands off me long enough to let me talk, sir."

"I see." Then, "Go on."

Her man had died, a common enough problem for a camp follower, but instead of taking another from among his mates as was usually done she had determined to quit the army. However, she had no other means of support, and she had come to ask for his intercession in obtaining the dead man's pay, which was in arrears.

It took him, even in this mood, aback. A private soldier earned sixpence a day, from which any amount his officers thought fit could be stopped for his uniform, ammunition, for offenses, or merely out of malice. He was not familiar with this man's situation, but if he had behaved like the rest of them it was likely the army owed him nothing at all. But his woman had had the courage, or the stupidity, to ask. Doxies had been flogged for less, and men too.

And yet she had not been bold, and stupidity was too harsh a word to apply to her. Innocence might have been a better; there was innocence in her eyes and in the haggard face, and he realized with guilt and a growing self-abhorrence that she could not be more than fifteen or sixteen years old.

"It was impertinent of you to come to me like this," he said, but not ungently.

"I know, sir. But I hoped you'd forgive that in me."

The name came to him. Granville. At the same moment, she sucked in her breath and pressed her hand to her belly. He half rose instinctively and she made a little deprecating gesture to indicate that he should not touch her. It was not proper, and she had no need of his concern.

"Are you ill, Granville?"

"No, sir. I miscarried on the road but I'm brave now."

"You don't look brave." He had thought himself hardened to the bitter life of women in the regiment; maybe he was less so than he had been. "Has anything been done for you?"

"Nothing they can do for me now, sir."

He dragged his thoughts back to the matter at hand.

"So you want your man's pay. What do you think the army owes him?"

"I reckon about two and six, sir. I've been adding it up in my head."

"You're certain."

"Aye, sir. Jack were a good man. He didn't do nothing wrong."

"You're a clever girl, aren't you?" She said nothing, trying to sense his mood, waiting for his amusement or his anger, whatever would come. Certainly not expecting or even wanting his pity. Two and six. Christ, what a thing to die for.

He said, very gently, "Why did you come to me, Granville? There are other officers who might have helped you."

"I heard you was a decent man, sir. There's others that ain't."

There was no answer to that.

Something began to form vaguely in his mind, and he said, "Do you know anything of service? What was your occupation?"

"I were a laundress in a magistrate's house, sir. But then I met Jack, and he looked so handsome I left it for him."

And now you have nothing, not even his child.

"Where do you come from, girl?"

"Bristol, sir."

"That's a long walk home."

"It is, sir, but I walked up here. I reckon I can walk back."

"Very well, I'll do what I can for you about this money. Do you want me to have a word with your sergeant?"

For the first time she revealed fear.

"Oh, no, sir, don't. He'd only make it worse for me. An' it please you, don't."

Her appeal touched him oddly, and, damning himself for the power rank and class gave him over her, he said, "I will not then, if you would prefer it."

She dipped him a curtsey that spoke of servants' halls...all those forgotten memories. She had not even a name to him, a woman's Christian name; she was only another unit of the army, a soldier with a womb.

"Granville." She gazed at him. "Do you have family in Bristol, some reason to return?" She shook her head. "If I offered you service... if my wife offered you service, you might find the employment suitable." She said nothing; the eyes doubted him; her experience with his class had taught her well. "I live in Teesdale— it is a peaceful house. I think you might be happy there. Come to me again in Fort Augustus and tell me your decision."

"I thank you, sir."

"I will not forget," he said, the eyes disconcerting him. "You need not think that of me."

She stood still, looking at the table now, her fingers twisted in her skirt, and he became aware that she was offering repayment in the only currency available to her. He had no doubt that she had served other officers before, to mitigate a punishment for Granville or herself, to secure favours of one kind or another, to hasten pay that was, then as now, always in arrears.

He felt nothing, not even a passing interest in what limited pleasure she could offer. He had been like this since Inverness, dead, drained, impotent, with nothing but a frightening desolation when he contemplated any aspect of sexuality.

The bleakness of his gaze must have given her his answer, and she returned to the anonymity of the ranks.

About five that afternoon there was a peremptory rap on the door. He called, "Come," and continued to read the despatches.

He looked up to find Brevet standing before him, face flushed, but otherwise as inscrutable as ever.

"Colonel Bancroft's compliments, sir, and he wishes to know your decision in the matter of Stirling."

"My what?" He was aware that his afternoon of dissipation was showing: he looked debauched, red-eyed, gaunt; although he had shaved that morning he felt unshaven, unclean. By contrast the boy standing before him was perfectly composed, correct in manner, inflection, stance; the only thing he could not control was the contempt revealed in his eyes. "My decision? What decision is that?"

Brevet's eyes did not change; his mouth tightened a little.

"You are to say whether you or I will go tonight with the warrant for the arrest of Ewen Stirling. Captain Campbell is waiting for the word."

"And what the hell is it to him?"

"The Campbells are to accompany us, sir, unless you have forgotten. They have business on the estate."

He thought, yes, and I have no doubt of what it is.

"Your answer, sir?"

"Since you are so intimately acquainted with the situation, perhaps you should go." Brevet's face fell, but he instantly recovered himself. "Take heart, Lieutenant. If you are out of pocket, as young men of your station usually are, perhaps you will find some trifle or other worth your attention in his house."

Brevet said, coldly, "How many men shall I have under my command, sir?"

"You may take a hundred, if you think your ability extends so far."

He watched the stiff, slim back. A devil was goading him.

"And another matter." Brevet turned. "Have you had any luck recovering your greatcoat? I seem to recall that a substantial reward was offered this morning."

"No, sir. I have not."

"Perhaps a guinea and the prospect of a back cut to ribbons is not sufficient incentive. What do you think?"

When Brevet had gone he laughed for what seemed the first time in months, and resumed his work.

The Scot with whom he had quarrelled over the deployment of the Campbells arrived shortly afterwards.

He neither knocked nor was announced; he merely strode in as if he had never stooped to courtesy in his life. He was a princely little creature with pale green eyes and auburn hair clubbed back from a weak-chinned face, and he wore skintight trews and a heavily laced green coat.

He stalked to the table and put a jewelled hand on the papers. He was flushed with rage.

"Where iss the escort you promised me? It wass to pe mustering py now!" The accent was strongly sibilant, with the inflection of his native Gaelic.

Mordaunt said, "I beg your pardon— Captain, is it?"

"Captain Murray Elcho Campbell. I am to take a traitor tonight. The pird will pe flown—"

"It is no longer my responsibility, Campbell. I suggest you take this matter up with the officer who is to accompany you."

"And who iss this? This Prevet? Where iss he to pe found? I haf had no word, I haf not peen informed—"

The door was still open. Mordaunt went to it and shouted for a sergeant, returned, and stood looking down into the cold, pale eyes.

"As for you, boy, the next time you come to my quarters you'll damned well knock on the door."

The Scot put a hand on his sword hilt and said stiffly, "If I haf given offense, I will meet you where and when you wish," and he said with ineffable weariness, "Oh, go about your business, Campbell."

He heard hooves and Brevet's voice shouting orders in the street, and Elcho swept his bonnet on to his hair and brushed past him.

He had some little peace, during which he sat considering his own plans, then Bancroft summoned him. He went, dreading it.

Bancroft was at supper, one of the Murano goblets before him, and the table laid with silver from his baggage. There was evidence, another plate, an untouched glass, that he had not been or had not intended to be alone.

For a moment he continued with his meal. The salt beef had been cut for him but his left hand was still unaccustomed to the task, and some of the wine had been spilled.

Mordaunt, inexplicably moved, said, "You sent for me."

The eyes came to him, luminous with opium, but whatever the drug had done for Bancroft it had not robbed him of his acute sensitivity. He pushed the plate aside as if ashamed to have been seen engaged in so human an act.

"So you came. I was beginning to think you wouldn't. A glass of wine with you?"

"Thank you, no."

Like Brevet, Bancroft missed nothing, neither his dissipated appearance nor the fumes reeking from him. There was a faint smile, cordial and acquiescent.

"As you wish, of course." He managed to convey the impression that he was seated in his London dining room. "There are a number of issues I want to discuss with you. I have this moment heard of your altercation with Captain Lord Elcho Campbell. I caution you against offending one of so powerful a family... you know who his father is, of course."

"I don't care if his father is the risen Christ. I don't tolerate that behaviour from my servants. I certainly will not tolerate it from him."

The smile was thinner now, and unamused.

"The second reason is selfish. I wish to apologize for what I called you last night."

"I've been called many a worse thing. No doubt what Elcho is calling me now would make bastard pale by comparison."

"You are nothing if not gracious."

"And your handsome apology was nothing if not sincere."

Bancroft gave a slight cough.

"Well. Since we have forgiven one another our trespasses, will you not have that glass after all?"

"I said I would not, thank you."

The hand arrested itself halfway to the bottle. It had been a peacemaking gesture. Now there would be no peace.

"Why so delicate of a sudden? Turning Methody, are you. Or do you think me contagious, Achill; won't you drink with a sodomist tonight?"

There was silence, then the gentle voice again.

"A man may eat and drink with a buggeranto and leave him without contracting his vice. I think you have done this before."

"You'll spare me nothing, will you?"

"What do you spare me? Do you consider my thoughts when you throw this at me every day, how loathesome I am to you, how repulsive? I am not a thing, I am not without sensibility!"

He rose and walked, full of an erratic activity, tapping his hand along the back of the chair; he showed fatigue yet seemed unable to remain still.

"I understand that you have plans to go abroad this evening."

"Yes. I had not thought that they were generally known."

The fleeting smile. For one who rarely left his quarters, Bancroft was remarkably well informed, but then he had eyes and ears in some one else.

"Where do you go, if I may ask?"

"To Glen Mor. The rebel MacNeil has a house there, according to the reports. I propose to go and question his wife, if she may be found. I shall give you a full account in the morning."

"When do you go?"

"I was on the point of leaving when you sent for me."

"You take— how many men with you?"

"None. I had hoped to come and go unremarked."

"There is no question of your coming or going anywhere, so far as I am concerned."

He said, "You misunderstand me, Colonel. I am not seeking your permission."

"You intend to go, in defiance of me?"

It had meant nothing to him before. Now, perversely, it had become an obsession, a symbol, a cause.

"If I must."

Bancroft gave him a long, contemplative stare.

"I think I should have foreseen this. But you're a gambler, ain't you… you like to live on the edge." He resumed his seat, leaned back. "Your behaviour has been increasingly strange over the past few weeks. I would willingly give you the chance to explain it before I come to conclusions I may in future regret."

"I am afraid I don't understand you."

"I think you do. You've been spoiling for something since we left Inverness— for a time I thought it was cunt. Now I see it's to be a fight. You should choose your antagonist with more care." His fingers began their fretful drumming. "When you undertook to defy something tonight, was it the army or was it me? And before you answer, Major, I must remind you that in the eyes of the Crown they are one and the same."

He said nothing. It was no longer clear to him.

Bancroft said, "*Damn* you. Why must you make this so difficult for me? I am not your enemy." Then, "Sit, will you." When there was no response he looked up sharply. "I desire you to sit, if you please."

When he had been seated Bancroft allowed him to remain so for a time; the silence was intended to instill apprehension, as the order to sit was a ploy to remove the advantage of his greater height. He was no stranger to Bancroft's subtleties and when they were understood they could not intimidate. He waited.

Bancroft began to speak in a quiet, conversational voice, examining the veins on his hand; the stump of the right wrist was hidden beneath the table. After a moment he picked up the unused knife and drew lightly on the table's surface, throwing the lamplight back from the blade in blinding, irregular flashes.

"I am going to say something to you, and I hope there will be no other occasion on which I must say it. When we begin to clash as officers we tread on very dangerous ground. I think I hardly need to warn you." The restless hand replaced the knife, tired of its diversion. "When you defy me you flout my authority, you hold me up to the ridicule of the men, you undermine my position with them and the respect they have for me. I cannot allow that to happen; I will not allow it. I will sacrifice my feelings for you if I must to make that clear."

He looked up: the grey eyes were pitiless. "Don't let it come to this, Achill. I've always dreaded it. You may abuse me as a man and perhaps you have a right to, but when you defy me as your colonel you do yourself deadly harm. You can ruin us both this way. Are we understood?"

"Yes."

"And will you continue on this course?"

"Yes."

"You know that I could have you arrested."

"I am aware of that."

The flames leaped at Bancroft's sudden movement. "Then, Christ, why do you persist!"

The wine quivered in the glass; its reflection stilled.

"I have tried to understand you— I told you I was not without sensibility. I know you are a moral man, I know that what you see here offends you and you must reject it. But I will not be your scapegoat."

"Nor I yours, Aeneas."

Bancroft sank back in his chair. The languour of the drug seemed suddenly to have overcome him.

"God's blood, do as you please. I've done with you." A new irritant presented itself. "What did that whore Susannah Granville want with you?"

His informant had been very thorough. Bancroft gave him that flickering smile.

"You need not imagine very much escapes my notice."

"I had not imagined that in the least."

"What did she want?"

"Granville's pay. I'm glad you told me her name. I had forgotten it."

"Insolent slut, what does she plague you for? Why don't she go to Brevet?"

"I do not believe Lieutenant Brevet is very popular among the men. And I am your adjutant, not he."

"I won't have any favours dealt out to the slut. And don't think you can pay her out of your own pocket without my hearing. You may have money to burn... there's no need to play Lord Bountiful with it."

"I had no intention of flouting your wish, sir."

"It is not a wish, it is an order. Endeavour to obey that one, at least."

Mordaunt ignored the barb.

"Very good, sir."

"No, don't get up. I haven't finished with you yet." The fingers drummed again. "I have heard distressing things about your conduct toward Lieutenant Brevet; your mention of him brought them to mind. You have been harassing him. I want it stopped."

"May I ask who was the bearer of this tale?"

The eyes were level and icy and something in their displeasure was not professional.

"I had it from David himself, and you damned well know it's the truth."

"Besides keeping you informed of my plans, does he make a habit of imagining grievances against me like some slighted whore?"

Bancroft said, "That is enough."

"I don't think it is. When a man makes an accusation against me, I prefer it to be made in my presence. And if there has been harassment, it has been on his side, not mine."

"Are you calling him a liar?"

"Of course it's a lie. And as for him, he's beneath contempt."

They were cutting at one another now with controlled, intense violence, always aware of the ears that listened.

"You admit that you despise him."

"I have never denied it. I think he's the devil's cub, and if you were any judge of men you'd know why."

"I am a judge of men. I have need to be."

"Then your judgment must be as blind as Eros."

Bancroft said fiercely, "By God, you overreach yourself!" He was on his feet again, possessed of that feverish tension. "Listen to me now and listen well. I will not have men savaged to humour you. I will not have my officers abused to gratify you, I will not tolerate vendettas between you and the rest of the world. You are a disturbed man and you cannot deal with your command— that is a pity. But if your personal weakness begins to affect the stability of my regiment, then I can promise you what you seem to want. You'll wish you was in hell for all the peace I'll give you."

He reached abruptly for the glass and drained it. His anger seemed to have exhausted him.

"For God's sake try to understand me. If we cannot govern our personal lives we cannot command others, we cannot hope to maintain order among the men. I had hoped we would support one another more, the three of us.... I thought you might put aside this thing between us. Instead, you even turn on *him*. What has he done to you? He has tried to approach you in the most friendly manner—"

"I was not aware of it."

"—but he insists you will have nothing to do with him. You throw him off.... *I* am accustomed to this behaviour from you, I am inured to it. But it is hardly necessary to inflict it upon other officers. It does you no credit." Then, in an odd voice, "He is very young. He has his share of hardships. He is isolated, he feels despised. We are to blame for that, you and I."

"I am sorry for his disappointment, but it does not alter my feeling toward him. Have we anything further to discuss?"

Again that haunting softness of tone. He began to understand what it meant.

Bancroft said again, "He is so very young...."

And he knew.

The face on the edge of the lamplight remained remote. A faint colour had risen to his cheek.

"I wanted—" and hesitated, seeming unable to recall the substance of his conversation. "I wanted him to— pattern himself after you. Officers of your age and experience—" His fingers traced the edge of the table; beneath the hooded lids, his eyes followed them as if the action fascinated him. "Officers of your age are meant to serve— as examples to the young. I have often— you know I have often pointed you out to Lieutenant Brevet for this purpose." He paused. "You can hardly imagine—"

He broke off again, staring at his hand, the shadows thrown by the lace, the auburn hairs on his wrist.

"My dear Achill, you must forgive me. I never meant to do this in your presence."

"What have you done, Aeneas?"

"I've just taken a drop of laudanum; I took it in the wine. I shall feel it in a moment, don't be alarmed." And laughed. "Before your very eyes, my poor Achill. How contemptible of me."

He was pacing now, uncertainly, the full flush of the drug in his face. "I daresay you think this is a pose too, another attitude. Well, by God, I'll strike one for you now, and you can remember it."

He leaned heavily against the wall, abandoned to some private ecstasy.

"Attitudes. I'll strike attitudes for you...."

Time passed. He had become profoundly still, supported by the wall. Imperceptibly, consciousness left him.

"Aeneas."

There was no response.

"Aeneas." The eyes opened, tranquil and unfocused. "How much have you taken, Aeneas?"

A flicker of annoyance, the spirit visibly reinhabiting the body.

"Not enough, if that was what you thought." Pause. "Or what you wanted."

It left him, inevitably. The silence appeared to distress him; he paced again. Twice Mordaunt rose; twice he turned and said sharply, "Stay. Stay. I do not give you leave to go." Then, as his mood grew darker, he came and sat, taking Mordaunt's hand in a cold, dry clasp and staring intensely into his face.

"I wish I knew you. I wish I understood you. I knew you once so well, but not now. Is it my fault? Am I to blame for this, too?"

By gentle increments, Mordaunt removed his hand.

"Are you to blame for what, Aeneas?" Bancroft shook his head and did not answer. Then:

"Do you think I wanted this to happen, that we should be forced to live together like this? Do you think it any easier for me than for you? No. You never think of that, do you, you only think of yourself." He was silent; it seemed he was drawing himself back with effort to thoughts he had gladly left. "What— tell me what I was saying— before."

"It was nothing."

"Don't humour me, damn you! What was it?"

"You were speaking of Brevet."

"To hell with him. Do you think I care for him? You are a thousand times more to me than he is."

He said, "I must go, Aeneas." Bancroft appeared not to have heard.

"I wish— you would let me help you. I wish— no, that ain't the way with you, is it? I cannot say to you, I wish, and hope it will be done. I wish

51

we might have been better friends here, we might have comforted each other more. I might have known that some one gave a God damn for me, but you don't, do you, and there's an end to it. Oh, God— we were friends once— I never wanted to change that. I want only to care for you, to be good to you—"

There was no sound in the room or in the street; his voice could scarcely be heard.

"Why should we live like this, having nothing of each other? We must make our own ways here, we must take human passion where it offers itself, otherwise we shall become... other than human. We are not strangers, you and I... but we behave like strangers now when we most need each other. We are not monsters, but if we go on in this fashion, indifferent to everything, we shall become monsters. I ask only for your comfort, and that you let me give you mine."

Was it not human to want it; to lose oneself for a night, for an hour, to want whatever peace there might be in its tenderness? And he had no doubt that there would be great tenderness; there might even be pleasure; surely for an hour there would be no past and no future.

Bancroft was saying, "That night in London... if it had ended differently.... I think you hate me for it. Don't you?"

"No."

"You pity me, then. I don't want your pity."

"I don't pity you either."

"Then what do you feel for me?" He said nothing. Bancroft said, "Well, that's pretty straight, ain't it," and reached for the bottle.

The hand paused.

"I said I didn't want your pity. I think I do. I would take it gladly... I would welcome anything from you, even your hatred, just to know you wasn't completely indifferent to me."

He was silent for a moment, then he laughed.

"Dear God, how wretched I am. I hope you never know a love like mine in your life, I hope you never suffer as I do. Or if I were a vindictive man I would wish it on you, that you might know a little of what I endure."

The brown glass vial that held his laudanum stood on the table beyond his reach. When Mordaunt did not oblige him he said, "Oh, for God's sake, man! Can't you see I am in pain?"

The characteristic bitterness of opium filled the damp air.

"I shall want to see you tonight when you return from Glen Mor."

The vial glinted as he set it down. At the far end of the table the other goblet and the plate sat forsaken.

A fleeting, acerbic smile.

"He thinks he takes your place. But he can't fill it."
Mordaunt left him.

One more memory rising out of the night, of all the nights he had left Bancroft: the night in London, the night in Inverness, and all the naked mornings that had followed them. After that night in London he had wept, and awakened in her bed with the taste of debauchery in his mouth, and the memory of another house and another caress receding with the darkness. And the night of Wednesday, the sixteenth of April, in Inverness, when he had gone to the Charity School, the army's makeshift hospital, and found Bancroft lying in his bloody uniform, his arm crudely bound and his gold-laced coat thrown over him, shocked, drugged, nearly insensible, but still attempting to speak. He had sat for half an hour with the cold, dry hand in his, then, when he had laid it down, Bancroft had clasped his fingers more urgently, as if frightened to be left alone.

Stay....

But he had gone, and walked through the town, ignoring the burial parties, the smoking torches, the shouts, the songs, the challenges, the prisoners shot in the churchyard, the drunken officers lounging in the streets. The hours of hard drinking that followed, to drive the horror from his mind; the whore he found in the dirty narrow street; the hovel near the river. The filth and the cold and the stench and the coarse sheets and the woman who was urging him with rough, unsubtle hands to an act he could not perform, attempting by every means to stimulate him, although he knew there would be no congress between them. Then she had offered fellatio, which had not aroused him, and a refinement upon intercourse which she undertook for greater pay, and, revolted and sick with alcohol and impotence, he had beaten her: she had screamed abuse at him, directing him to sodomy, as his taste was not inclined to cunt.

Knowing he would have killed her had he stayed, he had staggered back into the street and stood by the river with Bancroft's watch in his hand, crying, because he believed it was the truth.

Since then, nothing, save this sense of being damned, of intense sexual revulsion and perverse, erotic dreams, and this other bitter, relentless passion, which was every hour harder to resist. Tonight he had come close to yielding to it, as if by abandoning himself to it he could at last find peace.

From the dimness, from the calm night and the silence, came a memory of Catherine: a salvation, an ephemeral sweetness. He clung to it, attempting to recall it in exquisite detail, to recall everything of their brief time together, and of the times and the passions before her, Italy, and the rapture of music;

clinging to it, to the past and its sanity, like a drowning man, like a man without hope.

It was not yet nine o'clock, and Ewen Stirling was at supper with his first cousin, Coinneach Stirling of Carr, an officer in the French army. A young ghillie was serving them, and several other men, Ewen's bodyguard, were stationed around the room and throughout the house.

The house itself was quiet, and both men seemed at ease, but a pistol lay at half-cock near Coinneach's hand and only Ewen was unarmed; he glanced up once or twice to reassure himself before returning to his meal. He was a fair, frail man with greyish blue eyes and an ethereal face, and he spoke to his cousin with a pronounced stammer. He had lived in Scotland for only three of his thirty-one years.

He was devoutly Catholic, and he had prayed fervently in the night for guidance, knowing government troops were in Glen Sian, unsure of their purpose but suspecting the worst. He had sent his wife Elspeth and his son to safety, but knowing himself innocent of any involvement in the rising he had taken no such personal measures; only his cousin was privy to his political inclinations. So he waited, trusting in God and believing steadfastly in the innate decency and justice of all men.

The first member of his household to die was the keeper of his gates, who called out to the horsemen approaching in the dimness a little after nine. He did not see their faces, and he died without raising the alarm, his head cleft from skull to chin by a Campbell who replied to his challenge by silencing him forever.

The house was taken within fifteen minutes. The fighting was sharp and savagely cruel; the floors were running with blood, not in rivulets but sheets, before the last man died.

Coinneach Stirling of Carr, shielding Ewen, was cut down even as he threw away the pistol in his left hand and thrust with the broadsword in his right. His corpse in its handsome, hated French coat was dragged into the hall and robbed, stripped and mutilated, then spat upon, drenched with urine and decapitated. Ewen, choking on the vomit of horror, was beaten with the butt of a musket and kicked repeatedly in the groin. At length he lay still, and the soldiers took his wedding ring, and ripped the filmy Mechlin lace from his wrists as a gift for one of their whores.

He clung to the edge of consciousness, hearing the clash of arms and the screams of women and the voice of some one who seemed to be in command. He tried to raise his head, but the taste of blood filled his mouth and he fell into the darkness that was opening for him.

David Brevet halted in the domed entrance hall, looking about him with interest and some surprise. The house was a looter's paradise; Ewen Stirling had brought the elegance of France back with him to his inheritance and made this his own very gracious, very private world. Having shattered it, the invaders were destroying what they could not easily carry away.

Brevet picked his way among the corpses on the parquet floor. He had just come from the stables where three boys had been found cowering. He had looked them over distastefully, indulged himself a little, and had them hanged; their bodies were still jerking outside.

He paced through the hall, his sword still sheathed, his hands behind his back. His eyes narrowed coldly when they saw what remained of Coinneach Stirling, but he said only, "Gentlemen, I must urge you to show a little more restraint," and walked on.

The girl came from nowhere. Her gown and her face were splashed with blood, and when she threw herself on her knees, her arms fastening about his legs, some of the blood transferred itself to his stainless breeches. He regarded her for a moment, his mouth curled in contempt, then he kicked her away from him as if she were a dog and let the men who wanted her have her. They raped her one after the other, oblivious to his presence or indifferent to it, until the sight of their naked, rampant sexes became increasingly offensive to him, and he told them to hole the slut elsewhere.

"And you will oblige me by doing it in private. This is not a brothel."

Aroused and annoyed at his own response, he went on with his solitary wanderings.

On a table he found several goblets of Belgian crystal and a bottle of claret. He poured a glass and took it with him.

The house was full of little treasures. He went from room to room, looting with discernment: a lacquered snuffbox from a Paris jeweller, several miniatures in gold filigree, a pack of French playing cards of unusual design.

He came to a white-panelled door, pushed it open. The morning room apparently, a serene, wholly feminine retreat; the walls were hung with pale yellow silk and a bowl of yellow roses stood on the mantel; the furniture was of some pale wood, ash-grey, with a lovely grain. The room appeared to be full of sunlight.

Glass in hand, he crossed the carpet to the escritoire and pried open its locked drawers, splintering the wood. He rummaged desultorily, finding papers, letters, household accounts and what appeared to be a half-finished manuscript. His Italian was not what it might have been, and yet, rifling idly through the pages, he grasped the essence: a cycle of twelve sonnets in the Petrarchan mode. He tossed the manuscript aside to peruse more fully later.

More sound from upstairs, the shattering of glass. It was painful to his ears, and he left the escritoire long enough to close the white door against it. He caught a glimpse of himself in a mirror as he did so; his face was pale but composed, a study in perfect dispassion.

He wandered about the room, pocketing small, expensive trifles, running reminiscent fingers over the brocade of the chairs, recalling things and places he had not thought of in months. Eventually he finished his claret and put the goblet down, opened the door and went out, leaving the room, for the moment, to its peace.

The hall was quieter, and there were fewer, fainter sounds from the upper regions of the house, the soaring dome that sent whispers down the wide, spiralling staircase. He heard voices but by the accent he knew them to be Campbells, roaming the gallery like wolves in search of prey.

A man was still alive at the foot of the stairs; he had crawled a few paces, leaving smears of excrement on the floor. There was something hideous about his legless progress... relentless, obscene. It was almost a relief to Brevet when he died.

Someone was standing at his elbow, splashed from waist to gaitered foot with blood.

"We have Stirling, sir."

Brevet looked a last time at the dismembered limbs, repressed a shudder, and said, "Take me to him."

He was keenly disappointed in what he saw: a fragile, beaten man shackled hand and foot and propped up on a settee. His head lolled, and the blood from his mouth and nose and left ear were staining the brocade.

Brevet gestured for light and some one proffered a taper. He held it close to the ruined face and struck it sharply, twice, with the back of his hand to command its attention. The eyes opened, a strange, slate blue, and Ewen Stirling observed him with a distance and reserve that dismissed into nonexistence the irons on his wrists and the desolation made of his house.

"You are under arrest." The eyes did not lose their detachment, as if no humiliation offered his body could touch his mind or spirit, or the hidden recesses of his heart.

Brevet returned to the morning room and brought the sonnets from the escritoire. Only then did a painful incandescence leap into the eyes.

He burned them. Once Ewen cried out, half in English, half in French, pleading that they be spared. Brevet marked the accent and the stammer and mocked him delicately for both.

When the papers were ashes, Ewen turned his face away and wept. Brevet said gently, teasingly, "Oh come, sir, come, come. You unman yourself."

The quiet, anguished sobbing went on, like a woman weeping for the loss of a beloved child.

Brevet said, "Bring him out after me. As for the rest of this, burn it."

At about the same hour, Mordaunt reached the Bridge of Sian.

He had heard the waterfall: as he passed over the bridge he saw the Sian throwing itself two hundred feet into the dark gorge of Glen Mor. After its tumultuous descent it ran into peat-brown shallows; the air was close and filled with spray and insects. The silence, but for the roar of water, was intense.

He left the bridge and rejoined the track.

He had seen Glen Mor in a dozen guises, in other villages, near other rivers, in other glens of such stark beauty: a few scattered crofts, cattle standing in a sea of weeds, sheer walls of slate seamed with water and softened with mist or cloud or passing shadow. They were seldom prosperous, they were always isolated, straggling habitations on the edge of desolation. There had been, there would be, other Glen Mors. There was no reason to mark this place.

He found the manse; there were no other houses of any distinction. It was a bleak place of local stone, with another low lightless building, the church, adjoining it; the house was surrounded on three sides by graves, and a garden behind a wall.

He dismounted and drew his sword, and hammered on the door with the hilt. There was no response, and he repeated the action until its violence became an irrational violence of thought, outrage that he should be forced to behave in this manner, that whatever he knew himself to be he would be perceived only as the invader, feared and hated as if this bloody aftermath were the execution of some personal vengeance... then the bolts scraped back and the door was opened.

He thought her a child: a moment later he saw his mistake, but she was still no more than seventeen. In one hand she held a candle and it flickered in the fitful wind, revealing a cloud of dark hair and dark eyes; the other hand held a pistol, inlaid with silver, and almost antique.

"Is this the house of Patrick Inglis MacNeil?"

"Who are you?"

"I am Major Mordaunt-Collins, of His Majesty's Fourth regiment of foot. May I come in?"

She set the candle on a table, and he saw the wedding ring, then she was behind him again and the bolts were drawn.

"What do you want with me?"

"My business is with your husband, and concerns no other person."

"He is away. With a sick parishioner. I do not expect him back."

The eyes were grey, not dark, and he felt their hatred and suspicion like a physical assault.

"Unless your sick parishioner is a prince of the House of Stuart, I am forced to call you a liar."

Her face was expressionless, the hatred now concealed. A faint fragrance clung to her clothing, elusive and disconcerting.

"He has been gone for a year. They told me he was dead."

"He is alive."

There was the barest perceptible pause. Then she said, "I did not know."

The truth would be a simple matter, a little matter of pain: he sensed that she read his thoughts. Then she spoke again: her voice was indefinably accented; after years of service among men from every part of Britain, he could not identify it.

"I see you doubt me. Will you walk into my kitchen then, while I light another candle? You will want to search the house."

"That is not necessary."

"But I insist. I would not want you to think I was concealing my husband, or, God forbid, the Prince."

She preceded him, the fragrance clinging to the folds of her gown. They came into an ordinary kitchen, dark, stone-flagged, with flitches of meat suspended from the ceiling; he was obliged to bend his head beneath the lintel. She laid the pistol down and took another candlestick from the mantel; there was a blue earthenware jug filled with cranesbill on the mantelpiece, the papery petals falling. The peace, the perfect absence of sound was intense, almost unnatural.

"Come with me," she said.

The house was old, a warren of dark passageways and roughly plastered walls. She walked ahead, opening doors with deliberation, forcing upon him the search he had not wanted to make, and he followed, aching with fatigue and pain, his senses numbed, his sabre sheathed.

Another room; the pervasive fragrance. Among the sparse furnishings, a box-bed with wooden shutters and a child's cot.

"Come in, sir. This is my boudoir. My bed, my daughter's cot. You may search the bedclothes, there may be some one hiding there—"

He took her by the shoulder and terror sprang into her face. Fear of him, fear of rape, fear of murder, fear for her absent husband and for the child beside her; then it veiled itself and she stood as if turned to stone.

"Enough. Your point is made." The child was crying now, awakened by the candlelight or their voices. "Go to her."

She shrank away, trembling, her cheek pressed to the small dark head; her daughter was instantly silent, regarding the stranger over her shoulder with huge, solemn eyes.

"How old is she?"

"...Nine months. Have you children?"

"No."

She walked, deeply withdrawn, until the child's eyes closed and she seemed to drowse.

"What is her name?"

"Margaret."

"Is that your name?"

"....No.... Mine is... Isabel." Then, curtly, as if she had divulged some secret, "She will sleep now."

In the kitchen once more, she took the pistol from the table where she had left it.

"Is your business with me finished?"

"I shall wait with you a while, if you have no objection."

He sat near the fire. The dampness had reawakened the ghosts of Dettingen; the damaged eardrum was acutely painful. She sat watching him, the pistol in her hand.

After a time he said, "Do you mean to kill me with that?" She said nothing. "Then for God's sake put it down."

She did so, very quietly, and he knew as surely as if he had handled it that it was not loaded.

There was silence, and then a furtive rustling.

She said faintly, "Mice. What did you think it was?" and leaned back, her entire body surrendering itself to indifference.

Minutes passed; the hallucination deepened, the illusion of peace.

"What have they done in Glen Sian?"

"It was burned."

There was a long silence. Then, "Have you a watch? What is the time?"

He opened the guard and held it to the firelight. Not quite eleven.

"You were expecting some one, perhaps?"

"My husband's sister lives with me.... I only wanted to know."

"Another sick parishioner, no doubt."

"She is a midwife, and birth and death are at God's discretion, not ours."

Silence, and a faint sound of rain, and the sweet, elusive perfume. He opened his eyes; she was kneeling by the chair, staring into his face. She had not touched him, although the coolness of her fingertips was palpable on his skin.

"Are you ill?"

"No," although his perception had become distorted; he did not know how much time had passed. "No. I was merely thinking."

"I hope they were kind thoughts."

"Yes."

"I hope they were healing thoughts."

Her eyes held his, cool and luminous, then she looked away. After a moment, she withdrew her hand.

"I am going upstairs to see my daughter."

In her absence he examined the hearthstone; one of the roughly dressed slates had been disturbed. There was a scattering of ash on it, and congealed blood.

He lifted it and found what he had expected: louis d'or, a map crudely drawn on canvas, a letter. He broke the seal; it was written in cipher, and also stained with blood.

She was returning.

She paused in the doorway, pulling a shawl around her shoulders, lifting the hair from her neck. The hands came down slowly when she saw what he was holding.

"Did you know of these?"

"I knew they would be there, if not tonight, then another night."

"They cannot help him now, or his cause. The cause is lost."

She leaned against the door, her head bent. He allowed the letter to fall back into its place.

He became conscious of her following him in the twilight. Her face was shadowed: she might have been any woman. This might have been any night, any path.

The wind had not died, and it threw her hair across her eyes; she did not brush it away.

"You think I lied to you."

"No."

"You think I lied when I said he has been gone so long. I told the truth."

He brushed the concealing hair from her face; she did not respond, nor did she resist him. He touched the face, the brows, the lashes, the bones beneath the skin. She tried to speak; he silenced her with his fingertips, with the same delicacy, and kissed her. Her resistance was slight, and very sweet the small struggle to subdue it. She stood then, and allowed him to do what he wanted; her hair blinded him, its fragrance intoxicating, the warmth of her skin against his lips the bitterness of the perfume. The living body yielded to him, the mouth, the eyes, the breast.

It was enough. He caressed her once more, a slow, lingering passage of fingertips, of delicate sensuality, and then he walked through the gate into the dimness. There were no witnesses; the night was empty, and he was alone.

The sky was sullen, and thickly clouded; a few drops of rain spattered his cheek as he rode the last mile. There were torches burning below in the cup of shadows that held Glen Sian, and the picquets were strung out across the steep road with fixed bayonets.

He reined in long enough to throw back a curt countersign to their shouted challenge; he doubted if they had even seen his face. He put two hundred yards between himself and the muskets, almost expecting a bullet in the back, but they were notoriously poor marksmen, and the Brown Bess was useless beyond that range.

He did not know precisely where he was going until he reached the place. Brevet's quarters: he opened the door. Brevet and Murray Elcho Campbell were at cards, a bottle on the table between them. Brevet looked up with a wild expression of mingled dread and consternation, which he quickly extinguished, unfolding himself from the bench where he had been lounging and murmuring the appropriate courtesies. His fine, dark-eyed face was flushed, his mouth a little slack; his formerly immaculate clothing was bloodstained about the knees. Elcho remained seated, his short legs splayed, reddish hair pulling out of its stiff, pomaded side curls; the lamplight glittered on his jewelled fingers, which seemed to display more rings than before.

Brevet was making some languid gesture toward the bottle.

"Hard riding, was it, sir?"

Elcho tittered. He, too, was drunk, and his eyes were strangely glazed.

"Where is Stirling of Glen Sian?"

An equally languid smile.

"Want to see him, do you? Very well." To Elcho, with a graceful inclination of the head, "Y'servant, sir. Bear with me. This will not take long."

They stepped into the street, walked a short distance. Bastard, he thought, insolent young bastard. Two sentries stood by a door. At Brevet's command it was unbolted and opened.

The thing on the floor resolved itself into a man, sleeping, unconscious, or dead. He had been severely beaten, and his clothing was stained with the emissions of terror. He was shackled.

Brevet stood over him.

"Reveillez-vous, m'sieur! Bon matin!" His French was faultless, and he punctuated it with kicks to the groin and chest. When he received no response he leaned down and pulled up the head by its hair. The face was disfigured beyond humanity, a mask of blood with an opened mouth.

"Have you seen enough, Major?"

The mouth was smeared with excrement.

"Yes. Enough."

They returned to the street. The night seemed darker; most of the torches had been doused, although one was still burning. Brevet glanced toward it.

"Going in to him? I doubt you'll find him sensible at this hour— that is, if you can rouse him at all."

He did not answer, and Brevet left him. Another cold spatter of rain struck his cheek. He walked toward the light.

The room was as he had left it, if anything colder than before, closer, fouler, in every way more like a cell. Bancroft was sitting motionless, his back to the damp stone wall, one booted leg stretched out and his arm resting on the knee. He had removed his coat and the powdered wig as if abandoning with them the authority they represented, and his hair was disordered, the grey at the temples nakedly apparent.

"David?"

Some emotion flickered in the vague, brilliant eyes, then Bancroft shielded them from the flare of the lamp.

"Have you seen Stirling of Glen Sian?"

"Who? .... No. Brevet... brought him in, I'm in no state. I'll see him tomorrow."

"I think it only fair to tell you he may be dead by then."

The eyes searched him with genuine surprise.

"Dead? Why should he be dead? He was only—"

"Beaten within an inch of his life, and now he's lying in his filth where your little bum-boy threw him. Were those your orders?"

There was a raw, hideous silence.

"What did you call him?"

"What would you prefer? Catamite? But it's only boys who are called catamites, isn't it? Little, pretty boys. So I'll call him what I like, your shit-hunting whore of a Brevet."

The silence deepened, ghastly as a wound.

Bancroft said, "If you ever speak to me again in that manner, I will have you broke. *Broke.* Do you understand me?" There was no pain in the eyes, no affront; there was nothing. "I'll have your apology now, and not another word."

The silence went on.

"Say it," and then again, "Say it," and finally, "Apologize to me, God damn you!"

"I will not."

"Oh, but you will, or I'll have you before a—"

"Court-martial? Of what would you accuse me that does not implicate you, too?" Bancroft was staring at him. "So it's only another posture, isn't it, another attitude. They don't signify to me, Aeneas."

His hands were trembling, as they had sometimes done after action, when that fist of icy indifference unclasped him and naked fear took its place.

Bancroft was saying, "....No, by God, it don't signify. I've heard this too, from men like you. I knew you'd come to it."

"I want that poor bastard looked to at once."

The vague eyes blazed.

"When I want your God damned orders, I'll ask for them! And who in hell's name are you to tell me what to do? Is that all you have to say to me?"

Then he coughed, and when the spasm had passed he groped back to the bench.

"... Christ, always cold in this filthy place. I used to walk in the park in the summer evenings... watch the Household Brigade. All the whores used to come after me... poor bitches, they didn't know." His mind drifted. "My house... once in my house...." Then he paused, perhaps remembering, perhaps pushing away some painful thought. "I wonder has Revel paid my tailor yet. I shall want a new coat after this, all the blood and piss on the other...."

Mordaunt spoke but it went unheard, or perhaps not entirely. The eyes came to him again, reaching for him like hands.

"You came to tell me something. What was it? Why did you come?"

"I have just returned from Glen Mor."

"Yes. I remember. Go on."

"There is nothing else to say."

"Nonsense. What did you learn?"

"I told you, nothing of consequence."

"Did you see MacNeil's wife?"

"Yes."

"What did you make of her, eh? What did she tell you?" But the questions were desultory: the eyes had lost interest.

"Shall I report to you again in the morning, sir?"

Bancroft threw back his head.

"No, by the living God, you'll report to me now! Or do you think I'm too damned drunk to understand you? Or is it that you don't want to tell me about *your* little whore, eh? We've had mine, haven't we, so why may we not hear about yours?"

He said nothing, controlling what he knew was a fatal impulse.

"You fucked her, didn't you, that bitch in Glen Mor.... Didn't you?"

"No."

"You're a liar." There was silence; he was watched with a bitter, quizzical smile. "You bloody, bloody liar. What do you think I am— what the fucking hell do you think I am? Take me for anything but not a fool! You went for

63

a woman, did you think I didn't know? Any woman, any piece of cunt, that was all you wanted—"

"That is not true."

"It *is* true."

"It is not true, and if it were, it would be none of your God damned affair."

There were cards lying on the table. Bancroft began to rearrange them.

"Get out," he said. "You sicken me."

Mordaunt picked up his hat; the movement seemed to take hours to accomplish.

"Achill." He stood with his back to the room, his hand motionless on the latch. "Achill, stay. I thought you was dead, you was gone so long.... Christ, do you want me to grovel? Be a friend to me tonight, only for a little while."

He stood, the iron beneath his fingers cold now with his sweat.

"Help me. Stay with me. I thought such strange things while you was gone."

Outside, from the street, the faint sound of voices and hooves. The rain had begun once more, whispering in the darkness.

"Achill...."

He thought of sleep, and the release it would bring, from the memories of her face and the taste of her mouth. But it was not over, there would be more. He wondered if he could endure it.

Bancroft was staring at the cards, his hand moving among them; the patterns he made were known only to himself.

"I never asked for this. I thought it would pass. I tried to rid myself of it. Now I let it be. I think I have paid enough, but you make me pay more every day." He turned up a card, put it aside. "Sometimes— are you there? Are you listening?"

Mordaunt said nothing.

"I want to leave the army— I've thought of it, but I can't. I have nowhere else to go, do you see. I could live in London but I hate that house now...." He pressed his hand to his eyes. "Christ, sometimes I think I'm going mad— I go down and down to such darkness.... I dreamed of you dead tonight. And when I woke, my God, how I wept for you, and you won't even look at me. I would have died for you a hundred times— why can you not love me?"

"You must not talk like this. Not to me, not to any one."

"Why not? Are you ashamed? I am not. I would die for you, *die* for you, and you repay me this way, you give yourself to some poxy whore, some punk.... Can you doubt me? Can you think I would not love you? That I would hurt you, betray you? That I would do you harm? You go to some whore when you know that I... could... give you love, I could care for you—"

"You must stop this, Aeneas. I cannot listen to it."

Bancroft stared at him, anguished.

"Do you *fear* me? Have I given you cause to fear me?"

"No."

"Look at me."

"Aeneas—"

"Look at me! Yes. I see. You have tried to hate me, haven't you? And I have tried to hate you— but you still care for me, don't you? You was my friend once, you came to something in me, whatever it was.... *I* have not changed, I am who I was then, still the same man... I am still that man who was your friend."

"Aeneas—"

"Why, why do you hate me? Because this is unnatural, that I should feel these things, that I should want you? Why can there be no love between us? Why do you hate me for my love when I offer it to you with such— oh God— such... tenderness, when I would not hurt you for the world! You hurt *me*, again and again until you could not hurt me more if you should kill me."

"Aeneas—" It went unheard. "These thoughts do you no good. Nor me. Leave them."

But they could not be left. Bancroft was speaking again, vague, wandering reminiscences, shot with moments of horrifying clarity: betrayal, blackmail, degradation, names, places, acts committed, letters written and burned. A lost, agonized litany of things impossible to listen to, things no one should have heard... ending with a hopeless, bitter gesture of love, of desire, of submission, without caution, without reserve. When it was not acknowledged he said only, "I thought you had changed your mind."

Then, "Please go. I shall ask nothing of you. You may do as you wish about this. But I will bear no more from you. If you hurt me, I shall not be responsible for what I do. Go."

He said it again, almost gently, and Mordaunt left him, knowing that one way or another it was for the last time.

III

The twilight of night became the dawn; a fine rain was still falling. Margaret Campbell had not slept, although the children seemed at peace who lay against her, her son's back to hers and the heir of Glen Sian, James Gordon Gunn Stirling, aged five years, in her arms. There was no sound from the other side of the shieling where Elspeth Stirling was sleeping.

She was a white lily of a girl, Franco-Scots and convent-bred, and she thought Margaret a whore and a savage. Their only language of communication was French, which Margaret had almost forgotten. Neither spoke English.

Elspeth was fretful, restless, and pregnant, and obsessed with a privacy which could not be maintained in a single room. She had wept most of the night, and sank into an exhausted sleep an hour before dawn; small wonder, Margaret thought, that her son had left her and sought his bed among humbler company on the floor.

She touched his face now, and as if he sensed this small betrayal her own son Malcolm woke.

She stroked his sallow cheek and kissed him, although he did not like physical contact.

"Dhia dhuit, 'ille."

He ignored the blessing and said, "Where are you going?"

She moved silently, trying to warm herself; the fire had long been doused.

"Down to Ardsian. Be quiet now."

"I'll come with you," he said.

"No. And don't let her follow me, when God knows what she could find."

"I have a knife."

"I will not want your knife."

There was no further argument. He rose lightly, so as not to disturb the sleeping child, and pulled on his breeches; as always, he covered his nakedness as quickly as possible, and she found this dignity in one so young both affecting and amusing. She smiled at him with great tenderness. He did not respond.

"Go and wash your face, 'ille."

He moved like a shadow to the door. She whispered his name, and he halted.

"Are you frightened?"

He said, "I'm not frightened of anything," and went out.

Approaching Ardsian from the rear, she saw the smouldering piles of furniture and carpet they had burned to give their officers the impression that they had fired the house. She could not imagine what perverted mercy or indolence had prompted this action.

She went first to the stables, from which every horse had been taken. The three corpses were still hanging, drenched with the morning's rain; after obscene effort she cut them down. She sat for a time on the wet cobbles with the head of the youngest in her lap; eventually she left them to the curious peace, the rain whispering, and walked into the house.

The same grey soft peace, the silence of rain. She was shoeless and her feet made no sound, and her footprints were blood.

She found the dead, the man who had crawled like a bleeding snail, his bowels spilled on the floor, the decapitated Coinneach Stirling, his genitals hacked and placed in his hands. And others, men and boys, some little older than her son. She examined them all, searching for Ewen, and when she could not identify him she vomited with horror and relief.

The sound of the rain filled the house with whispers, the voices of the dead.

She came upon Siubhan MacGregor on a blood-soaked bed upstairs, bound with the cords of the hangings. The rain was running on the mullioned panes with a sigh like breathing, and she thought her alive, then she went further into the shadows of the room and saw the bone-handled knife protruding from her vagina. The red-gold hair had been cut from her head; it would fetch a fair price from some southern wigmaker, despite its unfashionable colour.

Numbly, and with a terrible dread, she freed the dead wrists and ankles, and took the wet plaid from her own shoulders and covered her.

The beauty of God is in thy face, the Son of God is protecting thee, the King of the stars is before thee ...

She walked along the gallery. The house seemed full of whispers, of the sound of the rain.

As she descended the spattered stairs she saw that she was not alone.

She knew who he was, although she had not seen him for several years, and time and war and privation had killed the youth of memory. But she recognized the eyes, and the tawny hair, and the chieftain's bonnet he affected, held loosely now, with the eagle's feather brushing a raw-skinned thigh.

"God and Mary be with you, Máiréad. Now, and in the days to come."

She gazed at him, unable to look away from the gently swaying bonnet. One of his fingers had been severed.

"You had better go on to old Caelighn's house now, and see what your kinsmen did there."

She dared not pass or turn her back on him, but he made no further gesture, nor spoke, and when she brushed by him he stood motionless, head bent, hand lightly resting on the hilt of his broadsword, staring at the mutilated corpse.

It was perhaps two miles' walk, and she encountered nothing, neither the living nor the dead. The doors were standing open. She entered, knowing what she would find.

She covered their faces and left them, fearing them in death, believing in their spirits. The sound of the rain went on.

When her tears came, it was not for them or for Murdoch or for Ewen, but for herself and her son that she wept.

The roar of Sian water seemed louder yet in the morning stillness.

They entered Glen Mor, leaving the sound of the waterfall for the silence of the track. Mordaunt rode without speaking.

The rain grew lighter and ceased; the sheer slate walls crept closer, and the crofts were visible. Brevet reined in with some inanity on his lips, and he swore savagely at him to keep quiet. Brevet flushed and said in a controlled voice, "I am a King's officer, sir, as you are, and I will not be spoken to like a dog." He spurred to the rear of the column and lashed out a command. The drum was silent.

Bayonets were fixed, although Mordaunt did not recall having given the order.

They had marched on dry bread and water, five miles on a cold morning at seventy-five paces to the minute. The air was unbearably sweet with the fragrance after rain, and a lark was mounting eastward into a torn sky.

Three children were driving cattle into a field white with weed; one was an adolescent girl, taller than the others, and they were all singing and shouting in high voices, driving the cattle with sticks while a dog ran bounding in the weed. Then they stopped, seeing the men and the horses, and the cattle were forgotten.

He killed the girl first, to spare her what a slower death would mean.

The rest was never possible to recall in sequence, or with clarity. He remembered approaching the manse, the fulsome, blood-red roses, the wall, the gate, the graves. His hands were running with blood, although he did not know how he had acquired it, and his clothing was spattered with blood: he seemed unable to speak, or reason, as though in the grip of nightmare. A woman was screaming, and the sound was unbearable; a child cried and was abruptly silent.

He stared down at the bleached knuckles on the hilt of his sword, blood congealing on the blade, the lanyard soaked with blood. There was blood beneath his nails. His arm and his shoulder were trembling.

He covered his eyes with his bloody hand, and there was silence... silence, and then, as though in nightmare or in madness, indistinguishable voices... an endless litany of voices, among them, unrecognized, his own.

Oh God, help me, help me.

She was standing on the doorstep of the manse, as if going in or having just come out. She wore the dark red gown of the previous night.

Her eyes seemed to hold his, and her lips moved, but whatever she was attempting to say to him he could not understand it. It might have been a plea for help, for mercy, or a curse, he never knew. Then she broke away and began to run; the heavy mud in the street sucked at her ankles and was clinging to her skirts. He fired once, not meaning to hit, only to delay her; she staggered, as though at some impact he could not perceive, and then was running again.

The second and third shots were fired simultaneously, by himself and by another. One shot smashed into her back. He thought she died instantly: the ball had penetrated her spine.

He could not remember going to her, how he came to be beside her. She was lying in the mud, her arms outflung, and he saw that the fingers of her right hand were a bloody tangle of bone and sinew. He touched her hair, which was wet with blood, and turned her face toward him.

One eye was open, the lashes fanned against the brow. The other eye had vanished; nothing remained but a gaping socket, fragments of bone, the matter of the brain. The socket steamed faintly, tendrils of blood and vitreous tissue welling from it, running over his wrist; and, subtly, from the hair he held, rose the sweet, bitter perfume.

Smoke caught at his throat. They were trying to fire the dwellings in the street but the heather thatching was soaked and would not burn. One man was standing at the manse gate with an uplifted torch. There was no sign of Brevet.

He came to his feet, loading mechanically. The ball struck stone with a scream and he heard the incredulous curse. No one else approached.

He bent over her again, staring into her face, closing the remaining eyelid. The lashes and the mouth, except where her blood and the humours of the shattered eye had splashed them, were as beautifully drawn as when his lips had touched them; he stroked the strands away from her cheek and turned the spilling socket into her hair, then he wrapped the wounded hand in a fold of her gown, taking an exaggerated care with the fingers. The hideousness of her death concealed, he left her and went into the house.

He walked through it, the lanyard stiffened around his wrist, the hilt biting into his palm. The kitchen. He bent his head to enter. The light here was grey, and the same candles were on the mantel, burning; there was a kettle on a crane over the fire, boiled dry. The papers were still beneath the hearthstone, the stone scattered with paper-dry petals.

He burned them, and extinguished the candles, then he turned his attention to the child.

In the years and the nightmares and the imperfect recollections that followed, he never left her: in nightmare, others fired the house, and he burned with her, as she would have burned; sometimes in dreams he killed her, as others would have killed her, with the point of the sword, by strangulation, by smashing the tender skull; sometimes, hideously, the dream of death was perverted by the memory of sexual abuse he had witnessed, and had been powerless to prevent. In his dreams, he died with her. He did not recall leaving the house.

Glen Mor when they withdrew was wrapping itself in a shroud, veils of mist descending from the heights to mingle with the smoke.

He rode to the rear, having given Brevet his place in the van. After one startled glance at him, Brevet made no objection.

In Glen Sian he dismissed the men and sent Brevet away; there was no doubt where he would go first; he would be more than eager to carry the news. He went to his quarters.

He threw his hat on the floor and sat, ignoring repeated summonses from a sergeant to attend on Bancroft. At length he became aware of a cold voice outside, demanding that he open the door; the latch came up and Brevet stepped in, flicking some indefinable speck from his lapels. His haughty young face was rather pale.

"Colonel Bancroft requires you to wait on him at once, sir."

"Tell Colonel Bancroft to go to hell."

Not a muscle of the face moved.

"With respect, sir—"

"Please carry my message, Lieutenant."

Brevet executed a stiff salute, turned on his heel, and went out.

Time went on, and the silence, and the rain. Brevet returned, his manner remote.

"You are ordered to report forthwith to Colonel Bancroft. I am to escort you there. I shall do so under arms if necessary."

He looked up. The face seemed to swim in his vision: the fine, girlish features and dark eyes, the full red mouth. His head was aching, his neck, his shoulder.

He stood. Brevet's eyes ran distastefully over his stained clothing.

"Your hat, sir."

"Leave it. I won't want it."

Bareheaded, he walked out into the rain, stood a minute outside Bancroft's quarters with his face uplifted to it.

Brevet opened the door and stepped back, to let him go in first.

By evening most of it had become obscured, and would never be remembered, no matter how often he was questioned. The first words Bancroft spoke to him, what he said in return, what he was asked concerning Glen Mor and his behaviour there. He remembered only that his answers did not please, and Bancroft struck him first, an open-handed slap across the face.

He hit back, not once, although once was enough, was criminal. Bancroft fell and attempted to rise, spitting blood and obscenities; he remembered dragging him to his feet and grinding with his body against the wall, the fluent curses in his ear, and, toward the last, Bancroft's knee driving up for his groin. He remembered his own hands, the fingers shaking and bloody, clenched in Bancroft's hair, smashing his head repeatedly against the wall; tearing the gorget from his throat and gouging his thumbs into the frantic pulse. The right arm, Bancroft's maimed and handless arm, came up in a grotesque, instinctive attempt to attack him; he took one hand from the throat and drove his fingers into the wound, forcing the stump into the rough stone wall.

A cry of unimaginable pain, affording him an almost sexual pleasure, then he was struck from behind; his grip broke, and he was dragged away. He carried one final image of Bancroft on his knees, cradling the weeping stump with his left arm and sobbing with anguish.

He was taken back to his own quarters and his weapons, pistols, sword, penknife, were confiscated. There would be no lamp lit tonight; they had relieved him of his tinderbox. The hours passed, and the day became darkness.

His thoughts were fluid and erratic. He summoned Evesham to his mind, fully aware that he would never see it again if the court-martial he would now surely face should convict him. He thought of Catherine, and of Isabel MacNeil as if they were indivisible, and relived the circumstances which had brought them together so briefly. He thought of Ewen Stirling, a prisoner like himself, and conducted imaginary conversations with him, not in French, for which he had no affinity, but in the Italian he loved. Then Catherine again, and the unresolved features; music played in another lifetime, shaping itself audibly in the darkness; volumes of erotica dipped into with a shuddering delight by a younger, infinitely more innocent self. His childhood, his brother; the crown of golden hair, the godlike nobility of feature, the corruption of the soul, the mirror in which he had more than once recognized himself.

His mind returned to Isabel MacNeil, and this time her death would not leave him; the image of the shattered face broke in upon his thoughts with a terrible clarity until he rejected it, numb with pain. He grieved as for one long loved.

Ewen Stirling, and Isabel, and her child, and his dead child, and Catherine, were woven with the night into a strange pattern which was not yet clear to him. He began to compose a letter to her, until he believed he had written it. Never at any time did he fear dying, although a sentence of death was a possibility that could not be discounted.

At some hour the door opened, and Brevet stood in the daylight, ordering him to come out. He rose, stiff with the night's inactivity, and followed him.

Even as his wrists were seized up to the halberds, he could not believe what was to happen to him. It was an unconscionable act of criminality, indefensible, the last act of madness in a nightmare which had consumed all sanity.

The first stroke knocked the breath from his lungs, and he choked on the taste of the leather strap. The skin flayed and the raw flesh clung to the knots; shreds of bloody fibre, tissue, muscle spattered the cobbles. He fainted. A bucket of water was thrown over him, and he was conscious of the sound once more. He had not cried out. His wrists were breaking.

A tide of blood obscured his vision and obliterated everything.

Evening. A drum beating faintly in the darkness. The fog had come down again.

He was lying on a pallet, his head pillowed on his arms; he was naked. Some one had loosened his hair and it was clotted with sweat.

He moved, and thought he burned with the child in the house; every inch of his skin was consumed by fire. The sullen tide of unconsciousness returned, and he resisted it; it receded.

A thin, tormenting stream, blood or sweat, ran across his ribs; the sheet beneath him was heavily stained. His lips were cracked, bitten at the halberds; his wrists ached from the ropes. Nothing moved in his mind but a consciousness of pain; no names, no faces, no knowledge of day or hour or circumstance. He heard the voice in the unremembered nightmare, animal, incoherent, and did not know it was himself.

Things, objects, atmosphere, manifested themselves. A guttering lamp. The earthen floor, spattered with liquid. Cloths and basin, evidence of a bloody sponging. Brine was the army's only antiseptic; the fire was the salt in his wounds.

The cat was mewing somewhere. Dimly, he understood where he was.

Bancroft was seated, leaning back against the damp stone wall. One leg was outstretched, and the slim hand lay across his knee. His eyes were closed, the patrician face disfigured by monstrous bruises. The cat was rubbing against his ankle, wanting to be lifted and held.

Other sounds. The rattle of the ghostly drum, beating in a distant world, a dream world beyond the walls of this; the sounds of men and horses, arms and orders. He was far removed from them here. This was all the reality that remained to him, this nightmare seamy with blood and sweat. They might already have been lovers for what lay between them now, a powerful eroticism born of his pain and his nakedness and his degradation.

There was some small sound. Bancroft's eyes opened and came to him at once, apprehensive, uncertain, intense.

There was a plate of something on the table. He offered it.

"Will you eat?" Silence. "No, I thought not. You won't even speak. Is that to be my punishment then, your silence?"

Outside, the endless rain went on.

"Take a little brandy. Please." He had added laudanum to it, several drops from the vial. "Take this. Take it, for God's sake, it will ease the pain."

Silence. He set the brandy down.

"Why did you force me to this? When you knew it was madness, you knew what I would do. Why were you not kinder to me? What would it have mattered to you? It was all I wanted."

Silence, the drumbeat stilled. Only the voice and the rain.

"I thought I could keep from you. I should not have come to you. If you tell me to leave you, I will go."

The rain again, but the sound was fainter. The tide of darkness was coming to take its place.

"Oh, my God, will you not even look at me? Achill—"

The fingers touched his hair, a long, anguished caress, and the rain ran like a sigh in the night, the last thing he heard.

IV

Ewen Stirling was taken from Fort Augustus to Edinburgh in late July and imprisoned without trial, first in the Tolbooth, then as the charge of one of the King's messengers, citizens who turned their homes into private gaols for prisoners of quality. He slept on straw in a garret with a dozen other men and boys, shackled hand and foot at night and only allowed such brief glimpses of sunlight as visits to the privy permitted.

His faith was all that kept him sane: prayers and conversation with two Irish Catholics who shared his imprisonment, and sometimes a little half-hearted merriment when the men sang or recited poetry. But most of them believed they had come to Edinburgh to die, and prepared themselves and one another for it, with few exceptions, with the grace and dignity of their class.

It was to death, or at least to trial, that Ewen believed himself summoned on the fourteenth of September, when the door was opened and his name was pronounced. Instead, he was released without explanation or apology, in the verminous clothing he had worn for weeks, and so ill that he could barely stand. He had no money, and no friends in Edinburgh; they had either been arrested or had fled for their lives to France. He slept that night in a close, with a bitter east wind bringing rain, and in the morning commenced his journey home.

He walked, begged and slept on the roads and in the ditches until he came in early October to the borders of his own land. He was wearing a coat given him by a Badenoch tinker, his stockings were in ribbons, his shoe buckles bartered for food and lodging, as the chased silver buttons of his evening coat had been cut off one by one and given away for meat and drink and fresh straw in the messenger's house. He watched the mountains until the light failed, and then lay down to sleep. In the night there was snow, the first of that year to fall in Glen Sian, and in the morning Ewen was found, and brought to shelter by his own people.

In his absence men and women had disappeared, and the fates of others had become known.

The remains of an infant were found in a disused well, discovered only when a stench began to rise from the uncovered water. Its sex could no longer be distinguished, but it was accepted as the body of Margaret, Isabel MacNeil's daughter, and buried in the churchyard beside her.

MacNeil's sister Deirdre went walking one August morning through the summer pastures to escape her brother's shattered parish for an hour. She was surprised there by a party of dragoons who raped her repeatedly, cut to the skull the hair which had fallen to her hips, wounded her with hangers and left her for dead. Toward evening she made her way, sometimes crawling, to Glen Mor, and when eight weeks had passed with no sign of her menstrual blood she spread the crude instruments of her midwifery on the table and aborted herself into a basin.

She had barely recovered when her brother returned, seeking shelter from the bitter weather with the rest of his fugitive companions. She gave him the news of his wife's death, and that of the child he had never seen. Her own poor story she never told him.

By autumn, MacNeil had preached again in Glen Mor, a devoted alcoholic, crippled more by grief and rage than by any physical infirmity.

Lachlan came and went among the MacGregors, sometimes passing like a phantom, sometimes rumoured to be dead, but always returning, a shadow in the eye's edge, seen and then gone.

And Margaret Campbell waited.

Murdoch refused to live in the house where his parents had been murdered, although she lived there now with her son; when he returned it was only to drink and to abuse her, and one night when verbal abuse was not enough he raped her.

The boy came to the bed in the darkness afterwards, when they were alone, and kissed her.

She clung to the slight, bony body in its nightgown, and wept with fear and with love.

A heavier snow fell on the eve of Samhain, the thirty-first of October.

Margaret walked in the darkness, skirting the lights of Ardsian. It was not a night for the superstitious; Samhain was the Celtic feast of the dead, when the year plunged into darkness and kings and heroes died, and the spirits of the dead and the divine daoine sìth rode until morning, wreaking what evil they wished. She had nothing to fear from the unearthly; it was earthly danger, flesh and blood, that threatened her, and it would seek her out wherever she was.

It was her son's eleventh birthday, and when she returned to the house she told him of it, how Murdoch, then compassionate, had prayed aloud to his Catholic deities and to older gods, and laid her on the earthen floor so she might draw her strength from the Great Mother. The child had come fighting out of her womb at midnight, wailing as if he knew all the sorrow of the world.

She leaned forward, picking up the poker. The circumstances of his own birth were merely preparation, but there would be no further revelations tonight.

Carefully, she wrote his name in the ash and encouraged him to copy her. He was vividly intelligent and committed whatever he was taught to a prodigious memory, although he remained illiterate, because she had no books.

The lights of Ardsian burned all that night, and in the morning Elspeth Stirling was delivered of a daughter. By evening they were both dead.

Margaret walked to Ardsian to attend the wake, and was refused entry by a servant who told her there was no room in the house, although others arrived and were admitted. She stood on the lawn for a time, a small woman pinched with hunger, understanding at last that it was not Ewen who was responsible for the funeral arrangements but his factor. Her head and body ached as she stood, and she clasped her arms to warm herself; her breasts, too, were painful.

She was already aware that she had conceived. What Murdoch would think of the child he had sired of his hatred she neither knew nor cared; it was her son's acceptance she craved, and the ugliness of the act she wanted to expunge from his memory before it poisoned him.

She took the bread and salt she had brought for the spirit of Elspeth Stirling back to the house, and ate it there with her son.

She broached the subject in the evening. He was watching the fire as if it held visions for him, and when she spoke his name he looked up reluctantly, turning those clear eyes upon her. She never knew his thoughts, any more than she had known Magnus, even when he and she might have been one flesh, as much a part of one another as this child was part of her.

"Come here," she said, pushing away the past.

He rose with that lithe, fluid grace, so much like the younger Murdoch, and knelt beside her. She held his unwilling hand to her belly, and told him of her pregnancy and, patiently and explicitly, the details of intercourse, describing it as an act of love. He said nothing, accepting it for the lie it was, and before that cool stare she felt naked, and degraded, and ashamed.

The year ended which was coming to be called Bliadhna Thearlaich, Charles's Year. It took without discrimination children in the glens and soldiers in the garrisons: some froze to death at their posts, cursing the white hell of snow and fog and a cold more intense than any they had ever known. Death came down like a starving wolf from the hills, and it alone fed well.

Margaret made a game of their survival until she saw that nothing juvenile remained in her son, and her painful efforts met only with his pity. She turned to him then as an equal, confiding in him her fears and her fragile hopes. They scavenged and he hunted, sometimes with a little success. The fetus quickened, and she lay sleepless at night and prayed for some premonition of the future, some sign that her children would survive.

The winter had brought her a strange certainty that she had not long to live, and in subtle ways she tried to prepare her son. Knowing that Murdoch had never loved him, she did not know who would care for him, and she feared the vengeance of her enemies. She had considered approaching Inglis MacNeil, but she was frightened of him and fully aware of the contempt in which he held her. Ewen, newly bereaved and under Murdoch's influence, was out of the question. There seemed no one else.

The boy was restless in his sleep, and she drew his head to her breast; he responded with a small, nestling movement. She embraced him and listened to the rhythm of his breathing, and let herself be carried by it into the sweetness of the past.

There was a new moon on the evening of the eleventh of March. She called him to the door to see it and recite the old prayer with her.

Greeting to you, new moon, kind jewel of guidance. I bend my knees to you, I raise my hands to you, I lift up my eye to you, new moon of the seasons....

They stood, her hands on his shoulders, not moving, breathing as one.

It becomes me to praise the Being of Life, for His kindness and His goodness....

He was still gazing at the moon, and did not appear disturbed by her silence: it was a paring of light, unspeakably pure, and he watched it with a visionary's eyes. At moments like this she saw the intensity of his spirit, and some of the beauty it gave to his face.

The wind was raw, and turning easterly. She brought him back to her gently.

"Come in now, my hero. It's cold."

In the kitchen, he tended the fire and swept up the chips for the next day's kindling; she had smashed a chair for fuel.

"Who told you to put that shirt on, Malcolm? It's torn."

He went on with his work, indifferent to his appearance, a thin child with long legs and a grave, preoccupied expression. His hair, although clean, was unkempt, uncut.

"Leave that," she said sharply. "We'll do it tomorrow."

He did not listen, and she went up to bed, leaving him for the first time alone and in anger.

Rain was falling when she woke, and she woke as she had slept, alone. He was like Murdoch in that, impossibly quick to take offense and unwilling or unable to forgive. She went downstairs in the grey light and found him patiently sifting weevils from a handful of meal.

"There's no more," he said. "I'll go and ask for some at the crofts."

She knew what that beggar's errand would cost him, and her heart filled. He was shaping the last of the oatcakes; his face was in profile, illuminated by the flames, and its beauty moved her beyond speaking, all the beauty of Magnus's face, in which she had never shared. He sat back on his heels, hands on his knees: Magnus's hands, slender and strong, now covered in oatmeal which in a moment he would eat to avoid wasting anything. But, for the time, he was watching the fire, seeing in it the visions she would never know.

Words of love had never come easily to her, but this morning she reached out her arms and held him, and he allowed himself to be held, and she stroked the unkempt hair and buried her face against it. She held him silently, passionately, until the cakes began to burn, and then she released him.

They ate without speaking, then he took a creel and a jar and disappeared into the rain. Lachlan came about an hour later.

He was not alone; seven of his minions were with him, wearing the rain-soaked rags of fugitives. Their smell was as intense as their hatred, and the strength of their purpose.

She remained in her chair, her hand resting on her belly, then she reached down to the hearth and picked up the poker.

"Put it down, àlainna."

She began to cry, quietly, as he took it from her.

There was a scar on his left cheekbone, a little below the eye, and she clung to the thought of it, that he could bleed like other men, that he could die. Some one whispered, "MacIain, have pity...."

The others did not interfere; it was a matter of pride that he should be able to subdue her. She fought with her nails and her teeth, and he groped for the dirk at his hip and wounded her in the hand; then he forced her to her knees and held her head by the hair, and another pressed a knife to her throat.

She trembled, crying soundlessly, and fellated him, and obediently swallowed his semen.

A voice was saying, *MacIain... an gille.....*

He kicked her away and she flung herself at the opened door, screaming *run run run....*

Her son was coming up through the garden in the rain; she saw him turn in the direction of her voice and hesitate, and then, instinctively, he obeyed her. Some one, she thought the one who had asked for pity, was running after him.

A fist seized her, crushed her from within. The onset of labour.

She was carried outside and her clothing torn off, and they raped her one after another, although his preferred act was sodomy. She did not know that she wept; she lay only wanting to die, and knew that she would die but it would not be quickly; they would not free her and allow her to go from them so soon.

She removed herself from them, withdrew her spirit.

Her thighs were running with blood and semen. Some one crouched close to her and pulled the hair away from her face.

She lay still, holding him with her eyes. He violated her yet again, with his knife, with the handle and then with the blade.

They left her.

Time passed, was nothing now. The blood became the substance of the fetus, expelled from her womb; it was lying between her legs when the agony of her living child recalled her to consciousness.

Twilight. He neither spoke nor moved. She formed Ewen's name with her lips, but, if he understood, he chose not to leave her.

With nightfall the rain ceased. The cold of winter was seeping from the ground.

He wept now, hideously, without tears.

She opened her mouth, attempting to say his name, to speak one word to comfort him, and stop the terrible sound of his grief.

The beloved name came from her on one long, final breath.

Magnus....

And death refused her no more.

V

Lachlan was arrested and charged with treason at Fort Augustus later in the spring.

He was shackled to another man and they were marched in pairs to Stirling, then to the Tolbooth in Edinburgh, and finally to Carlisle for sentencing. The dragoons prodded and herded them into every bog, and bewildered them with senseless cruelty.

He had lain in Carlisle prison for nearly a month. The gaol cell stank of urine and rotting excrement, and the butchers' offal which was thrown in to the prisoners as food. The days passed from darkness to darkness with nothing to mark their passage, except, at intervals, the cell door opened and a man came in with an upturned hat full of slips of paper, and ordered some of them to take one. Nineteen were numbered, the twentieth a black card that represented death. The nineteen went to America or the Caribbean in irons. The twentieth was hanged.

On the eleventh of July, 1747, Lachlan faced the lottery and drew the black card. In the night the man next to him, of similar colouring, died of dysentery. On the morning of the twelfth, nineteen men were removed for transportation. Lachlan went with them under the dead man's name.

The ships sailed from Liverpool. They were merchantmen, and their owners expected to show a profit on their human cargo. There was no accommodation for the men, women and children to be transported, so they were forced to lie on the earth and stones of the ballast. Many had been robbed in Carlisle prison until they were naked but for tartan rags, and some could scarcely crawl. They fell in the hold and died with their faces to the earth, their legs swollen in irons and their bodies infested with vermin. For the living there was foul water, frequently tasting of the sailors' urine, and sometimes something to eat.

Twice during the passage the prisoners were allowed on deck and forced to cleanse their bodies and their clothing. They were segregated by sex, and the women afforded the crew the pleasure of watching while they shivered and tried to shelter one another; salt water was sluiced over them when they refused to strip before the leering eyes. Consumption and lung fever rampaged among them, and when they died, drowning in their phlegm, they were thrown overboard into the sea.

Rebellion or defiance of any kind seldom occurred to them, as infrequently as resistance in the Highlands, and when it did it met with the same savage punishment. Lachlan was flogged for throwing a bucket of the urine-tainted water into the face of a ship's officer. They cut him down from the gratings and left him lying on the deck for two or three hours, the other prisoners forbidden to touch him on pain of the same punishment, and as the seamen passed they spat on him.

Thoughts came to him. His body's pain. Memories: mist, the cool light on the heights of Sian, the eagles wheeling and keening. The spray hissed, the wind thrummed in the shrouds and was no more to him than a dream that would pass with the night.

Another act of defiance— only by such rage could he keep his sanity— and for it he was shackled for hours in a tiny dark locker where he could neither sit nor stand nor lie. When he was taken from it, night had fallen. The men who had removed him took him out onto the deck and told him to wash.

When he refused he was stripped and subjected to icy water and soap with the bite of lye, his buttocks spread and his raw legs scoured, and his beard and hair were cut. He stood naked on the deck, his cheeks scraped, his face gaunt and pale and peculiarly young without its matted beard. Some one thrust a shirt at him, and breeches. Dazed, he put them on; he had never before worn the southern clothing. The men laughed and prodded him, and he could not understand what they were saying although he sensed that much of it was obscene; what little English he had once known had deserted him.

He allowed them to take him below, and aft to the stern cabin, where the violent dream from which he expected to wake became a nightmare.

He was overpowered, and when he resisted further sodomized as savagely as any act of vengeance he himself had committed. In the grey first light he was taken back and thrown down into the hold with the others.

It happened again, and again, and he learned not to resist, and on the final night when the business in the stern cabin was concluded he locked his hands around his rapist's throat and gave all his strength to the last act that would save him.

He was beaten while his attacker watched, until he thought he could never again be so violated, then he slipped into the darkness that waited so often to claim him; it had become his only home.

The next day, the ninth of October, heavily shackled hand and foot, Lachlan MacIain MacGregor of Glen Lyon and Glen Sian, and lately of nowhere but hell, came to Port Royal, Jamaica. He was twenty-one.

Business took Noel Coventry down the Palisadoes from Kingston to Port Royal harbour on the morning of the ninth, business and his craving for news from England, and the hope of letters that never came.

The brig *Royal Anne* had come in from Liverpool at dawn, past the guns of Fort Charles and round Port Royal Point, and was warping up to her anchorage: the wind veered and he caught the smell of her. A thousand memories crowded into his mind. He crushed them down.

He knew what she carried; he would have thought her a blackbirder with a hold full of Guinea slaves, but by her port of origin and the talk on the quayside he knew her cargo was white.

He had no intention of staying to watch English men and women sent up on to the auction block; it was a spectacle he had always avoided. But he was there by chance, and he was drawn by a terrible fascination with human bondage and the depths of soulless brutality this island required to make it prosper, so he lingered, even as his skin crawled at the sound of grating leg irons and the musty stench from the opened hatches. He saw the first figures struggle on deck, dazed by the harsh sunlight. Women, a ploy by the brig's master to attract the attention of potential buyers. Then the men.

He saw the face, recognized it with a powerful surge of empathy. The defiant lift of the head, the bitter, furious stare... a deep, visceral excitement stirred within him. He knew what had brought him here; he had thought himself done with it, but it had reawakened and once more it commanded him, and he could no more stop what he was about to do than he could still his own heart. He had made his decision. He was well aware that it could cost him his life.

He spoke to one of the crew.

"Who is that standing alone? He'll burn like hell with a skin like his."

"He come from Carlisle. I dunno his name. MacIain, I think. He don't answer to it. He don't answer to nothing. He don't speak, neither."

"Is he mute?"

"He's no bloody mute, that one. Just step over to him and make a bit of sport. You'll soon hear what he has to say."

Coventry returned to his horse for the rum, then he went forward, understanding in some obscure fashion that he himself was no longer free.

Lachlan watched him cross the quay, a dark man, almost Spanish in appearance, pausing only to take something from the slave who stood holding his horse. As he came closer, the object resolved itself into a flask and a cup.

"I've heard you called MacIain." His air remained lifeless, indifferent. "My name is Coventry. Will you drink?"

The cup was offered to him. He knocked it away. The dark face with its darker eyes and its drawn, tanned skin remained unchanged.

"If you behave like an animal, you will be treated as such. If you behave like a human being so shall I."

This time he allowed the cup to come close to his lips, then he spat and followed his saliva with a flood of obscenities in Gaelic. The man struck him on the fresh bruising of the previous night, and filled the cup again.

"This is the last time, MacIain. Think on it." His eyes revealed nothing; his voice remained without inflection. "You are not the only one to whom this has happened. It happened to me thirteen years ago. I lived through it. So will you."

He drank, not out of subservience but because he was thirsty, and the unfamiliar spirit brought tears to his eyes. The man laughed, not an unpleasant sound, nor mocking, merely amused.

"I should have warned you." The hand turned his face to the light, hard, but not ungentle. "Who did this to you?" He said nothing. "Did you make trouble aboard the ship, MacIain?" Silence. "Well, you won't make trouble for me, will you, not if you're wise. Now let us get this over with. We've a long ride ahead of us, and I'm anxious to be gone."

They had come to the hill overlooking the sea at dawn, the sea sweeping in a dozen different shades of blue and green to a white beach. The untidy straggle of Montego Bay lay ten miles to the west, ten miles of mangrove and swamp and the broken coastal road. The heat was unbearable, the air heavy and humid with the smell of secondary jungle.

The land closed in around them, fields of pale green flashing and rattling in the wind. The light was painful where it struck the narrow, sword-like leaves; it was painful everywhere.

They had ridden for days, how long he did not know. He had been allowed a horse but his wrists were tied to the reins, and Coventry rode fully armed with two slaves following, who watched the white man with a mixture of pity and contempt.

The sun was striking his uncovered head like an iron, a white-hot iron, and it had barely risen. He felt faint, sick; the edge of madness returned. It remained his close companion.

Coventry drew rein and looked toward the sea.

"This is my land, Ironshore. There's another plantation around that point at Rosewynd Bay, my nearest neighbour. What do you know about cane, MacIain?"

The darkness receded. All around him was the soft, smothering, opal morning. The words came, his English slow and heavily accented.

"He... slew... his brother."

That quick, pleasant laugh.

"No. Sugar cane. The plant."

"Nothing."

"Well, I know something. I broke my back in the cane fields for twelve years down Barbados way."

He gave his horse the heel. The tall plants brushed his thigh, mounted though he was, and the smell was overpowering. Lachlan did not follow him.

The white whips of the sun were stronger, the sea an endless glitter fretting at the edge of his eye... so close, so unreachable, so pointless to think of death that way. A shadow of wings fell across his face.

Coventry, waiting, said, "MacIain," once or twice, but made no move to touch him or intrude upon his thoughts.

He watched the birds overhead, the black John Crows, the vultures of these islands, with a fierce, passionate longing in his face, and bitter memories of golden eagles in their tumbling, spiralling dance. Remembering their harsh, mewing cries— these birds were silent, rising and falling like ashes, caught in an endless unseen river of wind over the hills and the shore.

He watched until his eyes ached from the glare, then, blinded by the light and his own tears, he looked down at the earth, let it enclose him, for never again would he be as free as they.

At thirty-eight, Noel Coventry was old for Jamaica; he would have been old at thirty. Men seldom lived longer than that in a country where death was commonplace from fever, rum or poison, ambush by runaway slaves, accidents in the fields, on horseback, or at the mills where the cane was crushed. Life was short and he knew it, and he lived recklessly and often brutally to wrest every pleasure and opportunity from it before it was gone.

His real name was not Coventry; whatever it was, he had left it behind him in Barbados with twelve years of his life. There were books in his library, jealously collected and displayed, to suggest that he had once been a student of medicine or botany, a gentleman of substance, or a naval officer, and gossip suggested a hundred things besides. The talk did not disturb him; rather, he encouraged it. It was amusing, and as likely to be true as not.

He was already a man of consequence on the north shore but he was not satisfied with what influence he wielded there. He wanted to extend it as far as possible, to Government House if he could; he had a compulsive desire to be recognized and acknowledged by the society he professed to despise. He wanted land and money and a great house of such beauty that it would set other men ablaze with envy. It was a house he saw already in his mind's eye, set on the steep hill overlooking the sea, to be admired from the coastal road, a gracious house, a social magnet, with terraces and porticoes and grand staircases of Jamaican mahogany, and gardens where he could indulge his passion for rare plants. For the time it remained only that, a dream. The foundations of a more modest house had risen soon after he bought his first two hundred acres, and he built much of it himself with hands hardened in the cane fields of Barbados, and brick sent out as ballast from Liverpool in brigs like the *Royal Anne,* and mortar mixed of molasses and dirt. It took a year to build, and it remained almost empty because there was no money yet to spare to furnish it. There was only money for more land.

But his latest acquisition was not land but flesh and blood, and he watched him with a fascinated dispassion, convinced that he would either break or die. He knew all of Lachlan's pain and outrage but it made no difference. He could not help him and he could not free him; he was held by a compulsion stronger than himself.

Pain and the sun were the only constants in his life.

And the cane. If Jamaica was slaves, and the sound of obeah drums in the hills at night, and the curling lash of the whip, it was cane above all. December to June. Burn the fields, cut the cane, haul it to the mill, crush it. Boil it in shallow copper taches until the sulphury, nauseating smell of sugar and molasses, molasses and rum, clung to hair and skin and clothing, until a man ate cane and slept it, smelled of it and dreamed it. Until he came to hate it more than anything else in the world.

He threw down the machete he had been given to hack away the undergrowth and huddled on the ground. He had gone down this torturous path to madness before, spending days neither eating nor working, crouched in a fetal curl in the dimness of his hut. He had run away once as far as Montego Bay, was recognized there not so much by his ragged clothing as by his hair and eyes and known for Coventry's Scot, was flogged by the local officials as a runaway and brought back at night manacled to Coventry's stirrup. He had tried to kill himself and was prevented.

Coventry was at first patient, then inflexible.

"MacIain, get up." A boot in the side. "Get up."

Curses flooded from him, half English, half Gaelic, and his eyes flamed with tears of impotence, because no language had words enough for his hatred.

Coventry listened to him without expression until his voice left him entirely and he could only crouch on the ground, his eyes searching for the blaze of hot metal where the sun was beating down on the machete. It was lying where he had flung it, closer to Coventry than himself.

Coventry said, "If you touch that blade I'll kill you. Now get up. I have work to do."

"You can take your work to hell, you bloody bastard."

It was a harsh whisper and whether it went unheard or not he did not know, but he was left alone, and the unknown terrors of the empty land, the sounds in the undergrowth and the sun overcame him. Three or four hours later Coventry returned in the heat of noon, threw his whip aside and leaned down, putting an arm around his shoulders, holding the cup to his lips.

"If you don't drink you'll die. Now swallow this and get up, slowly."

He worked beside Coventry for the rest of that day and the days that followed without end, sharing his water and his rum; he fainted from the heat and the searing light and was drawn out of that welcome darkness by Coventry kneeling beside him and Coventry's shadow blotting out the white sun; he was stricken with malaria, and Coventry's face swam above him in the nights of fever. The work progressed, the cane fields sloped to the sea, to the boundary of Rosewynd in the east, to within sight of Montego in the west, and miles back into the hills. The weeks became a month, two months, until he ceased to count them.

Coventry bought more slaves, Coromantees, and spoke of hiring a white overseer but none came. Their world remained what it was, strangely isolated, and they lived as if they were the only two inhabitants, bound by race and a common exile but nothing else.

Lachlan thought of death, and longed for it, and knew it was at his command now, he was no longer watched so closely. The machete and the cane knife were at hand if he wished to use them on himself. He knew that if he ever turned them on Coventry, Coventry would break his neck as dispassionately as he had disciplined him in the fields or cared for him in his sickness. He came to hate Sundays. His days were eating and labouring, his nights exhausted sleep, but on Sundays there was no work and he was left utterly alone. Coventry rode to Rosewynd or Cinnamon Hill, or to Montego Bay, and seldom returned before dusk; even the slaves sat and sang in the quarters or worked their gardens, laughing, making music in their own language, but he had no one. Sometimes he wept, sometimes he planned his

85

death; sometimes he slept and woke grateful for the darkness because it meant that the day was gone. Without his work, it had no meaning.

He did not consider, did not allow himself to consider, that it was without Coventry that the days were meaningless, but it was true. Whatever he had been before had died, and now he had no identity except what Coventry chose to allow him.

He had fallen asleep that night in February listening to the sea. It was a lonely sound and sometimes heartbreaking, but tonight it comforted him. He woke once and saw nothing, only the strong pattern of moonlight, and slept again. The second time he woke he found Coventry watching him, with a face bleached by the moonlight and eyes too deeply shadowed to be seen.

He had been drinking but he was not drunk, and he had brought the rum with him. "Will you drink?" He waited for an answer and when none came he drank from the jug himself and put it down. He was smoking, and the end of the slender cigar glowed and faded in the darkness. "I've been down to the sea. You should have come with me— perhaps we shall go later."

Lachlan lay still, trembling, his mouth filled with the iron taste of fear. Coventry said:

"It would be better for you if you drank."

One sharp, sudden move to fight, and it was aborted as swiftly. The voice remained gentle, but the hand was brutally strong.

There was pain, but he made neither sound nor movement, and his tears were never seen.

Coventry was at his desk, the wind from the sea disturbing his papers. It was a dull afternoon, heavy with approaching storm; the surf was audible. The season of calamity, he had always called it.

He had walked along the beach at dawn and seen the wrack thrown up by a passing hurricane; it might yet claw round and assault them with only slightly diminished fury. He had no cane to lose at this time of year, but there was Ironshore's safety to be considered, and the safety of Rosewynd on its seaward prominence to the east.

The palms lifted and rattled; the thunder was closer, reminding him of gunfire across water. The wind brought no freshness, only an unsettling chill that smelled of salt and the churning sea.

The papers stirred again on his desk and he weighed them down with a piece of coral. He had been writing to a young naval officer who had sought his advice on buying land on the north shore. Ships' officers were welcome guests in Jamaican society, fresh faces in an incestuous round, and were lionized whenever they strayed from the naval base at Fort Charles.

Upstairs louvres banged. A patter of bare black feet and soft patois, and they were secured.

The lines in his own handwriting stared back at him.

*17ᵗʰ September 1748. My dear St. James, I have the pleasure to acquaint you with a little news....*He sealed it and began another, to Lydia Seguin, the newly bereaved owner of Rosewynd.

My sweet love....

He had known Seguin since coming to Jamaica; it had begun as a casual acquaintance and become a friendship, with advice exchanged on cane and the shared ownership of a mill which served both estates. His liaison with Seguin's widow had begun the night of his funeral.

She was an attractive Creole from Haiti with black hair and black eyes and a touch of African blood, which excited him as the exotic always did. He had taken her to bed and they had found one another mutually satisfying, and he had spent many of his days and some of his nights at Rosewynd since. Her body was golden, small-breasted, pared of femininity, and her sweat and her ardour were what he had wanted from his other lover, who after eight months still offered him only cold submission.

The idea of their marriage had come as a matter of course; that it would be loveless did not disturb him. He had no doubt that their physical relationship would be as short-lived as it was violent. It was Rosewynd he was marrying.

His back was aching, and his head. He shouted along the gallery.

"MacIain!"

The wind took his voice and ran with it. A heavy crash from somewhere, a door blowing shut, and excited voices. The slave patois again, knowing he was within earshot, not wishing him to understand what they said.

"MacIain!"

He came eventually, the golden eyes without expression.

"Why don't you come when you're called?"

"Because I am not a dog."

Coventry let it pass, and began to gather the pages of his letter.

"I am going to marry Mrs. Seguin next week. I shall be riding to Rosewynd. In the meantime I want—"

Their skins were equally bronzed now, but the knuckles bleached on his wrist; he watched with an odd detachment as the veins on his own hand swelled beneath the pressure. The light was grey and flat; even the sea was grey and flattened, and rain obscured it like a veil.

"Take your hand away." There was no response. "Take it off me, damn you. Who do you think you are?"

Silence. The rain had reached the shore.

He said, "Well, what did you expect? I want a wife, I want a hostess, I want a woman I can be seen with. Who the devil should I present to the governor, some mulatto from Port Royal?"

The wind had dropped completely with the rain. It was curious how silent it had become.

"I've never stopped you from taking some wench to your bed, so long as she's clean."

The rain came in waves, at first driven, then dying away.

He said into the silence, "I shall want to see you tonight."

Lachlan said, very softly, "You go to hell," and was halted at the door only by the voice, which was as quiet as his own.

"I will marry her, MacIain, whether you care for it or not. I will do as I wish."

But he did not. Two days later he fell from the saddle with yellow fever and lay near death for almost a week, his skin cold and jaundiced, his vomit the characteristic black of the disease.

Lydia Seguin came as soon as she received the news. She arrived on horseback and entered the house uninvited, throwing her crop on the table and leaving her hat in the hands of an astonished slave who tried to prevent her from mounting the stairs. The smell of sickness hit her like a wall. She pressed on.

Rain was falling heavily, and the room was in a strange half-light; the pall of the storm was cast over everything. The bed was draped in mosquito netting. She went toward it without hesitation.

Then she saw that she was not alone with him; some one else was sitting by the bed.

"Get out, you Creole bitch."

She stared at him without speaking, then she turned on her heel and went.

The hurricane veered and ploughed out to sea, cutting a vicious swath toward the Bahamas and the coast of Florida. It passed Ironshore with only torrential rain; mudslides swept away the shacks of Montego Bay. There was no wind, only days and nights of smothering stillness, throughout which Noel Coventry struggled to live.

Two days had passed since Lydia Seguin's visit. Whether he lived or died now, there would be no marriage. She had left Rosewynd, or so the slaves were saying, to return to Haiti. Her overseer had orders to sell.

Lachlan had remained by the bed. It was 'dead time', after the crop was harvested and before the December planting, but had there been work in the fields he would not have gone to it. It was still raining, the eaves rushing with water and a sharp fragrance rising from the gardens. He had ordered the windows to be opened, unable to bear the stench of a closed room and doubting it would make any difference to the outcome. He had nursed roughly, with little instinct, neither knowing nor caring if the powders mixed by the slaves at his request would kill or cure.

Coventry was lying still, the tanned skin a ghastly yellow with disease. He had neither moved nor spoken for some time; it was either sleep or coma, the last long sleep before death.

Lachlan listened to the heart, the breath. Both were very slight.

He lifted the other pillow. The rain gushed; there was no other sound. He looked for the last time at the face, which was not handsome, although it could charm both men and women into believing it was. The strong, swarthy, irregular features, the heavy-lidded, sunken eyes: a parchment mask, no more.

He held the pillow to press it down; it would not take much effort.

He hesitated, his mind torn, and as he was struggling with himself the eyes opened, dark and endless, drawing him in.

"MacIain?" It was a thin thread of sound.

He put the pillow gently down, knowing now he would not use it, could not; perhaps he never could.

"I am here," he said.

VI

The Culloden battalions were recalled to Flanders, where they were once more engaged in bitter conflict with the French.

The Highlands were divided into four military districts, garrisoned, and harried by patrols of dragoons who routed out fugitives and rumours of spies with sullen determination. They came and went, staying in shielings and bothies, sometimes dirked or shot, mostly shooting, raping and hanging where they pleased.

There was talk of another rising. There was little food and less kindling in any of the ravaged glens, but the agents did exist, and where they eluded their pursuers they carried rumour enough to fire men's imaginations. French spies in the Fraser country were bearing letters from the Prince; French gold lay hidden at Loch Arkaig to finance another revolt; rebellion would come in the Isles with the spring. Perhaps some of it was true— most of it was lies, the beginning of legend.

They fed on it for a time. The first yearning ballads sprang up about the Prince, cherishing their vision of his return. The men who had crept home buried their broadswords in the thatches and peat hags, and waited.

They had been stripped of their dreams, their hopes. By late summer of the year after the rebellion, they were stripped of their very clothes.

The notices of the proscription of Highland dress were posted at every market cross, town house and church door in Scotland :

Some resisted. Some fled into the hills rather than surrender their arms or their dress, or the right to wear them. Some openly defied the laws and were imprisoned, transported, or shot. In Glen Sian they were mainly broken and sullen; MacNeil was sick and often drunk and Lachlan had disappeared, and the flame of rebellion had flickered out among them; those who had fought retired to the crofts and drank the raw spirit from illegal stills and surrendered themselves to their memories, to the shadows of what they had been.

Ewen Stirling heard them one night singing Jacobite songs forbidden now by law, with the recklessness of men who had nothing left to lose. Slowly and mournfully, voices in the dark.

Who will play the silver whistle
when my King's son to sea is going?
All Scotland prepare, prepare his coming ....
I will be dancing, I will be singing
and I will play the silver whistle ....

By autumn of 1747 many of them had rendered up their weapons and were forced to take the oath of disarmament. The more ingenious submitted pistols that appeared not to have been fired since the first rising thirty-two years before, keeping their newer, brighter swords hidden. Murdoch Scott took the oath like the others, swearing in the Irish tongue with his hand resting on the iron of an old knife which he later surrendered :

.... as I shall answer to God at the great day of judgment, I have not, nor shall have in my possession any gun, sword, pistol or arm whatsoever, and never use tartan, plaid or any part of the highland garb; and if I do so may I be cursed in my undertakings, family and property, may I be killed in battle as a coward, and lie without burial in a strange land, far from the graves of my forefathers and kindred; may all this come across me if I break my oath.

Then, like the others, he tossed a brace of rusted wheellocks onto the table, so clearly useless that it seemed unlikely his oath could be taken seriously. It was indeed a token submission: within a month he was openly carrying his steel pistols across his saddle again as he made his rounds of Glen Sian.

His rent rolls had decreased. From every glen the homeless were on the roads. Women went to the garrisons at Fort Augustus and Fort William, prostituting themselves for heels of bread; they were driven away by the provost guard and drifted on to Inverness, or to the squalid slums of Edinburgh or Glasgow. Young men went as labourers to the Lowlands, but it was brutal living: their speech was not understood, their clothing outlawed, and the pitiful rags they wore in place of the Highland dress mocked; they were rebels and savages. They endured the abuse and lived in misery, or they died of unknown diseases in the filthy, overcrowded towns, or they returned, not often, to the Highlands where no future awaited them.

There was no other rising. The chiefs were away, dead, or in hiding, and those who said the Prince would come again said it less often and with less conviction. But the rumours lingered, disquieting an already anxious Parliament, and as an alien and a suspected Jacobite Ewen Stirling was required to lodge bail of a sum that staggered him, against his own future loyalty to the Hanoverian. He paid it and was beggared; if his fortunes had been depleted before, they were entirely ruined now.

Before the end of the year another legislation had been nailed to the door of the kirk in Glen Mor. He read it and found he had lost his right of hereditary jurisdiction: what legal privileges, what power to try and condemn his own people he had possessed before the rebellion had been stripped from him by a jealous government. He had become nothing more than a petty landowner, with a title that was meaningless in England.

The loyal chiefs were paid compensation in cash for the forfeit of their hereditary powers; the great Campbell, Argyll, received twenty thousand pounds. And so it went, down the roster of Protestant Whiggish peers and the heads of clans who had fought for King George or kept their disaffection well hidden. Attainted rebels, exiled lairds and suspected Jacobites were not compensated. For the loss of his rights and his cattle, the forfeit of much personal freedom, and the theft or vandalism of many of his possessions, Ewen Stirling received nothing at all, nor ever would.

***

In the summer of 1748 Inglis MacNeil was arrested, and taken to the garrison at Fort Augustus. Ewen followed him, and by oaths and promises and humiliating bribery secured his release. MacNeil came home a bitter man, cheated of the death he had craved.

So it ended, the lost cause, as a song sung in the darkness, as a shred of tartan cloth, as a sword rusting in the peat hags awaiting a call that never came, as a sad tale told.

The desperate tragedy that was sweeping the Highlands affected Ewen surprisingly little: the estate was Murdoch Scott's concern. Ewen received news of it as he heard of each parliamentary legislation that stripped old powers from him, as distant echoes from a foreign land, a land which meant nothing to him.

From time to time he rode out in Glen Sian and observed his devastated fields, and Murdoch's difficult work of restoration, but he could not help his people and he had always held himself aloof behind the barriers of foreign birth and breeding. Even now, with his fragile world of grace and pleasure lying in ruins, he found it hard to understand them or the upheaval which had torn away the ground from beneath their feet.

He wept, often, and woke trembling at strange sounds, sudden shouts, passing hooves in the night. He slept with one of his Italian pistols by the bed. He could not bring himself to leave off mourning clothes, or to hear the subject discussed; he wore his wife's watch around his neck and carried always, on his person, something of hers.

He was sick, bodily, and as he came later to understand of that time, in mind. Sick, as Scotland was sick, as the whole world seemed, reeling and without purpose.

The year turned, and winter came.

The boys were playing shinty in Glen Mor. Not the great shinty game which had been played before the rising at New Year's by teams of men from the two parishes for the prize of a keg of whisky, but a lesser game altogether, for children only. Murdoch's son loitered, wanting to be asked to join, as the two teams marked their goals with broken slate, and one produced the ball.

There were eleven on each team: he had heard the captains quarrelling over players. A youth of about fifteen led off with a hard, clean shot and loped after the ball, and the others swarmed after him. Some girls smothered in the dyed-black plaids now required by law came out from the crofts to watch, but the cold soon drove them in. The game raged up and down, through oatfields gnawed by winter, down the track and across the bridge and out on to the frozen river; the child following heard the vicious thwack of camans and the ice groaning in protest. They scrambled off then, hitting the ball up over the bank. It bounded toward a goal; they surged after it, laughing and swearing. It sped between the marks. A brutal scrimmage ensued, stick cracking on shin, and one player emerged with blood dripping from his nose. The afternoon sun swung lower. The game with all its violence would continue until dark.

The child ran, his feet in their thin hide brogans too numbed by cold to feel the stubble. One of the players had hobbled off the field, dropping his caman; he seized it and ran out after the ball.

He saw it and bore down on it, carried it on the curve of his caman as he had seen the others do, and ran, the cold air stabbing his lungs. He fell once but scrambled up, his face a wind-scraped mask, his head thrown back, his heart bursting with joy. The black slate goals opened in welcome before him; he tipped the ball from his stick and raised the stick high above his shoulder and bringing it down in a long sharp curve hit the ball with a resounding crack through the goals. The others had reached him, pounding over the stubble; he turned to face them with shining eyes. He had done the right thing, he had won a point for them, he was part of them and one of them and the game was over, he had given the winning point to his team. He felt crazed with victory.

They came up scarlet-cheeked, heaving like horses, some twenty boys surrounding him.

"Give me my stick, you turd," and it was wrenched out of his grasp.

He was jostled; the radiant joy died in his eyes. He took a small step sideways, not enough to look as if he were scuttling away.

Some one laid a heavy hand on his shoulder and said with an oily kindness, "So you want to play shinty, do you?" and he turned eagerly, gazing up. "Then you can take my stick, you dirty tink!" It hit him across the back and he staggered.

"Christ, man, leave him alone!"

"I'll kill him after what that old bastard did to my—"

The child, who thought he had been forgotten, sidled away. The peacemaker gave him a hard push.

"Get away home. You cause nothing but trouble, just like your stinking da."

The first stone hit him in the small of the back; another struck his cold-numbed ear. He walked on steadily, glad of the darkness, that no one should see his tears.

He went down to Glen Mor again to see the Fastern's Eve cockfight, held every year in the school to mark the beginning of Lent. The darkness had fallen about half past four; he walked by the greyish glimmer of the moon.

He slipped in through the crowd. The benches had been pushed against the walls and the walls were stained with smoke and mildew. He had never before entered the school.

Gradually he saw more: Murdoch standing, one booted leg shedding dung on a bench; MacNeil; other men watching the coin Murdoch was tossing; the cocks, red and black, held in the arms of boys. Murdoch was considering the odds; then he said, "I'll be putting my money on the red," and from that moment his eyes, veiled, amused, and hard as steel, never left the pit.

The red, although it had shown promise, fought briefly and then refused. Murdoch said, "Let's be shut of this whore."

There was a brief consultation with MacNeil, who had withdrawn into the shadows as if he hated them and this desecration of his school every Shrovetide; the child saw him raise bloodshot eyes.

"You know the custom. A boddle a throw."

Seven or eight men had the coin. The child watched them batter the bird, breaking its wing joint, blinding its jewel-bright eyes. It fluttered and beat as the stones rained upon it; repulsed, he saw it die. When it was lying inert Murdoch held it up by the feet.

"Here's a fine kain-hen for somebody's supper. Who wants it, eh? Who'll take it?" And the dead cock was tossed aside; they raked away the stains and handed another bird to the pit, a proud thing with bronze feathers and fitted with steel spurs. The bets flew; the others made their brutal sport, kicking the bloody, blinded corpse until the child heard the scratch of its spurs along the floor, and then the man nearest him, its owner, cursing it for having lost, put his boot upon it and crushed its head.

The child pushed outside and vomited in the ruts. Then he stumbled on, but the old panic gripped him and he began to run. He ran and stumbled and ran again, five miles with the terror and the sickness drowning him: he burst into the house, bleating.

He huddled in the corner. The house was dark; the calm, the clear, the unspeakably pure new moon shone in beneath the eaves.

He shut his eyes and fell into a dazed sleep.

It was March and still cold… it was April and too early for sowing. The child went out, barefoot and shivering, and wandered the moors and climbed to the high corries of Creag na h'Iolaire, where the snow lay until midsummer, and returned with cut hands and chilblains and a deeper sense of calm and reason than any he had known throughout the winter. When the men were cutting peat he went down to the hags to watch them, feeling for the first time in months the need of human company.

He was startled by the violence of one who threw a freshly filled creel at him; it smashed, spilling the wet turf.

"There's your peat, you whore's son! Take it to Muireach on your own bloody back!" and there followed a stream of obscenity, which the child understood. Finally the more paternal of the men drew him away, saying, "Go home, boy. This is no place for you," and he went, but he did not go home.

He ran up to the birch wood, where the young birds of spring were calling. The ground was scarfed with blue, the wild hyacinth blooming, and where the sun penetrated the new leaves a shivering pattern fell.

Memory seized him, and a brief, bright joy. He had played here once, coming with flowers for his mother's lap. He ran in among them, and picked so many that he could scarcely carry them, and wandered deeper into the wood.

He was not alone. It was not unusual for Ewen to take his exercise here, occasionally with one of the dogs, although he hated the weather and was as oblivious to his surroundings as the child was painfully aware.

Fearful of him, the child kept away, and watched him with hungry eyes. He would afterwards remember Ewen's face, and hold the memory to himself like a secret, imagining him his guardian, a man to love, a man to trust; and the fantasy comforted him. And he wanted with all his heart to run after him and fill his hands with the wilting flowers.

But he could not bring himself to do it, and Ewen, unaware of him, walked on.

The spring advanced. The land quickened, giving first the weeds, thrusting from the winter's tangle to blow and blossom in the fallow fields, followed by the hesitant corn, the coarse black oats, the bearded, inferior barley. Giving the scent, later in summer, of sorrel and wild thyme, sedge and waist-high bracken and foxglove. On the moors there were hares, and adders, and the flashing runs of the hill streams, and the child walking saw cloud and rain drifting as low as smoke, and heard the day's thin high shrieking of eagles, and the evening's sad drumming of snipe.

He did not go again to the wood, but he looked always for the man and the dog. He did not see them on the moors: he never saw them again, and soon they too became part of the tangle of half-remembered things, and at last he forgot them.

His own, his private world, was full of nightmare. His vision had narrowed to the hearth where he slept and the rooms where his father abused him; he had begun to tremble at the very words, "Come here," and cringe at the sound of his voice. He was awakened from his sleep with a kick: he submitted passively when he saw the belt being loosened. In the mornings he could scarcely walk. He found blood in his urine more than once.

He spent his nights waking and in fear, watching his father drunk or asleep, unable to free his mind from anything but the wish that he or his father would die.

The slow meagre harvest was winnowed and milled. The nights drew in, the child shivered in the sharper air and wanted his brogans and a heavier shirt. But the brogans had been put away to save the leather; he was told he did not need them. And his father said there was yet warmth in the sun.

The year turned and darkened and began its plunge toward Samhain.

An hour or two after midnight he crept to the bed, crying softly. He had dreamed of his mother, and heard her voice. She was not there. He climbed in, huddled weeping, and slept.

He woke suddenly, every nerve tensed at the sound he had heard in his sleep. The light flared close to his face.

His father had come home and was staring down at him, the candle in his unsteady hand spilling tallow into the bedclothes. The child looked beyond the flame and saw the girl, not much older than himself, leaning against the doorframe. She was thin and dirty and drunk, and his father was also drunk.

He caught the child's hair in his fist and jerked his face up toward the flame, so that he felt the heat sear his cheek.

"Get out of my bed, you cunt."

He dragged him roughly out: the child, dazed by light and fear and shame, clung to him in a sweaty tangle of limbs. Stripping him of his nightgown, taking his belt off slowly, the girl all eyes, sobered now, saying, "No, Muireach, don't hurt him—" the belt singing and biting around his naked flanks. "Show her your cock, gallan," and to the girl, "Aye, there's his little prong, it's piss and the fear of me makes it so proud—" Then he had spilled his urine with fear and pain and was thrown back against the stained bedding, and the night was dark and quiet once more; his father pushed the girl out and they went downstairs for their purpose. Then he threw the girl out and went out again himself, and the child fell asleep in the tumbled bed in the first cold light of morning.

So Margaret's son spent his twelfth year.

No one was ever questioned or accused of the murder of Margaret Campbell. He never heard any other living being express a hint of shock, regret or condolence, or speak her name, or talk of her: he could not ask his father why because of their deep estrangement. His father pursued his own violent pleasures, and no one intruded into that life they shared but crofters and whores, whose eyes slid away from the child's face and who stood dumb as stones in Murdoch's presence. It was not as though Margaret had died. It was as though she had never lived.

So the child observed the world, and the world maintained its callous or its frightened silence, and he saw that it had no pity for him and no desire to comfort him or share his horror and his confusion. And so he became resigned to it, and regressed into silence, and thoughts came and went making little sense to him: faulty memories and questions concerning her death which came imperfectly and could not be answered or understood.

He knew he was crazed, his father had told him so. It did not occur to him to doubt Murdoch. He was not normal and he accepted that he had no normal perception of things: the rest of the world was content in the enigma of the twelfth of March, it was only another mark of his difference that he was not resigned.

He had never heard the phrase, conspiracy of silence, but he sensed an unnatural, silent compact surrounding those who should most vehemently have deplored his mother's murder. Inglis MacNeil... whatever his personal hostility toward her, Margaret was yet a woman of his parish. And no grave in Glen Sian could be found to bear her name. Why had she been buried where he could not find her, why had MacNeil allowed it?

And Ewen. Ewen would have known. Why was Ewen silent?

And Murdoch, who should have taken up the cause of vengeance; as the months passed and he made no loud outcry for justice, had not people begun to wonder, though their gossip, because they feared him, be confined to whispers at their own firesides?

Let's be shut of this whore.

Why had his father done *nothing?*

He remembered running, on stiff, insensate legs. Pounding feet behind him— curses— shouts. He ran down by the river, through the glen, hurtling into the foggy wood. Burying himself in the leaves, shutting his eyes in the deep bosom of the earth.

Lying, listening. The cold scent of leaves, soft rain wetting his back, the urine spurting between his legs. Breath tearing in and out of his lungs: his terrible panting.

The men came. They found him easily, kicking away the leaves. Their hands hauled him up. Whimpering with terror, he clung to their arms and knees.

He woke screaming. The house was dark. He threw himself out of bed and ran, on those same fear-numbed legs. Murdoch was standing naked in his room, a shirt in one hand, leaning down to snuff the candle with the other.

He flung himself at him, sobbing. He did not notice his nudity, only his immovable strength. Murdoch pried him away and held him, struggling, shouting at him.

"Ciod tha sin? Ciod tha sin?" But he could not tell him what it was: he could only cling to him, sobbing and gasping until his mouth and his father's neck and chest were wet with his saliva. Murdoch flung him away as though he revolted him, and his head snapped back and forth, and he cried soundlessly: spittle ran down his chin.

Da, tell me.... Why did you let them? Why did you go away?

But he could not speak, and Murdoch, beside himself with fury, was shaking him like a man possessed.

"Talk to me, damn you— why don't you talk to me? Why don't you talk like a natural bairn? You used to talk to me!"

He gasped, and slobbered, and shuddered, and tried to cling to him, and Murdoch slapped his face brutally, and put him out of his room and shut the door.

Ewen met the child in a birch wood called Sithean Oir, on the morning of the twenty-eighth of September. It was his thirty-third birthday, and he was contemplating suicide.

When his dogs deserted him he was at first indifferent, but as time passed and they did not respond to calls or whistles he became annoyed, and thought they had gone to higher ground, following the scent of the rut. Pursuit was not a prospect that appealed to him.

A frenzied barking erupted deeper in the wood, and he threw aside his walking stick and ran toward it.

It was not deer they had been stalking but a child, crouched on the ground protecting his face. A mangled rabbit lay at his feet. At Ewen's appearance the child snatched it and ran; the dogs chased him and brought him down. Ewen dragged them off and thrust them away. The child huddled with his arms around his knees, rocking himself, his urine streaming unheeded.

Ewen raised him. He was verminous, and his jaw was lividly bruised. There was no question of his identity: he had the woman's features in miniature, and, disquietingly, her eyes.

He was revolting, offensive to every sense, and Ewen, who had seen madness, wanted only to be absolved of responsibility toward it. Whatever Murdoch's reasons for this unconscionable neglect, he wanted to remain in ignorance of them; whatever pity and horror lay here, he preferred to leave it undisturbed.

But he could not, perhaps because in this wreckage of childhood he had found something he pitied more than himself.

"Let me see your rabbit, Malcolm." He spoke in French, but the gentleness of the tone was unmistakable. "Let me see this rabbit."

The eyes were opaque, the lashes lowered. His shirt was opened to the breastbone, the skin mottled with sores.

Ewen took the bruised face between his hands.

"Bha thu air do bhualadh," you have been struck, and the child grunted and twisted away. "Nach 'eil? Có aig do bhualadh?"

Another small struggle; in the hollow of his throat a pulse was wildly beating.

"Who has hurt you?"

The eyes were shuttered, without intelligence. Ewen released him and he scraped desultorily at the rabbit with his nails.

Ewen said, after several moments, "Am bheil t' athair an so?" Is your father here?

"Cha n-eil."

His face remained very quiet, very still. Ewen might have imagined that he spoke.

He crouched closer. The smell of blood and faeces was overpowering.

"Leave that," he said.

The fierce, light eyes burned into his face and the voice was toneless, as if he had forgotten the mechanics of speech.

"Is leam e." Mine.

There was a spatter of blood on his cheek. Ewen wiped it away.

"If you are hungry you shall be fed, but not like this." The child shook off his hand with real violence, and he said, "Leave it, or I will tell your father." The effect was instantaneous. The child almost threw it, then wiped his hands on his clothing as if he would be completely dissociated from it, and looked up like a dog, uncertain if praise or punishment were forthcoming.

"That is better. Now come with me."

The child allowed himself to be led, stealing wild, incredulous, frightened glances at him. He trusted Ewen implicitly: looking up into his eyes, something within himself had leaped in recognition, as if he had known this man and been waiting for him all his life. And so, whatever Ewen would do with him he was resigned... there was a strange peace in resignation... he had given himself to inevitability.

They had reached the gardens of Ardsian, and the grass was soft beneath his hardened soles, then he saw the stallion being led across the courtyard, and Ewen remarked, "I see that your father has just come in."

He faltered, and whatever else this beautiful man was he was not perceptive: he did not see his sudden unwillingness and the child did not presume to reveal it again. He allowed himself to be taken into the house and closed into a room where Ewen left him, saying, "I am just going away to wash my hands. Stay there." His nerves quivered with a haunted restiveness: images flickered in glass, his own and other reflections; motes of dust drifted in a vast, cold silence. The prospect of Ewen returning or Murdoch finding him here became unbearable.

He got the door open and ran across the courtyard, gulping the familiar, bitter air.

He ran until he was certain of no pursuit, then he flung himself face down, clutching the earth, barely able to comprehend what had happened to him.

He felt he had thrown himself out of heaven, but there was nothing else he could have done.

Ewen sent several times to the house but Murdoch refused to answer him, and finally he forced the confrontation he dreaded. It was a wild, wet night in the second week of November

The house was in darkness but for a banked fire in the kitchen; the door was on the latch. As his eyes accepted the absence of light he ventured further, speaking the boy's name quietly. The air was noisome with alcohol and neglect, the silence overlaid with furtive sounds.

Faint light, perceptible only on the periphery of his vision: he followed it and found Murdoch lying across a bed, the light of a single candle swaying over a semen-stained nakedness.

He raised his head, muttering, "Dé b'àill leat?" and Ewen, in an access of white fury, knocked the whisky from the table as he groped for it.

"Did he see you?"

"He did more than see."

Ewen said, "You unspeakable lecher," and turned back to the darkness of the stairs.

"So she learned him he has a cock. What of it?"

He returned to the kitchen, by instinct rather than vision, and controlled himself with effort when he became aware that the boy had emerged from hiding. He was sitting on a chair, bent forward from the waist, his elbows on his knees, his hands hanging loosely, the long black hair hiding his face. His body spoke of humiliation and shame.

Ewen approached him cautiously, and did not attempt to touch him.

"Malcolm." He was trembling; there was no other response. The head remained bent, the face concealed. He smelled of raw spirit and urine. "All is well, Malcolm. Have no fear."

For a second he saw the eyes, still, wounded, incurably aggrieved, then the lashes veiled them. He had begun to urinate where he sat.

"Take your coat and go outside, Malcolm."

He stood, shuddering, and walked toward the door. Murdoch had come down and was leaning against the wall, naked but for a soiled shirt, and for another searing instant Ewen saw the eyes. Ferocity, intelligence, outrage.

"Go on, brogach. Learn to lick lily arses."

The door opened and closed and the dead leaves settled. Murdoch spat phlegm on the floor.

"He's no son of mine, I tell you. He's a curse."

In the light of the opened door the burning eyes held him, unblinking, with rain-drenched lashes.

Ewen put an arm tentatively around his shoulders, and signalled to the ghillies to follow.

VII

He found himself in a dark red, candlelit room, facing a ewer and a basin. He had not spoken since they had brought him to Ardsian.

The verminous hair was cut by the valet; the flash of the scissors seemed to paralyze him with fear.

"Brûlez ceux-ci."

The hair was removed, followed by his clothes. He stood trembling, covering his genitals with his hands; he had been beaten and the injuries were fresh. He was desperately undernourished.

"Now you must wash. You know how to wash."

His head quivered. The fierce intelligence had receded, and the eyes were shuttered.

"Shall I help you?"

He recoiled, and Ewen gave him a strained smile and left him, and drank cognac in his own rooms and composed himself for several minutes, then he wrote in his journal, *Oh, my God, all is chaos. He is an animal*, before returning with a nightshirt.

The boy had laved his body and emptied the ewer over his head. As the nightshirt was pulled over his dripping hair he fought, uttering high-pitched cries. He refused the gruel Ewen offered him, biting the spoon and regurgitating what he had swallowed. Ewen abandoned the effort and took him behind the screen, indicating the chamber pot. He did not use it and eventually came out, and Ewen pulled back the bedclothes and gestured that he was to sleep, and covered him and leaned down to kiss his forehead. He shrank as if from an assault and, embarrassed, Ewen withdrew, taking the candles away.

He sat up, staring beyond the figured hangings; the darkness was alive with ghosts, his own or the indelible traces of the past. Eventually he dragged the bedclothes to the floor and made a nest, and fell into a chilled half sleep, waking to the sound of the rain.

He woke, his lungs raw with unremembered screams: he was drenched with urine. Ewen, in a dressing gown, was crouched on the floor near him.

"Tell me what you dream, Malcolm."

Of the sickness and obscenity, he could find language only for *m' athair*, my father.

"He will not harm you here. No one shall."

He had never known compassion, so he did not recognize it: the hands divesting him of the wet shirt were instruments of fear, and when they offered him only cleansing and comfort he wept, with great violence and without tears. It purged and exhausted him and he fell asleep with the abruptness of a child, and slept still when Ewen laid him down against the pillows, his face calm, averted, lost in a dream of peace.

MacNeil had been out all day visiting in the parish, something which, as he now had no horse, had to be accomplished on foot. He had walked twelve miles through rain and chilling wind, and the prospect of night was upon him, and his thoughts were comfortless.

He saw the lights of Ardsian and turned toward them. Here was an hour's hospitality, a welcome alternative to the dolorous silence of his house, and the answer to a disturbing rumour he had heard throughout the township.

He had hoped it was not true: as he stood in the entrance shaking the rime from his cloak, he saw that it was. The boy was sitting on the stairs, his face like a wizened painting, his hair cropped to the scalp. MacNeil stared at him coldly and the boy got to his feet and went up without haste, leaving his ill-fitting shoes on the stairs.

The drawing room was lit by fire and a few candles. Ewen half rose and extended a hand.

"My friend. What brings you here?"

MacNeil ignored the hand.

"I think you're a fool."

"That is nothing new."

"I think you want saving from yourself."

Ewen regarded him with pity, and with reserve. Throughout the years he had sensed an unyielding animosity, because he was French, because he was Catholic— although MacNeil had fought beside Catholics and led them for a Catholic king, in what was largely a Catholic cause— or because he had not opened his heart or his pockets freely enough to that very cause. He had wanted MacNeil's respect if he could not have his friendship, and had earnestly sought it, but always that nameless, immovable barrier repelled him, and he was no longer young or naïve enough to believe it would ever fall away.

"Were you fully aware of the circumstances?"

"Aye. I was aware."

"And yet you felt no obligation—"

"My help was never sought in that quarter."

"Need it have been *sought*?"

The eyes rested on him, reddened and unquiet. He had failed much in the past year, Ewen thought; pain and bitterness had burned compassion from him.

"There are some wounds, Glen Sian, that affection cannot heal."

They regarded one another across a distance of more than the dimly patterned carpet, and the silence was sharp with resentment.

"I take it you will not tutor him."

"He should be put to the plough. What his father's left in his head will never be worth teaching."

Another silence, intransigent on both sides. Finally MacNeil said, "And James?"

"He has always wanted a brother. I have given him one."

MacNeil walked heavily to the door, and on the stairs the boy faded from view, holding the secrets, the insults, the warnings to himself, nursing them like some fatal injury against the day when they, too, would be remembered.

"I hope you know what you do, to yourself and to your son."

"I have no fear."

"I hope you need have none."

***

There was terror in the house, which the boy confronted alone, of the dogs and the men, and of a meeting with his father, which waking and sleeping haunted him, but by chance or Murdoch's design this never happened, and he began to dread it less.

On Christmas morning Ewen gave him a rosary and a crucifix. He was ashamed, partly because he could not reciprocate, partly because he felt himself being forced into a metamorphosis beyond his comprehension. He knew Ewen wished him to lead a Catholic life; he had no inkling, then, of Ewen's fervent hope that he come to consider the priesthood, and when he learned of it in maturity the hope had become obscene.

Eventually he ceased to wear the crucifix. He clung to the rudiments of religion for a while, and finally rejected it, knowing that it offered him nothing: he would never find Ewen's god nor any other man's.

The Celtic year turned again, as inevitable as the progress of the stars, marked by Beltane, Lammas, Samhain, which Ewen with his calendar of feasts and saints did not observe and would never understand. Once the boy had been a part of them; now he watched from a window, divorced from something so essentially himself.

He grieved, without knowing it, for what had given him happiness: running out bare-legged in the mud, so joyous to see the new sunlight of April, watching the men of the township ploughing with cas chrom or horse-gangs, seeding the stony earth; the brown birds rising from the furrows, a child shouting to frighten them off. Women with kerchiefed necks and rough blue skirts beating linens clean at the river, the sun climbing higher, the days warmer, the nights shorter, and the first of May bringing the Beltane fires. The nights of fire had frightened and excited him: smoke roiling, men leaping, daring the flames for luck, women's hair in the red glow, fire licking at the skirts of the unwary. The cattle driven through the smoke to keep the plague away. And the children following the kine through the embers, then himself, Malcolm, when every one else had gone.

Then July, and the shielings, the songs of the dairymaids blown down on the soft wind, summer rain sweeping the lochan.

He grieved, and remembered.

Harvest... the hard flash of sickles, the grace of the dance of gleaning. The women sang at their work, the grain fell heavy-headed in the golden air; he heard the silken rustle as it fell. Bare feet, bare arms, bare heads, bare throats, dust and sunlight, chaff and corn; barley, oats; cool weather, warm weather, sunlight dazzling on the water. Run-rig fields. Winnowing. Lammas, the high point of summer. His mother's garden, tending it with dirty hands.

And Samhain coming, and winter, and night.

That night was not yet over for him. It seemed he had been sleeping, lying numbly in some dark place, unable to rise and free himself of the long dark dream which had begun with her death. Of that time he remembered no love and no kindness, only cold, and filth, and violence, and moments of obscene abuse, so he had thrust it all away from him until he saw and heard nothing, could feel nothing, as one dead, or who slept.

It seemed he had been sleeping a long time, and had only just begun to wake.

Reawakening, for him, was almost beyond endurance.

He remained illiterate in French and English, although they were languages Ewen spoke to him constantly. James loathed him and missed no opportunity to inflict humiliation: his arms and shins were black from pinches and surreptitious kicks under the table. The seizures and the tormented dreams continued, and remained his private hell.

Ewen wrote infrequently of him. There seemed so little progress, little prospect of rehabilitation.

He cannot learn, he cannot write. His anger is consuming him.

He cannot accept that he is not his father. He believes himself indelibly stained.

He confides in me occasionally, becoming more articulate, although the vocabulary of Murdoch remains his chief form of expression... he does not intrude but will loiter, with a quality of stillness, if I am reading or otherwise occupied... I know then that he wishes to speak.

He tells me that he hates my son, and I draw from him the little tortures James inflicts. I say it is no more than James deserves.

He continued his stoic endurance of James, but it came to an end in midsummer. James called to him to hold his pony: he refused, and James leaned out of the saddle and cut him across the face with his crop. Malcolm hauled him down and punched him savagely; a groom ran up to pull him off and he fought him with expert fists and feet and fled through the grounds to the eastern glen, where he had hidden in his childhood.

He sat in the heather, throwing stones into the river, blood coursing with fury and adolescence.

I want to be good. I want to be like you.

He no longer knew what he wanted, or who or what he was.

He was still sitting when he heard the hooves.

Before Ewen could speak he said, staring at the river, "I'll kill the next bastard who lays his hand on me, or shoves his boot up my arse."

His voice cracked absurdly.

"Come back to the house, Malcolm."

He got up, slowly, because his body ached.

As they walked, Ewen put his arm around him.

He crouched in the gallery, waiting for Murdoch: this had always been his favoured place for eavesdropping. He was there in a different capacity now, as Ewen's bodyguard.

James interrupted this vigil at his usual bedtime, trailing a velvet robe over his nightgown. Their conversation now was in an idiomatic Gaelic far more fluent than Ewen knew.

"Where's my papa? He didn't come to kiss me."

He was ignored, so he tugged dangerously at Malcolm's sleeve; he no longer dared to abuse him physically.

Malcolm said, "Go away, you little shit," not taking his eyes from the hall below, and James began a strategic withdrawal.

He stayed motionless for over an hour, saw the tray of whisky and glasses taken in. The drawing room doors remained closed, the voices were no more than a murmur. The dogs settled to sleep in the hall. Then the doors flung open suddenly: he heard Murdoch's voice, then Ewen's. Instantly he was on his feet, fumbling for the blade.

"Christ, you're like a fucking woman, what good is it talking to you?"

And he was gone, the hounds barking and snarling after him, before his son had time to draw his blood.

He found Ewen sitting, one hand to his eyes. The whisky appeared untouched.

"What do you want?"

"I heard my father here."

"And so?"

"Why do you let him speak to you like that?" Ewen raised his head and looked at him, but said nothing. He came further into the room. "Why don't you —"

"Why don't I— what?"

Subdued, he said, "Tell him to go."

Ewen said, as though it afforded him exquisite amusement, "Don't be so absurd."

"He called you— those names."

"Your father and I have dealt together for five years. I think I understand his way of expressing himself."

"But he—"

"Listen to me, Malcolm. You and I have become friends— very well. That does not confer upon you the right to assert yourself so familiarly, even upon my behalf. Do you understand?"

He went upstairs and continued to eavesdrop until he heard Ewen go out.

He waited all night; at dawn he came down and found him sprawled in his greatcoat before a dead fire, a dark rain rattling on the windows, a deerhound nearby. His hair was wet, his mouth slightly open, snoring; the peat on his boots had stained the carpet. He stank of smoke and pot stills.

The boy regarded him with pity and resignation, recognizing capitulation, dragged off his boots, and brought a cloak from the gunroom and covered him.

Ewen drew him into the very bosom of his family after that, and loved him without reservation.

Tentatively, in the evenings, he sought to establish himself, his history, his identity. Perhaps such disclosures were not decorous; perhaps a prouder or less lonely man would not have made them. But he imagined many similarities between Malcolm and that troubled, youthful self, and he did not want secrets in return. It was comfort enough to share some of his own.

He spoke of his family, all dead now, his brothers, the sisters lost to smallpox, his father, a vain, sensual man whom he had never loved, his gay, inconsequential mother, whom he had adored. He spoke of Rome and Paris, Tuscany and Provence, the silvered flicker of olive leaves in a bleaching sunlight, the wash of the Adriatic at the starlit steps of the Piazzetta San Marco in Venice. *You will see these places.* He spoke of himself with a deprecating smile, a shy and sickly child, a stammering, oversensitive youth gambling on the fringe of the demi-monde. He spoke of fear and hopelessness, and guilt because he hungered for music, art and pleasure; he spoke of Elspeth, and then because it would not be avoided, of sex, and encountered a frigid indifference.

He had expected this, but the disdain only heightened his own preoccupation, as if by seeking to sound the depths of a half conscious sexuality he had unleashed his own. He had begun to read and write pornography again, and encoded episodes of sexual activity in his journal with the single word *jouissance*: celibacy had been forced upon him, and he found it untenable. But there could be no prostitute from among his tenants; his own nature would not sustain it, and he remained acutely aware of James's innocent eyes, and the fierce, intolerant eyes of Malcolm.

So the nights remained lonely and stained piquantly with shame, the sins secret, the desire disdained. He denied both sin and desire, and was mocked by the eroticism of his dreams.

The year 1749 was drawing to a close.

He received a letter in the week before Christmas. A priest had come to the Great Glen for the first time in three years, and was staying at a house in Fort Augustus. All unattainted households had been informed.

It would be naïve to underestimate the danger. A priest travelling incognito through occupied country was almost invariably an agent, carrying substantial amounts of French gold and papers as well as the instruments of the Mass. If caught he could be hanged. If found with him a man, particularly a Catholic, a Frenchman, and a suspected Jacobite, could forfeit everything, including his life.

He took James and Malcolm and half a dozen ghillies, and travelled two days before Christmas.

They joined the River Moriston and rode through its narrow valley. By early afternoon he had seen enough to wish he had chosen some other route.

He had heard that of all Clan Grant only the young Glenmoriston and his tacksman Dundreggan had declared for the Prince; the Laird of Grant had always been royalist. He knew that for Glenmoriston's choice his lands had been ravaged not once but several times, by English raiders and then by Whiggish Highland lairds on their westward marches home after Culloden. He knew Grant of Dundreggan had been stripped and brutalized, despite a certificate of immunity, and left naked beside his wife with a halter around his neck, and that the great houses of Dundreggan and Glenmoriston had been burned to the ground. But he had not passed this way since the rising, and he had not known it would be like this.

If there were Grants still in the glen he did not see them. Nothing moved but a solitary shadow, a phantom-grey stag sniffing the scent of man and horse and springing away in languid flight. The river wound over stones, a black ribbon twisting between banks of rotting snow, and the quarrelling water was the only sound that disturbed the stillness. And then he saw the ruins, the fallen walls of Glenmoriston, blackened timber and charred rafters, the only movement a hawk rising from a branch, beating the air with powerful wings. He had prepared himself for this sight: he had not warned the others, and quietly, in the silence, his son began to cry.

Closer to the house he slowed his horse, recognizing human shadows; tinkers, he thought, living here in what shelter remained.

He reined in and one of the ghillies came to stand at his stirrup.

"Where are the Grants? Where have they gone? Who are these hellish people?"

"They are the Grants, Glen Sian."

He tore his eyes away from the roofless walls.

They had declared, while he had not. He had been secret, silent, safe, if safety was to be found in cataclysm. He had been discreet; for the sake of his people only, he had been discreet.

Between discretion and cowardice lay a fine line, for him too fine now to be discerned.

They lay that night at Invermoriston, and joined the road on the shore of Loch Ness in the morning.

A memory which had long disquieted him came once more to fret at the edge of his mind. The rain, the sodden red coats, the black, lonely country and the rattling beat of the drum. Women. Baggage. Pack horses, bearing plunder. And a prisoner, himself. The officers. He had watched them with a bloody vengeance in his heart, and he could not forget them even now. The lieutenant-colonel, a frail man with a Roman face and a maimed right arm. A boy whose beauty he had cause to know hid a monster of incalculable savagery. And the third officer, of senior rank, who rode at the rear of the column, and bore himself as though ill or in pain. He had acknowledged none of the others, although he had spoken once to Ewen.

We are two unhappy bastards, you and I, but they have done for neither of us yet.

They reached Fort Augustus in the bitter sunset. It was as he remembered: the pier, Crannog castle on its islet, the burial grounds across the River Oich, the Tarff, the desolate moors. A galley from Inverness with stores for the garrison lay at uneasy anchor where he had first set foot on Scottish soil. A sharp wind had come up and was churning the black waters of the loch.

The fort itself. Once square, thick-walled, with a dozen six-pounder cannon menacing the empty hills, it was a ruin now. The Prince's army had held it briefly against the Hanoverians and had blown it up after a week's siege with nineteen barrels of powder. The barracks had been demolished but cellars and stables remained, and damp cells he well remembered beneath the ground. The garrison was uncomfortably lodged there, and attempting to restore it with little success.

The daylight was seeping away, darkness coming from a threatening sky. The track, now joining Wade's military road from Inverness, led down toward the town.

They passed the fort, close enough to see the distinctive regimental lace on the facings of the scarlet coats, the light on oiled muskets. A mounted officer, approaching, kicked his steaming horse to a faster pace and overtook them, coughing into a stained handkerchief. The sentries, too, were coughing, and shivering at their posts. It seemed Fort Augustus was garrisoned by sick men.

Then they had left it behind.

A nondescript door opened; a young man in shabby clothing was seated in the room beyond, leaning toward the fire with a book. He could have travelled through any community and been forgotten overnight; he could pass unnoticed in any street.

Ewen bared his head and said in French, "I am Stirling of Glen Sian. My family and I have come to see Mr. Saunders."

The guest raised his eyes, and closed the book and smiled.

"Benedicite."

He gave his hands, and Ewen knelt and kissed them, and heard the calm voice speaking the words of comfort and sanctification for which he hungered unimaginably, and had thought never to hear again.

In nomine Patris, et Filii, et Spiritus Sancti.

And the sins of the lonely would be forgiven him.

They had eaten; they were lying in their clothes in the darkness. He was verminous from the dirty inn of the previous night, and the knowledge caused him acute embarrassment.

He lay, and the young man nearest the wall breathed softly, and James, between them, tossed and whimpered, and the vermin crawled from one body to another and a light rain fell, changing to snow overnight.

James woke in the middle of the night, needing but not knowing where to find in the stifling, shuttered bed the chamber pot which was always kept beneath his own. He whispered, "Papa," against the unshaven cheek. Ewen did not respond.

He lay desperately, trying not to touch the other man, who had shifted in sleep so that one hand was resting on his hair on the pillow, thinking, why didn't we stay at home, I can't put out my shoes for le bonhomme Noël here … and wishing it were not so dark, and that the stinging bites on his scalp would cease to torture him. He whimpered a little, and a tear trickled into his pursed mouth. He fell asleep briefly, then woke again in torment.

Then the shutter opened quietly and he heard the familiar, contemptuous whisper.

"Come on, then. I know what you want," and he was lifted out and over Ewen's body into the icy darkness of the room, and he felt Malcolm take and lead him, not ungently, by the hand.

Malcolm had not been invited to join the others in the parlour which had served as the confessional, and the omission and Ewen's failure to prevent it had hurt him briefly, although he had already begun his journey toward nonconformity and atheism, and had no real desire to participate in the rituals of the Church.

The Mass was celebrated at noon, following the arrival of four or five others. The boy stood outside in a slowly falling snow, and watched the road to the garrison with remote eyes.

Ewen refused to return home through Glen Moriston, so he took them by a different route, over the saddle of land that rose a thousand unsheltered feet from Fort Augustus. Their progress was slow: he was no horseman, and the ghillies were on foot.

By four o'clock night had fallen. They sheltered against rocks which broke the teeth of the wind, and the ghillies tried and failed to make fire. The horses swung their rumps to the weather, the men huddled on the ground. James cried and whimpered, complaining of a pain in his side. Snow began to whiten his hair.

In the night, Malcolm, who had been sheltering with the ghillies, came and rolled beneath the plaids. James lay still, embraced by his father and the slim, strong body at his back, and seemed to sleep.

They reached Ardsian in the morning. James had begun to cough blood.

On the third day, his bodyservant Coll MacGregor returned to Fort Augustus and came back with the priest.

In the afternoon, Ewen opened the door to his son's room. The priest, with great tenderness, was administering the ointment of extreme unction.

The colourless eyes lifted.

"Leave us," he said.

Ewen walked blindly through the house, found himself in the drawing room, in its frightening privacy.

My son is dying, he thought. Because of me, he dies.

And, putting his ravaged face into his hands, he wept.

***

He sat in the morning room, awaiting with apprehension the man he knew only as Saunders. It was the first day of the new decade.

"Your son has had pneumonia. The crisis has passed, and I think he will recover. Careful nursing will be needed to prevent a relapse. And it seems likely that the lungs will suffer some scarring, which will leave him susceptible to future infection."

"He has never been as robust as most boys. I was much the same at his age."

"I would urge you to send him to a warmer climate, at least until he is older. You have relations still in France?"

"My cousin in Paris. My brother-in-law in Provence. They have families of their own."

Silence. The fire smoked. He stared at his hands, twisting the plain band which had replaced his wedding ring.

"You have no other heirs?"

He could not speak; he felt crushed by some irresistible force.

"Will you consider what I have said? It may mean, quite literally, his life or death."

"He is all I have of his mother. I cannot send him from me."

Alone again, he stood a long while in the fathomless silence. The light was failing; the snow fell softly, shrouding everything.

This room had known so many tears: he had no more to give it.

He approached the scarred escritoire as he would an enemy, with hatred and bitter wariness, pulled a sheet of vellum from a drawer and began to write, filling the silence with the dry, hesitant scratching of his quill.

James departed for Provence in April. The weather was still uncompromisingly cold, and there was snow in Inverness the morning Ewen stood at Citadel Quay watching the ship for Rotterdam receive his son on board. James huddled at the rail with Coll MacGregor as the grey water of the Beauly widened between himself and his father, gravely waving and trying not to weep, although the wind made his ear ache and the uninviting sea was filling him with terror. Finally he put his hand to his ear, an odd little childish gesture seen by Ewen on the quay, and the grey water and the grey sky rushed together in a scathing flood of tears.

He hid his face in Coll's coat. The deck began to cant under the press of sail and the shore slid slowly out of reach and time began to take him into its flood, bearing him helplessly toward an unknown life. Coll bore his grief patiently until the ship cleared the roads and beat out into the Moray, then he turned his young charge to look back for what would be his last sight of Scotland for many years. Inverness lay behind them, river and town and bridge and quay, leaning houses and tossing fishing boats, the silvered hills of the Black Isle, the summit of Mealfuarvonie rearing above Loch Ness. It was the first landfall a homeward-bound mariner saw, tacking into the Moray a hundred miles away.

It was the last of his home James remembered.

VIII

The entry in Ewen's journal for the twenty-fourth of June 1750 read: *He disarmed me today, with a move I had not taught him. It was both instinctive and shocking.*

I have taken a young eagle to my breast. I will never forget his eyes as he contemplated this epiphany, his ability to kill.

Seen fencing by Murdoch in the library that summer, the son who had been a stranger to him since his birth was an enigmatic alien, matured beyond recognition.

The riposte faltered; some sound or sense of a presence focused the fierce eyes on the half-opened door, and he heard Ewen's impatient, "Fais-y attention!"

Murdoch let it close as though blown by the wind and walked away.

Their faces, all the faces from the past, haunted him that evening. He was not a superstitious man, had fought and overcome the Celt within himself to live in a house so peopled by ghosts, but this night he could not shake their clinging fingers. The wild swans flew over from the lochan: he sat, half drunk and half dreaming, listening to the beat of their wings.

The shadows deepened. He urinated in the weed-blown garden and stared at the glimmer of the lochan in the twilight and began to cry without any particular emotion, conscious only of a bewildering pain. He cried as he had not since the night Ewen had taken his son from him.

When his tears stopped he wiped his face on his sleeve and carried a candle upstairs and rummaged through Margaret's kist at the foot of the bed, the marriage chest for a wedding which had never been. After a time he found what he was looking for and crouched with it in his hands. It was very worn and the shape had never been plain, but it had once resembled a horse, and she had carved it as a toy for her son.

He held it, thinking, no, he would not be wanting this now.

He cried a little more, with his head down on the chest, then he replaced it gently and closed the lid on it.

He spent the next seven nights at his task, sharpening the bone hooks, tying the mottled feathers of grouse and curlew and making them fast with horsehair and wax. Cursing his unsteady fingers and the uncertain light, for these must be perfect, they were for his son.

When they were finished he laid them on the kitchen table and admired them, the large bright patterns for brook trout, the small dark flies for brown, and several spare hooks and a reed box in which to keep them.

He put them all in the reed box, awed by the sheer delicacy and skill of his own work, then, impulsively, he emptied them out and wrapped them in an unclean handkerchief and put the small carved horse in the box instead.

He closed it and folded the handkerchief and went to bed, filled with a lingering dread, and the strange, fearful pleasure of offering himself once more for his son's love.

At the end of the week, increasingly disturbed by Malcolm's isolation, Ewen took him to the shielings, ostensibly to inspect the herd but hoping, by exposing him to opportunity, to facilitate some sexual rite of passage. The girls were clean, shy, virginal, and despite the austerity of his manner, he was not immune to them.

In the event, he seemed more interested in the cattle than the women, and after a curt, "À bientôt," he was last seen at twilight climbing to a higher pasture; if he slept it was under the stars, and presumably alone.

The girl came with the brief darkness of the summer night. He dared not suspect Malcolm of complicity: to have done so would have attributed to him either a lascivious sense of humour, and humour he significantly lacked, or a degree of perspicacity Ewen was not prepared to contemplate

He had kissed her only once, the sensation piqued by shame and self-punishment like all his sexual experiences, and slid his fingers into the silken wetness he so desired to invade and violate: the ecstasy was premature, a second's spasm, followed by impotence.

He poured a measure of the cognac he kept in his dressing room and drank it now, stimulated and repulsed.

He knows me. I cannot hide from him. I touch what I love; I accuse myself.
He drank another measure.

Why you and not him? What did she see in you, her father?
His evening meal was waiting; he did not want it, did not want the sexless asceticism of Malcolm's company. He wanted only to think of the beauty and the despoiled innocence, and torment himself with it a little, exquisitely.

The candles were lower, the sky darker. He had been too long about his dressing; it was time he finished it.

He had been too long alone, in this room and in this house. Tonight, and too many nights before it.

Too many years.

The fly was lying on the boy's pillow when he returned to his room. He was admiring it, thinking it a gift from Ewen, when memory stirred. He let it fall.

He found the reed box in the pocket of one of his coats. It opened easily, and even in the dimness he recognized what it held. Its power to move him was undiminished, so he did not look at it again.

He went down to the dining room, where Ewen was already seated in one of his unconscious attitudes of grace.

"You are late."

He walked to the head of the table and emptied the flies on to the linen. Unlike Ewen, he had neither washed nor changed, and knew that, if nothing else, would give offense.

"I found these in my room." There was no response, so he pushed them closer. "I said—"

"I heard you. Is that any excuse for appearing at the table in this stinking state?"

"No... but... my father put them in my room. I knew they came from him, because he ties flies like these."

"I have never denied your father access to you, nor you to him, for that matter."

"But he had no business in my room. He had no right."

"If your father wishes to give you a gift that is his affair and yours. It is certainly not mine. Now, will you put those damned things down and let us see if we may eat a civilized meal, despite the shambles you seem determined to make of it."

"He had no *right*—"

Ewen said, "You are not the one to talk of rights, in my house, where you yourself have none except as I choose to give them. Now, will you put those things away? I am wearied to death of them and they have disrupted my meal enough."

A soft fluttering to the carpet. He threw the second after it.

"Pick them up."

The rain fell. A smell of mildew permeated the air, the familiar stain flowering on the silk wallpaper. The ormolu clock on the sideboard seemed unnaturally loud.

"Pick up those things. I will not ask you again."

An intolerable minute or two as their wills contested, then whatever remained of the child obeyed him.

"You make so much of nothing, you— you *bore* me!"

They did not speak for the remainder of the meal.

At the end of the evening the flies were still lying on the table. Ewen took them upstairs and left them in his dressing room, and went to bed, his nerves like wires.

His sleep was fitful, and his dreams appalling; he woke from travesties of lewdness. The rain still fell, and the flies had gone.

Murdoch found them in the morning among his papers in the estate office. Each one had been torn to shreds.

He slumped in his chair, his hair and clothing wet with the rain that was still falling from a white, spent sky. There had been some mistake. The boy had not understood; perhaps Ewen had influenced him, or his heavy-handed humour had proved offensive. And then he knew that there had been no mistake and no misunderstanding. He had had his answer; it was all the answer any reasonable man should need.

He sat still, chin resting on his hands, the rain glittering in his long wild hair as the light of the morning strengthened behind him, the pain of his rejection cast aside, even faintly smiling. It was when he found the small carved horse, the only remaining evidence of Margaret, where it had been thrown so savagely against the wall that the plaster was chipped— it was then, finding that, that he cried.

He rode south that autumn with the drovers to the Falkirk cattle tryst, as he had not done for years.

In his youth when he had followed the cattle they had been driven to Crieff, on the hilly borders of Perthshire, and as much as thirty thousand guineas had changed hands at one fair among the Highland drovers and the Lowland buyers. But more and more since the rising the buyers were coming from England, and the trysts had been moved further south to accommodate them.

They still rode the old way, over the familiar drovers' tracks southeast from Spean Bridge through Badenoch and Atholl, Dalwhinnie and the Pass of Killiecrankie where posts marked the route in case a September snowstorm should obliterate the road, and then through Pitlochry to Perth and Stirling and Falkirk.

They rode, breathing the dust, singing sometimes, sleeping among the cattle; with demand increasing reiving had become prevalent again, and more profitable than at any time since the '45.

The army was everywhere. Mile after mile the scarlet coats affronted eyes bred to the sombre beauty of the mountains: soldiers labouring on the roads, officers shivering in the fine, soft rain. They watched and were watched with suspicion and hatred.

Once in Falkirk nothing was the same. If he had thought to touch hands here with the past, he had been mistaken. Falkirk was not Crieff, where the air had been alive with the lilting voices of the Gaelic-speakers, the crowds brilliant with their blue bonnets and swaying plaids and silver buttons, and the flash of steel at every man's hip. Here the plaids were gone, and the broadswords hidden, and the days when they were worn by free men with pride were ended; they would not come again.

The sight of the soldiers on the roads depressed and saddened him. Scotland as he had known it was no more. The old ways were changing, the old world dying, and the new, harsh day was dawning, lighting a barrenness he did not know and did not understand: a Scotland shaken from her fitful dreams of the warrior past, thrust starkly and painfully into the hungry, grey world of the modern age.

He left Falkirk knowing he would not see it again, and he left without particular regret. He did not know it; he would not know even Crieff. Only the Highlands waited, offering their bitter, timeless welcome, where that cold wind of change had not yet begun to blow.

He came home to the black days of autumn in Glen Sian, rain, and then the first snow; he rode out and saw it lying in the furrows like some barren seed of spring. Samhain passed, and startled him with the recollection that his son was fifteen years old.

Martinmas dawned, mild and windless. It was his day and his dominion and he shared his authority with no one; he presided like a king in the estate office. Some of the tenants came with payment, some with empty hands: they were blaming the wet summer and it was an excuse he soon tired of hearing. Some brought quarrels and accusations against their neighbours, and he heard them out in a judicial silence. He was not liked, but he was not lied to either, and invariably he heard the truth. When he had heard it his judgments were also, invariably, fair.

By nine o'clock the estate office was empty. The strongbox was locked, its pitiful offering of cash uncounted. That could wait until the morning, and there were other, remote crofts he would visit, collecting his due in neither coin nor kind.

He ate in the kitchen, as always on a quarter day; he spoke to no one and no one spoke to him. As he stood in the courtyard whistling for his horse to be brought, he smelled the taint of burning in the night. The moon was low and hazed with cloud. It was still unseasonably mild.

He did not mount but twisted his hand in the stallion's mane and walked slowly, troubled: some shred of gossip had disturbed him, and his son's absence from the house. He had hoped to see him.

He had not known that Ewen was walking in the grounds until the deerhound bitch, his constant companion, padded out of the night, and he recognized the slight figure in its sombre clothes. The bitch slunk closer, baring her teeth, and he said, "Ach, shut your mouth, you whore," and she flung herself at his feet, tail beating. He fondled her ungently and thrust her away, and she sank down, tongue lolling, nose resting on his boot.

"You do not ride tonight, Muireach?"

"I've spent enough time on my arse for one day."

"How were my rents?"

"In arrears. You saw what the harvest was."

"Will they want grain for the winter?"

"There's enough."

"I hope there is."

"And I hope I know my trade, Glen Sian, because I was feeding the people when you were still playing with yourself in France." He hawked and spat. "Who was for going into my office while I was away to the south? The books are out of order."

"You know I do not go to your office."

"Was it the gallan then, eh?"

"I hardly think so."

"But he can read now, and do his figures?"

"He would not enter your office. He has no business there."

"Well, I'll tell you something and you can tell it to him. What's in that room is mine. Mine, and no one touches it while I'm alive."

"You may have to resign yourself to that in time."

"Eh?"

"I have considered bringing in another man." Silence. This, then, was what he had heard, the whispers, the rumours. "A man to mediate with you, a constable in effect, chosen from among the people, and a ground officer brought in from the south. What I mean—"

"I know what the hell you mean."

"The times change, Muireach."

"Aye, don't they just."

Ewen called the bitch and turned to go. The soft voice pursued him.

"There's none that knows your land like me. I've seen your land in famine, I've gone hungry with the rest. It's coming... not this year maybe, but the year after that, surely... and the people will be crying for me. There'll be no town-bred bastard will be able to tell them what to do." The bitch stopped nosing in the leaves and returned to him, whining. "I've seen famine. I know it. I can smell it when it's coming, and it's coming again. You think this is bad, a bad harvest. You wait until it rains from March until September and there's nothing on the land but rot, and you can see nothing but the funerals going by, and you hear nothing but the bloody women weeping. And when the bairns are dead the women start to die, and then the men. And there's such a silence, and such a smoke over the land, because you burn the crofts then, Glen Sian— there's not a living soul you can put into a house where a man's lain three weeks dead with his family."

He kneed the bitch away and slung himself into the saddle, and it was not until he had gone that Ewen remembered Malcolm's name had not passed between them, nor any of the things he had intended to say.

They met for the last time at a crofter's wedding on a winter night in the settlement of Glen Sian. The bridegroom was fifteen, the son of a man Murdoch despised; the bride was a year younger.

She was sitting with her friends beneath a smoke-encrusted rafter; on the beam, which glistened like jet with the carbon of half a century, a rooster was fluttering. She was wearing her Sunday kirtle of coarse blue drugget and her hair had been braided with white ribbons. She was waiting to be kissed for luck, and Ewen brushed his lips against her cheek and murmured something she never heard and he never remembered: she had been dancing, and the flat brass brooch on her slight bosom quivered; her skin tasted of salt. Then he shook the bridegroom's sweating hand, and was crowded out of the croft with the others to the drying barn where the wedding feast had been laid out: eggs and potatoes, cheeses, salt and oatcakes, and kegs of whisky, ale and rum. The same fare featured at wakes; even the same planks were known to serve.

The fiddler was seated on an upturned keg, a clutter of children at his feet, and on the chaff-littered drying floor young men were dancing the mocking, defiant steps of the seann triubhis. Murdoch was among them, dancing with a grace and arrogance they could not match, although they were shoeless and he had declined to remove his boots.

They danced in silence; the yelping shouts were for old men, observers, to quicken the pace of the music. The seann triubhis ended. They danced

119

the Reel of Tulloch, sweat soaking their faces, then they paused for breath and a swallow of ale and threw their coats in the dust and danced again, the foursome reel Gille Callum, until Murdoch broke from them, swearing, and pushed away through the crowd.

Another dancer took his place and the music and the voices flowed on.

He was not seen again until the bridegroom was going among the guests with the plate; he had been drinking heavily and was in a savage, sarcastic mood. When the youth reached him he took a piece of silver from his pocket; it was an English shilling, about the same value as a Scots pound, and a stupendous sum to people who seldom saw money of any kind.

The bridegroom raised mild eyes and said, "And what will you want in return for that, a Mhaoir?"

Murdoch murmured in his ear. The boy flushed and said nothing. Murdoch glanced at the bride, still smiling.

The moment passed. The fiddling resumed, and the women were calling for partners. The boy gave the plate to his father, shook his head when questioned, and walked away to lead his bride out into the reel. Murdoch leaned against the wall and watched them for a while, and then went out.

The drinking and dancing continued until midnight, when the bride was taken away to be undressed and bedded. When word came that she was ready the men carried the bridegroom on their shoulders to the croft, and he too was stripped and bedded. The candles were doused, leaving only a low firelight; the women blessed the couple and left, and the men came forward to the bed.

She accepted their kisses with a blushing sweetness, the decorous and those lusty with drink; general good humour prevailed. Overcome with shyness, Ewen kissed her again, and her eyes held his, radiant eyes, and she smiled as if she would have spoken. He murmured, "God bless you," and withdrew, knowing he was visibly drunk, wishing this strange, erotic ritual were over.

Murdoch was among the men waiting.

The girl saw him also, and the radiance died in her face.

Unlike the others, he did not lean down. He knelt. She gazed at him with those lovely, fearful eyes, and the boy in the bed watched him, and their blood kindred in the noisy, benevolent crowd were roused from alcoholic bonhomie and turned suspiciously. He saw none of them but the girl, to whom he whispered. She had withdrawn both hand and mouth.

Some one said, "That's enough, a Mhaoir, you're frightening the lass." He was caressing the averted cheek; he bent his head and kissed her hand. The older Cameron moved forward with a curse. Ewen said, "Leave him, he means no harm," and stumbled out into the night.

He walked, trying to clear his head; eventually the cold drove him back, and he paused to urinate against the wall of an outlying building. He was interrupted by a movement among the shadows.

"Oh, go about your business, avic. I'm not looking at your prick."

He fumbled with his breeches. There was no further sound from Murdoch, only an indifferent silence. He was drinking, and offered the flask.

"How's my fine vaunty son?"

"He is well. He would not come with me tonight."

"That was because of me. There's a thing for a man to know, eh, he's hated by his son."

Silence, bitter now, and a wind moaning around the wall.

"To hell with it. I wouldn't have wanted him with his damned cold face. I'm glad to be shut of him."

A door opened, there were distant voices; it closed and there was silence.

"What did you say to the girl, Muireach?"

"Eh?"

"You spoke to the bride."

"Give me your kiss. That was all I said. Give me your kiss, a chiallaich." He swallowed deeply and coughed. "And they threw me out. Out like a dirty tinker bitch on my arse. And there was no harm in me, I meant her no harm."

"I know."

"I'll break them for it, the bastards... the whoring sons of bastards. As if I couldn't have their flower if I wanted her, as if any damned man among them could stop me if that was what I wanted."

He leaned against the wall, wheezing.

"I met *her* at a wedding.... We danced to the Gille Callum... it brings bad luck to me now."

Ewen said, pitying him, "Muireach, come with me. I am going home. Let us ride together," but he did not move, leaning against the wall, head sunk, eyes hooded.

"I was never in love. Isn't that the shame and the pity of it, man. I was never in love." He passed a hand across his eyes. "Christ, I am so tired."

A greenish aurora was visible now: *fir-chlis* in Gaelic, the merry dancers. As a child he had feared these manifestations of energy and thought of them as shrouds, a superstition he had passed to his son. But tonight it held him with a perverse fascination, and he watched it, sobered, and coldly intent.

"They'll bring us snow tomorrow. You mark it."

A man and a woman out poaching hares at dawn found him. The stallion was attempting to rise, although one of its legs was broken: beneath its weight his ribs and pelvis had been shattered, and clots of blood had frozen on his mouth. The man ran for help; the woman took off her plaid and tried to cover him.

Ewen had reached Ardsian only an hour before.

He stood transfixed with horror as the ghillies struggled to free the crushed leg from the stirrup, watching their clouding breath and the new, pale sun and the snow beginning to drift from an opalescent sky; then he took the Italian pistol from its holster and shot Murdoch's stallion through the head.

He gave the smoking pistol to one of the ghillies and walked away and vomited the bitter excesses of the night. The others had lifted Murdoch and were carrying him, a strange, swaying procession across the winter-bitten moor. The woman plucked at his sleeve, showing him the bloodied plaid, and he had already laid his roquelaure over Murdoch; he had nothing else to give her. He began to take off his coat, then the ghillie with the pistol came and argued with the woman, pushing her away. She cried out; he left them, walking blindly through the sere, dead heather in the path the others had taken.

When he was certain that his father would not recover, Malcolm left the house and hid in the stables, with the metallic, warning taste in his mouth that preceded migraine or the seizure.

He closed his eyes against the aura's jagged prism, his other senses acutely heightened. He heard Ewen and smelled him, alcohol and body odour and the salt blood of Murdoch's vomit, before he was close enough to speak.

"You know what I have come to say."

"My father is dead."

"He is dying. It is only a matter of time."

He sat in the straw, shivering and nauseated, appalled more by this bloodshot debauchery than the imminence of death.

"You must come in." He moved his head on his knees and said nothing. Ewen took him by the shoulders with unnecessary force.

He raised his eyes. An indefinable nakedness of emotion passed between them.

"Why?"

"It is your duty. It is your duty to me."

He shrugged off the hands; the pain had begun, and every touch, every sound was unbearable. He looked up only once as Ewen stood, his face transfigured by pathetic hope and enquiry.

"His horse... how bad...."

"I shot it."

There was no response; in his own fatigue Ewen did not notice. From the doorway he said, "Come as soon as you may," and returned to the house.

The morning was soft with snow. Toward midday a pale sun reappeared, drifting in cloud, and was obscured again.

Ewen found him in his room, in a chair near the window. There was no fire and no light, only the pervasive luminosity of snow.

"He is asking for you."

No answer, only the intense quietness of snow. The sun had gone; the afternoon was passing.

"Please come. If not for his sake, for mine." He cupped the drawn face in his palms, stroking it, hoping for tears. The boy's hand came up with instinctive revulsion and pushed away the invasive caress. The dry eyes burned him to his soul.

Ewen left him.

The rosary was in his pocket. When he was alone, he tried to pray.

He prayed to grieve, to be given something to grieve for, some memory, something worthy of tears. But he could not weep and he could not grieve because he could remember no act of love that balanced the obscenity and the hatred; there was no emotion in himself that was a son's. Murdoch had no son, he had killed him, as surely in all those dark nights as if he had strangled him.

He remained in his dark room and time passed, and the snow fell.

The afternoon darkened. Murdoch asked for a priest.

His Catholic conscience lacerated, Ewen sent for Inglis MacNeil. When told of this Murdoch lifted his mouth in a rictus of a smile and a faint sound emerged from his throat. The haemorrhage that burst from his nostrils silenced it.

The hours struck and were gone: for him they passed for the last time, although he fought profanely to live. At half past six MacNeil raised his eyes.

"Is the boy coming? In a little while there will be no need."

Ewen went upstairs. The room was empty, filled with the pallor of the snow.

He sat embracing the dead, massive neck of the stallion. He had loved it, despite its brutal temper, had caressed it, confided in it, dressed its galls and spur cuts, had slept within the comforting sound of its movements, had cried with his face buried in its mane.

He had avoided its shattered head; he looked now in the twilight and was not repulsed, kissed it and laid his face against it, and, kneeling in the bloody snow, wept out his heart.

He returned late to Ardsian, through fast-falling snow. MacNeil had gone.

He stood in the hall, brushing the clinging flakes from his clothing, and did not see Ewen watching him from the opened doors of the drawing room.

What he said seemed to mean nothing. He repeated it, not loudly.

"Your father is dead. Will you come now and see him?"

Then, without waiting for a response, he went in again and closed the doors.

IX

The men who had carried the coffin stood now in the drawing room, shuffling feet in rawhide brogans, balancing plates in callused hands. They seemed disinclined to eat, perhaps too conscious of the atmosphere of death and the chill of Ardsian's hospitality. Ewen had no desire to be convivial, and they sensed it and obliged him by leaving as soon as was decently possible.

He stood at the door and shook each man's hand and thanked him, but his heart was not in it, and being perceptive this they also knew. He returned to the drawing room where MacNeil was still seated, and resumed a conversation which had been in progress since Murdoch's death.

"You understand that it was beyond me to force the issue. I could not... I cannot compel him to do anything these days. The truth is, I dare not."

"Time for him to be going into the world, surely."

"He can go to the devil for all I care. I wash my hands of him."

They sat in the long, shadowed room and the room became colder, and the afternoon went on. He found that he was listening, but no dogs started up in alarm, and no one came.

"The house is so quiet," he said.

Some one came and tended the fire after MacNeil left; the candles cast a tarnished light. The deerhound came and licked his hand, and put a paw appealingly on his knee; he pushed it gently away. He was summoned to eat and went and returned; Malcolm had not been at the table, perhaps was still out of the house. He brought a full bottle of cognac back with him and drank from it steadily. Some one came in hourly to trim the candlewicks until eleven struck, then he said, "Let them go out," and no one else disturbed him. The candles went out one by one and the fire died until the darkness immersed him and the cold was intense; he was very drunk now but quite lucid. He said once, "How many more, my God," and the glass fell from his hand and rolled on the carpet, its rim catching the firelight.

Elspeth... his daughter... Coinneach... in France his mother, his adored brothers, his sisters... finally his father in Italy.

He had received the summons and delayed; he went two or three days later with Elspeth. He found his father had been living with an Italian girl, a child of eleven or twelve; she was pregnant by him, a man of sixty. She had stood in the mean room drinking wine; she had darkened eyelids and a sulky mouth like a crushed flower and she wore a scarlet dress opened to her rouged, immature nipples; patches of sweat stained the dress at her armpits and beneath her breasts. He had asked for his father and she had said spitefully, "Go in there, signor, go in and see him now," and he had gone in; James Bécu had been dead for several hours. The sluttish child stood watching idly; he sent her away to bring a priest and knelt and tried to pray while the sickness kept rising in his throat, partly revulsion at the stench of faeces but mostly hate, the unspeakable sin of hatred for his own father.

Even with Elspeth in the still, foul room with the Italian summer heat burning beyond the shutters, lowering her face to kiss the dead, scarred cheek, he was tearless: he who had wept so easily when taunted and goaded by this man could not now forgive him and weep in grief.

He was your father, Ewen. Can you not have pity even now?

She had miscarried after the journey and he had blamed James Bécu for that also, and damned him for it.

The room was palpably colder, the fire ash, the deerhound by his chair deeply asleep. He stood; the darkness rose up like drowning water. The old dog stirred; he went down heavily on his knees and woke him, as gently as any old friend.

He reached the doors and got them open, the dog padding stiffly after him. There was a graze on the jamb where the coffin had scraped it. He had stood there that morning ... they had been waiting to close the coffin ... Malcolm had left the house. He had gone in and shut the doors and put the crucifix into the hands and kissed the dead, cold face. Everything he had never done for his father, every duty and observance expected of a son.

He stood, very drunk, with his hand against the jamb, the graze that marked the passing of a man, and his fingers moved up and down exploring this new wound to a house so often and so deeply scarred, then he began to think of his father, and cried slow, difficult tears as he found his way up the many stairs into the darkness.

His valet woke and came to undress him. He leaned heavily against him, crying.

And all night the old dog lay sleeping outside his door, as though it would never except by death be separated from him.

The child Malcolm had said to him once, "I wish you were my father," and he, masking his emotions, had answered, "Give your love back to Muireach. I am not worthy of it." And he had known then that he loved him, as a son and as more than a son, and he had betrayed James through it, and more heinous than that, he did not care.

He loved him. More than himself, more than his son, more than his wife. It was an envious, a jealous, a possessive love, at once paternal and erotic, protective and desirous. And the boy had that quality, that radiant quality of commanding love, of drawing love to himself.

He had sought Malcolm's love, had courted it, had wooed it and wanted to win it as fervently as he had desired any woman's: he had seen him month after month turning to him, and was elated and fearful. He had not thought Malcolm capable of love.

He loved him guiltily, half afraid of him, wondering what loneliness and deprivation had made of him, and tonight, in an anguished desire for poison, he sought it and found it in himself.

He wrote in his journal, *I have encouraged a filial devotion and bent it to myself, and defiled it. I have betrayed, as his father betrayed him, as my father betrayed me.*

The snows fell and the passes were closed; the isolation was complete. From time to time there was a death in the townships; the news was carried to him and he struck the name from the rent roll. There were always deaths in the winter; he had never felt responsible for them and he did not now.

A deposition of tenants was waiting in the estate office on the morning of January fourth. He walked in and placed his hands flat on the littered table.

"This is my factor's work undone, this is what fills my time. I cannot deal with you until I know the state of my finances."

Some one said quietly, "Will you not listen to what we have to say, Glen Sian?"

He marshalled his failing self-possession.

"I have expenses. I have a son to support in France. I have outstanding accounts."

"The children have no food," some one else said.

He turned angrily to that voice.

"Do you think I care nothing for your children? Do you think me so without a heart?" For a moment his command of this language so foreign to him was gone. "Those of you who wish to leave me may do so." He saw their expressions. "Surely some of you have trades, skills? You would be employable?"

Yes, there were craftsmen among them, shoemakers, tanners, millers, brewsters; almost every man was his own. But there was not a man among them who would go to seek work in the south.

"Who would be ploughing our fields when the spring came? Who would look after our families?"

"If any man among you spoke English you would find yourselves employable elsewhere. And your wives and children also."

At the door one of the men turned with his bonnet held low in his hand and said gently, "For God's sake, Glen Sian, will you do nothing to help us, or is it that we have offended you by coming?"

"You have not offended me, but I have nothing else to give you. I have done all I can."

It was not that he had no pity; he simply had no concept of the sharpness of their need. Glen Sian meant nothing to him. It was ink on paper, names on rent rolls, boundaries, yields, parishes. No aspect of it was human.

Another day, another delegation: a widow and her children. He took the infant on his lap, where it played with his watch fob, his hair and his lace.

"Your son delights me. How old is he? What is his name?" And when she told him, "I have a son of my own, you know."

He called for tea, "and pap for the babe. I shall feed him. No, I insist."

She drank her tea from the saucer with a dignified detachment.

"It was a man of this household was responsible for the child in my belly. I want nothing for myself, but for the child only. I think it is my due."

One of the older boys, sensing his change of mood, came unobtrusively and took his small charge from his lap, and at a word from her they edged away across the carpet.

He said, "It is unthinkable that you should come to me with this manner of accusation. And in the presence of your children, too... I am surprised."

"It is the fact of the matter. They knew the man, they were always seeing him coming and going." Then, "It is not that I would speak ill of the dead, Glen Sian, but is it known to you, the man I mean?"

He walked to the door and bowed, and opened it and went out. He met a servant in the hall.

"There is a woman in my drawing room. See her out, and give her money." It was not money she wanted; she would have no use for it. "And give her something to eat. I should not want them to go away hungry."

They were taken to the kitchens, wherein he had never set foot, and given a sack of meal and some salt, and although he did not go down again he sent four warm gowns from among James's baby clothing, causing his valet great annoyance in the search for them. He also gave her a packet of tea, not knowing that she did not know how it was prepared and would in ignorance stew and eat the leaves, and watched them go, his conscience eased.

He pored over Murdoch's ledgers.

Sometimes he had doubted him; now even he knew the extent of his debts. From Europe had come the luxuries of his household, soaps, candles, pomade, mirrors, patent medicines, books, cognac, shoe buckles... the rebellion had ended that by disrupting all normal commerce between the continent and the attainted gentlemen of the north, and few luxuries had been bought in this or any other house since Culloden. But Culloden had not expunged the debts. Plasterers, glaziers and carpenters who had repaired damage done in 1746 had placed their claims with his solicitor, who had sent them to Murdoch, who had thrown them contemptuously aside. Murdoch cared nothing for paper, and it was a rare man who would come and dun him to his face. Now they demanded payment.

He sat for hours in the estate office, staring at the figures. It had become an obsession, although in the room he accomplished nothing.

There's none that knows your land like me.

The rivers froze; there was no fresh water. The snows fell as deeply on his sheltered garden as the fields beyond. And no one came to the estate office; they had tested him and he had failed them; they had tested his strengths against Murdoch's and found him wanting. The room was not his, it was Murdoch's, its very silence was a stone raised to him.

He wrote to James, *Beloved son, the dearest of my bosom. Your silence pains me— you cannot know how much. I wish only to remind you of your love and duty toward me, that you do not forget your poor father who is so very much neglected and alone....*

He signed it, *your devoted father*, and it was not until he finished it that he saw how his tears had marred it.

He wrote beneath his signature, *you will not need to read this to know the man I am;* then, *it is better to be dead than to live*, and took the letter upstairs.

He laid out his will and wrote again, painfully and explicitly, to Malcolm, and left both letters with the will, and closed the connecting door, and in the candlelit privacy of his dressing room removed one of his razors from its case. There was a sound beyond the door, and a moment later his valet said, "Monseigneur..." and the door opened. He sat, wrists bared, and he and the man observed one another in the still light.

The valet said, "Monseigneur, give me that." He said, "As you wish," and gave him the razor, and the incident was not mentioned again. The pitiful letters were taken away, read carefully by the valet and burned, and the razors, Ewen noted in later weeks, were never left where he could find them.

The precaution was not necessary. Having seen the abyss, he retreated from it. He came out of his physical isolation; he received MacNeil one evening; he talked civilly if inconsequentially with Malcolm. It revealed nothing, resolved nothing; Malcolm had become very bitter toward him, for reasons which were never discussed. He told himself that it would pass, and meanwhile he could not afford to care so much for one when the lives of so many had devolved upon him.

He returned to the estate office, where from time to time he found something of Murdoch's which revealed to him a man he had never known. He had intended to give all such personal effects to Malcolm but he realized it was not now either wise or necessary, so he simply collected them and put them aside in a tin box: a paper covered with childish lettering which he knew to be Malcolm's, a crudely coloured religious picture of the kind hawked by tinkers at fairs, a luckenbooth brooch in a pattern of linked silver hearts, a lock of coarse black hair which might have been the boy's or the woman Margaret's. Then one morning he forced the lock on the lowest drawer and found the flies, feather torn from feather until he scarcely recognized them. Beside them lay the toy horse. It had been gouged with a knife.

He held the flies and a pity more intense than he had ever felt for any man overcame him. Eventually he burned them; they and the crushed reed box smoked an instant and were gone, leaving an acrid stench.

The toy horse he kept, wondering when he tenderly handled it why the sight of it should hurt him so terribly, why the violence of its rejection should strike so much like a blow to his heart.

X

The house waited. The rotting snow lay undisturbed; Ewen had sent no one here since Murdoch's death. He took a nail from his pocket, and with it and the blade of the sgian he carried in his boot he forced the lock.

Snow had drifted over the doorstone; he kicked it away and closed the door behind him. The house reached out for him, the darkness, the smell of frigid decay. His boots ground on the droppings of mouse and rat. He touched nothing, remembering all.

Peat still lay piled on the hearth. He knocked away the dead ash of Murdoch's last fire and set the fresh turfs in their trinity, the old prayers coming easily to him.

He crouched on the stone, the tinderbox in his hand.

I hated you. You unholy bloody bastard, how I hated you. The spark caught and grew with a curl of fragrant smoke.

Christ, I hate you still.

He lit the cruisie lamp and carried it into the passageway. He was sweating, a wild sweat that was partly fear, partly exhilaration. The room at the front of the house had been furnished sparsely before; now it was empty save for a chair and table.

The drawer was locked; he dealt with that with the blade of the sgian. The pistols lay where he had known they would be and he took them out carefully and moved the lamp closer, so that light fell on the glinting stocks. Highland pistols, steel from muzzle to butt, ball-triggered, prickers screwed between each ornamental ram's horn, and the finest black flint, wrapped in a strip of leather, still held between the jaws of each cock.

Strange to handle, older and more cumbersome than the brace of Italian duelling pistols Ewen kept hidden at Ardsian, and they were adamantly Murdoch's. His hand was trembling from more than their weight when he laid them down.

He came to the foot of the stairs. No sound but his breathing, loud in the stillness, and faintly, persistently, the rain on the roof.

He had feared it, coming to this house. Now all the things he feared began to stir and quicken, waiting for him in that place beyond the light. The past. The dark. The silence, alive with violence and the memory of pain; and the dead. He had never believed in their resting; he walked among ghosts as easily as in the solid world of his hand on the banister, his feet upon the stair.

He went up, leaving the lamp. The first door was ajar; he pushed it open with the toe of his boot. Even here the house was as quiet as death, as cold as death, and smelled of dampness and decay. The ceiling beams sloped close overhead; as a child he had braced himself nightly for the moment when the slates would fall in, crushing him. The roof had stood for nearly a hundred years; it stood still, against time and all his childish dread.

His bed was gone. Everything of himself was gone. Murdoch had succeeded in ridding himself of all the impedimenta of a son. But for all his efforts to remove the memory of the child who had slept here from his own mind he could not take him from his son's, and that child lived again, lying with his face pressed to the pillow, listening to the sounds in the night. The straining of the rope and heather mattress, the panting, the protesting ropes again as the man rolled away from the woman. And the smothering silence when the child knew they both slept.

Eventually he went to the room which had been theirs. It was as he remembered, a shadowed place where candlelight was always inadequate. Rain beat at the casements; beyond that it was very still.

Formless thought came; after a time he put a memory to it. *He raped her.* The word shuddered through his mind, striking alarms. He was weeping now, but the high, lonely sobbing might have been some one else, that ghostly child who was and was not himself.

He cried, kneeling with his face against the bedclothes. They smelled of Murdoch, of peatsmoke and tobacco, of his hair and his unwashed body. He had shed few tears in this house; they had been secrets to be hidden from Murdoch. He wept them openly now with his face resting on the bed which had been Murdoch's indisputable demesne: wept for all the things that were and were not, things that could have been, had never been, for that dirty, frightened child whose very presence here had been swept away like a hanging cobweb, for Margaret and his innocence, and then the tears began to come for Ewen, who would never come again to this decaying house to take him home, like a bright angel, an avenging angel, with the eyes of a man vehemently wronged.

For Ewen mostly, and for that child within himself who would always be crying in the dark.

He emerged from the dimness to find the lamp still burning on the stairs. He went down to it like a moth to the flame.

He carried it back to the kitchen and lit others from it, and washed the dishes left on the table, and scrubbed the floor and the hearth. When that was done he brought the pistols to the table and cleaned them, cautiously, and then with a growing confidence. It was perhaps seven o'clock when he laid them aside and left the house.

A meal had been kept for him at Ardsian, although Ewen was not in evidence. He ate with appetite, enduring the silent company of the ghillie who served. On his way to his room, driven by an odd compulsion, he knocked on Ewen's door. He sensed light and a wakeful presence, but he received no invitation to enter and he presumed no further.

He went out the following morning, back to the house. Within a week he had made it habitable; within two, he was hanging game there and cooking for himself. He had seen Ewen, only briefly, twice in that time.

He did not return to Ardsian on the last night, but slept on sheets he had laundered, on Murdoch's bed. Before he slept he masturbated, roughly and with shame, whispering obscenities to the dead, convulsed with rage and bitterness. Then he buried his face against the pillows and slept, for the first time he could remember, deeply, and without dreams.

Ealasaid Cameron starved to death during the week of Candlemas. Her corpse and those of her children were not discovered until the middle of February.

Ewen arrived at the croft in the blue, still dusk. The day's crowd had not dispersed; the low rise and fall of conversation died as he approached.

He covered his mouth and nose with his handkerchief and said, "Oh, my God. How long?"

Some one took his arm and turned him away, and he saw the cattle dead on their knees in the byre, and a voice spoke dispassionately of the dog which had torn out their throats.

The man who held his sleeve led him to another corner, and pulled back a fold of the blanket there.

"This bairn, her mouth was full of grass when they found her."

He closed his eyes, nauseated. The image persisted.

"The people are hungry, Glen Sian. The harvest failed, you will not have forgotten."

"I could hardly forget," he said.

"And there was no corn bought for us, there was no relief offered to the people."

"Why did no one come here? In Christ's name, why did not one of you come to her?"

They all looked at him. The man said patiently, "We all have our own families to feed, Glen Sian, it is the same case with ourselves. And she was not sociable after Iain died, she never wanted us to be coming to the door."

An infant had been lifted, living, from the breast; one of the women was offering it her nipple, although even he knew that it was futile.

In the silent crowd outside he encountered Diar Cameron, who had been married in December.

"The blessing of God on you." He had forgotten his name. "How is your wife?"

"She is well enough. There will be a child in the summer."

He flushed and murmured, "This is a terrible thing."

The fatalistic eyes met his.

"She was my cousin, did you know. I gave her the dog. After Iain died, I gave her the damned dog...."

Some one approached, and the boy said with an assumed callousness, "Have you been making yourself useful to the women, or did I bring you for nothing?"

She whispered, "What could I do, in the name of God, it is all over with them," and the boy said, "You will remember my sister Bridgid, Glen Sian. She was at the wedding, although she says you did not speak to her."

And he knew her. The shielings The vanished summer.

They stood, looking away from one another across the frozen ground.

He said, "Do you think it will live?"

"No, I think not," and then, "She is a child, not an it. Her name is Lili."

He could not have felt the reproach more keenly if she had beaten him with her fists.

She drew her shawl more closely around her body; she was shivering.

"O Dhia, life is so cruel sometimes. So unbearably cruel."

He said, "Tell your brother to take you home." She pulled the folds over her hair and face, hiding all but her eyes. Walked away; turned. "God keep you, Bridgid."

She said, "God and Mary keep you, Glen Sian," and held his gaze for a moment, although the language that she might have been speaking was not one he knew, or had long forgotten.

He went home and tried to sleep. He failed too at that.

He got up again and walked the dark house. He wanted to talk to Malcolm, but doors and more than doors were closed there against him, so he did not go. He took a candle and went and sat in the estate office for a time, drinking the whisky which was kept there, staring at the maps, opening the tin box and turning the things over in his hands. But he found nothing to comfort him, only dust and hopelessness, and Murdoch's spirit in the cold night waiting for him, so eventually he closed the office and came downstairs.

He seated himself at the escritoire; some one had forgotten to draw the draperies and he saw his ghostly reflection ... he began to write, listening to the uneasy stirrings of a house at night, a great house slipping without grace toward the half century of its age.

He wrote to his solicitor in Glasgow, authorizing him to select some suitable candidate as factor and send him north as soon as possible. There must be some one to take charge of the people... he had betrayed them and failed them time and again and they deserved better of life and of him.

There was another solution, and that was breaking the entail. He authorized his solicitor to investigate the possibility.

And, finally, there was the most complete cure. Other men were absentee landlords; in the Highlands after Culloden it was the rule rather than the exception. He had done his duty: why should he hazard youth, health, possibly sanity, for a land where he was not needed, not wanted, and a danger to himself and others through his ineptitude?

I am going home. I shall soon be in France. I will go home....

He signed the letter and pushed it away.

He looked up to find the ghillie Ruaraidh standing in the doorway in his nightshirt, with a coat buttoned over it and a pair of aged brogans on his feet. A nightcap hung out of his pocket.

Mon ange gardien, he thought. Pourquoi ne pouvez-vous me laisser seul?

"All is well with Glen Sian?"

"Yes." He turned the letter over. "All will be well now."

Ruaraidh came in with a proprietary, almost paternal air and began lighting sconces.

"It is cold Glen Sian will be... it is a coat he will be wanting. I myself will be going and getting one."

"I am not cold and I do not want a coat." The small man studied him benevolently, and began to draw the draperies. Sharply annoyed, he said, "Leave those."

"Ach, Glen Sian will not be wanting to look out into the night."

He sat at the escritoire and saw his reflection obliterated.

"This letter is to go to Glasgow. I shall want it taken to Fort William at first light."

"It will be done, Glen Sian."

"I expect there will soon be a new factor among us."

He said it with a certain defiance. Already the deep suspicion of all things southern was stirring in Ruaraidh's face.

"Will it be in Glasgow the gentleman is living?"

"Perhaps."

Ruaraidh was loitering, trimming wicks that did not need his attention.

"It is not my place to be saying—"

"I assure you I would rather you say it than think it, or communicate your displeasure to the rest of the household behind my back."

"Will the gentleman from Glasgow have the Irish?"

"I shall see that some one in authority speaks Gaelic." He sensed that Ruaraidh thought he meant himself. It would not do to tell him that by the time factor and ground officer were established he would have returned to France.

Strangely, the thought gave him no pleasure. He said irritably, "Besides, I do not yet know if this man will prove suitable. I must wait and see. In the meantime... I need some one. I cannot manage these affairs on my own."

He had said enough; his unseemly confidences only afforded fodder for gossip. But one thing more must be asked; he could not help himself.

"Is the boy at home? I did not see his boots in the hall."

"He is at home, Glen Sian."

Relief flooded him.

"Did he say... no, of course he would not say where he had been. How stupid of me."

Ruaraidh stood for a moment, silent. He had come to Ardsian after a chequered career as a poacher, a reiver and a petty lawbreaker in most of the shires of the south; he was MacGregor on both sides of his parentage. He had not given his devotion easily to this shy and lonely foreigner, and now that it was given it was absolute.

He said gently, "I had a son once, Glen Sian. I know how it is with the young men sometimes."

"He is *not* a man. He is only a boy...." Then, more out of courtesy than interest, "How old was your son when he went away?"

"He was sixteen, just. It was all the young men were for going away to the fighting."

An unutterable sadness filled him.

He said, "Was it not with MacIain that he went?"

"Aye, it was so. His mother was not made up with his going but MacIain told him to go. It was not that he wanted it, but that MacIain forced him."

Ewen's fingers moved on the brass lid of the standish.

"Do you think he may still live? That he may be in hiding?"

"It was not told to his mother and me that he came alive from the field."

"But surely one of his friends... must have known."

Yes, he had had friends. They lay with the rest, a wealth of strong young manhood, their bones and their beauty and their dreams, all buried together on the moor and rotting in their unmarked pits.

There was no answer to his question; perhaps even to ask it had presumed too far. His eyes were stinging: he saw that the candles had begun to smoke, but Ruaraidh made no move to trim them.

"And what of MacIain... do you think he lives?"

"I never think, Glen Sian."

It was the longest conversation they had ever had, the most intimate, and both knew it would not happen again; unwritten laws of pride and birth ensured that it would not. But the bleakness of the small hours, of lost sons and unassuaged grief made all men equal. Death was not the only leveller; there was also loneliness.

"Ruaraidh—" he said, but Ruaraidh had gone.

The deerhound followed, nose and tail low, stalking the imagined hinds of its youth through the forest of chairs, remembering the scent and the chase it would not know again.

And Ewen was alone, in the cold room with the smoke and the candles, and the smell of old dog and the empty crystal bowl on the mantel which had once held roses in their season. A shell of a room, empty, exquisite, a man with no spirit, waiting. Chairs ranged for visitors who would never come, mirrors that reflected nothing. And he among them, as dead and forsaken as they.

He fell asleep at the escritoire but did not recall it upon waking, only the sadness of his dreams.

The wind, which had been bitter, backed into the southwest, and carried a fog inland from the sea. It found the boy at the croft, where he had gone as a voyeur, and encompassed him, and damned him.

There was little left after the scavenging of neighbours, a dresser bare of plates, a knife. The crucifix was still nailed to the wall over the place where the mattress and the dead had lain. No sign yet that tinkers had occupied this holding, but if it was not allotted to some tenant they would claim it.

The fog had reached him, caressing his face. His hand hesitated over the knife, then he took it and went out.

The fog was heavier than he had imagined, the day hourless and lightless. Ground as familiar as his flesh had been transfigured, was alien, unknown.

He dismounted, ears, eyes straining.

It would soon be evening. Soon there would be no light.

He sat in the dead bracken, trying to conquer his fear of blindness, and the dread of remembered terrors in the fog.

He buried his face in his arms and whispered the caim of encompassing. In later years he remembered it, and that it had failed him.

Caim Dhé, caim Chriosda, caim an Spioraid, caim Mhoire... caim Mhicheil, caim nan naodh aingeal....

Time passed, under the hand of the angels; the fog was beginning to disperse. He saw a black moor stained with snow and heard the sound of water; he had ridden in a wide arc, like the circle of encompassing; close by, a shallow burn ran over rocks and spilled into the dark gorge of the Sian.

He followed the river. The air was cold, and filling imperceptibly with darkness.

He came upon her suddenly, sitting on a rock with her arms, as his had been, around her knees. Rags of mist were still drifting over the churning yellow water and he thought her a ghost.

She turned, and he saw her face.

"Go back. I have set a snare near you."

He spoke over the rushing of the water.

"You're poaching, ban-cheard."

"A woman has to live," she said.

"We'll see what Glen Sian has to say to that."

The snare was sprung, and the hare set up a shrill screaming. She swung unhurried legs from the rock and walked to the place and killed it with a blow to the neck. It hung, quivering, and she drew a knife from her belt.

"Are you lost, gallan?" She pointed with the blade. "Your way lies there."

And then she slit its throat.

Her name was Mhaire and she was what he had called her, ban-cheard, a female tinker. He knew nothing more of her, and after those few, fevered weeks he never saw her again, except in another face, in other eyes.

He came to her as he had known he would, not once but many times. She told his fortune, although he knew it was lies, beautiful lies promising him wealth and love and happiness. In return he gave her a button cut from Murdoch's coat; like many drovers he had worn the silver in case illness or death should befall him far from home; the silver would have paid for his physic or burial. She gave it back twisted into a crude ring, which he later buried. He stole a spoon from Ardsian and this she did not return but fashioned into a ring for herself, and he stole other things as she asked for them, a cup, a knife and fork, a shirt, a woollen blanket.

Sometimes she called him son, little son, other times other names, overtly sexual, which shamed him and brought the ache of arousal to his loins. She did not allow him access to her nakedness, and never fully revealed his; the pleasure of this debauchery, a stripping of the rags of innocence, lay in a slower sexual torment, in frottage, in interrupted masturbation, in the blind explorations of the tongue, seducing, corrupting, never satisfying, until he was repulsed and enflamed and crazed with rage and frustration. And yet he could not divorce himself from her, or from the uncontrollable compulsion. With her all memory of another life became faint; she was the only reality, and the past and the future subdued themselves to her.

On the morning of the fifteenth of March he saw her at the abandoned croft. He dismounted, and walked with fear and a painful eagerness toward her.

"You can't stay here."

"And who are you to say so? Are you the factor now, coming to put a poor woman out of her house?"

"It isn't your house."

"Maybe I will make it mine. It is a quiet place, I am liking it well."

"I don't want you here," he said.

She leaned forward and snapped her fingers in a gesture of crude contempt.

"I don't give that for your liking." The mouth smiled then, the irresistible invitation. "Come in, churaidh. You will want a drink after your long journey."

Closing the door, enclosing him in the brothel she had prepared for him. There was fresh heather on the floor, and the blanket he had stolen for her. The crucifix had been taken down.

She brought a cuach from the dresser. He drank, and then she, where his lips had touched. She walked to the bed, barefoot in the dimness, and paused there with her hands at her shirt.

"Come here." Holding out the hand, more insistently. "Come."

He allowed himself to be drawn down into the hot dark dream she offered him, the smell of arousal, the smell of the ground, of stone and of burning. He kissed the mouth with a fevered hunger, and the breast when it was given, and sucked it, trembling with exquisite shame. She was murmuring to him, stroking his penis, caressing his mouth with aromatic fingers, and he sucked them, sucking the essence of his sex and hers; and then, as always, the anguished, intolerable pleasure was withdrawn, the fingers injured, the lips cursed him. He fumbled with his clothing and with hers, calling her bitch, whore, cunt.

She said, "Come again tomorrow."

He stumbled to his feet, drugged, sick with fury and humiliation, calling her the most obscene of a vocabulary of epithets, and she raised herself on an elbow and mocked the failed erection, and lay back again, revealing the swollen nipples where he had tongued and bitten her.

"Come to me tonight. I'll give you what you want." He swore at her again from the door. "Do you hear me? I want you to come to me. I want you."

He stood at the door, tasting the tears and the semen, seeing the white mist on the furrows, knowing what the evening would bring, what blindness, what fears.

"Come," she said, behind him.

He turned once more to the smoke and to her.

***

138

In the depths of the night, under the influence of opium, Ewen dreamed of a voice and a sound. The voice spoke his name, only once; the sound could not be distinguished. He drifted into deep sleep again.

He woke once more, and held his watch to the casement to read the time, and opened his door. The stain on the panel was invisible in the shadows; the gallery was empty. He returned to bed, shivering.

When the valet woke him, only the bitter dregs in his glass reminded him of the night and the dream.

The mist had yielded to rain and the day was dark, the clothing damp which had been laid out for him. He complained of it fretfully and went to breakfast.

Malcolm was in the dining room, drinking bitter coffee. When he heard Ewen he pushed the cup away and rose, and remained standing in the shadows.

Eventually he slumped into a chair at the far end of the table.

"You do not eat, Malcolm?"

He said, "Will you let me alone," and the austerity of the formal *vous* was chilling, unyouthful.

"Certainly. I will... let you alone." Ewen poured coffee for himself; his appetite was gone. "I did not hear you come in last night. Were you very late?" He became increasingly aware of the sound of his own voice. "My God, am I talking to myself? Take that hand away from your face and look at me."

The eyes were burningly hostile, and bloodshot.

"Where were you?"

"I was out."

"So late?"

He stood.

"Sit down, Malcolm."

"I've said all I have to say."

"You have not heard all I have to say. You live in my house, you are subject to my wishes. I regret, but I cannot and will not endure this behaviour on your part, this arrogant flouting of me. If you wish to disport yourself like a young profligate, I pray you do not do it in my house."

"Then I'll leave your fucking house. That's what you want, isn't it?"

"It is apparently what you want. You neither know nor care for my desires, and if you did, in your present state they would mean less than nothing to you."

Craving solitude, he returned to his rooms. The valet was waiting for him.

"If Monseigneur will pardon me, there is something I think he should see."

It was the door to Malcolm's dressing room. The panelling was painted a pleasing greyish blue, there was a settee covered with fading silk and two chairs, and a scent of orris and cedar. A number of drawers were open, and on the carpet lay two or three crushed Turkish towels.

"It is blood, Monseigneur."

He left him and went into the bedroom. The rain was running on the glass. He sat down and watched it.

When he tired of the rain he studied the worn carpet with its pattern of lilies and roses, and the dark red damask hangings of the bed, and the enigmatic figures on the japanned screen in the corner. The rain stopped and a weak sunlight came. Somewhere a clock was ticking; the room smelled of age and time. A book in calfskin binding lay on a table, a ribbon marker halfway through. The candles had been replaced for the night.

There were few possessions in this room, little to indicate that the tenant was anything but a temporary guest. Perhaps because he had arrived with nothing more than the shirt on his back, the boy had never been acquisitive; it seemed sometimes to Ewen that he lived always in readiness to leave the same way.

Ewen sat, waiting for him, and the pale sun vanished, and the room became dim. It was nearly six o'clock; he had spent the afternoon waiting for Malcolm to return.

He thought, oh God, let him not be sick, or hurt— do not take him from me, let me not lose him now.

Twilight filled the room; eventually he left it. Malcolm had come in by the time he took his cognac in the drawing room. He did not go to speak to him but read through an old number of the Edinburgh Evening Courant, frowning in the dimness, then he folded it and left it on the table. He paused before closing the doors to look back at the room, the rotting silk wallpaper and the scarred mantel of Italian marble, and the far end where he had kept his vigil beside Murdoch. The sky held something of the afterlight. The days had begun to lengthen toward spring.

He closed the doors quietly and went to his rooms.

There was a knock on his door a little after ten, and Malcolm came in. He seemed indefinably older, drawn, and very composed.

Ewen offered him cognac. He refused it courteously. They sat, observing one another in the candlelight.

"I hoped, but did not dare to expect this."

"I was rude to you. I regret it."

"This is all that matters to me." He gazed at him. "How are you, Malcolm? Better than this morning, I trust." A dismissive gesture. "Well, I was young too once and I was no angel...." Silence. "You were bleeding. Why?"

Silence.

"The towels you had hidden in your room. You must have known that Guillaume would find them."

"I fell. I pissed myself. You would have been disgusted."

He remembered his own nights of sickness and disgust.

"My God, what do you think I am? A saint? A monster?"

The candlelight was falling on the rough black hair, the strong jut of the cheekbone. Ewen watched him, wanting to embrace him, restrained by the austerity in his face.

"You never want to know the truth, man. I told you what I was."

And whatever I am, I cannot be tolerated, or lived with, or forgiven.

"Well, we have never allowed one another much humanity, have we? You always thought I was a god and I thought you were an angel, and the reality is more than either of us can bear." He walked to the window, stared out at the clear night. "Do you wish to go now? You have made your peace."

The room was quiet behind him; he saw the reflected movement.

They stood together for a moment and he thought Malcolm would have spoken, and again he wanted to embrace him, but the eyes were remote, reticent, permitting nothing.

"Good night, mon cher. Sleep well. I am here if you need me."

The brilliance of the eyes suggested tears: perhaps he only thought he saw what he wanted to see.

The door shut. He listened until the footsteps died away.

The valet woke him. Beyond him a tranquil dawn unfolded; the sky of March was delicate, lucid.

He sat up, transfixed by the man's expression.

"Monseigneur—"

Malcolm had gone.

XI

A dream of France which had sustained him was dying, and without it he did not know how he should continue to live.

He submitted to the valet's tyranny, to fittings for clothes he could not afford, to having his brows shaved and his hair pomaded and tortured into stiff side curls, but he had no notion of what was fashionable and he was without influential friends; had he desired the pleasures they offered, the salons, the gambling hells, the elegant houses of prostitution were as closed to him as to the merest beggar. He went to the Tuileries, where the sweating, milling crowds were mostly English; he went to the Grand Boulevard and sat on a straw-bottomed chair drinking sour wine and watching the parade of carriages. He went to the Comédie-Française, and during the interval a beautiful woman tapped on the door of his box; he had seen her alone and, flushing, had returned her smile. She seated herself beside him, sipped the champagne he offered her and laid her hand between his thighs, and he realized she was a whore, not merely some forward gentlewoman. He left her, but not before she called him homosexual, and, more wounding still, bourgeois.

He went out no more in the evenings.

He went to the Marais. He walked up the Rue des Quatre-Fils and stood in the hot sunlight gazing up at the house where he had been deflowered by one of his father's mistresses, disporting himself in ecstasy in her fragrant bed only to learn later that his initiation had for an idle hour entertained James Bécu behind a spy-hole in the wall.

He was sixteen again and felt her moist lips parting his... then the taste of dust filled his mouth and the sun struck without pity at his sombre clothing and his fair, uncovered head. He leaned a moment against the wrought iron gate. A woman passed him with mincing steps, holding her skirts away from him, glancing back as she shut her door.

Sparrows came to flutter in the dust at his feet. The air was sullen; he heard distant thunder, and water playing languidly behind yet another impenetrable gate.

Eventually the faintness left him, and he made his way in the failing light to the corner. Disturbed, the birds fluttered up, then settled like dead leaves on the place where he had stood.

After the evening's storm there was music again from the neighbouring house, and he listened in the darkness of his room and wept, although he did not know why.

He followed the directions of a tradesman into the sordid heart of the Quartier St-Séverin. The spires of Notre-Dame were visible over the blackened rooftops; the stench of the Seine followed him into the alley off the Place Maubert where he found the lodgings he sought.

He sat in a darkened room with Elspeth's sister, sipping with polite distaste a red wine as bitter as misery. Two candles were burning on a graceful walnut commode, all that remained of the household furniture he had known.

"Why did you leave the Marais, Jeanne? When did you leave?"

"We had no money. Where else were we to go?"

"The pension...."

"There is no pension. You sound like her... she always talks of the pension. You think the King remembers his dead chevalier?" She twisted the limp flounce at her elbow. "Have you been in Paris long?"

"No," he lied.

"And how long do you stay?"

"A few days only."

"And where do you stop, this not long time in town?"

Ashamed, he murmured, "The hôtel Saint-Arnaud."

"Oh, yes, who could forget the so charming vicomtesse? Let me announce you to Maman, Ewen... she seems to be awake."

"Jeanne—"

"I shall not be here when you come out. I must go and buy bread. Such a pleasure to have seen you again, so good of you to remember us."

More candles, on either side of a mirror in a tortoiseshell frame. Janet Douglass received him. She was wearing a rusty black gown, a crucifix at her throat; and the hair he remembered was hidden by a grotesque wig. The mercury wash she used had begun to eat into her skin in a manner more often seen in old whores; she had brushed a hare's foot of rouge over the ravaged cheeks and it lay with a pounce box and snuff in a clutter of spilled powder and broken jet beads.

She snapped her fingers and he went to her, and bowed.

"So it's you again, is it, Stirling?" He carried the limp hand to his lips. "You still have that womanish face. What brings you back to France?"

"Your son proved himself unworthy of his charge."

"You talk in riddles," although he knew she had been fully apprised of Charles Arsène's activities.

"He placed my child like an unwanted parcel on the Lyons-Paris chaise and decamped with his wife into Italy. I understand from my cousin Honorée that his creditors had threatened him." Spots of shame were burning beneath the rouge. "I suspect he wrote to you for money?"

"You were a gambler too, Stirling."

"I came to my senses, madame, as soon as I was married. And had our positions been reversed, I would not have betrayed a trust placed in me by Charles Arsène."

After a time she said, with a fondness that was not for him, "How does it go for my dear child, my little grandson? He has a cough, if I recall....he wrote to me once and said so."

"He has inherited my family's unhappy weakness in the lungs."

"Your family's weakness was all here, Stirling, in the stomach and the loins. Your father was a lewd dog and your mother was no better, as silly as a girl. And all your brothers were the same." Again, his appearance seemed to offer an affront. "You dress beyond your means; I always thought so. Weak and vain and foolish, that was what I thought from the first. I told my daughter. The eldest child of a chevalier— she could have had any one." And then she began to speak of Elspeth, which he had dreaded. "She was only a toy to you, a plaything— and that monstrous letter you sent me, I shall never forgive you for it—"

He laid his hand gently on hers.

"Madame, my mother, please—"

She thrust his hand away.

"You were never my son!"

She turned her face aside. His reflection wavered in the clouded mirror, a stiff, slim figure, hair greyed by the candlelight.

"Permit me the honour of wishing you good-day."

Jeanne had gone out. He stood in the filthy street, blinded by the sun on the cobbles, wondering in which direction she had walked. But then he knew it did not matter, whichever way she had gone it would always be one where he could not follow.

He returned to the Quartier St-Séverin on the Thursday, to take his leave of Elspeth's mother.

She received him as before in her airless, darkened room, and he thought of the squalid Italian village where his father had died, and could scarcely control his sense of being entombed with her.

He had brought her a gift of snuff, of a blend she had once favoured. She inhaled daintily, indicating her dressing table. He saw what she wanted and brought it to her, an old silver watch and seal.

"Give these to my grandson— they were his grandfather Douglass's. I do not expect to see the child again." She dabbed her eyes and turned them on him without love. "You look frail to me, Stirling. You do well to guard your health."

"I do, madame, believe me."

"I shall have trouble with Jeanne now. She is always peevish when some one comes and goes... but at my age life is only just that, comings and goings."

144

He took the watch with a slight, courteous bow. "Keep it well, Stirling. It survived Sheriffmuir and it was given him by a king. A king, mind you, his sainted Majesty. Give it to my grandson and see that he knows its worth. Douglass had it of a king."

"He will be honoured, madame."

"You may go now. I do not keep your hours. I must soon be abed."

He rose.

"Adieu, madame. I do not think that we shall meet again."

Jeanne, sewing in the other room, looked up.

"Give my love to my little nephew. Ask him to remember his Tante Jeanne."

He left money on the table, his back half-turned so that she should not see what he was doing, and went out.

He arrived at Saint-Arnaud on the Friday afternoon. The chaise, spattered to the roof with mud, followed a carriageway through ornate gates, and the château's crenellated façade rose through the misty rain, fronted by two terraced gardens and broad, shallow steps. The doors were opened and his cousin Honorée de Salignac, heavily pregnant, was waiting for him.

He stepped from the chaise to the wet gravel and stood a moment, imagining he could smell the sea in this, the mild breath of the Loire.

She met him in the rain and kissed him. He was surprised and not a little moved to see that there were tears in her eyes.

"Oh, my dear Ewen... I would have known you anywhere. How long has it been?"

"Eight years, I think." He was unconsciously looking past her. "James? Is he hereabouts?"

"He is with my sons, visiting friends. They will all be back tomorrow."

"Oh," he said.

"So disappointed? They were having fireworks for some one's birthday. I could hardly refuse."

"Of course not," he said. "One cannot offer him fireworks in Scotland."

They went in, the footmen and his valet following. His eyes, starved of beauty, found satiety of it.

They supped at ten that night. The rain had stopped, the windows stood open to the humid smell of the gardens, moths flickered in from the darkness to the candles on the table.

"I have lost my sense of when to present these things. A small gift. It is really nothing."

It was a fan of red silk painted with peonies; he had not bought it himself but merely requested something suitable of the valet. She wafted it before her dark, vivid little face.

"How beautiful! And how thoughtful. You know red is my favourite colour." He did not, but he assumed an air of having remembered. She sat gazing at him with a lovely radiance; he had not seen his mere presence accord any human being such pleasure since Malcolm had been a child.

The first course was served. She talked of family matters; there were no revelations. He knew the unimpassioned state of her marriage, her singing, dancing and amateur theatrics at Versailles, her rowing, fishing and hunting in the country. And she was like her letters, brisk, direct, acute: he was emphatically not like his. He had distorted or omitted all details of his imprisonment, his suicidal depressions, his passions or his grief: he had found all that repugnant, and so denied her the opportunity of knowing him as he had changed, as life had changed him. So that now she sat near him and thought she knew him, but it was another man she knew; she directed her questions and her gossip and her affection to a man who had not existed for eight years, to a man who was essentially dead.

It was only toward the end of the meal that he began to suspect she had been lying to him as cleverly as he to her.

She took up the fan again; it had been lying by her plate.

"Saint-Arnaud told you, of course, that we no longer have the entrée."

He said, "No," cautiously. The subject of Saint-Arnaud, whom he had never liked, was one he thought best avoided.

"He is disgraced. We are both sent away."

"I am sorry. May one ask, how long?"

"Until His Majesty pleases. My husband's uncouth temper has finally bowed to a stronger censure than mine. It matters little to me, I never cared for Versailles. But it was a great blow to him." A pause. "He said nothing of it?"

"I have not had the honour of seeing the vicomte."

"But I told him you were coming."

"He had gone away. I assure you, I was better alone. Not in a companionable mood."

They sat in silence until cognac had been brought, and the servants had withdrawn.

"I seem to have intruded upon a personal quarrel."

"It is not a quarrel. We are estranged."

"I did not know."

"I never told you. I never wanted you to know."

"Has it been … long?"

"I've grown accustomed to his absences. The only things that distress me now are his returns."

"Is he physically brutal?"

"No. Nothing so crude."

"Why do you stay?"

"Where should I go? And where should I take the children? This is all they have ever known. And it is not intolerable, when he is not here, which is for the most part."

He said, "Do you prostitute yourself for Saint-Arnaud's money?" and she gestured elegantly, succinctly, around her.

"Yes. Wouldn't you?"

He splashed cognac into his glass, despising it, and drank.

"Tell me about your home, this Glen Sian in Scotland."

"It is a house which holds my possessions. I do not consider it anything more."

He left the chair and her eyes followed him, lingering on his hair, his stiff, still youthful back, his face, arrogant in profile. He reached the fireplace and examined the arrangement of flowers on the marble hearth.

"Perhaps you find it possible to forget, possible or expedient. But you have not lived here for nearly a decade."

He stared at the rose petal in his palm. It was dark, almost black, and his desire to taste it was intense, almost sexual.

"Do you know what you remind me of, Ewen? You remind me of a man in a small boat being blown out to sea. He pulls against the wind and he pulls against the tide, and he will never come back to the shore and he knows it... but still he rows, until he breaks his heart. Every year you go a little further with the ebb of things. One day...."

"Perhaps your man is rowing for his life."

Silence. So dark now, the scent of the gardens stronger. Moths coming in heedlessly to the flame.

He opened his fist; the dark petal was crushed.

"I hope they do not keep him up too late, watching these fireworks."

"Poor Ewen," she murmured, "do you fear you may be dwindling into a Scot?"

He threw it into the fireplace and sat again, avoiding her eyes.

"When I was contracted to Saint-Arnaud, it was you I wanted. If any of your family had known where you were...."

"Are you saying you would not have done it?"

"I wanted your advice. I wrote to you. You never answered."

"I was in Italy."

"And what did you find in Italy, Ewen, besides Elspeth, and a little of the river Lethe?"

"I paid for it," he said shortly.

"I thought you were happy."

"I thought so too, while she lived."

"I envied you. I never loved Saint-Arnaud."

Another moth flickered in and died, and he heard the hour strike: night had passed into morning.

"Have you never thought of marrying again?"

"I could never endure it. I would die if I had to so reveal myself again, and be so wounded. I could not bear it."

"My poor Ewen."

"I wish to Christ you would stop calling me that."

She came to him and caressed his cheek.

She said, "I wish sometimes we were not cousins," and left him.

In late afternoon Evariste de Salignac, the heir, arrived unexpectedly on horseback. He vented his fury at the gates he found closed on his mount, which he spurred toward the wall, on the carefully tended lawns, and on the footman who betrayed surprise upon seeing him: he removed his gauntlet and struck the man across the mouth with it.

He sent a message to his mother requiring her presence at his table; Ewen was to join them. He spent three hours in preparation, enduring the tortures of the toilette, and stared with a bizarre fascination at his reflection. The valet was watching with passionate approbation.

"This is how Monseigneur should always look."

He went downstairs. Honorée did not remark on his appearance.

"Ewen, I present my son. Evariste, you will remember your cousin."

He was almost insolently underdressed. He bowed, as inadequately as was permissible.

"Your servant, monsieur my cousin."

He did not paint, but he was as lavish as his mother with the scent, and he wore a patch near his mouth. He was very like Saint-Arnaud in his youth, with a bony, equine face and drowsy eyes. The heavy lids lifted slightly: the eyes were a surprisingly cold blue.

"Pardon me, monsieur my cousin. Madame," offering his arm, "shall we proceed?"

Ewen drank heavily at the table, but the boy drank more, and was flushed and incoherent long before he rose abruptly and left the room.

"Where does he go?"

"To piss," she said, and laughed, unamused. "He is considerate of you tonight. I have known him use a vessel from the sideboard, and his father with him. Go yourself, if you like... don't stand on ceremony for me."

He said coldly, "I am not one of your sons. Do not insult me by behaving as if I were."

"We all have such iron sensibilities in this house...." She shrugged. "When he has your measure he'll ask you to sit down to cards. He knows you were once... accomplished."

"I never play any more."

"Indulge him. You know what you were like at that age."

"I was never like him at that age."

"I don't think you care very much for my son, Ewen."

"Does that so surprise you?"

"No. Sometimes I hardly like him myself." She came around the table; the strong perfume overwhelmed him. "It's late. Are you coming to bed?"

"I shall sit a while and await your son."

"I don't think he will return. Not now."

She took his flushed, powdered face between her hands, and alcohol had dissipated enough inhibition to allow him a frisson of desire.

"Promise me one thing." And very gently the hands fell away, a brush of powder on the palms. "No more of this. You do not need it, and you do not wear it well."

Long after she had gone he sat, drinking cognac until it became obvious that the boy would not return, then he went to his silent rooms and threw the heavy coat on the floor and sat taking off his paint before the mirror like any streetwalker. His hair was filthy with pomade, his lips stained with alkanet; he felt hideously soiled.

He was still awake when the rain began, breaking the sullen dawn.

The children returned on Monday morning: Honorée's three youngest sons and, descending from the carriage last, a slight, fair boy. In return for her salute he executed a stiff little bow.

Honorée took him by the shoulders and gave him what appeared to be a small push of encouragement. He looked older than not quite ten, quieter, more contained, and very unlike the winsome child who had gone away.

He came up the steps; he had not lost his old sedate walk.

"James?"

He turned, as though his eyes were not yet accustomed to the shadows, and said coolly, "Oh, good morning."

He accepted the embrace but did not reciprocate. Ewen released him; James stepped back and gave him a curiously adult look.

"Dearest boy, how are you?"

"I am well, thank you." Then he scuffed his toe and said, with another of those upflung glances, "How did you know where to find me? I was with my uncle Charles Arsène."

"Your cousin Honorée wrote and told me."

James was looking past him into the shadows.

"Where is *he*?"

"Whom do you mean?"

"*You* know. Where is he?"

"James—" He was conscious of Honorée's hand on his arm. "Listen. We shall have to have a talk—"

An hour later she was reclining in the salon. He, still staggered by the chill of James's greeting, was staring blindly at the lawns.

"He looked at me as though he despised me."

She stretched out with a bored yawn.

"What an imagination— Jamie!" The sedate footsteps approached and waited politely at the door. "Here is your father with nothing to do, chéri. Take him into Saint-Arnaud's rose garden and be sure to show him all the new ones."

James stood with his hand on the high doorknob, his face shuttered.

"Go outside and wait for me there." James gave him the stiff little bow and went. "Honorée, you see how he is with me. I cannot... bear it."

"Oh, go away. You cannot mean to tell me you are shy of your own son."

They walked. He initiated painful conversation and it died; he tried another subject and that, too, politely dismissed. Did he enjoy himself here? Yes, Madame la Vicomtesse was very kind. What was he studying? Latin, Greek, algebra, trigonometry, music, and Italian ... he liked Italian. His tutor was a Jesuit. It was the only information he offered.

Then he mentioned bluntly that all the de Salignacs had allowances; madame sometimes gave him a little pocket money but he had none now.... Ewen gave him a livre.

"That isn't very much."

"It is all I have at the moment. If you must have more then you will have to wait until later, when I shall accommodate you." He watched him secreting the coin on his person. "How much exactly do you want?" James named a sum dispassionately. "I do not believe small boys have need of so much money, James."

"Anne-Claude—"

"Anne-Claude has Saint-Arnaud for a father. I must remind you that you are not in the same position."

James stood inspecting the toe of his shoe.

"I want you to tell me about Malcolm."

"He has gone. Apparently we meant nothing to him, you and I."

He was staring at the ground. His face had flushed.

"James, I do not say this to distress you. I merely wanted you to know."

James said, "I don't understand," then he blinked and said rapidly, "I'm not going any further. I was up at six o'clock and I haven't had any rest, and Madame la Vicomtesse said I'm not to overtire myself, or do anything I don't want to do."

Ewen said gently, "Then you had better go back to the house, hadn't you, and I shall see the rest of the gardens myself."

Ewen went up to see him later; he was lying on his bed, where he had sulked undisturbed all afternoon.

James lay face down and ignored him.

"Believe me when I say I knew nothing of what was happening in Avignon." The mattress gave slightly; he was sitting on the bed. "I should have arranged to send you to Honorée from the beginning. I should not have allowed my obligations to your mother's family to dissuade me."

James gritted his teeth. The gentle hand was stroking his hair.

"James, I never meant to wound you this way. Believe me, I never meant it."

One last late bird was singing; the moon was almost risen. "I understand that you have been writing to your grandmother Douglass. That was very good of you, James. I saw her in Paris." Another movement, another sigh. "She sends you this. It was your grandfather's."

He turned his head slightly. The watch was lying on the pillow.

"Your grandfather Douglass carried this at the battle of Sheriffmuir, in the year I was born. Your grandmother said it was given him by the King. She wanted you to have it especially." There was a heavy silence; he began to cry again quietly, hiding the tears in his pillow. "I named you for that king, James. You may have thought I named you for my father, but that was not so."

It was very dark. He lay face down, rigidly.

"I love you, James. Even if you think you can no longer love me."

He spoke, muffled by tears and pillow.

"Are you going back to Scotland?"

"I think so, yes."

"Why can't you live in France?"

"I cannot afford to." A slight cough; he remembered it, so many things he remembered. "Has Madame la Vicomtesse had you to the physician?" He mumbled an affirmative. "And what does he say? Is there any more blood, do you have any trouble breathing?" Silence. "My dear, you may as well tell me, otherwise I shall only ask madame."

James flung himself upright.

"Ask her, then! You never asked *me*, you never asked about anything! You just sent me away!" He groped wildly. "And you can take your horrid watch, I don't want it! I hate it! I don't want anything from you ever again. I wish you'd never come! I hate you!"

Ewen said, "I see."

Already he was scrambling, groping for him in the darkness.

"No, Papa, I didn't—"

"I understand. There is nothing more to be said." He was at the door, and the light from the hall outlined him and hid his face as effectively as a mask. "Good night. I shall not trouble you again."

Evariste found him on the terrace at three in the morning and brought him in to play cards. He was drunk and in a filthy mood; he began to lose at once, and he watched the money go with indifference.

The boy sat opposite, smelling of sweat and his lavish cologne, and dealing with practised hands. His conversation began lewd and became obscene; he availed himself of an apparently inexhaustible supply of salacious anecdotes, and glanced only once at the footmen standing impassively nearby.

"I appreciate your conviction that you invented sexual pleasure, Evariste, but I assure you it has been experienced by others before you. I am proof against such revelations as these."

Silence. Heat; the stench of cologne. The lawns swept away bleached by moonlight beyond the open windows; he heard the shriek of an owl, and then the vicious barking of dogs.

"Some poacher." The boy shrugged. "The keepers will see to it." He ate cherries and spat the stones with relish; his eyes were insolent. "My mother talks of you ad nauseam... she always led me to believe you were some manner of saint. She seems to think your prick doesn't harden when you look at her."

"I confide that none of my peculiarities escape her, and none of yours either, in case you flattered yourself that they did."

The candles burned lower, and stank; they both sweated. The cards shushed on the baize tabletop, the footmen stood motionless.

"For God's sake send these people to bed."

Evariste, dealing, said coldly, "They can stand. While a de Salignac wakes, why should they sleep?"

Some time later Ewen said, "I am finished."

"Put up your watch. I have a fancy for it." The old chevalier's watch had been lying on the table; he would not be sorry to see it go.

"To your...?"

"This ring. My father gave it me."

"You may have to buy another."

"I doubt it. I want to send you back to your smelly Scotland in a beggar's coat."

"I have worn beggar's clothes before. They do not offend me."

They played; the boy won; he was very drunk and his mouth was moist. They played again and he lost.

"You cheated, you bastard."

Ewen leaned forward and took the end of his stock between his fingertips; the silk was stained with cherry juice and wine

"Don't say that again, mon cher. I might take your sordid remarks to heart."

On the third trick he lost again, and stared across the table with glittering eyes.

"All or nothing. I'll have you... all or nothing!"

"On the turn of the card?"

"On the turn of the card! Do it!"

"You trust me?" Evariste swore luridly. "Very well, call it."

He called it and lost.

"It seems your luck has run its course."

"Where are you going? We haven't finished!"

"We have more than finished, you and I."

The candles had burned down in a haze of smoke. The footmen began to relax their inflexible attitudes. Ewen said to one of them, "He has a valet?"

"Yes, monsieur."

"Summon him. Have him taken to bed."

The boy was lying with his head on the table, the cards spilled on the floor. He began to vomit as the footmen carried him away.

Ewen walked out on to the terrace. The light was grey and sultry, the lawns white with dew.

He leaned against the wall, his mouth foul, his head aching. The footmen had returned, scraping back the draperies to show a room still dark and drifting with smoke, wine dripping from the table to the cards on the floor, the candlesticks smutted with tears of wax. A sullen gleam of dawn pierced the clouds.

It was sordid... God, how sordid it was. The stains, the smoke, the sour smell of vomit.... He had passed too many nights like this, burning the hours in self-indulgence: his father had led him and broken him to it as he had led him and broken him to whores. This was all his life in France had ever been; all life would offer now.

He was sick of it, sick of corruption, pretense, lies. He felt gutted and burnt, defiled by it: a broken-down gambler grown prim with age, appalled at the taint of an old debauchery.

He watched the sun rise across the lawns. His eyes ached, his wrist, the soft tendons between thumb and forefinger which once had been like steel from the constant exercise of the cards.

He thought, bonne nuit, France.... bonne nuit, mon ancienne vie.

The day flowered. The birds sang with inexpressible joy.

They sat on the terrace in the afternoon, she somnolent beneath a parasol, he with eyes closed against the assault of the sun. The children were playing croquet on the south lawn, and from time to time there were shrill complaints. The rap of mallet on ball seemed excruciatingly loud.

There was a more violent outburst from the lawn.

"You cheated!"

Silk, perfume, and the shadow of the parasol across his face. She had risen and walked to the steps.

"That will do, François."

"He cheated, madame!"

"Claude?"

"Madame, it was unintentional. My thoughts were somewhere else."

She murmured, "This one will be a diplomat, upon my life."

The youngest child was jumping up and down.

"Claude cheats! Claude cheats!"

"Oh, my God, I shall be a madwoman yet. Disregard it, then, and play quietly, or I will take away all the mallets." The silk returned. "They should all be little Englishmen, with this wonderful sense of fair play."

It was quieter. The parasol's shadow lay across his face, and he opened his eyes.

"Will you tell me now about that shambles in my drawing room?"

"What is there to tell? As you so accurately prophesied, the son of the house invited me to cards."

"And you won."

"Only at the last. It seemed not to matter very much."

"You have got old, haven't you?"

"Yes," he said, without humour.

The whiteness of her clothing and the light was painful, and he closed his eyes. The umbra and its coolness receded, the sun assaulted his eyelids once more. On the lawn there were jeers and laughter, and James's voice, almost hysterical with excitement.

"There will be ten of us at supper. Not Evariste, but friends."

"Why should you think I object to the presence of Evariste? I congratulate him for having the stomach. I certainly have not."

"You need not eat. I only want you to... talk a little."

He opened his eyes and said coldly, "Do you wish me to entertain them?"

"I would rather say enlighten... but yes."

"I daresay I *would* entertain them, a man who stammers. That would be very entertaining."

"Ewen, you are not going to be difficult?"

"No," he said. "Monsieur tenders his regrets. He will not be performing tonight."

She found him in one of the arbours before moonrise and sat beside him, crushing the sprig of aromatic balm she had picked on her walk through the garden.

"And your guests?"

"I cried off. In my condition I can be excused these little whims."

He said, after a silence, "Do you love all your children, Honorée?"

"Even my misguided eldest; yes, I love them all."

"My son hates me. He told me so last night."

"Oh, Ewen, he—"

"He thinks I wanted to be rid of him, to encourage some one else. And I know not what. I cannot blame him, really, but I did not take it well."

"Do you think you are making too much of this?"

"Perhaps. It's difficult to tell, isn't it, if children truly mean what they say."

"Ewen—"

"No. I don't want to talk any more. What I want is to be left alone."

"I know what you want. I thought perhaps I could change it. Now I see it was always what you preferred."

He did not look at her, but by the moon's faint light he saw her hands, flat, as if pressed against glass. "I feel... such a wall between us. I can't bring it down."

"Why? Because I would not laugh and prattle to your friends? I feel the world is sitting at a banquet, and I am the bloodstained ghost going from chair to chair. Some of you pretend not to see me— most of you do not see me at all." A movement. "Please— stay. To lose you too would be too much."

She sank back, and he was conscious of the warmth of her body in the chill of evening.

"Shall I tell you something of my life in Scotland? In summer it rains and is cold. In winter it snows. My valet airs my shirt before the fire before I find it dry enough to put on. My bed is damp, my books are full of mould, my rooms smell of rot and smoke, my chimneys are in bad repair." He felt her fingers through his. "Please don't. Or I shall weep, and shame you."

The fingers withdrew.

"We come to the people. They are primitive: this is putting it charitably. They speak neither French nor English but an uncouth language which in my poor way I attempt to understand... they live in small black windowless hovels. The roofs are weighted with stones against God's marvellous winds, which in that place never cease to blow. They share their living quarters with their animals, and in winter eat their blood to survive. The land gives nothing but stones and a little grain, from which they distill spirits; the rivers are full of fish. All this, rivers, land, fish and wretched people, all this is mine to possess."

"Oh, my dear...."

"You should profess yourself relieved that I did not entertain your friends. We come finally to myself, and this is very amusing. I could tell them any number of diverting things about myself. How my house was violated and my kinsmen murdered. How my wife died because there was no quack I could bring to her. How I sent my son to France, because in the dead of winter I saw him coughing up his life's blood in a house I could never keep warm. And shall I tell them how I wanted to take my life, because I was sick and cold and lonely and I hated it all so much, and even I thought there must come an end.... I do not see you smiling, Honorée, although I have made this as diverting as I could."

"I never knew you were so bitter."

"My dear, you do not know me if you think this is as deep as it goes."

She took his hand now, furtively in the darkness, and he did not reject her.

"I wish I were dead."

"No, Ewen. No."

"On the contrary, I do sincerely wish it."

She twisted on the bench, taking his face between her hands.

"For God's sake, what is this terrible malaise?"

"I think one calls it guilt. For living.... I have failed at everything, as a man, as a father, as a Christian. I don't love my enemies, I hate them."

"It takes no courage to die: it only takes courage to live. You know that I love you."

"It is not enough. To have loved one another as children...."

"I love you still. But not as my cousin."

"I have committed sins you cannot imagine. Must I now add incest to the list?"

"It happens between cousins. It does not go by that name."

"I could give you nothing. I have nothing left to give."

"Believe me, whatever you could give me would be more than I have ever had."

The moonlight was stronger, fretting the shadows.

"Perhaps it would not be so great a sin to love you. I would to God I could."

She had risen, and the moonlight lay upon her gown, lambent and ephemeral. The sweet sharp fragrance had dissipated, a wind had stirred the leaves.

"Go home, Ewen. And don't write to me again in this half-death, where you care for nothing and you feel nothing and you haven't the courage to live or die. Expect no sympathy from me."

She left him, walking beneath the trees, the patterns of moonlight on her gown; walking slowly, so that the white light deceived him, and when he thought he saw her still, she had gone.

He returned by way of Flanders, and from Rotterdam to Inverness. Bad weather and bitter cold and a lonely sea crossing; for a time he feared they would be wrecked, as the ship beat off course almost back to Holland, and stood off and on three days and nights before the wind allowed them to enter the Beauly Firth. It was late September before he reached Ardsian.

The table in the hall was bare.

"Where are my letters?" The letters were in the estate office. "Bring them to me at once." He did not want to read them there, confront that dead, accusing stillness so soon.

He took them to the morning room, rifling through them with his heart in his mouth. The room was silent, the wind rattled a hail of leaves across the terrace, the old dog lay at his feet. The letter was not there, no sign of that illegible, eccentric hand. He put his head back against the chair and thought he would weep but there were no tears, only the dead finality, the knowledge that however long he waited the letter would never come, the words *I am well, I am happy* or *I am sick, I am coming home* would never be written.

He read the others after a while; there was nothing of any importance, bills and commonplaces from his solicitor not worthy of his consideration. He left them in the escritoire and went to Malcolm's rooms. Shadow and sun, passing quickly; from the window he saw the darkness of cloud and mountain, the beaten gold of birches. The bedroom was as he had found it that first morning, with the delicate sky of March beyond the windows: the book half read, the clothing discarded, the rosary and crucifix abandoned on a table.

When he came upon the girl in the dressing room he was shocked, not so much by the fact that he was not alone but because she was a stranger, and committing a violation in these rooms so sacred to him. She was touching something; he did not see what it was, or even what she was, a servant hired in his absence, only that she was an intruder.

He said, "Put that down and leave at once. I never want to see you here again."

It was only after she had gone that he recognized her, and that he had spoken to her in a language she could not understand, as once her eyes had spoken to him, and were speaking still.

In the days that followed, the affairs of Glen Sian preoccupied him, and he felt once more the estate's moribund embrace. In the evenings, the girl Bridgid offered her body, and he exploited it, until their commerce in his bed had become an obsession and a necessity.

She had seduced him with unerring expertise: it had happened the night after his return and was quickly over, without words or tenderness. She came to him again the following afternoon with, he thought, the valet's compliance, and he had stripped her and taken her brutally on the brocaded couch in his dressing room where the child Malcolm had sometimes slept; it exorcised that sexless and tenacious ghost and he was savagely glad. Eventually he had intercourse with her on Malcolm's bed, in the sterile coldness of that room.

She was fifteen, he thirty-six, and he no longer considered the future; he lived only within the hours he was with her. If a child resulted from the liaison he would claim it: unlike Malcolm, who had never been possessed, or James, who had been lost to France, it would be wholly his. Secretly, he hoped for it. But there was no child; he suspected her considerable skills had ordained that also.

There was no affection, no familiarity; there was neither intimacy nor understanding. He knew no more of her than her body, and she gave no more than that.

She sat naked one evening in the disordered bed and combed her hair with her fingers, and turned on him opalescent, inexpressive eyes.

"Tomorrow my father is coming."

Strangely, he felt no dread.

"He knows?"

"Not of this. It is another matter will be bringing him here."

"And you know this other matter."

"We are leaving Glen Sian. There are many of us wanting to go."

"What do you mean? Your father? Your family?"

"It is wanting to go to America he is. Not Diar, he will not go. But it is myself and the others if you will give them leave. You will not prevent them because of me?"

He said, without rancour, "Is there someone else?"

"No… yes."

"Is he going with you?"

"Yes. He is—"

"I do not want to know his name."

She lapsed into deep silence, fingers in her hair. She looked very unchildlike: he wondered how he had ever been astonished by her youth. She would age quickly in the life to which she was going; neither here nor in that unknown country was there any pity for women.

"What do you want of me? What did you mean by beginning this?"

"I am going from you. I wanted this, while there was time."

The hair spilled like silk across her shoulder, as it had been silk to his face and lips, silk to his closed eyes and the tears he had shed the first time, and never since in her presence.

"I wanted the knowledge of you. I will keep it before me, if my life be long or short… I will have the thought of you and your face held in my mind. Because there is not another man like you in this land, you like a prince in all things, and the other men smelling of cattle."

Raining now, in the greyness of evening. The face and the silken hair bent close, the skin translucent, the pale mouth an invitation and a farewell.

She gathered her clothing; he lay watching her. He felt nothing, not regret, nor grief, nor resentment: she had exorcised those too. When she closed the door he left the bed and moved through the half-light to the window, stared out at the black hills marching away to the south, the garden below in the rain, shabby with November. The house was quiet. No candles burned; there were only shadows.

His hair had come loose; she had teased it from its black riband and it fell as fine as a woman's to his shoulders. She had laughed at the grey in his hair.

He gathered it and reached for the crushed riband and his hand paused; he had seen the reflection of the bed.

Oh my God... forgive me. All my sins... forgive me.

And yet... I was happy for a time.

She was gone, gone, gone: no sound from the gallery; the servants were unobtrusive, even the dogs were quiet. He still found himself listening on nights like this, when the rain was also a light step running in the darkness.

He breathed on the glass, looked through the rain to the garden below to see if she had lingered, but there was no one. The garden, the path, the stone bench, the fountain, all were deserted.

She had gone. The house was empty.

Interlude: Glen Sian 1758

The world progressed toward the declaration of a war which would continue, at intervals, until the century's end. Hostilities between Britain and France had begun in North America, with siege and ambush and the bizarre tactics of the frontier: now it became a war in deadly earnest, with the armies of Britain, Prussia and Hanover allied against those of France, Saxony, Austria, Russia and Sweden. The brilliant Frederick of Prussia raged through eastern Europe, attacking Saxony, Prague and Bohemia, smashing the French army of the Prince Charles de Soubise at Rosbach in November of 1757, and the Austrians under Prince Joseph of Saxe-Hildburghausen at Leuthen in December. His genius was not shared by that other royal general, George II's son William, Duke of Cumberland, who the same year lost a thousand men at Hastenbeck on the River Weser in Lower Saxony, and conceded defeat to a superior French force; on September sixth the victor of Culloden put his signature to the convention of Kloster-Zeven, surrendering to the enemy his father's ancestral lands of Hanover and Brunswick. Of him upon his return to England the King said, "Here is my son who has ruined me, and disgraced himself." Cumberland, pleading ill health, resigned his military appointments, and brought to that inglorious end a notorious career.

To Ewen the war meant nothing, a dispute over obscure territories for indeterminable reasons. His country now was a country forgotten, and coveted by no one.

The effect of the war upon the unimpressionable Highlands was slight. The price of beef had risen as the voracious army and navy increased demand. And there was a bleeding away of young men: Highland lairds culled Highland regiments from their rent rolls, armed and kilted them, and sold them into the service of a government which despised them and had recently suppressed them; and if any man saw any irony in the situation the little pay and small comforts of an English service perhaps offered compensation.

They did not go because they hoped for anything better; it was because they were hopeless that they went. There was no hope for them and no future, neither in the Highlands nor on the broad seas nor in the scarlet lines of regiments on distant, foreign shores.

He had never seen the girl again after she had left his house: she and her family had departed in the spring of the following year. There had been full-scale famine in 1756, with dysentery and smallpox in its wake; in Glen Sian

161

sixty people, one-tenth of the population, had died, and now it was autumn again, and the demarcation between hunger and starvation remained as fine as ever.

For himself and his household, by careful economy, there was enough to eat: game and salt fish, root vegetables and the unpopular potato, which the people could not be persuaded to cultivate. That was the substance of his table on this night, the twentieth of November. His breath clouded; on the fork, a fine silver with elaborate ornamentation on the back so that it could be laid tines down in the French fashion, his fingers ached with cold. At his feet lay the deerhound bitch, Juno; the old dog he had so loved had gone in the bitter winter after his return. Now she had taken his place, and like her predecessor was his constant companion.

Something had disturbed her: she rose and padded out of the room. He picked at his food and the silent Ruaraidh, standing behind his chair, moved from the shadows and refilled his glass.

She barked suddenly in the hall, and the alarm was taken up by the remaining two of her litter. Ignored, she belled hysterically, and finally Ewen put down his fork.

"What ails that dog? Has some one gone to see?"

Ruaraidh murmured, "The boy will be going, Glen Sian."

"I should damned well hope so."

Outside the deep, belling chorus had ended.

"It is nothing, Glen Sian. They will have been hearing something, maybe. It was only the wind."

He grunted and crumbled more of the foul cheese on his bread. Behind him, the boy had come in and was whispering to Ruaraidh. He said over his shoulder, "What is it?"

Ruaraidh said hesitantly, as though trying to prepare him for something:

"Glen Sian—"

And then he heard the voice, not loudly, and the footsteps, slower now than he had used to imagine them, and although voice and footsteps were unfamiliar his bowels lurched with dread and recognition, and joy, and he bent his head and stared at the tablecloth.

Between the dimness of the hall and the smoky light cast by the candles, some one stood, and the voice spoke his Christian name. He raised his eyes, and the face he had held in his memory was before him, but irrevocably changed; the child was gone from it, and all his memories of the child.

His voice faltered, as he had hoped it would not.

"Malcolm."

But not the child he knew.

162

The deerhound bitch had followed him in and was sniffing the leather of his boot. There was no animosity in her manner, and no ecstatic welcome; her behaviour was that of a dog acknowledging one who had but lately gone.

Ewen said, "Elle vous souvient," and knew immediately, and with an inexplicable sense of loss, that this was no longer a language to be shared.

"She has a long memory. And so have I."

He thought, so have we all, God help us.

"Come in and sit down, Malcolm."

He sat, and the candles illuminated features which had been obscured. The face was guarded, virile, the olive skin tanned, the bones prominent; the aquiline nose had been broken, and the smallest finger of his left hand; two fingers of the right were lividly scarred. He was only twenty-three years old.

There was movement and a shadow, and Ruaraidh placed whisky on the table and left. The piercing eyes followed him.

Ewen said, "Every one will know by morning."

"Let them know. I've come to make myself known to them."

Another measure splashed into the glass.

Ewen said, "Do you intend to stay," but this was ignored.

"Where's your son, Ewen?" He spoke in English, which had never been their language of conversation; the voice was soft and distinctive, and used the colloquial with the ease of familiarity.

"He is in France."

"What, still?" and Ewen cut across the inflection of contempt.

"At least he writes to me. Was it too much to expect that you put your hand to a piece of paper and tell me you were alive?"

"There was nothing to say. And after a while, there was too much."

"And how many years have you spent phrasing that? It has a polish of long wearing—how many times have you practiced it?"

As though he had anticipated this, Malcolm did not rise to it, merely sat, his face half in shadow, immobile, as in the past he had always detached himself from emotion and abuse.

"I thought you were dead. I have been in hell."

The eyes came up; the face was no more like Murdoch's than his own, and its resemblance to one forgotten teased his memory. There was nothing in it of the child he loved; nothing there he knew.

"Have you? Then we must have passed. I did not see you there."

He rose and went to the fire and replenished it, a leashed, restless, dangerous tension in the movements. He remained there, crouched, staring into the flames.

Ewen said, "I thought you had gone for a soldier."

"The day I fight England's battles will be a cold day in hell."

He tossed more peat onto the fire and turned, his face lit by the flames. "What's the matter with your son? Is he too dainty to get off his arse and put food on his father's table?"

"He returns in the spring, to study law."

"And what will that profit him? Will it feed the people?" Another turf; there were no more. "By Christ, I'll give you a decent fire if I have to cut the peats myself." And smiled, and the illusion of youth was disconcerting, ephemeral. "Do you doubt me? I've bent my back for pay since I left this house. Another day's labour is nothing."

Ewen said, "It will not signify," but thought he had not been heard. The green eyes were moving around the room, lingering on the stained silk as if seeking some familiar object. The homecoming of one whose home this had never been; of one who had no home.

"There was a painting there."

"I have had expenses. Your room at least I have never changed."

Only desecrated; but in this man, unlike that taut and nervous youth, there was no innocence.

"I owe you what I owe my son, Malcolm. Let me... give you what I can."

He had been gazing into the flames, his face harsh in repose. He turned.

"What would you give me? A place in the world? Would you give me money?"

"If money is what you want."

"You lifted me from shit. You owe me nothing."

The gaping boy had come in with his meal; he stared down into the flames until they were alone again. Ewen said, "It is poor stuff. My apologies."

He ate without speaking, and as though he were ravenous: when he had eaten he wrenched something from beneath the sodden greatcoat he had left lying on the floor, and spilled the contents across the tablecloth.

"Some of that my father took from you. The rest is mine. And there's more where that came from."

"And where did it come from?"

"My blood and my sweat. I earned it."

It was not all sterling, nor all gold. There were French coins, and others he did not recognize, and their total value represented more than his annual income.

The eyes were watching him, intensely clear.

"Do you not want it, man? Or is it no good to you?"

Ewen gazed at him, overcome, and for the first time there was a softening, almost a tenderness. "I brought you coffee and brandy, too. Do you want them?"

He felt old, old, exhausted and alone; the night had played with him and produced these things to torment him... the pile of coins, the shadowed, unknown face, the haunting knowledge that the child he had loved had died as surely as he had feared.

He said, "Tell me what you like. I will believe you, whatever it is." He pushed the coins away; the words failed him. "... I do not know what to say to you."

He walked toward the door. The soft, compelling voice arrested him.

"Do you still pray for me, Ewen?"

"Believe me... when I could, I always prayed for you."

"It was wasted on me."

He went out, leaving him seated between the light and the shadows, and only later recalled that he had offered no word of welcome or of affection, nor had Malcolm seemed to expect it.

THE HEIRESS

I

They are my ghosts. I was daughter, lover, wife to them, mistress and friend, rival and enemy; I was loved by them, and I loved them. They spoke to me, sometimes in a language unwritten: sometimes only instinct divines their secrets, the shadow and the substance.

They are the web and mystery of my past, and my voice is theirs.

This house, Evesham, has remained substantially unchanged, except during Catherine's brief regime, so that for me, after every absence, there has been comfort and reassurance in its constancy. A rambling Jacobean manor house of russet brick with a clock tower and a gilded weathervane, the north front faces the stables, the south the lodge, the gates, and a park of copper beech where thousands of narcissi turn the lawns golden as far as the river. There is a formal east garden of clipped yew and granite walks, designed by the landscaper Charles Bridgeman at the turn of the century, and west gardens which Mordaunt always preferred, and where I ran freely and cut the many flowers, sweet Provence roses and hollyhocks from Virginia, Carolina phlox, peonies and jasmine. These, lovely and ephemeral, marked the passing of my childish life, even as the angles and patterns of the shadows in rooms I had always known altered only with the progress of the sun, and in accordance with the seasons.

It is the only constancy, the only unalterable truth, to know that when I die I shall be buried here; and while I live I will see myself here, my younger self, that Margaret, always troubled, always uncertain, walking where the rose had an incomparable sweetness, which it does not now seem to possess.

Time and rumour have lent their dark patina to my reputation.

It is not true that Mordaunt raised me as his son, preferring an heir to the heiress circumstances provided. It is not true that I am lesbian. If, occasionally, I have worn man's attire, it was convenient, and if I have camouflaged my sexuality, suppressed it, it was in my own defense.

If feminine is coquetry, docility, submission, I know not femininity, only the essence of femaleness. I have never wanted children but I nurtured those who loved me, and would have defended them, even to the shedding of my blood. I have loved men, my destroyer, and he who was my redemption.

I have not committed incest.

I have killed.

He was my father, and I adored him. His were the hands that lifted me to saddles, first his and then my own, guided my small, stubborn fingers on the keyboard, mended dolls, fashioned kites, taught me marksmanship. His education had been limited, curtailed by the army: I learned what he knew, Italian, poetry, philosophy, history, horticulture. It seemed natural to me and I thrived on it, but I learned no limitations: I defined femaleness in terms unacceptable to the world, and perhaps it is because of the unorthodoxy of those years that I have always felt estranged from other women.

They were, for the most part, happy years. I was swung off my feet and tossed in the air and pick-a-backed like any child, and no buried shard of memory has surfaced to corrupt the recollection's sweetness. A certain inhibition tempered this boisterousness after she told him it was not decorous, but there was never any sense that I was not his flesh, and when I sought sanctuary with him on nights of violent storm I was merely a small girl in her father's bed, and my sleep was innocent.

I remained unaware of the army's legacy. I only once saw him unclothed, as a very young child surprising him in his bath. His valet was emptying a ewer over his head; steam and wet towelling obscured his nakedness. I remembered only the white claw of scarring on his right shoulder and bicep: I thought nothing of it. He merely asked me what I wanted, wiping the water from his eyes, and the Italian diverted my attention, and led me away affectionately by the hand.

I understood very young that their marriage had become a hell, and I was a solitary, sensitive child; what I witnessed injured and haunted me more than either of them knew. I hid the wounds and let them fester until they became monstrous, and like most children, perhaps more acutely than most, I feared that I myself was the cause.

She did not live with us. She kept a house in London, for which he paid, and my life was marred by her comings and goings. Birthdays were an event because of her letters and gifts, and when she came in person, which was not often; she brought me delicate, expensive little toys which were soon broken and cried over, and I wept too when she had been with us, even if they had quarrelled, and she was preparing to leave us again.

When I was eight years old I sensed that the tide had turned against me, for no reason I could ever discover.

I was watching her dress: her ritual and the objects on her dressing table fascinated me. She had given me a little glass coach and six with which to play, but I had forgotten it in my examination of her clothing.

She was applying rouge from a pad of human hair impregnated with pigment and complaining of his failings. The subject of her discourse this morning was his indifference toward the household liveries. "I should be mortified if any one from town saw them, not that any one from town comes here, or would be welcome if they did...."

I had heard all this before. I returned to my child's world of dreams and imagination.

Stand and deliver, as you value your lives....

"Come and have a sweet, darling."

Affection like this was rare from her, and I was starved of it. She gave me a sugared almond and allowed me to taste her liqueur, and the silk of her hair and her robe caressed me.

"Now tell me what scent I shall wear."

I chose it; I wear it still. She applied it to her throat and breasts, and touched her perfumed fingers to my earlobes.

"I must have your ears done, Meg, I have such pretty little earrings you could wear. I wore 'em at your age. And it's good for your eyes, too."

"Is it?"

"Well, mine are pierced, ain't they? And there's nothing wrong with *my* eyes."

Indeed. What could be wrong with them, so dark a blue that they were almost violet, and with those perfect features? What comparison could be made with a child like myself? There was no promise of her great beauty in me: I was no more like her than a shadow is like the light.

She rose and stretched, petticoats frothing around her knees, and told me to ring the bell for her woman.

I ran across the room to the bell pull, came back flushed with importance, and stepped on the glass coach and six.

She was beside me instantly, in a perfumed storm of silk, and I saw the manic violence which hitherto had been directed only at him. I was holding the fragments and she was trying to wrest them from me, screaming. The door opened; it was Mordaunt.

He said, "What the hell are you doing?"

They were the first words he had spoken to her for over a week. She dropped my hand; my blood was streaming to the carpet.

She said, "It's too late... it's too late."

He wrapped my fingers in his handkerchief. Whatever he thought had happened, he gave no further indication of emotion.

"I shall buy you another."

"I don't want another! Nothing is the same, you loved me then—"

He carried me to her commode, washed the blood from me and dried me with her towels. She threw what remained of her toy into the fire.

"You, God damn you, you love that child more than you love me!"

He told me to go and find my governess and closed the door against me, and I, who had heard the violence of their quarrels many times, huddled outside, torturing myself with yet another I had caused.

"Since you choose to make this ugly—"

"I didn't mean it."

"But you did. You mean it more every time you say it. This is simply the first time you've said it in her presence."

"I've cut my hand too. Pity it wasn't my wrist, ain't it?"

He said, "Oh, for Christ's sake," and then, "Give me that," and after a time she said, "Achill, don't send me away like this."

"I don't send you away. You do as you please— you always have."

"We have a little time.... Darling, come to bed."

He said, in a dry voice in which there was neither love nor pity, "It's a little late in the day for that now," and I never knew in what sense he meant it.

Their marriage was moribund. I did not precipitate its death throes, although I blame myself: I was the principal instrument.

In the spring of my ninth year there was an epidemic of measles; there were many deaths. My illness progressed normally for several days before complications ensued, and during one of Mordaunt's vigils I heard the doctor's whispered recommendation that my mother be sent for.

She had already left London; I knew nothing of this, only that she came. I still loved her then, and if she had not come forever, she would at least remain a little while. It was all that mattered to me.

She stayed, and my tenth birthday passed; the London season commenced. And still she did not go.

She began arranging a place for herself, not only between us but in the very house. The paintings were cleaned, the walls rehung with French fabrics, new and graceful furniture appeared and familiar pieces were relegated to the attics. The only rooms she did not touch were Mordaunt's library and the drawing room, which already bore the stamp of her relentlessly exquisite taste.

Mordaunt, whose resistance to change was as unyielding as mine, said nothing. Perhaps it seemed to him diplomatic, a silence in the interests of peace, or perhaps it did not matter to him what she did and at what cost, as long as she was with him.

I saw the selfishness of their passion for the first time in late September, and experienced its exclusion. They had been playing cards in the drawing room; she paused, and was staring at her portrait.

She said, "Sixteen years," and there was a silence. "Do I look old to you?"

He said, "You look like Catherine. How can Catherine be old?"

She gazed at her cards and did not speak.

They finished the game, and then he played for her. He seemed intent on his music, but it was Catherine of whom he was most aware, and it was Catherine to whom he gave its haunting beauty.

The moonlight grew stronger. He was playing familiar things from memory, a courante, a sarabande and variations by Handel, airs from the opera "Rodelinda". Then he paused and flexed his wrist, where the powder and filth of Dettingen had been sutured into the wound, and the scars twisted like some obscene attempt at suicide. I knew by this that it was aching, and thought he would stop, but he began to play again, some little cadence of notes only she recognized. She said, "No, not that. Not tonight," and he played no more of it.

Time passed. I was drifting, only half aware of their conversation, a murmur not intended for other ears, almost part of the rippling notes, one becoming the other.

Then the notes stopped and I was discovered.

They sent me to bed. I was not part of what was between them there, man and woman, and so I was shut out.

I lay in bed, dry-eyed with bitterness. He had not even kissed me good night. It seemed a final betrayal of me.

She conceived, of that autumnal flowering of desire. I wept when I was told, which prompted her to call me a jealous little bitch; thereafter I hid my resentment, recognizing that I had been displaced.

Their happiness was brief: it seems impossible to me now that I had ever believed it would last. A letter was sent from London and the footman gave it to him by mistake; whatever its contents, the consequences were appalling.

I had been out walking with my governess; when we came in we heard obscenities from the morning room. She was screaming at him, calling him a bloody Irish bastard, and then a door slammed, and perhaps because he had removed himself she too came out; she was sobbing dryly. I never saw him physically abuse her, although on that occasion it was evident by his face that she had exercised no such restraint.

Their son was born prematurely during the night. He lived perhaps an hour.

I woke before dawn; rain was falling. All the candles in the gallery were still burning.

Downstairs Mordaunt was crying, uncontrolled and uncomforted. I put my head on my knees and wept also, for his sake, sitting on the stairs, until Jane Neville found me and took me back to bed.

When I saw him in the rain-shadowed light of day, he was in the drawing room; he had not changed his clothing or shaved since the previous morning. I sat at the harpsichord and he began to teach me an obscure piece of renaissance music; he was patient and very composed, as if it were any other lesson. Sounds came and went: the arrival of a second surgeon, Jane, seeking me, and leaving us undisturbed. The afternoon passed, rain beating on glass throughout the hours of a dark spring day, that music, never again played by me, a cadence of remembered anguish. Finally he rose and stood staring out at the rain, and said, "God seems so far away to me, I wonder how other men find him."

Then he went once more to her, and left me alone.

They allowed me to see her in the evening; it was thought that she would not survive the night. Thackeray and his colleague were present, but they were obscured by the shadows. The scent of narcissi was overpowering: it did not mask the smell of a mattress soaked with blood and the effluxions of birth.

Thackeray led me to the bed. She opened her eyes and smiled at me.

"Come here, sweetheart." The smells of blood and narcissi mingled hideously. "Have you been good, Meg?"

I said yes.

"What do you think? Achill says you shall go at last." I did not understand. "To town. He says I may take you with me. You want to go, don't you?"

I could not believe what I was hearing. I said something she thought was assent.

"I told him you would. I'll take you to Vauxhall." It seemed to have exhausted her. "Go away, darling. I want to rest. Kiss me, and we'll talk tomorrow."

I had lied to her; now like Judas I kissed her, knowing there would be no tomorrow. Death would release me from my promise, as it would release him.

And yet, impossibly, she did not die. She clung to his promise as though it alone had sustained her, and by early autumn we were in London. He did not accompany us.

I think of that first morning as The Harlot's Progress. Her acquaintance, both male and female, sat conversing in her boudoir, tying her garters, holding her camisole, partaking of chocolate and scandal. She sat, half naked, before her mirror, drumming her fingers. "God's blood, does he think he can keep me waiting while he dresses heads all over town?" And then to the room at large, "You see, dear friends, what happens when a woman goes home to whelp? All the town forgets her, and her damned friseur don't come when he's called."

She returned her attention to the mirror and conversation resumed, blades and fops discussing politics, racing, their debts and the latest maidenheads they had had the pleasure of tearing, while the women, all witty little powdered faces under aureoles of unclean hair, talked of their lovers, admiringly, their husbands, disparagingly, and the latest modes from France. They did not notice me, until a saturnine man who had been sitting apart from the others looked up from a broadsheet and said, "Who the deuce is this?"

She said, not pleasantly, "My daughter."

They were all staring now, and their eyes shrivelled my soul.

"The devil she is. Where did she spring from?"

"Mordaunt's forehead, fully armed. And farouche, like him." And, turning from the mirror, "Come in, you goose." There was a ripple of amusement as they quizzed me, which I found intolerable. She said again, "Come in, damn you. Is this how you was taught to behave?"

He said, "Leave the chit alone, Kitty. She don't know any of us. It's no wonder she don't want to come in."

She rose, perfume and silk and powdered skin, and conveyed me to him. His eyes discomfited me: upon a blank innocence the first vestige of sex was imprinted.

I curtsied to him, and he said, "She has pretty manners, Kitty. You can't fault him on that account."

"Oh, very pretty. A year or two more under that influence and she would outswear and outshoot us all."

He continued his slow assessment of me.

"So. You are grey-eyed Athena, the maiden clad in armour."

I responded with the childish pomposity Mordaunt had always found amusing.

"You do me too much honour, sir. My name is Margaret."

"And mine is Harlesdon. Do you like town, my dear?"

I confided that I had seen nothing of it, and he laughed then, cruelly. It was the first of the humiliations of that year, until, listening acutely to the voices around me, I lost my northern accent.

He said, more meditatively, "I don't think you'll care for it. It's very different from the country. How old are you?"

Scarlet with embarrassment, I mumbled my age. "You remind me of my daughter. She looks a little like you, or used to. I never see her now."

Catherine was beckoning to me, and I glanced at him for leave to go, but he had already dismissed me. Her hairdresser had arrived; there were no introductions. He merely took a handful of my hair as if it belonged to some inanimate object and opined that it should be cut; she agreed, and instructed him to pierce my ears, and they discussed whether this wounding should take place immediately or be deferred until the following morning. My preference was not solicited, and no one heard my protest.

Harlesdon rose and announced that he was off to the 'Change; she acknowledged it and he left her. He carried himself well but he limped badly, and the shoe could not disguise the deformity of his left foot.

She whispered, "Don't stare at my lord. He don't care to be reminded."

Her hairdresser demanded her attention then, finding fault with every strand, attacking it with comb and scissors, tongs and pomade, and all the while telling her how to apply her cosmetics, removing her patches and affixing them to her breast and cheek with his saliva. When his ministrations were over she called to Regan to bring her a particular gown; the others left their chocolate and their lapdogs and their brittle, malicious gossip and told her it was out of fashion. She threw it on the floor and demanded another, until their approval was unanimous.

She was the most beautiful of women, more beautiful than any in the room, but they delighted in tormenting her, sheathing their barbs in polished wit and striking where they would most harm her. And yet they were so civilized, these people, so eminently civilized.

She saw me, and her eyes devoured me. Mine, too, would be this agony, this submission of body and spirit.

"God's death, are you still here? Go and tell that plaguey slut to get out of bed and have you dressed in half an hour, and not in that damned moth-eaten habit!"

I fled.

***

173

We drove in Hyde Park around the fashionable Ring, and she promised me that I should have one of her horses and ride with her in Rotten Row; and in the evening she went to Almack's. The pattern of our days and nights was set.

The ton gathered in her boudoir once or twice a week: men, titled and without titles, and women, actresses, duchesses, courtesans. Harlesdon was the constant. I did not want to like him, but he did not force his presence on me and he was kind in an unsentimental manner when we chanced to meet.

There were others for whom I could not say the same. Catherine courted strange and dangerous men, and I was careful not to be alone with them: roving hands and eyes and elegantly phrased innuendo, desiring to touch and be touched in return. They were beautiful and bored, like predatory birds, their dress exquisite, their manners fastidious, their morals nonexistent. That I was not yet twelve made no difference. I was female, and therefore meat.

When I had been clothed to her satisfaction she took me to her perfumer in Jermyn Street, her mantua maker in Oxford Street, Pickering the grocer at Number Three St. James's Street, the goldsmith in Cranbourne Street. The city was a labyrinth, a cesspit of terrors, and yet its spell was a powerful one, as pervasive as the stench of rotting garbage, the bloated corpses of vermin and strays, the relentless cacophony of vendors' cries and the screams of children and horses. Chairmen and coachmen cut through the crowds with a clear intention to do murder; the chairmen in particular were brutal and uncouth, many of them Irish, with their hatred of England written in their faces. If one escaped them there was peril from overhead, sewage flung into already teeming gutters and signboards low enough to decapitate the unwary. Danger was endemic. More than two hundred offenses were punishable by death, but the threat of execution proved no deterrent to those who had nothing left to lose. Crime became yearly more depraved, criminals more vicious, and, uncomfortably aware of the hunger and poverty in the streets, I did not wonder at it.

The Earl of Harlesdon was much in evidence. We observed the Guy Fawkes fireworks from a boat on the Thames, the slap of black water oily on the gunwale and the riding and masthead lights of the vessels in the port swimming above and below; I had never been in a boat or seen fireworks, and it seemed a great adventure. Three days later he took me to the Lord Mayor's show, and we all went to Vauxhall, where we drank punch, heard music, walked beneath the coloured lanterns through pavilions and grottoes, and mingled with pimps and prostitutes and the bucks and ladies of the town. There were other visits also, to the Tower, to St. James's, to Richmond.

I wrote nothing of him to Mordaunt, and little else of what distressed me, only of the frivolous things Catherine did to fill my time and her own, and he wrote curiously shallow and unaffectionate letters in return. They told me nothing of him, and the distance between us intensified until we might have been on opposite sides of the earth instead of three hundred miles apart. I had chosen London and I would have it, unadulterated by his influence: he had given me to it as completely as if he had committed me to the grave. So our silence grew, and but for Jane Neville I was more alone than I had ever been in my life.

Catherine's only gesture toward him was to send him the portrait of me she had commissioned of Joshua Reynolds. It hangs at Evesham still, bearing the artist's signature and hallmarks, the glowing treatment of light and fabric, the gauzy, romantic background, and for my immortality on canvas she paid Reynolds' fee of five guineas. In it I see myself, a serious grey-eyed girl in a deep red gown, hair a cloud around a childish face, and that face, which should have had a child's fresh colour, rendered as porcelain white as any lady's of the ton. And, like the portrait of that young, grave man in regimentals which hangs in the gallery at Evesham, there is something significant in it, some desire we share to preserve nothing of the years that followed, for, like Mordaunt, I have never had another painted.

He despised that portrait, but he accepted it. It was all he had of me. Of him I had nothing.

On Christmas Day, a Saturday, we went with Harlesdon to Westminster Abbey. The King passed, but as I curtsied I received only a glimpse of a red frog's face under a powdered wig, and a glittering entourage of obese Germanic courtiers: I saw nothing more.

The rare snow of London was falling as we came out. There was snow also on Monday night when the theatres reopened, and I was taken to Drury Lane to see "The Recruiting Officer". Catherine was wearing a dark red satin gown, her breasts all but revealed and a necklace of rubies at her throat. Mordaunt had not sent them; she had not looked at his gift. The play was considered witty but I remember little of it, only the stench of pomade and sweat, the guttering foot candles, the heavily painted actresses, most of them looking like the whores they were, and a distressing incident when two officers of a royal Scottish regiment came in, and were pelted with fruit and shouts of "No Scots! No Scots!" until they were forced to leave. I watched them go with pity and confusion, for they were soldiers of the King, but the brute instinct of the mob allowed for no such nice discrimination. They were Scots, and the hatred of Scots endured in London; the grinning skulls of Jacobites executed on Tower Hill would remain spiked on Temple Bar for thirty years.

Catherine's sister-in-law, Anne Lady Hatherleigh, was in London in January and called upon her one afternoon. My acquaintance with her was slight, as with all Catherine's relations, but she paid me kind, unfounded compliments and I thought I could learn to like her well given the opportunity. Then Catherine told me I might go to my lesson, which meant she wanted to be rid of me.

The conversation continued sotto voce as women will exclude children, and consider them deaf or without intelligence.

They were speaking of Mordaunt.

Anne murmured something. Catherine said, "Did you not hear me, miss? Go to your lesson."

I saw Anne Hatherleigh no more; she had returned to Westmorland, and what she had not said in my presence retreated to the back of my mind where it remained, becoming more disturbing as the winter passed.

In April Catherine took me to the races at Dachet, where the unspeakable cruelty of the jockeys to their horses and one another scored itself into a mind already numbed by violent impressions, and on a Monday morning in early May she completed her initiation by exposing me to London's ultimate entertainment, a hanging at Tyburn's triple tree.

Harlesdon was not in town for that episode; he had retired to his estate in Sussex. To do him credit, I think he would have prevented it.

I suffered nightmares afterwards, and Jane Neville wrote to Mordaunt, but it did not bring him to London, and if he censured Catherine for it I never knew. Neither he nor I mentioned it in the subsequent exchange of letters, and his communications to me became curt, almost perfunctory.

In September I lost what little innocence remained to me.

They chose for their assignation a couch in the drawing room, where the possibility of interruption heightened the sexual frisson, and from there I heard endearments, wild, obscene, raw with an unimaginable pleasure, which remained burned into my soul, so that, in time, when they were said to me, some vestige of that virginal child could not repress revulsion.

Months passed before I lost the sensation of uncleanliness. I never forgave her for her betrayal of Mordaunt, and Harlesdon became a stranger to me. My coolness hurt him, for he had grown fond of me, and his manner toward me became frighteningly harsh; I should have feared him for it, and had I been any other child perhaps I would have done, but aversion was all I wanted of him now, all I would ever want.

I had lived in London fourteen months. Mordaunt had written that I would be brought home shortly before Christmas; I was desperate to leave. My life had become intolerable, and no one knew, except myself.

In late November she took me with her to a salon. As was so often the case, there were no other children present.

She deposited me near an alcove and told me to disturb no one.

I was not alone; the other occupants were a cat, newly released from a travelling basket, and a soldier. His coat was scarlet and the facings the dark blue of a royal regiment, but the sash was yellow instead of crimson, the sword knot yellow and gold, and the waistcoat and breeches buff. Even after a year in Catherine's house, I did not recognize it as the uniform of an officer in the Hanoverian army.

He did not speak to the woman who was sharing the alcove, and when she departed I insinuated myself into her seat and gazed at the cat. He was playing patience; the broad, laced cuff of the right sleeve concealed a handless forearm.

To have called attention to myself would have been unthinkable, although I may have made some small sound to the cat. He looked up, and if he was surprised to find himself sharing the alcove with a young girl, he had the grace to hide it.

"So you like cats, do you?"

His voice was distinctive, and not without kindness, his eyes an extraordinary, brilliant grey.

"Yes, sir, although I have little experience of them," because Mordaunt had never liked them.

"Well, there never was a cat that was less than honest. They may share your bed for a plate of oysters, but they'll love you or leave you as they choose."

"What manner of cat is she?"

"An Abyssinian."

"Did you bring her all the way from Abyssinia?"

"Not today," he said with a little smile, and then relented. "But she came from Holland yesterday, and from Dover since."

The cat slept on. He seemed interested in me, and did not resume his game.

"I must go now. I only wanted to see your cat."

"You are an endearing child. What do they call you?" and when I told him, "Your name derives from the Greek for 'pearl'. It becomes you."

There was something in his voice, in his eyes, an unhappiness I found disconcerting. I returned the conversation to a safer topic.

"What is your cat's name, sir?"

"Dido. She loved Aeneas. Have you read the *Aeneid*?"

The cat roused itself enough to yawn. My longing to stroke it must have been apparent; he gathered it and put it into my lap.

"Have you et? Do you care to eat? Will you take a glass of something?"

I said the first thing that came to mind, which was a comment on my life with Catherine.

"You are too young for ratafia." He raised his hand, and a footman came. "A glass of lemonade for my young lady, and another of the hock for me."

The light burned with the passing silk of gowns, but none was Catherine's. My eyes returned to him and lingered on the fall of lace at the handless wrist.

He said, "The fortune of war," although he was watching the room.

When the footman came back he said, a little querulously, "Is his lordship still engaged?" A murmured assent. "Then make me known to him again, and beg the favour of an interview at his convenience."

The footman bowed, and for an instant he revealed an utter weariness.

"Never marry a soldier, girl. This is what comes of a man when his regiment is broke."

I did not answer. Some one had edged into the alcove, a young man with a faun's face, very much the worse for the alcohol of which he smelled.

"By God, in the flesh. And in a new disguise."

The soldier revealed no emotion, except to murmur, "We are not alone, sirrah."

"No, by God, not this time!" A tangible silence. "I never thought to find you here. I had it on good authority that you'd been sent to Rochefort.... Was my source mistaken?"

"Apparently."

"Damn me, what a piece of luck. The last thing you'd want is another court of enquiry."

"My affairs no longer concern you. And there is a child present."

"So I see. What a nice little pussy. Will you dandle it or shall I?"

"Keep your hands to yourself," he said.

"Why should I, when you didn't?" The perspiring fingers were fumbling beneath my chin. "Still, they're all of a piece, ain't they, little girls and boys—"

He said, very quietly, "I will have you thrown out."

"And who will throw you out, Aeneas?" And to me, with the sad confidentiality of the very drunk, "Don't go home with him, pussy. Don't."

He was removed. Conversation, so lately and crudely interrupted, resumed in the room. Between myself and my companion an intolerable silence grew.

I moved. He said, "Stay," as if to a dog.

After a time, I asked if he had known him. The brilliant eyes examined me as if seeking some hidden significance, then whatever he saw in my face seemed to mollify him.

"I knew some one like him once. My friend was not so cruel." Pause. "You was about to tell me something. Talk to me."

I heard her laughter, full of promise, before I saw her. The gown she was wearing was of shot green silk, and the colour ran in the weave like flame. She wore no jewellery; her beauty was her only ornament.

I said, "That is my mother."

My child's sensibility could not define what clothed this seismic recognition: hunger, craving, jealousy, as if her beauty both wounded and affronted him.

"Who sent you to me, to speak to me? Did she? Did any one else?" He seemed to remember where he was, and perhaps with whom, and his voice softened; I heard in it what I had seen in his eyes, eagerness and hesitation. "Did your father bring you to London? Is he here with you?"

"No... my father doesn't like town. He is at home."

He began to question me again, wanting news of Mordaunt. He gave me the cat again to stroke; and the pressure of this interrogation was so intense that I could not resist him. He had just asked me if I thought Mordaunt would answer a letter when Catherine came in again.

As I had seen in his face, so I saw in hers the immobility, the slow draining of colour from a lacquered, exquisite mask.

She crossed the room and pulled me to my feet; the cat spilled from my lap and disappeared.

Their eyes met, and some tortured thing passed between them, then she inclined her head gracefully; he did not acknowledge it.

"Colonel."

"Madam."

Voices with that deadly edge, as if they raked one another with broken glass.

She did not speak in the carriage. When we reached the house she closed me into the drawing room with her.

"What did you tell him? God damn you, what did you tell him?"

I became incoherent, not knowing what I had done. She jerked the bell pull furiously. Jane Neville appeared in the doorway.

"Take her to bed. And I want a glass of brandy."

It was not Jane's province to wait upon her, but she said only, "Yes, madam."

"And bring the damned bottle."

I rose to leave her, to escape. She was on me in an instant, her perfume and the smells of liquor and pomade and perspiration enveloping me like arms.

"Oh, sweetheart, why do you make me say these things? Don't tell Achill.... Give me a kiss, Meg, say you forgive me. Tell me I haven't been bad to you...."

She held me so passionately that there was pain in her embrace, stroking my hair and cheek, but it was neither love nor pain nor anything else she could offer that I wanted. I went to bed without speaking, because there was nothing to say.

The Abyssinian kitten arrived the following afternoon, with a letter brought by a footman in black livery. She sent it back with a terse command to "tell your master my daughter regrets, but she don't accept gifts of this kind."

Two hours later her servant brought her a card on a salver. She read it and said, "I am not at home to the Colonel."

He made no further overtures.

We met in Hyde Park on Saturday at the beginning of December, a soft, still afternoon with the taste and smell of smoke. It had been an ugly morning; Harlesdon had spent the night and quarrelled with her upon rising, then they had gone out, she desperate to placate him. I did not know when they would return, but I had had enough of domestic turmoil where her husband was concerned; I did not see that I should have to witness it between her and her lover.

Jane Neville and I were walking when we heard other footsteps. Whatever Jane thought his intention, abduction or robbery, she refused to allow him to speak to me. He said, "I served with her father, and I am known to her mother. Perhaps you would do me the honour of accepting my card."

She refused again, and he said, in the tone of one unaccustomed to defiance, "This is a public place and there are witnesses. I assure you I mean her no harm."

She relented, and he bowed to me. I thought it the act of a gentleman; I did not feel that it mattered to him that I was only a child.

Jane walked behind us, within earshot. His carriage was waiting, the footmen, the coachman, the black horses standing perfectly still. The leaves fell around us in a windless silence.

"I wanted very much to keep your gift, sir. She would not permit it."

"I should not have sent it."

"She threw your letter into the fire."

"It surprises me she didn't throw the cat in, too."

We walked further.

"If I gave you a letter for your father, would you see that he received it?" He must have sensed my hesitation. "I would not ask you to do anything dishonourable."

A single sheet, folded and sealed with red wax. There was no superscription.

He said, "I would prefer that no one else know of this," and how accurately he judged me. It was a measure of his understanding of human nature that only once had that unerring judgment failed him.

He drew out his watch; there was an inscription within the guard.

"I have an appointment," he said.

The carriage had been empty: now some one waited in it. A still presence, reminiscent of an aquiline face in an ill-lit portrait in an echoing gallery at Evesham.

Durham was bleak under frost, the roads iron hard and a light snow falling: the carriage lamps were burning although it was just past three o'clock. We had been travelling six days, and although Catherine's berlin offered every comfort, from seats upholstered in Pekinese silk to varnished leather chamber pots concealed in walnut chests, the rigours of the journey had exhausted us and we no longer spoke. We drowsed and shivered, the coals in the copper footwarmer having died out hours before, and drove on through the dimness, the view of a northern winter beyond the blue silk shades as unwelcoming as any I remembered.

It was dark when we reached Evesham. A delegation was drawn up in the entrance: Mordaunt was not present. I asked if he were out. He was not out. I left them in the hall and rushed ahead, so much a child still.

I found him in the library. There was a fire but it gave no light, only a suffocating smell of coal. He was watching the snow and did not turn until I spoke. I stood in my pelisse with my fur muff on my arm, eyes smarting from the smoke, wanting to be admired, loved.

"Well, well," he said. "The prodigal returns, the product of a wasted year."

I thought of the silence in the hall; they were all waiting.

"Please, Papa, won't you come and speak to Jane?"

He brushed past me abruptly, into the light; Jane curtsied, and although he did not smile there was a kindness in his greeting which he had not offered me.

"Did you like town, Miss Neville?"

Her pallor was gone, replaced by a painful radiance.

"No, sir. I am much happier here with... all of you."

His mood at supper remained withdrawn; he was not inclined to talk, or apparently to eat, although he drank. I had dressed in the dark red gown and had no more figure in it than a boy, but my hair remained in its fashionable crimp and I wore the garnet earrings Catherine had given me. He sat at the head of the table, and watched me without approval.

Since he would not talk I carried on a difficult conversation with Jane about the London neither of us had loved until the pressure of the silence forced me to stop, then he said sarcastically, "God almighty, a lady. I should've dressed for the occasion." And then, to Jane, "Where the hell were you when my wife took it upon herself to create this?"

She said, "Margaret has learned—"

"To ape the manners of a detestable society, and no longer speaks like a child of this county, or any child of mine."

He opened his watch.

"As for you, madam, you may go to bed."

"In town I never—"

"I don't give a damn." Jane's chair went back. "I do not give you leave to go, Miss Neville."

She was pale now; whatever had brought that tenuous beauty to her face it was gone, like a candle snuffed.

"I am not well, sir. I beg your pardon."

I left.

When I returned he was saying to her, with unexpected gentleness, "Are you truly not well? Off to bed with you, then." I heard her rise, and the sound of her skirts briefly stilled, as if he had detained her. "I've been alone too long. Don't judge me harshly."

I put the letter down on the table near him and went out.

I never knew what was in it. I never knew what effect, if any, it had upon him. It might have been destroyed; it might have been kept. I never saw it again and it was never mentioned, and whatever was written remains only in his memory and in the heart of the man who penned it.

Catherine arrived on the twenty-first. Curiously his mood, and the mood of the household, lightened and became festive. She was as passionate toward me as if we had not seen one another for years, and her warmth toward him sickened me.

"Achill, come with me and we'll walk in the snow as we used to. Just down to the river."

I was not included.

They were gone about an hour. She came in laughing, the snow melting in her hair, and whatever their conversation had been he had obviously not directed any criticism at her for her handling of me. He made negus for her and stood warming his hands, and she watched him cat-like from a chair.

"Achill, you're never forty."

"I shall soon be forty-one. Or had you forgotten?"

"I don't believe it."

"God, I do."

She glanced superstitiously at her portrait.

"Achill, play for me."

"Not tonight. Another time."

"Another time I shan't be here."

"Stay a little longer, then."

"I can't. I give a soirée on Twelfth Night."

"Oh, Catherine," he said. "Catherine, Catherine... will you never stop?"

"You don't care. You prefer me in London."

"You wanted it. And Meg, and occasionally even me."

"You could live with me."

"I don't care for the life you want. I've seen too much death: it makes me bad company."

Silence. Her hands were curved around the tankard, her head bent, her hair across her shoulder.

"Achill, I know what this past year has been to you. If we lived together—"

"We tried."

"I suppose that was my fault."

"And was it mine?"

She held her hands out toward the fire but dropped them. The warmth did not reach her where she sat.

"Our son would be eighteen months old now." He said nothing. "I wish to God he'd lived. You could have had your northern cuckoo and I would have had my boy."

He had not moved, staring down into the coals. She seemed to shiver.

"I'm going to bed, Achill. I'm cold."

He did not go with her.

We all appeared in the church on Christmas morning, she, beautifully attired in bluish purple silk, shivering in her furs; our breath mingled with the scent of putrefaction from a corpse recently interred beneath the altar. Later we entertained the vicar and his wife to fortified wines and cheeses. She was gracious and charming until they had gone, then she threw a glass against the wall.

"Christ, is this how you want me to live? In a tomb?"

He took her upstairs and came back alone.

She did not reappear until eight or nine that evening. She was wearing only a gauzy robe through which her nakedness was visible.

"Play the Scarlatti for me, Achill. Play it— darling— darling—"

Jane picked up her needlework and left.

"I want a son, Achill… I want a child, give me one, give me one…."

He said, very quietly, "You are behaving like a whore."

"Don't you ever want a whore? Achill of the cold, cold heart. You never used to be so cold." He said something, too softly to be heard. "You were ardent. God, you took my breath away. So daring... so hungry. And your body... your body was like silk—"

He removed himself from the clinging caress and came up the room, leaving her where she had knelt; then he saw me and took me ungently by the hand, shutting the doors behind us.

He said only, strangely, "The basilisk child. Why must you always see?" Then, "Tell Regan to put her to bed."

She was still sitting on the carpet when Regan went in with me; Regan lifted her, murmuring to her. The Scarlatti fluttered to the carpet: she had torn it to shreds.

In the morning there was a short, intolerably ugly scene, during which she called him every obscenity I had ever heard and accused him of things I could not comprehend, then she left for London and the new year of 1758 came in, like a breath drawn after pain.

But she had not done with him.

News of her affair with Harlesdon reached him on the nineteenth of February. Her brother, a naval officer waiting at the Admiralty for a command, had stayed at her house; she had taken care that he should know she did not sleep alone.

Mordaunt went to London for the first time in ten years, riding the twenty-eight miles to Durham in little more than four hours, changing horses and riding on to Darlington. The stage from Newcastle would have taken six days: he had neither the time nor the inclination to travel with strangers, so he rode on, through a winter bitter in the north to almost impassable with mud in the south, and reached London on the evening of the fourth day. He had changed horses every twenty miles, slept little and eaten less: he left the horse at a coaching inn where he drank with great purpose for an hour or so, then he walked the darkening streets in an indecisive snowfall and stood on the doorstep of the house he had paid for in the last light of day.

Had she not been alone he would have killed them both.

She was in the drawing room. She closed the doors and sat on the sofa and by this he saw that it was meant to be civilized. It did not begin in a civilized way and it ended as though both were demented.

"Which one is he, this bastard Harlesdon? The one who wrote you a letter when you were in my house, carrying my child? The cripple? The club-footed harlot's pimp? Is that what you enjoy, madam, going from cripple to cripple, exciting yourself with their scars?"

"I love him! He would marry me!"

He struck her across the face, and it gave him such insane satisfaction that he did not know he was also weeping.

"You can take that back to your table at Almack's and flaunt it for your friends, and your *lover*, and you can tell him, on my behalf, that if I ever find him in this house when I come, I'll kill him. Not like a gentleman— I'll kill him with my hands. And don't think I won't come, madam, even if it's never been my custom."

She was on her feet; there was blood on her mouth, and the memory stirred of another night, another place; here or somewhere else, her or some one else, in the dark years of war, or the black, spiralling madness of the years that followed.

"Our marriage was never legal— we were married by special licence, as much as married in the Fleet— I can prove it— I'll live with him if I must—"

"Then you'll see the town's hypocrisy, madam, you who love it so well. Every door will be slammed in your face. You can sleep where you please, and by Christ, with whom, but you'll live alone, otherwise you'll find yourself called a whore. And the town's well known for calling a spade a spade."

He remembered nothing of the journey home. She wrote a week later requesting a dissolution of their marriage on the grounds that their relationship had fallen within the bounds of consanguinity.

It had had the quality of a dream, an endless, twisting nightmare. With the letter it acquired reality.

He took it into the library, his sanctuary. It was March, and raining, like the day when this same man, like the devil's cub, had precipitated the birth of his child, the longed for son who had lived an hour; there would be no others. He watched the rain, as he had watched the snow and the sunlight and the passing of years, from this window and this house, unseeing.

Jane came down to him in the evening; no one else could be persuaded to disturb him. When she carried in a candle he turned his face from the light and put his head back down in his arms. Papers and books, letters were strewn on the desk and on the floor, drawers wrenched open. The letter from

Catherine was near his hand, blotted and stained beyond legibility. He had been drinking and crying all afternoon.

She said nothing; he did not want her to say anything, only to listen, and not to leave him.

"My wife thought... I had a mistress once. It wasn't true. There have been women but they were whores... I was a soldier, I can't help that." He had nothing now, no pride left; he had nothing left. "What is love? Why can't it die? What have I done that I should be so hurt? Why can't it die?"

There was no fear in her eyes, only virginity kept like a gift in silence, and now offered to a man long loved; and there was neither shame nor lust nor the memory of outrage in his heart, only a craving for peace.

In his room the candles were burning. He closed the door, closing out the world, all its pain, all its memories, and took her to his bed.

As his mistress she could expect only a position in the household made invisible by necessity; she knew that their affair could not last, and that she had ruined herself by it. For those few months' joy she had hazarded reputation and security, to love in fact one loved in secrecy for years, who had been legally bound to another woman when she had been a child, and whose husband by law he would remain until one or the other was dead.

If there was no hope for the love she cherished, so too was there no alternative: she had known almost from the beginning that there would be no other man to whom she would wish to give it, and now that fate had granted this impossibility, this time in which he might be loved, she regretted nothing. And so she lived for the moment, for the days and the nights and the hours spent with him, for the rare smiles and the intimacy, knowing she hoarded their memory against a future as empty as it was inevitable.

In the evenings, in the garden where on her first morning at Evesham she had met a small child in a dimity frock who had offered her daffodils, they walked now, and he talked of the past, of his youth and his love of an estate he had never hoped to inherit; of music and the Continent, where she longed to travel; of the army and the Low Countries, the experience of war, up to a point beyond which he would not admit her. If he spoke of his wife it was not often and never by name, and Catherine stayed incommunicado in London, for which she was profoundly grateful. She had no difficulty transforming herself from governess to mistress, but she did not think her serenity would remain unshaken in the presence of her rival.

She had no illusions concerning him. She knew him a difficult and troubled man, and if she could not bring him happiness at least she brought him peace, an interlude of calm in a life and a marriage which had offered little. If he loved her she never knew it: he never spoke of love, as though it, like the past, was a territory into which he could not permit himself to enter. But if the name of love was never given to their relationship its tenderness and poignancy suffused all, and the strength of his physical passion for her could not be denied. In the hours of daylight she cherished his daughter, teaching and advising: in the evenings which belonged to him she flowered under an exquisite tutelage. In the intimacy of those hours, after the urgency of passion, she found comfort in his presence, and she saw the sweetness of the youth he had been and the man he might have become.

She tormented herself with lost possibilities only once— if Catherine had made valid her threat to secure a dissolution of the marriage, if Catherine had not existed— and her resentment of the years she had never shared was so destructive that she never allowed herself to envision them again. She did not guess the depths of his own bitterness until one evening at the end of summer, as they walked by the water garden, and stood on the bridge watching a lucid twilight. He was leaning forward, looking at the lilies in the water; he had planted them for the child Margaret, as he had done so many things.

He said, "All this is mine," and she knew he did not mean the river, or the expanse of lilies. "I made it what it is. There was no profit in it when I inherited."

"Does it give you satisfaction?" and he stared down at the water.

"No man likes to see so many years of his life lying waste. This is all I have."

She waited for him to continue but in this as in so much, the past was riddled with secrets and enigmas, and she never knew if it was the answer to that anguished *What is love? Why can't it die?*

Perhaps it had, and the child Margaret was all that remained of that sterile, destructive union. Her love for her grew richer, deepened by her experience: she watched her with the memory of her own childhood and the love which had surrounded her in her father's vicarage, and pitied her in her loneliness, seeing her on the brink of an uncertain adolescence and unable to ease her passage to womanhood. Viewing her through a heightened sensibility, wondering, in the light of the physical richness to which she herself had newly awakened, whom she would marry, with whom would she discover that incomparable hunger and joy. She wanted, in the press of time, to teach her those lessons of maturity which could never be shared, to wait for love, to recognize and seize it... what right had she, she thought, a woman now dishonoured, who when she should leave this house would have no prospect of respectable marriage?

Time, which had brought her to this circumstance, was as surely bearing her away. One night she sketched Mordaunt, to his amusement. She had done this secretly many times, so that she had innumerable portraits of him: she said, putting this last away, with a wistful smile, "To keep for my old age."

He said casually, "I shall be dead by then," the only occasion upon which he mentioned the difference in their ages, although it was always in her thoughts, the years unshared, the years ahead that never could be shared; and she wept then, finding unbearable the thought of his death, but knowing it as inevitable as the fact that she would leave him, and that their gift of time had been too brief.

She left on a night in early autumn, when she knew he would be absent for nearly forty-eight hours. He had gone to Durham with some yearlings: when he returned he found a silent house and a letter on his desk in the library. He read its few uncompromising lines until they became meaningless, then he put the letter away with two others he had not had the courage to destroy, Catherine's last, and the first anguished entreaty for peace from a man who had written them at intervals for the past twelve years. Then, having locked all that remained of her away, a wrenching grief overcame him, and he gave himself to a bout of drinking so intense and prolonged that, as on the occasion of Catherine's betrayal, no one ventured to disturb him.

He emerged from it clinging only to the soldier's instinct, and waited for some unspoken order, some indication of how to proceed. The weeks became months. In the third month a letter arrived for me, a few lines scrawled as if she were ill or in haste with a bad pen on cheap paper, asking my forgiveness. He traced the letter to a Newcastle packet-master who had been given it in Falmouth; he did not say by whom and it could be traced no further. He kept the letter and carried it on his person. There was no other word from her. He never saw her again.

Catherine came from London at his request. There was the matter of my education to be considered, and he did not believe himself capable, in his present state of mind, of undertaking the curriculum. At the same time he could not bring himself to surrender me to Catherine; and he resented the necessity of this meeting and dreaded it as he had not dreaded anything since a rainy night in Scotland when he had walked to meet another obsessive adversary.

He had anticipated a lacquered, confident beauty: he was not prepared for her pathetic air of illness. She coughed into her handkerchief and complained that her lungs were bad, and the body which had always inflamed him was a rack of bones. If she had come to do mischief she could not have planned it more effectively than by this blatant appeal for his pity, and he knew, disgusted by himself and by her, how easy it would be to give it.

She followed him into the library and sat where and when she was told. He said, "Jane Neville has gone," and sat opposite her, turning a bone paper knife in his fingers.

She said, "The ungrateful slut," and he looked up from the knife.

"Don't speak to me of ungrateful sluts, madam."

The calculating brittleness came back into her face.

"Why did she go?"

He balanced the blade between his palms and looked across the desk until she could no longer endure his gaze.

"I don't believe it." The smile remained fixed as though painted on the mouth of a doll, then she almost consciously removed it. "You're lying, ain't you— you bastard."

He saw when she had gone that the paper knife had snapped in two. He laid the halves neatly on the desk and stood staring out at the early darkness, knowing that it was not finished.

He retired to the drawing room. Within the hour she came in, and paced until his patience was raw from watching her. At length she coughed so harshly that the brandy spilled from her glass to her bodice.

"Where's the rest of this damned brandy?"

"I drank it," he said. "I had cause."

A silence, inexpressibly hostile, then he summoned the major-domo for another.

When it came he put it on the table near her.

"Here. Drown your sorrows. Shall I tell you about my mistress to help it down?"

She stood as if frozen, her eyes never leaving him, and he remembered that scornful smile. "So you never thought it possible. How do you know she was the only one?"

She covered her ears but he could not stop; it gratified some impulse to use her violently.

"Had you thought of that, madam? How many years have you slept apart from me? Why should I dance attendance on your appetites— do you think I've none of my own?"

She took the brandy and went to the far end of the room with it, sitting with her back to him like a child, shutting him out. He watched her drink, and cough, and when she began to cry he watched that too until it was too much for him, and then he looked away.

Perhaps an hour passed. He heard her rise and come up the long room, dreading that she would fall. She came to him without speaking and laid her head against his knee. Her favourite attitude: she could make it an act of supplication, seduction, or sexual submission.

"Harlesdon left me."

Her capacity for alcohol was alarming: he had not taught her this, but he had not discouraged it, and perhaps it was he who had made it necessary to her.

"You always hated him, didn't you? Ever since he wrote to me here."

"He took you from me."

She put her hands over her face.

"Oh God, I want to die sometimes.... The night he left me.... Achill, forgive me...."

What have you done? What more could you have done?

"I only wanted to hurt you— to make you love me.... I almost died... and then they told me... I can never have any more...."

"I don't believe you."

The mascara ran in rivulets down her face: her eyes were burning him.

"It's true— my God, do you think I would lie? Why else should I look like this?"

Her eyes never left him, and in them he saw whatever truth she could give to this revelation. She could not have chosen a weapon more powerful than this, and for that reason he resisted it, refusing to allow himself to suffer as she intended.

She wept openly now, her face against his knee.

"I wanted your son.... why does God punish me, Achill?"

"God punishes us all. You have no monopoly on suffering."

She sobbed, and said something but he could not hear. Some time later she whispered, "I love you. Can you still believe me after everything I've done?"

He said nothing, sickened by contempt. She lifted streaming eyes.

"Give me your pity, for God's sake— can't you see I've nothing to live for?"

He had been betrayed and manipulated and she was using him again, in this performance, as she had used him in her bed and rejected him when it pleased her.

"Achill, pity me...."

"I've loved you always. God help me, I love you still."

She said nothing more. She had won, she had always won.

The candles were lit. She moved to snuff them, to begin this ritual which he did not want and could not resist, as though it were some drug.

"Leave them," he said.

"How can you want me like this? How can you love me?"

Because she was Catherine; and whatever she was, whatever she had made him, what eunuch, what cuckold, what contemptible hypocrite, he was still Catherine's slave.

II

Annus mirabilis, 1759 came to be called: the year of victories, although the portents at its beginning were not favourable. On the Continent the beleaguered Frederick of Prussia increased his demands for support from his British ally; in Spain the king lay dying, and his heir, Don Carlos of Naples, planned collusion with the French; along the coast of France spies informed their British masters of a feverish building of flat-bottomed landing craft, and thirty thousand men encamped in Flanders and Brittany. The fear of invasion, present throughout this long war, suddenly became acute, and by summer the Secretary of State, William Pitt, had directed both army and navy to increase their strength by bounties and impressment. Men of wealth were encouraged to raise regiments, and private citizens contributed to the ever mounting cost of maintaining a militia which numbered eighteen thousand by the end of that "ever warm and glorious year".

The victories, hard won and long awaited, studded the closing months: on the first of August the combined armies of Britain, Hanover and Hesse defeated a superior French force at Minden, and London celebrated with illuminations and bonfires. On the thirteenth of September, after a summer's campaign in Canada, an attack upon Quebec was launched by some four thousand men who had climbed wooded cliffs in darkness, hauling artillery with them; in the rainy dawn their youthful general arranged them in an order of battle to suit the terrain on which they found themselves, a tree-studded field to be remembered as the Plains of Abraham. The opposing French force under Louis-Joseph, General le Marquis de Montcalm, advanced and were broken within fifteen minutes by the perfectly timed British fusillades, and withdrew into the citadel with more than a thousand killed and wounded, among them the Marquis de Montcalm. James Wolfe, aged thirty-two, lay dead upon the field, wounded in groin, wrist and breast, the last a shot claimed to have been fired by a soldier bearing a grudge against the general, who was later hanged: the veracity of his claim could not be proven. Within days the garrison at Quebec surrendered, and only Montreal remained as a bastion of French power in North America.

On the nineteenth of October the news of Wolfe's triumph and death was published in London. His body was brought home by His Majesty's Ship *Royal William* on the sixteenth of November, and on the twentieth he was buried beside his father, the first General Wolfe, at Greenwich.

The year, Walpole wrote, was "still all gold... We have not had more conquest than fine weather: one would think we had plundered East and West Indies of sunshine. Our bells are worn threadbare with ringing of victories."

On the day Wolfe was buried, they were given cause to ring again. On the fourteenth of that month the French fleet under Vice-amiral le Marquis de Conflans seized the opportunity of foul weather and broke out of Brest, where the blockading squadrons of Admiral Sir Edward Hawke had kept them confined for six months; and twenty ships of the line put to sea to join French forces awaiting transport at Vannes. Their object was the invasion of Scotland. Before they could make their rendezvous, Hawke pursued them into the rock-strewn Quiberon Bay on the coast of Brittany, and brought them to battle in the closing hours of the twentieth. In squalls and heavy weather, from dusk to dawn, in constant peril in dangerous waters, some fifty ships of the line engaged, with losses to the French of several vessels, including Conflans' flagship *Le Soleil Royale*, and thousands of seamen. Hawke's losses were appreciably lighter: two ships wrecked and casualties of less than three hundred. The engagement broke the back of the French navy— the power of its remaining squadrons was negligible— and it ended forever the fading hopes of those few Jacobites who had seen in the prospect of a French invasion their last chance to revive a cause which had been lost at Culloden.

Of that year, so golden in the nation's memory, two events depressed Mordaunt profoundly: notably, the death of George Friedrich Handel in London on the fourteenth of April, Holy Saturday, and the death of James Wolfe at Quebec two days before my fourteenth birthday. Of Handel he said, oddly for a man who professed atheism, "God rest his soul. Nothing on earth has ever given me more pleasure than his music." Of Wolfe he said little, but the news seemed to oppress him. A man was dead who like himself had been commissioned absurdly young, and blooded in Flanders and Scotland; and with him seemed to die a bloody era, an embodiment of experience remembered and unspeakable, shared only by those who had known it. His interest in the war, which for reasons of his own he had been trying to ignore, deepened until it verged on the obsessive, and he studied its engagements and strategies as if they were his personal responsibility. He combed gazettes and newspapers for the army's casualties and promotions, as though he were feeling once more the influence of an association he had long since thought broken and discarded; and it is only in retrospect that I sense the guilt and self-abhorrence of a soldier in time of war who was a soldier no longer. I dreaded that in the flood of military fervour sweeping the country he would take it upon himself to raise and command a regiment of militia: when I spoke of this once I was curtly told not to be so absurd.

As Horace Walpole wrote, the year 1760 was not the year 1759. The French had not been defeated in Europe, only disordered by our victories of the previous year, and the fear remained that Spain, whose relations with Britain were becoming increasingly hostile, would throw her forces into the balance. The Secretary of State consequently committed more regiments to the German war, in the hope of forcing a conclusion to a conflict which was draining the country of men and of millions of pounds, with no apparent end in sight.

In Canada, Wolfe's sacrifice was rendered hollow by the inability of his successor, Brigadier James Murray, to consolidate his position and hold the citadel against those French forces still based at Montreal. In April, in a near disastrous reversal of the tactics of the Plains of Abraham, the enemy attacked in strength, and Murray pleaded for reinforcements to be sent up the still icy St Lawrence from Halifax. The navy finally relieved them, and Montreal, surrounded by three contingents of the British army, surrendered on the eighth of September, nearly a year after the death of Wolfe. So fell the last bastion of French rule in Canada, and British supremacy in North America was assured.

On the twenty-fifth of October the King suffered a fatal heart attack, and it seemed, as with Wolfe, that an age passed with him. I recalled the red frog's face at Westminster Abbey: the pathetic man who with tear-stained cheeks had asked for news of his son after Culloden, and when reassured of Cumberland's safety on that field of slaughter had declared, "Then all's well with me"; the man who had railed against that same son "who has disgraced himself" after the convention of Kloster-Zeven; the king who had taken the field at Dettingen at the head of his own army, the last king of England who would ever lead men personally into battle. His funeral took place on the eleventh of November, and in such a mood of solemnity and gloom the year passed into memory.

It had been gnawing at the edge of my consciousness for years. Now it stood out so starkly in the light of his adultery that I wondered I had not known it before. No matter what my relationship to Mordaunt, Catherine was not my mother.

Whether it was her beauty and my lack of it that convinced me, or her behaviour toward me over the years, it came as a relief to know that I was some other woman's child. The grudge she so obviously bore me was not a personal one. I was merely a reminder of the past, of a time she would prefer not to recall.

And yet I was still here. What did he see when he looked at me with that searching, unquiet gaze? My mother? Jane? Catherine?

No. Catherine's child would be golden, as golden as herself. The face that stared back from my glass was not hers and I saw nothing of beauty in it, because all the beauty I had ever learned to admire was Catherine's. Whatever I attempted to do for myself, touch some colour into my cheek, clumsily dress my heavy hair, Catherine's face mocked me and Catherine's voice seem to whisper, *so you'll try, will you? Well, you're no daughter of mine.*

I took refuge from too much pain and failure behind a freezing shyness. Had Catherine loved me she would have drawn me out of it, teaching me grace, but she did not love me and it fell to the man who did, as everything that would make me a woman had fallen and would fall to him. So subtly was I fashioned that I was not aware of how I had changed. Clothing arrived from London, in exquisite taste, and I delighted in it, not realizing that it was not my choice but his. I learned to play cards, and a dancing master came from Newcastle to instruct me in the difficult figured dances, the cotillion, the allemande and the country dance minuet, the true minuet being considered too demanding for a novice, and I continued with my French and Italian not because I wanted to, but because Mordaunt chose that I should, and it did not occur to me at this stage of my life to want anything else.

Catherine observed this from a distance, as she had observed my childhood, amused at first, then disapproving, and finally, when it began to disturb her, with cruel humour. She called us Pygmalion and Galatea, which touched some nerve in him, she sent me lacy black garters, and spoke of me to her friends over the tea table; one of them wrote me a pornographic letter. I burned it and never acknowledged it, but she knew I had received it, and no doubt knew its nature. Her conversation was pungent and sprinkled with obscenity, and it was suddenly too easy for her to speak of matters between "Achill and I". I knew they shared a bed when she came from London, and I was worldly enough to know that was one of the reasons she came, but I managed to put my distaste out of my mind. Except when she chose to remind me, sometimes subtly, sometimes blatantly, of what was done before they slept.

I understood her. Whatever I was to her husband, I was not and could not be everything. In one respect and one alone, she would have no rival.

The process of bringing me out continued. He who was seldom seen in society introduced me to a select circle of acquaintances, landowners and their wives: I had not overcome my shyness and these evenings were ordeals to me, but they were gentlefolk in the finest sense of that word, plain, hearty and sensible, and welcomed without pretension the gauche adolescent I was. And had it lasted perhaps I would have married into their world, and found myself a squire's wife with a pack of children, and a hunter to ride to hounds.

But it did not last. Sometimes I regret it.

In April of my sixteenth year Catherine's eldest brother fell ill in Westmorland; his wife Anne was seven months pregnant, and like Catherine had a history of miscarriages. Mordaunt had been expecting this news, and was not surprised by it. I was to send to Catherine; if the situation warranted I was to follow him to Westmorland. Then he was gone, a solitary horseman with twenty-five miles of the roughest terrain in England between himself and his destination.

He sent for me a few days later. I rode with Vennor, our steward, and two grooms, and we followed the old road and the course of the Tees from Middleton-in-Moor, passing a High Force obscured by mist. The track was bad, strewn with fallen rock and treacherous with mud: we climbed until it seemed we were crossing the roof of England, the rushing sky offering by turns hail, thunder and fleeting sunlight. By evening, twelve hours after leaving Evesham, we reached Kirby Thore. Our progress was thought remarkable.

It was my first sight of Moorfields, Catherine's birthplace, which she had left at not much more than my age. A disappointingly small Elizabethan house, the complimentary E fronted a courtyard which was dank and overgrown in the twilight. There was a black wreath on the door.

Mordaunt was standing in the courtyard, seemingly self-possessed, but he had been drinking, as though this place and these circumstances represented an ordeal the nature of which I could not imagine.

"Of what did he die, Papa?"

"Syphilis," he said.

It was darker, rain and night falling together. A few lights showed, sullen behind leaded panes.

He said, "Shall we go in?"

The house was dark and cold and smelled of death. Anne was drinking tea in her room, with the casement standing open and the wind from the night bringing the clean scent of the moors.

Her reception of me was as loving as anything I remembered of her in London, and her quiet, fresh prettiness was undimmed. She existed in a serenity far removed from grief, and I knew that she had not loved her husband, and the manner of his death was no more shocking to her than if he had been a stranger. She kissed me and said how tired I looked and how uncomfortable I must be in my sodden habit, and saw me to my room herself.

I changed into a warm gown and asked my way down to the drawing room. Mordaunt was there, still in his wet clothing, drinking brandy. I sat near the fire, waiting for him to speak, for something to happen, some one to come.

They arrived as buzzards to carrion, the Reverend Priam Hatherleigh from his wealthy living near Cheltenham, his sister's features honed razor-sharp in a jaded face and his cleric's clothing heavily laced and suggestive of Bond Street. He had buried two wives; his third, Frances, was barely twenty, and had never been told of my existence. I heard her asking him if I was Mordaunt's mistress.

Catherine came about ten that night, viewed her brother's body, drank his brandy and went up to see his widow. When she descended her mouth was bitter with jealousy: even a syphilitic child was better than none.

She broke when the hour was late and the brandy and her grief, not for her brother but for what she could not have, had begun to weigh upon her; and in the room they shared beside mine he must have made some gesture of comfort. There was a torrent of profanity, reminding him that her brother was dead.

"So is mine, but you didn't love him either— and you wanted me that night, didn't you?"

Some time later she called out his name, terrified that after such habitual abuse and reconciliation she had lost him. There was no answer for me in the silence, if he had gone or stayed.

Captain Harry Hatherleigh, who had been in Portsmouth while his command was refitting, arrived on the morning of the funeral. Catherine collapsed in his arms like a lover; he had neglected to tell her in his infrequent letters that he had lost an eye to a marksman off Toulon, and his disfigured face, once so like hers, was a nightmarish mirror that threw back images of her own mortality.

Neither Anne nor I attended the funeral. I ventured a little in the west wing, trying to discover something of Catherine, to sense what that golden, radiant girl had been, but all the phantoms of her childhood were gone, and there was nothing but the sound of the rain.

Golden lads and girls ….

I returned to Anne; she was tatting and began to teach me, and the time passed in gentle conversation until we heard the vehicles returning. She put the work aside.

"I must have my handkerchief out now, so Fanny can tell Priam if I've wept." Then, "Do I shock you, my dear?"

I said no.

"I knew little of him. And what I knew, the world took from me." I went to the door. "Margaret… stay with your father. He hasn't a friend in this house and he knows it."

Catherine was sitting in the drawing room, applying a vinaigrette to one pinched nostril. She told me she had fainted at the graveside.

All lovers young, all lovers must consign to thee, and come to dust.
I left her and went along to the library.

Priam was standing by the casement, taking snuff; Harry was seated, a slash of black silk bisecting the ravaged face.

"You're her husband— what ails her?"

"She has a taste for theatrics."

"You're a cold bastard, ain't you, Mordaunt?"

Priam turned from the rainy light, face like a pale stone under water.

"I should like to settle my brother's debt."

"My business was with him, not with you and not with Anne. It is null and void, as of his death."

A murmur, then, "If you must persist, give it to your sister. I know you think I keep her on a pittance, to say nothing of beating and starving her."

The rain was still falling, a bitter, insistent sound. The fragment of leg in my vision drew up, the blue and white uniform stood.

"If there's nothing else, I'll be on my way. I'll see Cathy...." Anne was an afterthought, Priam's wife recalled only for her tactlessness. "Do ye know what that silly chit said to me? 'What a pity about your face, Captain Hatherleigh. Cathy tells me you was such a pretty man.'" The imitation was almost as savage as his words. "I hope she's good for something, brother. She don't seem over blessed with brains."

Silence.

"You won't stop the night?"

"I will not. I command a king's ship and I serve my king and my country. Unlike some." He pitched his voice a little louder over the rain. "Good-bye, Mordaunt. I don't think you need my prayers. Durham don't come under fire very often."

He did not acknowledge me when he passed.

After supper, interminably graced by Priam, Mordaunt left the house: I followed him, and Frances called a servant for a pair of pattens and affixed herself to my arm. We walked through the gardens and caught up with him near a ruined folly, which she asked him to show her: they emerged after a minute or two, she having attempted a little flirtation to relieve the boredom of the obsequies. It had obviously been unsuccessful. She called us a grim pair, and said she didn't wonder that Cathy had gone to live in the south, where the atmosphere was a good deal warmer, then she flitted away like a moth on her pattens and we walked on through the rain toward the River Eden.

We stood there in silence; his eyes were very bleak. I wanted to slip my hand into his as I used to, but something made me hesitate. He was staring across the flooded fields.

"So much cruelty," he said, "to so small an end."

"Let's go home, Papa."

"Yes. Whenever I think my heart is broken, I can always go back to Evesham."

Silence, pervasive but for the river in the reeds. Then he said, "I am no example of love for you to follow. And whatever I have tried to give you, I have given you no example of marriage. I want you to think well of me, when you think of this in the future. Most people do not, as you will have gathered."

We left the river, walked toward the lights. His footsteps slowed.

"Why should some one have the right to deny another? Why should some one say, you cannot do this, you cannot have that, you cannot love this woman or this man, because it is against these laws, these precepts? Who has that right? Are they God's laws, or are they man's?" I said nothing; I did not understand. "Life is so short. Why should we not have what we want?"

We reached the house. The spiritual darkness, the smells of years, of rot, of the corpse, were a palpable miasma. I went up the stairs, passing the ornamental gates, now unused, which had been placed across the bottom to restrain the dogs. Passing myself in a mildewed mirror, seeing a stranger's reflection. Dark eyes, and a face older than mine, knowing something I did not want to know in this house where everything was dying.

Catherine met me.

"Where is Achill?"

"Down there." Her eyes went beyond me. "His mood is very strange. If you can help him, go to him. If you can't, leave him alone."

My skin seemed to be on fire, although I was wretchedly cold.

She went to the stairs. I closed myself into my room and hid.

He thought, oh God, what matchless irony, that you twist all these threads on the warp and weft of years, and the pattern remains the same.

"I heard your brother laughing a little while ago. I suppose he had his bunter on her back and was doing his duty by her... in memory of poor Laddy, I daresay. He liked his bit of scut as well as the next man, maybe more, since he died of it."

Silence, and the sound of the rain, and the fire of the brandy in his throat.

"Achill, will you not come to bed?"

"I thought you made it plain the other night that you didn't want me. I don't have to be told twice."

"I didn't mean it." He laughed. "I didn't."

"No, you never mean it, do you? You've never meant anything in your life. You told me you loved me that first time, and I think you were lying."

She closed her eyes. "You've never been a wife to me, and you've surely to God never been a mother to my child."

"She isn't—"

"You've hurt me enough this time. Don't begin that again, or I'll make you wish you hadn't."

His name, and the caress. "I don't want you, Catherine. Don't make me want you. I hate you when you use me that way."

She dropped her hand without resentment and poured a measure of the brandy. After a time she said, "You remember the date."

"I remember it."

"We were never happy married, were we? All our happiness was before. And that day... that night.... God, how I cursed the army. If you had been killed, I would have died."

He said nothing.

"I don't know you now, Achill, what hurts you or pleases you, what you do with your days and nights—"

"You were my days and nights, and everything that hurt me, and you made me love you for it."

"And now?"

There was silence.

Eventually he said, "I've bought nothing for you."

"Give me your love. Tonight, of all nights."

"My dear, how sentimental. But this isn't Cheyne Walk, or a house borrowed for three days from understanding friends."

She left her brandy and knelt beside him, face hidden against his thigh, a gesture at once suppliant and arousing, and he touched her hair.

The kiss was without design, without intention, but it would not be ended: perhaps this too was part of the debt, a final discharging of payment. She opened her robe; she was trembling in the sharp chill of the room and her fingers moved without their habitual assurance.

They had not made love with such yearning and hopelessness since the first time, when she had been committed to another man, and there was as little hope that they would ever come together again; when there had been no time but the moment, and the future was only as long as the night which had joined them. A tender, desperate night, it, and not this anniversary they observed with such graceful, empty gestures, had been their nuptial, and it had ended with the light as this, the last night of his passion for her, was ending.

She slept. He watched the dawn, and thought of who she had been to him in the darkness, and closed his eyes. Against the knowledge, against the morning, bleak and without promise, waiting to be admitted.

★★★

By May it appeared that the war, now in its fifth year, might be drawing to a close. France was still reeling from her defeat in Canada and, more significantly, the loss of her wealthy sugar island, Guadeloupe; the Duc de Choiseul, Louis XV's chief minister, had asked London for a conference of all the antagonists, Prussia, Britain, France and Austria, and presented proposals for a separate peace between Britain and France. Pitt, the Secretary of State, who had offered a fickle public no fresh victories, insisted there be no cessation of hostilities even as his meteoric popularity began to wane. Bute, prime adviser to the Crown, and the young George III wanted peace almost as desperately as they wanted to be rid of Pitt. But Pitt laboured on, agitating for war against Spain, devising secret schemes, and delaying. No peace was signed.

The war was moderately fashionable. Raising a company or drilling militia on village greens was a popular diversion. The towns adored their scarlet-coated darlings; black facings, buff waistcoats, gold buttons flashed at every social gathering. Men who had served with Wolfe sang "The Girl I Left Behind Me" and looked for any one to take her place for a night. Their officers, honorary colonels of militia or veterans of the regular army, were at cards, at dice and at large, in scarlet for the May hunt balls, hallooing after vixens of a different brush.

The invitation was waiting for Mordaunt upon his return from Westmorland. He read it with contempt and perspicacity: Georgina Lady Harrington was a whore, her stepson a fortune hunter home from the army with a half-healed wound, a pile of bad debts and a mind to make another killing far from the field.

He sat at his desk and considered for a time, then he wrote his acceptance and affixed his signet to the wax. His hand was sweating and the scars throbbed beneath his cuff, as they and his back and his leg had ached since his return over the fells, fifteen hours in the saddle in a constant rain.

He called a footman and sent the message.

He found the package as it had been left in his dressing room, still swathed in its London wrappings. He had been saving it for September, a gift for the birthday he had arbitrarily chosen. It would not wait now; he did not want it to wait. He laid it out on his bed, a gown of ivory silk with roses embroidered on the panels and Venetian point lace six inches deep from the elbow. With it he would give pearls which had belonged to his mother, the Irish beauty who had bequeathed to him more of the Celtic predisposition to tragedy than she would ever know.

There was pleasure in the feel of silk against his hand, in the delicate beauty of the fabric, in the thoughts that came, and he let them come, caressing the silk, until he recalled himself and withdrew unwillingly from the seduction they offered.

He paused before entering; he had not been in this room for so long that it was unknown territory, and ordinary things were possessed of so extraordinary an intimacy that to touch them was almost a violation. The dressing table, its white muslin cover tied with ribbons, was a pleasant disarray of perfume flasks from Floris; he recognized them as Catherine's. Two candlesticks Catherine had once kept on her own mantel. A trinket box of Bristol blue glass, chipped, also Catherine's. A pair of pearl earrings. A rabbit's foot with a dusting of powder.

A doll. It occupied the corner of the window seat, stiff polonaise gown spread out, unseeing eyes of black glass opaque in a cool bisque face. It was not a doll at all but a mantua maker's fashion baby brought from London by Catherine some years before, claimed by a child more lonely than he had allowed himself to know, and now not discarded but put aside in honourable retirement. Did all things, then, forgotten or discarded by Catherine eventually make their way to this room?

He had stood for some time; now he sat in the window seat, the gown heavy across his legs. Fleeting, indefinable emotions possessed him, too elusive to be identified: a certain day, a certain hour of sunlight and flickering patterns on a wall, clouds in a shifting, endless arc.....

He felt bereft, horribly lonely, and old, with the sun warming his hair and the side of his face nearest the glass. He would never be young again, never love again... love was a painful word, not to be thought of, not to be acknowledged in this virginal sanctuary.

The muslin stirred, the memory also. There had been a day like this once, of unbearable sweetness: what was it, what had happened on that day so long ago that it could not be remembered? Was it here, or somewhere else... with Catherine, or some one before Catherine? Was there any one before her, could there have been, before Italy at twenty-two and an illicit passion for his brother's wife?

Lost, intangible sweetness, almost touched, almost grasped. Almost remembered in this cool room full of delicate scent, as fragile as the moment of shadows moving on the wall, petals falling on a page. There was a clatter of hooves: a rider coming in. The tranquillity of the room had gone; volatile reality had returned. He rose and left the gown on the bed, caressing it with the back of his hand, not trusting his roughened fingertips. Then, unutterably shaken, depressed by the youth in the room and the time he had spent there and the impossibility of every thought they had brought to him, he went out, to the stairs, through the hall, to the stables, to be out of the house when I came.

***

The fan was an iridescent silk edged with Valenciennes lace; the wrist cord was gold, the ivory sticks worked with gold. It had been costly, and this expenditure by one who was not extravagant made me ill at ease.

He had been dressed before me, and as I reached the top of the stairs I disturbed him in a strange little scenario: he was staring at his reflection over the console. He was forty-four, and whatever maturity had taken from his face, what it had given was exceptionally attractive. But he looked at that moment like a man who felt twenty years older, and wished he were twenty less.

I went down. His eyes were an enigma.

"It becomes you," was all he said.

My sensitive soul recoiled, as it had that winter evening when I had returned from London, wanting to be admired, loved.

I held out the cameo on its ribbon and asked if he would fasten it.

"I don't want you to wear that. I want you to wear these." He took the pearls out of his pocket, where they appeared to have been carelessly thrust.

He rearranged my hair slightly, a few tendrils against my cheeks.

"Shall I wear something else? A flower?"

"No."

He said it so curtly that I wondered if he thought the gown immodest, and I said I would wear another if it displeased him.

"It is not the gown."

"Then what is it?"

"Nothing. Go and fetch a wrap. You'll want it."

I thought it unlikely, but I went.

The drive was not a long one, and neither of us spoke: by now I was wishing the affair over. We joined a procession of vehicles. The house was blazing with lights in the dusk.

He said, "I don't intend to tell you how to behave, but watch how much you drink. I've seen women twice your age come to grief on these occasions, and there's no cure for lost virginity."

We were announced; the crowd swallowed us.

The first dance was his, a minuet. Whether I danced it well or badly I cannot recall: all I remembered was the strangeness of moving in the intricate patterns with him, the strangeness of his manner, of his eyes, as if he were dancing with some one he had never seen before and would not see again. Other partners spoke: we executed the entire series of manoeuvres in perfect silence, and because there was no conversation I immersed myself in the music and allowed it to carry me to its graceful conclusion. It ended; I sank in the final curtsey; even that had its ceremonial movements, and was as strictly regulated as any figure of the dance.

The next was a cotillion, and he would have left the floor, but I knew this music also and persuaded him to stay. The several figures were linked by a promenade; during one of these, flushed with a happiness I had not expected, I said, "We dance very well together, don't you think?"

I did not hear his answer. The third dance was a bourrée, of which there were as many variations as there were melodies composed for it: one bourrée could not be danced to the music written for another, and at this I quailed, and allowed myself to be led from the floor.

He did not dance again. When I objected he said, "My leg is troubling me, and you'll have partners enough before long." And he left me to strangers, introducing and abandoning me, although I was conscious of his eyes upon me everywhere I moved. I danced an allemande with the local member of Parliament, a chaser of women, foxes and fortune, who eyed me throughout as if I were something on a bed of lettuce and told me to avoid the young men, they was all piss and hot blood and if they hunted anything during the season it was only cat. When the dance finished he beamed at me, said I wasn't as shy as I pretended, and returned me with effusive compliments to my unresponsive guardian.

Some one spoke then, a deep voice with the drawl of the ton.

"My dear Mordaunt, how good of you to come. And who is this pretty child?"

Her face was dead white, skilfully made up, a patch shaped like a crescent moon at the corner of her mouth, her hair powdered a faint blue to match her gown and the gown a diaphanous silk, baring her breasts to the rouged nipple. She was not at all beautiful, but it was not her face men looked at and it was not her beauty she offered them. She was offering now, with the cool assurance of one who is not often refused.

"May I present my daughter Margaret, my lady."

"Zounds," she said. "Even so?" then I was brushed off as if I were no more than a tiresome fly. "Perhaps I may claim you later for a contredanse?"

"It would be my pleasure."

"And mine, believe me."

When she had gone I said, "I thought you told me you would not dance. Why with her and not with me?"

He gave me a sarcastic smile.

"Well, well. Not jealous, are you?"

And he passed me to some one else, but who he was punishing, himself or me, I did not know. Other dances: she returned and claimed him for hers, obviously believing in the military tactic of divide and conquer. I watched until her campaign began to sicken me, and then I turned away.

I was not the only one who had been observing them. He stood so close beside me that I almost walked into his arms.

"God's blood, a seduction comedy. 'Virtue in Danger'. Are you the ingenue?"

He was a soldier, by his aiguillette a captain. I had seen him before in the company of a cornet of dragoons, circulating through the crowd as though looking for prey; he was alone now, and he had found it.

"Captain Harrington."

"Your servant. You look a little lost in this throng without your protector. Do you think Georgie will carry the day?"

I flushed, and he laughed gently.

"You shouldn't be a bad sport, Meg. She was my whore once, and I don't mind."

I murmured an excuse and tried to withdraw, but, as gently, he held me.

"Don't leave me, child. It isn't fair when you know I can't run after you. Take a glass with me."

He limped ahead of me, leaning heavily on a malacca cane. The temperature in the room had risen with the volume of music and voices, and smoke had begun to obscure the ceiling.

"You're a nice little jade, ain't you? Why don't you come out to play more often?"

"No one's ever asked me."

"Taste the wine. D' ye like it?"

"Yes."

"Dirt cheap. The pater has friends in the trade."

"Oh, vintners…."

"No, little goose. The free traders, in the dark of the moon."

"But… we are at war."

"I fight the frogs. I have no quarrel with their wine, or with the free traders either. And that's French silk on your back, or I'm much mistaken. My service to you."

He drank. I flicked open my fan, an affectation that seemed to amuse him.

"I heard that you were wounded, sir."

"How remarkable. I hadn't thought Mordaunt or any of his household gave a damn for the outside world." I sensed an insult and stood. "Oh, sit down, you're like a jack in the box." A winning smile. "Keep me company, won't you? All my friends have gone up to cards and I can't follow them."

"Why not?"

"Because I'm weak from hunger, and the damnable Georgie won't give us supper till midnight. You can't expect a wounded man to drag himself up two flights without sustenance, unless there's something more appealing at the top than a pack of cubs with some pasteboard. Do you play, Meg? You have beautiful hands."

"I think—"

"Oh, don't. It's so boring in a woman."

"—I'll go and see what's become of—"

"He can hold Georgie at bay without you. They tell me you're a judge of horses, Meg. Would you care to ride with me some time and give me your opinion of mine?"

"I should have to consider it, sir."

"My name isn't sir, it's Valentine. And if you should favour the idea, he's a stallion. You can try him if you like, he'll give you rare pleasure."

There was no hint in those light, cold eyes, but I sensed that this horsemanship was not a kind with which I was yet familiar, nor, at the moment, cared to learn.

He smiled, seeing that I knew, and leaned forward as if to whisper a secret.

"He can go all night, sweet, and there's nothing he likes better than a firm hand."

His laughter was as cool and metallic as his eyes, or his voice, or his fingers on my wrist.

It was now nearly midnight, and the noise was tremendous: as the drink flowed more freely there were obvious signs of licentiousness. The member of Parliament accosted me and swept me out on to the floor for a Sir Roger de Coverley in which most of the participants were drunk. In the course of it I followed the progress through the room of a tigerish figure in blue silk. She emerged, not in possession of Mordaunt but another, leaning on his malacca stick: he seemed to be listening to her, then he shook his head. She spoke again and he looked toward me, and eventually he nodded. My partner saw this, and when the dance was over kissed my hand wetly and delivered me to him.

"We have nothing to say to one another."

"If you so choose. But if you would do me the honour of accepting my apology, we might yet enjoy ourselves."

My eyes went beyond him. He must have read my mind.

"Georgie's taking him in, and you know he's such a gentleman he won't refuse her. So it's me or some boozy old magistrate, and I give you my word I'll behave."

He kept it, and proved a diverting companion although his wit and his language were vicious. The cornet of dragoons came up and was introduced as the Honourable Perce, and sent off with a cool, "Go away now like a good boy and see what Georgie's doing. Tell her I said she was to mind her manners and keep her hands out of strange men's britches." Then he apologized gracefully, and went on to another subject.

Some time later he took a twist of paper from his pocket and sprinkled the contents into his wine. There was a sheen of perspiration on his face.

"Help me outside, will you? I'll swoon like a lovesick maid in another minute otherwise."

We left the light and the noise and the heavy smells of the ballroom, and when he found a stone seat and drew me down beside him I did not resist.

His mouth was hard and experienced and mine was innocent. His fingers, as knowing and intimate as the mouth, were exploring me with great assurance.

"Let me go. I'm cold."

"God's life, you're no colder than I am, and if you are I'll warm you."

He kissed me again, murmuring his hard language of endearment and promises; his tongue probed, and he assaulted my breasts with such expertise that his own success must have astonished him. Sexuality in all its violence and power overwhelmed me; I was drowning in it, and I was not so naïve that I did not recognize the full extent of his arousal.

I ran, knowing he could not follow, toward the noise, toward protection, and it was not until later that I discovered I had lost my fan with the last bonds of innocence.

By midnight a sense of profound isolation had overcome Mordaunt. Having drunk more than he remembered, he watched the degrees of intoxication around him, the gross behaviour, the lascivious fondling, the uninhibited dancing, with an ineffable conviction that he was too old and too jaded for this, the self-indulgent frivolity of a society from which he had been absent too many years. Nor did he belong in the company of soldiers; he had spoken to none of those present, and if his rank was known to them they did not approach him. His war was not their war: his had been rendered meaningless by this new shifting of allies and partitioning of territories, and although less than a generation separated them he felt, as he had among younger men in Flanders, isolated and estranged.

And yet, the bonds were powerful. The fraternity of the army, the uniform's brotherhood, the habit of service and of command, the love of comrades, the strictures of duty, the exercise of insensate courage: the memories of a life which had taken a youth and forged and broken a man, giving a lifetime's legacy of atheism, cynicism and bereavement, illness of body and disquiet of mind… a life brutal beyond description, and yet so terrible in its compulsion that even now he knew he had never left it. He had been born a soldier's son, of a lineage of soldiers, and had he fathered sons he would have given them to the army as inevitably as his father had given him. He watched the uniforms, and the compulsion to submit to the habit of duty and service was as overwhelming as any sexual desire: it led unavoidably to his other obsession, and the fear tormented him that the war would end, and remove the only avenue of escape that he could imagine.

Some one spoke to him. He turned and saw that it was an officer, a captain by his shoulder knot. The uniform facings and lapels were deep yellow, bound with a silver lace in which diagonal stripes had been worked: only three regiments had ever been distinguished by that shade of yellow, and the silver lace had been plain when he had worn it.

He said, "I do not know your regiment, sir," although the sense of inevitability remained, and he knew the answer before the other spoke.

"The Fifteenth foot, sir. Captain Lascelles."

"Mordaunt." They shook hands without warmth. "I was a captain in the Fifteenth foot. It was my second regiment."

He had no desire to establish the relationship this man apparently wanted, to enumerate the regiments, or the campaigns, or the commissions; his past was private, and he had no intention of illuminating it for another's entertainment.

"Do you hunt, ah, Mordaunt?"

"No. I am the neighbour one always feels obliged to invite."

There was another awkward silence. He wished he were drunk enough to behave abominably and so free himself of this unwanted interrogation.

"What do you make of this peace, Mordaunt?"

"There's nothing in it. Pitt's a mad dog— all he wants is war with Spain and another laurel for his crown."

"You think Spain will come in, then?"

"I am certain of it."

"Well, I daresay we can give them hot stuff too, as the song says."

His eyes returned to the dancers and the luminous, opal silk.

"We have given them nothing else for the past twenty years. I don't wonder the fields of Europe give such a bounty of wild flowers— they've been fertilised enough with the blood of my generation."

He had had too much to drink and now he knew it, but he could not stop, and he no longer cared.

"And then when the smoke clears, we will all sit down peaceably and divide Europe like a chequerboard— a bloodied chequerboard— and all our blood and sacrifice will have been in vain. Until the next time."

"Do you not think France is finished, sir?"

"France is a many-headed Hydra. She will never die."

He watched the dancers then in a stony silence until the other man muttered his apologies and withdrew; a passing footman proffered glasses and he took one and drained it without noticing what it was. The dancers and the music he loved blurred and became a half-remembered tableau of names and faces from the past: the bored, complaisant women of the Belgian aristocracy in a hot salon in Brussels, in an officers' mess in Ghent. The lost faces... the four card players on the day he had returned from England, congratulating him on his marriage, the men he had seen die piecemeal, whose corpses he had held, whose blood had soaked his clothing, whose eyeless faces he had tried to cover, whose youthful bodies, obscene with gangrene, had become so intolerable that other men dying nearby had demanded they be removed... men he had loved, and had betrayed by living when they died. He closed his eyes, and the memories overcame him, and in the midst of the dance she eluded the hands of a drunken magistrate into whose care he had commended her, and he dared not look at her, lest in her face he see the anguish and distress of one similarly betrayed.

When the woman laid her hand with familiarity on his sleeve he opened his eyes. She was offering herself, for their mutual enjoyment, with such blatant invitation that the temptations of an honest whore seemed infinitely preferable to the sickness of his thoughts.

"My dear Mordaunt, I am faint with hunger, and I shall not sup with any one but you."

He said, "My daughter...."

"I have asked Valentine to take care of your pretty child."

This, too, was inevitable.

"I am your servant," he said.

"She's a fucksome piece. I like the way she walks."

"Who, Georgie?"

"No, the chit. The mad major's little bunter."

"She's not a bad little thing. Comes up all in a pretty colour if you talk bawdy. But touch her— my dears, you would not have believed it."

A brief, murmured interlude, punctuated by applause, then some one's wistful voice.

"I can't think of anything sweeter than a virgin's blush."

"I can. A virgin's cunt."

"Ecod, man, watch your language. You ain't in town now, you know."

Silence for a time from behind the white-painted door, and an acrid scent. Their voices were languid, as if they had been drinking, and were more than half drugged on the narcotic smoke and their own fantasies.

"Christ, I'm sick of virgins. They never know a damned thing and they always weep after, as if you'd ravished them into it, when you know they wanted it all the time."

"I wish they'd ravish Pitt into peace and free me of this deuced army. I haven't been so bored since Oxford, and I'm a damned sight poorer."

A desultory shuffle. Some one swore obscenely. The other voice murmured on.

"Your virgin is a curious creature, gentlemen. Think on your finest filly. You'd not ruin her with rough handling, would you? No more so with your virgin. If you ride her rough she'll throw you the next time you try to mount. You must bring 'em to it slowly, on a leading rein, with kisses and promises. Now, your virgin heiress is a different matter altogether... to be approached with exquisite caution. Out of this nettle, danger, and so forth. The flower of that maidenhead is gilded, my dears. 'Twill die if rudely plucked."

"If you want the chit, Val, why don't you take her? You know we'd all come in on it for the sport."

"Your idea of sport, Perce, is putting your cock where it ain't wanted, and you'll die with a foot of cold steel in your guts for it yet."

"You ain't frightened of him, surely, Val?"

"Yes, by hell, I am. I wouldn't cross him for a thousand pound, and neither will any of you if you have any sense. Now pay up, my dear. My temper's a little short tonight, with one thing and another."

"Bad blood in that family, mad and bad."

"Scandal?"

"In spades, dear boy."

The door closed, and the gallery was silent.

I had come upstairs and passed the painted door; I knew he had my fan, and I had almost been brave enough to confront him when he had commenced his catalogue of his activities. I could not have been more violated and ashamed if he had succeeded, and had I been able to find Mordaunt perhaps I would have told him, with what consequences I can only speculate. But he appeared to have deserted me.

I walked around the gallery, sick at heart. A man in dark clothing was coming toward me; the candles had guttered down to their sockets and I thought he was one of Valentine Harrington's companions until I recognized him.

"Doctor Thackeray."

He looked clean, austere, and uncompromisingly sober. A strained and bony face, dark hair, dark eyes: once the difference in our ages had seemed incalculable. Now I saw a man no more than thirty, and thought how young he must have been when he had attended me in my childhood.

He did not remember me.

"Do you not know me? I live at Evesham."

He came into the light where I stood, near the head of the stairs.

"You are quite transformed," he said.

His presence comforted me; perhaps he knew. He put down his bag and looked over the balustrade. Whatever he thought of the saturnalia below, he retained his professional discretion.

"Is the Major well?"

"He seems so, thank you."

"And your mother?"

"She lives in London."

"I know. You went to her, did you not?"

"I didn't care for it."

The smile came and went, so quickly that it might have been a grimace.

"So much the Major's child," he said. "I wonder that he brought you here tonight. I thought he despised people like this."

"If you know him, you know that he does."

"Perhaps that was why. So that you would learn to despise them, too."

"I have."

"In one sense, I am happy to hear it. In another, not."

"What do you mean?"

"This, unfortunately, is the world to which you were born, and one cannot escape one's destiny."

He was harder than I remembered, more abrupt, more cynical. Maybe the barren years in a bleak northern practise had done this; he was not a Durham man. Maybe it was some ironic social consciousness, when his voice and manner were those of a gentleman, and those he attended, although gentlemen in name, were sprawled insensible like louts in a gutter.

He said, "I must go. I can do nothing further here," and so Mordaunt found us.

"I trust I find you well, sir?"

"Is that a professional question?"

"Merely courtesy, on this occasion." But his eyes were keen.

"Old injuries, Doctor. Too old to be of interest, and irreversible, I assure you."

There was tension and animosity between them, and I did not know why. Thackeray took his leave and descended to the littered hall.

"You make yourself invisible at will, it seems."

"I came here looking for you." It was a lie, but I could not tell him the truth; his mood was volatile.

"Then we were both distracted." Then, "I saw his patient earlier. Seaton Harrington." And, when he saw that I did not know the name, "Your absent host. Or did you not think to enquire?"

"Is he ill?"

"He is dying. He has a cancer of the stomach and his pain is intolerable. When her ladyship can't bear the noise she sends for faithful Thackeray. He brings him opium."

"How did you see him?"

"I had occasion to ask his wife. I knew him as a boy."

"And she dances while he is dying?"

"She has her weeds to hand." It was the biting, sarcastic mood I could not endure: I wondered how much he had drunk, and why he had abandoned me; when her attempts at seduction had become this bizarre valediction. "He has perhaps a week to live. Then our gallant captain becomes Sir Valentine. God knows he will never be *saint*."

The contempt with which he said it suggested that if I wanted pity I would not find it here. I had, after all, been warned.

"Miss Mordaunt."

My saint was standing on the stairs, leaning on his malacca stick. His eyes were reddened but his dress was impeccable, and he held my fan.

"You left this in the garden. I had it at cards with me an hour past. It brought me luck."

I said numbly, "I am very glad."

"It is a charming thing. I knew you would be sorry to think you had lost it."

Movement beside me.

"I'll take that, Harrington."

He said, with equal coldness, "Your pardon, Major, but it is not your fan." He came down the stairs very slowly and conveyed my hand, without kissing it, to his lips. "Adieu, dear heart."

I said nothing, nor did Mordaunt speak until we had reached Evesham. A thrush was singing, the air was cold; the early dawn of spring leavened the night. I held the fan and stared at the fields, shivering in my silk; how radiant with pleasure I had been when I had dressed. Now I was going home like a dying moth, crushed and colourless.

He said, "It appears that you made conquests wherever you went. Up in the gallery with the leech, out with the pimp in the garden.... May I ask what so occupied you that you misplaced your fan? You seemed to prize it highly when I gave it to you."

"He said he would faint. We went out to take the air."

He said, "You silly child," with such contempt that tears came to my eyes, and I wept quietly in the dimness until the door was opened and the step let down. I stood on the wet gravel, holding the skirts of a gown I would never wear again, hiding my face from the grooms.

"Are you coming, Papa?"

He had walked away and was standing with his back to me, staring over the park, or perhaps at nothing: perhaps his own recollections of the night possessed him, or the memory of his own behaviour, which was not above reproach.

"Papa?"

He turned, and the grey light fell across his face, enigmatic, impenetrable.

He said, "Go to bed. I cannot talk to you," and I went in. He did not follow me.

Two days later Valentine Harrington sent me a white rosebud from his hothouse, and a fan of peacock feathers. I kept the rose as it would soon be gone, leaving no reminder, and returned the fan. Within the week I was sent a bouquet of Rosa Mundi, accompanied by a message: *O cruel beauty, like the rose, sharper than the thorn....* These, too, I returned.

He became a nuisance. He loitered outside the gates on horseback, alone or in the company of his confederate, the Honourable Perce, and when Vennor warned him against trespassing he replied insolently that he had as much right as any man to use the public highway. He accosted me twice, once near the village, once on the edge of the moor where apparently he knew I rode. On both occasions I was with a groom and Harrington was alone; on both occasions his behaviour, although eccentric, was irreproachable. The third time he and the Honourable Perce were found in the home park, within the gates of Evesham. Both were drunk, and what had appeared a series of troublesome coincidences now seemed sinister. I told Vennor, that saddened man, whose eldest daughter, had she lived, would have been my age. He said succinctly, "If ye doan't tell t' Major, ah will."

I did not tell him. There were too many aspects of that night I could not forgive, and something in my own behaviour seemed to have offended him so deeply that he seldom spoke to me. We existed in this stalemate until Harrington's father died. I did not attend the funeral, and to my relief the new baronet observed a period of mourning before continuing his harassment of me.

More flowers arrived, an armful of Persian lilac cut, he wrote, by his own hand, accompanied by a long, incoherent sonnet beginning, *Virgin pure, you shall be my sheath, and I shall be your sword.* The rest was pornographic. I took the lilac to the library: I had never previously hesitated before opening this door.

"Where did those come from?"

"Captain Harrington."

"Is this an affair you have encouraged?"

"I have not encouraged him in any way."

I laid the folded, perfumed paper on the desk beside the lilac. I think he knew what it was before he read it.

"This man is dangerous."

"I know, Papa."

He said, "Then I will deal with it."

Valentine Harrington came to Evesham in response to a letter, the contents of which I never knew, on a June morning. I was not at home. He was directed from the front door to the courtyard, into the cool shade of which he walked, leading his horse. He was in the process of resigning the commission he so disdained and consequently wore civilian dress, a newly acquired coat from the finest tailor in Newcastle, a cascade of freshly laundered linen. He was piqued to find himself in the midst of stable muck, and to discover his impeccable riding boots awash with the effluent of running pumps.

The man he had come to see was standing ankle deep in horse manure, wearing an old coat and wielding a pitchfork. When Harrington spoke, he drove it into the pile of manure and turned. Harrington said, "I had not anticipated this, Mordaunt. Surely we can discuss our differences in some more suitable place."

"This seems a suitable place to me."

"Very well. You wished to see me. I am at your service."

"Your attentions are unwelcome to my daughter."

"Have you asked your daughter if she shares your opinion? She seemed willing to learn more of me, aye, very willing."

"Your attentions are unwelcome. As is your poetry. As is your presence. This is the proper place for you, you bastard, shit among the shit."

Harrington said sharply, "It will be my pleasure to see you in the company of seconds," and attempted to withdraw. "And as for your daughter— the cuckoo in the nest—the cuckoo and the cuckold— there'll be a man in her bed one day, Mordaunt, whether you like it or not, and it won't be you."

He had deliberately provoked a response and had been prepared to enjoy it. He had not anticipated this, a slashing, potentially fatal blow from the edge of the right hand across his carotid artery. His windpipe swelled and his knees bent like paper; he crumpled forward and lay face down, manure soiling his hair and clothing. He fainted, and when he was conscious once more he was turned over by a booted foot, which delivered a final kick to his wounded thigh. Then the shadow passed away and he lay on his back on the cobbles; the sun moved imperceptibly and the impervious sky, delicate with cloud, shimmered above. A bluebottle explored his face: the stench overwhelmed him. He fainted again: no one came, although there were voices in the nearby paddock. He lay in the heat, vomited with terrible effort and began to cry with pain. The sun moved, and in the pearly, vibrant air a clock chimed many times. He dragged himself to his knees, groped for the rein of the horse standing patiently, and kicked its flank. It carried him safely, so safely that he never knew how many times he vomited or swooned in the saddle.

It had been dealt with, so finally that but for the disappearance of the man and the cessation of the gifts and the strangely stimulating poetry, it might never have happened. It was never discussed, and his name was never spoken at Evesham again.

I was in charge of the household at the end of the month, Mordaunt and Vennor having taken colts to Durham to sell.

There was little peace in solitude for me. The morning after their departure an accident occured, and the major-domo came to me as logically as he would have gone to Mordaunt. I rode up to the scene. A few men from our stables were already there, but they had not moved the victim; the nature of his injury was so horrifying that they did not know how to proceed. One of the boys was huddled by the body, holding his hand: it was his father, a groom I had known since childhood. The rest was a rider's nightmare. There had been lightning, the young horse he had been exercising had thrown him, and his boot had caught in the stirrup. The horse had bolted, dragging him until it cleared a fallen log. The impact had wrenched his boot free and broken his leg, and when I knelt beside him I saw that his face was impaled. The branch had torn open his mouth and emerged beneath his cheekbone; the cheek lay peeled open like a flap, attached to his jaw by a few threads of bloody tissue.

I dared not touch him, but I spoke to him. He seemed utterly alert. The boy was still sobbing, and I sensed that this was disturbing him; I told some one to take him away. There was more lightning, but no rain. I said to the most senior of the men that I was going for the doctor.

"Whit abaht t' rain, miss?"

"Cover him. And keep that child quiet, or send him back to Evesham."

I rode down to the village. He was washing his hands at the stone sink, his case lying ready and his horse saddled; I thought some one had had the foresight to send for him before coming for me.

"Why do you want me?"

"Haven't they told you? One of our grooms has had an accident."

"Your father will deal with it. I'll come later."

"My father is in Durham."

I described the injury; he was never still. In that darkened, humid room he unlocked cabinets, opened drawers, selected vials, removed a leather roll of instruments and put them in his bag.

He said, "I shall depend on you. I hope you've the stomach for it."

It was raining by the time we reached the wood, and the injured man had pulled himself or been lifted from the log and was lying on the ground with some one's shirt pressed to his face; another was holding a coat like a canopy over his head. The eye in the undamaged side of the face remained open, nor did he lose consciousness at any time during the proceedings. Thackeray spoke quietly to him; whatever his thoughts were, he was adept at concealing them.

"Keep the rain from his face. There is nothing more distressing to one who is in pain." Then to me, "Do exactly as I direct you. If you faint, do it elsewhere."

"I won't faint."

"We shall see."

He worked quickly, without opiates, holding out his bloodied fingers for the instruments: the blood ran and thinned, and the rain soaked our hair and clothing. He stitched impassively, a neat line of sutures from the swollen eye to the corner of the torn mouth, and from the mouth to the jawbone. The man groaned and retched, voiding a river of blood and broken teeth. Thackeray wiped his mouth gently and gestured for a fresh dressing.

"There will be considerable scarring, and there is always the risk of serious infection... I consider it fortunate that he did not lose an eye. I have known the shock of a blow force an eye from its socket.... You do not find my conversation too distasteful?"

"I find it interesting, in a peculiar way."

"You surprise me."

He applied the dressing; the injured man had fainted. The others moved forward with their door.

He said to them, "Carry him carefully to the house, and I will attend him further there," and began to gather the instruments; I helped him. The steel was extraordinarily cold to the touch.

"Was it as you thought? Or did you consider it a minor injury?"

"It was much as I expected." He rolled the case and put it into his bag. "But I hope you will apprehend that a burned child in Middleton went without my help, and that child may be dead by the time I reach her."

"Is that where your duty lies, Doctor, in Middleton? Or with us?"

"My duty lies where I am most needed." He closed his bag. "Still, it was surgeon's work, and I am a surgeon, not an apothecary. Perhaps my obligation lies where my skills are challenged."

We stood staring at one another while the rain dripped from our faces, then, unexpectedly, he said, "I admire you. Don't let them strap you into a backboard and make you read improving books, when you could be giving something useful to the world."

"What could I give?"

"Your intelligence. Your courage. You have great spirit. Not many women of your station would sit watching a man sew another man's face without blenching."

"So much the Major's child, you said."

He said enigmatically, "Perhaps. His influence is not always benign. You do well out of it."

I walked away. Whatever I thought privately of our relationship the observations of a stranger were heresy, even if they happened to be true.

Anne Hatherleigh was delivered of a son, and the strengthening flicker of his life was watched with disappointment by Catherine's brother Priam, who saw his hopes of a baronetcy dim in proportion, and by Mordaunt with an obsessive interest, and when he said to me, "Anne has a son," I heard an echo of great Elizabeth's cry, *And I am but barren stock.*

He rode to Westmorland to stand godfather to the child. I declined to go with him; one visit to that decaying house was enough. Apparently Catherine shared my views, for neither she nor her reverend brother attended the christening, and the others, as we had so scathingly been reminded, were in their country's service.

During his absence Thackeray called to attend his patient, whose eye he had saved but whose wound was infected: he feared some secondary paralysis of the facial muscles and wanted to discuss the case with Mordaunt. He asked me pointedly if the Major were never at home, and I told him that my father's affairs were none of his concern. He apologized almost grudgingly, and then to my surprise he laughed, and said, "Poor Margaret, between the rock and the hard place. What a devil of a thing is love."

When we met again it was warily, conversing like fencers, like adversaries. I began to put myself in his way, riding out alone at that hour of the morning when I knew he would be starting his rounds. He greeted this tartly with, "I thought fine ladies stayed abed until noon. Or is this another soldierly influence?"

He did not protest on the second morning. It was high summer, with dew and fog hanging on the pastures. He rode up the track at eight, saluted me with his crop and would have passed, but I kneed my horse up beside him and asked if I might ride with him.

"There will be gossip."

"Shall I go back? Do you want me to go back?"

"No," he said. "I don't want you to go back."

So it began. The sun burned away the mist, the moors unfolded, the day opened fully like a rose, and we rode together. I relished his company because he seemed to expect nothing of me: what he found in mine I could not speculate, but he must have thought me sympathetic because he talked of himself, and told me more of what had previously been an enigmatic background than I think he had any one since taking up his practise, and I sensed that they had been lonely years; perhaps that was the reason for his interest in me.

It became customary for us to meet, at that time and in that place, and to ride for an hour together. I never went farther or remained absent longer. He did not comment on the absence of a groom, but one morning he said, "Does the Major know you ride with me like this?"

"Would I deceive him?"

"Oh, yes, you would. Do you think for one moment that he would allow you to ride alone, knowing what might happen to you? Do you think my heart isn't in my mouth every time I watch you turn and ride away, when anything or any one could be waiting for you?"

I might have turned back. Instead I rode on, in a simmering silence, and had Mordaunt not spoken to me it is possible that I would have allowed the relationship to die. I continued it out of defiance, condemning us to the consequences.

It was evening, and raining, and I was sitting opposite him dealing for piquet. We played for money, he with a gambler's dedication. My temper was short; I was menstruating, and perspiring heavily in my boned corset. I envied him his freedom.

He had rolled up his sleeves, revealing the scars of Dettingen.

He said without preamble, "I don't approve of this unseemly friendship with Christopher Thackeray."

"In what way is it unseemly?"

"He is a man and you are not a child. And you have been seen together, in case you thought it had escaped my notice."

He laid the cards down, and again I saw the scars: how nearly they must have crippled that hand which now so seldom played.

"And if your taste is for long rides, then by God you can ride with me. You seemed to enjoy my society once. Now I have fallen out of favour."

I stared at my cards, conscious of the sweat running from beneath my hair to the nape of my neck. He laid his wrist flat on the table, deliberately.

"I have worse. You need not embarrass me by displaying your revulsion."

I left the money and the cards and went up to bed. Whatever devil drove him, I would not give it the satisfaction of seeing me weep for my loss of him.

The summer continued, and destiny shaped the course of all our lives.

Belle Isle off the coast of Brittany fell to the Royal Navy with heavy British casualties, and the blame for this costly and indecisive amphibious action was laid at Pitt's door. There was, fortunately, news of other victories to bolster his sagging popularity, from the West Indies, Germany, and in July from India, where Pondicherry, the last French outpost, had fallen to British forces on the fifteenth of January. Houses in London were illuminated, and bonfires lit in celebration.

On the eighth of July the King's betrothal was announced, to Sophia Charlotte, youngest daughter of the Prussian Duke of Mecklenburg-Strelitz. The young Charlotte came to London in September, where Catherine wrote that she had been well received by the crowds, but she was short, thin, pale, and large of mouth and nose. They were married almost immediately, and the coronation followed a fortnight later.

On the tenth of September I rode with Thackeray to High Force, and sat in the sun watching the play of foam and opening my heart.

"She isn't my mother, and you know it as well as I."

There was a long silence, and a curlew's cry, and the rushing of the water; spray drifted against my cheek.

"Have you been saying this to any one else?"

"No."

"Why do you say it to me?"

"You knew, didn't you?"

"Yes. I knew."

"Well, then, it doesn't matter."

"It does matter. It is indiscreet, and it would hurt the Major."

I sat in silence, the sun beating on my back.

"You are very unhappy, aren't you?"

"I think... he resents me, because I have none of her beauty."

"Great beauty can be a handicap."

"I shall not likely suffer it, then."

"Don't be so ridiculous." And I heard the contempt and impatience of maturity, and felt denigrated, childish. "She is a woman. She has suffered much, and loved much, and her face reveals it. Your face shows nothing yet."

I stared over the moor, resenting this unlikely championship.

"What has she suffered?"

"She's borne children and lost them, and she can never give him another, although she has almost broken her health in the attempt. And she has loved him, although that cannot always have been easy."

"How do you know what's easy for her and what isn't?"

"He is a difficult man, and life with him must be a difficult business."

It was true, God knew. He ignored me, or baited me; in my presence he was withdrawn and restless; he spent hours in the saddle, sometimes alone, sometimes with his steward or his keepers, whose society he apparently found more congenial than mine.

I said, "She's had to suffer me for sixteen years," and his answer was unexpected.

"Yes. I don't imagine that has been easy for her, either."

He took out his watch. I had no desire to know the time, or to return to a house where I no longer felt welcome.

"Can she carry a child to term?"

"I should not discuss this with you.... I do not say it is impossible, but I think it unlikely."

"Then I'm a bastard."

He said sharply, "Don't ever say that to the Major."

"Why not, for God's sake? If I am, he made me one."

"You do not know that is the truth."

"What other truth is there? I have no name, I have no rights—"

"You bear his name and you enjoy his protection, and you are heir to everything he owns. What further proof of any man's devotion have you any right to expect?"

The sun was weaker now, drifting behind cloud. I pulled on the coat I had discarded and mounted without waiting for him.

He was no horseman and I outpaced him, and came back to look for him through a sea of tossing heather. He was on foot; his horse had cast a shoe.

"You'll be hellish late if you stay with me."

"I daresay no one will notice."

We walked, and over the miles of desolation a wind roared that in this high place made speech impossible. There was nothing but darkness, the rushing darkness of the sky, the dark seas of the heather, and the tortured half-light flying over our faces from cloud that seemed close enough to touch. When the rain came it obliterated everything. We leaned against the horses and it beat like whips around us, and I saw him laughing at me through it, then it lessened and the moors unfolded, softened with mist. It had cleared by the time we came down into Teesdale, and we walked under a wide evening sky, suffused with the long light of summer.

He took me into his house as if I belonged there. His housekeeper appeared briefly with wine and biscuits: she knew me, and she would see that word of where I was reached Evesham before me, but Evesham's master would not be at home and no one else would judge me. We stood in his crowded sitting room and he offered me a towel, and I wandered round looking at his library as I dried my hair. *A Syllabus of Anatomy in Thirty-Five Lessons*, an old pamphlet, *A Dialogue Concerning the Practise of Physic*, several volumes by La Framboisière, many more bound in calfskin and printed in Latin. A full skeleton, its yellowed bones wired together, hung upon a frame in the corner. I looked away, and he laughed.

"Don't you relish the prospect?"

"Not particularly. Do you?"

"I expect death to unravel the last great mystery. I shall be disappointed if it does not."

I stared at the grinning, eyeless face.

"Have you no respect for his soul?"

"I doubt if he had one. He was very much one of the baser species— a convicted criminal. He was, however, quite difficult to obtain, so I respect his bones accordingly."

I sat with the towel around my shoulders, and we drank our wine.

"You have no fear of death?"

"I take a professional interest in it, as the logical progression. I suspect that birth and death are the same process, an emerging from one state of being into another. So I cannot say I fear it. I am merely curious."

"Why do you fight death, when you consider it a natural process?"

"I comfort myself with my philosophy, otherwise I could not endure the inequality of the contest." The housekeeper had left candles burning, their light stronger now against the dusk. "Everywhere I see ugliness, despair, disease, and degradation. If man is made in the image of God, then God's more of a monster than we thought." He drank the last of his wine. "No one should ask you to share that. No one should even think it."

The last birds were singing; the sun had set. I took the towel from my shoulders.

"Let me," he said.

He combed my hair, rather roughly. It was thick and undisciplined and I had not cut it since London. When he had finished my scalp was tingling.

"I should like a lock of your hair."

"For scientific purposes?"

"No," he said. "For love."

It had begun to rain again. Somewhere a clock struck, muffled by distance. He said coldly, "What, nothing to say? Or is it 'much as you expected'?"

I turned around and said, "Don't play with me."

"I don't. But you play with my life, and this is the result."

"What... must I do?"

"Nothing. I've played this miserable game before, the burning lover with all his hopeless passion. I can't do it again, not for some one I can't have. And I can't have you."

By the time I reached Evesham it was fully dark and the sound of rain was deafening. The stable boy who came to help me was clearly discomfited by something; there was a momentary lull in the rain, and more lightning, and I saw Mordaunt.

"Where have you been?"

"On the moor with Kit Thackeray."

"So it's *Kit* now, is it?"

I began to rub her down. The boy had vanished, unwilling to witness this confrontation.

"His horse went lame. It was late when we came back— he asked me into his house." I was conscious of his eyes, although I could not see them. "He has a housekeeper."

"And she has a tongue. I would be obliged if you would look me in the face when you speak to me."

I stood up and stared at him over the mare's back and said, "Did you not teach me to see to the comfort of my horse before my own? Was that not my first lesson?"

He came around and took the cloth from me and dropped it into the straw. "I have been looking for you. I have been on the moor, and I have been on this estate. I have asked for you at every door. I thought you had been injured. Now I see that you were taking your ease with *Kit*, and enjoying yourself at my expense."

"You never tell me of your comings and goings— you show me no consideration. And as for my absence, you're so seldom in this house I hardly thought you'd notice."

He said, inexplicably, "Don't play with fire, Meg."

I turned my back on him.

"Perhaps a month or two in London will cool your interest in him."

I should not have said it, but I was driven to it.

"Don't threaten me with London. When I recall your wife's behaviour there I wonder that you dare to question mine."

"You will not see him again."

"I'll see who I damned well please."

I found myself in the rain, the lightning on our faces. He had me by the shoulders, the rain pouring down on us; the strength of his grip was appalling.

He said, "I have never struck you, but if you ever say anything like that to me again, alone or in the presence of my servants, by Christ, I will."

He released me. There was more passion in that violence than in Thackeray's profession of love for me.

How thin the line between love and hatred: perhaps, for him, it had already begun to blur.

III

The summons came for Thackeray at the beginning of October, and on the evening of the fifth, before the appointed time, he rode up to Evesham.

It seemed very quiet. At the door the major-domo greeted him, with a pouched and inscrutable face, and a footman drifted away with his cloak and hat. There were flowers on the console where he had laid his crop the night he had laboured to save Catherine's life and that of the premature child she had borne: that loss had always haunted him, although death at birth was common enough. He thought of the frail, the unwanted and the illegitimate he had brought into the world, and wondered why he had failed, why this so desired son and heir should not have been allowed to survive. Although it could not save this sterile marriage, it seemed so little compensation to ask.

He touched the flowers: they were asters, in shades of blue and rose and purple, and he knew whose hand had arranged them here. The daughter of the house... as he had always considered her. Even that was false.

The major-domo was waiting.

They approached the drawing room. The doors were open, and from within came music, unexpected and scintillating. He did not recognize the composer or the composition, but he had a sensitive ear and the execution was flawless: it seemed touched by genius.

The major-domo said, with what seemed a criminal disinterest, "The master plays, sir."

He opened the doors fully and for a moment the scene was held before him like a tapestry: a long, candlelit room filled with the patina of wood, the sheen of brocade and satin and the glint of crystal, the luminous portrait of a young Catherine, vividly beautiful, and the harpsichord where the light fell, still and radiant, over the face of the man who had summoned him. An oddly intimate glimpse, like a secret revealed, then the major-domo cleared his throat tactfully and the music stopped. The last note seemed to shiver into the silence.

"Doctor Thackeray, sir."

The eyes rested on his face, at this distance very much greyer than blue. The strong, bony features were neither welcoming nor displeased: he did not rise from behind the harpsichord.

"You are early."

"I thought you would find lateness unacceptable."

"It is a pity you cannot teach that lesson to my daughter, who is utterly oblivious to time."

The major-domo withdrew, closing the doors. Thackeray said, "I apologize for having disturbed you in your leisure. I had heard that you were gifted. I did not expect that I would ever hear you play."

He did rise then, and came around the harpsichord. He did not offer his hand.

"So you've heard of my effeminate accomplishment."

"You demean it, wrongly."

"I do not demean it, I assure you. But others have."

At close quarters he dominated the room, and the eyes were clear and daunting.

"Are you fond of music, Doctor?"

"Yes. But I seldom have the opportunity to hear any... Margaret plays, does she not?"

His bold mention of her name had no noticeable effect, although he knew she was the reason he had been brought here.

"Yes. I teach her."

"She must be very—"

"She has no patience, and, I regret to say, very little natural talent. Will you take a glass of sherry?"

Thackeray regarded him with interest, still cherishing the intimate vignette. He must have played this way a thousand times, to these unhearing walls, to that portrait of a woman as indifferent as in life, to a house full of shadows, and memories, and secrets, for no one but his servants and himself. And for that time he had been at peace, absorbed in some joy of creation which must satisfy him, however briefly. But the peace, the absorption, had gone now: it was the face of a man both wary and controlled, and as always the impenetrable quality of his nature challenged and stimulated.

"Do you write music— do you compose?"

"No." And then, perhaps because even he was aware of the monosyllabic harshness, "I have no ability."

They drank the sherry standing, as though it were an unpleasant but necessary ritual. Thackeray sensed some pain of body or limb, and wondered why he had never on any occasion sought treatment for himself.

Mordaunt said, after a silence, "It was my ambition to become a musician. My father thought otherwise."

"Hence the army?"

"I was a better soldier."

"You had no notion of defying him?"

The eyes were faintly humorous, contemptuous.

"If you knew my father you would not say that. He was a captain-general and he ruled his family accordingly. And I was his second son, and not his favourite." He drained the glass. "Will you walk in, Doctor? I hope you find my table to your liking."

Only two covers had been laid.

"Will Margaret not be joining us?"

"Margaret has gone out. She is spending the evening with friends."

He doubted it. She was as reclusive as Mordaunt, and if she had been sent away he would have selected her company as stringently as he ruled every other aspect of her life.

They began with game soup and more sherry and progressed through crimped skate in onion sauce and salmon genevese in herbs and Madeira, accompanied by white burgundy. They discussed the war, guardedly: the reason for this interview was never mentioned, and the subject of their mutual concern remained oppressively unbroached. The wine was changed and a heavy claret poured; roast partridge with apricots and rice was served, followed by a compote of peaches, a plum tart, and custard in glasses, accompanied by a sweet canary wine. Thackeray drank only moderately, aware that the moment would come when he would need all his clarity of thought, but the wines were potent, and he observed with concern that although his host drank heavily, their effect upon him was negligible.

The meal and the strained conversation ended. Walnuts in a silver dish were brought.

"A glass of Madeira, Doctor? I prefer it to a rather mucky port."

"You must forgive me if I decline. Really, I exceed my capacity."

The major-domo, who had been overseeing the service, and the footmen withdrew. Thackeray sat in the flickering candlelight marshalling his thoughts. The long, roughened fingers across the table cracked a walnut without effort.

"I do not approve of your relationship with my daughter, and I do not intend to allow it to continue."

Thackeray said, "When Margaret is eighteen I am going to ask her to become my wife."

"When Margaret is eighteen she is going to the Continent with me. I do not believe this war will last much longer."

"When she returns, then."

"And do you think she will find you acceptable?"

"I hope that she will look favourably upon me."

"Have you spoken of this to her?"

"Not of marriage, and without your consent I will not."

"You trained in London. Why did you leave?"

"A love affair. My rival had money. There was really nothing left to be said."

There was now no subterfuge; the animosity was undisguised.

"You are much older than Margaret."

"I am thirty-two."

"Do you love her?"

"I have known a woman's love, in the fullest sense. Margaret cannot give me that yet." Then, gauging the effect, "Love is not summoned on demand. Her youth delights me."

The response confirmed his suspicions.

"And your desires are not carnal?"

"As I said, she cannot give me a woman's love. I respect her innocence above all things."

The fingers, which he watched with fascination, turned a fragment of shell.

"What sort of life do you propose to offer her after what she has known? Some hovel full of scurvy brats, while you bring all manner of disease through the door?"

He refused to be baited. His mind was active now, analysing, speculating, probing, the surgeon supplanting the man.

"I should go with Margaret to Bath or Cheltenham and practise there, or if she would prefer it, to London."

"To mingle with men and women of fashion? If I wanted her to have that life I would take her there myself, that she might do it at her own level."

"What is your desire for Margaret, sir?"

"Happiness."

"Cannot you allow her to find it in her own way?"

There was silence, overlaid by a virulent current of dislike. He waited, controlling himself, for the next attack: he had never met so formidable an opponent.

"You have asked for my permission to pay your addresses to Margaret. I forbid it. If I could forbid you seeing her I would do that also, but unfortunately that is beyond me."

Thackeray determined his manoeuvre: his only fear was that it was obvious.

He said bluntly, "I have lived alone, and I have had no companionship. I had hoped that you of all men would understand."

He was speaking of the governess and the nerve he touched was raw; he felt a surge of pity.

"I see that not only is Margaret free in discussing her own affairs, but she discusses mine as well."

"She is discretion's very self where you are concerned. I made my own deductions."

"And they led you where?"

"I thought you had found happiness. And I believe it is something of which you have known little, although I do not seek to know the reason."

"A man may love where he will. A woman may not." Yes, formidable, Thackeray thought; formidable and implacable. His admiration deepened, and his compassion. "You seem to prefer plain speaking. I will be blunt with you. Margaret is my heiress. You have no money. It is as simple as that."

"You cut deep, Major."

"No blade cuts deeper than a gossip's tongue. When you begin looking above yourself you'd best grow accustomed to it."

Another silence. It seemed that the interview was at an end.

Thackeray said, "May I speak to you as a man, putting aside our disagreement?" His compassion was overwhelming, but it was still necessary, compulsive even, to dissect, to probe even further. "I find your hostility toward me inexplicable. It is not, I believe, contempt for my profession. Although you have never required my services I have attended Margaret and your wife, I think to your satisfaction." Mordaunt said nothing; he continued gently, "I tried with all my power to save your son five years ago."

"It is not my son who signifies in this case."

"Thank God. I have always thought you could not forgive me, when I could only do what was humanly possible."

The moment had come: he had nothing left to lose. "I know why my suit is not acceptable to you. It is not because I have no family of consequence and Margaret is your heiress." He paused, hoping that what he was about to say would be enough: he had no desire to force into words what he now knew to be the truth. "I know that Margaret is not your daughter. I only wonder that no one has spoken of it openly."

The fingers selected a walnut shell, turned it over, and were still.

"Who told you?"

"Your wife's medical history is sufficient to assure me that she has never carried a child to term, and there is a malformation of the uterus which ensures she never will. The rest was speculation. The girl believes herself illegitimate."

"She is legitimate."

"Who is she?"

"I do not find myself obliged to discuss this with you, Thackeray. She is legitimate, and she is my child, as much as if I had sired her. That is enough."

"But not in your eyes."

"I will say good-night to you, sir."

Thackeray said, "You regard me as a rival, and your attitude is that of a lover. I think that concealment will not afford you much quietude, mental or physical."

There was nothing, not even a change of expression, and for a dreadful moment he thought he was mistaken.

Then Mordaunt said, "Does she know?"

"She is sensible of a change in your manner. I would be the last to tell her."

There was another silence, and he heard the rain. The strong, introspective face across the table remained as enigmatic as the day he had first seen it, and he watched it with pity and fascination, knowing he had been drawn into the labyrinth of its obsession as inexorably as she.

Mordaunt became aware of his gaze.

"Do you regard me as a specimen, Doctor? Do you think I am mad, perverted?"

"I think you are troubled, beyond my ability to help."

He wanted to rise from the table and go, leave this flickering circle of candlelight; the mind's dark territories were not his province, and this was not perversion. But he was as firmly fixed an element of this triangle as either of the others, and he could not break the peculiar intimacy of this hour and its revelations.

The long, musician's fingers played idly with the walnut shells, as if there were no haste now, no need for reservation.

"My wife called me Pygmalion not long ago. Do you know the legend?"

Thackeray, repulsed and compelled, said, "I have forgotten."

"Ovid tells this story. There was a young sculptor in Cyprus... some say he was a king... whose experiences with women had so disillusioned him that he swore never to love another living being. So from the purest marble he fashioned his perfect companion… whom he named Galatea." His voice was slow, as though foundering in memory or poignant imagination. "He brought her jewels, and he dressed her in silks, and he told her all his hopes and his fears, and he kissed her, but her mouth was cold as stone, and for all his passion she would never be anything but stone to him." The fingers moved again, examining a fragment, replacing it. "He was obsessed, and close to madness, and one day in the temple of Venus he cried aloud to the goddess that he might be allowed to find a woman he could love as he loved Galatea— and the goddess heard his prayer, and granted it. When he embraced his beloved statue that night her mouth was warm. His creation, his work of art, had come to life." He looked up. "So you see I have my Galatea. I bred her. I made her. And only convention stands in my way."

They stood, as if by some unspoken accord. The evidence of pain was there, in the lower back; Thackeray noted that it had worsened in the evening's dampness. Kidney— spine— a rheumatic disorder— a legacy of war?

They observed one another with dispassion and utter clarity.

"I can offer you no reassurance. I can only say that my life has been riddled with scandal. I hesitate to do the same to hers."

And yet it was inevitable: so certain of its inevitability was Thackeray that he could no longer resist it. He measured the strength of his affection against the power of this opposition, and recognized the unsuitability of the match and the untenable nature of his position. He made his decision: it was easier than he had expected. His conscience had been inclining him in this direction since the outbreak of war.

He knew his way now. He was certain of Mordaunt's.

He said, "This course leads you only to tragedy. There can be no satisfaction for you in it."

"There is no satisfaction in my life. I am its victim, as much as you or she."

They shook hands. It was as close to understanding as they had ever ventured, and the presentiment of an inexorable fate was such that they sensed its finality.

On the last, halcyon morning of October, in a sun as warm as summer's, Mordaunt sat in the walled garden watching the light on the lichened pond. He had built it himself, and laid out these symmetrical beds of lavender and phlox, lilies and delphinium, after he had left the army: as a refuge for himself, as a supplication to Catherine, who had not then approved of it and who now never came here. In later years it had become the child Margaret's retreat, and a sanctuary for her play; and here on scented evenings he had brought his mistress, of whom he still dreamed so poignantly that he awoke crying out her name.

On the other side of the wall the girl, the child, the woman, Margaret, was singing, in the voice no longer shared with him, as she cut the last roses that clung to the sun-warmed brick. He closed his eyes, and the sunlight fell red across the lids, as it had on that May morning when he had sat with the heaviness of silk across his legs, offering it like the lover he was, and waiting for her to discover him.

> Perché tacer, perché?
> Perché temer, perché?

He dreamed of Italy, the windblown cypresses, the heat, the sharp profusion of colour, the squalor and vice of his youthful months there, redeemed by the glorious flowering of music, and allowed himself the fantasy of returning, of making love in a cool room on scented sheets, kissing the ruched, silken nipples, caressing the secret hair... and the slow, familiar current of the dream carried him, languid and irresistible as some drug, into depths of eroticism so intense that he opened his eyes, shaken, on the point of orgasm. He had committed the irreparable violation; the innocence and the delicacy of the dream were gone.

> Che pena, oh Dio! ch'affano!
> Che fiera crudeltà!
> What pain, oh God, what anxiety!
> What fierce torment....

"Oh God," he said aloud, "help me."

> Dite belle alme amanti,
> se v'è piacer più grato....

He took the clasp knife from his pocket and cut the last, crimson rose from the cane above his head.

She stopped singing when she heard his footsteps, and turned as though surprised, with a steely, resilient grace that brought his heart into his mouth. She wore a fraying waistcoat and skirt and a severe, almost masculine shirt. Her skin was luminous from the wind and sun, the grey eyes radiant, but it was a radiance of their colour alone: it was not for him.

He held out the rose, saying curtly, "I thought you might want this." She accepted it, unsmiling, and when her brown fingers closed around the stem he clasped them and lifted her hand to his lips. The scent of the sandalwood oil she had found among Catherine's things was heady, almost sickening; he released her wrist and turned away abruptly. He did not look at her; he did not dare, not knowing what she might see in his eyes, or he might read in hers.

Thackeray had departed, like a coward, he thought, with no word of explanation: perhaps he could not have borne her tears, if tears there would have been. A letter came from Portsmouth entreating him to tell Margaret the reason for his decision; Mordaunt kept the letter, locked in the drawer of his desk which held so many secrets, but he did not tell her.

In the middle of December he took her to Durham to buy her Christmas gifts. He saw all with the clarity of a man who knows that time does not favour him, and he tried throughout their four days there to establish himself as an individual, that he might be remembered and loved. They walked in the cathedral and saw Cuthbert's tomb, that chilly repository of the saint's well-travelled bones, and the splendidly carved altar screen with which the Nevilles, lords of Raby, had sought to purchase their easy passage to a medieval heaven, and the thistled Castell clock, spared by Cromwell's rampaging Scottish prisoners when they had devastated the cathedral after the battle of Dunbar. He spoke of Scotland, knowing that like most Englishwomen the Scots meant nothing to her; spoke of his service, of the army. They walked the cold stone nave, and his breath faded in the frigid air, and she nodded politely, her mind elsewhere or purposely closed to him, and he ached with frustration and hopelessness, knowing that time afforded him no second chance.

He had lost her without possessing her: he would never know her, as surely as she would never know him.

He bought her gifts, a heavily caped riding cloak, a pair of leather gauntlets lined with fur; he went alone to a goldsmith and, anguished and irresolute, left without buying anything; he walked up the steep cobbles of Silver Street with the first hard flakes of snow cutting his face, and stared at the jostling, passing scarlet of the newly formed 68th, recruiting in the grey towns of the north where it had been raised.

On the night before their return to Evesham they sat in the assembly room of the Red Lion in the North Bailey, where he often went to hear music after attending horse fairs in Old Elvet, and listened to a selection of Telemann's violin concertos. He could comfort himself only with the knowledge that she was as sensitive to the beauty of what she heard as he was himself: perhaps in the future she would remember it had been he who had given her that sensibility.

Only on the return did she show any animation: she enjoyed the cold and the hours in the saddle. It was a grey, sharp morning and the air scraped his lungs like surgeon's instruments. He had had little sleep, and his back and his thigh were aching: he rode the twenty-eight miles in an acute depression, aware of his age, and the pressure of time, and the unbridgeable gap between them.

On Christmas morning she gave him a volume of Donne's poetry bound in a buff-coloured kid, which he would later read until it rotted in a tropical humidity. He gave her a pair of earrings, which he thought Chinese, and a gold watch with a mother of pearl face and her name and the date engraved inside the guard, and in the evening he drank himself into insensibility. On the last night of the old year he sent her to the vicarage to play whist, telling her not to disturb him on her return. From eight until ten he read the letters from the locked drawer, with their memories and their entreaties and their threats, then he wrote out lists of equipment he would need, horse furnishings and personal accoutrements, and made notes on their acquisition. He broke the seal on his will and read it through, and eventually resealed it. At ten o'clock he locked the desk and sat down with Jane Neville's last letter in his pocket and a full bottle of brandy on the table. It was half empty at midnight, and he heard the strokes of the old year die in the hall: the year 1762 had come, and in eleven days he would be forty-five. A man without heirs, whose memories of marriage were a bitter wasteland; a man without comrades or intimates, or hope, more than halfway on his progress toward death.

He did not attempt to rise when she came in; he could not. She had seen him drink, but he had never before been drunk in her presence, and her distaste was evident. She wore a crimson silk dress, and her cheek and the curve of her breast were like the petals of a Florentine iris, the pallor veined with blue; she had lined her eyes with burnt cork and her skin was scented with patchouli. The garnets in her ears were Catherine's.

"I don't like those," he said. "Why do you wear them? Why don't you wear the ones I gave you?" And he took her arms and drew her down beside him, until she was on her knees and the crimson silk spilled across his feet like a widening pool of blood, and he slipped his hand through her hair, removing first one earring and then the other. He heard her tentative, *please, no,* and covered her lips with his fingers, saying, "Don't speak— don't speak." He found the pins and removed those too, taking her hair down until it fell in a dark cloud around the strained white oval of her face, and he forced her head down against his thigh with a gentle, inexorable pressure. She lay quiescent under his hand, and he stroked her hair with restraint and sensuality, although he felt her trembling.

When he woke in the sour greyness of morning he found the earrings and the bottle on the table beside him. Only a single black hair caught in the setting of one of the garnets reminded him of what had happened.

231

In the first week of the new year Spain declared war on England; and he knew that the time had come.

At three in the afternoon London was dark with fog, and with the coming night; lamps burned here and there like lights in the underworld, and all things were distorted and monstrous. It might have been the last hour of the last day of the world, with some apocalypse imminent: the fog stung his eyes and filled his lungs with a sulphurous stench, and the faceless, silent passers-by might have been damned souls in Dante's rings of hell. He walked in the gloom, as blindly and as damned as they, like a man reliving the course of a long suppressed nightmare, until he found the street.

He remembered the house, although he had not seen it for nearly nineteen years. One of eight in a crescent, yellow brick with white stonework, and an elaborate lantern suspended over the entrance. There were glass panels on either side of the door, and they and the fanlight illuminated the stone step and the pavement where he stood.

He let fall the knocker, a Medusa's head. It had begun to rain, and the air, which had been cold, seemed milder. He stood braced as though for some assault, quelling a primitive fear. The door opened and a footman a third of his age stood with his hand on the jamb, wearing the black livery he remembered.

He waited, dripping on the Turkish carpet by the door, while the footman made enquiries. The response was negative. He drew the worn leather case from his pocket and proffered his card, aware of his presumption, his arrogance in supposing that the name engraved there still carried its powerful cachet.

"Be so kind as to ask again. You may discover he has just come in."

The card was borne away on a salver, up the stairs. He resisted the urge to look at his watch, but an intolerable amount of time seemed to pass. The silence was absolute, as it had always been in this house; even the appointments and the furnishings seemed barely changed. The hall was still papered in yellow silk; two orchids in exotic bloom spilled from a pair of terracotta Turks' heads on pillars, flanking the marble table where he had once laid his hat and gloves; the wall behind was hung entirely with mirrored glass, reflecting the golden silk and the carpeted stairs and a chinoiserie screen at their head.

He half turned, determined to go. There was movement at the top of the stairs and he looked up: an Abyssinian cat gazed at him with expressionless, lamp-like eyes and vanished. The footman reappeared.

"If it would please you to wait within, sir. The Colonel will receive you directly."

His cloak, studded with moisture and spattered from the journey, his hat and the heavy riding gloves within which his hands were sweating coldly were taken from him; he was not asked to remove his sword and he did not offer it. He was conducted to another white-panelled door, which was opened. He knew where it led, and he wondered what malice or insensitivity had directed that their first encounter in fifteen years should take place here.

It had changed unrecognizably: even the furniture had been replaced, for which he was grateful. He stood in the middle of the room with his hands behind his back and the unaccustomed weight of the sword on his hip: perhaps ten minutes passed. Then the door opened and the footman said, "If you will follow me, sir."

He followed the stiff, slender back up the stairs, his brain ice-clear, the composure of battle which had always come to him and would defend him now. Another door; he was announced. In a corner of the small, beautifully appointed room, a private sitting room, stood a tall bamboo cage with two small dull green birds, singing melodiously, and at the window with his back to the room, Bancroft.

The footman bowed and left them; the door closed. He did not turn, and Mordaunt did not speak. After a moment he said, "Forgive me. I do not dare to look at you."

"It is not the past which concerns me now. It is the present."

"That is not true, and you know it as well as I." Then he did turn, almost with effort: the brilliant eyes had lost none of their intensity. He could not imagine what they saw in him, what changes, what disintegration.

Bancroft said, "The years have been kind to you."

"I am not a young man now."

"Did you think it was your youth I loved?"

The afternoon had become fully dark; the birds had ceased singing in their cage. Bancroft seated himself, as though defensively, behind the inlaid desk.

"Please sit."

He sat, taking the weight of scabbard and hilt on his thigh. His back was aching, and this interview, barely begun, had exhausted him. But it was not unfamiliar; this was a conversation well known to him, and merely resumed after fifteen years of silence.

Bancroft said, "Why have you come?"

He had aged; he was now fifty-two or three, and the years had refined his features, sculpting the elegant bones; the close-cropped hair, which had been whitening in Scotland, was completely so. He was coatless, his waistcoat and breeches an indeterminate buff; his attire bore no marks of rank.

"Are you still a serving officer?"

"I command a line regiment, which is shortly to embark for the Havana. Why do you ask?"

"I wish to purchase a commission."

"Is this my punishment, after all these years? That you come to me?"

There was silence. The fingers of his left hand followed the contours of an ivory box on the desk: he seemed shaken, very much more so than when he had turned from the window. Without looking up he said, "You have an estate. You have commitments. You have... a daughter, I believe? You have a wife. What inspires you to this? What possesses you?"

"My affairs have reached a state at which it is no longer possible for me to remain in England."

"Are you in debt?"

"I am in love. I love where I should not love... does that signify to you? You once said as much to me."

Bancroft said coldly, "If you wish to kill yourself solicit the Hanoverians. It served my purpose near enough when it was politic for me to leave England." He pushed the box away. "For God's sake, what brought you to me with this? Have we not suffered enough, you and I, because of one another?"

"Perhaps this is the final stage in the process. There seems a justice in it."

"I have served out my sentence, believe me."

"So have I. But not enough, it seems." Then he said, "I am in hell. Out of pity, release me."

He remembered the gentleness of which Bancroft was capable: he received it now.

"Is there no possibility—"

"No."

"Is she married?"

"She is my daughter."

He closed his eyes and opened them, and before Bancroft could speak he said harshly, "For Christ's sake spare me your sentiments. It is incest in her eyes and mine. That is all that matters."

He sat staring at the sword knot where it lay against his thigh: when the glass came into the sphere of his vision he took it. Bancroft made no attempt to touch him, even to lay a hand upon his shoulder. He drank without tasting it, as he had at the hunt ball, and other times thereafter, to obliterate memory and guilt, to deaden all sensation. If Bancroft noticed he gave no sign, but the glass was not refilled.

"Do you still play?"

"Yes. It is not something I believe I can give up."

"And why should you?" Silence. "And do you not compose?"

"Perhaps you are remembering some one else."

234

"I have never in my life confused my memories of you with some one else."

He laid his hand flat on the sword knot, conscious of the dampness of his palm; the eczema of Scotland had recently returned and the fingers were cracked and painful. The dread, the sensation of inexorable pressure began to possess him: it had always been so in Bancroft's presence, and the years had not armoured him against it.

Bancroft said, turning the stem of his glass, "Occasionally I see your wife. She does not see me, or… appear to see me, if you will." A pause; perhaps he was judging the moment. "She has a lover. You knew."

"Yes."

"An affair of long standing, I believe."

"I do not care to discuss it," and Bancroft said with perfect grace, "Of course. Forgive me."

Some time later he looked up and found that piercing gaze still on him. Bancroft said, "Are you very unhappy?"

"Yes. And you?"

"In the main I am content. There is neither great grief nor great hope in anything." Then, with that same grace and simplicity, "Only occasionally, when I was with you, I glimpsed heaven… as it were, in passing."

He drew out his watch, opened the guard.

"Will you eat with me? I do not keep the town's hours."

Go away and don't look at me…. A watch taken into safekeeping, and held on the banks of the River Ness, a watch engraved with the name of an unknown boy and an inscription of passionate eroticism.

I would have died for you a hundred times— why can you not love me?

He did not remember what they ate, nor the conversation, only that there were candles alight on a round table laid for two, although Bancroft had not at any time in his presence directed that this be done, and that the meat, when it was served to him, was already neatly cut; he found it strangely distressing to watch the handless right arm at rest. At the end of the meal Bancroft said, "I am going out to hear music. Will you go with me?"

He protested; his protestations had never signified. He was once more carried, unresisting, with the tide.

It was twenty or so minutes' walk: the night was milder, most of the fog had lifted. They walked mainly in silence, through dark streets and past houses under construction, along the edge of a field hazed with mist and into Hanover Square: they had unconsciously fallen into step, as naturally as in the streets of Bruges and Ghent, and London on a night like this; the portico of the church loomed up. The interior was dimly lit and cold, the ceiling beautifully moulded in gilt and white; the altar was pillared, before a wall of stained glass. It was quite silent, the silence of anticipation; the several men and women already seated did not turn when they came in.

He walked up the aisle behind Bancroft, and saw his almost imperceptible genuflection: he himself stood stiffly and the moment was quickly over. They sat without speaking, and Bach's Toccata in C Major rose gloriously from the organ: steeped in the poisoned river of his own thoughts, he heard almost none of it. Bancroft's eyes were closed, his profile calm, distant, serene, as though he had found in this place and in these practises the peace he had sought in the dangerous, scented mysteries of the Catholic church, and in opiates, and in promiscuity.

He said, out of disgust and an inexplicable sense of betrayal, "Do you bring your other friends here?"

Bancroft looked directly at him, and for a blinding instant he saw again in the dimness the man of nineteen years ago, in the subdued light of Covent Garden: the gracious, classical face, the brilliant, calm grey eyes.

"No. But you have been here many times with me in spirit."

Time passed. The music ended. Bancroft said, "I generally go up and have a word with them. Will you come?" And when he refused Bancroft went alone to the organist, the choirmaster and the musicians: they appeared to know him well, and their pleasure at his attendance was obvious. They all shook hands, Bancroft spoke, and the choirmaster, looking toward Mordaunt, bowed. Bancroft rejoined him, and they left the church without speaking: it was raining lightly, and the mist had gone except around the lamps of carriages waiting for the women who were still inside. There were no bells; he could not determine what time it was; the night seemed to have no hours, it was like the river of his thoughts, without beginning or end.

They stood beneath the portico and watched the light flash on the spokes of the carriage wheels.

"You enjoyed it?"

"Very much so."

"I thought you would. I should have been disappointed otherwise."

"You once said you had learned to expect nothing of me— thus you were never disappointed."

The heavy doors of the church closed, and the bolts scraped into place.

"Where shall I send to you?" It was assumed, with delicacy, that he was not staying with Catherine.

"The George. Holborn."

Bancroft said, staring into the rain, "I consider your behaviour irresponsible."

"If you knew my situation you would not say so."

"I do know. By my God, I know. The army is not an escape. You should know that better than any one." Then, "I shall send to you when I can."

236

"I would be grateful."

"I don't want your gratitude. Only your forgiveness."

The rain fell, and in Conduit Street a linkboy and a party of walkers passed, voices carrying in the stillness. Bancroft said abruptly, "If you make haste you can catch them up. They go toward Bond Street."

"I'll walk a while. I have no fear of the dark."

"I shall say good-night to you then." He descended the steep steps to the road, the rain already glittering on his shoulder capes, an upright, frail, solitary figure turning back toward the darkness. The strange, disturbing sensation returned, and Mordaunt said, "Do you not take a chair? Your way is darker than mine."

Bancroft glanced over his shoulder and smiled ironically.

"Your solicitude touches me. I walked this road many times alone in the years when you wished me dead." And, drawing his sword, he walked into the mild night, the naked blade held casually in his left hand. He did not look back.

He received Bancroft's summons on the fourth of February, a date with its own significance, and was ushered once more into the sitting room with the chinoiserie silk on the walls and the dull green birds in their cage. Bancroft said, without preamble, "A colonelcy will cost you two thousand guineas. The transaction was completed in your name."

It lay on the inlaid desk between them, heavy parchment sealed with red.

"You embark in April. And I do not envy you the charge of this regiment."

In the corner the dull green birds were singing.

"What are those?"

"Charming, ain't they? They are from the Canaries."

"At least they sing in their captivity."

Bancroft said sharply, "For God's sake, Achill, reconsider this."

But he was holding it now, reading it: he was committed, and thereby freed. He said, "How strange that it should be today. On this day when I was fifteen years old I joined my first regiment. And now, a half-colonel. The Captain-General would be pleased— his son no longer disgraces him."

Bancroft wrote and pushed a slip of paper toward him. The scrawled, left-handed script had not improved with the passing of time.

"My tailor. You need not use my name."

There was another silence, of finality.

"I did not take you idly to Handel's church. I took a night from you, in the past... it was my poor attempt to give it back to you."

"I know."

"Did you recognize it as such, then?"

"No. Understanding came late to me, like most things."

Bancroft came around the desk, hesitated, and offered his hand. Mordaunt took it: the gesture was a caress which he did not now find offensive, only deeply saddening. "Good-bye." There was a pause, and an unflinching gaze, the emotion unashamedly revealed. "My dear Achill."

They would not meet again, and there would be no communication: death in the field was more likely, and interment in a foreign grave. But the intense, calm finality marked an end: there was nothing now, no revulsion, no sexual dread. There was no peace but there was an absence of bitterness, and of outrage: perhaps in this end there was also a beginning.

He said, "Good-bye, Aeneas," and did not see the gratitude in Bancroft's eyes.

"For God's sake, do yourself no harm."

He bowed and left; and the prevailing tide bore them, ever on.

Within three weeks he had been supplied with new uniforms, interviewed his subordinates and the regimental agent and made himself known to the men. He now understood Bancroft's comment. He had taken upon himself the charge of a sullen and depleted regiment perpetually on the brink of mutiny, which he was expected to bring up to strength before its embarkation in April. He authorized the distribution of bounties and recruiting handbills, paid the regiment's outstanding debts, and rode north to settle his affairs.

In his absence it had snowed, and the drifts lay along his route; in the frozen ruts the ice, like glass, cracked with every step. Also in his absence Martinique, St. Lucia, Grenada, all French possessions in the Caribbean, had been captured by Rodney and Monckton, and the German war, which was costing millions to continue, had lost its popularity; with the withdrawal of Russia under the leadership of the Tsar, Peter, peace seemed possible. A powerful sense of anticlimax and futility possessed him.

In his absence, too, a letter had come for me. It was from the captain of His Britannic Majesty's Ship *Telemachus* in the Caribbean, and it had been directed to me because my name had been found among the papers of the surgeon on board, who was Christopher Thackeray.

It had travelled remarkably quickly, for the distance. Only six weeks had passed since death had revealed to him its last great mystery.

***

There is no colour in the monochrome memory offers me, save the red brick walls of the kitchen garden, starkly overlaid by the espaliered branches of fruit trees which had nourished me for sixteen years. There were degrees of pallor: the dirty white cat I was stroking, the whiteness of my bare hands, the snow on the bleached straw protecting root vegetables in the ground. And degrees of darkness: in the wet, blackened foliage of all else killed by the bitter frosts, the grey light of February, my clothing and the shapeless garb of the gardener beside me, digging in the mud and offering me icy turnips. My fingers were numb, and my feet in leather boots caked with mud: I was not accustomed to this work, but it had afforded occupation during those weeks when inactivity and introspection had been unbearable.

I had had one letter from him in London, telling me that his business there was almost concluded, although I knew neither the nature of that business nor the date of his return. I dreaded it... I had loved him, but the night he had caressed me I had been sick with revulsion and fear.

I could give it no name, and I could not escape it— where was I to go? To Catherine, to whom all debauchery seemed second nature? To Anne in that decaying house, who would not believe me, much less offer me protection?

The white cat had gone. The sky was flat grey; the air tasted of snow. Where no colour had been was a brilliant splash of scarlet. Some one was standing there.

"Who is that man?" and the gardener hauled himself up and peered across the snow.

"Tha father, lass."

I remember that my feet and my skirt, caked with mud, seemed too heavy to move. That scarlet, so shocking in brilliance and implication, changed its position and approached, and I wanted to run, like a child in a dream before some oncoming monster. But I could not run, I could only wait, with a scalding rush of tears as it resolved itself into weathered bones and those clear, greyish eyes above an unfamiliar uniform.

In retrospect, I recognize its similarity to the uniform of the last regiment in which he had served, and how that similarity must have haunted him: scarlet coat and breeches, dark blue facings laced with gold in a zigzag pattern, crimson silk net sash and gold aiguillette on the right shoulder, and the old, heavy sword, a horseman's sword curved like a dragoon's sabre, with a new knot of crimson and gold on its half-basket hilt. But then I saw only with the shocked sensibility of a child, when what he wanted was the understanding of maturity. In this, I failed him.

He pried my fingers from the handle of the basket and set it down violently in the straw; I remembered then that officers must never carry burdens, nor be seen to perform manual labour while wearing uniform.

"Come into the house."

I followed him up the path, listening to his booted feet in the straw and the sound of his spurs. He had promised to build me a glasshouse in this sheltered garden; maybe as he walked he recalled it, or perhaps he had been driven to such a point that he no longer cared.

He would not see these pear trees bloom, which he had grafted and had taught me to graft. Not this year: perhaps he would never see them again.

In the house the atmosphere was vibrant with tension, as though the extremity of his action had shocked the household. His baggage lay where he had left it and he shouted for some one to come and take it.

To me he said, "Go and change your clothes. I don't expect to come home and find you out in the muck like a skivvy."

Still numbed, I hesitated.

"Go and do it! I want a bath— I'm too damned cold to talk to you now."

It was six in the evening before I saw him again.

He was in the drawing room, standing beneath that luminous portrait of Catherine, whose beauty it seemed no accumulation of smoke could diminish. He was drinking, and he was not in uniform.

"As it so obviously offends you," he said.

Had he told her yet? Had he told her before me?

"I have taken the colonelcy of the Eighth regiment of foot. At the end of April it embarks for the Havana, or so I have been informed."

I said nothing.

"I have made provision for you. You will live with Catherine, and the estate will remain in the care of Vennor, who will manage my affairs— our affairs— until I return."

Had he told her *why*?

I said, "Christopher Thackeray went to sea. Did you know?"

"Yes."

"Why didn't you tell me?"

"I thought the attachment unsuitable. I was glad to see it ended."

"He's dead now. Are you glad of that, too?"

He said acidly, "*I* may be dead by midsummer. Will you shed any tears for me?" and I heard that voice which was mine and not mine break on the edge of hysteria.

"Then why are you going?"

"I am a soldier. My duty is to the army."

"Your duty is to me!"

"Oh, no. I've paid my debt to you."

Some one opened the door, hesitated with a coal scuttle, and retreated.

"I should like to go now, please."

He did not prevent me. I walked out with my head up and my spine straight, as I had been taught, and reached my room, where I lay shivering and crying with my face buried in the skirts of the doll Catherine had abandoned, as she abandoned all things, praying the darkness would consume me before he came to find me: praying, for the first time, that I might die, and never hear what he had been about to say.

The library was almost dark. He was sitting in the leather chair he favoured; there was a full bottle of brandy on the table beside it, and beside mine the coffee and the spirit lamp. He said without looking at me, "Sit down," and then, "Sit down, for God's sake. Am I so repugnant to you?"

I sat. He drank nothing; neither did I, and the spirit lamp burned lower with its blue, flickering flame. Eventually he said, "You know that life, for us, cannot continue on its present course."

He sat at an angle to me in the dimness, the firelight touching his face; in the silence I heard the hissing of the lamp. A terrible sense of dread and entrapment overcame me, and I closed my eyes.

"You know the nature of my feeling for you."

And how pitiful my attempts to ward it off: stammering and choking, filled with a sensation of deathly cold.

"I must therefore protect you, as I have always done, and remove myself. I have been told that the army is not an escape, but it is the only possibility which presents itself to me."

The lamp was still burning with its small, demonic hiss: I thought that if he spoke again I would strike it to the floor. He did not move but I thought he would touch me: something in his manner suggested it, the terrible bleakness in his face.

"You regard it as incest. It is not."

Oh God... help me....

"I am not your father. You are not my child."

In my mind, I screamed; I saw my arm lash out and hit the spirit lamp; I saw the explosion of flames on the carpet ... anything, anything to stop this. In reality, I sat and watched the tiny, burning jet, and all the dark, unanswerable questions in my memory unfolded and were answered, and the room was silent and, despite the fire's heat, cold; and the world, which had been inviolable, had been destroyed.

"So contained," he said, "with so many tears to shed for Thackeray. Have you nothing for me? Not even contempt? Never mind... I have tears for both of us. God knows I've shed enough."

Then he leaned forward, as though my inability to speak goaded him unbearably.

"Say something, for Christ's sake. Why must you always be this way, like the basilisk, all eyes?"

Or the cuckoo in the nest? There were tears on my face, I felt them, but there was no pity and, now, no horror. "Who am I, then? Some bastard fed on lies?"

"You know enough: for God's sake leave it. I wish I'd never told you."

"I want the truth."

Whatever had bound us before this moment there was nothing now, only an abyss into which had fallen all the shattered wreckage of my childhood: all the joy, all the memories, all the sure knowledge of love.

"What is my name?"

"Your Christian name is Margaret."

"So that alone is true, of all the lies."

"My life is full of lies, and things done for convenience's sake, and things done for convention's sake, and things done and endured out of duty. My life is full of subterfuge, and pretense, and by God I pay for it— but the love I gave you when you came into this house was that of a father and a protector, and that was no lie and no deception."

Then he said with immense bitterness, "Do you think I wanted this to happen, that I would willingly inflict on you the very thing that made my own life hell?"

There were candles burning on his desk. I saw him move into their light, open a compartment and remove the key.

"You think you are the only who has ever been betrayed and wronged... my God, how innocent you are."

It held letters. He took out several.

"Read those. Then tell me how you suffer."

Letters from Catherine, from Jane, from Thackeray, unsigned letters in an angular, back-handed script: fragments, almost illegible and yet of searing frankness, stood out like ink on a burning page. Eroticism, abasement, accusation. And lines in the style of *The Art of Love*, in a Latin of such powerful clarity that their meaning was explicit.

I closed the page and my mind: it was not for me to read.

He was sitting at the desk with a broken paper knife, turning the pieces slowly: the condition of his hands had worsened, so that the skin appeared to have been burned.

"Did you understand what you were reading? Did you understand its significance?"

"I... don't know."

"You should know. You brought me one of those letters from London."

Colonel... madam.... Two voices with that deadly edge, and a woman refusing to look into the eyes of her rival; a woman flaunting, like a victor, a sexuality which had never been rejected.

"So you see, you have nothing to teach me on the subject— I learned all its refinements years ago. Although it seems appropriate to me now that I should find myself in the same pathetic role of unrequited lover."

The blade flashed and was still, and was turned again: there was a brief silence.

"Because of the conditions in which we found ourselves... and the difficulties attendant upon our relationship... Mr. Bancroft and I suffered extremely, as a result of which our association became unendurable, and I struck him, which is a grievous offense. I was ... unlawfully punished. Three days later we proceeded to Fort Augustus, where as a consequence the regiment was found to be in a state of mutiny. A court-martial was convened, and Mr. Bancroft was found guilty. He was broke. If it had not been for his family's considerable interest with government, he would have been sentenced to death." Then, seeing that I did not understand, "His offense was criminal. It has no significance now, except that it occured in the place where you were born."

One of the candles on his desk was guttering. He snuffed it with his fingers.

"Am I... a Scot?" He leaned back in the chair, turning the broken paper knife. "Who are my people?"

"Your father was a non-Jurant clergyman, and a fugitive. I had orders to arrest him."

"Is he alive?"

"I don't know."

"And my mother?"

"Your mother is dead."

"How do you know?"

"I may owe you explanations, but not the privacy of my soul. Grant me that much dignity."

A clock was striking. In this endless night there were still, somewhere, measures of time.

Eventually I said, "How did I come to be here?" as though we were discussing some casual occurence, and he said, "You were brought. By a camp follower, whom I paid. Are you satisfied, or must I continue with this sorry catalogue?"

"Why did you have me brought here?"

"Your life is a mote of dust, and of as much consequence to an army. In the destruction of my trade, I felt an obligation… which fate has now twisted to punish me further." He did not look at me. "Sometimes I think you are the only thing that holds me to sanity."

Then he said, "I expect nothing of you, only that you not hate me as I hated him for so many years. I am its victim, as much as you. All I ask is your forgiveness."

And I gave nothing. I could not speak, and to the end of my life I will see him there, one candle guttering on the desk amid the surrounding darkness, waiting for the cheap and easy words of forgiveness which would not come. I could not give him even that.

IV

The snow fell, changing into rain; time, like a river, gathered itself into a flood, and every action was touched with finality.

He had no reason to love these months: in the calendar of his memory they were coloured by the recollection of other springs, the dismal Marches upon service and in Scotland, the interlude at Bancroft's house on the night of "Messiah", the day with the shadow of a cold rain on the windows when Harlesdon's letter had provoked the birth of his last legitimate child; Catherine's demand for a separation, and the night he had taken Jane Neville's gift of virginity for his own comfort and satisfaction.

And April, the seed bed of all obsessions: his first meeting with Bancroft on Blackheath Common in 1742, the Wednesday night in Inverness following Culloden, the stench of corruption and the knowledge of his own lust in that dark house in Westmorland.

Oh God, what matchless irony, that you twist all these threads over the warp and weft of years, and the pattern remains the same.

He walked and rode the estate alone, dispensing reassurances until his hands and his emotions were equally wrung, and the depth of his tenants' affection for him had humbled and astonished him. He spent hours with his horses, for he would subject none of them to the sea crossing and the rigours of the campaign that lay ahead, until the morning when his favourite, the twenty year old Irish stallion Cormac, ceased to eat and refused to rise from the straw in his loose box. He sat with him until he died, and cried in the privacy of the box, as he had not in the course of farewells to men and women he had known since childhood. No one disturbed him.

Of his forty-five years some sixteen had been spent in absence, and the house was full of haunting reminders that time would bear him as finally and effortlessly away as all Evesham's other heirs and inhabitants. His father, unloved and unloving; the gay Irish mother of whom he cherished only a handful of childish recollections; his brother, in whose painted face he sometimes saw his own; the portrait of himself as a youthful captain, grave and clear-eyed, wearing the deep yellow facings of the Fifteenth foot; the portrait of the girl Margaret, rendered as pallid as a porcelain doll by the hand of Reynolds; and the tantalising beauty of the young Catherine as he had seen her at the age of seventeen: all ghosts, all shadows, and if he should die upon service, only a few scattered mementoes would mark his brief tenure.

He had never been an acquisitive man, the habit of the transient army life died too hard, and what few possessions he did not want to part with were easily assembled. He sorted his books and inscribed some, putting them aside to be given away: he had several conversations with the phlegmatic Vennor concerning the estate, and an impassioned confrontation with his valet of many years, the Italian Giacomo, who had married one of the housemaids and was now determined to accompany him. It was an exchange that began in English and ascended into Italian, rising in pitch and desperation until they were shouting at one another. He presented arguments and they were defeated; he spoke of responsibility and duty and had them flung back at him; he prophesied privation, heat, discomfort and the likelihood of fever, but his evocation of garrison life in the Caribbean held no terrors for a Neapolitan. At length he was exhausted, and the Frenchwoman Corneul's observation that no man was a hero to his valet had never seemed more true. The man who had known his scars and his drunkenness, his foul temper and, occasionally, his violence, would not be left behind like so much furniture, and such devotion shamed him— now he bore the responsibility for another shattered marriage on his conscience.

There was no need to state the reason for his departure. The servants knew. They had known of his adultery and Catherine's, and that the child he had raised from infancy was not the issue of his marriage; perhaps they knew the changed nature of that relationship. He felt no compulsion to explain or excuse it.

Or to conceal it. He loved. He was not loved in return, and he disciplined himself to anticipate nothing and, almost, to desire nothing: the intensity of an unwanted passion had marred his own life, and he was determined to subject no one else to its pressure. But he loved, with passion and with a hungry, unsated sexuality which he could not allow himself to demonstrate, and even the most casual, familial touch was now denied him. By his revelation he had gained only a measure of inner peace, that she knew, in the event of his death. As a lover he had possessed nothing and hazarded all, and had lost everything.

He remained aloof, allowing her time to think and to accept, to decide upon her course of action as the days carried him ever more swiftly toward his own. He walked the grounds in the rain down to the river and stood looking up at the house, as he had seen it in the nightmare-riddled sleep of the Scottish summer, a faceless Catherine and a lawn golden with narcissi... those at his feet were still in bud and would not open, even if he should take them into the house, an impermissible token from an unwanted lover.

He knelt after a moment, with the sound of the river and the softer sound of the rain in his ears, and pulled a dozen or so, and walked slowly to the house carrying them. He was a stranger now in that blue and white room close to his, and he did not presume to take them there: he went instead to the small bare room where Jane Neville had lived, and on which narrow bed, in the twilight of summer evenings, he had taken her. It held nothing of her in its sterile neglect, no crumbling rose petal, no fallen hair, no forgotten thread from any gown, no scent of her, no remnant, only the pale, patterned walls and the counterpane, and the grey light and the sound of the rain.

You must come and play for me some time, Miss Neville. Will tomorrow evening suit?

Very well, sir... You must not expect great things of me. I have not your gift.

I have not the gift you imagine, he had said, and gone out and closed the door.

He sat on the bed in his wet clothing, holding the wet, greenish buds. Stillborn also, and incapable of blooming: they seemed fitting tribute to a love which could not come to consummation, and this room was a fitting place to leave them, where they could die in secrecy.

He left them on the pillow, where he had buried his face in the fragrance of her hair, and felt the resistance and the yielding of a body as yet too virginal to have become accustomed to so intimate an assault. Here at least, he had been received with joy: here, at least, he had loved her.

We sat in the church of St. Mary and St. Edmund, facing the altar and the carved chancel screen, where the small Saxon windows in their timber frames had admitted this bluish morning light since thirty years before the Norman conquest.

He said, "If I should die, have that thing taken down. Its hypocrisy is more than I can stomach."

On the west wall the cold light illuminated the lettering of the memorial he had erected to his brother, *In Life esteem'd, in Death lament'd.*

"Was he not so admirable, then?"

"Ask his wife. She was only your age on their wedding night when he raped and buggered her."

No emotion in his voice; his profile was implacably calm.

"I married her when he was dead. So you see what a talent I have for blighting whatever love offers to me."

Then he gazed up at the vaulted ceiling, and I saw the faint cloud of his breath.

" 'And God shall wipe away all tears from their eyes; and there shall be no more death, nor sorrow, nor crying, neither shall there be any more pain: for the former things are passed away.' I should like that engraved on my memorial, with my rank. And I do not wish to be remembered as the admirable husband."

If it was his intention to inflict suffering on me for that which I had caused him he could not have chosen a better method. I knew the hell Catherine would make of my life once his protection was withdrawn, and that I could not now dissuade him from leaving me except by some desperate act, the nature of which I could not bring myself to contemplate. The only escape was suicide, and I had considered it.

"Should you wish to marry in my absence, I advise you to seek the protection of a marriage contract. You are an heiress, and upon marriage your property becomes, irrevocably, the property of your husband. If you should marry unwisely you would have no other recourse under the law."

"I have no... desire... to marry... any one."

"One does not always choose the moment," he said. "I sometimes wonder if one chooses anything in this life. It hardly seems so to me."

Another silence. From the flagstones worn to a silken finish by centuries of feet, the cold of ancient churches rose and settled in my bones. He seemed impervious to it, and disinclined to talk, so I huddled, shivering, with my hands in the sleeves of my riding coat, waiting for him to speak or move, and signal the end of this ordeal. The corpses buried beneath the aisle shed their sweet, putrescent scent; the cold northern light fell across the altar cloth and the wall where in an unknown period the hand of the faithful had crudely scratched marks I had seen many times: the letters *I K*, for Jesus Christ, surmounted by a cross.

Eventually he said, "The place where you were born is called Glen Sian. It is some twenty miles from Fort Augustus. The landowner was a man named Stirling, a Franco-Scot. I think it entirely possible that he may be dead now. I saw some of the treatment awaiting him."

"Why do you tell me this?"

"I thought it as well that you should know. I am a soldier. Soldiers live on borrowed time."

I kicked the first thing that came into contact with my boot, the pew before me: if he had thought me incapable of hysteria he saw now that he had misjudged me. I felt my wrists taken; it was the first time he had touched me since that night.

"Behave yourself, here of all places, and listen to what I say. There is no more time— there is *no more time.*"

I pulled my wrists away. His hands were on my shoulders now, but I could not look at him.

"I have no choice. Would you see me damned in the eyes of the world? What should I say to the men and women who know us— after sixteen years, this is not my daughter but my mistress, whom I have bred up for my pleasure? In God's name, you are not naïve. I have no love for society and I've carried scandal on my back for years, but drag you down to the level of a common whore I will not do."

I was sobbing, the dreadful incoherence of grief.

"No one... will know."

"No one will know what?"

"If I...."

"Is that what you think I want? Do you think that would make me stay?"

"I can't bear it— I can't bear it—"

"I don't want your sacrifice. I know that dark road too well." He drew something from his pocket. "Dry your eyes." Even I could not fail to hear the ironic coolness. "At least you have God's promise that all suffering has its limits."

There was a sound behind us. Some one was coming in.

"Go out the other door," he said.

I stumbled blindly toward the altar and the seldom-used door near it, fighting the stiffness of the rusted bolt, wrenching the door open to the windswept churchyard, conscious that even now he would protect me, and shield me from the curious and the insensitive.

He had risen, and he stood for a moment in that ancient light as the others, the intruders, entered the church, with his hand resting on the cold wood of the pew and the bones of his ancestors beneath his feet: then I saw him incline his head briefly toward the altar before he turned his back on it, and on all former things.

Like many final evenings, his was disjointed and dissatisfying: in spirit he had already left this house, and he could find recreation in nothing.

He was restless and in pain: the injuries of Dettingen, always vulnerable to weather, had awakened as if to remind him of the price of service, and he thought of sleep, or a hot bath and a massage at the experienced hands of his valet. But the Italian was spending these last hours with his wife, and no other servant saw his body; the privacy of its scars was closely guarded.

He read, but the favourite books were already among his baggage: he sat at the harpsichord and touched the keys, but the condition of his hands and the thickly scarred wrist made even that difficult. The heat of the Indies might lessen such discomfort... it offered, much more certainly, the promise of fever and summary death.

Then he read to me from Pepys for a time, and there was sporadic conversation: the finality of this night oppressed the household and there was no sound but the fire and the rain, and the hours striking inexorably. I refused to leave him, and although he said, "This is not sensible," he did not insist. There would be many other nights to sleep, and these hours in a house to which he might never return drained away like sand.

There is no more time.

So many things to say, so many truths to reveal, so many words of understanding or forgiveness to be exchanged, and like puppets in some stiff, unnatural play we could say none of them. The hours passed, carrying us from this place of safety into an unknown future, where if we should meet again we should meet without identity. We could no longer claim this past as father and daughter; we were not even nervous lovers, flinching at the sound of the clock; we were nothing, we had nothing. He was the man who could not love me, and I was even less; I was not even a woman who could accept that love.

So it passed, the last night of a life shared which had already been despoiled, the hours slowly dying in the guttering of the candles and the hands moving on the face of the clock. We played piquet, and my eyes burned with sleeplessness; the room became colder. He lit fresh candles and built up the fire; I had begun to shiver. We drank wine, and he put his coat over my shoulders and sat dealing in the candlelight in his shirtsleeves. We spoke of Catherine, briefly, and the arrangements for my removal to her house; his confrontation with her lay still in the future. I said it must necessarily involve me, and I had scant defense against her.

He said only, "I am well aware of her nature. I would not abandon you to that without appropriate safeguards."

I assumed they were financial, and I did not believe I could rely upon them for protection.

The clock struck three; the silence of the house was oppressive. He dealt with a gambler's confidence, the long fingers crimsoned with eczema, the strong bones of his face pronounced by fatigue and candlelight. I wondered how many nights had passed like this, dealing with luck and pasteboard, on the eve of battles, on the eve of leavetakings, with the hands of his dead comrades across the table. I had not known him as a soldier, or as a lover, or as a friend— if I had loved him it was without intimacy, and I had not known him in all the measure of time I had been given with him— I did not know him now. I did not know his thoughts or his secrets or his past or the nature or the depth of his emotions— the opportunity, once offered, would not come again. Now it was I who had been rejected, put aside, allowed to go, part of a life which must be left, and for him had already ended.

I had lost him, who had never known him, and the life and the secrets and the past had reclaimed the enigma they had created.

At twenty minutes to four we laid down our cards. I had lost, and I noted my debt to him as if it were any other evening. He had shuffled the cards and cut again as if for seats: now he laid out five cards and studied them. I asked what he was doing.

"Reading my fortune," he said.

"What does it say?"

"That I am unlucky in love." Then he turned up another card, and smiled. "Ah. An old friend, come to bid me farewell." He laid it on the table, the nine of diamonds. "They call this card the curse of Scotland."

It lay between us, a clean card in a pool of light, stained with invisible significance.

"Why do they call it that?"

"It was suggested that the nine diamonds represent the lozenges on the coat of arms of a nobleman responsible for atrocities against his fellow Scots. To me it simply serves as a reminder, a little accusation in every gambler's hand."

He took it and it was gone again, another card hidden in the deck. When I laid my hand on his wrist I felt the massive scars beneath his cuff.

"Did you know my mother?"

"I was the invader. It was not possible to know, or to be known."

Then, briefly, he closed his hand over mine.

"I have never told you that I loved you. I know I have no right." The fingers were cold, and held me with great strength. "I meant you no harm… and I am cursed in some manner, perhaps for the past, for things I did, for things of which I am guilty… perhaps we suffer in payment for sins I have committed. But I never meant this. I never intended—"

"I know."

"You don't know. This is all some retribution, some divine working through. And I, who would give you everything, have taken all away."

I released his hand and he withdrew it, as if some signal that I should not touch him had been given and received.

250

"I have nothing for you. Only half a dozen combs I bought in London—perhaps you won't want them now."

"I have nothing to give you."

"Give me your love. Give me your forgiveness."

"I do forgive you."

I unwrapped the combs, exquisitely carved in tortoiseshell and mother of pearl, sitting on the couch with his coat around my shoulders, and eventually I lay down, with the coat over me and my head resting on his thigh. And he spoke to me; I knew it was Donne, and I knew he was not reading; there had been no attempt to rekindle the fire and there was no light to read by.

> Let not thy divining heart
> Forethink me any ill,
> Destiny may take thy part,
> And may thy fears fulfil;
> But thinke that wee
> Are but turned aside to sleepe;
> They who one another keepe
> Alive, ne'er parted bee.

His hand stroked my hair. I no longer wept, and against my closed eyes the darkness lightened.

> Had we but world enough, and time....

There is no more time.

The air still filled with the northern chill, the sound of birds, the year passing into spring, the night passing into day.

> When in disgrace with fortune and men's eyes
> I all alone beweep my outcast state
> And trouble deaf heaven with my bootless cries
> And look upon myself and curse my fate....

The soldier, the lover, the comrade, the past; the memories; a chorus of silences and birdsong. The house was empty, empty....

> Yet in these thoughts myself almost despising,
> Haply I think on thee, and then my state,
> Like to the lark at break of day arising
> From sullen earth, sings hymns at heaven's gate;
> For thy sweet love remember'd such wealth brings
> That then I scorn to change my state with kings.

I woke alone, cold and dishevelled on the couch with his coat lying across me. I thought he had left me. I went out into the hall, the coat over my shoulders; the front door was standing open and the sun of April streamed across the floor. The carriage had already been brought round. The silences—the ticking of the clock— there was no time for words spoken and unspoken; there was no more time.

Then I saw the Italian descending: the process of departure had begun. I went to my room, stark in the morning light, washed my face and combed my hair; I took the fan he had given me the previous spring from my dressing table and went downstairs to the drawing room.

I waited there, where he had loved me with the words of other men, and stood with the windows open to the scent of the ploughed fields, Evesham's fields; the wind cooled my face and my dry, aching eyes. When he came it was in uniform, the hard scarlet and the gold shocking in the soft rose and green elegance of that room. He looked, strangely, younger, and at peace.

He held something out, keys on a thin brown ribbon.

"Keep these for me."

The drawer; the letters. Entrusted to me as far as any one could be entrusted with knowledge of him.

Once more, the hand on the harpsichord. One note, as if to test the instrument, the trueness of its sound. Then he left it, and stood for a moment in the doorway, looking at the pale sunlight streaming over the polished floorboards.

Never look back....

We left the room together, and walked toward the open door. There were no servants present; he had requested this. We stood on the broad steps, and in the carriage his valet waited, his eyes red with weeping.

My fault, I thought. My fault.

I gave him the fan.

"Please take it. I have nothing else to give you."

I remember that he opened it, and the opalescent silk shimmered in the sunlight before it was gently folded and put into his pocket. He said, "I shall bring you another, from the Indies." Then, "I am your servant, as long as life is in me, and my house is your home and your inheritance. Whatever you may think of me now, remember me – with kindness – and with affection."

He kissed me on both cheeks and on my forehead, as if I were his child, and then he stepped back and bowed, as an officer, as a gentleman, a little lower than he had bowed to his god, and he left me. He had spoken no word of farewell, as he had spoken no word of love, nor had he said my name.

***

By the end of September 1762, news of the surrender of the Havana reached London. After forty days' siege under the command of George Keppel, the Earl of Albemarle, this vital port and lynchpin of Spanish trade had fallen to a combined naval and military force of twenty-seven thousand men. Fourteen Spanish ships of the line were destroyed or taken, and treasure worth three million pounds.

On November twenty-fifth a conference was called of all the adversaries. On December ninth, a Thursday, the terms of the peace were debated in Parliament, and carried by three hundred and nineteen votes to sixty-five. Among the dissenters was William Pitt, who had spoken in the House against a cessation of hostilities for three and a half hours, in agonizing pain of body. But he had misjudged the temper of the nation, and in February of 1763 the Peace of Paris was signed, ending nearly ten years of war.

Thursday, May the fifth was a day of thanksgiving. By then I was in Scotland, and Paris might have been in another world for all the difference this peace could make to our shattered lives.

Interlude: Glen Sian 1763

There was silence here, and cold: no wind. The earth, in the grey, scattered stones, showed its bone; against the shoulder of a mountain grey as slate and wreathed, dreamlike, in cloud, a sapling quivered, brilliant yellow in the pale light. The quiet water lay dark, reflecting as in some nether world the perfect, unbroken image of the land.

It was utterly empty and without sound but for the trickling of water. No bird sang; there were no birds, only a solitary hawk, soon gone. The land diminished everything by its stillness and its magnitude. A road was a thread, a horse a pinpoint; a man was nothing at all.

She walked toward him without haste. There was no speech, nor would there be until later. He had brought her salmon and venison, but she did not thank him, nor did he expect thanks; they were given and taken as she was, as a matter of course, in the manner of an old habit.

His son was in the croft, a boy of three. She put the child outside and closed the door, unfastening her bodice. He was stripping completely; often he did not, and she was gratified to see the swiftness of his erection. She lay on the coarse sheets and opened her legs, allowing herself the small satisfaction of knowing that for this moment only she possessed what this man who was as God in Glen Sian hungered for: in this moment alone, in her body and his own climax, he submitted to a force more primitive and more dominant than himself.

After the act he smoked in silence, and she lay listening for the child outside and drifting in her thoughts, and the memories of the first time he had come. He had selected her with the dispassion of a man buying cattle: she was relatively young and had been childless, and her smallholding was isolated; he would not be observed there. She assumed that when her usefulness had passed he would transfer his attention to another woman, or women; she knew as much and as little of him as any in Glen Sian, and if there were other women now they were unknown to her. He would not be questioned, nor held to obligation, and it was the framework of a relationship she had come to accept, if not understand. Her only mistake in the past had been her attempt to clothe it in the guise of tenderness.

She watched him now, the callused hands, so lately the instruments of a delicate pleasure, the old scar on the knuckles, the rough black hair and broken-nosed, bony profile, and the olive skin so strangely foreign in so Celtic a man.

He seemed abstracted, not sated with sex but deeply withdrawn, as if she did not exist. She raised herself on her elbow.

"Will you eat?"

"No." The smoke drifted, blue in the cold air, and outside the child cried. "Christ, I told you to get rid of that. Why do you never do what I tell you?"

"He is your son."

"I have no sons," he said. "Only bastards, like myself."

He rose and walked naked to the bucket, washed the semen from his body and dressed. She left the rough bed and stepped into her petticoat, tying the tapes, pulling the linen blouse over her head. He was knotting his neckcloth; in a moment he would be gone.

She said, "Is it true this thing that is out among the people?"

"What thing?"

"Of MacNeil's daughter, that is come back from the dead."

"There is an English bitch at his hearth. That is all I want to know."

She knelt, and handled the splendid leather of his boots with reverence, and as she crouched at his feet she felt the heat of his seed gush between her thighs. She hesitated, and the moment was lost; he opened the door and passed the child sitting on the ground without a glance.

There was no farewell, as there had been no greeting, and she held his son in her arms as the immensity of the land enfolded him and took him from her sight. Then she left the boy outside and went in again, and with the rag and the water he had used washed his semen from her thighs, and caressed the womb, and within the womb, the undesired child.

THE LOVERS

I

I had come to a country of which less was known than of the Indies: a country of which the climate was said to consist of nine months' winter and three months' bad weather; a country so trackless, so uninhabited, and so primitive that thirty years before an army officer employed in the construction of roads to penetrate its desolation had written, "One might as well think of making a Sea Voyage without Sun, Moon, Stars, or Compass, as pretend to know which way to take, when lost among the Hills and Mountains."

I was fourteen days, by fast horse, from London; I might have been on the other side of the world. I had arrived in the Highlands in the midst of a decade plagued by failed harvests, famine, dysentery, scurvy, smallpox and consumption. There was no fresh meat until September, when a few of the prized cattle upon the sale of which this economy was precariously balanced were slaughtered and salted down, and no fresh vegetables until the brief, wet summer. Nothing was green until May, nothing was harvested after September. There was no tea, sugar, tobacco, tar, staves for barrels, iron, salt, soap, wine or brandy, except as they were imported and carried at enormous cost and irregular intervals over inhospitable terrain. There was little money, and I seldom saw coins passed from hand to hand. There were few books, for this was an illiterate community whose traditions were oral, and to whose culture I was never admitted, barred by an impenetrable language.

There was no joy, no Cead mile Faílte, no hundred thousand welcomes of the Gaelic greeting for the prodigal daughter who had returned from the dead. And yet I had come to it freely, even eagerly. By the end of 1762 I would have sought refuge in hell had some one offered me shelter there.

I fell into this monochromatic world like a brilliant bird of passage, preceded by a letter which must have shattered the strictured existence of my natural father like a thunderbolt. I had written first to the landowner, whose name like the keys on the ribbon had been given to me with such casual deliberation. Five months later he responded, enclosing a stiff communication from the Reverend Patrick Inglis MacNeil. I was the daughter he had buried in the churchyard, and I cannot blame him, in retrospect, for the staggering coldness of his greeting. I was no more welcome than if I had indeed risen from the dead— the stench of England clung to me, more noxious than any odour of corruption.

And yet, I went. I drove to Edinburgh, and in a private room at the White Horse I had an interview with Ewen Stirling.

Unaccountably, I trusted him. I would come to love him, as a gentle and ephemeral bond between myself and Mordaunt, whom circumstance had placed so briefly, and with such disaster, within the same sphere. Perhaps I sensed even then that his protection and his influence would be transient. But I remember him now like some bright angel in the squalor of that place, with the clatter of hooves on the cobbles outside, and a cold sun straining to pass through the dirty window. I remember his grace, and the cleanness of his clothing, and his eyes, which spoke to me, recognizing in my uncommunicative numbness and disdain the shock of the exiled, with which he had most intimate acquaintance.

Two days later I dismissed my grooms, and sent them back to a house whereof I had been stripped of my right of abode, and went with him into that dark country from which, like Persephone, I had abandoned any hope of returning. Ten years would pass before I heard an English voice again.

Whatever restrictions on her behaviour or sureties her husband had employed, I had not expected them to afford me protection, and they did not. Catherine's conclusions were quickly drawn, and her vengeance as speedily executed. Within a week of Mordaunt's departure I received a packet of letters accusing me of unspeakable things, the most innocent of which was my seduction of him. And then she came herself, when he was safely out of the country, and assaulted me with threats both financial and physical, and gave me notice, like a hated tenant, to remove, or to marry. She could not disinherit me, but from her circle of acquaintance she could easily have conjured a bridegroom who would offer me the life of humiliation and sexual abuse she herself had endured. She had all rights and all strengths on her side, and in his absence I had no protection. She was his wife, and, if she chose, the world would know me as his whore, the corruptor of an honest man.

Without truth and without scandal, without shedding the unwelcome light of public speculation on our already suspect reputations, I had no defense against this campaign, and so I left, abandoning her to her empty house and her obsessive uncertainty and her endless, wooing, self-abasing letters to him, pleading for his return and his forgiveness, torturing herself with the dread that the lies she had fabricated might in fact have been true.

And I committed myself to Scotland, and to silence. Perhaps she thought me harmless now, or hoped some aspect of that country might remove me more permanently. And the letters, and the remembered accusations, remained my weapon and my comfort ... and the years passed, but the memory never softened. One does not forget when one is called a harlot before a houseful of servants. One does not forgive.

There had been no need for me to prove my identity: MacNeil saw his dead wife in every line of my face, and perhaps that was why he never loved me. After the first, stringent interrogation he understood that I had not been abused in England, but cherished and bred to a luxury he found even more offensive, and he regarded me thereafter as some excruciating punishment, the embodiment of a past he hated and an enemy he could not forgive. He gave me shelter out of duty, because I was undeniably his child: the pressures of his conscience did not oblige him to give me anything more.

If he was hard, his sister Deirdre was harder; she had not even the fire of his Calvinism to redeem a natural coldness. She was his senior by three or four years, a tall woman with high cheekbones and a face of stark beauty. Her eyes were dark, framed by strongly marked brows, and her hair, like his, was a thick, greying black. She had no femininity whatever, except for a rarely heard and oddly girlish laugh. I believed she had no emotion and no pity, and like her brother she showed me no kindness, as though she were testing me to see if I was worthy.

Of the first foreigner who had shared their lives, there was no evidence. I saw no portraits of my mother, Isabel: I had nothing of her but her face. She had left a loom and two charming but untutored watercolours, which were eventually given to me; if there was anything else, letters, books or journals, I never saw them, nor ribbon nor handkerchief that was hers. It was as though she had never existed, as I felt I existed only marginally, as an irritation in the eyes of my family which, if ignored, would go away, and I wondered if the oppressive atmosphere of this house had chilled and blighted her as it did me. Nor was I to be acquainted with the circumstances of her death: that unenviable task would fall to Ewen. I merely found her grave among others in an untouched wilderness, where by Highland custom the nettles grew undisturbed and the rank weeds were never cut. There was no date on the stone, and only her name, although I knew she shared this grave with the child who had been accepted as my dead self. Had I read my own name there I could not have felt more keenly a sense of my nonentity, my responsibility for this and other, more recent disaster. The act of preserving my life, however much for Mordaunt an act of personal expiation, had thwarted a natural destiny. I had been ordained to die, and to have wrested me from that fate had forced a violent alteration in the course of lives already predestined. He had believed this himself, had believed in retribution, some divine working through, and the process had not yet finished. By our flights, by our cowardice, we had merely prolonged it ... perhaps that too had been ordained, and the aberration in the pattern would only be corrected and exhausted by our deaths.

There was no sense of him in this alien place. His presence here was unimaginable, and like my mother he belonged to an unmentionable past; I could not speak of him. So I repressed the memories of him and of Evesham, and disciplined myself with the recollections of the final months of shame and dread. And in my waking hours, I succeeded. When I slept I dreamed, and loved him as I had always loved him ... saw him, spoke to him, heard his voice ... and woke in the cold, confining darkness with tears running from my eyes.

The ink froze in the well, the water froze in the jug, the frost lay inches thick on the window; the necessary visits to the earth closet at the bottom of the garden, so that all the world should know when we emptied our bowels, were odysseys of discomfort, to be delayed as long as possible. If I wanted a bath, I must bathe in the kitchen where the only fire was, and I must do it in a shallow tin in water only slightly warmed from standing on the hob. My behaviour was considered eccentric by the others, but I persisted, stubbornly, stupidly, throughout that first winter, until I felt myself becoming indifferent to the squalor of my appearance; I had begun to submit to the grinding, destructive influences of the country and the climate. And then, cursing and shuddering on a night in February, I immersed myself in icy water and scoured myself raw— I had not bathed in over a month. The next morning I cut off my hair. Deirdre said nothing, but she had seen the state of mind from which this desperate act had proceeded. She did not offer me immediate kindness, but her severity was tempered, and gradually she acknowledged me in a way that her brother did not.

The ice rotted, the snow yielded to fog and rain, the hours of daylight lengthened gradually until the sun fell across my cheek as I was milking, and I felt its warmth.

It was April, 1763. A year had passed since the Major's daughter had become the heritor of so much bitterness.

At the end of April, Ewen Stirling invited me to Ardsian.

I rode up alone; it was not possible to lose my way as there was only one road, and after a winter in MacNeil's household I did not fear solitude. The sound of the waterfall faded, the path widened although still running with the river; across the shallow, stony water I saw broad meadows, and beyond them fissured walls of slate, drifting, inviolate, abruptly close, inexpressibly remote. Nothing moved but the clouds and the water.

I rode on, grateful for the warmth of the horse beneath me, and eventually the track divided, descending on my left toward the village of Glen Sian, and twisting back upon itself to begin an ascent, gradual at first, toward the heights of Sian. The air was cold and sweet. I rode through a light wood of birch, and heard a cuckoo, distant, monotonous, melancholy.

Why must you always be this way? Like the basilisk, all eyes?

Or the cuckoo in the nest— cuckoo— cuckoo— cuckoo—

The road, ever mounting, turning east, brought me to open moor. The clouds passed over my face, the light racing and fading... I was an infinitesimal mote in the landscape, and my life or death mattered nothing.

Your life is a mote of dust, Mordaunt had said, and of as much consequence to an army. To an army or a country; and this was my inheritance.

I rode on, chilled and buffeted, and not only by the wind, and the track led me through stirrup-high bracken, which in summer would engulf it like a sea. It was not a road for amateurs; it fell off on my right with a breathtaking suddenness into a wall of scree, which rattled away beneath my gelding's hooves, and ended in a narrow cleft of broken rock and water. In these few yards death was as close as a misplaced step, a moment's inattention in the saddle.

Beyond, the track widened and swung away over moor; snow lay not only on the peaks but in patches on the ground. There were trees to my left, and the iron gates of Ardsian: the track continued past them, rutted and overgrown, and I left it and entered an arrow-straight avenue, where for the first time I saw the fresh prints of another horse.

I had arrived within an hour of the appointed time and I considered that acceptable, and I was exhausted by a journey which would have been merely an hour's diversion in my former life. I halted, irresolute, wanting only to go home. But there was no home.

The house lay perhaps half a mile from the road: I did not know what I had been expecting, Evesham possibly. This was a newer house, built at the turn of the eighteenth century, faced with grey stone and with a roof of locally quarried slate, three storeys high and surmounted by a curious dome-like cupola. I thought it bleak, but my eyes were bred to Evesham.

I dismounted. Before my foot had touched the ground a servant had come to help me. I sensed that he judged me, and passed no judgment;

perhaps he pitied me. I was of England but I was not English: I was Scots, but I was not of his people. He took the rein without subservience and, unnerved, I turned away.

I was received by another servant with that same nonassertive dignity and conducted through the house. It was larger than it appeared, and the soaring cupola surmounted a stairwell and gallery. I stood beneath it, staring up as though into the heart of a nautilus while the pale sun and shadow flickered over proportions of an astonishing beauty, until my guide, discreetly and with a certain gentleness, indicated that we should not linger.

He brought me eventually through some warren of the servants' into a glasshouse. Ewen stood in profile to me, coatless and immersed in potting. He was wearing carpet slippers, and his feet were grotesquely swollen.

"My dear child ... I thought you were not coming."

I curtsied to him, which seemed to please and embarrass him, and he raised me with affection, as though he knew me better than he did. By his kindness he offered me an intimacy that hours of conversation would not have achieved, and I felt that I had known him always, and would never again need to suffer the devastating loneliness of the past.

I apologized for my lateness: he apologized for his slippers, as he could not put on his shoes. There were several dozen clay pots, into which he had been transplanting seedlings, and I asked him what they were. He smiled quizzically, as if he thought they could hold no interest for any one but himself.

"This is the work of a year. Do you like roses?"

The roses in the courtyard, the roses on the wall, the crimson, autumnal rose in a scarred and roughened hand. *I thought you might want this....* The fragrance, the vanished summers, the now-dead life, not to be remembered, not to be mourned, never to be relived.

And I had not thanked him for the rose. I had never thanked him for anything, not even my life, which by his compassion or his guilt, he had given to me.

I became aware of his scrutiny: eyes so similar in colour, indefinite blue, indefinite grey, kind but very keen.

"My dear Margaret, you are not ill?"

"No.... I remembered something."

He said, "I sometimes think a memory is a curse in Scotland," and began to put on his coat.

But I did not want to go in. I had known peace here, and for the first time in months had heard that voice, long suppressed, reasserting itself with a poignant intensity: I looked up as though I could see him in another face, in other eyes.

261

He was saying, "I know not which is worse, to be troubled by the past or to forget it. But you who are so young, you should have no past to forget."

To divert his attention, I asked him what the seedlings were; the pots were illegibly labelled in pencil.

"My dream of roses which will bloom throughout the year. They have so brief a season— so few will flower only six weeks at the most. This newest, this China rose, is the only rose said to bloom until Christmas. I have never seen it bloom so myself, although," another self-deprecating smile, "that should come as no surprise to you."

"I marvel that roses will bloom at all in this climate."

"The albas thrive upon it. The white rose, the ... Jacobite rose ... will survive even neglect." He had stammered for the first time, and in the diffused light his face was flushed. "I do not make a ... political statement. If the cause were as hardy as the rose, the disaster would be never ending. Perhaps it is, in any case."

We had approached the edge of something: we drew back from it. He allowed me to examine the seedlings and translated their scrawled labels: Damascena Bifera, the autumn damask, crossed with Alba Maxima, the Jacobite rose, the once-flowering Belle de Creçy with its rich scent and the new, scentless China rose, which upon its introduction had caused a sensation in Britain, the late-flowering Apothecary's Rose with Centifolia, the hundred-petalled Provence rose which Herodotus, four hundred years before the birth of Christ, had described growing in the gardens of Midas. The roses of my childhood were there, the Rosa Mundi of Henry's mistress, the Holy Rose of Abyssinia, roses of great antiquity which had lived their vivid season at Evesham and scattered petals on the walks in transient profusion. That they should survive here amid starvation seemed not only a miracle, but perhaps an insult.

"You wonder why I should play here with botany when we none of us can eat roses. I cannot improve upon the reality of my situation... I can at least attempt to make it bearable." He smiled: a delicate face, like a mask in ivory, and I saw how he had aged since our last meeting, and knew that whatever I had suffered in the winter, he had suffered more. "And now, please come indoors. It was not my intention to entertain you so shabbily."

In a long, light room that smelled of mildew, I took off my hat and gloves and gave him the Voltaire which was in my pocket. By his obvious pleasure I knew he had not read it, although it was four years old.

"*Candide*. I know nothing of it." I thought perhaps he had not had many books from France because of the war. "My dear, I have nothing from France any more, and not only because of the war. The war is over, by the way. The peace was signed in February, in Paris."

I had not known.

"You could not be expected to know. The world could end in this place and one would not know. I will give you my newspaper if it interests you— it is, of course, out of date."

So Mordaunt had gone for nothing: a useless, futile gesture.

"So there will be peace."

"For a time," he said enigmatically.

Then he asked me, with the greatest delicacy, if I would like to wash my hands, like a man used to dealing with quiet, difficult children, and apologized that there were no women in the household to wait on me. He conducted me up the broad staircase, to the doors of what I presumed were rooms set aside for guests, although God knew what guests had or did come here, and once inside I found the dressing room and knelt on the carpet heaving my heart out into the flowered porcelain of a close-stool until I thought I would faint. Time passed, the light came and went at the windows; I retched bile and eventually got up, trembling and weeping, and attempted to comb my hair in front of the first cheval glass I had seen since leaving Evesham. My reflection, staring, gaunt, obscene, was unbearable; I could not acknowledge it as myself.

The water in the ewer was warm, the linen fresh. On a small table a pot of blue hyacinths bloomed, shedding a scent like heaven: on the washing stand there were little intimacies of occupation, toothbrush, tooth powder, a half-empty vial of eau de cologne. It was his own dressing room.

When I returned he dismissed it with grace, saying the rest were not habitable. There was a drink waiting for me, cream and honey and spirits, and the yolk of an egg, which I had not had since the beginning of the winter. Its calming, restorative influence was the only indication that he had guessed the extremity of my reaction.

He drank brandy with a little water and talked, with great charm and vivacity, of his gardens and his son James, four years my senior and pretending, as he said, to study law; and of his deerhounds, one of which came in and lay at his feet after a cursory sniff at my hand. Then the meal was announced, and we sat down in a dark dining room with the cold sun refracting from clean knives and goblets. There was a vase of flowers hiding the threadbare linen: lady tulips, rose red and cream with a purple base.

"I force them in my glasshouse. My factor thinks I am mad."

"Then he is a man without a soul."

"Perhaps. They are a great comfort and a joy to me, nonetheless."

The meal was served by a wizened man with greying hair to his shoulders: like the rest of the household he seemed to speak no English. The food for all its plainness, fish, boiled potatoes, creamed onions and a good wine, was a banquet to me, and Ewen watched me as though I were an invalid, plying me with titbits. Then followed the inevitable oatcakes, with dishes of honey and butter, and oranges, and afterwards walnuts and coffee: unimaginable, almost unendurable luxury. When we were alone once more, with only the coffee and the tulips remaining on the table, he said, "Thank God I have brought some colour to your face. I have never seen a child so stricken in all my life, save once."

"I am not a child."

"I know how old you are. Why did you cut your beautiful hair?"

"I could not keep it clean." He said nothing, as though knowing there was more. "Sometimes … I think I will go mad if I stay here."

"Plus ça change," he said, "plus la même. I did not come here willingly, you know. It was an inheritance, a most unwelcome gift."

"How long have you lived here?"

"I can scarcely credit it. It is twenty years."

Outside, the spring afternoon was waning. There was a thump at the door and the deerhound banged in and thrust his muzzle beneath my elbow, and lay down with his head resting on my boot. He said, "If only they would close the doors," and on his slippered feet he crossed the room and shut it and returned. I saw for a moment the grace of his youth.

"It is an unwanted refuge. Like a convict, I serve my sentence here."

He drank more coffee, contemplatively. It was not very good, thin and bitter, but like Johnson's female preacher the miracle was that it was there.

"I beg you to reconsider, and go back to the life which you have left."

"I choose not to."

"There is a point at which free will is lost. One is overtaken by circumstances, and it is no longer possible to choose. This is no life for you."

"I have no other life. Not now."

"I presume very far upon our friendship, but perhaps some day you will tell me the truth. I cannot believe that any responsible person encouraged you to this decision." Then, with another of those keen, speculative looks, "I do not mean to undermine your family's authority. I care for your welfare, that is all."

"If by my family you mean MacNeil, I am merely an obstacle in his household. The sooner I were removed the better, in his opinion."

"That is not fair to your father."

"My father hates me, sir."

"That is not true. Your father has suffered—"

"We have all suffered. I have found more charity in an atheist than in him, who purports to be a Christian, and given encouragement I shall hate him equally."

"He has suffered," he said again. "Not more than any one else, but …
in the pursuit of an unwinnable cause. Loss and grief leave their mark on all
of us."

"He committed treason."

"He had a vision. A … hope … a commitment to something perceived
as worthy of restoration."

"Did you perceive it as worthy?"

"I had a clearer vision of the truth, the clearest I have ever had. I saw that
it would lead to disaster."

The edge of the past offered itself, and he turned aside from it. The room
had darkened and he noticed it with, I thought, relief.

"You must go. I meant to say so much … Perhaps you will come
again?"

Outside there was still sunlight, throwing leafless shadows. The air was
colder with the approach of evening.

He handed me into the saddle and stood in his slippers on the damp
stone of the courtyard.

"Come back at Whitsun. I will have roses for you then."

"Thank you for your kindness, sir."

He reached up and clasped my gloved hand as if he were reluctant to let
me go, and I wished that I had ventured to kiss him on both cheeks, but, as
yet, I did not dare.

"Good-bye, my dear. Good-bye … good-bye."

And I left him to his dream of roses, and his folly of beauty in the midst
of desolation; and, homeless, I rode home.

It rained at Whitsun: the rain changed to snow. The roses he would
have given me, the Rose du Saint Sacrament, offered their small flowers in
a gnarled display against the wall of his garden, where they were beaten and
blown by the bitter wind until they died. So tenacious was the grip of this
terrible winter that patches of snow lay on the fields until late May, and in
sheltered, sunless corries and on the high ground it was visible throughout
the summer.

There was rain for the next month, sometimes violent, with sullen thunder,
sometimes caressing, drifting like mist through the long hours of daylight.
Undeterred by the appalling reluctance of the land to give them sustenance,
the people pursued the timeless rhythm of their lives. In April they cut peat,
in May they drove the staggering, infirm cattle to the summer pastures, and
ploughed and sowed their stony fields, their backs bent to the rain. I could
do nothing here, neither sow nor harrow: this was masculine work and my

presence was not wanted. And the women's world of the shielings was a private one, from which by language and by breeding I was subtly barred. So I watched from the back of my horse, always the spectator, always the intruder, and the pattern of the year unfolded, and the grudging warmth coaxed life from the soil. The yellow and blue flags bloomed, the deer moved like shadows on the land, the grain showed green in the warp of the fields. The rain ceased: there was sunlight, sometimes. My aunt, as taciturn as ever, walked one afternoon to the summer pastures to deliver a child at the shielings, and was absent for three days: she did not invite me to accompany her, and my father, whose resentment of me possessed him like a fever, watched me with reddened eyes over the table during our meals, speaking as little as possible. The responsibility for all domestic tasks during my aunt's absence devolved upon me, and I hated both the enforced proximity to my father and the curbs upon my freedom: he would lift no hand to help me, even to empty the chamberpot beneath his own bed. On the Sunday he walked five miles to Glen Sian, where he preached on alternate weeks; his congregation there was small, for the inhabitants of that shattered village, which unlike Glen Mor had never recovered from its devastation, were mostly Catholic. He was from home all day.

I went out on horseback, Sabbath-breaking. I returned about nine in the evening. The kitchen fire, that cherished flame so superstitiously venerated and so ritually extinguished and rekindled at Beltane, was dead, cold ashes and there was no supper ready laid, and MacNeil had come home.

He had walked ten miles, he was in pain, and he had been drinking. I blamed that for what occurred, and perhaps he regretted it; he drank noticeably less for a time. But we had violent words, and I remember telling him that even Christ had not indulged in such pride that he would not feed himself and his followers.

I turned my back when I had said this, and was pouring water into the sink when I felt his hand on my shoulder, then he slapped me on the ear and across the cheek. My nose began to bleed.

"You godless, lazy, slothful bitch, is this what they taught you in England?"

Our shared blood, which we so despised, spilled between my fingers. I felt as though every bone in my face had been broken.

He slapped me again with the flat of his hand, with his knuckles toward my face.

"Honour thy father, you arrogant slut! Honour him, *honour* him—"

And then my aunt was standing in the doorway. Only her hand, at her breast in the folds of her shawl, moved.

"Oh mo Dhia, am bheil thu mearanach?"

Her voice was without inflection, but he heard it and thrust away from me, and stood blindly, stupidly, shaking his head like a man awakening.

I reached for the edge of the sink and raised myself. He was watching me with eyes like reddened glass.

I said, "You are not worth the honouring."

It was still raining the next morning, when I went to Ewen.

We sat in a room hung with yellow silk: on the table between us a bowl of white roses, marked by the rain, shed their exceptional fragrance. The windows overlooked his garden, and through the gloom I saw the rose bushes, bowed with rain, covering the ground with a confetti of fallen petals.

He said, although we both knew it was unnecessary, "Who did this?"

"My father."

"Why?"

"He finds me indescribably offensive. I am not submissive ... and I am not a Scot." It was raining more heavily than ever: it fell like steel bars. "Did you know my mother?"

"Yes. A little."

"What do you know of her?"

"She was Manx ... she was very young ... I thought her ... rather beautiful. I gave her roses .... She was fond of them."

"When did she die?"

"In July, of '46."

"How did she die?"

He said, "This is a long story, and a painful one for me."

"I should like to know. I should like to know what I am being blamed for."

So he told me.

We walked in the house, and its benevolence and its peace fell like scales from my innocent eyes, and its rain-shadowed rooms were peopled with the dead.

"It was a Saturday evening ... it had been raining. They came to this house about nine that night. It was the twelfth of July."

The rain had stopped. We walked in the rose garden, and his ghosts walked with us; we walked amid the petals and the fragrance and he paused, examining the dishevelled heads and describing the poisoned brew of Scottish politics which had produced this horror; we sat on the stone bench among the lavender and he spoke for the first time of his wife, Elspeth, and the sun was briefly, almost blindingly hot. He sat, his hair silvered in the sunlight, his right hand where the roses had scratched it studded with blood, and spoke, unconsciously now in French, of the officer who had arrested him, sequestered him in irons in a tiny, squalid room and given him wine, and then, by the light of a single candle, beaten him, arousing himself to a sexual frenzy.

267

"Il était très jeune … vraiment garçon … perverti. J' n' sais le nom …"

He coughed for a time into his handkerchief and wiped his eyes and his mouth with it.

"Vous souvenez-vous les autres? Les noms des officiers? Vous souvenez-vous le nom, 'Mordaunt'?"

"He was not … that man."

"Do you remember him?"

"I am sorry," he said. "I regret. I should not say these things to you. I told you … it is difficult for me."

He sat staring into the hot sunlight. There were bees among the lavender; he reached down and pulled one of the tough greyish stalks.

"I miss the roses of my childhood … the sun of France, the scent of lavender. This is not the same."

"Tell me about my mother."

"Why do you ask these things?"

"Because no one else will tell me."

"She was shot. By no one, by any one. No one saw, no one knew. Those who saw and knew were also dead."

I may owe you explanations, but not the privacy of my soul. Grant me that much dignity.

He was stripping the stalk of its greyish buds, extracting their acrid, nostalgic fragrance, then he scattered them on the gravel.

"I was told… many months later, as Inglis was told. He had not seen her all that year. He had been from home since August of the previous year… he did not return until October." Then he said, with difficulty, "You understand that he apportions blame, where blame cannot be laid."

The sun had gone. He looked up at the cloud, as though surprised that his hand cast no shadow.

"Come. I will cut you some roses, and then I will take you home."

He said it as though the inexplicable had been explained, the unforgivable forgiven. But he could never take me home.

He cut me roses and sat me down to a dinner neither of us wanted, and an hour later he rode with me down that empty track, with the bracken lashing our stirrups, in a fine haze of rain. At the bottom he hesitated, then he pointed with his crop.

"That is Glen Sian. Do you wish to see it?"

Like most Highland settlements it lay untidily grouped within the depression of the river, its strips of cultivated land weed-blown and neglected. There were newer crofts, far-flung on the crumpled slopes, but here the houses were roofless, plundered for wood and stone: subsequent years of wind and rain had finished what the army had begun. Much of it had been burnt, and in the reeking shells there was no movement. We dismounted and walked, the rain drifting like smoke, and once he stopped and laid his right hand on the stone of a nondescript building, and said, "I was held prisoner here."

He did not seem to feel the rain: his profile was utterly calm.

"I was here ... two days, I thought, although it might have been more."

"What do you remember of the officers?"

"There were only two... senior officers. They never spoke, not to me nor to each other."

I struck him, which is a grievous offense....

"What happened here?"

He shrugged.

"What you see. Only the commonplace."

"What happened ... among them?"

"I do not know. I know only what happened to me."

The rain fell on the stones, on the coping of the well, on the weeds growing at our feet. The hooves startled echoes from the walls, which bounded and rebounded in the street.

We left it, and the rain obscured it; and the fragments of conversation from another life were similarly obscured, unanswered and inexplicable. And at the heart of their enigma, as surely as among those ruins, dwelt that enigmatic ghost, discoloured scarlet and gilt tarnished with verdigris, whose eyes, offering me their impenetrable riddle, watched me now; would always watch me.

Where flags had bloomed, curlews nested in the marshes; the horizon shimmered in a haze of late summer heat. On the high ground there were eagles, and red deer, and the dappled fawns which had been born the previous month. On the lower, clouds of midges hung in the humid air, tormenting any flesh exposed to the luxury of the sun.

On a hot afternoon at the beginning of September I sat among scabious and butterflies, watching the wind move over the grain. Within a fortnight the reapers would work in echelon over such strips, cutting and binding and stooking in the fear of rain and the hope of a substantial harvest, for upon it the mere fact of their survival depended.

I closed my eyes, the red heat beating on the lids, and opened them again: a man was walking amidst the grain, and at the edge of the field a black horse stood with the reins loose on its neck, a heavy horse, with a hide like polished stone. And in the grain the man, the sun bleaching white on his shirtsleeves, pulled what must have been several heads from the stalks; at this distance I could not tell whether he had sniffed or tasted them. There was no sound, only the rushing of the wind: a cloud passed over the sun, and I was cold.

Then he mounted and rode away, and the field lay under the empty skies and the sun, disturbed only by the wind.

We harvested from sunrise on the thirteenth of September until Wednesday the twenty-first. The grain was damp, and would be carried to drying barns before it could be flailed and winnowed.

As the light strengthened the heat increased: I sweated and my back ached, my thighs were trembling with the strain of the steps of this primitive dance, the necessary curtsey to the earth with every gathering of sheaf, every cutting twist of straw and every binding.

The work was uninspiring and relentless: there was little communication among the reapers, and only occasionally a few words of encouragement from my aunt. The wind blew, the sweat streamed from my neck and armpits, the dust and stubble worked beneath my gloves and clothing. The other women had kilted their coarse blue skirts up to their waists in the wet grain. The gaunt youth who led us cut a last swath and paused, sharpening his scythe; in other parts of the field other men were doing the same. The women rested, calling to one another; there was raillery, rivalry, a sleeve drawn across the face, a kerchief retied, a neck rubbed. The scraping of the stone on the long curving blade ceased: the terrible monotony of labour was resumed.

My mind drifted. My tongue was parched with thirst, the sweat ran stinging into my eyes; the scythes whispered and glittered. The sky darkened; a little rain fell. A sigh ran over the field. The rain passed. Somewhere a voice sang, and the others took it up.

> 'S a' Mhaire 'g am bheil a' ghruaidh chiatach
> 'S glan am fiaradh th'ann ad mhalaidh....

I asked my aunt what they were singing.

She shaded her eyes. Unlike mine, her palms were neither blistered nor reddened.

"A love song. I will show you how to stook, so you may rest your back."

> Gun chuireadh air mhisg le d' ghaol mì,
> 'S mear, aotrom, a' ghaoir atà 'm bhallaibh....

"What does it mean?"

"It means I am mad with passion," she said; then she gestured sharply at the youth, who had stopped and was leaning on his scythe looking back at us. "Ochan! Togaibh an aird!"

"I delay you, Aunt."

She was binding unhurriedly, her face unsmiling.

"It is not a day's work. You are fast enough for me."

They sang of lifting their hearts with song, although their work was heavy, and heavy it certainly was. I stooked with indifferent success until midday, then we sat in the stubble, on the stony ground, and the women picked ticks from their legs and the men lay on their backs, and we all ate bannock and cheese and butter and honey, and drank water and the potent local uisguebaugh. I tied up my hair with the stock from my throat, a spotted lawn I had been given in that vanished life, ever receding, increasingly unclear ... the last swallow of brackish water from the stone bottles, the last moment of leaden weariness on the ground, and then the scythe's silken rustle began the dance, and all the reapers followed.

On the second morning I went stiffly, in my stained shirt and stubbled skirts, into the wet cut furrows, following the scythe once more, and in the chill of evening stumbled back to MacNeil's house, and my bed. On the third morning, my aunt brought me salve for my hands, and offered me clean clothing of her own: a drugget blouse and a skirt of the now familiar local weave, a coarse woollen cloth dyed with indigo, which repelled water as if it were oiled. Then she tied a kerchief over my hair, and I felt that some obscure rite of passage had been performed, and I had gained in stature in her eyes.

We walked in the soft light of the mornings to the fields and joined others walking, who now greeted me shyly as I had learned to greet them, with the blessing of God on the day: we walked back from the fields in the long shadows of evening, when after a day of bending beneath the sky all I wanted was to lay my head on a stone and sleep. The fields varied in nature, configuration and altitude, and in some the work was uphill, and the grain had been flattened by wind and rain. There was little privacy for bodily functions. The skin on my forearms was scarred from the stubble; the blisters broke and bled inside my gloves.

On the fourth day Ewen rode up to the field where we were working, thirty reapers among the hundred who were harvesting in that area, and my heart gave a curious leap of pleasure and anticipation. My aunt saw me and said, "He will be thirsty. Take him water from the bottles."

"I, Aunt?"

"Go on, so. You will be his friend ... do him the office of a friend."

I crossed the stubble, between the standing sheaves: the sun was in his eyes and he did not recognize me until I came up to his horse and pulled the kerchief from my hair.

"Good morning, sir."

He peered down from the saddle, and if I had ever seen astonishment in any man's face, I saw it now in his.

"My God. What are you doing here?"

271

He dismounted, and I thought he would have taken my hand, but seemed to reconsider it.

"How can any able-bodied person refuse?"

He took the stone bottle from me, and for a moment his fingers touched my glove: then he drank, and gave it back to me, staring over my shoulder into the hard light.

"You are not my servant, nor even my tenant. And the harvest scarcely warrants it."

Again the image of a bleached white sleeve, the outflung arm scattering grain.

"Does it not satisfy you?"

He said gently, "I am grateful for what there is. Will you come to see me when this is over?"

"If I may, sir."

"I have missed you," he said. "And I wish you would not call me sir."

Insects rustled in the dry stubble at our feet; from the higher field the melancholy song of the reapers drifted down on the wind like the crying of gulls.

"I must go. I gather it is some disgrace to fall behind, or to be last."

"I do not expect this of you, Margaret. I dislike it. It is not right."

I said lightly, and with great affection for him, so great that I thought I could tease him, "Perhaps I am confronting the life I was born to," and I was surprised by his vehemence.

"You were never born to this. And I do not want you to … *confront* it."

I felt eyes upon us. I had stayed too long with this cherished man, for whom those I worked among had a love so deep it verged upon the superstitious: they would think I presumed, by my familiarity with him, that I had no modesty.

"I must go…."

He said, "You are the only person I can talk to, the only one to whom I can open my heart. A woman once said to me … my cousin in France … did I fear I was dwindling into a Scot. I do fear it now, for you."

Then he took my hand, and kissed the back of the damp, scarred glove: the intimacy seemed to surprise him as much as myself, and a faint flush coloured his face. He turned his back and thrust his boot into the stirrup.

"Good-bye, my dear. Thank you for my drink."

"Good day, sir."

He looked down from the saddle, with those grey, familiar eyes.

"My name is Ewen," he said.

The days followed as one, relieved only by the nights, by fleeting rest, by changes in weather, by fragments of incident. A woman went into labour in the field, and her companions came stumbling over the stubble. I was binding again, twisting brittle stalks – anything would break the monotony.

"Shall I come with you, Aunt?"

"No." She was rising unhurriedly. "Bind and stook both, as I showed you."

"Perhaps I can be useful."

"No. It is not fitting."

I watched her long, narrow back, unbowed by the days of reaping and patched now with an uncharacteristic darkness of sweat, then the gaunt youth stopped and sharpened his sned and ventured to smile at me. We had barely a word in common. I stooped and finished the sheaf I had been binding and his air of expectancy vanished; he resumed his task with a mournful determination.

The end of the harvest approached. I followed the scythe as in a dream, mesmerised by the silken rustle of the blade. The flowers fell with the oats, the tangled weed with the barley; the sky in the west darkened and a litter of white birds swirled across it like ash. A fine, needling rain began to fall.

My aunt had hung the stone bottle around her waist. I walked down toward her.

"Whose horse is that?"

"It is the factor's. He is down among the men, measuring the sheaves."

"And if he does not approve?"

"Then they will bind them again to suit him. He has been here before. He came to test the sickles, to see were they too small."

"Is that all he does?"

"He earns his bread," she said briefly, "for all that he is not a good man."

"Why do you say so, Aunt?"

"He is a strange man, with strange ways, and better left unknown."

On the final day of the harvest we ate in the stubble with the corncrakes rasping around us, and the murmur of Gaelic conversation enfolding us in an intimacy I did not think would survive the circumstances of our daily lives.

"Have you always lived here, Aunt?"

She gazed up at the sky, a harsh blue painted with mares' tails, and I wondered if she were relishing its beauty, or warming herself in its unseasonable sun against the certainty of winter.

"Your father and I were children on Gigha. I remember the sea.... I carried your father on my back on the shore, above the reach of the tide. Now all that is no more."

"Have you never thought of marriage?"

The corner of her mouth lifted unexpectedly, and she smiled, showing stained, even teeth.

"Who would be wanting me, an old hag like myself?"

"You weren't always so. And you aren't old."

She laughed outright, that high, girlish laughter, so strangely imprisoned, so seldom heard, and briefly touched my blistered hand.

"Well then, a hag only."

She withdrew her hand and relapsed into silence, her eyes hooded once more. After a long time she said, "I could not have the man I wanted, and who wanted me. And that was an end to it."

So ended everything. The slowest reapers cut the last standing grain, and bound it: they decorated this, which they called the Cailleach, or old woman, with the fading flowers they had reaped. The cutting of the Cailleach was considered either an honour or a disgrace, I was uncertain which, but I was glad it had not fallen to me. I had been, for this brief interlude, part of this unknown and unknowable community: I wanted nothing to mark me out from it, not yet. I would resume my solitude soon enough.

For the moment I could delude myself that, like Ruth, I had foresworn my past, and embrace these as my people who reaped among this alien corn.

I rode to Ardsian on the last day of September, a Friday. There had been frost, and the wind was scattering a hail of golden birch leaves; on the higher ground the rutting stags, plundering one another's hinds, issued their bellowing challenges to warn off younger interlopers.

I found Ewen in the garden, sitting in the sunlight on the stone bench near the fountain. He had been reading a paper, which he held now folded on one knee. I spoke, and his eyes opened: he looked jaded, and deeply saddened.

"I thought I asked you not to call me that." I had called him sir. "Please sit by me. I will ask Ruaraidh to bring you some coffee presently."

I leaned forward without thinking and laid my hand on his knee.

"What has happened?"

"My cousin Honorée is dead. This is from her son." I heard the wind in the trees, like a distant sea, and leaves fell around us. "Ten years ago I would have wept. Perhaps all the tears are dried in me— perhaps I have no more to shed." The leaves fell onto his knee and the stone bench between us and the granite at our feet. "How hard the light is," he said, and then, "She is as dead as this," and closed his fingers on a leaf and crushed it, and let it fall to join the others.

"I would say so much," he said. "To you, to her, and now it is too late."

"What would you say to me?"

Again the wind, like and unlike the sea; like a long, drawn out, ebbing tide.

"Does your guardian know where you are?"

"I believe so."

"Believing is not enough … When did you see him last?"

"In April, a year ago."

"Is he in England?"

"He is in the West Indies, with the army. I don't know where."

There were clouds now, and the sunlight was infrequent.

"I am cold," he said. "Come and walk with me."

After a moment's hesitation he offered his arm. He was little more than my height, and his pace was slow: I thought how similar we were, clothed in our shabby gentility.

We reached the garden, littered now with yellowing leaves as it had been earlier with rose petals.

"Who would know where he was?"

"His wife… I daresay."

Across the broad swath of grass, some one was burning something.

"And where is she?"

"In London, most of the time."

"You do not write to her."

"No."

He said, "There is no love lost, it seems." The smoke was peculiarly acrid: I felt it in my throat and eyes. "We will go back, I think."

We turned away from the smoke, but we did not go back.

"Does she prevent your letters to him, or his to you?"

"There are no letters."

"You were a favoured child. Why then are there no letters?"

"It was … agreed. It was … difficult. Life was difficult."

"He mistreated you?"

"*No.* Very much … the opposite."

And as if I had said, *Too much the opposite*, he said, "I see," and I thought that he did see, some truth which he had hitherto only suspected. "I beg you to write to him, and tell him where you are."

"I cannot."

"Why not?"

"I can't explain. It's finished. It must be finished."

He said nothing more. Beyond and above, light and cloud drifted endlessly over the peaks, painting and obscuring them. He said eventually, "Christmas falls on a Sunday this year. You knew, of course."

I had not known: I had a Lady's Complete Pocket Companion but I seldom consulted it any more.

"I would be honoured if you would spend it with me. The kirk does not keep Christmas as you have observed, and I thought it might be my privilege to offer you some … festivity."

I thought he had been going to say 'happiness'.

"I should like it very much."

"Such a good child," he said, with a little, ironic smile. "As though I had offered you sweets."

"I should like it … Ewen."

"I will speak to your father concerning it," and I saw that my use of his name had disconcerted him.

We had returned to the bench and the fountain. He had left the letter here: it had blown onto the ground, and spray had spattered it. He picked it up and held it, closed: I knew he would not read it again.

He said, "Life offers … a gift, not very often. One rejects it, and one comes to regret. Life is very short. I ask only that you consider this. One day, this is all you will have."

The winds raged without respite, and those trees which did not fall were stripped early of their leaves: there was hail, snow and the bitter, relentless rain. The season had begun which would kill both men and beasts.

There were rumours of Ewen's illness. I could not go to him. The rivers, which had risen two feet overnight in the rain which had preceded the snow, had frozen and the way was impassable. The hills above Glen Mor were blinding wastes; the wind and the terrible cold and the snow continued. The garrons died, the delicate sheep died, the old and the frail began to die, and the ground was frozen too solid to bury them. The cattle died, in numbers that would be noted in estate records throughout the Highlands as exceptional. The very birds, starved, fell from the sky. And in the white, pitiless hills, under the blinding sky, the deer died: drowning, starving, riddled with parasites, in leafless woods greyed by falling snow or in conifer woods where they sheltered. They died in the high corries where only the eagles found them, they died on the slopes and on the moors, and in the outfields, where they scraped the stubble for a sustenance the land could not afford them. They grazed, covered with snow, with their legs folded beneath them, until they were disturbed, then they rose like living hummocks, shaking the weight of snow from their coats and turning bulging eyes on any predator: too weak to run, and easily killed.

I see myself, in some hallucinatory landscape of winter, under a grey smoky sky: I am wandering. I thought I was walking, exorcising demons, escaping the noisome claustrophobia of a house and a village gripped by a fearful blockade; but I am stumbling, directionless and lost, falling into the crusted hardness of a drift, moving my feet like weighted blocks. The snow is rain and the rain changes to snow: I see how a man can be obscured completely at a distance of less than a hundred paces. All blacks blend into grey... the hush of falling snow muffles all ... it whitens hair and clothing. The living deer rise around me like silent beasts in a dream, some trembling, some collapsing with blood issuing from mouths and nostrils ... like myself the man among them walks without haste and without sound. Here he cuts a throat, and a black torrent gushes steaming into the snow ... when I move toward him, he holds a hind in its death agony ... the roe are small deer, and easily held. He holds it until it dies, and also cuts its throat. And all the while the snow clings to us, in a landscape without substance, without colour, except where he kills and bleeds the deer, and the gralloch steams in the snow. He kills perhaps four, perhaps five: the sun in a pinkish, delicate sky now shows itself, and the drifting snow is glittering as it falls, on my clothing and my arms, and in the air between us. The sun is behind him, as exquisite as a morning although it is almost setting, and his breath is an opalescent cloud. I cannot see the colour of his eyes, but he stands with the knife in his hand and the blade smokes, and his bared hand is bloody.

And he cannot know who I am: he cannot see my muffled face. But he says, in the only language I understand, "Go home. This is no place for you."

And I say, over and over, until the tears freeze on my face, "I have no home— I have no home—"

And I am lost; lost; lost.

II

On the first mild night of spring, he walked by the light of the new moon, contemplating the land. He had entered his assessment of it in the previous day's estate records.

> In three out of every five seasons, the Springs are wet, the Summers cold, and the harvest abounding with drenching rain. Even where the land has been thoroughly drained it often happens that from the long and continued heavy drenching of winter, the land is too wet for the plough until the middle of April. But it is chiefly in harvest that the principal danger to the Corn Crops arises, in Slopes and exposed places from the effects of tempests of wind and rain, in shaking and lodging the Corn, in its late Ripening, and the great uncertainty of drying and securing it in any usable condition when cut.

He walked without haste, with a long, tireless step, despite the dimness of the light. He knew the land in the darkness or otherwise, with an intimate familiarity; knew its contours and its distances, its repetitive disorders and its dreadful, continuing malaise. It did not pay and it did not support: it was improperly managed and misguidedly used. He did not love it but he was obsessed by it, and his hunger to subdue it was intense, almost sexual. And like a man premeditating rape, he had already decided upon his method. He awaited only the opportunity.

He walked more heavily now, knowing the limits of his strength, and the time and the distance he would walk. He had never been known to be ill, and he had never shown fatigue— if his breathing quickened with exertion, he ignored it. He had no pity for the weak, and only contempt for the dead, the winter's toll that marked his failure to control the land as they marked it every year.

The winter's fury has slain us, the winter's torrent gushes forth, mountainous and raging … righteous Lord of the Feasts, only protect me from the mighty blast, from the cold hell of the winter.…

The last trees fell away behind him. The moon swung in the leafless branches, a paring of silver unlucky to look upon unless blessed, unless offered homage. He offered none— he prayed to nothing now. The night was as empty and as ancient as the prayers, and bereft of superstition.

Greeting to you, queen of the night, beauty of the skies, new moon of the seasons.

There were no gods here; if there were gods in Glen Sian they were embodied in himself. The prayer, like the night, was empty.

He walked on in an immensity of silence, and the moon rose higher, giving little light. The stars moved overhead; sweat broke on his face and the douce night dried it; he walked in the dull tirelessness learned in his childhood, measuring out the days and miles of Glen Sian with the callused soles of his child's feet. The clods of earth beneath his boot gave way to barren moor.

He crossed the stream. Beyond the rushing water the croft was dark against the vast night sky, and the stars also gave a little light. When he found her, lying on the ground outside the door, he could see her clearly enough by it although she could not see him. Somewhere inside the boy was crying, a high-pitched, cat-like mewing.

He crouched beside her and slid his arm beneath her shoulders; the grizzled hair spilled across his sleeve.

"Grania."

"O mo Dhia— cia tha sin?"

"It is myself."

"Go ... go, and leave me."

He carried her inside. In the foul, stifling darkness the boy, his son, wailed pitifully.

"Fan sàmhach," he said brutally, and the sobbing subsided into a terrified silence.

He lowered her onto the mattress and crouched over the fire, pushing the peats together. The child watched him, clad only in a little shirt, eyes brimming with tears. In the face of his son he saw his own.

"Go to sleep," he said. "I am with your mother."

He said it without gentleness and without menace, and the eyes of the child, with strongly defined brows and black lashes, flickered beyond him to the mattress where the woman lay as she had often been seen to lie, and the agony of labour convulsed her body as had the spasms of orgasm: the child associated one with the other, and both with this fierce, elemental presence. And it was not unfamiliar: he knew it as he knew the rain and the sound of the wind, so he submitted to it, and to his mother's whispered entreaty.

"Go to bed, Conn— like a good lad. Go to sleep. Oh God, have mercy—"

She forgot him, and the man had always ignored him, so consigned to oblivion the boy cried and then huddled and slept throughout the hours of her travail.

He kept the fire going and the lamp: there was a stench of blood and secretion in the smothering air, and of unwashed linen. Fastidiously, he unknotted the clean stock from his neck, and wiped her face with it.

"If I die ... you will not harm the children?"

"You will not die," he said.

Her eyes closed, sunken eyes in a gaunt, unbeautiful face. Again the probing memory touched him.

"Why did you not call one of the women? They know more of this than I."

"Who ... would be coming to me?"

"That MacNeil hag. Or Mairi."

"It is not fitting ... a lass should see ... her own father's whore brought to bed."

He said coldly, "If you know that, a ghràidh, then you know more than I."

The peat settled. He leaned forward and pushed another turf into the fire with the toe of his boot. Behind him she gave another guttural cry, and her bowels contracted. The stench of faeces overlaid the odours of birth and fear.

"I will clean it," he said.

He removed the stained sheet, taking it out into the darkness. The April night filled his lungs with a sterile cleanliness. There was no suggestion of dawn. He returned to her: she had fallen into a chilled stupour, broken only by the hideous dream of pain.

He smoked for a time, watching her: the stars wheeled overhead. Perhaps an hour passed, perhaps less or more. Her eyes opened and fixed on his face.

"Seircin ..."

"Don't say what you don't mean."

"Mo seircin," she whispered again, with great resolution. "What they say of you ... is a lie."

He smoked, ignoring the fingers, slippery with sweat, that grasped and hesitated, then they were still. She turned her face away from the smoke and grunted stoically.

When he had finished the pipe he leaned down and tapped it out, and swore as the clay broke against the hearthstone. Behind him she cried out. He straightened without haste, putting the fragments into his pocket, and pressed her thighs apart: they opened willingly for him, as they always had. The child's head was presenting itself, waxen and cauled with membrane.

"Bi làidir— tha e tighinn."

She convulsed, gasping, "O Chriòsda ... Mhuire nan gràs ..." If she thought, she thought of sin, and of this as payment for that sin, many times repeated with him, and she had tried to tell him that for the joy of their brief and infrequent couplings she would pay it willingly. She had called him in extremity what she had long called him in private, beloved, and he had cast it aside, her last offering, with contempt and pitilessness. And now she was drowning in his eyes, cold light eyes seen dimly through smoke and shadow ... in a cold, green sea. And without pity, without pity....

It came, a bursting agony. Then the squalling thing in a rush of blood and mucous, and an expelling of slimy afterbirth and dripping, greyish cord.

"An caileag," he said.

A girl. Born alive, out of the privations of winter, kicking now in protest at the cold breath of the dawn.

She closed her eyes, weighted with exhaustion, and listened to his movements. The lamp still burned, and the fire, paler in the growing light.

"I will get up later," she said.

She felt the damp, piercingly sweet air of the morning lapping at her face, like a slow, incoming tide. "I will get up, a chiall."

She continued to murmur to him although she knew that he had gone, until drifting on the tide of exhaustion she slept, drowning in the cold, bright sea.

***

By ten o'clock the brightness of the dawn had given way to rain. He sat in the estate office listening to its rhythm against the opened windows. The last snow melting, the rivers now in spate, the furrows turned to mud beneath the plough: *the long continued drenching rain of winter.*

The room was unheated, and consequently damp: it was also small, concentrating the mind upon the minutiae of management, and cluttered with the debris and impedimenta of generations, the shelves lined with ledgers in green and brown leather or bound in marbled covers, the paper spotted with mildew, the table littered with candle stubs, goosefeather quills, a tinderbox, and a flask of the local whisky, newly confiscated from one of half a hundred nearby stills.

He sat in the darkness of the spring morning, the pages closely written in his own hand lying on the table before him.

> Farm 7th. Glenkill. This Farm is occupied at present by 3 Tennants and extends to the No of 62 Acres, 30 of which is arable and the remaining 32 Acres of very fine pasture interspersed with a great deal of shabby wood which tho it takes up some of the ground, yet affords much shelter, and naturall Grass that at an average its value may be taken in with the ploughed land. These 3 Tennants sow yearly 12 Bolls grain and hold 6 horses, 12 Milch Cows, 12 Yell do./ and 2 Score sheep for which they pay of yearly Rents £8.4.3 d. Sterling.
>
> Farm 8th. Monnymore. This Farm is occupied at present by 6 Tennants and Extends to the no of 265 Acres....

He drank deeply from the flask. He had drunk this particular water of life since his childhood, for sustenance, for warmth, for oblivion. It was all three now, or merely habit, and its fiery assault on an empty stomach was also familiar. The rain swept the courtyard below. The wind, searching, stirred the papers slightly. He turned the pages. Backwards or forwards, it made no difference. This tune was always the same.

> 15th August, Falkirk tryst. Small cattle, no money offered and many left unsold. 30th September, Falkirk tryst. Lean cattle very stiff to sell. Prices offered very low and as such would not remunerate the rearers of stock. 19th October, Falkirk tryst. High prices for sheep. The numbers of cattle from the north unusually short. The losses sustained by north country dealers are immense ... some sales are effected but at considerably lower profits then previous markets.

The litany of disaster continued like a melancholy chant.

> 1763, December (cont.) Mortality in the Parish unnaturally great.
> 1764, January. Sickness and mortality esp. among the old, much beyond the common average.

February.	Two deaths reported of Absolute starvation. Much sickness prevailing.
March.	Disease, the result of insufficient and bad food, is committing great ravages. Deaths frequent among the old, bloody stools always present.
April.	Purpura present. They are attacked with languour, pain of the arms, then ulcers, generally on the Legs and body – There is also pain in the mouth and throat, swelling of the limbs with discolouration. Number of deaths averaged 40 in a population of 1,650 (est.)

The people are in very poor Circumstance.

He looked up. Ewen stood in the doorway, with a lighted candle in his hand.

"It is as dark as the Apocalypse. I do not know how you see what you are doing."

"There's no need for me to see it. I have it all by heart."

Their conversations were now almost invariably in English. Ewen's enthusiasm for Gaelic had dwindled with his abjuration of responsibility toward his tenants, and French belonged to the past, as dead and vanished as that graceful, eager boy.

They sat in silence: Ewen studied him. The olive skin, closely shaved, the long, broken nose, the black hair falling roughly to his collar; he noted the red-rimmed eyes and the whisky on the table, and as if sensing his disapproval Malcolm slopped some of the spirit into a dirty horn cup and drank it.

"You begin early."

He said nothing, feeling in his pocket and pulling out a small roll of tobacco, tied with tarred twine. The sgian was in the top of his boot where he always carried it: he drew it and cut off a lump and began to shave it into shreds with the razor-sharp blade.

"What do you want?"

"Only to see you. I do not see you often, Malcolm. I merely wondered how you were."

He rose, leaving the records where they lay and moving the candles nearer.

"You had better look at these, since you've come."

Ewen came around the table and sat down, leaning close to the pages: when he looked up Malcolm was standing at the window, the bones of his face sharply pronounced in the greyish light.

"I am a cursed man. Surely we are cursed."

"The mortality of your cattle should concern you more."

"There were five buried yesterday."

"Aye, and another born this morning."

"For which you are responsible?"

He smoked and watched the rain: it reminded Ewen of the intractable silences of his youth.

"Why do you not marry her, and put an end to this sordid liaison?"

"Do you perceive it as sordid?"

"I do so perceive it. Yes."

He turned, with the roll of tobacco in his hand. "This is the only prick of mine I show publicly. What I do with the other is my own affair."

Ewen persisted quietly, bravely, hearing the echo of another conversation had in this room with Murdoch thirty years before.

"The woman has no status in the community; she has only the contempt of her neighbours. Your children are illegitimate. Will you not give them the benefit of your name?"

"Give bastards the benefit of a bastard's name?" He smiled, without humour. "And what status would I confer on her by making her my wife? At least in her present state she can always claim that it was rape— which I have no doubt she does when it seems convenient."

"Do you not consider marriage? I do not mean at this level of society."

"Who would have me, for Christ's sake?"

Ewen's pity deepened, and his sense of futility. The morning was stale with it.

He laid his hand on the ledger. Like the room, it smelled of mildew.

"What am I to do about this?"

"I will tell you, when I know."

And he heard himself say humbly, "Thank you."

I had the dream again, as I had dreamed it at irregular intervals since coming to Scotland. It was always the same house, a house I did not know, which was neither Evesham nor Ardsian, and they were always the same darkened, secret rooms in some upper region which was kept hidden, a mystery. Sometimes I was alone, searching in the shrouded rooms for fragments of the past, which caused me unbearable pain and grief when I found them, but for which I searched with a morbid compulsion: diaries, mementoes, a lock of hair, a lover's explicit letters. Once, in the labyrinth of those rooms, I found them together and watched their intercourse, and woke hitting the pillows with indescribable violence.

Now I was standing at the bottom of a narrow stair, which I knew led up to that darkened storey and its inevitable torments, and he was leading me with a hand of cold, raw strength. It was Mordaunt's hand, although he never turned his head or spoke. We climbed through the shadows and came, not to those shrouded rooms, but into a painful intensity of light… and he attempted to pull me against him, although his face was obscured by a bright mist. And I struck him, and woke, shivering, in the first glimmer of the dawn.

It was the fourteenth of May, almost Whitsun; two years had passed since he had quit Evesham. And I knew with an utter conviction that he was dead, and in the guise of this dream had come to me one last time, and rejected, had finally left me.

Still numbed by the dream, I rode to Ardsian: it was a little past ten o'clock. I went up alone, into the heart of the nautilus, knocked and pushed open a door; and the sunlight blinded me. The room was long and luminous, with windows from highly polished floor to ceiling – Ewen was there at a table, with the radiance of the morning behind him, and he was not alone. There was a man with him who seemed all darkness, dark clothing, dark hair, whose face I could not see and did not need to see. I knew who he was.

I stood, with my hair clubbed untidily back from my face, in my shabby, stained riding clothes, gaunt and graceless and as taut as a wire about to snap, and Ewen said gently: "Come in, my dear. You do not know my factor."

I said, "How do you do." I could not offer my hand, because Ewen held it, and the man to whom he had introduced me made no attempt to approach me, or to offer his.

He said, "We have met."

His eyes were some light colour, green or grey, I could not distinguish which; nor had I been able to distinguish it in that drifting, glittering snow, that hallucinatory twilight.

I said, "I think not."

An interminable time passed: it seemed we stood in crystal, in that bloodied, drifting snow; then Ewen said, "My dear, if you will do me the kindness of waiting in the garden … we will take coffee presently. If you will excuse me—"

He was gone, with a surprising lack of subtlety, leaving me alone with that still, silent shadow against the light, who was watching me with eyes I could not see while motes of dust, instead of snow, drifted in the broad bars of sun between us, and somewhere a thrush was singing in yet leafless branches.

He said, "I see you have recovered your wits, from which you seemed briefly parted on the occasion of our last meeting."

I stared into the light for a moment; then I walked out and closed the door behind me. Ewen was not yet in the garden. I sat, shaken, on the stone bench by the fountain, and eventually he came, wearing his coat and his shabby boots.

"You do me an unexpected honour," he said.

"Thank you for receiving me … with such grace. For not making me appear a fool before your man."

He smiled a little, as though something in my turn of phrase amused him. "I should not like you to feel that you must always be invited.... I would prefer you to use the house as if it were your own." Then, "What is troubling you, Margaret? What has brought you here?"

And I wept. I wept so easily now. Perhaps he recognized in it and in me something which alarmed him.

"He is dead—"

"Who is dead?"

"Achill. I dreamed of it."

"You have never spoken his name," and I thought it had brought something to his mind, some fragment he would share with me.

"You remember ... him."

"What I remember I have told you."

The thrush was still singing, as it sang in the gardens of my memory, and at the bottom of the garden a wild cherry, white with blossom, dropped its petals on the barren ground.

"Will you tell me something, Margaret?"

"Yes. Whatever you wish."

"Why did he leave his house, and why did you leave it ... for this?"

"He loved me."

"Who could not love you, Margaret?"

"I could not love him. I was ... frightened. He had—"

I did not finish it. He sat for some moments, deeply reflective; then he said, "To take the love of a child, and to betray it, is not easily forgiven. But I cannot judge him. One can only pity him, and perhaps, understand." He said nothing for a while, as if hesitant, considering. "Thirteen years ago... I had a mistress. She was fifteen. I had been betrayed and deserted by every one, and in the end I was betrayed and deserted by her. But I was happy. I imagined ... that it was possible ... that she could love me ... that she would not find me ridiculous, or disgusting ... and for a time I thought ... I myself loved her. And there was some light in hell— and I was in hell then— I had been in hell many years. And I thought ... perhaps if you can understand, and forgive me, then perhaps you can also understand ... and forgive him." He rubbed his hand across his eyes. "I should not tell you these things. I talk to you as if you were myself."

Then he touched me, tentatively, laying his hand very gently on my sleeve, so that it should not be intrusive; I could ignore it if I wished.

"Can you forgive him?"

"No."

"One day you will."

"No... Perhaps I am blighted. I cannot love— there is no love in me, no ability to love."

"You are very young," he said. "My little one."

The wind moved among the cherry branches, scattering the petals like snow.

"Where is he now?"

"I told you. He is dead."

"He is not dead. This is mere fancy, mere distress. Did you know where he had gone?"

"No.... The Havana. I don't know."

"You know the regimental agent?"

"Yes. Mure, Son, and Atkinson, in London—"

"Why do you not write to him? I will have it carried for you to Edinburgh, for the post."

"I cannot."

"So," he said. "C'est finis. L' pauvre."

And I never knew which one of us he meant.

In the evening Ewen sat staring at the luminous sky, and phrasing in his mind the elegant courtesies of the letter he believed time had granted him the maturity, and the wisdom, to send. After several attempts he finished it, signing himself *Ewen Hilaire Gunn Stirling, of Glen Sian,* and folded it; and wrote on the cover, *To the Garrison Commander, the Havana, in the care of Mure, Son and Atkinson, London.*

He drank brandy and water and watched the sun set, and the sealing wax harden on the letter. Then he tore it neatly in half and burned it, and wrote instead to his son, informing him that his season of dalliance in Edinburgh was at an end, and summoning him home.

And so he came, James Gordon Gunn Stirling, twenty-three years old, a fair-haired chameleon of charm and immense insecurity, with an accent which drifted from French to Scots as he himself had drifted, belonging nowhere. Born in Nice but possessing no European sensibility, and reared in the Highlands, where he had acquired no sensitivity to Gaeldom, he had passed the years from nine to eighteen in France, and emerged neither corrupt nor innocent. He had travelled on the Continent for two years thereafter, funded by a dying vicomtesse as a gift of love to his father, knowing that Ewen could not afford this, the accepted climax of a young man's education. With the Peace of Paris he had kept his deferred promise to his father to return to Scotland, and had glided without distinction through two years in Edinburgh in the blue and maroon gown of a student. Fifteen pounds a session, board, lodging and tuition, from November to April: he left eagerly, with no interest in law, halfway to his degree. He had accomplished what he had intended in Edinburgh, and he planned to return as soon as the opportunity presented itself to claim his prize: the hand of an Episcopalian heiress three years his senior whom he had cheerfully seduced after ascertaining the extent of her dowry. He had neglected to tell her of his family's chequered history of Jacobitism, and he had renounced Catholicism out of boredom— he saw these as minor considerations, so minor that he did not find it necessary to inform his father, and when he did perceive the necessity, he found he had not the courage.

And so, for a time, chameleon-like, he altered himself to blend with his surroundings, playing the part his father wished: the adoring son, rapt with delight at his homecoming and eager to learn the affairs of Glen Sian. And he played another part, almost to perfection, when gossip and judicious enquiries had afforded him all he wanted to discover of my past, and my own inheritance.

"Are you the beauteous Margaret, of whom my father has told me so much?"

"Your father exaggerates, if indeed he said it."

"I like a rose with thorns," he remarked with a little, knowing smile.

So he began his campaign.

It was a silly, shallow little interlude, and ultimately wearying. As his pursuit of me intensified, so his father withdrew and observed it, and us, as it were from a distance, with a cynicism I had not seen in him before. His coolness hurt me, and I saw him very seldom throughout the summer. I saw only James.

I rode with him; I walked with him; I fished the peat-stained, icy waters with him. I played the spinet, out of tune and out of practise, and he played the flute in the white summer evenings. Once, in a secluded corner of the garden, he attempted to make love to me, but I found him curiously asexual, and after a few desultory kisses he seemed to concede that I was similarly unappealing, so our relationship became casually filial. His fumbling, boyish ardour had neither frightened nor disgusted me, and evoked no memory... I merely found it, and increasingly him, an encumbrance of which it was suddenly imperative that I be freed.

I lived in a miasma of disapproval. My father's eyes burned me like acid, burned the perfume from my skin and the pearls from my ears, burned what was feminine and renascent in me and left me scarred by his contempt. My aunt, enigmatic as a stone, commented neither upon his behaviour nor my own, but she watched the emergence of the woman from the gaunt and slovenly chrysalis of the girl, and assessed her strength. Even James, for a strange, brooding interval, left me alone: our marriage had become, from a

287

matter of crude speculation in Glen Sian, almost a foregone conclusion, and perhaps even he was aghast.

In the last week of September I wrote to Ewen: such formality had descended upon our relationship that I felt I must speak to him. I received no answer, and chilled by his silence I rode uninvited up to Ardsian. There was fog on the road, and a clinging quietness that persisted throughout the house. I went to the library, where James was sometimes to be found lounging, and pushed open the door: at the end of that lightless room, where the sun had streamed through glass on a May morning, the casements stood open. The air was intensely cold.

He was sitting at the table, coatless and smoking: the scent of the tobacco in the damp, cold air was curiously sweet. Behind him, as in a milky sea, the world lay shrouded and indistinct.

"Whichever one you want, he is not here."

He was writing, a difficult script that might have been any language, even some private shorthand: the sound of the quill seemed unnaturally loud. Eventually he paused, consulted one of the piled sheets, wrote again and looked up.

"Unless your business is with me?"

His eyes, which had watched me through that glittering, drifting snow and the glare of spring sunlight in this room, were a stark, clear, disconcerting green. They could not be mistaken for any other colour; nor could their expression be misconstrued.

I said, "You do not approve of me."

"You do not seek my approval, nor I yours. But I'll tell you something, Miss MacNeil. Choose the whelp or the dog. Glen Sian has no patience with whores."

There was nothing more to say.

I broke with James.

He sat in the estate office, smoking and writing, conscious of the silence and the hourless quality the falling snow gave to this, the last afternoon of the year.

Abstract of the Foregoing Accompts

Discharge:

Branch 1st   Repairs and Buildings divided thus

Repairs of Ardsian House	17.13.10
Building a house to the gardner	22. 4. 5.

288

	Repairs of Sian mill	10. 3.10
	Repairing the mill offices	5. 7. -
	Repairs to Stables and Greenhouse at Ardsian Hse	9.13. 2.
Branch 2nd	Improving Farms by burning, plowing & harrowing	32. 7.36
	Sundry Articles of Improvements	2. 2.11
Branch 3rd	Price of Tools and Repairs	23.12. 4.
Branch 4th	Factors sallary 2 years to Marts 1766	£70.
	do. Candles, paper, pens, ink	11. 9.37
	do. Incidents and Traveling Charges	14.10.11
	By 2½ years wages as factor from Martinmas 1766 to	
	Whitsunday 1769 at £35 a year	£87.10

He had raised the rents, experimentally. There had been pathetic protests but they had had no power to move him, and the tenants had paid. He had requested credit and received it. He had adjusted the figures of several years' accounts and made good the shortfall from his own capital, the extent of which was unknown to Ewen. In the years of his administration Ewen's income had increased, and so had costs, and so had expenditures.

His pouch was empty and the pipe was cold. He put them into his pocket and shook the ink from the quill again, scoring out the final lines.

The snow fell, and the hour passed, and the glow of the greasy stub on the table became inadequate even for his keen eyes, so he snuffed it and sat in the cold dimness, with the scent of the smoking wick and the smell of stale tobacco, and mildew, and degeneration. The short northern day passed into the white darkness of a snowy night— when the flask was empty he left it, and the room, and the year's accumulation of debts and deception and frustration, and went to see Ewen.

Ewen was indisposed; sleeping; not to be disturbed. This intelligence was imparted by James, who leaned against the drawing room door displaying a substantial amount of Mechlin lace and exuding spirits and bonhomie.

"Oh, for God's sake, man, unbend a little. For the New Year— it's the least you can do."

"I drink when I like, and in what company. Yours does not appeal to me."

Behind him the voice, so like and unlike Ewen's, lost its affectation and its civility.

"You graceless lout. Go off to your drab then, since you prefer her society."

He turned back, with no change of expression. As he had in their childhood James hungered for his approval and dared to hope for his friendship, both of which he withheld: as he had in their childhood, James feared him.

He said, "You may see a cock pheasant when you look in your glass, but I still see a snotty wee bairn. And I still carry you on my back. Christ, I carry all of you."

He went out of the house, leaving behind the lights and the smell of roasting meat from the kitchens where, by midnight, the gillean caillaig, the New Year's men, would gather, disguised in cowhides, with their torches and their rituals and their demands for whisky and bannock, and their invocations of the Trinity and of darker spirits, and their *deisal* walk in the direction of the sun, and their passing of a flaming torch about the head of the oldest woman in the house, while all the inhabitants beat the torch with sticks and tongs and burned the cowhide worn by the leader, and sniffed the burning flesh: pieces of the hide were even carried to the beasts to smell. He knew who they would be, what faces were hidden beneath the hairy hides: but this night transformed them into a force inexpressibly sinister, and their presence would infect Ardsian like a malignancy. Their rituals were reminiscent of witchcraft and sacrifice, and the ancient Celtic custom of king-killing; and he who feared nothing felt a primitive frisson, as though his skin had been touched in passing.

He rode home in the drifting whiteness, and the bitter cold burned his lungs. He kicked the snow from his own doorstep and made up the fire and drank, walking the house. The snow stopped, but the pallor of the air and sky illuminated the night.

Near midnight he went out, into an intense cold and the unearthly glow of a land without horizons, and a sky suffused with veils of light through which few stars penetrated.

He rode north, under the flickering bands of the aurora. The snow lay on the peaks and on the moors, an infinity of white.

He closed the door on the pallor and the clarity of the night, and on the northern sky, alive with its baleful fires, and the musty darkness embraced and smothered him: the smells of confinement, human and animal, of dung and poverty. The smells of childhood.

He quoted the guisers' Gaelic at her, unaware that he swayed where he stood.

" 'This is the night of gifts ... I am the servant of God's son at the door. Arise thyself and open to me ...'"

She said, "What do you want?"

"I ascend by the door lintel. I descend by the doorstep. I bring you the gift of eternal life—" He threw the sprig of evergreen on the fire and followed it with a broken clod of peat. "I bring you fuel. I bring you the holy gift of salt ..."

"You're fou," she said, with contempt.

"What the hell is that to you?"

"The flux is on me."

"Then there'll be no damned bairn. I don't want any more damned bairns."

He woke before dawn, his penis and his clothing spattered with blood and semen. She had not lied: she had not protested. Nor had she responded, and she lay now rigidly, her face averted, her clothing, like his own, stained and disordered. She had endured him; he did not remember how many times, only that he had fought with his sex against fear, and that fear possessed him still, and there were no words in any language to describe it, or to offer explanation or apology.

The sky was cloudless, the deep blue before dawn; the air was bitter and silent. He watched the first transparent rays strike with geometrical precision, dimming the morning star, bathing the high serrated peaks with a sharp, unnatural gold. The sun was not yet visible, only the wash of green and the precise division between light and darkness in the sky. The moor before him lay still in shadow, a wasteland, and as trackless as the sea.

Possessed by dread, he rode forward into it: into the wastes of the unknown year.

III

In Edinburgh on a cold forenoon in May, 1765, in a chapel of the Episcopalian church, James Stirling and Charlotte Amelia Hardy were married. The ceremony was witnessed by forty of the bride's family, and by the bridegroom's father, who observed the proceedings as in a dream. He never afterwards remembered the exchange of vows, or any other sound.

He was a part of this assembly, had been a part of it for days, and yet he was divorced from it, by birth, by religion, by the bitter legacy of memories that poisoned his stay in Edinburgh. In these filthy streets he saw himself, cringing and faltering like some drunken outcast, stumbling in the gutter in the first steps of a journey that would take him from imprisonment to the resumption of a shattered life in Glen Sian. Yesterday he had seen the Tolbooth and the messenger's house where he had been detained, and the snivelling caddies touting for brothels outside it, who had prodded and mocked him when they discovered there was nothing worth picking from his pockets. He had felt the same probing east wind from the salt wastes beyond Leith. He had heard the many bells of Edinburgh's ordered day, from the noon chimes of St. Giles's to the kail-bell at two o'clock, the hour for fashionable dinners, and the tinkle-sweetie at eight that marked the end of the working day for master and apprentice, and signalled the beginning of the shivering night for prisoners who dreaded time's passing, lest it summon them too soon to judgment.

Now the bells rang and the cold sunlight flickered down into the street, and the bustling throngs of Edinburgh tradesmen jostled past to their collops and mutton and herring and some hours' hard drinking in the many fetid taverns in the Canongate, and the brilliant, moving tide of wedding guests pushed and laughed and eddied through the streets, bearing him among them, until they spilled through the door of the fashionable Fortune's Tavern. There they crowded into a private room upstairs and consumed a gargantuan wedding breakfast, throughout the course of which the day passed into dusk, and the hours struck monotonously from St. Giles's.

There was music. There was an unending supply of porter and fine claret. There were dubious jokes in an ever more impenetrable dialect, which Ewen found distasteful. There was an atmosphere of strained hilarity among those whose objections to this marriage had been made clear, which became riotous as the plates were changed and the glow of alcohol rendered all things more acceptable. There were countless toasts: this intemperate society relished any excuse to raise another glass.

"May the hinges o' frien'ship ne'er rust— nor the wings o' love lose a feather."

More winks and nudges. Another heavy ruby face beneath an elaborate curled wig.

"Aye, aye. May the pleasures o' the evening bear the reflections o' the morn!"

"Aye— may the winds o' advairsity ne'er blaw open oor doors!"

A staggering, magnificently laced velvet coat: yet another anonymous relative.

"Tae the trade o' Leith, an' the outward bound!"

Ewen watched the bride, flushed and brilliant-eyed, her thick fair hair dressed with ribbons and white flowers, her long mare's face tolerant, amused. But plain, so plain. Taller than James, and some three or four years older— why had she consented to this? Did she not scent a fortune-hunter? Had she no experience of life? Had she regarded James as some last resort?

She smiled with a singular sweetness, and he, overcome by shyness and his festering dislike of her and her family and Edinburgh and this entire brittle charade, engineered by a son for whom he no longer felt the slightest trace of affection, looked away; and did not see the deference in her eyes, the willingness to love him, and her discomfort when her boozy, magisterial father stumbled to his well-shod feet.

"We've nae heard frae *you*, Glen Sian," and he felt that it was an accusation. "Although bein' as ye are a Roman gentleman, maybe ye find oor ways a thing different frae yer ain. Hae ye onything tae say?"

Even James, lounging drunkenly at the head of the littered table, made some untidy effort to sit upright. The bulbous face and broad shoulders, frosted liberally with powder, swam in Ewen's vision like some distorted moon.

"I drink to my son," he said, and his stammer overcame him. "And to… my daughter." He did not look in her direction: he did not want to see her gratitude. "I think your God and mine, sir, will join in blessing them. They are not so very different as you choose to believe."

The voices rushed back like some roaring tide, carrying with them the flotsam of *James* and *Charlotte* amid the froth of hilarity. He retreated into a shaken, embarrassed reverie, ignored by his neighbours. Then the corpulent face with its map of red veins descended once more into his vision.

"A Frog an' a papist in one— ye canna deny ye were a Jack."

He looked up and said coldly, "I do not deny it."

Hardy seemed satisfied, prodding him in the shoulder with a forefinger.

"I kent it. I speired aboot for it— they said ye were taken up. Weel, there's nae doot ye would hae been hangit had I sat in the Sessions o'er ye."

"How very fortunate then that you did not," Ewen said. "Otherwise we should not be here together on this happy occasion."

Hardy stared at him truculently, searching for insult. Finding none, he was disconcerted, and then jovial.

"Weel, weel, 'tis deil-be-lickit— 'tis a' forgot the noo." The stabbing forefinger became the flat of a massive hand thumping his shoulder. "I'll nae bide here gabbing on the arsccockles o' the past. Take anither dram, man— ye're o'er sober for me, an' I ne'er trusted a man wha didna drink— nor nae papist neither."

The sun set; he saw the suggestion of its colours through the smutted panes. Spring twilight, May twilight. Why had they married in May? *Marry in May, rue for aye….* He had married in November; and he could no longer remember Elspeth's face.

I do not deny it.

Was this what it came to, he thought, was this how life ended, as an object of pity and ridicule? An old rebel burnished by the passing years, acquiring a patina of respectability? Had time which had rendered him an historical curiosity also drawn the potency and the power of that cause, so that, obsolete, it was no longer to be feared?

When the cool, pale hand came to rest upon his sleeve he gazed at it without recognition; then he looked up, and thought the colour on her skin like the blush on a sun-warmed peach.

"I beg your pardon for my father, Glen Sian. He is not—"

A gentleman, he thought.

"Your father is a fool, my dear. It is my good fortune that I need not suffer him, gladly or for any length of time."

"James and I wish to retire." She said it with no false modesty, without any innuendo whatever, and squinting through the smoke and candlelight he saw with a faint, fastidious dislike that James was in fact too drunk to lift his head, let alone indulge in carnal excesses.

I apologize for my son.

She lingered, curiously tentative. The white blossoms in her hair had wilted in the noisome heat, and the blond silk of her gown was crushed, but she retained a luminous quality of grace: not a bridal innocence but maturity, accomplished and serene.

"Shall we see you at dinner tomorrow at my father's house?"

It would be as it always was, a noisy, protracted affair in a household always crowded with people, whose conversation, often shouted, consisted of music, politics, the new Stamp Act which was little understood, the falling off of trade on the east coast, and the minutiae of one another's lives, which he found indescribably boring. But only two days remained before they commenced their wedding tour, lavishly planned by James and funded from Charlotte's considerable dowry, and it would be autumn before they arrived in Glen Sian, James, he hoped, having been guided into adulthood by this clear-eyed girl.

"Yes," he said, reluctantly. "Yes, I will see you there." Then, "You look very pretty tonight, Charlotte. I do not believe I have ever seen so pretty a bride."

He had never called her by her Christian name before; he did not know if she had noticed. There was movement in the room now: the ten o'clock drum was beating. He slipped out quietly before the process of reviving James began, and other staggering shadows followed him, relieving themselves with audible gasps of agony when they reached the street. Charlotte's sister and sister-in-law, with several nieces and female friends, teetered past the urinating figures, shivering in the cold night air and pointing out the shadow cast on the moonlit cobbles by the spire of a neighbouring church.

"A river! A river!" they all cried, and Ewen, who found the spectacle of drunken gentlewomen particularly offensive, looked away in embarrassment as they clutched at one another, tittering and lifting the rich stuff of their gowns to reveal their gartered thighs as they waded across the shadow.

The drumbeat stilled, and the moonlight flashed on the glass of a hundred casements opening in the vicinity to discharge the contents of close-stool and chamberpot. There was a pitiless chorus of "Gardy loo!" and anguished shrieks of "Haud yer haun'!" from the ladies, who teetered even faster. The indifferent moonlight shone on their progress, shimmering and giggling, and then on the torrents of urine aimed after them— the spring night sickened at it. He took refuge in a close, overcome by nausea, pressing his handkerchief to his nose until the deluge was over and the casements slammed shut, and the cobbles lay spattered with the day's accumulation.

He walked a few paces, his shoes slipping in excrement, and retched into his handkerchief, until he could control himself no longer and leaned vomiting quietly against a wall while a loitering prostitute, assessing the cost of his clothing and the ripeness of his pockets, jeered at him.

"Awa' wi' ye, ye dirty dog! Are ye too fou tae staun'?"

What is it to you, where the shit falls as the rain? What is it to all of you?

He lifted his head, but she had gone: and the east wind, which had tortured him when he had lain in these rain-swept wynds on the first nights of his freedom, now scoured away the sour taint of his sickness, and refreshed him, and allowed him to walk on.

I was not accorded much reputation by Glen Sian but my father, a picture of moral rectitude, informed me that I had tarnished what there was of it by my wanton behaviour with James. And my former unchaperoned visits to Ewen were not to be resumed, lest they be misconstrued. I realized that my sin was not my intimacy with the heir but my failure to marry him, and I did not know if Ewen himself regarded me in that light. By the half-spoken phrase and the significant look, my father encouraged me to think so.

So, out of loneliness and perhaps some final desire to prove myself to this narrow society, I made my last attempt to conform and drove MacNeil's cattle up to the summer pastures in June. After three weeks of living in primitive conditions I had had enough: the girls were kind but pitifully self-conscious, and the difficulties of language remained a source of tension. I left the cattle and walked back down to Glen Mor.

There was a letter waiting for me from Ewen; the wax had been broken and resealed. There was not much in it, only that he missed my dear company and that of his son, and if I would visit him he would be honoured, and would give me roses (if any were still blooming) and news of the wedding.

In the morning I went to him; my father was from home and so could not provoke a confrontation.

He had been pruning the Rose du Saint Sacrament, which had long since passed its season: the others bloomed in fulsome extravagance, littering the soil with fragrant petals. He laid his secateurs on the grass and picked up the coat he had tossed on the ground.

"Come and take a glass of wine with me, and then I will cut some for you."

We sat in the sun on chairs brought out from the house and drank claret; he regretted the absence of any hock, or the means to chill it. And he spoke of the wedding, and Edinburgh, and of the bride.

"You are not jealous? It does not offend you that I mention Charlotte?"

"I never loved him. So how should you offend me?"

"The convolutions of a woman's mind. I thought perhaps you had, and did not know it." He gazed at me with penetrating eyes. "You will take more wine? This is bought of my pocket money." And he laughed, ironically. "First the father bestows money upon the son, then the son marries and gives to the father. I remember giving James a livre in my cousin's rose garden in France some years ago. He said it was not enough. He was truly an objectionable child."

The sun warmed the wine, striking a hard light from the rim of the glasses. "How rare," he said, "to be so warm. The sun is like Italy." Then, "Did I tell you how I planted a slip of Alba from this garden on my mother's grave at St. Germain-en-Laye? James has promised to go and see it ... I do not suppose he will."

We sat in silence; the air was heavy with perfume. I sensed that he did not want me to talk.

After a while he remarked, "I do not feel I have known James since he was a small boy. I feel I have lost him, that we are strangers, polite strangers. Always I hope to encounter my son somewhere yet but I have never seen him. Perhaps I will some day, but I doubt it."

He finished his wine. The glasses dried in the sun.

I said, "How I wish it was always like this."

His eyes opened, like eyes opening unexpectedly in a mask.

"Allow me the honour of showing you my roses. Otherwise I lead you into decadence."

"Is that what you call this?"

"My dear," he said with a curious sharpness, "in this place where even God is a Calvinist, you need not doubt the answer. A little wine, a little sunlight, a few hours of regretted pleasure, and then we die, and we are dead forever." Then he shrugged. "I am out of sorts. This wedding business— I find it tiresome."

We walked; he cut roses and spread them in his trug, and his mood, so inexplicably disturbed, lightened again. Once he pulled the hundred scented petals from a rose of Provence and scattered them over my hair.

"Voyons! I make you a bride," and we laughed as they tumbled from my head and shoulders. "I should like to have seen you a bride, Margaret."

"I daresay I have missed my chance, and I shall be condemned to a useful spinsterhood."

"That is ridiculous. Moreover, it is obscene."

"Who would marry me then? Who do you recommend?"

He said in an odd, strained voice, "Mys—" and the rest failed him. He flushed and swore, which emerged with great fluency, and finally managed with immense difficulty, "My ... son."

He had scratched his hand; he brushed the blood away angrily. "I know you do not ... love him ... but I hoped he might love you. He needs your strength, although you deserve ... better than his weakness." He cut another rose, still trying to overcome it, but his impediment was worse than I had ever heard it. "It is nothing. I have said nothing... and even that I cannot say... except as an idiot."

He walked further away among the roses, cutting randomly; he returned after some time with a great many flowers of exquisite beauty and fragrance.

He gave them to me gracefully, with a slight bow. He seemed breathless, and his colour was high.

"There are no roses on your little rose bush, the one I bred for you. Maybe there will be later, or next year. I name them Margaret. I regret... I cannot give them to you now."

"But these are so beautiful. I have no need of more."

Again that little lift of the shoulders, so inimitably Gallic.

"Why should you not enjoy them? God knows their season is brief." I had knelt on the grass to arrange them: he was watching me. "They tell you something, Margaret. Here, at least ... I speak without interruption."

"How shall I interpret your message?"

"Oh, I shall write it down for you some day."

"But these will be dead by then."

He said, "So... they will. Well, I shall tell you one or two. This one is beauty, unconscious beauty— that is you, because you do not know you possess it. And these, arranged so, represent a secret."

"Are you telling me a secret, Ewen?"

He did not smile.

"They are merely a little cipher, a curiosity. On certain glasses— treasonable glasses— you will see a full-blown rose engraved above two buds.

The rose is James, the two buds his sons Charles, the young pretender, and Henry." He had never spoken of this subject before: he had always avoided it. "So all Jacobites are reduced to cabals and secret symbols, by which like Freemasons they identify themselves."

I had never wanted to know the depth of his bitterness: I had never sought this confidence.

"Oh yes," he said. "How bitter. How bitter is Mordaunt?" That name, which was also never spoken, was shockingly unexpected. "Sometimes, Margaret— sometimes now I see so clearly— that everything seems very stark, like the light before a thunderstorm when you see the sun, and then look up and the sky is black. I see everything... I see how we are fools, how time manipulates us all. We are used and discarded in the enterprises of other men— in the affairs of armies, and nations— and we are like puppets— and how like so much rubbish we are discarded when we serve their purpose."

He walked, and I walked with him, and his arm was in my arm, but he was not with me, and although he spoke, it was not to me; and I listened, and did not understand.

"I think sometimes of other men whose lives, like mine, have been despoiled— men I might have known. And I ask myself, for what? For a rose engraved on a glass? For a pack of kings we can shuffle like cards? Should we have a French king? Should we have a German king? What does it matter? When we are dead, what does it signify, any of it?"

We had reached the steps: the heavy perfume of the roses surrounded us.

"I have become cynical," he said, almost casually. "I think of the past, and I regret it, because it was taken from me. I did not waste it— it was taken from me. And instead of coming to terms with it I am raging at it. I do not slip easily into my old age, although I thought I would."

"Ewen ...."

"I am merely tired. I think of my youth, and I regard the future. I do not like the prospect. Now come. I will give you supper."

"I shall not stay if you are tired."

"It is only ... disillusionment. Now come, put these in water. You will permit me to put on a clean shirt before coming to the table? Perhaps you will play something. I know you played for James."

We ate salmon for supper. He apologized for it, in case I should think it common. And we talked of many things, he of his youth and France, and his wife, with great poignancy; I of my childhood and my loneliness, my sense of isolation both then and now. He sat with his back against a cushion and did not eat very much.

At the end of the meal he gave me bitter coffee, although he did not touch his own. The room was very still, and cool with evening: although there were candles on the table their light enhanced, but was not needed.

"My dear child, I would keep you here forever, your talk is so pleasant to me. But your father will wonder where you are."

"He knows. He opened your letter."

"You do not need my intervention, Margaret. You are more than capable of dealing with your father."

I said nothing, wondering if it were true.

He sent for my flowers, and for my horse, and walked with me into the courtyard, into the scented night.

He handed me into the saddle and held up the roses for me to take: I laid them across the saddlebow.

"I shall probably be away in late August or September— I will have business in Fort Augustus. Will you come and prune my rose bushes when you finish reaping, if you insist upon reaping, that is?"

"I do; and yes, I will, of course."

"I cannot but disapprove of your labouring in this manner."

"It satisfies an instinct within myself to serve you. Medieval, if you wish." He frowned. "By it I repay your many kindnesses to me."

He put up his hand to the rein as though, as on that first spring evening, he would delay me.

"I do not want your repayment. Nor do I expect or ask any service of you." He released the rein then as if his arm had tired. "You may discharge all your imaginary debts to me later, if you would." I thought he would say something delicate, humorous. "If I should die, scatter my grave with rose petals. I read that they did so in ancient Persia, at the tombs of honoured men. If," a little smile, "you honour me."

I leaned from the saddle and kissed his cheek. Despite the smile, there was no humour in his face.

"Good night, my dear. Good night ... good night."

I rode through the twilight, with the extravagance of roses on the saddlebow; a mile or two later the light dimmed and the sky was overcast, and the jingle of bridle metal came to me clearly in the stillness that precedes rain. I checked my horse and backed him into bracken that frothed to my stirrup, and Ewen's factor, for whom I had left the path, passed me on that heavy stallion, lifting a hand in acknowledgment.

I went home troubled, and the perfume of the roses I had carried through the rain haunted my sleep; and later I pressed one as a memento of the day, although I did not know why.

***

In late August Ewen made a slow circuit of the estate, alone on horseback. He had deliberately chosen a time when Malcolm would be absent at the first cattle fair of the season.

He had delayed this small odyssey for several reasons, not least the reluctance to confront his own thoughts in a period of enforced solitude, but he came to realize that he was always alone, even in the midst of a household of servants, and no solitude could be more profound or frightening than in the hours of night, when all his fears thronged the darkness by his bed and gazed into his face.

So he left the house on a Monday morning, seeking an acquaintance with the land he had always regarded as foreign and unknowable. Nor had he ever considered it his property: eternal, it could belong to no one. Now it became a rough, personal canvas over which were scrawled tiny signatures of memory: only on this scale could its immensity be reduced, rendered human, and possessed.

He rode in the green silence of the birch wood on Sithean Oir, where that ghostly child crazed with neglect and degradation would forever run; he rode in the glen through the heavy undergrowth by the River Sian, where the branches were bowed with the previous night's rain and the sound of birds and rushing water was almost deafening. He rode into Glen Mor, past the huddled stone dwellings that clung to the road and the scattered upland crofts. The sun, still low, was in his eyes: the corded strips of run-rig lay now on either hand, rippling in the wind. Here he walked briefly amidst the grain, running the unripe heads through his fingers. The harvest would be late again, and the condition of the grain troubled him. He mounted again and left it behind: Glen Mor, its fields, its crofts, its petty prosperity, its demands. Left it and abjured his responsibility toward it, and rode further into the silence, and the land, and into himself.

He felt its rain, wind, cold, heat, fog, sunrise, a country of cloud and light, shadow and substance, patterned by wind-driven cloud and the fleeting ghosts of deer and grouse; eating drammach and drinking brandy and peaty water and occasionally buttermilk at the doors of isolated crofts. If they thought his appearance and behaviour strange, they would understand it later. He sat on their low stools, beneath their smoke-encrusted roofbeams, and while their children gathered to stare at him he listened to their fears and preoccupations, and entrusted with their secrets like a priest he shook their hands and took his leave of them; and saw the next crofts, and the next, until the burden of their complaints became overwhelming and their faces, like the faces in distant memory, were indistinguishable from one another, and he allowed them too to go.

300

He sat one afternoon on a sun-warmed rock, in sunlight under a sky slate-blue with approaching storm, and gazed at the ruins of the crofts abandoned by those who had emigrated. As far as he knew no tenant had offered for them, or perhaps they had not been offered, Malcolm choosing to let this land lie fallow for some purpose known only to himself. He had long suspected Malcolm of some plan but it was too inscrutable to discover; and in the meantime the wind sang among the scattered walls, and weeds grew through the hearthstones.

The sun lay on the grass, golden with summer: he saw his shadow before the clouds obliterated it, another small signature, another memory. *I was here. She was here.* But ephemeral, as wind over grass.

He cometh forth like a flower, and is cut down: he fleeth also as a shadow, and continueth not....

He found himself walking among the fallen stones, as though there could be something of her left to find.

To whom do we belong, if there is neither marrying nor giving in marriage? To those we have loved most dearly?

The rain began, uncertainly. It seemed very dark.

There was nothing, not a button, not a broken shard, not a rotting thread. Only the grass beneath his feet, and the white splashes of bird droppings.

He wiped the rain from his eyes and wrapped himself in his wet cloak. This place could offer nothing, not even shelter.

He rode down from the hills through the ruins of Glen Sian on the Sunday evening; and as always the blackened, scorched walls and the staring holes of the doorways filled him with inexpressible terror. He left his horse at the well and walked, his back braced against pain and fatigue, aware that his legs and hands were trembling, until he reached the place of his imprisonment.

Here, too, there was nothing, except a reek of excrement— tinkers using this close, foul cellar as an earth closet. No trace of his brief incarceration, where the English boy had beaten him until his excitement at the success of the interrogation had become uncontrollable and he had ejaculated into a handkerchief. No trace there, in the drifting rain, of the white, sullen faces of the soldiers, the moisture blackening the harsh red of their coats, the drag and stroke of the drums, the drummers spattered with shreds of living flesh. No sound, only silence, and the whisper of the rain, as there had been no sound that morning. Only the drums and the lash.

What happened among them?

Margaret's face, strained, unyouthful in its obsession: so eager to know the depths of a man's dishonour; so oblivious to the truth, so many truths that could never be told her.

Mys— my son....

He closed his eyes, shaking with fatigue and a physical nausea. The rain was heavier, the light strange, fleeing, haunted. He walked back up the street, picking his way over the broken cobbles.

What happened here?

What you see. Only the commonplace.

He rode out of it in the rain, leaving to it its ghosts and his own.

When he came up the steps at Ardsian every servant in the house appeared to be waiting for him.

"Glen Sian, Am Maor is back from the trysts—"

"Glen Sian, there are letters from your son—"

"Glen Sian, the minister was here ... it is a new roof for the kirk he is wanting. He says it will not wait."

He stopped in the hall as they pursued him like dogs, and his voice cracked.

"In Jesus' name, I am fifty years old, and I am not accountable to any of you! Now go about your business! Guillaume—" as the Frenchman was insinuating himself toward the stairs "— I am going into the garden. When I return I will want your services. See to it."

The olive eyes flickered over him, taking in wet clothing, wet hair, filthy boots, unshaven face.

"Monseigneur is cold. He will catch his death."

"I should not concern myself overmuch on that account."

He walked in the garden, cutting roses he knew would be the last: the damaged heads shattered when he touched them. Dark red roses and candlelight, the heat of France, the moth immolating itself in the unwavering flame. Honorée ... Honorée ....

Seeing his days are determined, the number of his months are with thee, thou hast appointed his bounds that he cannot pass.

Turn from him, that he may rest, till he shall accomplish, as an hireling, his day.

And now, younger than he, she had gone before him into that dark country, through that same dreaded gateway of pain.

It takes no courage to die. It only takes courage to live.

Wait for me, he thought, wait for me a little while, and I will tell you.

When he rose from the hip bath there was a little stain of blood in the water.

"I am much troubled by haemorrhoids, Guillaume. What do you recommend?"

There was dark blood too on the towel.

He said, "I wish to see my factor tonight. Tell Ruaraidh to send a message."

The dark eyes slid away from his.

"Yes, Monseigneur."

"I do not care how late. Tell Ruaraidh to send a boy to wait at his house if he is not at home."

He sat drinking brandy and water, waiting, listening to the rain. It was darker, the darkness of summer declining into autumn, toward a mortal winter. He found himself listening for Malcolm's step as he had throughout the years, all the nights when the rain was also a light step running in the darkness....

He heard the steps finally in the hall, as familiar to him as his own heartbeat. Slower than he imagined they would be: the man who walked was no longer the graceful youth of memory. The knock on the door panel, the gilt handle dropping, the candleflame bent in the draught. He stood on the periphery of the light, the impassive stillness of his childhood in his eyes.

Ewen said, "Come in and close the door. I want to talk to you."

I had gone up in September to prune the roses; Ewen was away, and the harvest was to begin the following week. When I reached Ardsian the rain which had accompanied me had become so heavy that I took refuge in the glasshouse, with the secateurs in the pocket of my riding coat and my clothing so wet that I was shivering.

There were rows of pots on the benches, some draped in black cloth: bulbs to be forced for the house. I walked along attempting to read their illegible labels. I don't know what caused me to look up. Perhaps he spoke my name, although he had never used it before I think this unlikely. I only know that I became aware of a presence, and when I turned Ewen's factor was standing at the end of the gravelled path. I don't know what I said, or if I spoke at all. He merely said, "That can wait. Come with me." And I followed him.

He walked through the dim house and I walked behind him; he opened the door of the morning room and I entered it after him; he waited for me to sit and I sat, in my sodden clothing. The room was cold and there were no flowers on the mantelpiece: Ewen was not in residence. I noticed these things with a peculiar clarity. I noticed the brownish stain left on my fingers by the dye from my wet leather gloves; I still had them in my pocket with the secateurs. I sat and he stood: behind him the haze of rain blotted out the garden and the roses I should have been pruning.

He said eventually, "I know he gives you coffee. I will have some brought to you."

"I don't want any coffee, thank you."

"Because I offer it?"

303

"Because I want to know what you want."

He said, "Ewen is dying. I was asked to tell you."

And the rest is fragmented, incomplete. My mind obliterates it, as the rain blurs the colours beyond a window, as one breathes upon cold glass and clouds it; and in my animal pain I saw nothing, and knew nothing, not even that he also suffered, not even that he could also grieve, uncomforted, like me.

They had met like conspirators in the same fusty parlour, in the same house in Fort Augustus: he believed even the same furtive Catholics had crept down from the hills to receive the absolution dispensed by an indolent Irish priest, rather too worldly and too well-dressed, and significantly lacking in the qualities of grace and humility. Ewen spent the night and left, realizing that whatever he had hoped to find within the framework of a religion he had almost abandoned had not been offered here.

On the ridge known as the Saddle he paused and looked back without regret: at the grey turbulent waters of the loch, the sails of the supply sloop from Inverness very pale under the dark sky, the untidy straggle of habitation, the moving scarlet at the garrison. He suspected that Trapaud, the deputy governor, was aware of every popish practise within ten miles of his little outpost and now, twenty years after the rising, viewed them with disdain if not actual indifference.

He rode on, staying that night at the disgusting inn at Glenmoriston, which was full of drunken soldiers who had been working on the roads. He left at dawn, and by noon saw the eagles' rock, Creag na h'Iolaire, Carn Dubh, Saobhaidh, Beinn Ceòthach, the mountains of Glen Sian; and as he rode throughout the afternoon they moved closer, enfolding him. And he knew that however he conceived home and death, he had found them both here, represented in a final consummation. He had come home to die.

It snowed lightly, without menace. James and Charlotte returned, impoverished and replete with anecdotes, which they would tell over and over with embellishment for several weeks. They were accompanied by James's valet Coll MacGregor, Charlotte's maid Lucille, and a collection of pack ponies, baggage, musical instruments and other pleasant rubbish as mementoes of their wedding tour: there were also two thousand tulip bulbs packed in straw from the Low Countries as a present for Ewen. He smiled, and had some one take them to the glasshouse, and later asked the gardeners to dig them in. His composure left him as it always did with the approach of night and he slept badly, waking in the darkness to pain and terror, and the tinctures of opium in the bottles by the bed which were beginning to afford the only respite from either.

No one noticed. After the excitement of the wedding tour Charlotte plunged into depression and homesickness. Although she had never been a devoted daughter, she missed her sisters, and James's inadequacies as a lover and perhaps a friend had obviously been laid bare by five months of his unadulterated society. In disconcertingly frank conversation, she expressed the desire to become pregnant as quickly as possible, to assuage her loneliness, and in this wish she was not fulfilled.

She turned increasingly to Ewen for diversion and solace, even as he was attempting to withdraw from the world. He found her situation sad, and the timing of her disenchantment with James ironic; she was too late to receive his help, too late for everything he might have offered, and still she did not see. Neither of them saw.

The estate functioned, unaware. Malcolm came and went, hostile, strained, by report drinking heavily, avoiding him. Ewen understood this, even as it grieved him: he himself was rejecting the world and Malcolm was rejecting him, severing him like a gangrenous limb before death's amputation. But he had not thought that he would find himself so completely abandoned, and he feared solitude; and one afternoon he wrote to Malcolm and had the letter taken to the estate office, where he assumed it was found and read. But Malcolm did not come.

For a time he wondered if he had been mistaken; the gnawing pain eased, and he no longer vomited in secret. But in December he passed blood again in the night, and the following morning found the valet staring at the contents of the chamberpot, and overcome by shame and fury he struck him across the face, shouting, "By the living God, is not even a man's shit private in this Christ-damned house?"

He thought of suicide that evening, but he who had once courted death with an open razor could not bring himself to empty his assembled bottles into the glass he had brought for the purpose, so he merely left them in his dressing room as a choice that could be made in the future, when his lingering concern for honour and family might be less strong. He left them openly, knowing that the valet would not this time attempt to hide or destroy them, and went down to the morning room.

He sat for some time with a glass of watered brandy beside him, until the door opened and James wandered in.

"What are you scribbling, Papa?"

La fin de ma vie.

"It is nothing," he said, closing the covers of his journal; and it was nothing. He had closed them for the last time, having written indisputable instructions as to whom his diaries and letters were to be given. "I have written to Margaret. I want to see her, and she does not come. Will you send this down?"

James lounged against the desk, expansive with satisfaction and affection.

"You send it, Papa. None of these louts pays me any heed."

"Then it is as well that they learn. I would be obliged if you would send it tomorrow. And they are not louts."

But James had wandered away again with benevolent disinterest, and had neither taken the letter nor was listening to him.

He received me in his private sitting room with perfect courtesy: I sat in the chair nearest the fire, as he had seen that I was cold. He had given me brandy and told me to drink it; the brandy neither warmed me nor stopped my shivering. He sat opposite me, his legs in dark silk stockings, his feet encased in shabby slippers. I could not bring myself to look into his eyes, so I stared at the bowl of forced bulbs on the table by his elbow. They were hyacinths, dark blue like the upholstery of the chair on which his arm rested, like his coat and the veins on his hand; and their scent was like heaven, like Evesham on the first warm days of my childhood.

"They are my spring," he said.

We talked of inconsequential things, like two strangers who do not dare to venture upon intimate disclosures. We talked of the cold, the previous night's snowfall, which still lay lightly on the ground, and of James and his new wife, whom I had not yet met. We talked, and my mouth moved and words formed themselves and were spoken, and I heard none of them; and the hyacinths blurred from time to time, and their scent, so like heaven, would ever after evoke that memory. I never loved it again.

Eventually a silence fell, as will happen in conversation: a reflective silence, as strangers think of something else to say.

"I expect it will snow again before nightfall. You must not stay too long," and I said something in agreement, and all the while I was thinking, please God, spare me this; please let me wake and find none of it is real.

I saw the tears drop on my skirt and tried to brush them away without being seen. He said, "Why can you not bear to look at me? I am not so very frightful. I am not... so changed."

I looked up into his eyes: he gave a little, apologetic smile. Death had already begun to make him over into its image.

"Be strong a little longer. If you weep, I will weep with you, and then what will they think of us?"

Whom he meant by *they* I did not know until afterwards, but I was beyond caring for anything. He chafed my hands, peering into my face with those loved, familiar eyes.

"If you behave like this now, what will you do when I am gone? Grieve yourself to death? Is that what you want— for me, for my sake?"

"I cannot live here without you."

"You would have come to this place if I had never lived, if you were intended to come. And if you are intended to stay that is nothing to do with me. My life is not your life. My death is not your death." He was wiping the tears from my face with his handkerchief: it was very clean and scented with his cologne. When I took it from him he did not ask for it again. "I want to give you something, Margaret." I shook my head. "I have left it to you in my will. Please take it from me now."

"James's— wife—"

"There are other pieces, not very many. This is not for her."

He did not know that I could hear him faintly, retching and gasping, behind the white-panelled door of his dressing room. I sat staring at his handkerchief: its scent was his scent, and for that reason I would not give it back to him. He returned.

He had with him a satin-lined case, which he put into my lap. On the satin lay a suite of necklace and earrings, so dark a green that they were almost black; the three strands of the necklace were clasped by an oval pendant of the same dark green, and gold, and pearl. "They belonged to my mother, who was dark like you. They were never worn by my wife."

They were cold to the touch, some cold stone: agate, I saw later.

"I know you cannot care for them now, but perhaps later, when this is over ... And maybe you will think of your friend a little, who will always love you."

When this is over.

"My dear, put them in your pocket."

I put the case in my pocket. He stared out of the window with his back to me.

"It is snowing." And then, "Will you do something for me?"

"Yes. Anything."

"Go home."

"I will come again."

"I don't want you to come again."

Then he said, still without moving, "I have nothing more to say to you, no secrets to tell you. I ask only that you be ... kind to... Malcolm. Life has never been very kind to him. And I love you, and bless you with all my heart. Now... go, for God's sake."

The door opened. It was James.

"Papa, you sly dog— I was coming to ask you to take a dish of tea. Bring Margaret down with you."

And I knew he was utterly, stupidly oblivious, and I hated him. He stood smiling facetiously at his father's back and at me, and he saw nothing, and sensed nothing, and he kept patting my unresponsive hand and urging me to come and be introduced to Charlotte; and Ewen, still with his back to me and his hands clasped beneath his coatskirts, said, "I will not take any tea, James, but perhaps Margaret would care for some before she leaves."

I remember the proprietary way James tucked my hand through his arm, although it resisted him.

"Adieu," he said.

I pulled from James and went to him. I saw his profile, blanched with pain, then he turned fully to me. Grey light, grey eyes: in them I saw his soul.

He said, "I would kiss you, but my breath is foul. I am ashamed."

James said from the door, "What are you two whispering about?"

"I kiss you on both cheeks," he said.

They were his last words to me.

I do not remember leaving him, or James shutting the door, or any comment except something clever about my place in his father's affections, and Charlotte, endless mention of Charlotte; then I jerked my hand from his imprisoning arm and said I had forgotten something, and left him proceeding down the stairs in the direction of his tea.

And I see myself now in that empty room, with the chairs and the bowl of hyacinths, and all the doors are closed against me, and all my words remain unspoken.

On Christmas night Ewen sat in the chapel, after the day's ghastly charade. There was light only on the altar, where votive candles were burning. He was alone.

I know in my heart that God is a lie. Even up to Heaven we are betrayed.

He held the rosary so tightly that it cut into his fingers, trying to focus his mind on the illuminated figure, on its blank benevolence.

Mary Queen of Heaven... grant me the grace of thy peace....

What had he to fear from this, who had been robbed, tortured, imprisoned, ill and suicidal: death had shadowed his footsteps and worn the guise of friendship. Why should he fear it now?

Why do I cry unto thee? Why hast thou turned thy face from me, why are my prayers unanswered?

There was nothing: there would be nothing: there had been nothing for years. Religion was only the vinegar on the sponge, offering merely acid torment to one in extremis.

He said aloud, "If this is dying, give me death, and let there be an end to it."

And gradually, as though he were stepping from a shattered, hollow shell, he rose and stood trembling in the darkness. The votive candles he had lighted and blessed with the names of his dead had guttered out: the skin of his face was drawn with the dried salt of his tears. The pain, which had consumed him, had cast his body back to him, gnawed, weightless, and without sensation; he floated in its absence. He felt the iron latch on the door and drifted into the night: the intense cold enveloped him and his shoes slipped on the snow. He found himself in the garden under leafless trees, staring up at an immense moonless sky. The night was brilliant with stars. He drifted among them, transfixed by their icy light, which seemed to enter and suffuse and cleanse him: freed now of all anguish, of the agony of regret and memory and rage and bitterness, no longer haunted by the faces, dead and living, or by his love for them. And he saw the insignificance of their grief, and the futility of their tears.

He had felt the last keen bite of winter: it would trouble him no more. He left the garden, knowing that he had walked there for the last time, and in the privacy of his own rooms lighted his candles. He had exchanged books continually with Margaret; it was not surprising that at the ebb of his life he should still have some of hers. He had never liked Donne, had considered him an apostate and too sepulchral for pleasure, but he opened the book now to the place he had marked earlier. The words *Christmas Day, in the evening, 1624,* suffused him with recognition, and he held the page to the uncertain light.

> … He can bring thy Summer out of Winter, though thou have no Spring; though in the wayes of fortune, or understanding, or conscience, thou have been benighted until now, wintred and frozen, clouded and eclypsed, damped and benummed, smothered and stupified till now, now God comes to thee, not as in the dawning of the day, not as in the bud of the spring, but as the Sun at noon to illustrate all shadows, as the sheaves in harvest, to fill all penuries, all occasions invite his mercies, and all times are his seasons.

He allowed the pages to close gently.
And let my cry come unto Thee.

***

He had gone into the morning room on New Year's day to take something from the escritoire: Charlotte found him lying on the carpet. He had haemorrhaged severely from the rectum, and screamed when any of the household tried to lift him.

She remained with him, cradling his head in her lap while James wandered uselessly in and out. Eventually there were footsteps in the hall.

"What the hell does *he* want?"

She said, "I sent for him."

She became aware of the scent of winter, of a clean outdoor coldness that clung to the rough clothing. He knelt without speaking and took Ewen's weight. Ewen opened his eyes briefly, and fainted as he was carried.

She ran ahead, opening doors, running back to ask unanswerable questions. At the sounds, the valet emerged from Ewen's dressing room with cries of horror, and the man she had always thought courteous, if withdrawn, swore at him in fluent, obscene French. Sick with shock, the valet effaced himself, and Charlotte retreated to the hall.

James came and waited with her, wiping his eyes on his shirt cuff. When the door opened he took Malcolm by the sleeve.

The reddened eyes passed over him as if he were invisible.

"Madam, my thanks, for your care of him."

"He's *my* father, damn you—"

"Then go to him, and be his son."

James pushed past him, leaving the door ajar. Charlotte remained in the hall, twisting her rings and listening for some sound from within, although there was nothing.

She said, "Is he dying?"

"You know he is."

"Will nothing help him?"

"Let him die in peace."

As James had done, although gently, she touched his sleeve. His clothing was stained with blood and excreta, and her hand on the stains surprised him as nothing else had had the power to surprise or unnerve him. It was a large, square hand, unfeminine despite its many rings, and although he sensed her uncertainty she was not intimidated, either by the force of his presence or whatever reputation had preceded him: here was no weak-stomached delicacy, no contrived, silly girlishness. Her manner was as sexless as her hand, and in some strange way he found it comforting.

"You will not leave us, Mr. Scott?"

Now? In the future? It was not possible to know what she meant.

He said curtly, "No," and walked away toward the end of the hall, and the obscurity of the shadows there.

He heard her open the door gently and enter the room, into which he knew she had gone to rescue James. James would not long endure the slow business of dying... no one but himself and Ewen would endure it to the end.

He was dying, but he did not die, and the days passed intolerably. He was kept alive on a mixture of cream and eggs, warm wine and watered brandy: he strained to evacuate but his bowels had closed, and he excreted only foul-smelling blood. He remained vain of his appearance, and the valet attended him morning and night: occasionally he sat up, supported by pillows. More frequently he drifted in a sleep induced by the opiates he had provided for himself. Charlotte sat with him, and James paid brief, morbid visits, fearing contagion by disease or too much raw emotion.

And throughout the nights, while they slept and quarrelled and made miserable, guilty love, and even the valet, wounded by grief and the scathing animosity of Ewen's guardian, had crept away to shed his tears in private, Malcolm sat in an armchair by the bed, with a few candles alight so that if Ewen woke he should see he was not alone. And later, as they came less often, he was there throughout the days. In the mornings he relaxed his vigil only to shave and change his clothing in the dark red room.

Sometimes they talked; sometimes he read to Ewen; often, in the night, he held Ewen's hand, which comforted them both. When Ewen asked for opium he administered it, measuring the drops with care and wondering why he counted them, when so very few more would offer peace. When Ewen could no longer suppress the need to urinate, he held the stone bottle he had acquired for the purpose, and as Ewen's strength failed he cradled his body, and guided the scanty flow of his urine.

He whispered once, "I am so ashamed."

"There was no shame in your care of me. This is nothing more."

There was snow, rain, snow again, the brief bitter days toward the end of January. He sat in the grey, filtered light one afternoon, immersed in the darkness of his thoughts as he believed Ewen, drifting on a darker tide, was sleeping under the influence of the drug, and did not hear him speak. The skeletal face with the living, sunken gaze was smiling at him.

"You tire yourself on my account." He made a gesture of dissent. "What is the weather?"

"Snowing."

"How are the people?"

"Well enough."

"I care for them."

"Yes, you care, and much good it has done you."

"You care, too." He said nothing: he cared for nothing beyond this room. "Malcolm … do not put me in your records. I am not one of your purpura cases."

He said savagely, "For Christ's sake," and turned his face away, then he left the chair and went to stare out of the window, feeling Ewen's eyes on his back.

"Do not let Margaret see me like this."

He said, "No," and the voice went on, the stammer very evident.

"I have written instructions. You have read them, I believe." He did not answer. "I wish to be buried fully dressed, even to my shoes. I do not want a shroud."

He said nothing, staring out of the window.

"Do you hear me?"

He closed his eyes and thought, may I blow out my brains before I die like this.

He went back to the bed and sat on the edge, sensing that this was what Ewen wanted.

"Malcolm, be faithful to James. I leave him to your conscience… that you be tender with him."

"You are my conscience, Ewen."

He turned his face away again, but the dimness of the room could not hide his tears.

"Do not let the people see you weep."

He said in Gaelic, "The people be fucked," and instantly regretted it: he had not thought Ewen would understand, but the hand that held his admonished him.

"I hope you will forgive me one day for this… for the manner of my dying."

"You need not ask my pardon for anything."

There was silence. He thought Ewen slept, then the fingers moved once more.

"Tell me something, now, in this hour where there are no secrets."

He had anticipated this, and said with the gentleness so unnatural to him, which only Ewen had ever managed to elicit, "What would you have me tell you?"

"Why did you go, where did you go? Was it …."

"There was a woman."

He sensed Ewen's distress, and, perhaps, his relief. "Oh, foolish boy. Foolish, foolish boy. Why did you not come to me? I would have… helped somehow."

"I was beyond your help. For that matter, I still am."

He left him, rising abruptly from the bedside, and stood at the end of the hall staring out at the snow until he heard the rustle of expensive clothing.

She spoke with her now familiar directness, in her soft, schooled Edinburgh accent.

"How is he?"

"He fails."

As she had before, she laid her hand upon his sleeve.

"You do not delude me as to your good nature, Mr. Scott."

He said, "Don't be deceived, madam," and inclined his head to her stiffly; and went downstairs, to seek the obscurity of whisky and shadows until his vigil should be resumed.

He did not sleep again, and his premonition of death was strong. The hours were eternities, the days undifferentiated from one another. He opened books and read unseeingly, although he never knew if Ewen heard or understood: he had lost reason and coherence and his thoughts were random snatches of the past, names and incidents given up like flotsam from a dying brain, and relived with an absurd and terrible immediacy. Unconsciousness followed, but he remained aware of the pressure of the hand that held his, and once he said distinctly, "J'ai la vie dure," I die hard, I am hard to kill, and then, with great clarity, "Ne m'oublie."

I will not forget you.

He sat alone, in the chair from which it seemed he had barely moved for weeks, on the first night in February. He heard the hours strike past midnight, carrying himself and Ewen into Candlemas, the feast of the purification of the Virgin Mary: a quarter day for the collection of Scottish rents, a day for the blessing of candles. He would collect no rents today, and he had seen death too often and too closely not to know that it shared the room with him. Ewen's breathing faltered and laboured on, and gradually the darkness lightened, not with dawn but snow. It fell soundlessly, the only movement in the night, giving its pallor and its stillness to the room. He could see without effort, and he watched Ewen's face with burning, sleepless eyes, incapable now of love or grief or the violent, conscious striving of the past few hours: trying to persuade his spirit to linger, trying to will him to die.

He sat without moving, holding Ewen's left hand, on which the ring was bound with soiled thread; the tide of night had turned and ebbed. He heard the next hour strike and closed his eyes, but he did not sleep: when he opened them he saw that the snow had ceased, and Ewen was dead.

He watched the sunrise with great bitterness; it would end this vigil and this servitude, which he was not ready to relinquish. He moved stiffly, light-headed with hunger and the days and nights of sleeplessness, turned his back on the spreading light and sat again by Ewen, imagining for a moment that he lived. Then he laid his cold hand on Ewen's cheek and kissed him, with love and reverence.

"Go," he said. "Go— theirig thusa a'chadal— a churaidh," and wept, harsh tears that burned his eyes like acid. And then, having sent him to his rest, he asked his pardon, and knelt by the bed and laid his head in his arms, where, for an hour, he slept.

IV

When the news of his death was carried the snow, which had been falling for three days, became the subject of sombre reflection. It was believed to be the white wrath of God descending upon his bruised soul, and there was disquiet and apprehension among the people, and speculation upon the nature of his sins, which had so invited this divine displeasure.

My mind recalls these images and, exploring them, cringes still. Their pain has never subsided.

The road to Ardsian, a barren waste of snow. Myself riding ahead of MacNeil to break a path, and he, having refused for years to provide himself with a horse, following me stolidly on foot. The short day, and the cold, and nightfall, whitened with snow, and the house, an alien place, a shell that offered me no welcome. I did not want to enter. I was a stranger now, alone, and no one here loved me.

More images, the monochromes of memory. James, extinguished in mourning and redolent of spirits, with a swollen face and a conversation limited to curt monosyllables. Charlotte, wearing dull black silk, too thin for this savage winter and cut in what to my rusticated eye appeared the latest fashion: this mourning was an expensive business, and nothing if not flattering. I had no clothing now that was appropriate except a dark grey poplin, over which I had sat in the bitter evenings unpicking every trace of ornamentation lest some one accuse me of vanity when I wore it. James's only comment, from behind a soiled handkerchief, was, "You look like a Quaker."

I left them to their whisky and their seedcake: they would not notice my absence and I wanted none of their society. I had not come to revel in the conventions of the funeral visit and offer my condolence— I had loved him more than they, and they would offer none to me.

I drifted in a hideous nightmare from room to room. All were shrouded in white linen and filled with the haze of dripping, untended candles, and where fires had been lighted soot from the unswept chimneys showered onto the hearthstones and into the sullen flames. In every room a little knot of tenants had gathered, restive and anxious, women with shawled babies at the breast, carried here in anticipation of the usual open-handed funeral hospitality which was nowhere yet in evidence, children, quiet and mannerly, men cleanly dressed in good clothing. One group had brought a fiddler with them, but his instrument was silent. There was no laughter, no gossip, no music, no joviality, and although drink had been laid out on side tables, none of the customary drunkenness of the wake. An infant crying was instantly hushed, a ripple of conversation self-consciously stilled when they heard my footsteps.

The door of the morning room was locked: this place alone no one could desecrate. And it seemed to me that he must be there, behind that door which was locked against me, and if I could open it I would see him seated at that small grey desk, from which he would rise ... and if I could find him in this hellish, labyrinthine dream I would wake, and he would live.

I pushed at a door and it opened, and I shut it against the unseemly brilliance of the house; here darkness pressed my eyes, and I had found him, although in his presence I was still alone.

They had dressed him in the sombre clothes he favoured, in a dark velvet coat, and a film of lace spilled on his breast and covered his hands to the knuckle; his fingers clasped his rosary. His body was shrouded in translucent lawn, which did not conceal its emaciation: it was not a man that lay before me but a wizened doll, a doll of softened, shrunken wax, with silvered hair and a ravaged profile blurring even now with decomposition. There were sores around the discoloured mouth.

The odour of putrefaction seeped across the floor, and beyond the burning spears of light the darkness was alive with shadows, shadows that moved and did not move and were his ghost, his spirit. I wept, not with restraint but with a primitive frenzy, an uncontrollable sickness of grief. And eventually, although I knew I was alone, one of the shadows came and lifted me, and took me away from the candles and the stench, and compelled me to sit in the darkness. The flames flickered; my resistance had disturbed them. Now I and they were still.

Time passed, must have passed: there was no measure of time, only pain. He said nothing, and he sat beyond the reach of the light, no more visible than when I had come in. Although we were in one another's presence, our solitude was profound.

When he did speak, it might have been only a voice in my mind.

"It was his express wish that you should not see him."

"Not even you could have prevented me."

"Then let the memory be your curse. As it is mine."

The night and the nightmare were alive with fitful murmurings, voices like the doleful whispers in MacNeil's kitchen, murmuring of the bruised soul's passing.

He said, "Death with oil, death with joy, death with light, death with gladness. They wish him that. I wish them all in hell."

The shuffling footsteps had come closer. He rose, and I saw his face for the first time, harrowed by grief and sleeplessness. He laid his right hand briefly on Ewen's and walked into the darkness; he met the women at the door with a stream of obscenities and went out. They took no notice, as if, after three nights of vigil, this behaviour had become commonplace. They genuflected, and assuming grief as easily as they pulled the shawls over their heads, began the first prayer of the rosary. Although they knew I was there, no one acknowledged me.

And in the interval between their departure and Malcolm's return, I went to Ewen, and kissed him; and when I left that dark place I took him with me, in my heart, as I had loved him, as I would keep him forever: I did not leave him there.

At eleven in the morning we assembled in the chapel, where the coffin had been placed on trestles before the altar. James laid a white handkerchief over the decaying face to signify the beginning of the funeral. There were no rites familiar to me. My father merely offered a long psalm, consulting a small, dirty volume and drawling the words in the sing-song peculiar to the kirk, and gave a lengthy eulogy in an idiomatic Gaelic, throughout which we stood. I did not raise my eyes from my own book of Common Prayer.

Comfort the soul of Thy servant, for unto Thee, O Lord, do I lift up my soul.

I was conscious of Charlotte's breathing beside me, of the cold seeping around my feet, of my father's sonorous droning and the murmurs of agreement among the Gaels who crowded this tiny chapel, rubbing their homespun shoulders against the high-born silk. My father was speaking like a man in love with the sound of his own voice.

O Death, where is thy sting? O grave, where is thy victory?

Here, I thought. It is here.

Give rest, O Christ, to Thy servant with Thy saints, where sorrow and pain are no more, neither sighing, but life everlasting....

And I saw myself again in Evesham's church of St. Mary and St. Edmund, surrounded by the ancient scent of Norman stone and incense, with the cracked leather of a boot on the periphery of my vision and a rough sleeve not touching mine.

Neither shall there be any more pain.

I became aware of the black silk pressing close, and the powdery scent she used: Charlotte was whispering to me. She had veiled herself against the eyes of this male congregation, and had drawn me defensively close. Beside her James stood stonily white and silent, swaying slightly on his feet. The droning voice went on, punctuated by snorts and mutters of approval and the blowing of noses.

"I am an Episcopalian, and I cannot understand what he is saying."

I gave the book to her: it held nothing more for me. Then MacNeil, by much throat-clearing, signified that he had finished, and men with nails and hammers came forward to seal the coffin. The noise was ghastly and insulting, and a moment's paralysis followed, as if the congregation were transfixed by its finality. James stood by the coffin, having abandoned his wife to me, and seemed to be waiting for some direction, then Malcolm emerged from the crowd and he turned with pathetic eagerness to speak to him. I had neither seen him nor sensed his presence throughout the funeral, nor had his name been mentioned, and as he took the weight of the coffin on his shoulder it was obvious by his hair and clothing that only the sound of the hammers had brought him in from the rain.

Some one kicked over the trestles on which the coffin had rested: it seemed only another act of barbarism in this barbaric charade. They were leaving now, led by MacNeil.

Charlotte said I must not go.

And I saw that, although one or two women had indeed paid the rare tribute of attending the funeral, they would not go on to the grave; they would remain behind in deference to custom. But their customs were not mine and I was not bound by them. I was not one of them.

I withdrew my hand from hers and followed the silent procession. The tenants, with their delicate sense of propriety, were still marshalling themselves in order of precedence. I walked among them until I found James: after one startled glance at my face he paid me no attention. We halted where the ground was trampled and stained, and they had hewed out the frozen earth, and the snow had blown away from the stones and the weeds were frost-bleached and unkempt, and those who had carried the coffin laid it down among the clods, and the dark, straggling knots of men arrived behind us and stood coughing in the silence. Then MacNeil drew out his sordid little volume again, and in the course of turning the pages glanced up; I still remember the scathing disapproval in his eyes. I remember, too, the other eyes, which had watched me from the shadows the previous night, settling without compassion on my face, then they dismissed me, and Ewen's coffin lay between us like something unreal and meaningless, and his grave separated us like an abyss.

The drizzle stopped. The wind tore the clouds into passing blue, and there was hard sunlight, which hurt my eyes.

> Awake, thou that sleepest, and arise from the dead,
> And Christ shall give thee light.

The shadows swept across our faces. MacNeil coughed and was silent; I realized that his service of committal was finished. James lurched forward and knelt, laying his hands on the coffin, and for the first and last time behaved, out of instinct or piety or a sense of occasion, like the Catholic he was, chattering through his teeth fragments of the absolution no priest would speak over his father. "Misereatur tui omnipotens Deus… et dismissis peccatis tuis…." His voice faltered. "Perducat te… ad vitam aeternam." He crossed himself abruptly and rose, and there were similar gestures throughout the crowd. Across the grave that bony, hawkish face remained utterly withdrawn, nor did he move. Then men took the ropes and prepared to lower the coffin; the light came and went, and the wind blew, and brought the sound.

In my childhood I had heard Northumbrian smallpipes, a shrill, festive noise. This was not the same. It was indescribable, a thread of blowing sound, without source, from no direction, as thin and insubstantial as the rain. In my father's face there was a passionate uplifting, as though he heard again, across the bitter gulf of years, the siren song which had called him to die, and for which he would still gladly die. James was trembling, with cold or emotion. Across the grave, in that other face, there was no expression.

It was coming more strongly on the wind now, and the Celt in my blood was moved by its passionate grief.

"What is it?" and James whispered, "It is a coronach… for my father," and openly he began to cry.

It threaded the wind with its ineffable sorrow, a lament for him and for the years, and their indelible heritage of bitterness, and then it stopped. It had not been heard in Glen Sian for twenty years. I never heard it again.

We sat in the drawing room, which was littered with crusts and greasy plates. Every portrait and mirror was covered with white linen, and a fire burned fitfully in the grate. Such was the apathy in the room that none of us moved to replenish it.

Most of the participants in the wake had gone home, or crowded into the kitchens for the remnants of the boiled mutton and blood puddings which had finally been provided, or were loitering in groups on the expanse of rotting snow beyond the windows. MacNeil had accepted a last enormous draught of whisky: now he stood with every indication of imminent departure and said to me with unnecessary authority and familiarity, "Well, lass, I am for home. Are you?"

I said I would come when I was ready, and if he could ever be thought to have indulged in such careless behaviour as a shrug, I would have said that was his response.

James saw him out, with mournful civility, leaving Charlotte watching me across the littered carpet.

"How brave you are. I wish I had come with you. I did not think I should."

"I care nothing for what people think of me. I only cared for Ewen."

Her eyes filled.

"I shall miss him sorely. I hope… you and I may be friends."

Perhaps she sensed my utter loneliness. But it was not the moment, and if she might have said something else I never knew, because James returned.

I stared at the carpet: the wretchedness in his expression was too private to be shared. I heard Charlotte rise and make some excuse, leaving me alone with him.

"You have nothing to drink. You must be cold," and pouring something, he brought me a glass: it was the most revolting sherry imaginable and I later left it on a table somewhere. Then he said, "Margaret," in that choked and fervid voice he had used when making his advances to me at the bottom of the garden, and fumbling in his pocket he drew out a handkerchief. In it lay three locks of his father's hair, and I made some involuntary gesture of rejection.

"Keep them for yourself, if they comfort you."

"I thought you would want one." He was flushed and unkempt, and his linen appeared not to have been changed for weeks. "I thought … you loved him."

"I shall always love him. But I don't want his dead hair."

He folded the handkerchief and replaced it in his pocket, and wiped his eyes on his sleeve.

"You know if you had married me none of this would have happened."

"I would not have been able to prevent it, even if I had married Ewen."

He gazed at me. His face was blotched like a child's, and I saw jealousy and suspicion there.

"How disgusting," he said, and I could have hit him. "Did you want him, then? Did he ask you?"

Charlotte returned. I would not have answered in any case: there were no answers, and if there were, they were for me alone.

"James— some of the people wish to see you."

He said, "They can go to hell. I don't want to see *them*."

They left me with the sherry and the shrouded mirrors and the sullen fire, and no ghost came to comfort me, only emptiness, and the lengthening shadows of afternoon. I made up the fire because no servant had come to do it and because by a single word of encouragement to either the father or the son it would have been my hearth, and as I knelt the muddy skirts of the grey gown spread around me, and I knew that I would burn it; I never wanted to see it again. As I rose from my knees, I saw that dark figure standing in the doorway as though he had been about to come in.

"I am sorry. I thought no one was here."

"You need not go on my account."

He had come from the grave, where he had remained until the last shovelful of earth had been thrown onto the coffin: his boots were spattered with mud and melting snow, and left stains from the door to the console where he splashed whisky into a tumbler, and then to the window where he stood, drinking it. Then finally, without looking at me, he said, "It went off well, I thought. Did you find it entertaining? Something to write to England like Captain Burt?"

"It may surprise you to learn that I loved him as you did. So please spare me your sarcasm."

He refilled his glass and another which, disconcertingly, he held out to me.

"You're MacNeil's daughter— you'll have his liver." And when I demurred, "Oh, take it, for Christ's sake. This is what you want, not some damned foreign muck."

My lips were cracked, and the raw spirit burned them. He watched me with those pitiless eyes.

Eventually it seemed warmer in the room, and I attempted to talk to him.

"The music— was that of your doing?"

"No."

"I thought— and James thought—"

"That would be a new departure for James. As for you, you can think what you like." Then he said, still staring out at the grey afternoon, "I have something to give you, which I was asked to keep for you. I will bring it down to you if you cannot bear my company to go with me to my office." I said nothing. "I don't blame you. I am not fit company for any decent woman."

I waited for him until I doubted he was coming back; and I drank, which only made it easier to cry hopeless, self-pitying tears.

When he came in he was part of the miasma of whisky and grief; he had brought with him several volumes bound in morocco. I knew, although I had never seen them, that they were Ewen's journals.

"There are others, and letters. This is all you can carry away with you now."

"Have you read them?"

"They were not left to me."

"That wasn't what I asked."

"I gave you your answer, unless you call me a liar." Then, with the characteristic scorpion's tail of sarcasm, "But you would believe any ill of me, wouldn't you? Anything you were told."

I sat with the books on my lap: I could not bear to open them. He had put on more peat and was staring into the flames as if fire fascinated him.

"It is late, Miss MacNeil. You will lose the light."

"I don't give a damn for the light."

There was silence. No one came with fresh candles, or to question why the door had been shut so long: it was though the whole household had died, and we were alone.

After a while he said, "Well, are you not grateful for his little gift?"

"Not particularly."

"Why not? At least he'll speak again to you. He will never speak to me."

He felt for something in his pocket. "He gave me this when I was young." It dangled from his hand, a rosary of some dark wood. "I left it behind once, in this house, to hurt him. He kept it for me, and gave it back. Do you know what I think of it?"

He let it fall into the flames, where it burned acridly. There were tears on his face.

"I curse heaven," he said.

On February ninth, two days after the funeral, he made his rounds of the crofts in the northwest, and discovered that the rumour of smallpox was true. He had no fear of infection: he had moved so freely among the living and the dreaded dead in previous outbreaks that he believed himself immune, and as he rode from one croft to another and saw where corpses were laid out, or graves were freshly dug, or the dying lay in smoke-filled darkness, he merely glanced at them and noted their names to be struck from the rent-rolls later. He had lived Ewen's death; no other could hold any terror for him.

He went from place to place, uncertain of how the virus was spread and impervious to it himself, but carrying it on his clothing as it had always been carried and as the ignorant would carry it in the future, from the dead to the living. In the late afternoon he approached his mistress's croft with the stillness of premonition in his mind, and saw that she was sitting on a stool with her hands, uncharacteristically idle, knotted loosely in her lap. She seemed to be watching the draught scatter ashes across the floor, and did not raise her head when she heard him. The croft was silent, bitterly cold, and foul, and across the end she had drawn the curtain that separated the bed from the room.

She said, "My children are dead. All that I had of you, and they are dead."

Nothing moved in him, neither fear nor pity. He closed the door, allowing his senses to accept the dimness, the claustrophobic, familiar smell.

She said, "You cursed them, and they died. Go away and leave me in peace."

He went home, and drank and smoked incessantly as he had since Ewen's death. In the morning he brought the boards and the spade, and laboured for three hours in the rain. They were buried as they had been conceived, in silence and with resignation, and they were never again mentioned: and in time, deliberately, he forgot their faces, and no longer remembered their names.

It was the twenty-ninth of May, evening, and raining, although the sky was as bright as day. He watched the rain from the estate office. The previous week it had been snow.

He turned at the sound of James's footsteps. For so small a man he had a remarkably heavy tread, and he was expressing his annoyance at the prospect of this discussion and the inconvenience of climbing several flights of stairs in pursuit of it. He stalked in and flung himself uninvited into the only other chair.

"Can you shut the damned window? It's cold enough to freeze a man's stones in here." He resumed his childish habit of thudding his heel against the leg of the chair. After a moment, aware of the disapproval across the table, he desisted.

"This meeting has been long delayed because its subject is distasteful to me, as I assume it is to you. It can be delayed no longer. I want your instructions on how to proceed— or, if you have none, perhaps you will listen to mine."

"I am all ears."

"What are your plans?"

"My wife and I will remove to Edinburgh. I intend to buy a house there."

"With what?"

"I leave that in your more than capable hands. Glen Sian is your responsibility, not mine, thank God."

Malcolm gave him a curious, quizzical glance, searching for the sarcasm.

"Your father was in debt."

"My dear fellow, the world is in debt."

"I am not. And I need not remind you of certain expenditures and forfeitures resulting from his death."

"I am obliged to consider Charlotte."

"You are obliged to confront the truth. You have no wealth but the land beneath your feet, and if you want money then money will be had from it, but not by the established methods."

The rain was beating on the roof. James shivered and huddled deeper into the chair.

"I have several propositions to put to you." He paused, and shut the streaming window. "The potato will provide a source of nourishment from August, two or three months earlier than oats, and its yield is proportionately higher. I anticipate a return of ten to twelve barrels for every one planted. It can also be stored throughout the winter, and not only will it support life unsupplemented if necessary, but when eaten to augment the customary diet it will help prevent scurvy, which, as you know, is prevalent... are you listening, damn you?"

James said, "Yes," in a small, startled voice and attempted to contribute some sensible remark. "And— what if they resist the cultivation?"

"Then they will be persuaded."

"What else do you propose?"

"Turnip, rye grass, clover— compulsory sowing. One field of every three to be under clover, a deeper method of cultivation for the soil. The cas chrom only scrapes the surface. I want no shallow fields."

"I fail to see the benefit of all this fodder, unless it will pay me."

Malcolm studied him. The dark blue eyes, the pale, boyish cheek, the bony hands protruding from the cuffs of his plain black coat... there was a flicker of Ewen in his face, elusive and distressing.

You selfish little bastard, he thought. Always me first: always *me*.

He said, "There remains my final proposal. I suggested it to your father. He would never consider it."

"Why should you think I would consider it then, if my father would not?"

The resemblance was gone, to his relief. He said coldly, "You haven't his stupid attachment to the land. That at least is one hypocrisy of which you cannot convince me."

James crossed his legs, uncrossed them, stared at the uneven floorboards, thoughts chasing one another across his transparent face. Money... insult... resentment... money.

323

"What is this proposal?" He outlined it briefly. "That is absurd. We have enough of the damned things as it is, and they serve no useful purpose."

"This is an experiment, conducted with some success in Perthshire and in Ross."

"Well, I have not the benefit of your expertise in these matters, but I daresay the climate will not support it. I don't fancy the expenditure in any case; and I want nothing to disrupt the status quo. I don't want the name of an improver with the vilification that goes with it."

"You want— you don't want— but mostly *you want*. Christ, man, the very deer are dying underfoot. Do you think I can wring blood from stones?"

"I am never surprised at what you can do. I know you believe yourself capable of anything. So do I."

He said harshly, "Then free my hands, and I'll give you money. That's what you want, isn't it?"

James shrugged, another little mannerism recently adopted from his father.

"Please yourself. I intend to go to Edinburgh this summer whether you proceed with your projects or not. My wife wishes to consult a leech: it seems we cannot all breed as effortlessly as the peasants." Malcolm had risen; he saw only the rim of a light iris staring impassively at the rain. Tentatively, like a child, he touched him on the sleeve.

"Forgive me. That was thoughtless."

His apology was not acknowledged, nor rebuffed with the sarcasm he had feared. Malcolm said only, "Instruct your servants in that case. I am away soon myself."

"You ... what?" He felt his hand tighten on the unresponsive sleeve. "You cannot leave me. You cannot abandon Glen Sian—"

"I could vomit Glen Sian, I am so sick of it."

"But ... but where will you go?"

"Ross-shire, Perthshire, maybe further south."

"But you will come back?"

The harvests— the trysts— the cattle—the columns on the page— the voices always crying, crying. *A Mhaoir, what shall we do?*

It was dark now: beyond the glass the rain fell, the sound strangely lulling. He watched without seeing it, felt the hand on his sleeve, heard the anxious, persistent questions. And he was tired, so tired ... he wearied of it, and of them.

"If it rains like this much longer, there'll be no harvest to concern you."

"But you will come back?"

When he said nothing James faded away, fearful and uncertain. Let him gnaw on it, he thought, and learn the bitter taste.

They had all gone, and I who had nowhere to go and less reason than any to stay, remained in Glen Sian and fed on the very dregs of grief.

I discharged my last duty to him in midsummer. I went up to Ardsian on one of those rare hot days in the Highlands, and walked in the gardens. My head was aching, and I was thirsty and would have asked for some water, but although every door and window stood open no one emerged, so I did not approach the house. I merely cut his roses and sensed that I was being watched, although I saw nothing but the empty, open windows and the flicker of curtains in the wind.

I took the roses to his grave, and the same hot wind scattered the petals from my hand, and carried them, like him, away.

V

In the spring of 1767, long after Charlotte and James had returned to colours, I removed the black bands from the sleeves of my riding coats. The habits had faded and were greyish from rain and sunlight, but the places where I had worn my mourning remained as green as memory.

It was the year that the first Gaelic New Testament was printed, which gave MacNeil scope for many bitter complaints, with reference to my supposed inheritance, that he could not afford to bring this word of a Celtic god to his parishioners: the year of the death of Telemann: the year of Charlotte's first pregnancy, which ended in an uncomplicated miscarriage in the early weeks. To console herself she altered everything in the house. The morning room was rehung several times until it was finished to her satisfaction in a figured dark blue silk that removed forever its impression of sunlight, and my memories and perhaps her own. The crystal bowl which had held roses disappeared from the mantel, and all of Ewen's furniture and the fittings in his room were changed, burned or banished to the attics; James now occupied that suite, and his freckled Scottish manservant the adjoining quarters. The Frenchman who had served Ewen for nearly thirty years was given notice, and left the house between one of my visits and the next: neither James nor Charlotte concerned themselves with his eventual fate. He was merely another of Ewen's furnishings, to be disposed of as quickly as possible.

It was a year of famine, which affected other areas and left Glen Sian untouched, and rumour abounded that James was under pressure to institute sinister changes in the pattern of land use and practises. But nothing happened, no catastrophe occurred, and the monotonous cycle of the seasons progressed undisturbed.

It was the year when the estate absorbed, in addition to Charlotte's extravagance, the expenditure of £82.16.3 for a new roof for MacNeil's kirk, and the local slates, locks, hinges, doors and three arched windows were installed by Calvinist tradesmen who would not so much as pick up a fallen nail if it rolled beneath their shoes as they walked to the services MacNeil doggedly held in the open air every Sunday. In return for their piety MacNeil fed them in the kitchen, where they often sat long over prayer, but he never offered even a cup of water to the factor who rode down several times to observe the progress of the work.

It was the year of the letter, which had been directed to Ewen's solicitor in Glasgow, where it had lain for several months before being collected with other post for Glen Sian. It was very dirty, and the superscription was well written but badly spelled, in an unfamiliar hand. Inside were several lines of abuse that began, *You wicked hoor*, and ended with the words, *you killed my husband, so may it be dun to you*. There was no signature but I knew it was from Catherine's housemaid Rose, whose husband Giacomo had gone with Mordaunt to the West Indies. There had been fever, and the Italian was dead, with much of the regiment.

> I doant blame the Major he was ane onest man and may bee ded now too but may God damn you I will tear out yor hart if ever I see you agen

The page was blotted as though with tears.

I knew it was genuine, and that she had written it with Catherine's connivance and perhaps at her instigation. Only from Catherine would she have learned where I was.

When my father went through my papers, as he did when I was out of the house, disturbing even Ewen's journals in his search for the letter he had seen me receive, he found nothing. I had burned it, and whatever suspicion he cherished he never knew what it had contained, nor who had written to me.

Glen Mor was very empty throughout the summer, with most of the women at the shielings, and the harvest still some weeks in the future. I dreaded my aunt's absences, because although I offered my help she would never allow me to assist her, claiming I could not be spared from the house. So I remained at home with MacNeil, laundering his shirts and cooking and serving his meals, which he ate in solitude at the kitchen table with a book in front of him before retiring to his study and his smeared tumblers of whisky. He seldom spoke except to criticize what I had prepared, or my general ineptitude in domestic matters, and when this happened I went out, and remained out as long as I dared. Sometimes I went to Ardsian, until I sensed that my visits were becoming too much of a habit, accepted too eagerly by Charlotte and James: I was providing the only diversion in a rapidly cooling marriage and becoming, uncomfortably and inevitably, the unwilling confidante of both.

So I rode a good deal, and the estate became like a map to me, crumpled and familiar, and it was also inevitable that if I saw another human being, which was seldom as I rode so far from habitation, it should be my old antagonist. Sometimes he saw me, and distance made our evasion of one another easy, and socially acceptable: sometimes I suspect we passed within minutes of one another, seen by nothing but the same hovering eagle. I had woven fact and gossip and rumour into a potent web by this time and thought I knew him, as a troubled man, misjudged and isolated, trying to hold chaos together. If he came to these desolate wastes merely for peace and solitude I could not blame him; nor would I disturb him. God knew what he thought of me, nor what I hoped to find.

I went up to Ardsian in late August, and discovered that the tenor of my life was changing, and would never be the same.

I found James in the garden with papers on his knee. The sight of the sunlight on his hair still caused my heart to lurch, but as I approached the resemblance vanished, and he looked up guiltily. Whatever he had been reading or writing, he did not want it seen.

He came to his feet, stuffing the papers into his coat pocket.

"My dear Margaret, what a surprise! How enchanting you look."

I looked as I always did, faintly threadbare, and I was by now immune to him.

At the mention of Charlotte the charm slid from him like a garment.

"Supine, my dear, till five or six. Until her head clears, or so I gather."

He never listens, she had said to me once, he never cares.

"Shall we walk, and take tea afterwards? You'll want to see the famous roses, or what's left of them."

"Does Charlotte not —"

He took out a penknife and began to saw vigorously at a browning spray.

"Charlotte don't care for things like this. She's only concerned with paint and paper."

Eventually I had to beg him to stop. He seemed intent on destroying them; and when he came back dishevelled, with scratches on his hand, he thrust the lot carelessly at me.

"You might as well take them. No one else seems to care."

They were shattering even as I carried them, and were full of greenfly and earwigs. He walked stiffly beside me, licking his hand, and as we neared the house he said, "No, not there," and turned me in another direction.

He wanted to talk, and he knew where he wanted to do it: on the stone bench which had been his father's favoured venue for conversations he did not want overheard.

"I hate this place." He was staring up at the house. "Let's run away together."

If I had thought it was one of his twisted attempts at humour, his expression convinced me otherwise.

"You are not serious."

"I was never more so, on my life. I could make you happy, Margaret. I know you ain't happy here."

Again the sensation of being watched from behind those glittering casements.

"You can't even make Charlotte happy, and she's more suited to you than I."

"Oh, we're suited, you and I. You would be surprised how well."

"And who should fund this escapade?"

"I have something of the dowry left. And you, of course —"

"Come well provided for, or so you think."

He stroked my hand with a blown rose, and something crawled from the petals to my skin.

"I merely put forth a proposition. We are sophisticated people, Margaret. You have some beauty, and I have family connections— the world's our oyster. No one would raise the issue of marriage." The rose was stroking me, and beneath it his fingers caressed me. "And if, in time..." He paused delicately, and I removed my hand. "Well, we should see. But we need not be prisoners in this damnable place. I know you share my sentiments— they were your words, not mine."

I said, "You have no honour," and he threw the rose onto the gravel, where it fell apart.

"You haughty jilt, who are you to talk of honour? You should be a man!"

I left the roses on the bench beside him. At my back he shouted, "What the hell am I to do with these?"

And because, in that world which had taught me grace, one might quarrel but not like this, like drab and pimp in a public place, I returned to him; and he watched my movements with lidded eyes and a half-smile of satisfaction, as though he thought I had relented.

I said, "Give them to your wife. You may enjoy her gratitude."

I did not look back because I knew he would resemble Ewen, surrounded by rotting flowers in the midst of that small, corrupted Eden.

The August trysts. Cattle culled and shod, driven the dusty miles, bought and sold and too often rejected, and driven back to await the next market. The prices were low and showed no sign of rising: the prices of corn and fodder mounted.

God, give me a war, he thought, to feed England's mouth. This sterile peace profited no one.

On his return from Falkirk he went to his mistress's croft. She was not there, but she had left bannock cooking, so he walked up to the potato beds to inspect them. The sprawling stalks lay on the ground, their insignificant flowers long faded. There were nettles in the trenches. There was no curl as yet; the winds where he had dug this bed were too strong for the disease to spread, and heavy rain had washed the plants clear of the greenfly that carried it. None of the tubers had been pulled up.

She was returning, idly switching the flanks of the cow as it meandered towards him.

"So?" he said, not ungently, because it seemed absurd that they should stand in this complete silence. "So, Grania?"

She gazed at him fully for the first time in months, not the haggard, sidelong look he found so infuriating.

"What do you want of me?" He saw the brown fingers move to the strings of her dirty bodice. "Is this what you want?"

"Cover yourself," and she stood staring at him with that terrible, empty gaze. "The beds are full of weeds. Do you think I broke my back for nothing? What in Christ is the matter with you?"

Nothing changed in her face: nothing moved in the deep, summer blue of her eyes.

She said, "Would I eat of the ground you dug with the spade that buried my children? The self-same spade? Would I eat of the dirt that came from their graves?"

Every tenant will plant a boll of potatoes... and a boll of potatoes will plant an acre of ground, properly manured....

He said, very softly, "You lazy, ignorant whore. Do you think I shovelled the shit from your byre for nothing, and bent my back in the rain— *for nothing?*"

The beds being 5 feet broad and the Trenches 3 feet Broad, in the month of April, about 4 inches deep....

"Do you think I dug an acre of this Christ-damned earth with my hands, and my boot on my spade, and shifted the rocks and drank my own sweat for nothing— for not even a word of thanks out of your mouth, only your damned children's names?"

"They were your children, and they are the only seed you will sow in this earth. Your things may rot— you will not make me eat them— not if my mouth was full of grass."

He was already in the saddle, otherwise he would have struck her, and gratified some primitive need for violence to relieve the months of frustration and failure. There had been no intercourse before Ewen's death, and nothing since but this inanimate resistance, this passive revulsion. She said nothing; she did nothing; she wanted nothing; she tolerated him only because he made no demands on her, and as the months passed she had sunk deeper into an unmitigated depression. He had tried to lift it, with uncharacteristic patience, with offerings of food, with the gift of his labour which no one else in Glen Sian could command, with lengths of soft cloth which were folded away and never replaced the stained garments she wore. And pity... he had pitied her, having thought that the plight of no human being could move him any longer; and some twinge of a dying conscience had not allowed him to abandon her.

Now he had brought her another gift, the novelty of which he had thought would please her: a Spanish orange, one of a dozen he had bought in Falkirk. She would reject it as she had rejected him, with the same inarticulate repugnance; and knowing this he tossed it on the ground.

Some instinct must have told her what it was, although she had never seen such a fruit before, and it appeared scarcely edible.

"Let your children eat it. You never brought such things for them."

So it lay untouched, until it shrivelled and became only another greenish, indistinguishable stone on that shallow, stony ground.

Another woman in the weeks that followed, and another after that, the first a prostitute who was known to men in the outlying crofts in Glen Mor, the second a crofter's wife, on the ground near the bleaching linen. Five minutes, and withdrawing in the midst of spasm in case she should fall pregnant. No more bastards, he thought, Christ, no more bastards, although he had gone to her again and coupled with her without speaking, losing himself in orgasm as though it were some needed drug. And as if he stood apart from himself and watched, he seemed to see some one else, some fragment of memory that was sordid and familiar.

The days, and the nights: the empty miles, the hours of darkness, the hand clenched on the rein, every rein controlling Glen Sian. And the failures, the delays, the frustrations, the balances, the demands, the subterfuge. Money on paper, money vanished into thin air, money rattling in a box: money in cattle, in corn, in the ground, in the lowering skies, in profit and loss— loss and hunger— hunger and starvation.

> In order to prevent all frauds, of any persons Butchering Cattle and Sheep not belonging to themselves, it is thought Necessary that no Cattle, nor Sheep, shall be, for the future, butchered without calling a jury of three of the nearest Neighbours, who shall be satisfied that the Cattle or Sheep belongs to no other Body, and if any person shall be found acting Contrary to this Beneficial Regulation, the Cattle or sheep if found shall be returned to the person to whom they belong, and if any person is found guilty of killing Cattle or Sheep not belonging to themself, he shall immediately be committed to the local Officer, to undergo the pains of Law....

On an evening in September he was alone in the estate office, smoking and preparing the cattle accounts for the second Falkirk tryst, in the futile hope that they would impress themselves upon James's fluid memory: any account rendered up for James's inspection might as well be written on water.

The light was falling in a cold, tawny sky, and the air was sharp; there was no sound from other parts of the house. He closed the books. His mouth was dry and foul with tobacco and he had eaten nothing, only drunk a little water during the course of the day.

He left the house, intending to go to the stables. He found himself instead walking through the courtyard toward the gardens. Some of the upper casements were alight, tightly fastened against the night's harmful vapours; in the garden there was only a scent of apples ripening, a dampness breathing from the grass, and some one working among the roses, in a pale shirt that flickered like a moth in the dusk. A man digging, turning over the soil in the rose beds: he imagined he heard the scrape of the spade, and he said, or thought he said, in a natural, unsurprised Gaelic, "What are you doing?"

And the pale, flickering shirt turned, and raised an arm as though in greeting as he had seen it so many times, in welcome and salute and occasionally farewell. It was Ewen. In the uncertain light, he knew with certainty: Ewen in the disreputable clothing he favoured for the garden. And he tried to speak, although he knew he should not speak to the dead, and tried to move, but he who seldom felt the cold seemed paralyzed by it, and the sensation overwhelmed him. When he opened his eyes the garden was empty, and although he went immediately to the place and examined the ground, no one had disturbed the earth; and no loved spirit came again, nor memory comforted.

The rains came, and the gales of autumn, stripping every tree, wreaking havoc with fields and roofs. The Sian burst its banks, the lochan below his house rose eighteen inches in a single night. The sunless days were snuffed out by an increasingly early darkness, and the nights were long and full of turbulence.

He told no one what he had seen: there was no one to tell, no one with whom he conversed, only a series of floating faces like masks that came and went, swimming into the dim circle of lamplight in the estate office by day with mouths always open, always moving. Sometimes he heard them individually, other times he did not, and there was only a deafening clamour of voices demanding answers, instructions, advice, issuing complaints against neighbours or enemies, or pleading. Always pleading: for time, for loans, for leniency. And as time, the one commodity he could not rent or buy, passed and ran out, they would be pleading for grain, not to sell but merely to keep themselves alive.

15th October 1767
We have not had 5 fair days and had these been running or following one another, it had been happier for the Tenants, for in that time they would have got in all their Corne with safety, but as these happened not above one fair day at a time, rendered this Harvest to be as bad as any remembered. Yesterday was the first for drying the victual, and the day looks so well, it gives me hope that the whole crop may be got in, tho not in the best of order, the bear and oats have suffered much.

Any such hope was futile. The rain resumed, and fell by day and night.

He sat in the estate office, watching the darkness beyond the lamp. *Come to me then— tell me what you want*, although the dead, he knew, never spoke. Listening to the wind in the hours of the night, the rushing as of dark water, some dark tide rising, carrying them all to the edge of irrevocable things. Sitting during the day in the grim, leaden light, while the wind threw the rain like stones against the glass: listening to the faltering voice of the crofter on the other side of the table, and trying to drown it with the scratching of his pen.

"A Mhaoir, there are tinkers in Glen Sian...."

And the wind, like the sound of the hated sea, always rising, like sea on shingle.

"I will deal with it."

The crofter's hands moved around his bonnet. "They are stealing the cattle, A Mhaoir. The wife and myself, we lost three. It is bread in our mouths, A Mhaoir."

"I said I would deal with it."

"Aye. Thank you, A Mhaoir. Thank you."

He rode down later and found what he expected: five of the neglected cottages along the single street occupied, with garrons and dogs and sullen children and the usual accumulation of garbage. There were two or three adults in a doorway, speaking to one another in shelta. They fell silent when they saw him.

He dismounted and stood in the sewer of the street, the rain drifting against his face. One of their dogs ran up growling, and he kicked it away before it could fasten onto his leg. The men muttered to one another, and some one else came out swearing into the street.

"It will be your arse next, if you're here when I come back."

From the dark interior a woman called, "Ach, away and shit," and he said coldly, "I'll kick your arse too, ban-cheard. I'm not particular."

He looked down at the man with the ringletted hair who had pushed out in defense of the dog.

"If these are your people, move them from this place."

"Move them yourself, you bloody bastard. Who do you think you are?"

He said, "Who do you think I am?" and the man, obviously reconsidering what he had been about to say, spat on the stones near his boot.

"Then you can be buggered. And you can bring a warrant."

He thrust his boot into the stirrup, and surprisingly no one moved, although he had turned his back on them hoping to provoke some violence.

"I will bring you a warrant all of you can read," and he heard their contemptuous laughter, until it became as insignificant as all the other voices, and could be as easily ignored.

By the end of the week there were four more families, with their mangey garrons and dogs and children infested with lice and ringworm, and another complaint in the estate office: another yell cow missing.

"A Mhaoir, you said you would be carrying any of us to an officer of the law. How is it that you pronounce on us and not on these stinking cairds?"

The rain stopped, the dark tide of the wind died away, and the moon rose at a later hour. He collected what he wanted and waited for a dry night, which came at the end of the month.

He rode down after midnight. There was no moon, but hundreds of bright stars paved the black wastes of the night. By the starlight some one stumbled out onto the greyish stones, released a flood of steaming urine and staggered back inside: nothing else moved, no dog barked, and the gusting wind carried all other sounds away.

The tarred canvas smoked sullenly and bloomed; the couples and side-trees were already alight. He watched until the roof collapsed; and the blistering heat warmed his skin, and the bitter stink filled his nostrils.

It was dark on the road, and he thought it quiet: although the wind had not died its fearful velocity had lessened, and it no longer assaulted him. After the violent light of the flames the stars seemed diminished, but his eyes became accustomed to the darkness, and as he rode in the small hours of the morning the moon rose, huge and scarlet, changing slowly to white until it threw a light as pale as day, and all the birds, awakening, sang uncertainly.

VI

I was alone in the house, so I had laid out my possessions and was looking through them for something to give to Charlotte for Christmas.

Books, too scarce and too dear. Jewellery: there was not much, and every piece was heavy with memory. Garnet earrings, Catherine's gift; pearls with a diamond clasp. A satin case I did not open: Ewen's only bequest to me, which I could never love but never give away. And my watch, with *25th December, 1761* engraved within the guard, while the delicate hands crawled endlessly around its mother of pearl face, marking the hours and years of my life and moving, as my life moved, without rest or progress, always in that same dismal circle.

It was snowing, a soft, dry sound, no more insistent than a whisper; the harbinger of that deathly whiteness, that dreaded, starving season.

How many winters? How many years? How much bitter lovelessness? My very friendship with Charlotte was at risk; James had withdrawn his companionship, which was all I had wanted of him. I had nothing else, only a dead man's letters and meditations and a living man's pencilled likeness.

One day, this is all you will have.

I put the garnet earrings aside for Charlotte— they would not suit her but Mordaunt had never liked them— and there was a volume of sonnets which could be given to James, although he had not an ounce of his father's sensibility. Then I wrote in my journal, although my fingers were stiff with cold.

What will become of me?

And I wrote nothing more, because there seemed no answer.

***

She had been writing letters in the morning room, where she received me and gave me coffee from Ewen's silver pot. She sat at his escritoire in a fulsome déshabillée with her hair down her back in a dishevelment which appeared not to have been combed, and turned over her gift with a little delighted smile while I tried to drink the scalding liquid and remove myself as soon as possible from the room. She sat gazing at me like a kindly but insensitive mare, and knew nothing of my discomfort; if there were memories for her here, they did not haunt her as they did me.

Beyond the foam of lace on her shoulder I saw that the morning's rain had turned to snow.

"I must go," I said.

She turned her head and glanced at it.

"I used to love the snow," she said.

My gelding faltered before I had gone a mile; it was a stone, wedged between the shoe and the frog of the hoof. I pried at it while the snow, now sleet, soaked into my back, then a greatcoat brushed against me and an ungloved hand took the hoof and worked briefly with a pick.

"Walk him home."

His face was deeply withdrawn, and I thought then that I had never seen him smile.

"Thank you. That was kindly done," and he began to walk away. He said over his shoulder, "I will walk with you a while, if you have no objection." The sleet had lessened, and the air seemed lighter; the sky was torn to rags. "I don't see you much by Ardsian now. I used to see you coming and going," and there were too many answers, too many reasons, which I suspected he already knew.

The silence was unbroken except for the roar of distant water; we walked steadily, keeping pace, not looking at one another.

"I used to hear you chattering away like a magpie... you don't have so much to say nowadays."

And you, who speaks to you? Who knows your mind at Ardsian?

"I used to hear the pair of you laughing. I wondered what it was that you were laughing at."

"I have little cause for laughter now... no more, I think, than you."

The sun had come out, and in its harsh light everything glittered: the stones, the dead bracken, the heavy broadcloth of his shoulder capes; and the clouds were blacker by contrast in its exceptional brilliance.

He said, "I saw him," and I misheard or misunderstood, and the light was hard; so hard. Like his eyes, I thought it pitiless, and I did not want him to see my tears.

I don't know what he said then; I don't know what I answered. Perhaps it was beyond my comprehension, and I was never told again. All I could think was, why you and not me? Why you?

A flask came into my hand and he told me to drink, and I began to question him, absurd questions about death and resurrection and the soul's immortality, until he said, "When you see the things I've seen you'll know there is no God." Then he capped the flask; I no longer felt shock or gnawing cold or incredulity. I said, "Shall we walk on?" and he said, "No. Go alone from here." I remember that I held out my hand to him: I don't know why.

And only for a second he touched me, touched my cheek, with a cold hand I scarcely felt.

"Your tears will freeze," he said.

He left me, and I walked four more miles while the sleet froze in my hair and the tears froze on my lashes, and the reins were frozen to my glove by the time I saw Glen Mor.

Why you and not me? Why you?

One does not always choose the moment.

Perhaps we never chose.

On the feast of Candlemas, An Fhéill-Brìghde, he sat in the estate office, and the voices were heard or not heard according to his mood. It was Wednesday, the second of February, the second anniversary of Ewen's death, and he hated the hard, pure light that filtered through the frost and insulted the darkness of his memories.

They stood across the table from him, an old man with rheumy eyes and a pimpled youth. The man was barely fifty, the father of eleven; his son was in his early teens.

"Failte na maduin duibh, A Mhaoir."

He cut across the elaborate preamble of Gaelic conversation.

"What do you want, MacBean?"

Their hands were all around their bonnets, their eyes everywhere but on his face.

"It is not for myself I am coming, A Mhaoir, but for the boy only."

"What do you want?" he repeated, less patiently.

The boy said in a cracked voice, "I am wanting to be married, A Mhaoir."

Marriage, he thought, what do you know of marriage, with the pap still in your mouth?

"That's no concern of mine. Either you do or you don't."

The boy watched him with eyes so pale a blue that they were almost white.

"It is wanting to settle on my father's land we are," and it was said with so little deference that the old man whispered audibly, "Uist! Uist!" in rebuke, and Malcolm, who had been shaving shreds of tobacco from the iron-hard lump he carried in his pocket, paused with the knife balanced in his fingers.

"Your father's land is Glen Sian's land, and Glen Sian's to dispose of as he pleases. And it is against the policies of this estate to subdivide without the factor's consent. I do not give my consent."

There was a silence.

"This is hard news, A Mhaoir."

"It is the policy of the estate."

The boy said, "Aye. It is your policy."

"Keep your mouth shut, churaidh, until you come into this room with rent. When you work like a man then you can talk to me, and maybe I will talk to you."

MacBean's eyes were running, or perhaps they were tears: he wiped his nose on his sleeve and turned to go, but his son held him back, and seemed to force him to some further, unwilling defiance.

"I will be appealing on behalf of the boy to Glen Sian. He will put this matter straight."

"He will merely repeat what I have already said. Two families are strictly prohibited from living upon one croft, and if one of a family marries, he must leave the croft. This is policy. It has been written and published. If you take him under your roof you will pay for the first offense a fine of one pound Scots, and for the second, *you*, churaidh, will be removed from the estate— and I will send such a black name after you that no other landowner in the Great Glen will give you shelter."

The pimpled face was mottled with fury, the pustules more enflamed. The old man coughed with a violent rattling of phlegm.

"It is a cruel man you are, A Mhaoir."

He said nothing, and they left. He listened to the outburst of furious whispering outside the door until it died away, then he sat in the cold, shadowless light, smoking, and considering the nature of cruelty. A cruel climate, a cruel winter; the cruelty of pain and hunger and death; the cruelty of bereavement; the cruelty of abuse and punishment; the cruelty of rape; the cruelty of murder. What was cruelty? In all its refinements, its infinite shades and subtleties, it was, like passion, unknown to them: like passion, or some insoluble question of philosophy, like God or the limits of the universe, it was beyond their experience, beyond any hope of their understanding.

***

He was summoned just after three o'clock. He went from the coldness of the estate office through the coldness and dimness of the house, down the stairs to the morning room.

Charlotte was seated at the escritoire, with a teacup on its polished surface and a litter of paper stuffed into the drawers.

"Ah, Mr. Scott. At last."

There was a lacquered tray on the table, holding a dish of savouries and the teapot, and another cup with its accoutrements, but she did not invite him to join her.

Plus ça change, Ewen.

"Will you sit down?"

"I prefer to stand, if it is the same to you. I have been sitting all day."

He stood with his back to the fire. She remained at the escritoire, her hands folded in her lap.

"I have sought this interview with you for some time. I do not see you often in this part of the house."

"I don't like the colours," he said, and she flushed visibly.

"You are an impertinent fellow."

"I am not your fellow, madam, nor anybody else's."

The big hands unclasped, displaying a collection of antique rings which had survived the depredations of debt and invasion; then she laid them along the arms of the chair and said, "I wish to be apprised of the state of affairs— our affairs. And do not refer me to my husband— this is done without his knowledge. I trust I can rely upon your discretion."

"Oh, depend on it," he said.

It was darker beyond the windows, and the room itself was dark; her gown, of some dark striped stuff, spilled across the carpet into shadow. He found himself staring at the place where Ewen had lain, and barely heard her when she spoke.

"I will depend upon it, Mr. Scott. Now tell me the accumulation of rent."

At some time during his discourse the door opened a fraction. Imperiously she waved it shut.

"And your propositions for improvement?"

"I am opposed on every point, if not by him then by the tenants."

"I will give you my support. And you, surely, can subdue the tenants?"

He watched her face, one side of which was illuminated by the candles. Even her eyes seemed dark, and devoid of the expression which might have indicated sarcasm or approval.

He said, "I propose a census, and a new rent roll to include the married offspring of tenants farming a subdivided croft. The practise has been discontinued, but the problem remains. I consider it an invisible population, uncounted and unaccountable. They pay no rent, and yet they enjoy the privileges of accredited tenants, if privileges we may call them."

"How many people do you find in this situation?"

"Perhaps a thousand, with their dependants."

She said nothing for a while, while the tea cooled in the cup, and he heard the first brush of snow on the glass, invisible in the early darkness.

"And your second proposition?"

"There is a piece of land in the northwest— several families abandoned it and went to America some years ago. I want it."

"For what purpose, Mr. Scott?"

"I want to put sheep on it."

She gave him a pitying smile.

"Lawks, man, we have enough of those!"

"I propose a different breed. The Border breed, which can be managed by a few men with dogs. It is in every way superior to the native breed— it produces four times the wool and three times the mutton, and guarantees a substantial profit."

"And you put this to James."

"He found it amusing, as you do. But then, progress is sometimes ridiculous to the ignorant, is that not so?"

She moved, and the hollows of her face and throat swam in the light: on her left hand the listless stones of too many rings threw back no brilliance.

"But you believe this is a profitable venture?"

"I have seen it put into practise. There is an experimental sheep farm at Ballachulish which consistently profits. I have visited it."

"And you recommend this to us?"

"I recognize it as a profitable alternative to a black cattle economy, which I hold to be archaic."

She said bluntly, her Edinburgh accent very strong, "I have access to money of which James is not aware... an annuity paid by my father. How much is necessary?"

He leaned down casually and tossed more peat on the fire, turning his back on her.

"I would prefer a thousand, or better still, two thousand— that is breeding stock and wether stock. At, say, ten shillings a ewe and twenty-five or thirty a ram. I would consider that a flock of moderate size."

He listened to the brief activity of her quill and the silence that followed.

"This is... an expensive proposition, Mr. Scott."

"I do not expect you to support it alone. I would regard it as a useful investment."

She said, as though uncertain, "I may... put it to James."

"Aye, you put it to him. Put the alternative to him as well: he can starve or sell."

He replaced the poker and stood with his back to the flames.

"You are a hard man, Mr. Scott." He watched her with enigmatic eyes. "But make no mistake. I can be hard too, very hard, if it is to protect my husband's interests."

"I am no enemy to your husband's interests, or to him, or you."

She changed the subject, with so little subtlety that he took a perverse pleasure in eluding her.

"What do you make of this business in Glen Sian? It could not have failed to come to your notice."

"What should I make of it? A pack of drunken cairds— what else could be expected? And there'll be more of it, if the situation is allowed to continue."

She said, so quietly that he could barely hear, "You take too much upon yourself sometimes."

He said, "Take it then. Take it and carry it, and see if it does not crush you. This is Cloutie's Croft, this place, a few acres for the damned." She did not answer: her face was swimming in the uncertain light. "And you can carry James too. Don't think I don't know you already carry him."

She was twisting the rings around her fingers as he had seen her do that morning, when the silk on these walls had been a discoloured yellow, and the carpet had been stained with blood.

"If there are repercussions, all improving measures must be stopped immediately, for the people's good."

The wind was rising, driving the snow: he heard it like a faint, demented song.

"You are not an independent agent now, Mr. Scott, whatever liberties you took upon yourself before."

He said, "Is that all?"

"Yes, that is all. You may go."

"Thank you." And as he turned his elbow caught the edge of the hideous Italian vase on the mantel. It fell, and smashed into gaudy fragments, and he glanced down at the pieces but made no move to pick them up.

"A pity," he said.

He had been climbing for three hours, through snow and sleet and equally blinding explosions of sunlight, from the leafless wood where the dead deer lay in the drifts that bore the signatures of visiting predators: the sharp encircling prints of foxes, the brushstrokes of wings and the gaping holes

340

between the ribs where eagles had torn out hearts and lungs. Then across the empty hills, following the tracks of the deer, climbing until he had surprised a dozen ailing hinds huddled in the snow, and farther on thirty stags together, driven down from their accustomed wintering place by the cold.

He climbed now with effort, sucking the clean harsh air in laboured gasps. To fall was to die: to slip, to die more slowly, broken by the teeth of many projecting rocks in an endless, icy descent. Now at eight hundred feet there was nothing, only the bitter gnawed ground called with ironic significance An Reithe, the Ram. Here he would burn in April, to force tender new growth from the heather: here, among the fallen stones of crofts long unoccupied, sheep would graze, and force from this uninhabitable country the profit no other method of husbandry had ever provided.

He flung off his coat and sat sweating in the bitter air, eyes narrowed against the glare of sun on the snow of the closest peaks. Eight hundred, nine hundred, a thousand feet high, their Gaelic names evoked with understated clarity a country's resistance to man. The cold hill, the bare hill, the little hill of struggle, the place of the sharp dry stones, the hill of no shelter, the ridge of the mist, where the scree fell away into eternity. It was not a country made for men: it was not to be subdued by men. It was not meant to be farmed; it was not meant to be cultivated. It was primitive; and until men ceased to farm it like some verdant upland, attempting to wrest an easy livelihood from it, it would break them... it would break their hearts and their spirits and their fortunes, and sometimes, indifferently, it would kill them, until they acknowledged its grandeur and its brutality and left it alone in its solitude.

He believed it utterly. He believed the land uninhabitable, and unfit for cultivation. But he could not abandon his attempts to subdue it. He knew he would not lose his life to it; and he would wrest profit from its barren stones.

The sweat dried on his body, and the fingers frost-bitten in his childhood bleached to insensibility, and still he did not move, staring across the ground. Indigo shadows, black rock, drifting snow hardened and sculpted by the wind. As sterile as rock, as clean as rain: no frost-blackened fields, no rotting bere, no bloated carcasses, no human voices crying.... There was nothing between himself and infinity but the wind, and a pair of eagles in the sun. Spiralling, tumbling, diving at one another in their ritual courtship flight, the shadow of their great wings crossed his face, and mocked him with their freedom.

VII

When time has dulled the memory of pain, these pages resurrect it: my book of dreary hours, of commonplaces, of proprieties and drudgeries that hedged my screaming soul.

7 o'clock. Rise. Air bed. Window frozen. Dress. Bring water to kitchen, sweep, clean fireirons, make up fire. 8 o'clock. We break our fast. 9 o'clock. Wash breakfast things. Half nine. Cows, hens, stable. 11 o'clock. All rooms swept, dusted and arranged, water cans full, brush my father's boots (not to his satisfaction). One o'clock. Dinner, boiled potatoes and tea. Half one. I make black pudding with my aunt of yesterday's dead sheep. Singe head and trotters for soup, clean heart and lungs. Salt and hang meat. 5 o'clock. Lay table. Half five. We eat supper, a hard fried liver. 7 o'clock. Bed.

By night I wrote, to preserve my sanity. The blowing snow scraped like sand against the glass and collected on the sill, and lay on the page of a shabby book cracked with much reading.

I am Duchess of Malfi still....

The draught blew my candleflame, and in the silence of the sleeping house a board creaked beyond the door: MacNeil, emanating disapproval and whisky fumes; but even he did not dare to disturb me.

Return, fair soul, from darkness, and lead mine/ Out of this sensible hell....

I had lived in this place for five years and five months. I was twenty-two years old.

On a day in late winter, the date of which I could never remember, I stood in Ewen's glasshouse, where neither I nor any one else had come in the two years since his death. It was full of desiccated plants, cracked panes of glass overhead, a litter of twigs and leaves and moss on the roof. Beneath one of the benches a few bulbs had bloomed and shrivelled unnoticed. Among the empty pots I found a label in Ewen's hand: the sight of it, unexpectedly, could still bring tears to my eyes. Then I closed the door and went into the house, where I thought I might be welcome for an hour, and coming out of the servants' warren into the cold hallway I heard James's voice.

They say listeners never hear well of themselves. Certainly ever afterwards I recalled my sense of outrage and betrayal.

"... as you intend to display her to your relatives, perhaps it would not be too much to ask that you have a word with her concerning her appearance."

She said only, "Oh, James," as though the entire subject were an unnecessary interruption in a trying day, then he said, "Well, I do not know how I should tolerate it. Some one who claims to meet me with equity, to look like such a guy— one feels one should toss her a penny for a new shoe. Cannot you give her something of yours? You seem to throw enough of them out."

And my shabby coat hangs on the peg, and my cracked boots, patched and soled by Glen Mor's tanner, sit on the floor beneath it; and my clothing smells of neglect and smoke, and in my chests the silk gowns rot, and against my skin the greyish linen of a boned jump fitted to the breasts of a sixteen year old girl frays and strains; and the cuff of my shirt and my stockings are greyed, and the snow falls outside the window as it fell on me that morning coming out of James's house, whispering to this poor tatterdemalion ghost, this diminished heiress, *A penny for the guy, a penny for the guy.*

And I write, and I write into the night.

O death, rock me asleep....

I came in one evening and found a stranger sitting in the kitchen. It was my only indication that our contact with the world had once more been established.

He was a lank, ill-made man, badly dressed, with hair of a nondescript brown tied back with a snuff-coloured ribbon: where the firelight touched his cheek the skin was pitted with smallpox scars. He was not a man of consequence, otherwise he would have been entertained in the parlour instead of lounging at the table with a coatless MacNeil, who sat in slovenly disarray nearest the fire in his stockinged feet. But his manners were impeccable: he rose when I appeared and MacNeil broke off in mid-discourse and said, "My daughter."

He spoke in Gaelic, and his guest bowed and addressed me in that language. His voice was pleasant, but the general atmosphere of dissipation and MacNeil's air of sly expectancy, as though he had conjured this little scenario for his own amusement, disgusted me; so I turned to that eager, pitted face and said, "Go back to your boozing-glass, sir. I do not understand you."

And I left them in the smoky kitchen, amid the smell of feet and whisky and drying laundry. I neither knew nor cared for my father's response, and in fact he made none. Perhaps it had added an unexpected savour to the drama, or perhaps I had genuinely shocked him. But nothing he did or said signified any longer to me: nothing any one did or said would now govern my behaviour, save myself.

Such was George Cameron's first experience of me.

He took up lodgings in the derelict school, which it was MacNeil's intention that he should reopen, and where he himself had been educated before the rebellion.

His father, in the final days of a dying feudalism, had called himself a bard. In truth he had been a failed farmer who had followed MacNeil into revolt and died a fugitive. George had inherited his father's fine tenor voice, his rusting broadsword, and a starving patch of kale on the hill: when his mother died he was passed like an unwanted parcel to various hungry relations, and lodged in the end with cousins. When he was fourteen he had fed long enough on his uncle's contempt and announced he was leaving Glen Mor. MacNeil, lifting his head briefly from his miasma of drink and self-pity, had subjected him to a thorough course of study and sent him to Edinburgh to the house of a ministerial acquaintance, where for some years he had laboured and attended the university, which he had left abruptly and without his degree.

He told me all this one day at the school, to which I had been despatched with rags and buckets and broom to render it habitable.

We were sitting two or three rows apart on the hard, scarred benches in the dusty cold, breathing in the sweetish odour of mildew: we were permitted to be alone because my father sanctioned this acquaintance, and all the doors were open.

The conversation was conducted in English; he never again attempted to speak to me in Gaelic.

After some hours we ate together: cold mutton and bannock and cheese brought by my aunt, who stayed only long enough to inspect my efforts and the walls, which he was washing with lime. When she left she shut the door behind her... more complicity, I thought.

He said, "It was my intention to serve the Kirk."

"What prevented you?"

"I fell into evil ways." And he said it so drolly that I laughed.

"You are a strange man, Mr. Cameron."

"I would be honoured if you would call me George." He was painfully ugly, but his ugliness was relieved by a wistful charm, as though he apologized for it.

"What an unfortunate Christian name for a Scot to bear."

"Alas," and he gave me that ironic smile, "we do not choose our names, any more than we choose our relations." I laughed again, more than I had for months— or years— and found myself liking him.

"Were you christened George?"

"No... but I prefer the English version."

"How odd."

"No odder than you: a Scot with a Saxon tongue."

"I believe there is a proverb to the effect that although a man be born in a barn, it does not make him a horse."

"Are you not a horse then, nor even a Scot?"

He said it whimsically, as if he knew the depth of the wounds; and maybe he did, maybe MacNeil had presented some bent version of the truth. But I told him nothing— why should I tell him?— and he changed the subject.

"So Jamie Stirling succeeds the old man."

" 'The old man' was dear to me."

He flushed, which intensified the pitted scars.

"You must forgive me, Miss MacNeil. I stumble at every step."

He said it with great sincerity, and even offered his hand as schoolboys ask for Pax. His fingers were as bony and as pale as his face: they clasped mine across the gritty floor and the greyish scum of the water.

"I have prayed for the friendship of some one like you."

Does God hear your prayers? Or do you cry in the wilderness, like me?

But I did not say it. I did not say anything, only sat in a permissive silence while his fingers ventured upon their first intimacy; and he called me Margaret, without my consent.

Malcolm sat in the estate office at seven in the evening: he had risen fourteen hours earlier, and ridden and walked thirty-two miles in the course of the day conducting his census: he had no lieutenants and he trusted no one else to do this accurately and impartially, uninfluenced by family pressures or pleas for favour.

When they were registered they signed or made their marks, taking responsibility for the mentally deficient or infants housed among them. Some refused, having heard the rumour that to mark his paper was to sign away their tenancies. These he brusquely recorded with a cross and bracketed "illiterate". At one croft which supported fifteen adults and children, some from other impoverished townships, he had given members of the extended family notice to quit, in accordance with the policy of non-subdivision. They had stared at him with no show of resistance, while beneath the dense fug of smoke an old woman, clearly senile, huddled and moaned, hugging herself and shuddering whenever one of them spoke his name.

Eighteen families, seven of which had never previously paid rent. How many more? Three hundred, four hundred? How many hours, how many miles, how much profit?

He closed his eyes. Heavy rains had delayed the burning and clearing of heather; the fields were a sea of muck; the Sian which meandered through James's garden had burst its banks, and flooded the orchard with a foot or so of fast-flowing water. And solutions must be found to every such act of God, and must originate here, must proceed from behind this table, from behind his aching eyes.

There was movement, and he raised his head. The figure drifted toward him through the dusk.

"How fortuitous to find you here. Your little exercise continues, I trust?"

He tossed the sheaf of papers across the table, and felt for his tobacco while James squinted at them in the gloom.

"Very progressive. I congratulate you."

Still light in the sky, and the cawing of rooks. He waited for James to speak further or go, and allow him to do the same, but James merely studied his silken legs and settled deeper into the chair. Irritated, he pulled the papers toward him and closed them into their marbled covers; then James said, "I hope this business proves as profitable as you say. Because come the autumn I shall have a son to inherit."

"Or a daughter to dower."

"I thought I might have your felicitations."

"You have them, if you need them."

The light was dying now. How rapidly the air became cold... the season was early yet.

He became aware of the hostility with which James was watching him.

"I might have expected that from you, as you sow your bastards so freely. The bloom is rather brushed off the experience for you."

"Have you anything else to say?" and James stood up jerkily like a beautiful puppet.

"Yes, and it may prove of passing interest. You are no doubt aware that our mutual friend George Cameron has returned from his travels."

"George Cameron is no friend of mine."

James's hands came within the periphery of the candlelight. On the smallest finger of the left, he wore Ewen's long unused signet.

"Well, it comes to my attention that your other little friend, the one you had in common with my father, is seen about a good deal in his company."

He put the quill down and looked over the candleflame. The light seemed to burn his eyes.

"I am not Miss MacNeil's guardian, any more than I am yours."

James said diffidently, "Oh, well, in that case, perhaps I should not have said." There was no response, only the burning, inexpressive eyes, and he felt as though nothing he had been saying had been heard since he had entered this room, and nothing after he left would be recalled but the insignificance of his interruption. "You do take a certain proprietary interest in her, I collect?" The quill was moving again, trailing its stream of ink, indecipherable hieroglyphics upon which his future relied: as it had yesterday, and the year before, and all the years before that, as it would like the line of Banquo's progeny stretch out to the crack of doom. And nothing changed, and its claustrophobic sameness and futility smothered him, and made him want to scream.

"I never thought you would come to this. Everything you were, and everything you wanted to be, now reduced to the margins of a ledger. I never thought to ever see you pushing a quill on my behalf."

This, he thought, this is mere shadow play. I make this with my fingers against the wall.

He replaced the quill, the papers, the ledger, in a red haze of fatigue. Even James seemed to waver in the heat rippling from the flame, and when he stood James retreated slightly, as though his movements held some inexplicable menace.

"I am everything I was, and everything I wanted to be, and what I am is not this, and is not here. Only a fool would think so."

He went out, leaving the candle burning. James said after him, "I concern myself only with your welfare, Malcolm, and your happiness."

When there was no answer he flicked open a page of the ledger, but the columns and calculations bored him and he let it fall shut, and conscientiously snuffed the candle, remembering the cost.

The moon was late in rising. By three in the morning it was at its zenith, casting the cold, greyish light by which the woman saw him.

There was no conversation, only a moment's cursory groping: he came at once, in silence. When he had gone she picked up the coin and returned to the croft where her husband slept: she had heard the recurrent whine of his snoring even in the midst of intercourse.

She turned away with contempt and slipped her fingers into the wetness, the unsatisfied mouth he had filled so brusquely: then she fell into a heavy sleep, as if she had been disturbed only by some violent, passing dream.

VIII

I cannot recall the exact moment, or precisely how it happened. He was always there, and his name and his presence run like a thread through my remembrance of all those years. I resented those who insulted or criticized him, and there were many, although fear kept them circumspect; I began to cherish every memory, however slight, of his kindness or attention. In Ewen's journals, too, I cherished every mention of him, although they were infrequent or unrevealing: perhaps Ewen had not trusted his affection to paper, as I neither trusted nor recognized what was so slowly happening to me.

Other matters disturbed me. My relationship with George Cameron bloomed luridly into desire: I rejected him and he became resentful, with a mouthful of picaresque names for women who encouraged honest men and then offered them indignant rebuff. We avoided one another after that, and MacNeil speculated but said nothing.

In the middle of May James wrote, inviting me to tea. I had seen neither of them since the overheard conversation and I was friendless without them. Charlotte, indiscernibly pregnant, spent much of the afternoon drowsing on the terrace with her white cat on her lap. James had summoned various shabby men whom I was expected to instruct in the care of Ewen's neglected roses and followed me restlessly, making inane observations as I pruned and pointed and spoke passable Gaelic, to every one's surprise. Occasionally one of them glanced at the cloudless sky, and the irony of the situation was not lost on me: I purloined their time, which would have been more constructively spent manuring their own fields.

Finally James said I must see the orchard, and we walked through a rain of blossom until we were out of sight of the house.

"Do you know, when I look about the place, knowing I possess it, I confess I find myself falling victim to ridiculous bucolic sentiment."

I said I thought that was commendable, and waited for him to come to the point.

"Although it meant nothing to me as a child, you know, Margaret. I never interested myself in his concerns. The young are so thoughtless, ain't they." Then, in a different tone, "I'm glad you came. I've wanted an opportunity to speak to you privately." He subsided into the damp grass; I controlled a ludicrous impulse to spread my coat for him. "I wanted to ask you about money. I take it you're fairly flush?"

"And if I am?"

"Would you be prepared to advance me a hundred or so against my new investment?"

"I don't know what your investment is, so I can hardly say."

"Sheep," he said. "It was not my decision, but these things never are." He stared into the sun, and his profile seemed young, drawn, tight with anxiety and resentment. "My wife thinks money drops like manna from heaven and spends accordingly, my creditors bay like hounds for my blood, and others devise schemes for the sole purpose of ruining me. If this venture fails I shall very likely emigrate, trailing my debts behind me." He turned, and for a terrible moment, in the flickering shadows, I saw his father in his face. "I know not what you were accustomed to from your acreage, but I count myself lucky if I see two hundred a year."

We sat; the petals drifted. Then he said with a strangely apposite poignancy, "By God, I've never missed my father more. And it's my wedding anniversary today... three inestimable years."

"At least you are not alone."

"My dear Margaret, we are all alone."

"You have a wife who cares for you. You have a capable agent—"

"He tells me what he wants. God help me if I don't agree." Then, "I don't want you to think I don't understand the man. I know his position is difficult— no factor can hope to be popular, it accords ill with the office. But he damns these people, Margaret... he holds them in contempt. And he feeds on their hatred... it nourishes him. I can't stomach it."

"I think he is a man of principle. And he has always been kind to me."

Perhaps he had known, or suspected: perhaps it was toward this he had been leading me.

"So he speaks, does he?"

"He is courteous. Otherwise, he pays me little attention."

"Well, you're better off beneath his notice, and that's the truth from me."

"I don't know what you mean."

"The man's a lecher, and he sows his seed in every ditch. He had at least two bastards, and he's illegitimate himself.... I thought some one would have told you."

"What do you mean, 'had'?"

"Smallpox... or some manner of pox. Not uncommon at that level of society." He stood, brushing petals from his clothing. "I must go. People will wonder where I am." He broke several blossoming twigs from the tree. "I'll give these to Charlotte... must do the pretty on the anniversary."

I said they would not last, but he was admiring his token and did not appear to hear me.

"Take some if you want... I know you like your posy. We can discuss the money later." He was waiting. "Are you coming?"

I said that I would follow him, and he walked away briskly, carrying his twigs.

I sat for a long time with the impression of his body in the damp grass beside me, and the sun, like a many-pointed star, flickered through the branches: the hidden earth was still cold beneath me, and the petals drifted like snow. I heard Charlotte calling me from the terrace, as though calling a child from its play: as voices had called me, loved voices, loving voices, in the fragrant twilights of my past.

The petals fell... one rude wind would shatter them, but the everlasting revolution that would carry me to the grave would only bring them to fruition. I had seen them last year, as I would see them in the future: every time these trees bloomed I saw another year of my life dropping with their blossom, scattered to the wind.

349

Charlotte was calling me, in a high voice like a girl's.
Stay me with flagons, comfort me with apples....
I was sick, and James had poisoned me.

They were buried under the bleached grass in a place scoured by winds; moss and crotal had begun to obliterate the piles of stone. In another year these cairns would be no more than undulations in a broken landscape.

Behind me the dark hole of the door was empty; no smoke tainted the wind. The croft was as dead and forsaken as these children, and she might have been away for an hour or forever: there was nothing in the place to evoke her for me, and nothing, thank God, of him.

The sun went in. A shadow of rain was sweeping the flank of Riabhach, but where I stood no rain fell yet.

Like her, time did not encompass me... I might have stood there for an hour or a heartbeat, while the curlews flickered across the sky and the wind sowed these graves with nettles, the flowers of neglect.

Then I left his children to the rain's tears; and I went away.

Malcolm left Glen Sian twice in the remaining months of 1768, the first time in July, when the pack roads were dry and shimmering with heat and the taste of sere grass filled his mouth at the end of each day's riding, and the horse dozed, standing, in the broad moonlight while he lay with his head on his saddle staring at the immeasurable wastes of the night. He carried no letters, no grocery lists, no money but his own and no commissions from James, and as the Highlands released him and fell away into tumbled folds of blue on the horizon, his life and perspectives emptied into a void which contained only dust and miles, and at night, the restless current of his own thoughts.

There were few other travellers, only, occasionally, pack ponies laden with two hundredweight of lead or coal or grain, licensed or smuggled, jingling into view and disappearing as the ground dipped and enfolded them. The jaggers neither spoke nor acknowledged him, and no one interfered with his passage.

He reached Kendal on a Wednesday afternoon when the town was full of packmen. By Monday his business was concluded, and he knew the state of the market, the breeds, the breeders and the quality of the shepherds offering themselves for his money like the prostitutes in the streets. The town disturbed him like a half-remembered dream. Without regret, he left it.

He dreamed of her that night, waking on the hard ground with the dampness of sweat in his clothing: dreamed with a violent, bitter sexuality which he had thought himself able to discipline, and expurgate from any contact with her.

It had been possible once. It was not possible now.

He rode north. Even the air seemed colder, and the summer brief and transient. The disturbance on the eye's edge resolved itself into familiar country, secretive with rain, and as the Highlands had released him with every mile, so now they enclosed him. He slept badly, waking every hour in the yellowish light of a waning moon, and rode into Glen Sian the following day. Nothing had changed but the deeper colour of the grain and the luridness of his dreams.

He spoke to her for the first time in weeks in the courtyard at Ardsian on a humid morning, with the filtered sunlight already reddening for storm; he remembered afterwards with a peculiar bewilderment and pain that she had not even acknowledged him. She had merely turned those eyes upon him: grey eyes, grey as the morning, grey cool eyes like rain, on his body and his face as if he were shit to be scraped from the sole of her boot before she walked into the dim cool hall to meet James, who was waiting there for her.

Trying, then, to maintain the semblance of normality, to accept insult with courtesy. To control the beating blood, the rage, the jealousy, the hunger to touch her, touch her skin, to lay only the heat of his hand on her coolness, to invite even her contempt.

"Nothing to say today? Or has your friend the ugly dominie tied your tongue in school?" and when she ignored him, lust and anger and frustration seized him so violently that he wanted to hit her. "Well, I'll tell you something. He's an unhealthy fellow and he has an unhealthy past, and you'll do well to remember it."

"And you?"

"And I what?"

"Is your own life above reproach? By God, I don't think so," and as she turned once more toward the house he became aware of the pallor of James's clothing— clean shirt, clean skin, clean conscience— swimming in cool shadows like an attentive spirit; and involuntarily he put his hand on her sleeve.

He had never called her by her Christian name before: he could not later recall if he said it then or merely heard it in his mind.

"Margaret—"

"You go to hell," she said, with an intensity of emotion which could not have shocked him more if she had abused him with some terrible obscenity. He knew only that he had removed his hand and she had walked forward into the waiting house, as if she had been only momentarily detained by a stranger.

351

Since then, nothing. She absented herself from the usual places, and where he knew he would find her he did not go, avoiding Ardsian on the days when she was expected, and even those fields where he knew Glen Mor reapers were working. He directed his increasingly ferocious energy into preparing accommodation for the shepherds, whom he proposed to house in the abandoned crofts on An Reithe, and for which he needed and requested the labour of fit men in the area. They refused, as courteously as he had asked them, and when he suggested that they reconsider there was no threat, only an implication of consequences. Conscious of the insult he was affording them, he offered money. The harvest provided every man with an excuse.

He laboured alone for a week, gathering and setting stones until the calluses on his hands bled in the rain, and he cursed them and the stones and the rain and the harvest and the whole abortion of the land until he was hoarse. Now, in the twilight, he sat with books and papers scattered and tobacco spilled on the table: an open watch, barely visible in the gloom, had stopped at nine o'clock. He had been drinking for hours, and the light and the rain and the evening seemed interminable.

He thought he slept. When he opened his eyes the light was a little greyer, and the rain was steady: the house and the silence seemed fraught with whisperings, stirrings, half-heard voices. He locked the door and went out into the night.

He found himself standing outside his mistress's croft, with the rain soaking his clothes: he expected the same passive resistance from her, the infuriating silence of the past three years, and he was prepared for it. As his father had beaten his childish self to release so many years of inarticulate fury, so tonight she was Glen Sian to him, to be violated and subdued. He pushed open the door and bent his head beneath the lintel, and in the shadows something moved as if gathering itself.

"Is it you?" Her voice neither welcomed nor denied. Her nakedness swam in his vision. "Is this what you want?"

And she waited, unresisting, while he fumbled at his clothes.

It was quickly over. He was impotent.

After a while he dragged his coat from the bed and felt in the pocket, and smoked, staring into the fire.

Eventually he said, "They've done for me, Grania."

"You? Never," she said.

"I'm done for," he said again.

She leaned forward and saw the glitter of his eyes in the firelight.

"They fear the sheep, and they fear you. This is nothing new."

"Do you fear me, Grania?"

"Have I cause?"

He said nothing, his eyes without colour, reflecting the flames.

"What did you expect, when they think you want their land? Not this year or the next but the year after that, until there are no more men...."

"The price of everything goes up, and the price of nothing falls— except beef, since the war. Do you understand?"

"Maybe. But what is it worth to you, an acre of stones? Is it worth more to you than to them?"

The smoke seemed thicker, stinging his eyes, and the pipe was foul and bitter.

"I am so tired," he said. "Help me sleep, Grania."

In the grey evening of another day, in the same drifting rain, he bent his head beneath the lintel of another door and sat down at the scrubbed table at the place indicated to him, and stretched his boots out towards the fire, contemplating them. He was aware of the eyes, and the wary gaze of children quick to grasp an atmosphere of unease. He took the knife from his pocket and began to shave shreds of tobacco with its razored edge.

"So, Diar? What do you say?"

The eyes across the table flickered towards the woman at the door, who left her wheel and set out whisky with an unnecessary amount of noise.

"Will you take a dram with me, A Mhaoir, while we talk of it?"

They drank; he smoked, always conscious of the disapproving stare and the silence from the doorway, where the woman, spinning in the rainy twilight, was listening intently.

"You don't like me, Siubhan."

Her fingers continued to feed the wheel; her eyes, the dark blue of the Celt, never left him. He remembered her as a girl with a face like an opened flower, a delicate vein in her cheek like a tracery, and beautiful hair, always clean and braided with coloured ribbon. Now the hair was hidden under a soiled breid: she had lost teeth, and the iris-like cheek was sallow. Over her features, like a transparent mask, he saw the old woman she would become. She was the same age as himself, and Diar was only two years older.

"I don't care for you one way or the other," she said.

"Then take my part, and tell your husband to make something of himself."

She said, "Why do you try to buy his labour when you know you could demand it? What do you want of us that is not right, that you want him to do in secret?"

The man was listening. Inarticulate, and perhaps less clever than she, he had allowed her to speak for him and voice his deepest misgivings.

" I could have gone to a dozen men—"

"Aye, and they refused you."

"I didn't offer them what I offer you, avic," he said, and the silence was apologetic, even nervous. "I know you, Diar. I knew you when we were bairns, and you were always kind to me in those days— there were many who weren't, and I have not forgotten them, as I have not forgotten you. And I think enough of your labour to pay for it, and pay well. You see what I'm putting on the table... you see it, Siubhan. To set a few stones for me, and to do other things maybe, as I need them."

"For the sheeps?" Diar said, with a bitter slyness.

"For the shepherds; and maybe later in the village. And there's more in my pocket for you and a gang of others— you choose them, you run them, your friends or your kin, as you like. You sweat for me a few days out of the month and your bairns eat well. I cannot say fairer to any man."

The coins lay on the table, dull in the duller light. In a corner one of the children whimpered, but neither of the parents moved to comfort it. There had been twelve, one almost for every year of their marriage: five had died in infancy, and the rest ranged in age from fifteen to a few months. He drank the whisky and poured another measure for himself, then pushed the jug gently across the table.

"It wasn't much of a life for us then, was it, Diar... when they drew the blood from the cows' necks and we ate it with the chaff, and you could feel your teeth rotting in your head and your shit spilling out like water— do you remember, Diar? Do you remember the red soldiers? Do you remember that winter, when your cousin Ealasaid died on Riabhach, with the grass in her mouth and the belly of the wean alive with rats?"

"Take it." He had not seen her move, but she stood now so close to him that her mud-spattered skirts brushed his boot. "Take it, for God's sake, for the sake of the children. I never asked anything of you— take it now for them, if you love me."

Silence, the moment hanging, to be turned upon a word.

"Take it, or be damned for a coward," she hissed.

"And my rent?"

"I gave you my answer. You must take my word."

"Ask him about Coinneach." Siubhan, prompting.

"What about my son?"

He searched his memory. The firstborn son, a pimply lout more given to boozing and idleness than was necessary even in these miserable circumstances, who was not at home this particular evening and whose expressed desire for land and marriage was thwarted by the policy of non subdivision.

"It is the same case for him. If I cannot subdivide for others I cannot subdivide for him. Policy binds me as much as the next man."

You make it; you can break it, the eyes said.

How much dissent do you think your services are worth to me, Diar?

And in his mind the other voice, like the voices whispering in the rain: *What is it worth to you, an acre of stones?*

He said curtly, "I can promise nothing."

Diar said, "Then I am your man."

"You will not regret it, Diar."

"No, A Mhaoir. No." But his voice was bleak, unsure: he seemed to expect something more, something binding, perhaps something honourable. When they had shaken hands at the door he seemed satisfied, even reassured. And his wife was already counting the money on the table, so there was no need to take a formal leave of her.

In the weeks before his departure for Kendal he went to the estate office only in the evenings. The house was filling with Charlotte's relatives in anticipation of an autumn christening: with any luck, he thought sourly, they would be condemned by the snows to a season's malnutrition in Glen Sian. James, presiding over their expensive entertainment, professed himself disinterested in the imminent purchase of sheep, saying only, "I place myself entirely within your hands, Malcolm," before returning to the genteel clatter of teacups and women's voices and music from an out of tune spinet behind a white-painted door.

He rode south. At the end of the Kendal market he had bought a thousand sheep, half a dozen shepherds, eight dogs and a woman, one of the shepherds' wives, who would later go mad in the brooding silence of An Reithe and hang herself from the crossbeams of one of the the crofts. The sheep were Swaledales, a small, active, hardy breed with coarse thick wool, similar to the Blackface but for the lighter mouth: if they throve he would cross them with another breed, Cheviot perhaps. The seller took him by the arm in the melee of sheep and dogs.

"Dos knaw owt abaht sheep?"

"Aye. I know something of them."

"Weel, forbye, here's summat ye divvent knaw. When they ails, look at their teeth."

"I'll remember it— and don't sell me any broken-mouthed ewes, old man, or I'll come back for yours."

Kendal to Penrith, on the familiar packway, with the jaggers' Galloways coming up through the mist and the bells on the leader's harness jingling a warning; narrow baskets of coal shouldering through the moving tide of sheep; badgers, wholesalers of farm produce licensed by local government, pushing past with teams of muzzled ponies led sometimes by women, their faces so heavily muffled that they passed unspeaking, like phantoms. Watling Street, avoiding the toll of five pence per score on the sheep that the turnpike would have cost, and always impelled by the weather: the stretch from Penrith to Carlisle became impassable with the onset of winter, and sleet if not snow was almost always a possibility on this roof of England. The sheep moved slowly, the ewes showing every sign of readiness to stand for the rams, so the sexes were segregated and driven sometimes three or four miles apart. He rode from flock to flock, aware that he was only one man with a valuable asset against half a dozen strangers, Borderers, who were entering their own country, not his.

Across the Cheviots, on a track frequented by drovers and criminals, with the welcome pressure of the curving blade in its scabbard beneath his boot. Every night a freezing fog, every morning a white tracery on the ground, like snow where it lay throughout the day: the route sometimes paved with stone, sometimes heavy with mud, visibly deteriorating even as they left Stirling. And then the pass of Corrieyairack: the leaves furred with frost every morning, a constant ache in the bones, the harsh warmth of whisky passed from hand to hand.

The sheep carried him with the inevitability of a tide into Glen Sian. It was the last day of October, his thirty-third birthday, and a bitter snow, the first of that season, had just begun to fall.

On the sixth of November Charlotte gave birth to a son, after forty-eight hours of labour. I saw him when he was four days old, and even to my critical and inexperienced eye he seemed a perfect child. He was christened Henry James Hilaire by a dissipated Episcopalian priest who had accompanied Charlotte's family, and slept angelically throughout the procedure while his godparents, of whom I was one, shivered in the chapel; then we repaired to the comparative warmth of the house for a christening feast which would have sustained several families for a week, and I suspect that much of it disappeared into the servants' pockets. A few days later, in fear of a snowfall which would hold them prisoners in Glen Sian until spring, this gay company departed, and on my next visit to Ardsian I missed them; I would have missed them more keenly still had I known what was to follow.

On November twenty-seventh Henry James Hilaire Stirling was three weeks old. On November thirtieth, he died.

My father buried him, with a compassion I would not have accredited to him, and them he was dismissed by James. This left me alone at Ardsian. It was expected that I would stay.

So I stayed, at the hub of a wheel of chaos. I went prepared for a few days and ended by remaining a month. A hellish month, during which gales assaulted Glen Sian, and the frozen ground was littered with wreckage, slates, branches, panes of glass, old bricks, and in the infrequent lulls when rain or snow hurled against the windows I heard Charlotte weeping. James offered her no comfort; she accused him of not wanting the baby and he accused her of neglecting him, as it was Charlotte who had found him dead in his cradle. She still slept near it in the nursery, and I often found her there holding one of his little garments or his carved ivory rattle. James slept wherever unconsciousness overtook him, and his servants collected the bottles.

The sun rose on Christmas morning, giving its light like a gift: snow had fallen in the night, and the wind had dropped. I persuaded James to walk in the orchard, now white with snow more mortal than that drifting sea of blossom. He had not been out of the house since the funeral, and he blinked bloodshot eyes at the sky and groped and fumbled like Lazarus.

He reeked of drink despite the earliness of the hour, and the bitter air was clean; I supported him and dragged it into my lungs as though I had been dying for it, and so, I think, did he.

Further on the way was blocked by fallen branches, throwing blue shadows across the snow; the orchard might have been a battleground, the wind had savaged it like cannon. He wandered here and there, picking up twigs and staring at the damage, then he recognized one of the trees and whispered, "My Pomeroy, my Pomeroy...."

It had been split down the middle and lay in the drifts, like something pitifully dead. I turned him away and spoke soothingly of grafting and tying and perhaps saving it. He wept inconsolably, as he had not wept for his son, and, putting my arm around his shoulders, I led him back to the house.

As though he hated the light, he hid from it for the remainder of the day, nor did I see Charlotte, who preferred to be left alone. I never knew how the time passed, or at what hour I went down into the drawing room: no one had attended the fire and my breath hung in the air as I replenished it. I sat staring at the book in my lap and listening to the intensity of a silence in which, for the first night in weeks, no wind could be heard, then the handle on the door dropped and James came into the firelight. He was very drunk and had been crying, and in his shapeless mourning clothes he looked frail, and pathetically young.

I said, "What have you there, Jamie?" and he stumbled down onto one knee and upset the box, spilling its contents over the carpet. Lead soldiers, blue and red... I guessed they had been his own.

"They were for him," he said eventually. "His first Christmas present."

He balanced one on his palm, gazing at it.

"My son," he said, "my *son*," and covered his face. After a long pause he whispered, "Didn't you think I knew it was Christmas? Did you think I was as far gone as that?"

357

"What does it matter, in the circumstances?"

"It doesn't matter, does it? In the end— nothing matters." Then he said, "I'm going to kill myself... quite soon, perhaps tonight. I don't want you to be unhappy. I only wanted you to know."

There was not enough light to read his face, but there seemed no expression in it, as there was no inflection in his voice, or in mine.

"Do you love Charlotte so little?"

"I've never loved Charlotte. I don't think she loves me. I don't think I can love anybody— no one ever taught me to love."

"Your father loved you."

"No. He loved Malcolm more."

He put the lead soldier down and groped for me.

"Help me up, Maggie."

"Why? Where are you going?"

"You know where I'm going. Help me up, damn you."

He sat on the carpet with tears running down his face, and I, God forgive me, ignored his reaching hands and said brutally, "Get up yourself, if you must."

And because he was too drunk to stand, he crawled to the fall of drapery and tried to free the tasselled cord.

"This will do. All I need is this... I know how it's done."

The rest is fragmented, indistinct. He put the cord around his neck and a struggle ensued, during which I tried to restrain him and he hit my breast and cheek and scratched me, and then I left him, crawling on the carpet searching for something from which to hang himself. Ill-fed and deathly tired and aching in every bone, I did not think myself capable of running but I remember the sensation if not the act, running as though my feet never touched the stairs. Other fragments: interrupting his valet, who was reading his own room, moving his finger slowly across the page and forming the words with his lips... the comprehension dawning in his eyes... James slumped on the carpet with his soldiers lying around him, his valet taking the cord from his neck and giving it to me. When he had led him away, James still weeping those soundless tears, I restored it to its hook and drew the draperies with a self-possession I did not know I could command, and picked up the fallen soldiers, and left the box on the table.

And then, having tidied away all the pitiful evidence of human frailty, I closed the door and went out into God's silent, holy night.

There was a moon for me to see by, pure and cold, occasionally masked by drifts of cloud, and the black sky was pierced with the burning stars of winter, flashing their bitter, jewelled light. There was no wind, and what snow had fallen had been scoured from the icy road. I walked, oblivious to the cold, bareheaded and without gloves, and eventually I came to the place where I had been going.

I hammered on the door. There was no response at first, then it opened a fraction and the light, dim as it was, dazzled my eyes. In his right hand he held a pistol. Strangely, I was not surprised.

He said, "No one visits me at night," and then, "You had better come in."

I came in, and stood in the hall. It was not warm, but the heat of shelter after intense cold seemed to embrace me. I heard him lock the door, then he picked up the candle from the table: it threw a pool of uncertain light over the other pistol lying there.

"What do you want?"

"I've been at Ardsian."

"I know." He did not say how he knew.

"I thought I should tell you. James threatened to commit suicide tonight."

He said abruptly, "Come into the kitchen. I have a fire there."

The shapes of furniture emerged and were ordinary: a dresser lined with blue and white Prestonpans pottery, creels of turf and potatoes, hanging meat, a fowling piece, not old, over the mantel, with a pair of brass candlesticks and unlit wax candles beneath it. A masculine room, unadorned and vaguely unloved: a room spartan and orderly and, like his person, very clean.

He was lighting the candles; he had left the pistols on the table in the hall where, perhaps, they always lay.

"You look like death," he said.

"The wind keeps me awake."

"Don't lie to me; you didn't come here to lie. I want to know what happened, as if I can't already guess."

He seated me on a seise near the fire and splashed something into a glass: it was, as I expected, the harsh local whisky, his elixir. When it had all been said there was silence, and the sound of the flames, like the sound of blowing silk.

He was still standing, staring into the fire.

"Why do you do this?"

"Why do I do what?"

"Stay there, watching this little charade. James plays the grieving father and gives you nightmares... don't you think it would benefit them more if you went home? They won't perform without an audience."

"Is that how you regard it?"

"James is a charlatan, and he does things for effect. You saw that at his father's funeral."

"I stay out of love, and I don't consider what I saw tonight play-acting. They need me, perhaps in different ways, and they have no one else who cares for their interests, with the exception of you."

"I don't have the influence you suppose. James and I are not close, as you may have noticed."

"Your acquaintance is a long one— and you serve him."

"Duty." He seemed to imagine disbelief in my eyes. "Well, what else should I do with my life? I've seen the world, what I wanted to see of it, and what I saw left no favourable impression. Where else should I serve out my time?"

"You loved Ewen."

"Yes, and maybe I still serve him. But if James dropped dead tomorrow you wouldn't see me weep, except for lost opportunities."

"You don't perceive his intention as real."

"I perceive it as a bid for your pity, as if you haven't already fed him enough."

"Do you believe that?" He said nothing. "Then there's no need to give you this." The key to the gun room; I had taken it as I left.

He said, with a disconcerting gentleness, "I could have put a gun to my head a dozen times in this life, and so could you, but never James."

I put it back into my pocket. He smoked, watching the flames.

"I need not have come, then. You must think me... very forward."

"I think you've had enough. I think your friends are leeches, and you give them your heart's blood and call it love. I don't ask that of you. I don't ask any damned thing."

He knocked the pipe against the fireiron. In the rush of light as the tobacco burned his face seemed deeply strained.

"What is this attachment between you and James? Were you lovers? Are you lovers?"

"I am not responsible for James's imagination, or yours, if it comes to that."

"And Ewen? Did I imagine that, too?"

Brilliant eyes, implacable eyes... that delicate relationship, so pearled in the nacre of grief, was not for his nor any other scrutiny.

"You do not have the right to question me, your own affairs being what they are."

The wind, so still when I had walked that dark road, was rising, and it was difficult to hear his voice.

"Oh, I see. Was that the poison some one dropped in your ear, when you told me to go to hell in the summer with James for an audience? What did you hear that you didn't already know, and who was it if not our darling Jamie who whispered it to you?"

Sometimes, in the depths of night, things are done which are regretted, immediately or later, and truths are spoken which otherwise would remain unsaid.

"You have a whore." His eyes, cold eyes, never left mine. "And children."

"They were never wanted."

There was a silence, then he said, "I have lived rather longer than you, and my life and yours are not lived within the same sphere. You were not there." If he were waiting for some sign of comprehension or acquiescence, I gave him none, and he remarked caustically, "I once said you would believe any ill of me. By God, I never spoke a truer word."

"People tell me things they hope will hurt me. Usually they succeed."

"I never pretended to be other than what I was, to you or to any one. Ewen tried... I failed him. Like you, he was easily hurt."

He bent and tossed peat on the fire, and I sat within its light and drank his whisky; he seated himself in the shadows and smoked, and did not disturb me with conversation I did not want. Time passed, and held me there: whatever the consequences of my coming here I could not change them by leaving now. The room swam in a firelit haze: the wind buffeted the house and tore the minutes of this grotesque Christmas night toward a new and violent day. Eventually he refilled my glass and I talked, of things which seemed to matter then but cannot be remembered now, except that they did not touch the raw nerve of sexuality. I did not notice that he drank uncharacteristically little; I knew only that I needed the illusory strength it gave me, and whatever strange, ephemeral comfort this house and this night could offer.

He had been so silent during my monologue that I thought he had fallen asleep, and it had become so private and painful to me that I hoped he had.

He spoke from the shadows, startling me.

"Listen. The devil is passing."

The dark, formless violence rushed on: its howl ebbed in the night.

"You didn't go to the funeral."

"I was not wanted. James made a point of telling me."

"It was so pitiful... so futile. Why are children born only to die? What kind of god ordains that?"

"Children die. That is a fact, and some of them are better off. They'll have another. They have nothing else to do."

And you? Will you?

The firelight beat against my eyes; alcohol and misery washed over me.

After some time he said with that unnerving gentleness, "Save your tears. Nothing is worth them, not even this. Not even all the other little deaths, yours or mine," and I stared at him, trying to penetrate the enigma of his eyes. "No, you don't understand me, do you? I thought not."

And God shall wipe away all tears from their eyes; and there shall be no more death, nor sorrow, nor crying, neither shall there be any more pain. Dry your eyes, Mordaunt had said, as if sexual intent and calamity had signified no more than some passing, erotic dream: as if then, as now, I had not been drowning, resisting this dark, compelling current.

"Don't be kind to me. I can't bear your kindness."

"I can bear yours. You feed me on it so infrequently, I starve for it."

Nothing in the words, no warmth, no nuance, no significance, only emptiness. The red heat seemed to sear my face. I closed my eyes against it.

I thought he had spoken my name. I imagined it. Only on one occasion, in the six years of our acquaintance, had he ever used it, and I had never once called him by his Christian name.

"Why do people say such vile things of you?"

"People believe what they want to believe." A pause. "What do you want to believe?"

"The truth. The truth...."

"I'll give you the truth, if you want it."

"Are there children?"

"The children are dead."

"Are you a lecher?"

"I have been." Perhaps he saw my revulsion. Perhaps, if he had a conscience, it moved him. "For your sake I regret it, but I told you, you were not there."

He did not speak again, and the silence became volatile.

I said that I would go.

"I think that would be wise. Did you tell any one you were coming here? Did you mention me?"

"No... there was no one, only James's man."

"He's James's creature. Your little secret is safe with him."

"You dislike him...."

"I have cause."

He snuffed the candles, and was only a darkness within darkness; there was nothing in his voice, neither pain nor introspection. "My life was taken. Ewen found what was left."

The moment held us in an inviolable stillness; what he said held no meaning for me, but I said, "I understand."

"No, you don't understand. My life has been a sewer. Circumstances damned me to it, or maybe I offer them as an excuse. I never wished it were otherwise, not even for Ewen's sake. I wish it now, for yours."

I could not see him, obscured in shadow. Reality and unreality flowed into one another as the hours of night and morning had become this indistinguishable pallor, and this hour would never be remembered as truth, but only the waking dream of imagination.

"You have always been a good friend to me. I hope we shall always be friends."

"I don't want your friendship, Margaret."

We did not touch. Throughout the whole of that night we had not touched so much as a hand, and I had never spoken his name. We stared at one another with wary eyes, neither strangers nor, yet, lovers.

He took me back to Ardsian. The wind, like a tide, obliterated our footprints, so that we might never have walked together as far as the gates. I walked the rest of the way alone, and let myself into the house by the door to the estate office with the key he had given me.

I left it on his papers in the stale room that confined him as this dying house stifled me, and stood there for a time; but there was nothing of him, only the grey and violent remnants of the night against the smutted glass, and the key, and the cold filtering of dust, as though he and I had long been dead, and no one else came here.

IX

January. The faoilteach began, the days between the middle of the month and the middle of February: the storm days, the wolf month, the dead month. The cold was unremitting, the snows heavy and frequent and sculpted by the bitter arctic winds. Whenever possible he rode and walked, climbing once a fortnight to An Reithe, and often as he approached he startled deer scraping the blown snow among the sheep. The shepherds were hard men, inured to the weather, but they were dourly pessimistic; and in the privacy of his journal he reflected upon the nature of that pessimism.

> Sheep are easy to kill: subject to tetanus, dysentery, pulpy kidney, braxy, gangrene, louping, scour, worms, fluke, footrot, scald, abortion, prolapse of Uterus or cervix, dropsy as the result of feeding pregnant ewes on kale or turnip. They are vulnerable to lice, ticks, struck and poisoning, pine, swayback and Lightning stroke. Some are diseases of malnutrition and fatigue, some are parasytic in origin. Some affect the Mature Animal, some the newborn lamb. Some are peculiar to location or season; many are contagious; almost all are incurable.

February. The white light of the snow at night, the colourless sun of a snowy morning. The lines on the page, the coldness of the estate office, the stiffness of his fingers on the pen.

> Having now digested our whole Observations on these 24 farms presently to sett and having with the greatest Care and Diligence not only investigated the particular value of the different farms with regard to their sowing and to the staple soil and bottomes; but also the system of husbandry we lay them under restriction of, and having ordered the Severall Tennants by an advertisement on the Kirk doores to attend us tomorrow, we are determined on the following Articles.

> That we again repeat to them our Resolutions already told them in our survey. 1ˢᵗ: That we shall be at one word as we expect the same from Them 2do: That whatever no. of Tennants may agree for one Maillen they shall have Liberty of ploughing no more than one third part at a time, and that only for the space of 3 years. Each third part will go 3 years for resting Six: that with the Third crop of grain Each Division will be sowan down with Rye grass & Clover at least all the Croft Land of said Division and for their own benefit to sow all their field Land with plain Rye grass and the ground dressed to our satisfaction....

March. Rain. Wind. Flooding. Decomposing deer in the leafless woods, weakened by the continual wetness, and brought down by starvation and parasites. Their flesh was inedible, their hides ripped by the claws of badgers. They were reduced to clean bone within a month by birds of prey and maggots.

When will you come to me, O skin like flowers....

Sex, so brutal and so frequent that he disgusted himself, sometimes violently coerced from his mistress, sometimes lasciviously wooed, seducing this familiar flesh as if it were a virgin's. Taking her in the darkness, covering her face with her hair, never looking into her eyes, because they were other eyes and another face; until, dazed by his turbulent moods, she loved him abjectly and pitifully and subjected herself to ever deeper degradation, because she knew for whom she was a substitute, and allowed herself to be so used.

> 1ˢᵗ March 1769
> We are of the opinion that Glen Sian's expired farms cannot be brought to the rents they might bear, till the present setts of the persons be fairly ejected, and the lands lie unlaboured for at least a season.

"Is this an attempt to divest me of profit?"

He stared through the drifting smoke at James, who, muffled in heavy mourning and displaying hollows beneath his eyes, had acquired a belated interest in the estate's affairs and now considered himself an expert.

"It is an attempt to adjust rent and productivity. I have put this proposition to you before."

"And what do you expect these people to do while their land lies fallow? Who will provide for them? Myself?"

"They will farm under the terms of the new lease, in a system of divisions. If that will not content them, then let them go, and I will consolidate the land."

James said, "You will what?" and when he repeated it, leaned into the candlelight and laid his hands, mottled with cold, flat on the littered table. "By whose authority, by God? I never gave you the right to talk of dispossession! Balance your books on the backs of your damned sheep, and moderate your behaviour, or you may not find yourself so indispensable as you imagine!"

He sat smoking in the silence after the door had slammed, bemused by this show of defiance. James was certain now of what held him to Glen Sian, and thought him vulnerable to abuse.

10th March 1769
Heads of Resolutions
All the farms out of Tack in the townships of Glen Sian are to be sett on the following conditions:

That for and after Whitsun next the whole farms in the townships of Glen Sian now out of Tack shall be sett to such a number of Tennants as Glen Sian shall chuse for 9 years provided the Tennant agree to the terms aforementioned, that each Tennant shall have a separate part of the farms allotted to him which he shall possess by himself and for the Rent of which he shall only thereafter be found, the Divisions of Land and Rent being made by the factor, and in case of the Tennants not being satisfied therewith, the several divisions shall be rotated among the Tennants of the Farm in order to prevent any disputes that may arise in the Choice of these Divisions.

All subsetts to be wholly excluded without the consent of Glen Sian or his factor under the penalty of paying Double Rent for what they subsett without consent.

"Your little friend is ill," James remarked, paring his nails and drawing what he chose from the silence.

"How ill?"

"I'm damned if I know. The hag told me it was influenza— you know she gets that regular." He scraped something from beneath one of his nails and brushed it off his knee. "Of course, the paysans are quick to speculate otherwise."

"What do you mean, otherwise?"

"Oh, for God's sake, man, there's no truth in it! I used to cough blood all the time. I daresay she has some inflammation." He shifted restlessly. "If

365

it so concerns you, go down and see for yourself; I imagine MacNeil would enjoy that. Is there any other business?"

After the first three years, the Tennant shall at no time of the Lease have above one third of the arable ground in grain; the other two thirds being always laid down in the best manner with Clover & Ryegrass seeds, under the penalty of voiding the lease.

That at no time of the Lease, the Tennant shall have Liberty of taking up any part of the grounds, without a sufficient quantity of Dung, of Marl, or of Lime, under the penalty of voiding the lease.

That no Tennant or Cottar shall have Liberty of planting or sowing Potatoes upon any ground that have been planted with them before, or upon any ground that have been laboured by either plough or spade: But shall plant or sow their whole potatoes upon new ground, taking no more than two crops of the same ground, under penalty of confiscation of the whole.

That at any time of the Lease it shall be in the power of Glen Sian or others employed by him to inspect the sowing of each Farm, and to reduce the same to such Quantity as shall appear most conducive to the general good.

By the first of April forty-eight ewes had aborted, thirty lambs were stillborn, and one hundred and fifty-three had died in the snow within the first week of birth: such bloodied effluxions fed the vigilant predators that followed the flock. Four hundred and sixty-seven ewes had come to term successfully. A dog had been put down, the woman had committed suicide, one of the shepherds had developed a consumptive cough, and the others, who had never met James Stirling and knew only one employer, pleaded to be allowed to shoot the eagles sometimes seen through the boiling mist. But he had never known an eagle to take a living lamb, so he refused, and considering him a man both obdurate and driven, they decided he was not to be challenged. It was further agreed that this country of fogs and storms was a hellish place; but the money was good, so they stayed.

Whitsun. Raining, and the dirty casements stood open to the cold sweet air. It was just after dawn, and in the branches, faintly veiled with green, chaffinches sang and skirmished.

We ordered the several Tennants by an advertisement on the Kirk doores to attend us this Whitsunday, and we again repeat to them that we shall be at one word as we expect the same of them: that whatsoever number of Tennants make offer for one maillen they shall have Liberty of ploughing no more but one third part at a time, and that only for the space of three years running.

If the present Tennants do not come near then we shall next take in all offers promiscuously; if none of these come up to our Estimation we shall then proclaim that as of Martinmas next all Maillens that stand unaccepted of shall be divided into 60 acres for one Tennant only and laboured according to our general system.

He sat with the ledgers and the strongbox and the keys, waiting. Some months had passed since he had issued his notices of evaluation and adjusted each rent according to his survey, and he had recently been offered eight pounds four shillings and threepence for a farm he calculated was capable of generating rents to the value of twenty pounds sterling. Another more belligerent group who had crowded into the estate office, reeking of pot stills, had offered him nine pounds five shillings and seven pence for a farm worth four times that. He had told them to go to hell.

The light strengthened. The rain stopped and lay in pools in the cobbles, reflecting a soft sky: the bare heights, grizzled still with winter, dreamed, unmenacing, in cloud. Across the courtyard a white branch described arabesques of blossom, dropping with the weight of rain. Around him the household was stirring: smoke in the damp air, feet crossing the wet cobbles, women's laughter and fluting voices. When they found his horse in the stall a manservant would bring him breakfast, ale and bannock and the cold leavings of the previous night, and then the tenants would arrive, singly or in groups, having risen, like himself, before dawn to walk the long miles to this appointed place. Men and boys with uncombed hair and ill-made clothing, many of them afflicted with that common Highland complaint, the itch, scratching and shuffling in their rawhide brogans or on dirty bare feet, to stand opposite this table and submit their rent.

The meal came at the expected hour: he could have timed it by his watch. He drank the ale, hating it, hating the confinement of this room and the futility of the day's wasted efforts, and wasted they would be. An icy prescience had warned him on this, as on other occasions.

Noon. Up and down the scarred stairs to ease the cramp of inactivity. The sky had cleared, and patterns of sun and shadow marked the passing hours. He stood for a long time with the sun's living heat on his face, then he went back indoors.

By late afternoon another servant had brought something else, and taken the other away: with the sun's lingering descent the air seemed cooler. In the early hours of evening James drifted in, sunburned and refreshed by a day's recreational riding. He tossed his gloves on the table.

"Well? Malcolm?"

He raised the lid of the box, and allowed it to fall shut.

James said, "What is the meaning of this?"

"We shall see."

"There is a conspiracy."

"Perhaps."

The twilight was a lover's time, imbued with a poignant sadness, an indefinable melancholy... only a lover could relieve him now of this unbearable sense of isolation and hopelessness.

James was staring owlishly at him in the shadows. He continued to write.

Whitsun 1769. We sat this whole day with patience, and although all the Tennants should this day have appeared, with their Rent, yet not one of them came.

"This is your damned persecution of them!"

"This is what comes of moderation," he said, and closed the journal and got up stiffly. James barred his way to the door.

"But what shall I do? This is your responsibility, your duty is toward me! I can't live on that— I shall have to declare myself a bankrupt! For God's sake, Malcolm, if you ever loved my father, do something...."

"I am going home," he said.

Once, during my illness, I imagined I heard his voice, but no one ever indicated to me that it was anything more than a dream. Later, one evening, I saw him pass through the village, encircled by the candlelit frost on my window, the horse drifting soundlessly through the snow, the rider so heavily muffled as to be unidentifiable; but it could only have been he.

Then there was fresh fish, of which, to my aunt's obvious disappointment, I could eat only a little: at the time I was too ill to question its origin but subsequently, in the long hours of recovery, I knew who had conjured it out of Glen Sian's starveling winter. My comfort became a matter of concern to my family. For the first time in all the years of my tenure in MacNeil's house a fire was kept burning in my room. Deirdre pressed concoctions upon me: cream with honey, or beaten with oatmeal and whisky. There was salmon; there were delicate broths; there was rabbit. I was told that they came from Ardsian, and indeed Charlotte visited me once and brought me some indigestible invalid's jelly, but I was well aware that she was not my benefactor, and the rest of the household knew it also. Whatever reservations they harboured in no way prevented them from sharing in Malcolm's bounty.

Charlotte came again, wrapped in furs and offering desultory conversation. Since the loss of the child she was subdued and introspective, and now never spoke of him. James never called, and was seldom mentioned. George Cameron remained a faithful visitor, coming from the school every evening and providing me with books and gossip. My aunt duenna'd me on these occasions, knitting stolidly on a chair at the foot of the bed while George sat like a tailor on the floor and entertained me. His company was gay and stimulating, and I was grateful for his kindness in so closely attending one who was rumoured to be dying of consumption.

Nor was my aunt immune to his irreverent humour, and by the softening of her manner toward him she signalled her approval of the affection he still so clearly cherished for me. Once, when she left us on a pretense of going to the kitchen, he rose and sat on the bed in an uneasy breach of decorum and took my hand.

"Is it still the same between us? Is there any hope?"

But he knew there was not, and I was too ill and too weary for the repetitive futility of these arguments. I said, surely there must be some one else, some one suitable. He shrugged, and the light was very cruel to the ugliness of his face.

"There's no one for me but you. And if you don't want me, I don't want any one else." He smiled as he said it, that odd, wistful smile. "Maybe you care without knowing it. Maybe I can make you care."

And then my aunt was heard returning. He folded himself back onto the floor and watched me with a sphinx-like expression. He might never have moved or spoken, and his body had left no impression on the bed, nor lent any warmth to mine.

In April, on my first visit to Ardsian, I entered by the door to the estate office, determined to express my gratitude for a protection I was very aware of having been offered. The room was as stale and cold as it had been in the dregs of night; and now, as then, there was no sense of him, nothing of that harsh, vital presence. And so I left, but before I went I found paper and ink and wrote him a stiff little letter of thanks, which I folded without superscription and placed between the pages of a ledger where the dates were recent.

It was not acknowledged, and I suffered an attack of embarrassment and was convinced I had behaved precipitately. On my next visit, hoping he had not found it, and being certain that he was not in the house, I went to the estate office to retrieve it if possible. It had gone, and an unfolded sheet of vellum had been closed into the same page, and for the first time I saw my Christian name in the difficult, sloping script that filled the ledgers.

Perhaps I was not meant to take it. Upon reflection, I think not. It was a private meditation, left out of a sentiment and delicacy no one had ever suspected in him. Distilling it from the Gaelic in which it was written, as though it were a precious essence, gave me an exquisite joy... even after so many years, so many passages, even obscured with tears and crumpled in

369

attempts to deny or forget what was expressed or promised or betrayed, I
have it still.

> When will you come to me, O skin like flowers,
> and breathe a breath like summer against my eyelids,
> closed, too fearful to look at you?
> When will you lay the little gift of your bones
> within my arms,
> and come with me to that place where I will drink your tears
> and you will sing the sweetness of unknown songs
> against my hair until I sleep?

At the end of May, we met. Five months had passed since we had seen
one another.

There is a moment in one's life of deliberate undertaking, a point at
which one hesitates, recognizing the significance of the decision to be made,
knowing that afterwards nothing will ever be the same. For me it was this, and
every detail of recollection is heightened to an unnatural clarity. The smell of
the corridor with its greasy, wavering stain where crofters had leaned against
the white-washed walls waiting for an interview; the heat of the spring sun on
my back; and the cool draught flowing down those narrow stairs, refreshing
my hot face and bringing the fragrance of tobacco. He was there, and in a
moment I would go to him, and my life, which had been one pain-filled
metamorphosis after another, would change again, change irretrievably and
never be the same: neither should there be any more pain.

The room was shadowed still, unlit by the bright sky beyond the window.
He sat with his back to it, his head bent over his papers, smoking. I must
have made some small sound; he looked up, and for a few seconds only the
smoke moved, drifting sweetly between us. In the silence birds were singing;
there were voices in the courtyard. Then he said, "Why can't you come in like
a woman instead of a ghost?" and stood, shuffling the papers together and
pushing open the dirty casement like a man in the throes of some violent,
controlled anger. He stood there with his back to the light, the smoke eddying
around him as it escaped in tendrils to the sun.

"Well, what do you want? Have you brought another letter for me?"

"I was very sensible of your kindness. I merely wished to say so."

He said, rather more gently, "What did you expect me to do, with James
prating about consumption and MacNeil feeding you on nothing but prayers
and the bread of affliction?"

"As a matter of fact, he never prayed. Perhaps he thought it wasted on me."

The wind stirred his sleeve and his hair where he stood by the opened casement, and for the first time the sun, reaching this room, touched his cheekbone and one green, clear iris.

"Why did you call me 'Mister Scott' in your letter? Is that how you think of me, as 'Mister Scott'?"

"You know how I think of you."

There was no acknowledgment, no softening, then he said, not urgently, "Come here," and I went to him. He lifted my face into the sun's warmth, a cool, rough hand without passion against my burning cheek.

"Look at your little face, all wasted away to nothing."

What my eyes willed him to do, he did: what my body, in all its tension and hunger, told him I can only guess. That at twenty-three I was virgin, and frightened, and ashamed of my innocence; that I knew nothing more of sex than fumbling, unwanted kisses and the shameful pressure of a drunken soldier's arousal against an adolescent thigh, and other shame, all of it attributable to me, shame and disgrace and hunger and confusion, of which only a lover with patience and compassion could heal me.

I remember that I disengaged myself, or perhaps he allowed me to go: the heat of the sun was on my skin, the smell of dust, heat, blossom.

"I'm afraid...."

"I know."

"There was no one else."

"I know that too."

"Look at me... how can you want me like this? What can I give you? I don't know how to love you."

"Let me teach you," he said.

Whatever preceded, whatever follows, these memories retain their sanctity.

What he had promised I learned, in another cool, shadowed room, on a bed where the sheets were clean and uncrumpled and smelled of the sunlight in which they had been dried. The room was in his house and the bed was his own, where no other woman had lain with him, and where no woman's voice but mine learned to cry out in joy and astonishment.

I remember... I remember... the stillness and tranquillity of that spartan room in the heat of the afternoon.... the uncertainty of touching and being touched, the indescribable shock of joy when, undressing me, he kissed me, lips, eyelids, throat, nipples, and loosened the pins from my hair, letting it fall slowly, as in a dream... the slow, deliberate sensuality of everything, every caress of lips and fingertips, as if there were no time, no hours that signified; time in this room and in this house was suspended, and nothing mattered but this languorous exploration.

My clothing fell like shadow to the floor, and his mouth and tongue and nakedness touched my naked skin, and I was ashamed. Of what was happening, of the power I had to command this man in this manner, of my body, which I had always believed was ugly, and which seemed so poor a gift. And I was afraid— of pain, of risk, of pregnancy, of the unknown act of sex, of loss of self, of him. And he gave me the great gift of his understanding, for which I knew I had loved him deeply: there was no haste, no interruption, only the sweet, drugged languour. I could not give of my body, or look into his eyes, or touch him, and he did not insist; perhaps what little I gave and what he took and savoured with so deep a sensuality was enough, and satisfied him.

Only once he felt my fear, as he led me from one delicate act of lovemaking to another more intimate, which as yet, for me, could afford no pleasure. I pulled his hair to stop him.

I lay in his arms then, with my face hidden: he did not touch me again, and I thought he could not forgive me for my naïveté and my revulsion. After a long time he said, "Why do you flinch when I kiss you there? Who was there before me?"

"You know there was no one."

Silence. I watched his face in profile, the bones, the broken nose, the beautiful, thickly lashed eyes. Eventually he said, "You came to me last night. I thought I dreamed, but I was waking."

"Tell me."

"You stood there... you were clothed in moonlight and in your hair, and I knew your body before I knew it today." There had been no moon last night, but this was not fantasy; he believed it, and it was as real to him as I was real now, and he spoke of it not with surprise or affectation but with perfect conviction, and regret, and longing. "I thought something had happened to you, that you sent your spirit on me. I could have touched you. I cried out to you but you left me... I called your name. I wonder you did not hear me, in your sleep."

"I wish I had."

"I came then, wanting you."

My hair brushed his face. He held it to his lips.

"I disgust you."

"No."

"Give me your love then. Give me what you can."

But it was he who gave, who urged me, and who held me in the drifting half-sleep afterward. For him there was neither sleep nor satisfaction, but his hand caressed me with great gentleness, and I sensed in him a curious repose, an uncharacteristic peace.

"Now you will never leave me," he said; and I slept in his arms.

Is it possible that it can be remembered as I remember it: that there could have been such passion, that there could be, briefly, such perfection? That love remembered is the ghost of a lost perfume, once powerful and rich, so that the senses swooned at it: now faint, sere, crumbling almost to the touch, like rose petals pressed in an ecstasy of reminiscence and evoking a poignant melancholia, but oh, sweet, sweet....

Perhaps the greatest folly was my own, for believing that this relationship could survive the oppressive secrecy in which it was conducted. To be seen with him, even in protracted conversation, was to invite gossip; had we given any deeper cause for scandal his reputation alone would have guaranteed the end of mine.

So there was no careless lovemaking in the open air: there were no sunlit trysts, only these hours, hurried and stolen from the too-short days. Throughout the burning months of June and July when little rain fell, and the weather oppressed him so that he became withdrawn and irritable, we loved, secretly and sometimes unsatisfactorily, with hesitation and diffidence and a lingering uncertainty on my part, in that room in the heat of the afternoon when his movements need not be accounted for, and Ardsian provided a well-worn excuse for mine. The sun burned and the rivers dried and the clods of earth in the outfields crumbled into dust, and the fear of fire was ever-present, and a woman followed me through the burnished twilight as I carried milk from MacNeil's cow and asked me conspiratorially to intercede with the factor on her behalf, as her man would not be capable of making up his rent. How gossip, like smoke, had been carried on the wind I never knew, and I never told him. The stags retreated to the high, cool ground; the cream soured in the jar; there was thunder, and grey rain seen in the distance which never fell. MacNeil slammed doors and indulged in fits of unwarranted temper and avoided speaking to me: he knew or suspected, and I prepared myself for a confrontation which, like the storms over a parched Glen Sian, only threatened on the horizon. My face and hands and forearms darkened with the sun, the smell of heat and dust was on my skin and upon my lover's skin when I embraced him in the stillness of his house, where we found our only assurance of privacy, and our only peace.

I loved, and knew love: knew now the depth of my ignorance, and with what intolerant eyes I had viewed those lives lived close to mine, which had been scorched by this white heat. I understood Catherine, desperate to the point of self-abasement for a man she could not hold; and Mordaunt, torn between morality and loneliness, obsessed by her beauty and her faithlessness and groping for a substitute neither a servant nor an adoptive child could have given him. I understood my father, still driven by an impious love for his murdered wife, whose death he perceived as the price of that fanaticism poisoning him yet, like a sickness in the blood; and Bancroft's life, lived in barren solitude, reflected in those unhappy letters which had been flung into my lap as explanation and bitter education. And Ewen, who had seen in me some evanescent spring, who had once said *my son* when the word *myself* had refused to leave his lips... *like you, he was easily hurt.*

Dear child, I send you a rose, he had written across the last page of his journal, knowing I alone would read it; leaving me, even in death, the sweetness of his nature and his love.

And my lover, who brushed ignorance from me like an obscuring web, so that all things were heightened or deepened or intensified or clarified or made known: my lover, who led me deeper into mysteries, and so seldom revealed himself. He cursed subterfuge even as he preserved it in his own nature: a man habitually secretive, who had so hidden and concealed and armoured himself in secrecy for so many years that he was now incapable of intimacy.

In his bed, I knew him. He gave himself to me, and taught me every refinement of sex from a considerable experience, and no other woman had known that skill and tenderness, it was for me alone. He gloried in his strength and his sensuality and in mine; as my innocence delighted him, so even more his initiation of me into a sexuality as intense as his own. My mouth learned his body, spare and heavily muscled, the contours of his face, the heavy, corded genitals. I learned the taste of his semen and the taste of myself on his lips and his fingers; I learned to caress him, although my hands and lips faltered; I learned to touch myself, and the first exquisite joy of orgasm, to give myself pleasure and to receive him in the only way in which he would love me— there was no intercourse, no penetration, because I would not accept the risk of pregnancy.

He was mine, then. Later, sometimes immediately, he became remote, frustrated by a relationship so explicitly sexual and so impossible of consummation, which he blamed himself for having initiated and by which he believed he had stained me.

And I saw that he was vulnerable, although vulnerability was not an impression he cared to give the world. He suffered seizures, although this he never told me, insomnia, migraine, and rheumatism in a knee injured on the hills and never allowed to rest. His right hand was lividly scarred, the little finger of his left had been broken and so crudely set that he could not straighten it, and there were other lingering injuries, emotional and physical, which he would not discuss. He could never speak of Ewen without pain and hesitation: he asked me only once what he had written of him in his journals. I never knew if what I told him comforted him or gave him peace. He seldom spoke of James. He never gratified my jealous, female hunger to know the deepest secrets of his sexuality, the loss of virginity, the experience of other women, although I laid my own past open to him in all its bruised innocence.

He was deeply convinced of his own ugliness, and although I never knew through what dark glass he viewed himself his perceptions remained distorted, and he would not be convinced that I did not find his genitals repulsive, or the manner of our lovemaking, which was both tender and erotic, unnatural or degrading.

He would not speak of his childhood, except that fragment which had been in Ewen's keeping; there were scars on his buttocks, relics of that abuse which was, as yet, only a shadow and a suggestion to me. When I asked him he merely said he had been burned, under what circumstances he did not tell me, then he laughed as if it were some sarcastic joke.

"Poor wee bugger, eh? What a pity."

The rest of his past, distant and recent, remained an unknown country, into which I was not invited.

Once, after orgasm, he slept, in an attitude of peace and abandonment; the years fell away from that guarded, hawkish face and I saw youth in it, and the grave sweetness that must have been his in childhood. Then he dreamed, and seemed to be trying to speak: his breathing was anguished. I brought him into my arms and stroked his face, and he woke and stared at me with wide, shocked eyes.

"What is it?"

He said, "Nothing, nothing," but I had never seen him so shaken. I said again, "Tell me."

He said sharply, "I've told you, nothing, and that's the God's truth. Don't you ever dream?"

I never knew; and he did not sleep again while I was with him.

***

The days of that endless summer passed: perhaps he could not be blamed for counting them as days that imperilled the harvest, like dry grains of sand running out of an hourglass. For me other faces were dim in the shadows revolving around the burning sun which was Malcolm.

James, sitting in the dry garden in his shirtsleeves, complaining of Charlotte's lassitude. "I'm damned if I know what she does all day." Apart, I thought, from overseeing the kitchens, the laundry, the dairy, the stillroom, the pantry and the gardens; as I, rising at five with the sun in my eyes, replenished fire and water and milked and baked before MacNeil appeared, crumpled with sleep and ill-humour, at the breakfast table; and after weeding or laundering or whatever other domestic work was necessary, gathered my remaining strength for a seven-mile ride and an hour in another house with a man for whom I sometimes waited in vain.

And Charlotte, separating cream in the dairy, lifting a yoke across her shoulders. She was breathless, and dismissive when I remarked upon it.

"Oh, I lace myself too tightly— James cannot bear to see me fat," although her colour troubled me, and I tried to dissuade her from her heavier work, carrying the rest of the milk myself.

And Deirdre, another face in the dimness, another cautionary tale. This one I invited, on a grey sultry evening when my father was out in the parish and I felt the need for another woman's company and confidences.

"You know my situation, Aunt."

We were sitting on the scrubbed doorstone. She, never idle, was carding greasy fleece with which she would teach me to weave in the winter.

"Aye. It is clear to me."

Was it so clear that every one knew, that they saw him in my eyes?

"I am happy... the first happiness I have known since coming to this place."

She said, "How does he use you?" and it was explicit enough.

"We find... great joy in one another."

"Do you consider the consequences?"

"There will be no consequences."

"And how long do you think this unnatural state of affairs will satisfy him?"

"As long as it satisfies me."

"You are not the first to say so, and you will not be the last." Then she said, surprisingly, "Child—" which she seldom called me, and there was a lengthy pause, as though she weighed carefully what she had been about to say. "I have known this man all his life. I have not always liked what I saw."

Then rain spotted my pristine doorstone and we went inside: MacNeil came home with dank hair and dour looks, and nothing further was said.

In the night the rain continued intermittently, and sleepless, I listened to it, knowing that in that other bed which was now also in some sense mine, he was listening to it too.

But it was not enough to save us.

Even as I was losing him I knew an increasing joy, and abandon, and jealousy that I had not shared his past or alleviated what was then only my naïve perception of its injuries. And I knew a different jealousy, which I had brought with me to this bed and of which I could never be freed, a bitter and uncompromising hatred of other women who had preceded me, and who, if I failed him, would receive him again, and afford him the depth of pleasure and fulfillment I feared I could never give.

There was an afternoon of madness, of licence, and it was I who seduced him, and urged him, in the language of whores or lovers, to do what he wanted with me. I was mad... I enfolded him and felt him poised to enter me, and lost myself in orgasm. He withdrew as though the contact had burned him and ejaculated, and lay staring at the shadows on the ceiling; and the absolute of sexual pleasure was poisoned, and what had been an exquisite fervour seemed shameful and disgusting.

Eventually he said, "Don't ever do that to me again."

"I thought... you wanted it."

"And what would we have later? Tears and recriminations and you protesting, 'Oh, I never meant it'?"

Stung by the sarcasm and sick with jealousy, I said, "Is that what they all say?" and he turned and took my wrists, quite gently.

"Is that how you still think of me, after all this time?" I became aware of pain, although he held me with only a suggestion of his strength. "I told you, I regret the past. Now let it go, or we will have no hope and no future. None."

He released me and began to dress, and did not answer when I spoke to him. I touched him. I might have been some importuning whore: his body, which had been so passionately responsive to mine, rejected me with an astonishing coldness.

"Does this mean nothing to you, that you think you can play with me?"

"I thought it was what you wanted."

"And marriage, if I wanted that? Would you marry me?"

"No." Not when it was so sordidly offered, flung at me like an insult across dishevelled sheets, in a bed stained with semen spilled in anger and frustration.

377

I had hurt him, and I was losing him, to something, some intolerable pressure: I could not help him or myself.

"Why do you come here, then? For this, for sex play in my bed? Is that all I am to you, a stiff cock?" The crudity hurt me, and the eyes, and the bleak, burning silence. "You never speak of love, Margaret. In your soul, you never love me."

I could not give it the name of love: I feared it. Its price was my freedom, my very sense of self.

"Love me. I want you to say you love me."

"Do you love me?"

There was no answer. He was no more capable of saying it than I, resisting still that final commitment of language when, with his flesh and his fierce spirit, he had already married me.

When we met publicly, it was as strangers. He passed me one morning at Ardsian, leaving as I arrived: he acknowledged me with one of those spare gestures, barely lifting his hand from the rein. Nothing more was necessary now for me, or apparently for James, who was waiting on the steps.

He greeted me with a dry little unaffectionate kiss on the cheek, and murmured, "My dear, why this pretense of coyness? Everybody knows."

I took offense, which he seemed to enjoy. He goaded me a little more.

"Oh, you lie very well— you must have learned that from him. You almost convince me."

Charlotte was waiting. We would drink tea on the terrace and talk of ordinary things, and play with the cat, and when James had departed she would slide another letter from her mother across the tablecloth between the cooling teacups: some crumpled missive spotted with tears, urging her to separate from James and resume a life among civilized people. And while the fountain played and the browning rose petals scattered on the grass, she would offer me small female revelations and ask me my opinion, expecting a secret for a secret, my confidences for hers.

He was still holding me, with a little too much familiarity.

I said, "Your wife attends me, and there are others watching."

He released my sleeve and smoothed the creases his damp palm had made.

"You do well to remember it, my girl."

I sat in my lover's kitchen in the white twilight: he had just come home. I had not seen him for a fortnight, and loneliness and apprehension had brought me here at an hour which would require invention and excuses on my part later. The evening was heavy, charged, sullen: there was no dampness even of dew in the air or breathing from the earth.

"James knows," I said.

He was washing the dust from his face and arms at the stone sink. His eyes burned like a cat's against the darkness of his skin when he looked up.

"James knows nothing."

"He told me everybody knows. He thinks to school me in discretion."

He said, "James should be cracked between somebody's nails, like the louse he is."

He came to the table, which I had prepared for him— in such small intimacies had I made this house my own, and myself, by degrees, a wife— but he did not eat. I laid my hand over his and felt the heat of the dry, tanned skin.

"What is it?"

"I never wanted this. This is no life, living like this."

Heat. Stillness. On the mantel where the white candles always stood the flames, scarcely needed in this evening light, burned unwaveringly, and the cranesbill I had arranged there in a blue and white jug dropped papery petals on the hearthstone. His hand beneath mine never moved, but I sensed he did not want me to touch him.

"How shall we change it?"

He said, "You know how," and there was silence, fraught with tension and significance. He did not speak of marriage now because he knew I feared it, more and more inexplicably than that other consummation we had never known.

"Is it me? Is it what I am, all my little sins? Or is it that I am illegitimate, and you stand to inherit property?"

It was all those things, and it was more. It was the dread of entrapment; it was more than anything the point of no escape, the point at which free will was lost.

Silence. A dry, powdered wing against my hand and his where they lay together on the table: moths coming in from the twilight, seeking the bright, flaming death.

"I don't want your inheritance, whatever it is, or your property. I leave that to scheming bastards like James— he has the tongue for it. I want you, and I want you openly, not like this, like a whore in a corner. And if you want me, say so— if you don't, then let me go. I won't wait forever while you decide what you want more, me or your soldier in England."

His hand left mine as though it had never touched me. I heard another moth beat feebly against the window.

"That's the truth, isn't it?"

"No. That is obscenity, not truth."

Were these our voices, dry whispers full of such bitter vehemence?

"What is true, then?"

"I shall go mad if I spend the rest of my life in Glen Sian— and so, I think, will you."

"Go home, Margaret," he said, and I went, leaving the door open behind me; and although I knew he called me back, I pretended not to hear.

One last ounce of sweetness left, all that would be pressed from those days. He took me to the eagles' rock, Creag na h'Iolaire, and we stood on the top of the world.

A country lay beneath us, uninhabited and limitless, without boundary or road to the horizons, pearled with a shining mist until the red sun burned the distance clearer. Rivers laced it like silvered veins, the Doe, the Moriston, the Sian, the Loyne, and their tributaries, whose names rang like unfamiliar music: Allt na Dubh-claise, Allt a' Chroin, Allt na Dour Oir, and the shimmering waters of lochs and lochans reflected the sky like shards of glass scattered on the contours of the land.

Where there was sunlight there was beauty, a glorious, changing colour: where clouds obscured the sun the country was sullen, almost threatening. Sun and shadow crossed it in succession, conferring beauty and imbuing it with menace; the danger here could not be underestimated, where one false step, one act of folly would mean certain death.

There was no wind: a wind of any force at this height would have scraped us from this barren resting place and sent us over the edge into oblivion. And there were no birds, although eagles nested on the rock faces below us. Now, in September, their young had long since flown, and their prey was found in softer places.

We spoke little at first, resting our backs against the lichened stones. The sun steeped us in healing warmth and dried the grasses and campion and saxifrage that clung to this shallow soil. Then for some minutes I searched for a suitable stone, and finding one put it into my pocket.

"I want to remember this place."

"You're a sentimental fool, Margaret." But he said it with a certain affectionate contempt, and found a stone himself. I thought he would keep it, as I had; instead he walked lightly to the edge and sent it spinning into space.

He said, "I've often wondered what it would be like to throw myself off here. Do you think I would die before hitting something, or slowly, afterwards?"

"I don't know. Come away, for God's sake."

He came back and sat beside me, stretching out his leg, took the flask from his pocket and gave it to me, and drank where my lips had been. We sat in silence, my shoulder against his arm, the sun, burning free of cloud, warming my face and my closed eyelids. I wanted to hold it: this day, this absolute solitude, this smell of thin shimmering air, the play of light on that face, so loved and so remote. I wanted to absorb it with every sense, every pore, every fibre of being, to retain it and cherish it against a winter of separation, the first coolness of which was already in his manner. He who had turned upon me the full force of an uninhibited sexuality like the sun at its zenith, was withdrawing from me into a physical and emotional austerity in the presence of which my own desire for him seemed an inexpedient insult; and here, where for me an act of love would have been a consecration, I could not invite it or initiate it. And the hour passed, to be remembered only for its silence and its failure.

He seemed to recall himself from whatever thoughts oppressed him.

"I used to come here as a lad. No one else has ever come with me." I wondered what woman would have allowed her son the freedom of such perilous places, then I understood that by the time of which he spoke he had been no one's child. "I sat twelve hours here once, I think. The eagles came to have a look at me, to see if I was worth their trouble."

"Good God. They didn't touch you, surely."

"No... oh, no." A shadow of reminiscence crossed his face; whatever terror or communion he remembered of that moment, it still moved him greatly. "But if I had been dead they would have torn out my heart." Then he said, still staring into that intolerable brightness, "I have been faithful to you, Margaret. I know you sometimes doubt me, but I wanted you to know."

"I never doubt it."

"You give me more credit than I deserve."

"You deserve more than I give."

There was silence. He found another stone and threw it into a thousand feet of emptiness.

"If I could choose the manner of my death, it would be here, like this, with you."

"You'll never die, my love," and for a long while I thought he had not heard me, that this small epiphany had passed unnoticed, then he smiled.

"I'll prove you wrong one day."

"I don't think we should be talking of this."

"I think of it. I have no fear... I was dead for years. There can be nothing worse than that, no life, no death, no hope. Would you ever leave me, Margaret?"

"If you hurt me, yes."

"I would never hurt you."

"Then why should I have reason?"

"If my actions seemed strange to you. If I behaved with what you thought was unnecessary force— if others came to you and lied, and told you I had used them with inhumanity. Would you judge me? Would you condemn me, if all the world should come against me, and you had only my word against theirs?"

"What are you trying to tell me, Malcolm?"

"I have little hope of this harvest. Maybe some of it can be saved, if nothing else happens, but I doubt it."

Had I known the full implication of this, there would have been no joy for me in the day, but whatever the hard years had inflicted upon me they had spared me the experience of real hunger; and he did not elaborate.

"I will do what I can, but as usual James harps on money and claims I persecute him, and very little is accomplished."

"You know I have money. Take it, if you think it necessary."

"You would be wiser to take it yourself and go."

"You ask if I would ever leave you. Is that what you want me to do?"

"What I want is never given to me." The light changed; the haze was hard and dazzling. "If I could always see Glen Sian this way. Clean and silent, not swarming with maggots like a dead dog."

This, then, was the poison, this apprehension, this responsibility. I remember laying my hand on his sleeve, the strength of the arm beneath it. I remember how he smiled, with great poignancy: every gesture and expression seemed touched with finality, as in the last moments of leavetaking.

I would have spoken, but whatever comfort or reassurance I could have given was interrupted. Above us, in that dazzling space, the sun burnished an eagle, which soared like Icarus into cloud so incandescent the eye ached at its brightness.

It was gone; but he watched the cloud with a passionate intensity.

"How I envy it," he said.

And so, imperceptibly, separation came, and he put me gently aside. I saw him less; and finally MacNeil, seizing upon what he perceived as a withdrawal of that harsh protection, accused me openly of fornication with "that pandering whoremaster" and advised me that on the following Sunday I should be examined and disciplined in the kirk as an example to other wayward young women, and obviously, to save his own face before his congregation.

He said all this in a cold room on a cold morning, with his breath hanging in the bright air, and he watched me with a terrible sanctimonious sobriety, as though he sincerely believed that by such public humiliation he could cleanse me of the obsession which was Malcolm, and so redeem my soul.

There was no such discipline: there was no such public chastisement of me. He was reminded that if he wanted scandal I would give him excess of it, by living openly with Malcolm, and that my profligacy would cast such aspersions on himself that he would find his own position untenable and be compelled to resign his living, or be stripped of it by the unforgiving Synod.

There was no more talk of fornication. He expended his spleen on that subject in a vituperative outburst from his pulpit, during the course of which a blood vessel burst in his forehead, but I was spared this spectacle and this petty vengeance. I had left his congregation.

And I read and listened to the rain, as I read and listen now. *By night on my bed I sought him whom my soul loveth,* but the night and the rain fell together, and Glen Sian was devouring him. *I opened to my beloved; but my beloved had withdrawn himself, and was gone; my soul failed.*

Oh my love, my love, my love, what will become of us?

I sought him, but I found him not.

On the night of Sunday, September twenty-fourth, with plans to salvage what remained of the harvest in the coming week, and two hundred and fifty-six cattle returned unsold from the second Falkirk tryst, he sat at a battered secretary desk in his own house preparing the accounts for submission to James in the morning. Their failure to sell had dashed any illusory hopes of easing the problem of cash flow, which had become acute. As he worked only the slightest draught disturbed the candleflames.

At half past ten he went to bed, and lay in the darkness for hours before an uneasy sleep overtook him. He was awakened by the wind's screaming force a little after one.

He closed his watch and replaced it on the table where it lay at night with the pair of pistols, and, naked, carried the candle through the howling darkness to the study. The accounts left on the desk now stirred as if by invisible hands. He held up the candle and consulted the barometer he kept there, frowning at the level of the mercury: it had fallen so steeply he could not recall ever seeing it so low. Within the hour the wind was blowing a full hurricane.

He made up the fire in the kitchen and sat watching the flames, smoking, listening to the windows rattle under the onslaught of rain, and the slates shatter from a roof which had withstood the gales of autumn for a hundred years.

You bitch, he thought. You bitch— why must you always turn on me when I have you in my hand?

At some time in the depths of the night the wind died away and the moon came out: he went to the stable to quiet his crazed stallion and walked around the house examining it for damage. Then the wind and the slashing rain resumed from the opposite direction; by morning every window was caked with dirt and salt, blown thirty-five miles inland from the churning sea.

He rode out in the greyish dawn. Some ways were impassable, blocked by uprooted birches or the shallow stony streams feeding pot stills, which overnight had been transformed into raging torrents. But the first fields were sheltered and gave him hope, where there was no hope: as he rode farther the scale of destruction chilled him with its magnitude.

Here and there humanity stirred, emerging from eyeless hovels to stand stricken in the rain, staring at the havoc wreaked in fields already blasted by drought and frost; he might have been dead, passing among them like a ghost, for all the notice they took of him. That would come later, the voices crying like agitated birds, *A Mhaoir, A Mhaoir, help us, feed us, tell us to do.* In this first pitiless hour, as they balanced on the edge of catastrophe, they prayed.

O son of God the father of vast hosts, protect us from the horror of wild tempests; the wind has broken us, it has consumed us; the winter's fury has slain us.

When he reached Ardsian James was still in bed. He left a curt message and retreated to the estate office, where he sat in his wet clothing with the dirty horn cup full of whisky, haunted by what he had seen and his own inability to predict or prevent it.

More bitter than death, O God, is the great wind that blows, that consumes us like twigs in the red heart of fire, that carries us like ashes to heaven...

At eleven o' clock he snapped the watch shut, cursed James lividly and got up. At that moment some one tapped on the door and summoned him to the morning room. He was unsurprised to find it occupied not by James but by Charlotte.

She was seated, as on the occasion of their first interview, at the escritoire, the drawers of which were stuffed with what appeared to be household accounts. Untidiness was now a feature of her large person, the fair hair brushed into an uncertain pompadour, ribbons untied among the elbow flounces of a blue and white gown brilliantly splashed with chrysanthemums. There was a tray holding coffee cups and pot on the table: he recognized

Ewen's Sèvres service and spirit lamp, and Ewen's crystal bowl, empty, had been restored to its former place on the mantel.

"Ah, Mr. Scott. Come in. You will sit down?"

He said, "You see the state of my clothing," and remained standing, with his back to the door. The room, darkened considerably by its redecoration in deep blue silk, seemed to have grown smaller, and the heat and smoke of a carelessly laid fire rendered it oppressive.

"I offer my apologies for my husband's absence. He has a heavy cold."

"Yes," he said, "I know how frequently he enjoys ill health."

"You are sarcastic, Mr. Scott."

"I am tired, Lady Glen Sian, and the situation is very grave. Grave enough, I would have thought, to rouse your husband from his bed."

She said bluntly, "Is this the end?"

Oh no, the end comes by hair's breadths; the end has been coming for years. This is not it, but nearly so.

"Your position is precarious, and only a fool would pretend otherwise. You want money and there is none readily at hand. I cannot sell cattle at Falkirk, and if the prices remain at their current level and our cattle are still stiff to sell I will be hard pressed to pay Glen Sian's accounts, or for that matter my own."

She had been studying her hands, which were folded decorously on the papers before her: the display of heavy rings lent no delicacy to their masculine proportions.

"And you will want grain. That is the normal practise in these circumstances."

The Sèvres cup at her elbow cooled unnoticed. She did not invite him to take refreshment with her, although he knew that if Margaret should join them some subtle distinction would be made between them, lover and mistress, and she but not he would be accorded the privilege. So status and presumption and the essential futility of his love were expressed in coffee cups.

"What provisions have been made?"

"I have purchased two thousand bolls of grain— wheat, peasemeal and oats— from a chandler in Aberdeen with whom I have dealt in the past. We will want more. And it was to have been financed by the sales at Falkirk... I shall ask for credit, but in the event I doubt it will be offered."

"Should he sell?"

The sheer naïveté of the question might have amused him on another occasion. He said shortly, "He can try. Who do you think will want it, with the devil's hooves printed all over it last night, and property going for a song from here to Inverness?" She sat staring at her hands as if she had not heard, or considered this. "And the land is bound by entail— I don't fancy pouring money into lawyers' pockets to break it. There is no time."

"What shall we do, Mr. Scott?"

The voices always crying, crying. A hard wind was still blowing, driving bitter rain, and the light of too many candles swelled and beat against his eyes.

"There are established patterns of distribution and allowances at subsistence levels: a pound and a half per man per day, three-quarters of a pound for women, half a pound for children. I will insist that that be supplemented by the consumption of potatoes, which will support life if necessary, and will provide a defense against scurvy, and the other diseases of deficiency. We must anticipate rather a high level of mortality— this need not prove a disadvantage, the imbalance of population being what it is."

She was watching him with a peculiar intensity, and he could not remember what he had said to bring that expression to her face.

"You asked for my opinion. I am giving it."

"Continue then," she said.

"I do not propose to adhere to the established custom of promiscuous distribution, offering relief to every non-paying cottar. Those who farm on their kinsmen's land will be supported by their kinsmen; otherwise they can flit. The entire practise of subdivision is to be discouraged by any means, and to rid ourselves of that class is the object. There will be little enough to spare at the present allowance for rent-payers and their dependants."

"You have given this matter considerable thought."

"Believe me, I have had little alternative."

"And you earnestly propose to allow tenants— non rent-paying tenants and their dependants— to merely slip through our fingers as the result of this unequal distribution? That is a measure which would appear to want common humanity, Mr. Scott."

He repeated, "There is no alternative."

"What is your intention, Mr. Scott? I mean generally, not only in this situation."

"I intend to reduce the population of this estate by fifty per cent, and so secure the future of the remaining tenants at better than the present pathetic levels of subsistence. If they farmed adequately the land might support them, but the land is overburdened and those who farm it are inefficient and ignorant, and ill-served by those who would cosset them for their own smug satisfaction."

He opened the door. As a child this gilt handle had filled his hand: now it seemed no more than a toy.

"When your husband recovers from his cold, perhaps you would ask him to wait upon me in my office, where the matter may be raised again."

In the estate office he tossed the cattle accounts aside and opened the current journal; the rain was still falling, interspersed with hail, and the clean page swam before his eyes as though he watched it through dark water.

He wrote *25ᵗʰ September, 1769,* and paused. His fingers on the pen were shaking. *This day we have had nothing but hurricane and storm.*

Then he sat and waited, not for James but for the tenants who were even now assessing the extent of their losses, the damage to property and stock. The page, still drifting in the darkness of noon or perhaps only his vision, was blank. By nightfall it would be filled with the catalogue of disaster.

James's response, offered through a sodden handkerchief on Thursday evening, was to order the sale of a hundred cattle at Martinmas, and to categorically forbid discrimination between tenants and cottars in the matter of grain distribution.

"I have a moral obligation to support and relieve the distress of my people in these tragic circumstances." There was a silence, during which his factor smoked and watched him with cold eyes through the resultant haze. "Well, what are you gaping at, man? See to it, before the damned snow starts."

"You misapprehend the point."

"And what is the point? You want money, you demand money— sell the cattle. At what, four or five pounds a head? Surely that would content you."

"The market is depressed."

James stared at him over the balled handkerchief, then opened it, examined it, and filled it again with a revolting rush of mucous.

"I don't give a toss for the market. Sell the kine and take what's offered."

"It would be a sounder proposition to slaughter them and put them on your table."

"And what will the people eat?"

"Let that be my concern, not yours."

James stuffed the handkerchief into his cuff and leaned forward into the candlelight. His hands, pressed against the edge of the table, were mottled with cold.

"It is my concern. My inheritance was a solemn undertaking, and I am bound by honour. My father...." he seemed to seize upon it like a talisman, unassailable and sacrosanct, "my father would turn in his grave if he knew what you proposed. And this is not the first time I have had to correct you in matters of administration, when your judgment seemed clouded by absurd and intractable prejudices." His hands flexed, and he leaned slightly closer. "Don't think I don't know what animates you, and debits and credits and two thousand bolls of grain don't cloud the issue in my view."

Malcolm said, "You don't know. You wrap yourself in your father's name, and you feed your wife on your father's dreams, and he was full of mawkish sentiment and so are you, when you find it convenient. But he believed it, and you don't. That makes him honourable, if misguided, and it makes you a liar."

"You are an insolent bastard."

"And what are you going to do about it?" James was staring at him. "Do you want me to go? Because I will go. I will take my money and my sheep and my woman, and I will go. And they are my sheep, until you pay me for them, and if you ever read the accounts I gave you you would know what you were putting your hand to. And, by God, she is my woman, and I'll kill any man who touches her... even you, Glen Sian."

In the silence he heard the rain again, black rain, shining in the candlelight, turning to ice where it ran. James had moved to the door; his eyes were shocked dark smudges, and affront and anger had wiped the boyish satisfaction from his face, giving it an austerity and a pallor that were starkly reminiscent of his father.

He said, "I shall not forget this conversation. And one day you will account for it, either to me or to God."

"I don't fear either of you."

James went out, leaving the door open: the tapping of his slim, polished heels seemed to echo for a long time, before it was drowned by the sound of the rain.

He sat listening to it, splashing more of the vile spirit into the cup and over the pages of the journal; the barley was already sprouting in the ear, uncut and unsalvageable, and soon there would be little enough even of that, and the oblivion it offered.

In his mind, he often spoke to Ewen, as he spoke to Margaret when the terrible hunger for her mere presence became insupportable. On this night, which would have been Ewen's fifty-fourth birthday, it was upon Ewen that his thoughts dwelled, reliving suffering and bereavement with a morbid compulsion, then eventually he said, as if Ewen were sitting opposite him, "One day I will strike your son, and that will be the end of me."

He watched the candles until they guttered out and the darkness enfolded him, a stifling, airless darkness like a tomb, which seemed to vibrate with spirits that gave no comfort, ghosts who gave no peace. Around him, beyond the barriers of passageways and walls, the house slept; for him there was nothing, no refuge, no destination. Nothing waited for him but the night's rainy wastes, nothing spoke to him but the rain.

There were other gales, followed by a killing frost. The grain, rotting and useless, was ploughed under at his insistence, and the first murmurs of disaffection were heard. A string of pack ponies arrived from Aberdeen with little more than half the oats, peasemeal and wheat he had ordered, and not even his fury or the threat of violence would yield more from either jaggers or chandler. Demand had outstripped supply, and the price had been exorbitant. There would be no more.

The grain was deposited in a drying barn and secured under lock and key, which, in a community that prided itself upon its honesty, occasioned great resentment; the weekly distribution was overseen by himself, assisted initially by the gang led by Diar Cameron. For their efforts they received double the standard measure, the same ration he allowed himself, on the principle that his was the guiding brain and presence, and any illness or failure on the part of himself or his lieutenants would result in chaos. But as time passed and suspicion and hostility deepened, he lost them. Unable to withstand the pressures of family and community, they made their mumbling excuses, shuffled from one foot to the other and refused to meet his eyes, and left him, until only Diar Cameron waited for him in the bitter mornings, goaded by loyalty or greed or his wife's complaining tongue, his eyes shadowed with the dark rings that preceded scurvy, his lips and eyelids and facial skin roughened and flaking. He had been told, as every tenant had been told, by word of mouth, by notices nailed on the door of MacNeil's kirk which were later defaced or torn down, and by Malcolm himself, to eat large amounts of potatoes, to boil kale and turnip and dried peas and to drink the cooking water. Diar merely smiled and shook his head, preferring the Highlander's staples, cheese, pron, sour milk and the blood of cattle, to the consumption of root vegetables he considered fit only for fodder, and which he was now feeding to his animals.

There was no distribution to those who paid no rent, and after the first few occasions when they were denied an allowance of grain they ceased to appear. Their pleas, bribes and excuses had no power to move a man whose decisions were known to be adamant, and his lieutenants had dispersed so that they could not be intimidated. Appeals to James by representatives were useless: his vanity craved popularity, but he valued his own comfort more, and he saw in these straitened circumstances a threat to his own table; he was already complaining of flatulence and diarrhoea and an insatiable hunger, and in the belief that any acid would prevent scurvy was sprinkling vinegar on the rough vegetables he found so unpalatable. He had slapped Charlotte for feeding bowls of milk to her cat, which provoked her, not to the tears he expected, but to hit him across the face; and when he was heard to declare that he would rather hunt than starve she had stalked away and returned with the keys to the gun room, which she had thrown into his lap. He had led an inept foray over the winter-bitten moors, but the black game which had formerly leaped from beneath the foot had become appallingly scarce, and returning with a raging hunger he had gorged himself on salt beef and claret, and charged his ghillies with supplying meat for the table, abusing them when they failed. He had lost the fat he so easily acquired and was a thin, coughing ghost of his father; his eyelids and tongue were scarlet with incipient cheilosis, which, after weeks of malnutrition, was appearing across the estate. Charlotte passed the days in bed with swollen legs; her Edinburgh maid was in similar case. Of the household, only Coll MacGregor and the ghillies remained relatively unaffected.

In the first week of the new decade, the expected diseases of deficiency were reported; by the end of January they were rife. Scurvy, anemia, oedema, cheilosis, bronchitis, pneumonia: where there was smallpox, as there was every winter, the afflicted families were too frightened of losing their allowance to make it public. When the weather and the condition of his horse permitted, the factor rode abroad, threatening, encouraging, instructing the ignorant, those tenants who still refused to eat what they considered a poisonous tuber. Dispassionately he watched the deterioration of his own health, the fatigue, the breathlessness, the swollen limbs he blamed on rheumatism. He followed those practises which had always been his, eating quantities of kale, potatoes, onions and sprouting wheat, game when it was found, and infusions of pine and nettle. This he suggested to Diar Cameron, whose nose was bleeding into a soiled square of linen as he weighed and measured the allowance.

"Go home, Diar. The scurvy's on you. A sick man is no good to me."

The roughened lids flicked up at him, and a steam of foul breath, thought contagious by the misinformed, assaulted him.

"And what would you know about it?"

"I've had it. Now do as I tell you." Others had stopped to listen, lingering, hesitating, shawled women with the folds drawn across their faces, men shambling, insensitive to the cold. Everywhere the flecks of skin flaking from the cheek, the fetid breath, the odour of diarrhoea that seemed to pervade their clothing. He knew they had overheard and shouted at them, "And you, and you, you miserable bastards, before you all die like cattle, and a damned good riddance to you!"

Nothing moved in their eyes, no shock, no resentment: they had become inured to this abuse, which, as the uncertainty of his temper increased, had become habitual. One or two drifted closer, haggard and anonymous, among them a woman of no particular age who held a gaunt, staring child by the hand. Its neck was caked with a discharge of pus which had dripped from scalp or ear.

"There are no more potatoes left to me, A Mhaoir. What shall I do?"

"Eat grass," he said, and a sigh seemed to pass over the group, although he had not spoken callously but with perfect truth.

"For the children's sake, A Mhaoir... for God's sake, give me a little more."

His head and body were suffused with nausea, and his vision was disordered: the pain, exacerbated by fasting, would soon begin. A hand fastened on his cuff; he imagined its coldness, although its flesh did not touch his own.

"For God's sake, give me something... for the sake of what I was to you."

The face might have been any age from twenty to fifty: the eyes were grey, inflamed, and a trickle of blood issued from one nostril, unnoticed and unfelt.

What souls are these? No life, no death, no hope.... Their faces stream with gouts and clots of bloody pus and tears, which dropping in the dust the writhing worms consume.... I come to lead you into eternal night, to that sunless shore.

"Who are you?"

Her face might have been Margaret's face, wasted and suffering; the violent pattern of light disfigured it. But the voice was not Margaret's voice, although perhaps in some brief and unremembered intercourse she had been Margaret to him.

"You know who I am. You know me, you used me. Feed me now, give me something, out of pity—"

Weeping and cursing they come eternally... into fire and into ice.... What is it that you read, Ewen, he had said, staring at the incomprehensible Italian, the rough voice of the youth cracking with maturity.

She whispered, "May the curse of God and all his saints light upon you," and the foulness of her breath brushed against his face, "and may you die of a wasting disease with your guts spilling from your mouth and your children dead under the ground."

It is The Inferno. Beloved voice, beloved voices. The hand, like a claw, still held him.

"Go to hell," he said.

Life was darkness, a dark, turgid current upon which he drifted, forever drowning and unable to die. The brief dark hours of daylight, the endless hours of night, dark rain, dark fields, black frost, black ice, the torrents of wind in the darkness carrying all away: roofs, walls, branches, clouds, the spirits of the dead, which in ever increasing numbers slid from suffering flesh into oblivion. This was not the exodus he had hoped to provoke; but those crofters who received relief shared their meagre rations with destitute relations, a tenet of human nature he had not entirely anticipated. Such charity merely prolonged the inevitable, and ensured hardship even for those sectors of the population his measures had been designed to protect.

By now the veneer of civility had been stripped from his dealings with them. Upon the death of a principal tenant, his holding was laid waste and his dependants were obliged to seek shelter with relatives. On the quarter day of Candlemas, the fourth anniversary of Ewen's death, when again he sat all day in the silence of the estate office, and no rents were forthcoming from any tenant, he was determined to poind cattle where necessary, and sent for James, who after nearly an hour shuffled in with his feet in carpet slippers and subsided into the other chair.

They seldom spoke now; these spurious civilities, too, had been abandoned.

He sat smoking the tobacco which, of late, had made him curiously light-headed, and waited for James to finish a laborious decoding of the ill-written lines in the journal.

"You agree?"

James said indifferently, "Do as you wish," and covered his mouth and nose with the familiar soiled handkerchief. "Must you do that? It nauseates me."

A silence followed, punctuated by the hiss of snow on the darkening glass. At half past three this day was ending, and he who had always possessed a cat's vision in the darkness now saw very badly at night, a condition which proceded from deficiency: he began the first slow preparations for departure. James, watching him with heavy eyes, said, "My wife had a letter from our mutual friend this morning. She rashly sends an enclosure for you." He laid it on the table, and sat back, observing attentively. "Your connection is finished, I gather."

It lay in the candlelight, a single sheet, folded and sealed. There was no superscription.

"Is this some jest?"

"Assuredly not. My wife was charged with its delivery; you see that I have delivered it. Shall we anticipate your reply?"

He groped for it, tore it across and thrust the pieces into his pocket.

"No. There will be no reply."

***

When, in the ebbing hours of night, sleep came, it brought her voice, which awakened him: sometimes he saw her in burning dreams, when the vision of her was more real than any living face, and he imagined she touched him. And he spoke to her in love's language, aloud, in his thoughts, in words written when drunk which when read sober were so obscene that they shocked even his hardened sensibility, and he destroyed them.

He had never read her letter, nor burned it, but he kept it as he kept other tokens, obsessively, even superstitiously. Cheap fairings, a lace handkerchief, a music box, small gifts of jewellery he had never made, a linen stock taken from her neck to which her perfume still faintly clung, and which sometimes he spread on the pillow where her head had lain, and sometimes on his own. The silver brushes she had brought to this unfeminine room to make it a boudoir, with which he had brushed her hair; the rose oil he had rubbed into her skin, anointing her nipples with it, and sometimes her pubic hair; a handkerchief stained with her menstrual blood, which more than once he had tasted, and once, ritualistically, he had stained with semen. He kept it now as a powerful charm, a fetish, beneath his pillow, but such sympathetic magic was no more than a symbol: the need for her, which in the early months of separation had consumed him, was now exhausted. Sexual hunger had subdued itself to a physical which could not be satisfied.

Nothing mattered, nothing signified, not Margaret, not himself, not the dull, repetitive struggle of each day, the futility of leaving a bed which now offered neither rest nor peace, only a few hours' respite from pervasive cold, not the effort of maintaining an appearance of sanity and order. His hair came out in handfuls; the cold razor scraped a strained, wolfish face with bloodshot eyes, which no woman could have ever loved, nor would ever return to love, so powerful, to him, seemed its ugliness. The effort of eating exhausted and revolted him, although he craved meat insatiably; what little game could be found was riddled with parasites, and those organs which would have afforded the most nourishment had to be discarded.

By March, on An Reithe, evidence was found that two or three rams had been slaughtered, and their carcasses, each yielding some hundred and eighty pounds of mutton, butchered on the spot; but neither dogs nor shepherds could discover the culprits, and in the heavy fog that followed unseen predators disposed of what remained. The incidents became almost a weekly occurence, and the stumbling appearance of the shepherds' boy at his door another recurrent phantom in a shifting, unreal world.

The roe died; the sheep died; the hunger gnawed at his backbone like a cancer; the veiled eyes and gaunt staring faces, steeped in sullen ignorance, feigned deafness when he spoke. Men refused to labour for their allowances and stone walls lay unrepaired, cattle bled from the neck collapsed and died and were torn to pieces. He carried venison to his mistress, abandoned since the advent of Margaret, and found her crippled by weakness and almost blinded by ulcerated corneas. He remained there three days, feeding her and bathing her eyes: she offered only stolid silence or recriminations, and eventually he left her.

The cattle impounded at Candlemas were slaughtered, and he sensed the outrage at this ruthless confiscation and disposal of other men's property. Those who were offered meat refused it, so a large proportion was consumed by James's household, which had no such scruples. Some was carried to Glen Mor, ostensibly as tithe for MacNeil, but intended for Margaret; some he kept himself, and as though it drew a predator to the scent of blood, Mairi came down from the hills to be fed.

She did not come out of love. As it had never characterized his immature liaison with her mother, so it never entered now into the disordered current of emotions that flowed between them, and except when she came, infrequently, to move the grey dust in his house from place to place, he seldom saw her, and preferred it so. That she was Mhaire's daughter was not in doubt; that she was his was only a possibility. She had been conceived in promiscuity and born premature and deformed; the socket of her left hip was undeveloped, and her left leg was shrunken and shorter than the right. Her face was Mhaire's, fiercely dark, with a feral little smile: he saw nothing in it that resembled him, although like himself in childhood she possessed an hysterical intelligence and sensitivity. Isolation and poverty and the peculiarities of her upbringing had made her erratic and unworldly, and given to inarticulate rage and fits of violence. He himself believed her crazed, and when he had first been made aware of her existence he had found any contact with her unbearable. Now, out of necessity, it was only barely so.

They ate in silence. She had lived alone since the death of Jonet, the midwife he had paid to keep her, and Jonet had never schooled her in the social graces; her manners were abominable. Eventually he reached across the table and rapped her knuckles with the handle of his knife. Then she simpered, mocking him, and crooking her little finger.

"Oh, I will be like English Margaret, so."

"Shut your mouth," he said.

She bared her little teeth, which unlike his had never bled or loosened, and drew out a crumpled paper, which she smoothed elaborately before pushing it into the candlelight where he could see it. It was a crude caricature, drawn with pen and ink and blotted where the rain had spattered it, the head of a wolf on a horseman's body, recognizable as himself by the oversized thigh boots, the caped greatcoat and the meticulously blackened mount. Another hand had added a further refinement in pencil, an exaggerated, erect penis. Underneath was printed in an educated hand, AM MADADH NA GLEINNE SINE, The Wolf of Glen Sian. He became aware that she was watching him, as if, like James, she would find his response entertaining.

"Who gave you this?"

"It was not given to me. It was nailed on the door of the kirk in Glen Mor for every one to see."

Not even MacNeil would permit this, or encourage it.

"And I saw who was putting it there: the ugly dominie."

Yes, he thought, the gifted, clever hand, the quality of paper, the means and the motive but no wisdom and no scruples, only enmity, and a moment's puerile satisfaction.

She wiped her plate with her fingers and licked them.

"There have been others. There will be more."

He said, "You are a hateful child," and she watched him, grinning with perverse amusement, but the face that swam in and out of the shadows was no more a child's than his own... nineteen years had passed since her conception, and he thought that all her perceptions of life, like his own, had been stained and distorted from that moment.

She settled herself uninvited on the seise, turning her face to the fire's warmth: he sat at the table with the thing crumpled under his hand until she remarked from the firelight, "She is thick with Cameron. They say so in Glen Mor," then he crushed it in his fist and threw it into the flames.

There was no further conversation. She coughed twice and fell asleep, like a bundle of rags on the seise, while he sat in the darkness staring at nothing, sifting truth and lies, and listening to spring's gift on the glass: sleet instead of snow.

On the night of Saturday April seventh, small dishevelled groups of men drifted in and out of the squalid public house where they habitually met to buy measures of the raw spirit distilled by the surly proprietor. In the eye-watering haze of a peat fire so small that the flame could be covered with two hands, they leaned or sprawled against the blackened walls or on the bare earth floor, men who would upon the morrow appear in kirk with vile tongues and tempers after this night's brawling, vomiting or assaults on their women.

Some were singing, until others cursed them into silence: some talked of an epidemical fury of emigration which would bleed the country white after this winter's starvation; some entertained themselves throwing knives into the floor, for a man could honestly be found with a knife in these hungry times, but a firearm was not so easily excused, even if they could have afforded

them. The songs began again, out of alcoholic melancholy and boredom—
the proposed cockfight, for which spectacle they had gathered, had not yet
materialized— and the voices rose and fell, guided by a clear tenor which
on other occasions produced the waterfalling descants of the long psalms in
Inglis MacNeil's kirk.

> O, gur mór mo chùis mhulaid,
> 'S mì ri caoineadh na guin atà 'm thìr...
>
> O, great is the cause of my sorrow,
> As I mourn for my country's wounds...

They sang of Culloden, and the songs became so maudlin that several
men who had fed on this cherished grief since childhood wept in the smoky
darkness, and the proprietor cursed them aloud. Then some one said harshly,
"The land is full of misery— Christ, who should bear it? We should all go to
America... it is our destiny to go there."

Then a rush of cold sweet air disturbed the dense fug of smoke and a space
was cleared in the middle of the floor for the cocks, which had arrived. Wagers
were taken, coins thrown into a wooden plate carried among the lounging
figures by the proprietor, and the cocks were flung together without ceremony.
They killed one another with unsatisfactory haste and disappointment rippled
over the spectators. The bloodied rags were picked up by their wings and
tossed aside, the floor raked to cover the fresh stains, and another jug was
broached. A filthy joke circulated, a man lurched to the door and vomited
noisily on the threshold, and the psalm-singer offered a new variation on an
old tune, which soon commanded their attention.

> B' e sin fitheach gun àgh
> Tha air tighinn an dràsd';
> Umaidh àrdanach, cruaidh,
> E gun taise, gun truas, gun tròcair...

As the words grew in significance one or two men thought it prudent to
leave. The others shouted their encouragement and the singer, emboldened
by the response, threw aside all caution.

> A haughty, harsh brute
> who has come to us now;
> without compassion,
> pity or mercy;
> 'S nam bu fada fear buan dheth sheòrsa,
> And may his kind be short-lived!

But like many amateur performers, drunk upon his own success, he did not know when to stop, and he could not resist launching into a further verse to which he had devoted considerable talent and malice; and when an electric silence seized the room he was singing with his eyes closed and did not see the cause. When the silence persisted he presumed it was out of respect for his art. He ended, and when there was no applause or display of appreciation from his audience he opened his eyes, peering around. Then some one said gently, "That's enough now, Cameron. Shut your mouth and go home, like the fool you are," and through the acrid haze he saw the man so lately and obscenely caricatured standing by the door. He said loudly to the room at large, "This man is killing us! Are you women that you sit snivelling while he tears out our hearts?" And groping on the stool beside him he picked up a jug and threw it, and had the satisfaction of seeing it explode against the doorframe, and its flying shards draw blood. Then he stood waiting for the approval and encouragement of his peers, without which he dared nothing, and briefly they gave it. Hungry men, emasculated men, men who hid behind the anonymity of smoke and darkness and the fumes of whisky hurled a shower of projectiles, as they paid on Fastern's Eve to throw stones at crippled birds, with only the most obscure and primitive intent to humiliate and injure; then gradually they fell into silence. Their victim was still standing. The nostril bled, the cheek bled, but men bled easily these days; the skin of the arms could be bruised with a fingerprint, teeth bled and could be pulled out with the fingers and brittle bones fractured without effort, and this man's blood, which they had all feared to shed, ran as red as any.

Malcolm remembered it later, remembered every face, as he remembered the faces on other occasions, other variations of this, and imprinted them upon his mind for some moment of consummation which had not yet come. From the door he said, "You pack of whores. Are these the odds you favour, one man against so many?" and then when no one moved, "Oh no, you won't, will you, you cowardly bastards— all you can do is sit in the smoke with your hands around your cocks, like brave Highland men. Come, you cunt—" and George Cameron, too drunk for judgment, flung himself on him, aiming the object he always carried on nights like this at his face. Expecting a knife, he threw up his right hand to deflect it and the razor opened his hand from fingertip to wrist; pain and rage and insane strength possessed him and Cameron was down, writhing and screaming as he cut him with precise, deliberate strokes, until the cheekbone gleamed in the mask of blood and some one was pounding his shoulders and shouting, "Malcolm—Malcolm—" as he had not been called by his Christian name since they had all been children; since the blood and snot had poured from his nose in the ringing winter twilight and they had assaulted him with stones and shinty sticks, and Diar Cameron had then as now pulled at him, telling him to go.

"Christ, man, Christ... leave him... leave him..." in a hysterical refrain until consciousness left the writhing body and he stared into the bloody face and said, "No songs, my hero? No pictures?" and let the razor fall, and spat on him. He pushed through the crowd, now hushed and stricken, and at the door he stood with the blood streaming from his hand to splash on the broken shards and mingle with the vomit. They stared at him, some with a kind of repellent hunger, others trying to dissociate themselves from anything which might have consequences for them.

"O brave Highland men," he said.

He woke from a dream of vermin crawling on his skin, which was trickling sweat: before he slept he had laid her stock across his pillow, to hold against his face. He found it in his bandaged hand. His blood had soaked through its delicate overlay of lace, and her perfume had gone.

Sometimes, still, I see the wound in my sleep, like the lips of an obscene mouth. Occasionally my needle is jerked away and dangles from its wet black thread, and his agony tears my careful stitches, which then I set again.

In my memory a book lies open, directing this activity: it is Churchman's *Practise of Surgery*, and its minute print occupied me in a moment of idle curiosity in Christopher Thackeray's shadowed study.

> ....Wounds of the face, owing to the great vascularity of the parts, readily and rapidly heal. The edges of the wound should be approximated as accurately as possible, especially near the eyelid, where there is danger of contraction, and united with horsehair sutures: means should be taken to render this aseptic.... Locally nothing answers better than dusting the part with equal quantities of oxide of zinc and starch powder and enclosing it in a thick layer of lint....

This wound, which extends from the temple to the jaw, seeps blood continuously: this and the puncture wounds with which I perforate its length may already be infected, by the air, by the weapon, by my needle or my thread, my hand, or organisms present in the vinegar and oil of thyme which are my only disinfectant, or the powder of comfrey root with which I dust my crude attempt at surgery, or by the lint, stored in a wooden press of uncertain age, with which I dress it. Every stitch, every drop, every particle carries an intrinsic threat of sepsis, which may manifest itself in a variety of forms within two or three days, and progress from a localized suppuration of the wound to a general affection, and death.

They had brought George Cameron to me in a condition of shock, passing in and out of consciousness. All three smelled revoltingly of drink, and his cousin Diar, who spoke no more English than the words, "missus, missus," could only wander up and down the kitchen in a frenzied agitation, while the third man, a loutish youth who must have been his son, huddled in the doorway staring at me while his teeth chattered in his head.

Eventually, when my butchery was finished, they moved him closer to the fire where he lay in a swooning doze. The others crouched near him and drank the whisky I gave them, passing it back and forth, while I, nauseated by the stench and substance of blood, washed my hands and arms at the sink. Perhaps an hour passed, then they began to talk, whispered fragments of a Gaelic riddled with local dialect. There was no sound from the rest of the house: my aunt was in bed with dysentery, and my father had secreted himself in his study as was his habit on a Saturday night, with his smeared tumbler and bottle. At midnight I pushed open the door to ensure that he had not set himself or his papers alight and found him dead to the world.

They were still in the kitchen when I returned. They stayed into the small hours, whispering at George's feet until I knew it all, while he shivered and sweated and tried to claw his bandaged face: occasionally they restrained his hand. I sat opposite in the firelight, ignored and perhaps forgotten.

At about three o'clock they carried him home, leaving the kitchen littered with the bloodied paraphernalia. I heard the scrape of George's shoes as they half dragged, half supported him, the sound of the gate closing, and then nothing. The kitchen was empty, the night was empty, my hands, folded over a blood-stained apron, were empty: my mind was alive with dry whispers, like vermin, and a still, silent cry, which was my own.

It was not confirmation I wanted: I knew what I had heard was the truth. Perhaps I went in an attempt to force explanation or apology from a man who never gave them: perhaps my outrage on behalf of George was merely the burning-glass that focused my own bewildered pain after months of silence and indifference.

I asked one of his shepherds where he could be found: I remember how strangely, after so many years, the Border accent fell upon my ear. I remember the place where I found him, even to the stain of snow lying on the ground, and how I waited for him as he crossed the broken slope beneath me, walking from one to another of those small heaps which might also have been patches of rotting snow, but which were premature lambs, all dead. I remember the moment when he hesitated, seeming to feel my eyes on him, and staring up into the cold drifting rain saw me and stood still, as though some decision either to ignore or approach me had to be consciously made. Then he came on, climbing with the old, harsh vigour, and when he was near enough to be heard he stopped, and stood with his hands behind his back, as was sometimes his habit, and said, "What do you want?"

His face, which hunger had made gaunt, was drawn and badly shaved, and cut and discoloured beneath the left eye; the eye was bloodshot.

"We were lovers. Has it come to this, that when you see me you say, 'what do you want'?"

His right hand, which was now visible, was wrapped in a soiled bandage; even as I watched the blood began to soak through, and he thrust it into his pocket.

"Yes. It comes to that. And is this what it comes to, that you spend a summer in my bed pretending you will when you won't, and when I turn my back you open your legs to Cameron, and put his cock in your mouth where mine was?"

He was close, and I hit him. At the force with which the ring on that hand struck his face one of the wounds opened and bled, running grotesquely in the rain.

Mindless, mindless words of abuse... obscenity and accusation. I called him a bastard, brutal, bloody, vicious, everything I had wanted to believe was a lie; everything said of him was the truth. He called me a whore, and other names, once heard as endearments in bed, then he seized my shoulders and then my head between his hands and held me as though he would crush me. I felt his blood running with the rain on my forehead.

It was so quiet, no sound but the rain.

He said, "It was all I had of you, and it was my life. My *life*— and it was nothing to you. *I* was nothing to you. You picked me up and put me down when it suited you— like a dirty glove— or maybe you told your friends, and sat over tea and tittered, and all the while you took everything of me and gave me nothing— not even your love. Not even your faith."

I struck his hands away. They were shaking, and the blood was seeping through the bandage.

"I wrote to you. You never answered. What was I to think? What was I to do? I was dying for you— just a word from you— and you flung me away like a used trull in a doorway...."

He was watching me as though he hated me, and God knew what was in my face. If I had ever loved him, I could never forgive him now.

"Couldn't you have waited for me? Is your love so frail? You saw what was happening, and you knew what I was doing. Is that what you were dying for?"

He shook me with a terrible strength, again and again, until I thought my neck would break. "Didn't I ask you to be faithful to me? Didn't I ask you to believe me, if all the world should come against me and it was only my word against theirs?" His strength possessed me and I was nothing: nothing in his hands. "Christ, I would have sheltered you, with my body, with my blood.... I kept myself from you and you knew why I was doing it, and you couldn't even wait for me, could you, you faithless bitch."

Out of pain and rage and the need to hurt him, I said, "Why should I be faithful to you, when you were never faithful to me?"

Sometimes, lovers play at games: we had, once. Sometimes in the heat and stillness, in the privacy of his bed, things were done and said in the abandon of sex which had nurtured passion: a pretense of rape, undertaken in absolute trust, a wrist restrained, a nipple roughly sucked, the invasive rasp of clothing on nakedness, the resistance and submission. Lovers play at rape sometimes, but not like this... not like this. I was on the ground; I had been thrown there, and I was in pain. He held me down, and asked me if this was what I wanted, and if I had wanted it of Cameron, because this was Cameron's hand now, this instrument of my pleasure: and he violated me, not with his penis but with the fingers of his gashed right hand, and the blood and putrefaction flooded from the wound; and he said again and again, "Is this what you want? Is this what he gives you?" until his nails tore the tissues of my vagina, and I screamed, but no sound emerged. And then I bled, and it ended; everything ended, and I could not see his face, although I knew he wept.

I left him. I could barely walk. He made no attempt to restrain me or to prevent my going. I went to Ardsian. By that time it was late afternoon and the light was failing, and I had had a riding accident, which, although I had no visible injuries, explained the dishevelment of my clothing and my disordered behaviour.

Charlotte cherished me like a sister, plied me with brandy and would not hear of my leaving before morning. To comfort me after my accident, and as a dainty acknowledgment that she had guessed my relationship with a man whose tenacity of purpose she had come to admire, she put me to sleep in my lover's bed, in the dark red room which had housed him. So that all night, although I had left him, he remained with me, and while I woke I imagined him watching me, and when I slept, exhausted, he came to me, waking me in terror; until the night was gone, taking with it his dark spirit, and the empty squares of sky beyond the windows had greyed with the approach of dawn, and a mild wind brought early rain.

X

I told no one. No one knew, and nothing happened. The revulsion and horror ebbed away, leaving me drained and insensible and possessed of a lingering sexual dread, but my nightmares and my thoughts were private, and only one man could have known them.

I never saw him. For several weeks I seldom went out, until my reclusive behaviour caused comment and I forced myself to walk the perimeters of the village, and sometimes beyond; but every track, every mile, every shadow was imbued with his presence, and I dreaded the possibility of our meeting, although this never happened. If his business brought him close to Glen Mor, or if he passed through the village, I never knew, and my father and my aunt, who had access to every rumour and every shred of gossip, were peculiarly reticent, and neither by name nor by allusion was he ever mentioned.

It was Charlotte who forced me to leave this self-imposed isolation and return to Ardsian. In early May when the road was still awash with melting snow she had ridden down with a groom running at her stirrup to call on me at the manse. We sat in MacNeil's unheated parlour, with neither curtain nor carpet nor cushion to relieve its Presbyterian starkness, and drank glasses of the elderflower cordial she had brought me, while she probed me subtly for the reason for my absence. I hoped she could not even dimly imagine the truth. Then, mercifully, the talk turned to other subjects, and she gave me books and a Lady's Pocket Companion only recently arrived from Edinburgh with the winter's accumulation of newspapers, and a pair of kid gloves. There were no letters for me, from England or anywhere else. Eventually she departed, perched in the saddle with her knee hooked up and the hem of her expensive habit splashed with muddy clay; a week later, coming to see me again, she fell from that same saddle and miscarried of her third child. As James's blotted message informed me, I was responsible.

And it was James whom I saw first: I had seen no one else, neither during the course of my ride nor in the courtyard, except servants, all wearing the mask of hunger we shared like some common disguise. The sun on this particular morning seemed cruellest because it shone upon a starving land, where nothing edible had yet been produced, and only weeds quickened.

I found him tense and bitter, seated in the drawing room with all the windows shut. He did not rise when I came in, and I thought this boorish and insulting.

I asked how Charlotte was.

"Sleeping. Is that what you came for? She'll be awake presently."

"And you, James?"

"Oh, admirable. Like yourself, the picture of health and happiness."

I was no longer capable of suffering fools, gladly or otherwise. "I shall go and sit with her."

He said acidly, "No, you don't want to waste the journey, do you? A pity you can't go up and dally with the demon lover in his lair," and then, observing me, "Oh, how smart a lash that is! So you have broken with him, haven't you? I should have guessed it from his manner."

I said, "That is none of your affair," and he rounded on me.

"Oh, yes, it damned well is! When my wife intervenes in your sordid little quarrels—what was she doing, carrying your letters? And what do you care, the pair of you, squabbling like ferrets in a bag while she's brought to bed at eleven weeks, and for what? For you, who can't make up your mind which one of your lovers you want? For that vicious maniac upstairs? Oh, you needn't worry, he isn't here. He's gone, to Inverness or hell. And I don't give a damn if he never comes back."

He sat staring at the carpet, with the newspapers scattered at his feet. I retrieved the gloves I had laid on the table: *you picked me up and put me down like a dirty glove*, and I shut my mind against the voice and everything in this room and this house that reminded me of it.

"I shall walk a while until Charlotte wakes. Perhaps, if you find yourself capable of behaving a little more graciously, we may talk later."

He seemed to wilt then, dissolving into self-pity.

"You don't know... you don't know what it's like... everything I touch is cursed.... And now this. I was forced into this business, I was coerced. And it was lies, all lies... and I can't support it, truly I can't—"

I tried to disengage my hands. I could not bear to be held.

"I cannot help you, James."

"Because of him?"

"I cannot intervene in your affairs. And whatever support I could give would be wholly artificial, a stopgap. Do you understand? I cannot offer you a panacea. If this is bankruptcy, nothing I can do will prevent it."

"I want to buy stock. Charlotte's father made seven thousand last year. I need seven thousand, and I intend to get it."

"What kind of stock?"

"East India Company."

"I don't think that's a very good idea."

He regarded me with contempt.

"Why not? What do you know about it?"

"The dividends are always a cause for complaint among the subscribers, or so they were when I was in England."

"Things change. I have it on the best authority— why should Hardy lie?"

Because he was a liar by nature, I thought; he was a boastful, swaggering, pompous ass, who might have made seven or seventy and added the noughts to impress the gullible. I had not liked him during our brief acquaintance; and Mordaunt, a shrewd investor, had never touched East India Company stock.

He still held my fingers tightly entwined in his. As if it fascinated him, he began to twist the ring on my right hand.

"I have mortgaged my soul," he said. "I don't expect you to understand."

He remained there, half seated, half kneeling, with the newspapers underfoot and his lashes down on his cheek: the sunlight streamed through the glass and his resemblance to his father haunted me. I said nothing, and neither moved nor took my hand away: I could never tell him how well I understood, but, by my silence, he knew.

The newspapers and periodicals which had been brought from Edinburgh were more than eight months out of date. The portents of war they carried were no less obvious for being communicated with such inevitable leisure.

The English newspapers bore the obligatory stamp, which had long been required by law and was affixed to every pamphlet, journal, legal document, magazine or pack of playing cards. The institution of a similar tax in the Americas as of November first, 1765, as a means of raising revenue from colonies which had already provided some two million pounds towards the cost of the Seven Years' War, had provoked organized rioting, looting of government property and premises and vicious attacks on government and customs officials. For the first time, to a populace already disquieted by trade restrictions and a more efficient pursuit of smugglers which offended those colonists who regarded evasion of duty as a legitimate and profitable business, the words "rebellion" and "liberty" became synonymous. In the same year another Act of Parliament enabling the army to billet soldiers in public buildings, taverns, inns and uninhabited barns, and requiring civilians to afford them victuals, kindling and other necessities of life, was regarded not as a measure designed to protect the persons and properties of citizens in increasingly disorderly towns, but as yet another subversive effort by the Crown to force and enforce unpalatable legislation upon an unwilling public. That there should be no taxation except as devised, drafted and democratically agreed upon in their own colonial legislatures, by their own elected representatives, was held to be the inalienable right of every freeborn Englishman. A Parliament wherein they were not represented and which was increasingly regarded as foreign and disaffected was not, it was thought, entitled to levy taxes upon its colonies.

The agitators and pamphleteers found an unlikely champion in William Pitt, now the Earl of Chatham, who campaigned throughout the following year for the abolition of the offending acts. Perhaps perceiving that an ally little understood and less attended to had begun its drift into a chain of events which would culminate in a calamity far greater than the still rankling Seven Years' War, he spoke passionately and presciently in Parliament in defense of Britain's intransigent child.

"A great deal has been said without doors of the power, of the strength, of America. It is a topic that ought to be cautiously meddled with. In a good cause... the force of this country can crush America to atoms. But America, if she fell, would fall like the strong man. She would embrace the pillars of the state, and pull down the constitution along with her... is this your boasted peace? Not to sheathe the sword in the scabbard, but to sheathe it in the bowels of your countrymen? Will you quarrel with yourselves, when the whole house of Bourbon is united against you?

"The Stamp Act should be repealed, absolutely, totally and immediately... At the same time let the sovereign authority of this country be asserted in as strong terms as can be devised... we may bind their trade, confine their manufactures, and exercise every power whatsoever-- except that of taking their money out of their pockets without their consent."

The Stamp Act was repealed. In America mobs shouted "Pitt and Liberty" in gratitude for this assertion of their right as Englishmen not to be taxed without due representation in Parliament, and even more felicitously, "George, Pitt and Liberty," but in the main the Act, the anger its initiation had provoked and the jubilation when it was repealed, were no more than a source of passing interest or irritation in England— 1766 had proved a disastrous year, with harvest failures, food shortages and rioting at home, and when new taxation measures were imposed upon the colonies which included duties on glass, lead, tea, salt and other staples, the renewed outrage in America was discounted as mere reactionary fervour, and disregarded.

Once again in the colonies the hated Townshend Acts provoked rioting, mass refusal to purchase British goods, more abuse of customs officers to the extent that the army's assistance and protection were requested and two regiments, the 14th and the 29th, were quartered in Boston alone; and inflammatory pamphlets protested against everything from the billeting of troops upon the populace to the powers of colonial government officials. There were no more cries of "Pitt and Liberty" and no warmth toward monarch or mother country. The King had suffered the first in a series of debilitating illnesses which would climax in madness, and Pitt had suffered a complete physical and mental breakdown, and could only be roused from his delusions and melancholia by what Walpole called a therapeutic attack of "gout, and the smell of war". France had seized Corsica, reinforcing her position in the Mediterranean, and was rapidly rebuilding a fleet shattered in the Seven Years' War; although this newly belligerent stance gave cause for alarm in Parliament, an envoy was dispatched to Paris to ensure that diplomacy prevailed. And other threatening behaviour by Spain, in forcibly expelling the British from their station at Port Egmont in the Falkland Islands, seemed to indicate that peace, for the world as for myself, had been but a resting place, an illusion.

So the shadows were lengthening, and as the situation in America deteriorated still further these two old adversaries, the Bourbon powers, considered how to turn the most recent, ominous developments to an advantage which would, as always, lie in intervention.

On Monday March the fifth in this year of 1770, on a snowy night in Boston, local passions, running high, exploded into violence. Some thirty or forty bully-boy labourers, apprentices and tradesmen had baited and assaulted thirteen soldiers of the 29th regiment, who fired a scattered volley in self-defense. Three of the mob were killed outright, two others later died of wounds. The soldiers were charged with murder. Their officer, a captain named Preston, and eleven of his men were acquitted; two private soldiers were found guilty of manslaughter and branded. All were condemned as murderers in the deluge of inflammatory broadsides and engravings which followed, and long after the drums of the 29th had ceased to beat in the streets of Boston, radical pamphleteers heard the "innocent blood" crying from the cobbles in front of the Customs House, and exhorted a people ever more disposed and eager to avenge it.

In April, three years after their institution, the Townshend Acts were repealed, leaving only an insignificant tax on tea to generate revenue. The King, recovered and perhaps endowed with the prescience of his ailing chief minister, called this "a fatal compliance".

So, as on a summer's afternoon, no one noticed the darkness on the horizon, until like a storm rising suddenly from the west it was upon us, and its vast, threatening clouds overwhelmed us, and the light was blotted out.

A party of twelve arrived from Edinburgh in July and remained until the end of September. It consisted of Charlotte's sisters Henrietta and Grizel and their spouses, a merchant and a petty laird of Perthshire, her brother William and his wife, my namesake, her youngest sister Mary, who was only fourteen, and a coterie of children and servants. They brought with them their own cook and bed linen, an insult to Ardsian's hospitality of which James seemed blissfully unaware.

Throughout the summer I was invited to join them, walking, riding, sketching, fishing, for music, meals or conversation: the women remembered me and penned me persuasive letters. I found excuses excruciatingly painful, and finally exhausted them. To have continued to demur would have offended Charlotte so deeply that I would have lost her friendship.

There was much to disquiet me. The house was thronged with too many people, and the infusion of the novel was too strong, as though strangers had exploded into the monastic peace of some isolated retreat. I found the women shallow and worldly, and their concerns and conceits insignificant. James, meanwhile, was bored and restive when the centre of attention was diverted: too much the snob to engage in a liaison below stairs, he was amusing himself with Charlotte's sister-in-law Margaret, while a compliant William introduced himself to more bucolic pleasures, and doors opened and closed with a furtive regularity throughout my troubled nights. James knew that I knew, he had always been transparent to me, and when I surprised him one afternoon emerging dishevelled from one of his places of assignation while a giggling Margaret hurried away in the other direction, he merely dropped me a lewd wink. Later, on a pretext of kissing me good-night, he whispered into my ear, "There's no need to look so crabbit, sweet. You know where to find your cockerel."

The house haunted me, made oppressive by Malcolm's presence. That we should meet was inevitable, and yet we did not meet. If he came or went, I never knew; I could only anticipate; and found myself paralyzed by shadows, a movement, a step which was Boyd or Paterson, one of the husbands, or James himself, whose game this was, and whose pleasure in sexual intrigue was heightened by these crude attempts to exploit what he recognized was a violent severing of relations between Malcolm and myself.

I remained another day, watching the children tease the cat until it hid, and ridicule and mimic the Gaelic-speaking servants; the women walked on the moors in their thin town shoes and mixed their paints with peat-stained water to produce genteel washes of this pitiless country, and a spaniel, surprising basking adders, died convulsively in its mistress's arms while the rest of us distracted the children. The men, exuberantly drunk, shot at eagles in the sun and mist and returned in the evening hung about with trophies: forty-two moorhens, fifteen partridges, a brace of snipe, three magpies and twenty-seven trout. Vignettes of such casual cruelty formed and faded throughout the days, and every day they ate and drank and played and hunted and disported themselves so carelessly among a people too squalid for quaintness and too grotesquely poor for grandeur was an ebbing tide in those ledgers I had seen in the greyness of a winter's morning; and when they had returned to the comforts of Edinburgh the thin rain which had fallen on them would fall still more coldly upon us, and the cool wind that fanned a powdered cheek in August would freeze our living flesh in December.

I passed another night in the dark red room. The white lilies with which Charlotte had filled it exuded a perfume of nauseating sweetness, and in my dreams I was held and raped until I thought my mind would burst. I woke screaming: the screams were inaudible cries, and my hands and nails and the bed linen were stained with menstrual blood. And in the bed which had sheltered him in his childhood, where he had wept, I wept, until morning came and delivered me from the night's shadows, and his memory.

On the first of October they closed the house for the winter and went with their guests to Edinburgh. I was invited by cursory note to accompany them; I sensed that my refusal disappointed no one.

I began to see more of George Cameron, who previously had avoided me and all female society. He had taught only briefly following his accident— how bitter a euphemism that had become, not only for him but for me— before the land's demands for labour had robbed him of pupils; nor, in these closing weeks of autumn, had he yet recalled them. So he sketched and drank to fill the time, and occasionally I met him, coming down in the early twilight from the outfields where he had sat for hours with pencils and bottle: he no longer so obviously shunned conversation, or averted his face when we spoke. I could not be unaware of the dissipation in which he had passed the summer and I was pleased that he was once more interested in exercising his considerable talent, until I saw what he had produced. Strange, cruel, sarcastic drawings, caricatures of his family and friends, crude cartoons of village life: death and burial, a marriage, a christening, himself, a grotesque in his dirty little schoolroom, applying the taws to a naked backside. They were all brusquely labelled, "A Highland Calendar", and tied into a pair of marbled covers, and he showed them to me one afternoon, watching with an enigmatic smile as I leafed through them.

"You don't care for them."

"I thought you capable of better things. This is prostitution."

He took them from me negligently, and tossed them onto the table. We were in the school, with the same gritty floor underfoot, the same gouged and splintered benches, the same odour of mildew staining the stale air. On a board dully painted black and propped on a trestle against the wall a graceful hand had inscribed in English, "The fear of the Lord is the beginning of wisdom." Nothing else had been written there for months. On the table, jarred by his careless disposal of his sketches, was a tureen of hough which I had brought: he was notoriously indifferent to food and seldom ate unless it was supplied to him. He was similarly careless of his person. Since his disfigurement he had lost what little interest he had had in his appearance, and his untidy clothes, infrequently laundered, hung upon a ramshackle frame as though they had been thrown there.

He was still watching me with those yellowish eyes; the low sun penetrated the dimness, throwing his scars into relief. He pushed open the door of his living quarters, which, like the school, were singularly slovenly and incommodious.

"If you don't like those, tell me what you think of these."

He had reserved his most malicious talent for this, a series of self-portraits pinned to the damp plaster walls. One, entitled "The Coxcomb", featured himself, crudely naked, hiding his face behind a fan.

"I thought they had a certain verity. You admire truth, don't you?"

"Is this truth or self-indulgence?"

"I prefer to think of them as part of a process. I am infirm of purpose, my dear, a natural coward. And one day I may want to avenge myself. These will strengthen my hand." There was a pause. "What do you want me to do, for Christ's sake? Should I practise Christian virtue and turn the other cheek?"

Then he muttered an apology and sat on the unmade bed and covered his face. I watched him from the doorway, unable to cross this or any other threshold and comfort him, unable to leave him. Eventually he whispered, "I don't know what to do. God help me, I even pray," and wiped his eyes with his sleeve: the left cheek, hideously scarred, was running with tears. "Why should I have suffered this? Why should God who made me ugly choose to make me uglier still?"

"God had nothing to do with it," and he began to sob. I left the doorway and knelt on the filthy floor.

"No, don't touch me. You never wanted to before."

I put my arms around him: his body remained rigid. He seemed frail, insubstantial, his body was unfamiliar, his hair, uncertainly caressed, was not Malcolm's rough, clean hair.

"I love you, Margaret."

"Don't, for God's sake."

"I had to tell you. You knew."

"I've had enough of love. I don't want yours."

"And you could never thole an ugly man, could you? He aimed well, the bastard," and then, with a painful hesitation, "You love him."

"No. I never loved him."

"Why did you go with him then, when you knew I would have loved you?"

Then he put my hands gently away, somehow contriving to withdraw from me while remaining in the same position, his head bent, his expression veiled, his feet in their down-at-heel shoes neatly placed together on the floor.

"I used to watch you coming back, when you had been with him. I saw you with the eyes of love... with my heart. I always knew." He blinked, staring at the floor. "I wondered what he did to you, to make you break with him."

Revulsion and sickness touched me and passed, leaving their familiar stain.

"We quarrelled."

He was the cause and he knew it, as surely as I was responsible for him.

He said, "I want to kill him. But, God help me, I haven't the strength."

He remained that way for a long time, staring at the floor, and his fingers held mine, unresisting, in a cold embrace that reminded me of no one.

It was a dark year, with mortality in the yellowing leaves and in my own morbid thoughts, in the uncertain harvest and the dreaded prospect of winter. Money was scarce: the price of beef fell again, and the trysts at Falkirk were bitterly unprofitable. And then, in November, the arrival of plague from Prussia off the west coast of Scotland prompted quarantines of ships and islands, and savage Orders in Council to the effect that "any master of Vessels, or any of her Crew refusing, or neglecting to repair with all convenient speed to their Stations appointed for them performing their respective Quarantines, shall be judged guilty of Fellony; and shall suffer Death as a fellon, without Benefits of Clergy." An itinerant tailor on his way to Glenmoriston brought this information, and instilled such a primitive fear of contagion in the village that for his own safety he cut short his visit, and left under cover of darkness.

He had carried with him, also, old news of America, which had stagnated in the seaports since the quarantine. The situation inspired an ever deeper pessimism. The world drifted indifferently toward war.

There was no hope, no peace from memory, no possibility of anything: no future I could contemplate, no past I could bear to remember. War threatened, and would surely touch Mordaunt; winter was now synonymous with hunger, and my health lacked the resilience of youth. I was twenty-five years old, a spinster of dubious reputation with no prospect of honourable marriage or, now, of happiness.

I have youth, and a little beauty.

But they would soon be gone.

I had nothing, I could hope for nothing, nothing was certain except death, and death in those dark months seemed very near: by disease, exhaustion, famine, by the breaking of my heart.

With the world, I drifted toward disaster. I knew that what I considered was a mistake, moral and physical, and yet I undertook it, out of pity, in defeat and despair and loneliness. I came to regard it with a sense of inevitability, as a natural progression. I gave it nothing but myself, in a manner I now see was sacrificial: perhaps to make amends, perhaps because there no longer seemed any reason for refusal, or reason or purpose in anything.

If Charlotte had been at Ardsian I would have gone to her, unburdened my troubled mind and told her what had happened and was about to happen in consequence, and implored her, with her stolid frankness, to stop me. But there was no Charlotte, no loving woman's counsel: only a cold half-hour in the grey December light kneeling by Ewen's grave, where he who had always given me comfort could give me nothing now, and on the winter-bitten ground a hand I knew had recently laid one last, decaying rose.

I gave my virginity to George Cameron in the last hours of Thursday, December thirteenth, when wind and snow held MacNeil in Glen Sian five miles away and duty called my aunt, with inviolable calm, into the white wastes of the night. I prepared myself, poor fool, like a bride, washed and perfumed in secret places; fought the wind and followed the light through the snow to the school and found him, unkempt and smelling of whisky, construing Latin amid the remnants of a half-eaten meal on the table that served him as both study and kitchen.

There was little pretense of conversation. He induced me to perform fellatio, and penetrated me; he did not sense that I had no experience of intercourse, and though bitterness and resentment should have been quieted by time, I never forgave his comment in the course of his crude exertions that I was as tight as a nun's cunt.

There were no tears: they would not come. There were only images, fragmented and blurring, and a memory of passion so profound that it was the sun to this smoking flame: it was a crucible, a god's love, incandescent and intolerant, and it would suffer no rival, and it would never release me.

The night and the shame faded into a pale unreality: only the snow remained.

There are no versions of what followed which are easy for me, no terms with which to convey the absoluteness of my physical isolation. Life was concentrated upon the microcosm of Glen Mor, beyond which, in the blinding wastes, nothing moved but hissing snow. Frosted glass, frozen water, a fetid gloom in an airless household, the taciturn silence of the inhabitants, who spoke only from necessity, and never touched except inadvertently and with an epilogue of apology. There were no letters, there was no news, there was no communication except among the closest neighbours; movement was restricted to the house and the path of trodden snow to the privy or, occasionally, the school. Those I loved were absent, dead or unaware, because I chose that they should remain unaware, of my guilt and desperation. I was alone; I was vulnerable; my strength failed, and in that momentary weakness of will he pressed the issue further.

He could be clever, he could be charming, he could be amusing, and in that grim and lightless winter he did amuse me. He offered mental stimulation: he was my intellectual equal, which could not be said of most men in Glen Sian. And he could be persuasive, when the object— myself— promised sufficient recompense for his persistence.

I struggled, convinced of my own failures, my inability to give or receive sexual love. He visited more frequently, the only face I saw in those weeks unrelated to me by blood. Sometimes he came sanctioned by MacNeil, whose complicity I suspected; sometimes he arrived unexpectedly, and sat by the fire with his rag-stuffed shoes placed neatly together, following my movements around the room. Sometimes he brought books for me, sometimes he waited in the school when I was sent there on increasingly unwilling errands. Waiting, always waiting with the smile, the chaste kiss, the persuasive voice affording me vignettes of my future without him, coloured with a painter's skill and touching so accurately upon my most secret fears that I must on some occasion have confided them to him. And in the claustrophobic blackness of my nights came the memory of Malcolm, with whom sexual congress had not been this hurried, dirty act but a consummation essential and elemental as flame. And there would be nothing else: I would never know it again, and I could judge no other man and no other relationship by an obsession which had so scarred me.

We had intercourse again on the last Saturday night in December, after appearing briefly at a local wedding and leaving, separately and unremarked, to meet at the unlighted school. The act was painful and disgusting, conducted in a smothering darkness and rendered obscene by his clumsy attempt at withdrawal; when I left him he returned to the wedding. On the last occasion, he watched the New Year's shinty match through a cleared patch of icy window while guiding my hands and my lips. The shouts and hilarity of the game pursued me as far as the stubbled wastes of the outfield, where I rinsed my mouth with snow and sat on a drystone wall until the shouts died down with the coming of night and my numbed hands and feet forced me back to my father's house.

He considered himself my lover, with indisputable rights of possession and access, and nothing would induce me to subject myself to that degradation again. He flung his final insult at me: that if I could not learn to accept male attention with better grace I was unnatural, and probably sapphic. By this time I had passed the point of vulnerability to such attacks, and my mind, sickened by a new conviction, was approaching a greater crisis. Neither he nor any one could help or harm me now.

My menses were late. I had been due at the end of December. As January drew to a close without blood, I knew I was with child.

Memories of a winter afternoon. Nothing moves but the snakes of snow, twisting like sand across a desert, white on whitening ice.

The ice cracks; my courage falters. And descending night, which is not darkness but snow, brings a softer prospect of death.

Then, confusion. The remembering mind fails. I was alive, who had sought death; I was lost and had been found, by some one who had brought me here, to this unknown place, and laid me carefully under these rough coverings, and forced raw spirit down my throat; the blankets were damp where I had regurgitated much of it.

The firelight dimmed. A hand laid itself on my forehead, and some one spoke in a slow deep voice, heavily sibilant. Understanding eluded me. The hand withdrew, leaving an impression of gentleness. I drifted in the sleep of exhaustion.

And dreamed, in fragments of the past, dreamed of Malcolm with unbearable poignancy and woke with tears on my face: strange that, in this shadowed hour, I could forgive his transgressions but not mine against him. It was lighter, quieter, the wind had dropped, the flakes spiralling through the smoke-hole in the roof had settled on my coverings. The fire was very low, burning among stones, and a woman was watching me through the smoke. God knew what she thought of me, or saw in my face— some taint of the unspeakable days and nights which had preceded this, or the nightmare of renewed consciousness. Perhaps she had discovered me near the ice: perhaps I had told her what I intended. Perhaps she knew me. I sensed that I should have known her.

She spoke to me, and although I could not respond I understood, as we understand the incomprehensible in dreams, that I was safe, it was not yet morning, I was to sleep again.

I was safe but not yet saved, and morning would come inevitably, presenting me with the same grim triptych. Confession, abortion, marriage to a penniless lout worth a shilling a quarter per annum; and disgrace and exposure would take my life as surely as suicide. So for this moment, the darkness and the pretense of sleep… the congestion in my lungs suggested illness to follow, and the tisanes, the douches, the blunt instruments still awaited me at the end of this long dark mile. The faintest light showed at tiny windows stuffed with peat: the blankets, unfolding from obscurity, became blue, and woven with the bird's eye pattern common in the Highlands; the shape in the corner was a cupboard of planks and wickerwork; the shape on the wall was a crucifix. The woman, plastering oatcakes on a blackened baking stone, glanced up without expression. I remained where I was, feigning sleep until the restive movements of cattle in the adjoining byre and my own hunger roused me.

Morning then, in an unknown place, with an unknown companion who had given me my life.

She brought me my boots and stockings, and knelt to hold them for me. She might have been any age, fifty, forty: she might have been any Gaelic woman, with the fair skin of the Celt seamed by labour and weather and bouts of malnutrition. Her hands were small and venous, without rings; she wore no ornament or jewellery, not even the flat brass or silver brooch favoured by Highland women, nothing to indicate, except by her poverty, her status as individual or tenant.

She gazed at me, without smiling and without deference; her eyes were beautiful, the colour of still water in September. Cool eyes, reflecting nothing, like water reflecting sky. I might imagine their hostility or their warmth, but the reflection concealed all.

She offered me water in a jug and a place to relieve myself, then we ate together, squatting on the bare earth with the eye-searing haze and heat of the fire in our faces. She gave me porridge, and oatcakes scorched from the stone, and milk still steaming from the cow, and although she glanced at me from time to time she made no further attempt at conversation; she believed, apparently, that I spoke no Gaelic, for which I was grateful.

When we had eaten she took me to the door, and opened it upon a pristine world to point my direction to me. There was no need; I knew where I was. The shoulder of Riabhach, had been curtained with rain on that other occasion, and the rain had flung sullen drops into my face like unshed tears for Malcolm's children, who were buried here beneath this untrodden snow. Nothing else, no suggestion of his presence, no physical evidence of him: only the woman standing beside me breathing whitely of the bitter morning air, who had been Malcolm's whore for the past dozen years, and who knew me only as a jealous poison in the blood, as I had known her.

What was she? Older, more primitive, less remarkable than I could ever have imagined her, a compliant prostitute or a submissive victim, used and discarded as men discard whores— what was she to him? What had she given him that I could not give, what was she still to him? What did she know of me: what had he told her, what would she tell him? That I had spoken his name in the night and wept with regret and grief, that even now, with my recognition of her, he who had been so severely absent from this place was now suddenly manifest?

She knew, and had the grace to look away, averting those inexpressive eyes which now, for me, reflected his nakedness and the unbearable secrets of their intimacy.

She was his lover: she was himself. What was bred in the bone was bred into both of them, the peasant's harsh resilience, and although he would never acknowledge her she was of the self-same earth as he. She had not my delusions, my useless refinements, my anguished dedication to a graceful past: she was a whore but she was a more honest woman than I, and a more suitable wife for him than I would have ever been.

The snow, touched with beauty, was still drifting in the sun; she unknotted the shawl she had been wearing throughout the night. The logic of this was plain. I had had a shawl; it was now lost; the snow was settling on my hair. I refused it. She ignored me and wrapped me in it as if I were a child, draping the folds over my head and shoulders. It was of fine, combed, undyed wool, an indefinite greyish black like that hour of shadows, neither night nor morning, through which she had watched me, and for all its plainness it was a valuable garment. I would return it as soon as it was possible to meet her with equity, when memory and jealousy had released me.

She was watching me again, with those eyes the colour of summer. There was nothing I could give her, either now or later, except my thanks, and she received them with courtesy and the conventional response, Is e do bheatha: literally, It is your life.

I never knew for whose sake, hers or mine or his, she had given it to me.

I woke in my own bed, with clear twilight beyond the window. Some one was sitting near me but it might have been a thousand miles, so vast and unbreachable was the gap between my hand and his, my fears and the protection he could offer me. My father.

The strain and sleeplessness had not left his face although he had scraped the white stubble from it, and combed his disordered hair since meeting me in the blown and drifting snow, after a night searching for me with others on foot and on garrons until the weather had driven them back, only to resume their search at dawn on this Sunday morning.

And now, evening. After excuses and explanations and recriminations far milder than I had any right to expect, this silent vigil, which might have proceeded from love had he ever been guilty of that emotion. And yet... when my strength had failed, it had been my father who had carried me.

There had never been a silence so difficult to break, so full of unasked and unanswerable questions.

Unexpectedly he said, "I saw your mother's face while you were sleeping. I was... taken by surprise."

Thou art thy mother's glass, and she in thee/ Calls back the lovely April of her prime.... By my present age she had been dead six years. What unlived life did he see in me, what resemblance between her face and mine?

"Am I very like her?"

"No. Not waking. Her nature was very different from yours—" Then he paused, as if upon some painful reflection. "Perhaps— not very different. She was young when she married me, and when she came to know me—" Another hesitation. "She was dutiful. Nothing more."

Nothing more. Only the implicit admission of his failure as a lover and a husband. He said, "We never knew one another as we should, any more than you and I," then the glacial eyes hooded themselves and he lapsed once more into silence and uneasy memory.

He was now in his middle fifties. Had my mother lived she would have been forty-four. I would never know the circumstances of their meeting, or where or when they had been married, where on Gigha he had been born and why he had forsaken that desolation for this: those were his secrets, and he did not consider it necessary to share them with me. Perhaps he never would, any more than he would ever divulge the nature of his estrangement with my mother or the guilt and frustration of the intervening years, of which, with not inconsiderable success, he had attempted to obliterate all recollection. His hair was streaked with iron grey, his long, clever, elegant face deeply lined with dissipation and what I now recognized as an incurable unhappiness. He had never been heard to phrase an endearment; he had never in all the years of my tenure in his house touched me, except to strike me on that infamous occasion, after which I had fled to Ewen. So much grief, so much lost never to be regained or restored, and he had lost as much as I. Perhaps he had lost more.

When he spoke again it was with the same precision, his beautiful voice still tinged, like a stone with the sea's salt, with a Hebridean accent.

"I know you have been troubled of late, more so than usual. And that a connection of which I disapproved has been broken." Any other man would have given it a twist of salaciousness, but he was not any other man. "Is he the cause of this reckless behaviour?"

And, surprisingly, I was able to answer in the same explicit language. We would never again converse with such unflinching honesty.

"I loved him. It ended. Perhaps grief is cumulative."

"I thought your affections were centred upon George Cameron."

"No."

"Good. He is unworthy of you." He unclasped his long hands and drew up his long thin legs in their shabby black stockings, and, only for the second time, gazed at me directly. "As to that other business— I hope that time will show you, it was for the best."

There was neither condemnation nor benevolence in his voice: my folly had been acknowledged and dismissed; no further judgment would be pronounced. He stood a moment longer with the candlelight at his back, as though he had forgotten something, or something remained to be done; but the moment passed and the words remained unspoken. He had given what he could, and was incapable of more. That I must accept, and could accept.

He said curtly, "I thank God for your safety," and with an odd, dignified little inclination of the head, left me.

It was enough.

The pain came later, bringing blood. I lay listening to the wind and the silence, my mind rinsed and hollow and fragile and blown like an eggshell down the waste of years, which were mine now, and would be mine. I was free— free— and all the years were empty.

On Monday the twenty-second of April I rode up to Ardsian to visit James and Charlotte, who had returned the previous week. James received me in the morning room and sent for coffee for me: he was alone. Charlotte had remained in Edinburgh, where she would stay until the roads improved. He said, staring absently at the lowering sky, "I thought that was the best thing, given the circumstances."

"What are 'the circumstances'?"

"Charlotte is ill. She was ill when she was a child, she was ill when she married me, and she's been ill ever since. And I was advised by various leeches in Edinburgh, all clutching fistfuls of Hardy's money, that it would be unwise for her to bear any more children— so you see where that leaves poor Jamie. In the lurch, as always."

The coffee came; and on the terrace beyond the white-painted windows a gardener, shambling and purposeless, began to sweep the dead dry leaves which had lain there, ignored, throughout the winter.

"Shall I pour?"

I heard him sigh, then he leaned forward and turned up the lamp. The same lamp, the same tray, the same blue and gilt cups, the same fair, waving hair: almost, in this light, the same face, maturing now into a blurred copy of his father's.

He said, "Strangely enough, I care. Oh, not for the children— I don't give a damn for the place after I'm dead. I'll leave it to my cousin; let him fight the other jackals in the family for it. That was how it came to us in the first place." He stirred aimlessly until the sound grated on my nerves. "I... care for Charlotte. I don't expect you to understand. I... came to love her." He seemed surprised. "And God knows why, she loves me. I didn't marry her for love— one doesn't. You know that. It... happened. And I can't bear the prospect, having only just found her."

He sat staring unseeingly at the cup, his face faintly illuminated by the candles: a cameo, lifelike and yet lifeless. The dark day darkened further, enclosed by these dark blue walls, the blue flame of the spirit lamp fluttered. A bowl of narcissi on the table, breathing their heavy perfume: myself (such a guy, my mind whispered cruelly) sitting across the patterned carpet from him, the polite nonsense of the coffee ritual punctuated by the dry sweep of the broom on the terrace and the fragment of an incongruously cheerful song, which came and went until the rain, suddenly falling, drove the gardener away. Hail, wind and darkness... the northern spring offering its welcome.

"I don't know why you didn't come with us," he said.

"I have no great love for Edinburgh."

"Nor I, after this." Rain swept the terrace: the singer and the song had gone. He said slowly, "I wanted to come home. I wanted to think. I mean, I want her here with me, but not yet. I... wanted to be alone. I wanted peace. I thought I could find it here. I think I can." A little smile. "Maybe I've become a contemplative like my father. Poor Papa... one can't help but see the divine hand in this, as if God had a sense of humour."

He rested his elbows on the arms of the chair and linked his fingers lightly, gazing at me. He still wore Ewen's signet ring on a hand which had become thinner, and less attractive.

"I found your friend in the usual vile temper, needless to say. I gather he had a not particularly happy or prosperous winter."

"I am not in a position to know. I keep myself to myself."

He said, with a flash of the old spiteful James, "Don't delude yourself that it agrees with you."

"I didn't. But it was kind of you to remind me," and he smiled for the first time, and taking my cold hand in his colder ones, kissed it with affection.

"I have missed your bracing company."

"And I have missed you, James."

"Don't concern yourself too much over this business of Charlotte, will you? She's perfectly well, or was so when I left her— in fact, a damned sight bonnier than you."

Later he stood in the darkened hall, offering me a packet of Charlotte's letters and holding my hand again, talking inconsequentially above the sound of the rain to delay me, as though, despite the hard new maturity in his face, he were still that golden child, and no candle lit his night.

I remember the terror of that blowing darkness, where the wind, which had slammed me against a wall at Ardsian, became my living enemy, and tried to throw me from the horse, and blinded me with rain. I fought him, forcing him to go on while he shied at the noise and the tearing trees and the narrowness of the track: I was alone in the rain and darkness, and then I was not alone. Malcolm was waiting for me. A moment later I recognized it for the coincidence it was, but the pain and terror of my memories had not diminished, and I could not control my irrational panic. Nor could I move, except to pull a rain-soaked fold over my face; I shut my eyes against the rain and the force of the wind, willing him to leave me. When I opened them he was still there, motionless, blurring in the dimness, then slowly he withdrew, giving me the right of way.

I passed him, seeing nothing of him: he saw nothing of me but my eyes. There was nothing, nothing in my path, only blindness and darkness, the malevolence of the wind, a thrashing violence in the trees.

"Jesus Christ, how many more years must I suffer?"

Even the anger and profanity, even the bitterness, even, when it came, his hand closing on my rein and my own inability to prevent it: all so familiar. So inevitable.

His knee was almost touching mine, although I thought afterwards that he had taken some care to avoid it; the rain streaming from his boot in the stirrup and the sleeve of the old caped greatcoat, the ungloved hand controlling the rein... that much I saw of him, nothing more. The rain was blowing into my eyes, and I refused to look at him.

His hand was uninsistent, no more than a token detention which a word or gesture on my part would have ended: it neither touched nor attempted to touch mine. He said, very quietly, "How many years must this go on? How much punishment is enough?" and in the silence a roaring gust passed overhead. The horse, shying beneath me, dragged away, breaking the contact, and back again, throwing my knee against his. "Margaret, look at me. I have been in hell—" and I stared up into the blowing rain, into his eyes.

"How much was enough for you? How did you determine the degree of *my* punishment— until it gave you satisfaction?"

Nothing changed in his face; nothing had changed, in the nineteen months since we had been lovers, in the year which had so ravaged me, leaving

419

him untouched. But he was still vulnerable: something in the light, impassive eyes told me I had hurt him.

"I hope this gives you an equal measure." There was a brief, final silence, torn by the wind. "And if you have no consideration for your own neck, at least get your horse to shelter. There's worse than this coming, and soon."

There is nothing worse than this.

He had kneed his horse away as if to conclude our conversation. He came up beside me again.

"What did you say to me?"

"I said, there is nothing worse than this. Can you imagine anything worse?"

He answered but it was thrown away by the wind, and his left hand came out to take my bridle; my horse jibbed and flung up his head and I brought him under control with difficulty. He spoke again, more urgently, and I knew that what he had been saying was, "Come with me." I said, "No," and he shouted at me over the wind, then something crashed down near us and I followed him.

Remembered slates, streaming rain, remembered stones underfoot; the gate, kicked open from the saddle, blowing wide to receive me; I dismounted without his assistance, nor did he offer it to me. The door was on the latch, the fire banked, the silence, after the tumult outside, profound. I stood waiting for him a long time, or so it seemed, knocked breathless by the wind and dripping rain onto the polished floor. The room was unchanged: the same brass candlesticks, the pot of paper spills, the oiled fowling piece, the absence of any ornament or personal possession, as though he were merely a tenant here, uncertain of his lease. And my own brief sojourn, expressed only in a blue and white jug filled with flowers on my visits and kept between those candlesticks, might never have been.

He came in. The silence was so intense that I knew he had stood a moment, as I had done, with the rain streaming from his clothing; then he removed his greatcoat.

I said, "What have you done with the jug?"

A click, and the sound of some heavy object being placed gently on the table, followed by an identical pair of sounds: his pistols, taken off the half cock.

"I broke it. Accidentally, as it happens."

"I daresay that, too, gave you a certain satisfaction."

Another, sharper sound: the knife he carried in his boot, less gently discarded and now also on the kitchen table.

"If I'd wanted such a childish diversion I would have broken it deliberately." Then, "Will you do me the honour of sitting, or is that too much to ask?"

I sat on the seise and listened to his movements and the clink of glass; it came within the periphery of my vision and waited to be acknowledged. His hand was so close that its scars would have been clearly visible had I focused my eyes upon it: the old white scar of the knife across his knuckles, the razor's scar from fingertip to wrist. I could not touch him, and I could not bear his touch.

His fingers moved slightly; I saw the amber of the spirit. He said, "Don't be a damned fool. What do you take me for?" and the glass came into my hand; his withdrew, and he walked away to the other side of the fireplace and stood there.

"I don't know what to take you for. The devil sometimes, I think."

Silence, and in that silence, which I had thought unchanged, a new intrusion. In this house where time, the enemy of lovers, had had no measure, a clock was ticking: time was, and lovers were no more. There was only this oppressive silence, divided into endless seconds and minutes of hopelessness.

He said, still with that gentleness I had always thought unnatural, "I must come and see to the fire. If you will permit me."

I sensed the faintest hesitation, as though the movement caused him pain: only my eyes would have recognized it once, and recognized it still. He remained there, with the firelight burnishing that hard, hawkish profile, then he turned his head and caught my eyes upon him; the force of his gaze was physically shocking.

"Will you not take off that wet thing and let me dry it?"

"I shall not be here much longer. I will not presume upon your hospitality."

"Abuse me if you must, but for Christ's sake don't insult me."

"What do you want of me, Malcolm?" and something, perhaps my use of his name, brought his eyes to mine again, not with hope or surprise or gratitude or suspicion, only an impenetrable calm.

"Peace. I don't ask for your forgiveness, I never expected it. But I thought that— if we met— if we could speak once, like this, I would be at peace. I can never close my eyes without seeing your face." Then he said with the old scorpion's sting of sarcasm, "Which is no more than I deserve," and rose, this time with effort.

He sat opposite me and straightened the offending knee, an habitual gesture. The leg was encased in doeskin, the boot of polished Spanish leather, the coat unlaced, of some blackish material with black buttons. The clothes, like the boots, were old, and expensive, and functional, and well remembered; I had never seen him wear anything new. His hair needed cutting badly, something he did himself; and the firelight, thrown across that face I had thought unaltered by the last, lost year, had shown me strands of white.

He said, quite without humour, "Do you see that I am harmless?"

"You are anything but that."

He smiled, and youth came briefly to his face, and with it something indefinable, which I had loved.

"You remind me of the first night you came here, all eyes and uncertainty." The smile was gone, and the illusion of youth. "Oh, take it off. Is that what you think of me?"

I unfastened the clasp and chain and laid my cloak on the seise: my habit was damp, and the unmoving air seemed cold.

"You are very thin, Margaret."

"I have been ill."

"And are you well recovered now?"

"Yes. Thank you." Another silence: his eyes were disconcerting, disturbing. "I see that your knee has not improved."

If this venture upon familiarity surprised him he gave no sign; he accepted it, as though it were a polite progression in the conversation of people of long acquaintance, once friends, but lately strangers.

"I ignore it. That usually serves."

"Does your business prosper?"

"Nothing prospers with me of late, as I am sure James will have told you— you saw James, I take it?"

"Yes."

"My dear, there's no need to look so troubled. The opportunity presents itself… that makes it convenient all round."

No intention, then, of obeying the rules of this social game: no intentions toward me that were good, were safe, were predictable. Only this: sarcasm and innuendo, as before; everything as before.

I said, "Charlotte is ill. Did you know?" and the sardonic little smile left his face.

"How ill?"

"Her heart is diseased. James fears for her life."

His opinion of Charlotte was unknown to me, but he had never spoken of her with the contempt he reserved for James; and her acknowledgment of him as my lover had been deferential, even nervous. At length he said, "This bloody place is cursed— and my bloody tongue."

"I had to tell you." He said nothing, staring into the fire. "I could have told you anything once. I wanted to tell you this."

"Have you been so much alone, poor Margaret? Did you find no other comfort?"

"No. Although I know you did."

"Yes, that's only fair. You owe me an injury, don't you?"

"More than one, I think."

"Will you speak of it? Or must it always remain vile and unmentionable, like all my other little sins?"

"You said everything imaginable on that occasion, and some things I could not have imagined."

"And I remember what you said. I thought you'd learned your language from your other lover, when he took my place."

"There was no one else."

"I was told otherwise."

"It was a lie."

"Was it?"

"Yes." It had been, then.

"I believed it. I was sick. I was drunk. I went mad."

There was a long pause, which he seemed to find as intolerable as I did; I heard him rise and sensed him standing in front of the fire. When he spoke again it was with the same dispassion; perhaps it was indifference.

"Nothing in this life could have taken you from me— because I think you loved me then. Only myself— only I, myself. And the pity of it is that I have always loved you. I love you still."

It seemed very dark; it seemed we had always been here in these shadows, insubstantial and unreal; it seemed he could never stop setting one cold word upon another, like a weight of stones: intolerable, intolerable.

"I have led a hard life, and many things have been done in it, cruel things— to me, and by me— but nothing in my life has ever wounded me so much as the loss of you. Now nothing can hurt me— there is nothing more."

"My love," and he looked at me, without surprise, without suspicion, without any discernible emotion.

"It's too late for that, for you as well as me."

"What remains then?"

He said, staring into the flames, "Nothing. We say good-bye, like civilized people. It was all I wanted."

It was darker, darker: there was nothing to say. The sound of dark spring rain, as cold as winter. Darkness and light, peace and hell: an afternoon, a lifetime. There was nothing more. I had only to go.

"Let it end, Margaret." I had only to leave him. "You would never forgive me, and if I hurt you again you would turn it on me like a weapon, and we would kill everything between us. You loved me once. Let me remember it, but not like this."

It was he who touched me, my hair, my lips, my fingers, and held them: they did not resist him.

He said, "Don't do this. You trusted me. It was not for this."

"I love you."

"For God's sake, if you play with me—"

"I love you. There is nothing else."

Only the kiss, the end and the beginning. Only the shadows of rain on the glass, the cold, remembered room, the shadowed bed. At the last, he hesitated, and there was pain, and I feared it and flinched from it, and it did not leave me, but he lifted me above it, moving deeply and slowly within me until my very womb convulsed for joy. His love possessed me and filled me and lifted me, as with great wings, into ecstasy. I was Leda, ravished by joy; I was his— and his— and his— forever; I was not myself, but him.

XI

On the morning of Friday September thirteenth, 1771, the packet *Worthy* out of Falmouth and carrying passengers, stores and mail from England and from English Harbour, Antigua, stood off to await the dawn before entering the anchorage at Barbados. With the sun and on a negligible tide she anchored, and was immediately attacked by ravenous lighters and bumboats poling out from shore and hawking rum, fresh fish and fruit and bags of coarse brown sugar.

In the hour after sunrise she was clearly visible, riding above her own reflection as though painted on the shimmering sea, and providing a source of speculation if not excitement for the garrison. Standing on its promontory outside the town, this commanded a panoramic view of beach, hillside battery, anchorage and commercial shipping: island traders, vessels carrying sugar, Barbados' lifeblood, to Bristol from Speight's Town farther up the coast, a litter of tiny scavengers and fishing boats, or the familiar colours, in this alien light, of passing men-of-war. *Worthy* had been expected: she had arrived. She would discharge her cargo and her duties and she would go, beating back across the Atlantic into English gales and winter, leaving these islands in their perpetual sun, and their inhabitants in exile.

The morning, although young, was hot. The newly risen sun, piercing jalousied shutters, struck the floor and the papers and the table as though it were glaring off metal. The ink well was hot, the glass and its astringent contents, an infusion of weak tea and lime juice, were hot... the onshore breeze which had carried *Worthy* through gem-clear water and under fair-weather canvas to her resting place had not yet refreshed the stale air of this room where, away from the glare of the slatted sun, the commanding officer of the Eighth was drafting orders to be read at Assembly the following day.

September 14th. It is ordered, that upon no account whatever any future indulgence be given to such of the working men as have misbehaved, contracted debts, or appeared dirty and slovenly, and they are strictly forbid to appear in a state of drunkenness, at any time of the day.

The colonel expects to see the men sober; and it is his orders that they parade without noise, and in a soldier-like manner. No man is to be seen without his regimental coat, waistcoat, and breeches, without the leave of his commanding officer.

The pen hesitated, and immediately the ink blurred as it soaked into the page. In the momentary stillness the life of the garrison intruded: voices, footsteps, the soughing sea, the smell of baking bread, the smell of the salt tide, the smell of mildew like a taint, progressive and destructive, the tang of sweat, which no amount of laundering could remove from clothes grown threadbare and sun-bleached after nine years in these latitudes.

The camp necessaries that are wanting of what was delivered to each company is to be made good, except such as the officers can certify to have been worn out in the service, the rest is to be paid for by the men that lost them.

He paused again, swallowed half the contents of the glass, which constituted his breakfast, and opened his watch. Another hour, perhaps half an hour, before Mainwaring's arrival.

The colonel has been told that some have pretended illness to avoid ordinary exercise. Soldiers are to understand that constant and regular exercise is as necessary for their health as it is for their instruction; and that an army of men undisciplined, untaught and unused to any fatigue, is an easy prey.

At the edge of his vision there was movement—a cockroach the size of a man's thumb scuttled across the floor and disappeared into a damp crevice. He continued to write, in the disciplined hand that had filled the order books of the Eighth regiment throughout its slow progress from England to the Havana, to St. Christophers, to Antigua, to Barbados, since 1762.

If ever the colonel hears, or is informed, that a soldier expresses himself to be dissatisfied with exercise or work, or marching, or any other duty that falls to his share, or that he drops words intending to discourage the young men, or finds fault with whatsoever is ordered or appointed, he will particularly take notice of such soldier, and will treat him as so pernicious and villainous a conduct deserves; and if any thing of that kind is ever discovered in a non-commissioned officer, he must expect no mercy or forgiveness. It is the distinguished character of a good soldier to go through every part of his duty with chearfulness, resolution, and obedience; for the good of his Majesty's service.

The Eighth had never been cheerful, resolute, or obedient. One battalion, understrength, less than three hundred men, the second battalion having been lost to the mania of renumbering and disbanding regiments which had swept the army in 1758: its regimental character had never changed since the day Mordaunt had assumed command. It remained surly and mutinous no matter how many men died, deserted or were transferred—every recruit seemed to put on defiance like a garment with its blue facings and blue and white zigzag lace, and the days were punctuated by drill and the lash and the dreary round of work. Building, repairing, shifting materials or stores, offloading cargoes: when the Eighth worked it was sullen; when it was at rest it brawled, whored, drank and thieved; when it fought, as it had done only once under his command, it had given its courage and its blood with a brutish dedication, and he had been appalled by the depth of his gratitude and his affection for them.

He heard the scrape of the orderly's chair in the anteroom, the exchange of voices, and his adjutant's boots crossing the floor. The door opened, and as the orderly's sleeve receded he prepared himself for the sight of Smallpiece's face, which he regretted that he had not yet, even now, learned to look upon with detachment.

Captain Henry Stanhope Smallpiece, called Codpiece or Janus by unsympathetic brother officers, was perhaps forty, old for his rank, and although of good family apparently lacking funds, influence or ambition enough to improve upon it. He had been Mordaunt's adjutant for eight years, returning to the regiment upon his recovery from wounds suffered in the great amphibious assault on Havana in the closing months of war. He possessed all the attributes of that office: he was disciplined, scrupulous and methodical, and their relationship had become such that communication between them was often reduced to a verbal shorthand.

"Colonel."

"Any news?"

Smallpiece had removed his hat, out of courtesy; as they had acknowledged one another earlier at Assembly no further salute was required. His hairline was irregular, receding from the scar tissue: where it was possible for hair to grow on his left temple and above the eye it was yellowish white. The eye itself, although both he and Mordaunt pretended otherwise, was blind, and lidded only by a transparent fold of skin in the burned and melted ruin of the left side of his face.

"Captain Mainwaring has arrived, sir, and presents his compliments."

"Ask him to present his person, at his earliest convenience if you please."

"Very good, sir."

426

"And, Harry—"

"Sir?"

"Is Mrs. Mainwaring in attendance?"

An infinitesimal hesitation. He already knew the answer.

"Yes, sir."

"Acquaint her with the quartermaster's accommodation and servants, will you? I'll see Mainwaring directly."

Smallpiece said with characteristic inscrutability, "Very good, sir," and returned to the unforgiving daylight. Mordaunt waited, controlling an immediate dislike of the unknown quartermaster, who had obviously been incapable of concealing the revulsion attendant upon any introduction to the adjutant, with whom he would be expected to work closely. There was a theatrical pause, and then with an excess of noise Captain Philip Hallwood Mainwaring appeared, stamped, and swept off his hat in the traditional salute, which in the interests of keeping the lace on the men's hats cleaner had lately been superseded by a new fashion of merely raising the right hand to the brim. His face, beneath immaculately powdered hair, showed a red crease of sweat.

They shook hands.

"Sit down, Mainwaring."

He groped for the edge of the other chair and sat carefully in it, bringing his scabbard onto his thigh and settling on his lap the sealed canvas bag he had carried in with him. The salt stains of what Mordaunt suspected had been an undignified departure from *Worthy* were drying whitely on his boots. His face, youthful, painfully sunburned from his passage through the islands, and entirely forgettable, was a study in hopeless perplexity. He seemed transfixed, after the shock of Smallpiece, by the irregularity of this greeting and the informality, even dishevelment, of his colonel's dress, as if he had woken from a hot dream of some weeks at sea to find himself in a chaotic hell where he had expected paradise.

Mordaunt said with a degree of patience, "I gather you have mail for us, Captain?" and Mainwaring visibly collected his wits and delivered himself of the canvas bag.

"From Mure, Son and Atkinson, sir. I took the precaution of sealing it myself after inspecting the contents. They appear to be in order, although, alas, sadly out of date." He blinked. "There are several for your especial attention, which have been in the hands of the agents for some time." Another pause. "I will gladly resume this interview at a later hour if that would prove suitable, sir."

"I assure you I am all eagerness to devour my post, Mainwaring, but we must necessarily subdue our personal desires to the needs of the regiment. You agree, of course."

Mainwaring blinked and agreed.

"Good passage?"

"Ah, yes, sir. Very fast, I'm told. I confess that I was heartily sick, and gave fervent thanks to God for our safe arrival at Antigua."

Oh, God help me, he thought wearily, he's not one of those as well.

"And your wife? I trust she found the journey not too much of a trial?"

"Alas, it was the same case with her. This life makes many demands upon us, but life upon service is lamentably hard for the fairer sex." Mainwaring blinked again: his eyes were pale and curiously expressionless, and a thin trickle of perspiration had stolen down from his powdered hair. He added ingenuously, "I only hope she does not damn me too heartily for persuading her to accompany me here. One anticipated… rather more."

"This is not English Harbour, Mainwaring, and the sooner one resigns oneself to that, the better." The cool, pebble-like eyes flicked up rather guiltily to his face: Mainwaring had been staring at the massive scars on his right wrist, revealed by his rolled shirtsleeves. "There are compensations. The climate is temperate, and society reasonably civilized— there is a large population of Africans, but they are in the main well disciplined and amenable, which cannot be said for other islands similarly dependent on black labour."

Mainwaring said, on cue, "I am bound to say that I believe the institution of slavery to be unChristian."

"It is unChristian to kill other human beings, but it is implicit in our profession. That is why we are soldiers, Mainwaring, and others are politicians." A small rivulet of sweat was shining on Mainwaring's forehead. "I must advise you that your views, while heartfelt, will not prove popular in Barbados, and it would be in your best interest not to air them. We are here as a presence and a protection, not as a conscience."

"I will be guided by you, Colonel."

"That would be wise. Having come so recently from England you will find yourself the centre of attention for some time— we and the Navy provide the only novelty here, and in some cases the only entertainment. I have just the one comment on that score: the rum is powerful and the women bored. The potential for disaster is everywhere. Your predecessor was shot by a jealous husband— and he was a freethinker too."

Silence, across which the sea was a brushstroke. In the anteroom voices murmured, and the outer door opened and closed again: Smallpiece gauging the progress of this conversation, and diplomatically refraining from interruption. Mainwaring surreptitiously wiped the trickling sweat from his sunburned face.

"It's... hot, isn't it, sir?"

He said, "Yes. The summers are hotter," and watched Mainwaring diminish at the prospect, then, knowing full well that he was fulfilling his reputation as a difficult superior, he said abruptly, "How do you support a wife on a quartermaster's pay, Mainwaring? I merely anticipate the others' curiosity."

"My wife has... ah, means of her own, I am happy to say."

"Children?"

"Sir?"

"Did you bring any children with you?"

"Yes, sir. Two little boys, aged five and seven."

"Hm. Better have a few more— they don't last long out here." The rigid mask of perplexity which would have been comic in any other circumstances had sealed itself again over Mainwaring's features. "There's no point in beating about the bush, man. Ignorance won't change the situation."

Mainwaring said faintly, "I will bear it in mind, sir."

Again the silence, now pierced by a repetitive hammering that bit painfully into Mordaunt's damaged eardrum. He covered it with his left hand and rested his elbow on the papers.

"You extended the hospitality of the mess to Captain Godden?" Mainwaring seemed to rouse himself from a contemplation of enforced intercourse and gave the habitual blink. "The packet master, whom we are to thank for your safe arrival."

"I... thought he would prefer to seek his own comforts ashore, sir. It would seem more, ah, in keeping with his nature."

Mordaunt said curtly, "Good God, man, these *are* the comforts," and stood. The air seemed suddenly fetid and he threw open the jalousied shutters, admitting the smell of the sea and the ripe profanity of soldiers at work. It was instantly quelled by the measured tread of Hackett, the sergeant-major.

He said, still staring into the sun, "I shall not instruct you in your duties, Mainwaring— you recommend yourself admirably in your letter, and you are necessary to the regiment. I trust that your brother officers will make you welcome. We commemorate the fall of Quebec tonight, so that will provide you with an opportunity to meet them en masse, as it were." Mainwaring seemed to swim to his feet in the dimness beyond the sunlight and was murmuring something appropriate. "I commend you to my adjutant, who will be pleased to introduce you to the geography of the garrison and answer any questions you may have. You will find him invaluable— he is acting-major here, and I intend to have him gazetted as such."

Mainwaring cleared his throat discreetly, the preface to a confidential whisper.

"He is... pitifully disfigured, is he not?"

"Captain Smallpiece was wounded in a magazine explosion during the siege of the Havana in 1762. And while I am very sensible of the cruelty of his injuries, I would caution you against allowing them to blind you to his qualities. He is a brave and honest officer, and a very kind and honourable gentleman."

Mainwaring said, still in that sepulchral whisper, "I understand you perfectly, sir. He simply... serves as a warning to us all."

He said dryly, "Really? Some men flinch from mortality, but not many soldiers, I think." He turned, so that the sun's heat soaked into his back. "I wish you good morning, Mainwaring. Acquaint yourself with your duties, and we will discuss them further tomorrow."

"Yes, sir. Thank you, sir." Again the theatrical salute, arrested in mid-movement. "I beg your pardon, Colonel—"

He looked up again, having already dismissed him from his thoughts.

"Yes, Mainwaring, what is it?"

"My wife desires to present her compliments to your lady, when it suits."

"That will be difficult, as my wife chooses to reside in England." Then he added with unnecessary sarcasm, "Perhaps you see her point. Occasionally I see it myself," and Mainwaring fled.

The sun moved imperceptibly over the floor until a single blinding bar lay across the corner of the table, bleaching the piled papers. The ink soaked into another softened page. These were his personal accounts, to be submitted later to the Paymaster-General for reimbursement. As colonel all regimental expenses devolved upon himself, and he kept his records with the meticulousness of the adjutant he himself had been in Scotland.

> To Ann Reynell, being His Majesty's Bounty for herself and her Four Children, in Consideration of the Loss of Her Husband
>
> £198.14.6
>
> To Alice Lucas, being His Majesty's Bounty in Consideration of the Loss of Her Husband
>
> £85.3.4
>
> To Mure, Son & Atkinson, for Vinegar sent to the Barbadoes, for the Service of the Forces there
>
> £260.10.6

As though he had suddenly gone deaf, the hammering ceased, and in the resounding stillness he heard every syllable of his sergeant-major's appraisal of regimental roofing skills. It was quiet, but quite crushing.

"Yew idle, useless, motherless lot— was none o' yew born beneath a roof? First puff o' real wind will take that straight off— now see to it, Corporal!"

In the peaceful interval while they conferred, the harsh rasp of the quill seemed unnaturally loud.

> To John Trotter, Esq. For Hospital Bedding for the 8th Regt in the Barbadoes in the Year 1770
>
> £214.15

In the cells some one was idly playing a flute, ex tempore, and not without talent. Jessup, he thought, a hardened offender, idler and genial thief, whose chief sources of pride were his service at Quebec and his endurance of the cat, of which, in his twenty years as a private soldier, he had survived two thousand lashes.

> To Geo. Granier, Esq., Apothecary Gen'l, for Medicines furnished for the 8th Regt of foot in the Barbadoes in the Year 1770
>
> £171.18.3

Smallpiece had come in and was hovering near the door with his hat under his arm, in an ostentatious attempt not to disturb him. By choice he shunned the sun, because he said "it makes me look inhuman": he stood now with his ruined face slightly and unconsciously averted.

"There's some post, Harry. Deal with it, will you?"

Smallpiece dispensed with his hat and advanced to the edge of the table, slit the bag open and sorted the contents. The hard scarlet of his coatskirt intruded into the bar of sunlight, and his left hand, no more than a framework of bones over which the scar tissue seemed too tightly stretched, came into Mordaunt's vision holding several letters. It arranged them neatly and withdrew: a faint scent of bay rum accompanied the gesture. He found Smallpiece's fastidiousness in dress and person singularly moving.

He closed the accounts. The flute produced an arpeggio of startling beauty, which they both ignored.

"What have you done with our new quartermaster?"

"I left him with his wife, sir, consoling one another over the state of their lodgings. He plans an assault upon the victualling yard tomorrow."

"Perhaps he should practise a little Christian forbearance. I gather his inclinations are in that direction."

"I shall endeavour not to shock him, then. Your letters are here, sir."

"Yes, and I can imagine what they are. Be glad you're not married, Smallpiece."

Smallpiece said distantly, "I am, sir," and seemed to withdraw a little from the hot sunlight.

"I am very sorry, Harry."

The right side of Smallpiece's mouth lifted slightly.

"Think nothing of it, sir."

But I do think something of it, he thought. I think of it all the time. I think of you, you poor, half-faced, courteous, gentle-mannered bastard, living out your life here because nobody can bear the sight of you in the family home. I think of the whores you can't pay enough to sleep with you. I think of all of us, the whole bloody, pitiful lot.

"I hoped I might acquaint you with the details of tonight's meal, sir, if that would be acceptable."

"If you think it necessary."

"I should welcome your approval, sir. While we do, of course, make every effort to remind the officers to pay their mess accounts, the ultimate expense is yours. I propose to start with a turtle soup... and the driest sherry, which seems to have kept reasonably well. It would be quite delicious lightly chilled, but unfortunately that is impossible."

"You should be hanging out a vintner's board in St. James's."

Smallpiece remarked, "Yes... my family has some marital connection in Jerez," giving it the Spanish pronunciation with unaffected grace before continuing his epicurean recital.

"Your guest tonight was to have been Captain Hartree, if I am not mistaken, sir."

Mordaunt roused himself from a drifting inattention. "Yes?"

"I think you will find that he sent his regrets, sir. They have received orders to proceed to Jamaica forthwith."

"Well, send to poor old Godden then, if he has nothing else to do. Our quartermaster neglected to invite him into the mess this morning... Captain Mainwaring was no doubt overwhelmed by the rapture of his safe arrival."

The flute once more embroidered the air, like a thrush's song at twilight; but there were no birds here so close to the sea, only predators. The mewing gulls cutting the sun, the frigate birds endlessly circling on motionless, scimitar-like wings. No thrush, no liquid cascade of notes, no lingering English twilight....

"May I speak, Colonel?"

"I do not for a moment believe that it is necessary for you to air your thoughts, Smallpiece."

He looked up; Smallpiece was watching him steadily. His undamaged eye was a frank, disarming blue, in the remains of a face which was thin and youthful and attractive in a pleasant, undistinguished way.

"I do not think Mr. Mainwaring and I will agree, sir."

"I am hardly surprised. However, Mr. Mainwaring has been visited upon us by Mure, Son and Atkinson for our sins, and will have to be endured until either you or I or he sells out, or it pleases God to take him hence. We shall simply have to tolerate him, like mosquitoes." He was gratified to see the ruined mouth lift again.

"There is another disquieting prospect, sir."

"I am not certain that I have the fortitude to endure it."

"We may be required to receive the French, sir. The lieutenant-governor seems to think it would be politic if we entertained them with suitable magnanimity. We are after all at peace, as far as we know."

He said, "We may be at peace, but I will be damned if I will entertain in my mess men who have been trying to kill me since I was fifteen years old, and I would have thought you would concur."

Smallpiece said with gentle humour, "This is not a Christian sentiment, sir," and suddenly he was tired of it. The badinage, the pretense.

"I am not a Christian, Smallpiece. That part of me died in Flanders. There was no joyful resurrection."

The hideous face remained impassive.

"Nor for me, sir."

There was no point in it, no point. He dragged his mind away from the useless, repetitive thoughts: that bitter avenue had long since been exhausted.

"That will be all."

Smallpiece responded, "Very good, sir," with grave formality, bowed and turned away, his carriage upright, his grizzled hair tied precisely at the nape of his neck with a pressed black ribbon, a small dark patch of sweat beginning to soak through the thick scarlet of his coat at the base of his spine.

Mordaunt thought: we have made a covenant with death, and with hell are we at agreement.

The connecting door closed; he was alone. He swore under his breath, pushed the accounts aside and broke the seal on the first letter. Voices drifted in and out of his thoughts, the sounds of hammering now distant and otherworldly. In the reeking dampness of the cells the flute played on.

> A north country maid up to London had stray'd,
> Although with her nature it did not agree;
> She wept, and she sighed, and she bitterly cried,
> 'I wish once again in the north I could be...'

They had been, in the past, letters from his steward, bills, communiqués from the regimental agent, inebriated letters from Catherine, who wrote as she wept, copiously and without an ounce of sincerity. Her abuse and accusations had been easier to bear than the more recent professions of love, which seemed obscene in their passionate explicitness. He had twice in nine years received letters from Bancroft, now nearly sixty-five and last known to be in ill health in the garrison at Gibraltar. He had kept them all, as he had always kept letters that disturbed him, but he had answered nothing for two years, as time and distance and memory and isolation and bitterness fell into the breach between himself and the past and became immovable barriers.

> 'Oh! The oak and the ash and the bonnie ivy tree,
> They flourish at home in my own country...'

The last letter, sealed into a soiled cover, the superscription in an unfamiliar hand addressed to Lieutenant-Colonel Thomas Achill Mordaunt-Collins, commanding officer, the Eighth Regiment of Foot, at the Garrison in the Havana, and forwarded by Mure, Son and Atkinson in London. Like a dead hand, he thought, touching him from the past. Four years had elapsed since he had been appointed to the full colonelcy of the regiment in Antigua. He broke the seals and unfolded the cover. There were two documents inside: a letter, closely written in that elegant, teasing script, a single side of a single sheet to make up for nine years of silence, and a copy of a marriage contract, signed, witnessed, and dated thirteen weeks earlier. The script and the signature were Margaret's. The other names meant nothing: the phrases swam in and out of focus and blurred, and also meant nothing.

He crumpled the letter, but he would not destroy it: there was so little left, and he knew how many times he would read it later, as he had read and still read all the others, as though the endless repetition of pain was necessary, and served some purpose.

In the shimmering, heated air the flute played on, and was suddenly intolerable.

> 'No doubt, did I please, I could marry with ease;
> Where maidens are fair many lovers will come,
> But he whom I wed must be...'

He did not afterwards recall having moved, but he found himself in the outer doorway with the white glare of the sun almost blinding him.

"Sarn't Major!"

Hackett, huge and fiercely scarlet in the brazen noon, snapped his heels together.

"Sah!"

"Shut that damned fool up, will you?"

"Sah!" and then, turning, "Jessup!" A muffled reply from the stony confines of the cell. "Colonel says if 'e 'as to stray up to London with yew once more 'e'll shit through 'is teeth, so stow it!"

Silence ensued from the cell and from the men, but even in the absence of any disturbance the office remained unbearable. He groped unseeingly for his undress coat, which had been hanging since daybreak on the back of the chair, putting on with it the safety and authority of rank and a familiar identity. He thrust the crumpled letter into his pocket and went out into the sunlight: the heat struck him like an anvil. He walked blindly toward the opened gates and the picquet beyond, and as he walked the desultory conversation of two bored young lieutenants pacing the parapet together drifted to him in fragments.

"...father thought he wasn't fit for it. So he took offense, charged their guns, made a man of himself. He was killed of course, had his head blown off, but his father was very proud."

He walked on, deaf to everything but his own measured footsteps— so many to the sanctuary of his quarters and the solitude offered there. The junior of the lieutenants, a rather piggy young man, peered after him and remarked, "What the devil's the matter with the Colonel?" His companion barely paused.

"Post from home, my dear fellow. Hadn't you noticed, it takes some people that way."

They resumed their steady pacing in sun-faded uniforms, to the sound of the sea creaming onto the beach.

In the dimness of his quarters there was respite from the heat, but no solitude. His servant Patenall, the replacement for the Italian Giacomo, dead these several years, was polishing the gilt buttons of his dress uniform coat in anticipation of the evening. A discreet man, civil but unsentimental, and unlike his fellows neither a professional soldier nor a hardened felon, he was a Devonian, a draper by trade, who had taken the shilling during an evening of drunken despondency after his business had gone bankrupt, and although no friendship had developed between them a mutual respect existed. There was no intimacy: Patenall was a competent subordinate but he was not a valet, and the privacy of Mordaunt's body and its injuries remained obsessively guarded, and kept secret even from him.

He removed himself politely now with the coat and the polish and the button-stick into the adjoining room, which sometimes served as his colonel's dining quarters, and pretended not to hear the clink of bottle against glass. He had left the room in its accustomed clean austerity: the camp bed draped in white mosquito netting, the copper basin burnished, the table and green leather chairs in order with the telescope and writing case and candles within reach, and the bookcase opened to allow air to circulate among the leather covers. Donne, rotting in buff-coloured kid, Shakespeare, Pepys, Ovid, Pope, a battered copy of Cleland's *Memoirs of a Woman of Pleasure* borrowed in Antigua and still unread except, secretly, by Patenall himself. He had obviously been polishing the sword as well, and had left it lying on the dressing case, unsheathed as usual to prevent it rusting in the damp scabbard; the blade, with its cabalistic engravings of crescent moon, phoenix, stars and locked hilts, had been honed, and the old sword knot replaced with an opulent gold and crimson cord. On the bed were laid out fresh articles of clothing and the accoutrements of rank: the gold gorget, the crimson silk net sash and heavy gold aiguillette. A tiny lizard clung to the wall near the shaving mirror on splayed, delicate toes like an insect. Mordaunt ignored it, staring at his reflection, and it remained where it was.

A bony face, drawn and unsmiling, tanned to the colour of leather, and deeply creased about the eyes and mouth: his eyes were bloodshot, from strain or sun or sleeplessness or grief; his hair, which had always inclined toward fairness in a climate more favourable than England's, a little bleached, and greying. He was fifty-four years old, older than any man or any officer in the regiment, older than any Englishman on the island, older than the present lieutenant-governor, a sodden forty-seven. An aging atheist nursing injuries and grievances a quarter of a century old, a landowner who had forsaken his land, a husband whose only home was the regiment, whose only sons were its fever-ridden soldiers, buried across two thousand miles and in a glittering waste of sea; a lover whose love was as unmentionable as lust, as secret and dishonourable and ineradicable as the scars upon his back, and as hopeless as the hope of God, or peace, or consummation.

"You bloody fool," he said aloud. "You bloody, bloody fool."

Her fans were in a locked drawer of the dressing case— her old fan, given to him that April morning, its golden silk now greyed and perishing, and the new, bought in St. Christophers and kept in an anticipation of their reunion which he now found contemptible and ridiculous. Its beauty was proportionate to its expense: a brisé fan, with sixteen tortoiseshell and mother of pearl blades inlaid with leaves, lilies, roses and a fantastically detailed peacock. He took it out of its silk box and put it in his pocket with the letter, shut the drawer, and locked it.

Patenall was still polishing the buttons with dedication in the other room.

"I'm going out."

"Very good, sir," and then, following him a step or two, as though disquieted by the fumes of rum and the peculiarity of his behaviour, "Colonel, your hat—"

"Leave it. I don't want it."

Down the road to the beach, on to the white sand, the heat thrown up into his face and striking his uncovered head. He could not remember the last time any one had spoken his Christian name... the sound of it atrophied in the mind: like Italian, spoken to no one since the death of Giacomo, like the divine gift of music in hands that never played, like desire, repressed until it died. Sex was a desiccated memory, something dried, dead, pressed between time's leaves like the browning rose from the garden at Evesham: there had been a woman once, in the early years, when the sensuousness of the climate had been both new and stimulating, and the heat of the sun had freed him from pain, and the miles between himself and England had freed him of guilt and responsibility, but he had been incapable of carrying it to its conclusion, and mistaking his physical reserve for inadequacy, she had taken another lover.

He walked on, in the heat of the afternoon sun. The sounds of men and horses faded into the silken rhythm of the sea: if only it could wash his thoughts, wear them down like coral into shapeless, unrecognizable fragments.

Margaret, Margaret....

There was nothing left of her. Only a face imperfectly remembered, like an illuminated portrait, only luminous eyes and an indefinite beauty, immature and unremarkable, which might with time have become arresting. Only a waste of years, of life, of hope: only this, now.

He walked on, on sand like wet satin laced with the tide's edge, on sand pitted with recent rain and drying, crumbling underfoot, in the flickering shadows of palms growing almost to the waterline. The drums beat for dinner at three, as they beat for reveille in the sudden vivid sunrises, as they beat Tattoo in the swift, scented darkness and the sharp, equally sudden rains. Everything was sudden here: dawn, dusk, rain, storm, lust, satisfaction, men's tempers, the ends of affairs, violence, death.

There were no graves here, no shallow trenches: the only grave was the sea. The dead were taken out by the Navy and disposed of beyond the thirty-fathom line, to which depths he himself would be consigned if he should succumb to the constant enemy, the typhoid, yellow fever, dysentery or cholera that lurked, beauty and menace, beauty and death, everywhere in these islands. He had already had malaria, from which he would suffer at intervals for the rest of his life.

Bury me in England.

The dream of an English winter, a cold rain, a cold wind, snow, a green spring, the scattered gold on the lawns at Evesham, the scent of roses, instead of this: the lush monotony of Barbados, the sphinx-like profile of Antigua, the green hills of St. Christophers, the prospect of the autumn hurricanes, the

437

calendar of military anniversaries observed by alcoholic men in a primitive mess on an island that was both paradise and hell.

The shadows lengthened. The peacock's wing of the water changed colour with the sky, the current, the nature of the bottom, the making or ebbing of the tide.

Tonight the Colours would be brought into the mess, unhoused and crossed and displayed with the drums, and the regimental silver, salvers, candlesticks, plates, bowls engraved with the horse and garter and "Nec Aspera Terrent" would be on the table: and the Eighth's battle honours would be only history and geography to drunken, half-grown officers, but to him they were names and faces and dead friends and his own blood and inexpressibly painful memories of his years of service in Flanders. And the relic, in a glass box, would be produced: a dried, gingery wisp of hair allegedly cut from the head of the dying Wolfe. He thought sourly that if every lock of Wolfe's hair were collected, like pieces of the True Cross, they would thatch an elephant.

There would follow an indigestible meal, soup, the local fish, and suckling pig, devoured by men who ate as though they were in England, with no regard for the steamy climate, and later Smallpiece, who was blessed with a melodious voice and who preferred to sing with his profile to his audience, would offer "The British Grenadiers", the risqué "Hot Stuff", "The Girl I Left Behind Me", and various tender ballads of the time, sending every one into a maudlin, reflective silence which would invariably degenerate into hilarity, horseplay and violence to themselves and one another, during the course of which the Colonel would retire, and his servant would discreetly convey a bottle to his quarters.

He halted. The pain, the legacy of lacerated muscle and nerve and damaged vertebrae and kidney, the companion of a quarter of a century, had returned: the pain was the memory of Glen Sian made flesh, as Margaret had been.

He had walked far enough. Nothing lay ahead but the barking dogs and shanties of Holetown, and the broken necklace of shells at the extremity of the tide. He took the fan from his pocket, snapped it blade by brittle blade, and threw it far out into the sun's burning track across the blinding sea.

XII

Malcolm and I were married on the sixth of June 1771. The parish register of Glen Mor records our ages, thirty-five and twenty-five, and our signatures, blurred as though with tears where the split quill touched a damp page in the presence of a crowd of unofficial witnesses.

He was thought old, in years and sin, for this pledge of fidelity. There was a minor revival of unpleasant gossip, and every aspect of his life and mine became the subject of avid discussion. But the speculation was as brief as it was intense, and whether out of nervous respect for him or deference to me, by the time of the wedding public dissection of our private passion was no longer so audible.

He had come on the rainy evening of April twenty-third to ask for my hand in marriage, and unlike the young men of the district he brought no gille-suiridhe, no lover's spokesman with him to extol his virtues to his prospective father-in-law. As he remarked rather poignantly to me later, he was not young and he had no virtues, and no friend but me, so he came alone. My father received him in the inhospitable parlour where they were closeted for nearly an hour, then I was abruptly summoned. When I opened the door I saw that whisky had been offered and accepted, and as I came in Malcolm drank from the glass and held it out to me. So, by this crude local custom, my father signalled his consent. He never verbally gave it, nor conferred his blessing.

In the weeks before the wedding I signed a marriage contract, which in the event of our separation guaranteed my sole possession of my property; copies were witnessed, sealed and despatched to solicitors in Glasgow, Evesham's solicitors in England, and Achill. With this last I enclosed a letter, no part of which I wish to remember except the formality of its salutation and the endless capacity to wound in its cruel little valediction. *I am, Sir, your most dutiful friend.* How that last word must have hurt him. How impossible, now, to describe myself in any other terms.

I prepared my wedding gown, a green and white striped silk. Although it had been seen by no one except my aunt, its cost was already a source of conjecture in the village, and I was well aware of the sensation its unlucky colour would produce: even Deirdre had had no comment. I packed my few possessions, removing myself without regret from a house which had never offered me more than a cheerless accommodation, and very little remained of me, only a mirror on the bare wall to reflect my bridal image and the narrow bed which had known my loneliness and my unhappy chastity. I set crooked pins and clumsy stitches in the hem of a gown my aunt had unimaginatively cut from the fourteen yards of grey tabby I had given her, and in the lengthening twilights of spring she sat by the fire, sewing into it thoughts she did not share with me. Apart from the preparation of legal documents and the removal of my goods to his house I saw very little of Malcolm, and in the atmosphere of stifling propriety surrounding our marriage we were never alone: I never visited the house even to sow a packet of seeds in the garden, or arrange my own books and clothing when they were taken there. He was withdrawn and notably short-tempered, and I thought the intense pressure of public scrutiny was becoming intolerable, or the enormity of marriage disturbed him as it had once haunted me.

And one last shadow, from a year spent in shadows, stepped out and touched me coldly. George Cameron, on hearing of my betrothal, came to wish me well.

"Is it true?"

I was on my knees scrubbing the hearthstone, and I was alone. When I did not answer he kicked the brush out of my hand with the toe of one of those familiar shabby shoes. "Are you going to marry that bloody bastard?"

His neckcloth was stained and fraying, and he had not shaved for several days. At the thought of him teaching in such a condition I shuddered mentally.

"Yes."

His face crumpled as if I had stabbed him. He looked sick, sick and shattered.

"Why? Why? *Why?*"

"I love him."

He stared at me with those burning, bloodshot eyes as if I were something loathesome.

"You whore," he said.

He halted at the door, his fist clenching and unclenching; then he turned and cursed me in a soft whisper, with unbearable anguish.

"I would sooner see you married to the devil! I would sooner see you *dead—*"

His voice broke, and he stared at me with wide, streaming eyes, then he stumbled out. When he had gone I retrieved the brush from the corner and scrubbed the floor where he had stood. It seemed indelibly stained.

The morning of my wedding dawned shrouded in a cold grey mist. My aunt dressed me and lingered, reflected in my wavering glass, as if she would give me something, some final word or token or some trinket of my mother's. But the moment passed, as all the moments passed in this inarticulate family, and was irretrievable. She rearranged the tiers of lace on my sleeve and gazed at them critically, as though she were embarrassed, then she said, "You will do, so," and left me. The slow, silent minutes passed, the last minutes of a sour spinsterhood in a room which had never been my sanctuary... I stood with Ewen's necklace still unfastened in my hand and the knot of white ribbon and white rosebuds at my breast where her uncertain fingers had pinned it, and the reflection of an unknown bride gazed at me: a woman with cool eyes, wearing her composure like a silken garment. The room was cold; my perfume hung here like a ghost, like the memory of my past life... too many memories, too much and too little of everything. Beyond my window, beyond the sea of graves and neglected grass and nettles a slight, brilliant figure lounged with one foot up behind him against the kirk wall, squinting at the clouds: James, who would give me in marriage. Except for the negligence of his stance he might have been his father.

I prayed to be blessed, as no one else had blessed me, fastened the necklace, and waited for Charlotte.

She came, beautifully gowned in blond silk and laughing breathlessly, pinned the roses more securely to my bodice and gave me the kiss which had been ungiven, then she slipped her arm through mine and together we walked to the kirk. Some one had raked the stony path before my feet in their thin morocco shoes should press it. I remember the unfamiliar hiss of silk as I moved, and her pale, elaborately dressed hair and straight, tightly-corseted back preceding me through the narrow gate; then she said to James, "Here's our darling Margaret!" and he awakened like some gorgeous marionette from his trance and held out his hand to me. His was very cold and damp, and on his little finger where he had placed it for safekeeping I saw my wedding ring.

Charlotte entered before us, and the murmur of conversation within was silenced. In the sudden lull he whispered, "I wish you well... but if you need me, come to me. I say this in all sincerity. Regard me as a friend."

"I do so regard you, James."

"He doesn't," he said.

There was no more time: for memory, for intimacy, for apprehension or reassurance. He led me into the dimness, where Malcolm stood with his back to the pulpit, immobile and impassable under the gaze of half a hundred witnesses. My ringless hand was given and received with a cold formality, and I thought of nothing else, except that we who loved had met like strangers; a man who had possessed my body but whose soul was never mine had given me no lover's welcome, and his eyes denied me the private communion I wanted.

We were married in Gaelic and in English, with the still obligatory benediction upon the House of Hanover at this conclusion of this, as any other religious service. The kirk was so crowded with spectators whom we had been powerless to keep away that it would have been impossible to seat any one else, or so I thought until, toward the end of the brief and curiously unmoving ceremony, a draught stirred the stiff panels of my gown, and I knew the door had opened to admit yet one more witness: my former lover.

He was dishevelled and already well gone in liquor, and did not raise his head when we passed.

As we came out there was sunlight, and James, behind us, pulled out a brace of pocket pistols and fired them into the air. I felt Malcolm's arm jerk in reflex, and the rest was lost in the unexpected outburst of cheers and shouts around us. Fragments of the bridal garland scattered over our hair and clothing and young girls scrambled for the pieces, which they believed would bring them luck; Malcolm picked up one of the crushed white flowers, although I never knew if he kept or discarded it.

For the first day since his youth he had worn no weapons, not even the favoured knife: it was his attempt to consecrate himself in the little innocence that remained to him. In his pocket with that fallen flower he carried Ewen's silver watch and the rosary from his dead hand; he showed them to me in the first moments of privacy we salvaged from the endless bright hours of afternoon, when the festivities, which had been marked by their decorum, were becoming more raucous with the advent of evening. We had left the table and its stilted conversation and James's rather too fluent wit and returned to the graveyard, and I was laying the white alba roses I had carried on my mother's grave. When I looked up he was holding Ewen's rosary. He held it, for a man who professed atheism, not carelessly but as though it meant something to him.

"I wanted his blessing," he said.

"I wanted hers. Or theirs." I saw the cynicism in his face. "I would marry you without a blessing from any one."

He said shortly, "You have," and thrust the rosary back into his pocket. Against the whiteness of the holland ruffle at his wrist his skin was very dark, and his hand with its scars and swollen knuckles seemed to despise the frivolity of its adornment. "I don't find this very easy. Perhaps you think that strange."

"I understand it. We are private people in a public place, and for the moment public property. Is that what you meant?"

"My life has always been public property, or so my enemies seem to think. And God knows there are enough of those. You see them all around you." He smiled faintly, although not at me. "So you see why the role of jovial bridegroom sits somewhat ill on me."

"Do you regret having done this?"

"I regret— the past. What it made me— what I made myself— things I did, injuries to you. I am not a good man, Margaret. I may break your heart."

"You've broken it before. It mends."

442

I thought he would have said something else, but in the street the fiddlers, who would be paid a penny a dance for this evening's entertainment, were scraping untunefully. I took his hand, making my familiar mistake of presuming upon our intimacy. He said, "no," so gently that I thought I had misheard, or this was some new idiosyncrasy, some obsession with dignity that my persuasion would assuage. When I persisted he said less gently, "I don't— so leave it, will you?" and there was a chilling little silence.

"Even for me?"

"No. Not even for you."

It was no darker: the long light of June would linger until almost midnight, but dampness was rising from the ground. I was cold, and my bridal silk was stained.

He said, "Don't go. I should have told you." He had taken the rosary from his pocket again, and the beads were twined through his fingers. "My father danced," and there was a lengthy pause: what he said was only a fragment of the thoughts and the memory and the life underlying the disconnected phrases. "He thought they loved him for it. I hated him."

Then he said in a different voice, "Don't tell James I have this, will you?" and returned the rosary to his pocket. Like the bruised white flower from the bridal garland, it was never seen again.

I danced with James, and with other men who barely dared to touch me, conscious always of their own acrid sweat and of the cold green eyes that watched them: I danced sedately face to face with Charlotte, whose serenity I envied. I danced with my aunt, who kissed me with dry lips like paper and held my hands briefly and secretively, as if emotion were something to be strangled, and whispered, "The house will be so empty now... I will be missing you at the milking." The shadows lengthened: the tables, planks on trestles that fed celebrants at weddings and mourners at wakes, were cleared of the picked remains of fowls culled from the neighbourhood, oatcakes, eggs, new cheese and old potatoes, casks of rum and whisky and the scraped bones of an entire bullock. Men and women anxious not to give offense, or curious, or merely eager to partake of such general hospitality drifted in from the twilight, from the hills, from the fields, from the shielings where many of the youths and children had been living since May. They ate and drank and threw the planks on the ground and danced on them, and on the grass, and in the street. Young girls fingered the cascading lace and ribbon at my elbows and blushed, and some of the older women kissed me, but none of the men. And Malcolm was always there: in the shadows or on the edge of the light, sometimes seen through the low resinous haze of burning pine torches, sometimes speaking to some one but usually alone, drinking James's astringent claret and watching me, following me like a guardian, like a predator, waiting until I tired. Occasionally he smiled at me, but I knew that he had already gone, withdrawn himself in spirit from this place and this spurious display of camaraderie with men and women he neither loved nor trusted.

At eleven o'clock I left the noise and smoke and returned to the manse to lay out my riding clothes for my departure. As I walked through the twilight some one who had been standing against the house wall stepped out and took my arm.

"Dance with me, Margaret."

Only the faint slurring in his voice betrayed him, and drunk or sober he was the last man with whom I wanted to be seen. I tried to ignore him and he shook my arm slightly to command my full attention.

"One dance… you cannot deny me that. Even he can't deny me that."

He stroked the silk of my sleeve and the knot of roses at my breast. His hand was as tremulous and uncertain as the fingers of young girls who had never touched silk in their lives: his fingers touched silk with a delicacy and wonder and diffidence they had never shown my skin.

"This isn't wise— you must know how unwise it is."

His face was intense, preoccupied with the silk and the knot of roses.

"He has all your sweetness now… is there nothing left for me?" I spoke his name, but he ignored me. "Come and dance with me. One dance. I'll bless you for it. I'll remember you in my prayers…."

I removed his hand gently. It was stiff and cold, and his fingers clung to mine.

"Go home, for God's sake. Go and live your life and leave me to mine."

He bent his head over my hands and kissed them with a terrible passion.

"My love, my love, only a minute. I will be good. I *will* be good…."

So we were found, with his lips and tears moistening my fingers and his explicit words of love made incoherent by drink and by a language I alone understood. The man and woman who emerged from the scented night stood staring at us appalled, as though the bride were Babylon's whore importuning an innocent man; then at a curt nod from the woman Diar Cameron prised his cousin's clinging hands from mine, and they took him away.

I closed the door and went upstairs to my room and sat shivering on the bed. There was torchlight on the bare wall and reflecting from the mirror, and a plaintive voice in the street singing of an old tragedy until it was drowned out by derisive laughter. Glass shattered somewhere, followed by obscenities: the dancers' heels thundered on the boards and the music carried them on toward dawn or insensibility.

Perhaps half an hour passed, and eventually he came, as though by the force of my will or my sharp, inexplicable loneliness I had summoned him.

He came without sound and without hesitation through the darkness of the house, my demon and my familiar, a shadow a little more substantial than the night's flickering shadows on the wall.

He had come, ostensibly, to divest me of this bridal silk and clothe me for the saddle, as in so many secret hours he had undressed me lingeringly, like a man savouring some exquisite gift, and clothed me again with regret. He undressed me slowly, and I was still that secret treasure, and that aloof sexuality quickened and burned, and was subtly offered: what I wanted of him now he would give. Then he released me and lit a candle. Its light seemed unbearable.

"Take me home," I said.

I woke and found myself in his bed. He had gone, and I was alone. A white rose drenched with the rain's bright tears lay on the pillow, the candle melted, the pearls taken from my hair scattered on the table: the knot of white roses I had worn at my breast, in dying, had perfumed the night.

XIII

Sometimes, in the innocence of dreams, my hand still reaches for him and expects to touch his skin. In the pallor of summer nights, in the firelit cold of winter, in the indefinite hour between darkness and light, sleep and sensibility, the fingers search of their own accord. There is no sound, no presence, no living warmth, no breathing but my own: my fingers touch the emptiness, my waking eyes confirm it. I am alone.

But so it was from the beginning. His absence from our marriage bed was my morning gift, and the rose left lying on my pillow no apology for it. I will not pretend to have understood his behaviour, or to understand it now; whatever knowledge of him I gained as his lover was infinitesimal. At the heart's core there was darkness, an impenetrability which repulsed any attempt at intimacy, which refused compassion, which was impervious to my own pain, and pain he had always caused me and would always cause me, often deliberately. At the heart's core, I never knew him. I was endlessly wounded and rebuffed by a mystery, an enigma, an emptiness, and my loneliness that morning was the first and least significant of the injuries this marriage would afford me.

I left the bed, and the memory of the night, and took possession of myself and my house.

At some time throughout its hundred years the room in which we slept had been two rooms, and while he clearly inhabited a small part of it and that aspect was familiar, he had given the rest of it to me and prepared it with freshly whitewashed walls and deer and sheepskin rugs, and furniture: an armoire, an inlaid oak chest of drawers, a screen painted green and white and fancifully adorned with peacocks and flowering prunus, which concealed ewer and basin, and a pair of silver-backed hairbrushes I recognized as my own. Apart from my riding clothes, folded neatly on a chair, there was nothing else of mine.

I went in search of my possessions. Eventually I found them in the room across the passage from Malcolm's study. It had always been unfurnished, and there was very little in it now except a turkey carpet, my chests, still locked with the keys I had give to Malcolm lying on the top, and my books in a handsome open bookcase. All the furniture appeared French and had obviously come from the attics at Ardsian: some months later I learned that James had sold it to him. In time a writing desk and chairs and a sofa from the same source would come to grace this, my sitting room, and here and throughout the house I would hang heavy draperies and curtains, and lay other carpets, and light fires to drive out the indefinable chill of neglect. On this mantel, as in Ewen's morning room, I would keep a crystal bowl filled with flowers, and the blue and white candlesticks from my childhood, and my doll, and in this room my papers, my journals and my secrets. But for the moment it was almost empty, and the air was stale and cold. I opened the window with difficulty and unlocked my chests.

My life was here, on this unfamiliar carpet, scented with a rotten pot of dead rose petals and nostalgia, and memory clung like a cobweb to lace and silk and folded letter. Here was the gilded pencil attached by a discoloured cord to the ivory tablet on which the names of my partners had been inscribed at my first and only ball; here was music, yellowing and torn, which played itself in my mind; here the case of childish trinkets, and the keys on the thin brown ribbon which had locked Mordaunt's secrets into a desk drawer at Evesham. I should have sent them back to him in that letter, so regretted as soon as despatched. His portrait was hidden in a volume of Ewen's journals. I thought neither would resent the propinquity.

And my mother's watercolours, all that I had of her: views of the bridge and waterfall of Sian and a sombre wash of peak and moorland which might have been anywhere in the Highlands. The chill of memory and disquiet and a peculiar nervousness had settled upon me, and only some noisy act of self-assertion would dispel it. I went in search of a hammer and nails and found them among Malcolm's tools in one of the other rooms upstairs where, with characteristic meticulousness, he kept his stores: lumber, glass, lead, varnish, tar, rope, gunpowder, shot and shot mould, coffee, a dusty rack of claret, candles, quires of writing paper and half a hundred quills, an array of patent medicine bottles which seemed mainly physic for horses, spare tack and saddle, and the greatcoat, boots and sheepskin jerkin worn in colder weather. The room opposite held only household linen, neatly pressed and folded. Small as they were, both had fireplaces, so they had obviously not been intended as storerooms: I wondered if one or the other had been his in childhood, and if he had chosen to obliterate the memory by using them for other purposes. There were two other rooms, smaller still, behind doors which were closed but not locked: they were utterly empty and somehow disturbing. I left them as I had found them, furnished only with the light, and took the hammer and nails downstairs.

I hung my paintings, my small stamp of self, and continued my exploration. With Malcolm's study I had only a passing acquaintance: his presence was both palpable and aloof, as it was in the estate office. It too had been freshly whitewashed and there was a threadbare carpet on the floor, but it was sparsely furnished, and there were few concessions to comfort. The walls were bare with the exception of a mercury barometer inscribed *Spano & Figlio, Napoli* and the mantel shelf held nothing but a pot of paper spills and a bracket clock in an ebony case; like the furniture it was French, although it was not old. The chair was scarred and uncushioned, the secretaire also oak: the fall front was open, and the drawers and pigeon-holes crammed with papers. A pewter tankard held a dozen quills and a stiletto. I sensed that it did not function as a paper knife, and I never saw it used for that or any other purpose. I replaced it carefully, and glanced toward the door. There was nothing, of course: the house alone was observing me.

I carried my clothing upstairs and arranged it in the armoire. This room, which faced south-east and received its only direct sunlight in the mornings, was now as I had always known it, in the dimness of afternoon: its shadows had been our refuge during the hours of illicit lovemaking, its silence had given peace. I had been happy then, a happiness I thought he had shared. Subterfuge had heightened the sensuality of those hours, and restraint their drugged, erotic sweetness. There was little sweetness now in the recollection of my wedding night, only the memory of unexpected pain, and my failure to find the joy I so hungered for in this, only my second experience of intercourse with him.

The coat in which he had been married, a dark green velvet, was lying across the armchair near the bed. I opened the wardrobe and replaced it among others I recognized. The rest of the contents were ordinary, and yet peculiarly intimate: two pairs of shoes I had never seen him wear, an embroidered waistcoat, a tin hat box, and, suspended from pegs, a leather baldric and a brass-mounted scabbard housing a sabre, the hilt and sharkskin grip of which were visible. He had the Highlander's fondness for weaponry and I knew the pistols and the knife he carried, but I had not known he possessed this. I drew it, and some dormant memory stirred: I had sensed what I would find and it did not surprise me. It was not new, but the blade had been recently polished and the edge was keen, and like many army swords the scabbard was reinforced with bamboo. There was no engraving: it revealed none of its secrets, and nothing of him.

I sheathed it and returned it to its peg, where it balanced perfectly. I knew now what was taking place, and I had had this dream before; I had made this obsessive and methodical search through a house which was and was not familiar. I was searching now, for fragments of a buried past, for confirmation of nameless fears, for secrets I could not share, the knowledge of which would injure me. And I could not stop until I had found it. I thought it was the only thing in that house that could injure me, and that having found it, the wound would heal.

It occupied his chest of drawers with the two dozen shirts which were his only extravagance, and it was folded, like everything else, with a fastidious precision beside the faded grey-green silk brocade of Ewen's dressing gown. It was my stock, taken from my throat in one of those hours of delicious pleasure, and never returned to me; it had been laid away here as a woman lays away her bridal silk, as though it were some secret treasure. Only the stiffness of the blackened blood in which it had been soaked held the threads of lace together. Fourteen months had passed since it had wrapped his hand in its violation of me.

I became conscious of sounds and movement in the house, and heard his voice downstairs.

I met him in the kitchen. He half turned when I came in, stripped to the waist and drying his face with a towel. I had seen this ritual cleansing so many times that I merely gave him the fresh shirt I had taken from the drawer and lifted my cheek to be kissed, something he did without passion.

"There's trout for your supper. Peel some potatoes, will you."

I peeled them with my back to him, at the stone sink. I heard him hesitate, as though my presence here could still surprise him.

"Will you take a dram with me, Margaret?"

We drank standing, self-consciously, speaking of little of consequence. Later, I set the table and lighted candles, although they were not needed. We sat in our accustomed places, he at the head, I at his right hand, as we had sat whenever we had eaten in the past.

"Did you sleep well?"

"No— not particularly."

"I am sorry to hear it. I hoped you had."

"The furniture... it was very good of you."

"If there is anything else you want, you have only to ask."

In the silence the clock in his study struck some uncounted hour, and the minutes of this endless day crawled toward evening, and aroused a strange, lingering disquiet at the prospect of night. Fear of failure, fear of intimacy, perhaps the shadow of a fear of him, the staining of a sexual fear, unthinkable and absurd.

He was boning the fish with delicate strokes of his knife. His manners were impeccable: I imagined they had been taught him by Ewen.

I said, "This is a pleasant house."

"Is it? I never notice." Then he laid the knife on the plate and looked directly into my eyes. "What's the matter with you, Margaret?"

"There is nothing the matter."

"I would have said there was something."

"There is *nothing*. Why should you think—"

"That because you refuse to talk sensibly to me there should be something the matter?"

As a lover he was neither reserved nor inarticulate, and I felt that he could read my soul, and see reflected in my eyes the failure of the night and the afternoon's reawakened memories, the association of his sexuality with pain and fear.

"I know that I hurt you last night. God knows I never meant to."

"It was my fault."

"No, it was mine. You were tired. I was tired. It was not... what I intended."

"Was the rose an attempt to make amends?"

"You cried in your sleep. I thought it would comfort you."

"Why did you leave me?"

He said abruptly, "I have work to do. I'm not paid to lie in bed all day."

"I had not noticed that it interfered with your pleasure before we were married."

He had picked up his knife to resume his meal. He laid it down sharply.

"You have the devil's own tongue, Margaret."

"So have you, when it suits."

After a moment he said, "That's true. Sometimes it seems the only language I know."

Very gently he pushed the plate aside and rested his head in his hand. The room was very still.

"I have been so sick of life," he said.

***

In the coolness of another afternoon, in that shadowed room, I sought him in the detritus of a sexual past which would always be veiled and obscure. I found my letter, still sealed and torn in half; the vial of oil of roses with which he had anointed my body in lovemaking, empty now, and filled only with a ghostly perfume; the bloodied handkerchief enfolding my pubic hairs; the sheaths, whose usage only instinct told me; the petals of a discoloured rose, pressed as thin as silk into the pages of a volume of erotica almost illegibly written in his hand. Much of it was pornographic, much hauntingly beautiful: perceptions, emotions, evocations of the sexual experience of myself. I read it in a secret ravishment.

Perhaps he knew: perhaps he sensed my odyssey into his soul. When there was clothing to be folded and replaced there, that drawer was empty. He never spoke of it, nor I.

How shall I speak of him, who never seemed my husband, who never diminished into familiarity, who was never my easeful companion but always a turbulent, difficult, vengeful and possessive lover. I lived with him, cooked for him, shared his bed and his nights, and watched the light restlessness of his sleep and never knew his dreams. He who had led me into mysteries led me deeper still, into the mystery of myself, and the flowering of a richness and sweetness and guiltlessness which was my own sexuality. I loved his body as though its beauty were a god's, and received the essence of his virility, and knew joy: joy without pain, without guilt, without the staining of the past; received him, drank him, cried out with him, became him, died with him the infinitesimal death of orgasm, and gave him joy of myself.

I loved him. I desired his body and I cherished and nurtured it as I sought to comfort his spirit when its terrible loneliness and vulnerability were revealed. One night, in his sleep, he wept: the nightmare I could never know preyed upon his mind, and although there is no single word in Gaelic for 'no', he cried out, denying something. Nothing in the words made sense, or perhaps they were words which would never have come within my vocabulary, and they were anguished, terrifying: he who feared nothing was trembling, and his terror frightened me and filled me with inexpressible pity. I held him, caressing him, until his breathing quietened and he turned away from me: but as always he was restless, and as always he woke with the greying of the light. He was more than usually uncommunicative that morning, and knowing it was what he wanted, I left him alone.

I did not often wake before him, or see him leave the house; the dawns came earlier than four o'clock and he had always gone by five, sometimes to remain away until six in the evening, but on a particular morning in July something awakened me. He was shaving, naked before the glass. Although I believed I had healed him of his conviction that I must find his masculinity repulsive, he guarded his bodily functions with an obsessive dignity, and casual nudity was not usual for him; and to watch him in this small intimacy was very appealing. He dried the razor and turned slightly away to take a clean shirt from the drawer. The scars on his buttocks were starkly apparent.

"Malcolm."

He was never talkative, but he was even less so at this hour: I had disturbed his cherished inner silence, his hour of meditation, during which he had once told me he arranged the furniture of his mind and scheduled his daily business. He merely said, "So," in a voice which did not invite further conversation.

"How did you come to be burned?"

"I told you."

"Only that it was an accident. Were you very young?"

"No. And it was not an accident."

"What happened?"

He pulled the shirt over his head and took a stock from the drawer, still with his back to me: he dressed without narcissism, as though his body were of no interest to him.

"The fire was burning in the hearth, my father pushed me down, I fell into the flames and burned my arse. It was thought a great joke, at the time."

"Your... father pushed you?"

"He saw to it that I fell."

"But why...."

"He enjoyed it."

He finished his dressing in silence. I spoke his name softly.

"What now, for Christ's sake?"

"Was... Ewen aware that you were beaten?"

"Yes. He knew."

"Why did he make no attempt to intervene?"

He was picking up small objects, putting them into his pockets: handkerchief, tinderbox, then the pistols, taken off the half-cock as they always lay at night on the table within reach of his pillow. He hesitated with his boots in his hand, then he came around the bed and sat down near me, his face in profile, pulling them on.

"Sometimes, some things are not within the power of a man to do. Or a child. It could not be done. And it matters nothing. I lived." He looked at me fully. "Now that's all I have to say on the subject. If the scars offend you I will try to ensure that you see them as little as possible. I know how such things disturb you."

"I would kill anyone who hurt you."

He smiled faintly, and disengaged the hand I held. I saw for an instant, in that hard, guarded face, the shadow of the vanished youth: the child was long dead.

"No one will hurt me now, Margaret."

He kissed me and left me, but the lost child remained, uncomforted: the nightmare wore a face, or so I imagined, and he who was my lover was my son, the child I could not have protected, whose injuries I could not heal, nor wash clean with my tears.

The weather deteriorated gradually. The mornings were often shrouded in mist, the land invisible and secretive, the rain drifting over the weed-blown fields, drenching the poppies in the unripened grain, the bitter corncockle in the oats. In my garden, where I staked and tied and weeded and manured vegetables and a few summer annuals, the flowers of peas and beans and potatoes were reluctant to open and quick to drop, rotting in the rain. Rain soaked my skirts where I walked and rode, and when Malcolm returned in the evenings his clothing was often wet; rain dimmed the interior of the house, and dampened linens where they were stored, and ruined laundry when it was hung out to dry. The light was grey: the luminous grey of clouded sunrise, the opalescent grey of evening, the indefinite grey of midnight, the sifting twilight before dawn, when I lay pretending sleep, knowing that the whisper of rain on the roof had occupied him more than the night's lovemaking; and then his shadowed nakedness rising from the bed, dressing in silence and leaving me, becoming another figment of the grey and shadowed morning.

Four days passed without rain. I left the house and rode for miles, and for hours I saw no one. The wind was at my back, driving over the striped warp of the fields: the grain glistened in the hurrying light, and beyond, on the hills, there were vivid patches of red where the early heather bloomed. But the weather could not hold. By late afternoon the wind was cold, veering and dropping, and the opaqueness on the horizon had spread, and the sun overhead was haloed.

Whose crop it was I do not know, but an hour from home I came upon a field like any upland field in Glen Sian: undulating strips of run-rig where the barley was blowing and choked with flowering weeds. The wind moved endlessly like waves upon a sea, engulfing the body of the man who stood there. The track where he had entered the field was imprinted on the grain: I followed it, although I did not think he heard me come. As I approached he pulled several stalks.

He did not seem surprised to hear my voice, and I thought then that he had some sixth sense that always told him when I was near.

Without turning he said, "What brings you here?"

"The ride appealed to me."

"You should go home. There'll be more rain soon."

"Come with me."

"Aye, maybe."

A corncrake rasped on the edge of the field; the heavy unripe heads crowded against me. There was bindweed here, twining the stalks, and prodigal drifts of scarlet. This seed would be bitter when harvested.

"There'll be no scythe on that before October, if the frost doesn't kill it first." Then, with no appreciable change of tone, "Do you pray much, Margaret?"

"You know I don't."

"I don't know what you do. I don't know what you think half the time."

"Sometimes I pray for your safety." His lips curved slightly, but his eyes remained on the field. "I try to believe that something hears me.... What do you pray to?"

"Nothing hears my prayers. Nothing ever has." There was no sound but the wind and the corncrake, and then that too was silent. "I was taught a prayer once, during a summer like this. I was thinking of it when you came. 'The eye of the King of hosts of the living, the eye of the God of glory, pour down on us generously in thy season...'" The haloed sun had veiled itself, and there was a flicker of movement overhead, a dull flash of silver as kite or buzzard rolled upon the wing. "I care nothing for myself if this fails. I only care for you." Then, as though we were discussing some commonplace, "I think sometimes that, as a man, I fail you. You are not very happy, Margaret."

"I never see you."

He turned those piercing eyes on me.

"Is it so simple? My mere absence?"

"I preferred life as your mistress. You gave me more of your time, and you gave it more intensely. Now I seem to have dwindled into a wife. You have your freedom, and I keep my house."

"You can keep your freedom, I don't want it. I didn't marry you to wash my shirts and bide by the hearth with a smile on your face."

"Why did you marry me?"

"Expediency. The unconventional are not readily forgiven here."

"Perhaps it was foolish of me, but I hoped you might have said something else."

"What else do you want me to say? Do you want me to tell you I love you? Is it necessary for me to say it?"

There was a fine, blowing mist now. He seemed not to notice it.

I said, "Sometimes you make me wonder."

"You possess me, Margaret, and you were capable of that before you ever spoke my name. And I have never thought of you as my... wife." There was a brief, caustic silence, and I turned to leave him, but his next words arrested me. "I wanted to ask you to lie with me here, but for so many reasons it hardly seems appropriate."

He closed his eyes against the drifting rain and opened them again. I touched him, although I would never reach him: he had withdrawn from me into that inexplicable remoteness.

"Malcolm— come home."

"In a minute." He was removing his coat, and the handkerchief from its pocket. "Take this and wait for me."

I took his coat and asked what he intended.

"Just go... and wait for me."

The grain, like some darkening sea, surrounded me as I walked, and the wind ran over the field: it seemed I was very alone. Then an irresistible compulsion overwhelmed me and I looked over my shoulder and saw, not some natural bodily function but the removal of the knife from his boot: he rolled up his sleeve and drew the blade across his forearm, so that when I reached him blood was streaming from the wound. He watched it impassively, clenching his fist to quicken the flow and parting the grain with his boot so that the dark stain trickled down to the soil. Then he pressed the handkerchief over the wound, and I knew that this was some ritual he had come to this place to perform, perhaps because there had been no possibility of that intercourse which would have been the salt gift, the life-gift, the libation of seed and sexual energy he would have preferred.

He turned away without disturbing the place where the rain, already falling steadily, had washed the blood into the soil.

"Now let the land feed us," he said.

I returned to Glen Mor for the first time since my marriage on Wednesday the seventeenth of July. The air was close, humid and bitterly cold, but I had become so inured to the summer of 1771 that I barely noticed it, and was irritated only by the cloud that drifted as fog from the moor and obscured my vision for the first hour of my journey.

I reached the Bridge of Sian about midday, and from this sheltered glen it was possible to see the stain of snow in the high corries of Saobhaidh before the cloud closed over it again.

The village had emptied with the annual migration to the shielings, and with so many women absent I was relieved to find my aunt at home. I had invited myself, and I did not think an hour's unsolicited visit with my father would be either welcome or comfortable. He came in from the kirk in his shirtsleeves, with several sheets of blotted paper stuffed into his waistcoat pocket, and gave me neither the ordinary courtesy of a greeting nor the kiss with which my aunt had met me. Eventually he seemed to become aware of her displeasure and stopped eating long enough to stare at me, as he might examine a stranger at his board.

"Well, daughter?"

"Well, father?"

"What are you doing here?"

"Dining with my aunt, and you."

His response was a grunt, both dismissive and disapproving, and he said nothing more until the end of the meal, when it was noticed that I had been unable to reduce by any appreciable amount the heap of boiled mutton on my plate.

With another of those indescribable grunts he remarked to my aunt, "Hmph— breeding. And no wonder," and I saw the quick flush of embarrassment stain her bony cheek. He did not expect me to understand, but he had reckoned without the effect of cohabitation with a man for whom Gaelic was the essence of daily life, the language of business, thought, dream, lovemaking: in that atmosphere some osmosis was inevitable, and the implications of his comment and its obscure undercurrent of jealousy were not lost on me.

I said, "I understand that you find speculation irresistible, but I would be obliged if it were not indulged in in my presence," and without another word he scraped his chair back and left the table, throwing the napkin onto the plate. He went out, with his usual habit, where my relationship with Malcolm was concerned, of slamming the door; and the odd, delicate, female intimacy of my reunion with my aunt was poisoned, as though I were a prostitute returned. It was not until we had cleared the table and washed the dishes together that she ventured upon what she considered an unpardonable impropriety.

"Child— is it well with you?"

"Yes, Aunt."

"And... himself is well?"

"He is extremely well, but then, he always is."

She was drying her hands vigorously. Absence had sharpened my eye: she seemed if possible thinner, a gaunt, aging woman with a knot of greying hair scraped aggressively back from her face.... Who saw that luxuriant blackness unbound, now that I had gone? Who rinsed her hair with herbs as I had sometimes done, who brought that elusive, half-guilty smile to her lips with some sarcastic observation, or encouraged her to sing in a reedy but melodious voice at the cow's flank during the morning milking? She had chosen her life, or it had been chosen for her, to be in truth her brother's keeper, and she had grown old in the sterility of that life. I wondered what had moved her to so bleak a decision, so complete an obliteration of self.

She said, still drying her hands in that paroxysm of shyness which had first occured on the morning of my wedding, "You are not with child," and to spare her further embarrassment I said as gently as possible, "No, Aunt. I have had incontrovertible proof," and to my surprise she gave her high, girlish laugh.

"Oh, you are a forward lass! It is a providence your father cannot hear you."

"I imagine it would bring on an apoplexy."

The preparation of the evening meal followed: more water drawn, more fuel brought, more vegetables dug and chopped. There were weeds in the garden I had tended, and everything was glazed with rain. I returned to the firelit dimness of the kitchen and found my aunt stooping over a damp shirt on the table, carefully pressing the sleeve with one of the flatirons which had been heating on the hob. This too had been my work during my nine years in this house, and for an hour I resumed it, while relieved of this labour she immediately found something else to do. There was a little, difficult conversation, then it lapsed. I exchanged one flatiron for another, and the rain drifted against the window, and the kitchen filled with the smell of freshly ironed linen.

Unexpectedly she said, "George is not well, and not happy."

"What concern is that of mine?"

"He asks for news of you constantly. I said I had not heard."

"It is not within my power to grant him happiness."

"A kind word would be a Christian act. He pines for you."

"I am not appointed by God to succour his soul or anything else."

"I thought... at one time, you cared for him. Perhaps it was a fancy of mine."

The iron felt like lead, and my arm was aching.

"Perhaps it was."

"Aye, perhaps." She was too wise, too shrewd; and yet her voice was neutral, implying nothing. "He was bringing some books to the door the other week. He said you had lent them to him. I put them upstairs. Maybe you will want to take them away with you."

Another iron: another endless expanse of crumpled linen.

"You said he was not well. What's the matter with him?"

"He has your father's illness."

"And no doubt for the same reasons."

She said, "If you are happy, Margaret, spare a thought for him, out of pity."

"I can spare him nothing, and I want no contact with him. Perhaps the next time he brings books to the door that may be made known to him." Another iron: too hot, and the linen quickly scorched. "This is too much work for you. Why don't you hire some one to help you?"

She said slowly, as though her thoughts were elsewhere, "Aye, maybe when they come back. Your father will have something to say about it."

I sponged the scorched linen and left the rest; the afternoon was growing late. I went up to my box-like room and found George's present to me, wrapped in crushed brown paper, on the floor near the narrow bed.

I returned with it to the kitchen. Deirdre was stooping over the table, thumping one of the heavy irons against another shirt.

"I must go, Aunt."

She said, "I had hoped you would stay to supper, despite your father's lack of courtesy."

"I cannot. And I would prefer to preserve peace in the house, for your sake."

She put the iron down and stood in the rain watching me mount. There was no embrace upon my departure.

"You should not ride so." I had not used a side-saddle since coming to Glen Sian. "It is not seemly."

"The road is no place for decorum, Aunt."

She stood, ignoring the rain.

"The books are with you?"

"Yes, Aunt."

"And you will be coming again?"

"If you will have me come."

She walked beside me, then she held out her hand to delay me.

"Child— be a dutiful wife to him."

"It is no duty, Aunt. Believe me."

"I hope you may always say so."

I rode down the rainy waste of the street, feeling the eyes of Glen Mor upon me from every smoking doorway: passed the school, where every pane was dark, crossed the bridge into the dripping gloom of the gorge, where the cataract roared down from the heights. And then the road running by the river and the river swollen with rain: a road forever haunted for me by that ghost in discoloured scarlet, the younger Mordaunt whom I had never known, who had ridden here in a similar cold dimness in a July a quarter of a century ago. And then Glen Sian, stones still blackened by smoke the rains of twenty-five

457

years could not cleanse, and haunted for me by another ghost, and the anguish of another loss: Ewen, again in July, the cold summer of yet another year.

What happened here?

Only the commonplace.

And in that haunted place where the ways divided, and the road to the dead descended into the shrouded stillness of Glen Sian, and the road to my past lay along the river behind me, and the road I must ride was a rutted track ascending into the fast-falling rain, I dismounted, and tore open the wrapping of the parcel that was a weight of stone, a weight of repulsive memory dragging me down like an incubus. The books were indeed mine, and the price I paid for their return was the letter placed between the covers. An hour later, with the desolation of the moor on my right, I halted and opened it, and rain spattered the single page, and blurred his raving flood of passion and threats of exposure if I did not see him again. I tore it into fragments and scattered them the length of the last mile.

By then the rain had stopped. There was no one at home.

It was ten o'clock in the evening before Malcolm returned, abrupt and irritable and soaked to the skin: the stallion had thrown a shoe on the hill, and he had walked eleven miles with him. He groomed the horses for his usual hour, came in and refused everything but whisky, and slept immediately and heavily. I lay awake, unable to still the flood of memory, and at some dark hour of the night his hand touched my face gently, almost as if, in sleep, he knew; and in the darkness the rain began again.

My position at Ardsian had altered subtly with my marriage. I was a guest of the landowner and his wife, and my husband was their employee: I was a friend, and Malcolm neither considered himself nor wished to be considered in that light, and more than once he reminded me of the difference in our status. A period of uneasy hesitation ensued, as if we were all players who had blundered into some impromptu social drama and no one knew what behaviour was now appropriate, what conventions should be observed, what invitations issued or withheld. The coolness of Malcolm's manner toward those whose friendship I held dear signalled no desire for inclusion, and invitations were ungraciously rebuffed until they were extended to me alone.

So it was that on the afternoon of Thursday August first I took tea in the garden at Ardsian, while in the estate office, where he had sat since daybreak, my husband was collecting the Lammas rents, and interviewing complainants who refused to pay, and mediating with less than his customary grace in the usual disputes between neighbours. Charlotte and I sat in the sunlight, partaking of berries and cream and teabread and butter and a host of sweet dishes all alive with wasps and laid out on queen's ware and mended damask on a table on the lawn, and so pleasantly did the time pass that she invited me to stay to supper, and to convey the invitation to the estate office. I could think of no plausible excuse or alternative, and it was something that was best done alone. I left her waiting for James and wafting an indolent fan at the wasps, and went round to the side of the house. Even that dark stairway and the passage beyond were crowded with men and a few shawled women, leaning against the walls and talking quietly while the procession shuffled forward. An immediate silence fell when I appeared, and then here and there I heard a murmured greeting, and shyly and self-consciously they made way for me. The office was occupied, the door ajar, and as I approached there was a hostile exchange of voices. Then a man I did not recognize shouldered out, and from within the estate office came a sharp summons in Gaelic to the next tenant. An expectant hush had fallen over the passageway, and it was audible even when I entered the office. I closed the door behind me.

He was seated, in his shirtsleeves, his coat draped over the back of the chair and the chair at an uncomfortable angle to the table so that it would not confine his long legs, which were crossed in a position he must have changed constantly throughout the eleven hours he had sat here. On the table were two quills and a standish, the relevant ledger and rent roll, and an opened strongbox displaying very little money. There was no sign of refreshment, only a heavy pall of tobacco smoke, and despite the opened window the air was stale and noisome. He looked tired, although only I would have recognized his fatigue.

He spoke in English, conscious always of the ears that listened.

"So, Margaret?"

"I've been drinking tea in the garden."

"I know what you were doing. What do you want of me?"

"I have been asked to sup here tonight. The invitation includes you."

"I have not dined, or been asked to dine, in this house for twenty years. I don't intend to begin now."

"That is your decision."

"Yes," he said. "It is."

"Very well then. I shall tender your regrets."

He was writing rapidly and did not look up.

"I have no regrets," he said.

Strangely, I could still be hurt. I said rather coldly, "I apologize for having disturbed you."

He plunged the quill into the ink again, pausing only to rub his forehead with his left hand. I had not yet seen the onset of migraine, but the gesture, a weakness he despised in himself, always preceded the many lesser headaches to which he was subject. I turned back, instinctively, protectively, repressing the desire to touch him.

"Shall I have something sent to you?"

He said harshly, "Aye, nightfall, and an end to this bloody business."

I went out, composing the mask of my face for those who were eager to see it; and behind me, I presumed he did the same.

The table was as I had left it except that a fresh pot of tea had arrived, and James had presented himself, casually and expensively dressed, in a gesture toward the afternoon's heat, in a new cream satin waistcoat and pale breeches. He rose with a little sarcastic bow when he saw me.

"My dear Mrs. Scott, I hope I find you well?"

"Very well, thank you. Please sit down."

He returned to his plate. Charlotte was observing me with a slight, ironic smile.

"And his answer?"

"He regrets that his work will prevent him from joining us."

James, eating busily, said, "Oh, I shouldn't worry about that. I've often known him sit up there till ten or eleven at night."

"But this is monstrous! The man must have some leisure," and she began to rise. "Perhaps I may succeed where you fail, Margaret."

"I should not attempt it if I were you. His temper is a little short today."

James said, with his mouth full, "I can never tell the difference," and Charlotte, snapping open her fan to avoid glancing at my face, sat down again and said abruptly, "That will do, James."

He merely smiled and turned his attention to the preserves, cursing the wasps under his breath.

There was talk: gentle, unthreatening discussion of fashions and furniture, of a carpet in the attic in which I had expressed an interest and for which Charlotte would not let me pay; talk of America, the suspension of hostilities both actual and political which might prove the breathless hush before war or merely the preservation of a brittle peace; talk of the weather, while the sun, gloriously, radiantly hot, threw our lengthening shadows over the golden grass, and struck a burning light from the silver and the glasses and the many gems in Charlotte's rings. She sat opposite me in a yellow and white striped silk, with her fair hair tied up in a muslin cap beneath a ribboned straw hat, and the diamonds were a blinding, restless pattern as the fan flickered back and forth across her face. She had put on weight, which, like James, she did easily, and although she was not a pretty woman she possessed a quality of stillness and serenity and grace that became her more than beauty. I suspected the reason, although she had given me no hint, and during one of her absences from the table James confirmed it.

"When is the birth?"

"January. However... one never knows what may happen in the meantime, so perhaps you would oblige me by saying nothing to any one else, for the present."

"Of course."

"My thanks." He toyed with the sugar tongs and stirred his tea loudly, aimlessly. "I daresay she'll tell you when she thinks the time is right.... It came as a shock to me, for one reason and another. I thought it was no longer an issue."

Then he assumed the negligent pose again, lay back in the chair and gazed at me with eyes half-closed against the sun. "So let us speak of other things. How is life with the demon lover?"

"Very happy, thank you."

"You must think me very gullible."

"I am sorry if I disappoint you."

"Well, better you than me. I wouldn't care to live with him." He steepled his fingers and watched me over them. "So, my child, apart from a pinchbeck ring and a few hours of unearthly delight, what was his wedding gift to you?"

"You presume too far, James."

His face changed and he leaned forward, taking my left hand.

"I would presume further. If you were mine I would shower you with diamonds."

"And whose money would pay for them, yours or mine?"

He released my hand.

"Touché," he said, and picked at a thread on the tablecloth until a wasp, brushing the back of his hand, annoyed him, and he attacked it viciously with the fan Charlotte had left lying by her plate.

He said, staring out over the lawn, "I had a brief interview with your spouse the other day. We discussed this and that, and in the course of our conversation I remarked that the August trysts are almost upon us and ventured to ask what number of beasts he was taking to market. He informed me that it was not his intention to attend the trysts, and that the market would prove more favourable next month. I said I hoped he knew his business, because I was rather short of the ready, and his answer was, and I quote, 'I do, and I'll thank you to mind yours'. So, my dear, the unprecedented sweetness of temper observed with cynicism by some of us over the past several weeks has dissipated. I hardly dare to ask what he intends instead. Have you any idea?"

461

"None. He does not discuss the business of the estate with me."

"Nor with me, by God." Then he said idly, watching me, "I saw your friend the tosspot the other day as well, in Glen Mor. I sometimes question his fitness to teach. Have you any thoughts on the matter?"

"Your dealings with him are your own affair, not mine."

"But my dear Margaret, I value your opinion. You know the man more intimately than any of us. Has he a brain in his head, or is it more or less permanently pickled?"

"I suggest you consult my father." He snorted. "I believe in his time he was a considerable teacher, and a scholar of some renown."

"Hmm. Well, perhaps I will. Better than having the fellow here— I don't think he'd prove a popular guest in some quarters." He glanced again in the direction of the house, but there was no one in sight. "I don't suppose you were unaware of... various rumours that came to one's ear over a period of time. I don't want you to say anything— don't confirm or deny— but I know you take my meaning."

I said, "Why don't you come to the point?" and, surprisingly, he flushed.

"I will, then. I will. I've always tried to keep your interests at heart, Margaret, ever since Papa.... Well, I know he would expect me to continue to offer you my protection and my counsel. I chose to overlook a certain ugly incident, but charges could have been brought if the injured party had desired it, and God knows where that would have led. So if I may offer you a piece of brotherly advice, in which spirit I hope you will take it... if there was any connection in the past, I suggest you keep it very quiet. Malcolm has a nasty turn of mind, and the prospect of him jealous is most unpleasant."

"Rest assured, then, that I shall not tell him the finer points of this tête-à-tête."

He said without irony, "I would be obliged to you, Margaret, and you may come to see the sense of it yourself." There was movement on the terrace: Charlotte returning, as though she had been waiting for her cue. "And mind, I've said nothing about the other business. It's quite natural, after all— all women come to it, even you."

He rose languidly to his feet as she approached and kissed my hand and then her cheek, she stooping to receive it, then he absented himself on some imaginary errand to avoid any further exposure to female conversation. Unlike his father, he could never credit a woman with the power of serious thought, so he would never know the substance of that conversation, or the depth of his wife's philosophy, or her religious conviction, or the true joy in the revelation of her pregnancy, of which she spoke as we walked in the garden, or the strength and reassurance she conveyed to me, who knew her vulnerability and feared for her. He could never know that it was the essence of life to her, the essence of her identity as woman: that I needed no such fulfillment but to her it was life itself, her very being, the ultimate gift and perhaps the ultimate sacrifice. And of that day it is not James whom I remember, nor even my lover, whose power to injure me was always as profound as my love for him. It is Charlotte, beloved Charlotte, burying her face in the blowsy, silken petals, cutting the last roses of the summer and sharing them with me: the sound of silk on the sunlit grass, the golden light, the perfume.

On this summer night the casements stood open, and moths haunted the candlelight: the wine warmed in the goblets, the flute played and carried in the stillness. In the coolness of evening the earth breathed, perfume and decay, the eternal cycle, and after the heat of the day the dew lay cold on the grass. There was a slow staining of sunset, overlaid with leaves, and as yet no moon.

As on that September evening when he had seen that in which he utterly believed, the spirit of the beloved dead, he had been drawn or summoned to this place against his own inclination; his only desire now was solitude and sleep. He had no ear for music or recognition of the piece or knowledge of the language in which it was sung; it had come to him faintly as he had stood breathing the air after the day's imprisonment, and the voice had been a thing of beauty, which had ravished the soul with loveliness. And he followed it, moth-like, to the source: the mullioned panes of the south-facing windows standing open and the candlelight spilling over the terrace. He stood, unconscious of time, unconscious of fatigue, surrendering his soul to it with a most perfect joy, lost in the soaring ascent and its delicate accompaniment, the immense purity of every note. Then, unbearably, the thrush sang, the music ceased, the voice was silent, and a shadow came to the casement and closed it, and he was alone in the darkening garden, always, always alone.

I carried the perfume of summer home at moonrise, wrapped in a web of introspection and troubled reminiscence. There was no one in the house although the door was unlocked and candles were burning on the table. I found him in my garden, digging the footing of a wall against which I had proposed to espalier fruit trees. The moon was copper in a clear sky over his shoulder, rising even as we spoke, and staining a solitary veil of cloud with light. The night was distinctly cold.

He was digging in his shirtsleeves, with a powerful, effortless energy although in the estate office he had looked deeply fatigued, and for a time he seemed unaware of my presence; then, as though he sensed he was no longer alone, he thrust the spade into the damp earth and raised his head. Seeing me, he resumed his work.

When I reached him he continued digging, his body beautiful in its strength.

"You asked me to do this for you. I have not had the time."

"Why is it necessary to do it now?"

"I choose to," he said.

"Have you eaten?"

"No."

The spade scraped on stone and thudded deeply again. "You had a pleasant evening, I trust?"

"I would have enjoyed it more if you had been with me."

"Diplomatic, but untrue. Who brought you home?"

"I came alone."

He removed some obstacle visible only to his eyes and left the spade in the ground. The moon, blood-red in its rising, had paled perceptibly.

"And what ill-mannered bastard decided that?"

"It was my decision." Then, as he moved once more, "Will you leave that and come inside? I want to talk to you."

He left it, surprisingly without argument, and came with me, carrying the spade. The perfume of the roses was a haunting presence in the house.

"What is it?"

They were lying on the table. He touched one, with one of those long, callused fingers, and a blood-red petal fell into his palm. With unbearable poignancy I was reminded of my wedding night, the dying fragrance of discarded roses, the lover's morning gift.

"Nothing. Only a ghost." Then, "I always used to think of Ewen when I saw these. Now they always bring you to my mind." Another petal fell, and he closed his fingers gently on them. "That was a pretty thing you sang for James this evening."

"Where were you?"

"Taking the air." He opened his fist and let the petals fall. "Maybe some night you will sing to me." There was a pause: he was still, very still, everything was still, the candleflames, the night. "What was it called, your song?"

" 'Lascia ch'io pianga'."

"Italian."

"Yes. And I sang it for Charlotte, not for James."

"Maybe some time you will tell me what it means. I never learned Italian from Ewen, although it was his pleasure to teach me French." He smiled, that faint, familiar, bitter smile. "I spoke French before English, did you know? And I spoke no word of English until I was thirteen. I remember your father's comment on Ewen's efforts in that direction. He said I should be put to the plough, as there would never be anything in my head worth teaching." I said nothing; no words would diminish the injury and the insult to a child whose sensitivity was never suspected. "So now my field is a hundred square miles, and I plough it with economics, and I sow it with my brains and with my money, and if I closed my hand upon it I could make it mine. Not bad for the bare-arsed bastard, eh?" He looked up, with that hard, piercing stare. "You said you wanted to talk to me. The last time some one said that to me it made my blood run cold."

And suddenly, in this mood and in this manner, it was impossible.

"It doesn't matter."

"It must have mattered if you made a point of saying that you wished to talk. What was it you wanted to say?"

I said, "Charlotte is with child," and there was a silence; then he said, "When?"

"January."

"That's a cruel welcome for any bairn."

He leaned back, and the candlelight was not strong enough to dispel the shadows or to illuminate his face. "Well, well. You had a most enlightening evening. What else did your friends have to say?"

"James is trying to divine your intentions this month."

"James can mind his own damned business. I leave for England Monday week, and you too, if you'll ride with me. And I go on my own affairs, and yours, not his."

The impact could not have been more shocking. I thought I had misheard.

"Cumberland, maybe into Westmorland. I believe you know it."

The grey moors of Durham reddened with summer, the smoke of High Force, the flowers of Teesdale. Thirty miles, after a mere ten years. A day's ride from Evesham.

He must have known what it meant to me. He must have known what he was asking.

"Will you ride with me, Margaret? Or will you stay here and keep your house?"

Perhaps it was offered to me with an open heart, out of an honest desire for my company. Perhaps it was some excruciating test; perhaps a challenge, perhaps a gift.

Whatever it was, there was only one answer; and he already knew.

***

He left Glen Sian on Monday the twelfth of August, and was gone for twenty-two days. He travelled alone, because in the darkness two hours before our departure I had allowed myself to recognize the truth. If I had gone with him to England, I would not have come back.

He did not seek to know my reasons, and I did not delude myself that, with his uncanny perception, they remained a secret from him.

So he left, and every hope or pleasure or diversion or intimacy the journey might have afforded us fell into the breach and was lost forever: ours was not to be that vivid, optimistic life but always this moribund silence, Glen Sian. I would never know the man he was when he left it, nor would he know the woman who might have been. I put the world from myself, and denied myself, perhaps out of love for him.

He left me, but remained with me, as his powerful spirit had always possessed me in his absences: such was the strength of his personality in the house that I never felt alone, and occasionally I imagined that I heard him, or caught myself glancing up as though he had come into the room. I wrote a good deal at his desk, and read the letters in the pigeonholes: he had told me to take what I wanted and open what I liked, he had no secrets from me. He had many, but they were now too carefully concealed, and their mystery confounded me; the letters at least were ordinary, communications from tradesmen. The ledgers and his journals both here and in the estate office were almost illegible even to me, and occasionally evolved into a private shorthand. The language of business was invariably English, and the entries over a period of years so pessimistic that I found myself walking the house, asking him aloud why he had never told me, never shared the bleakness of that responsibility he documented with such unflinching precision.

The spirit, ever enigmatic, ever elusive, gave nothing, and the man would never confide in me. All I had was paper, and the sound of the rain, the shadowed desk, the silent room. I was alone, and there were no answers, only the insoluable riddles of the past, the repetitive patterns of economic failure, financial crisis, climactic uncertainty, and the narrow margin between subsistence and outright starvation. The mind that played here with figures and surveys, and corresponded with southern graziers and proponents of agricultural improvement, was not merely progressive but also deeply Celtic, and immersed in a superstition he did not find incompatible with the age of enlightenment.

Now let the land feed us....

I slept that night with one of his coats on the bed beside me. Eventually, haunted by the bleakness of his vision, I buried my face in it for comfort. The house was cold, and filled with the constant whispering of rain, and his spirit, my companion, had left me, and was neither mine nor his but always lost upon that dark road, always lost in the darkness between us.

In the estate office my conviction of impending disaster became a certainty, and I wondered that no one save he and I could see it. Perhaps James was disinterested in his own affairs, or was not permitted access to these records.

I rearranged nothing and disturbed only what was necessary, in the guise of dusting, polishing and waxing. The room appeared not to have been thoroughly cleaned for years, and this was not extraordinary. Although fastidious in person, he was utterly indifferent to his physical surroundings, and discomfort and untidiness were irrelevant unless they interfered with the execution of his duties.

In his papers I attempted to read the future, and found only the failures of the past, the bitter frustration and the despair, and the infuriating shorthand. There was also a list of James's debts, dated December 1770: it ran into the hundreds, and a second page was missing. There were deeds, maps on folded parchment overwritten with browning ink, calfskin volumes discoloured by mildew, a piece of veined, broken granite: nothing more personal than these. No keys, no coins, no strongbox, few letters and none other than from tradesmen, no record or evidence of Malcolm's own debts or the extent of his finances. He had taken no wages from Glen Sian for nearly ten years, and he was adamant that my own money should not be touched: perhaps he was contemptuous of it. And yet, we lived; and he had invested heavily in the flock of Swaledales. Not only that, but his business in England was the purchase of more sheep, or at least an investigation into the potential of another breed, the newly improved Cheviot.

His papers told me everything and nothing. In his place of work the trappings of his life were ordinary. The vital knowledge, the secret intentions, remained his alone. As always, I sought him as I sought the truth. As always, they eluded me.

I drifted across Glen Sian, on foot and on horseback. I felt a curious compulsion to observe and record, as if some impartial account would have to be rendered up on his return. I watched the haying, and was watched from the fields by men and women who must have recognized me; I might have been a shadow for all their acknowledgment. By my marriage I had divorced myself from these people, or been divorced by them, and Malcolm's absence was now widely known: to them I was Malcolm in absentia, and I tasted the isolation which had always been his life.

And what was Malcolm, animate in me, drove me restlessly to the fields and opened my eyes to what I found there. On the edge of an upland expanse of barley the heads soaked the leather of my glove, and the grains were bitterly inedible; the leaves were mottled with rust or some other discolouration that left traces of powder on my skirt. With a gardener's instinct I pulled up the plant and took it home, where I burned it. A week later there were signs of the same infestation in a different part of the field, and further unscientific gestures on my part would not alter the outcome. The entire crop was affected.

There was a brief interval of sunlight, during which the midges were a torment, then great winds that damaged the standing grain, furious squalls of rain that caused the lochan to rise nine inches in a single night, and days of fog so impenetrable that I remained at home, unable to see my way with safety even to Ardsian. A sharp cold followed, the nights were intensely clear, and the aurora descended more vividly than I had ever seen it, twisting and flickering for hours across the northern sky. Malcolm from childhood had thought this phenomenon sinister, a portent of war or disaster: I had always dismissed this as mere superstition, but in my dark garden on the curve of the earth I felt uncomfortably close to that torment in heaven, and it was not difficult to perceive the insignificance of my own humanity in the vastness and indifference of that night.

I was tired and dispirited, apprehensive of the future, and physically and spiritually lonely: for Malcolm's voice and the sounds of his occupation in the house and the patterns my life assumed when he was with me, for his companionship, acerbic though it often was, for the mere reassurance of his presence, the sense of an abiding protection, for sexual love, which had been a revelation to me. I never suspected him of infidelity during his absence. I sensed that his sexual activity in the past had been provoked more by unhappiness and alienation than any physical hunger, and if it was possible for any human being to assuage that unhappiness I had done it, had given him as much as I was capable of giving. Our physical satisfaction was mutual and intense, and I believed him at peace in our marriage.

The date of his return was uncertain, and the weather became ever more unpredictable. Strong winds, sudden squalls, sharp cold assaulted Glen Sian. I lit fires upstairs, expecting every morning to see the first disastrous frost upon the ground. Domestic irritations plagued me. Slugs infested my potatoes, a clean sheet hanging to dry was inexplicably stained with mud as though a dirty hand had grasped it, a row of Michaelmas daisies coming into bloom was uprooted, I thought by some marauding badger. The night of the twenty-eighth of August was windless and bitterly cold, and although there was no frost by daybreak I saw that snow had fallen on the higher ground.

I dug potatoes all morning, until the sun with the fickleness of August was scorching my back through my coat. There was peace for me in labour on this, the first land that was truly mine— although I had not planted this crop I had weeded and tended it, and the care of Malcolm's garden and what I harvested there for my table gave me immense pleasure. I worked, oblivious to time, in the heat of the midday sun, from potatoes to salad vegetables, and equally oblivious to my ungloved hands bees and small azure butterflies explored the glistening leaves around me. Peace and sunlight, and then a shadow fell across me and there was peace no more.

I had not seen him since my wedding. He seemed somehow shrunken, as shabbily dressed as ever, and deathly pale. He was wearing a hat, which he swept off and tucked beneath one arm; under the other he held one of the marbled portfolios he kept his sketches in. His voice was perfectly sober, perfectly courteous.

"I hope you will forgive this intrusion. I was passing, and I wanted to see you." His eyes, strange, amber, near-sighted eyes, flickered toward the house. "Is he at home?"

"You know he is not."

"That's true. A general sigh of relief was heard over Glen Sian when he left. I have not yet heard the weary sigh that heralds his return."

"What do you want?"

"Only a moment's conversation. I saw you from the road— I knew it could be no one else."

"Will you come up to the house?"

He said with dignity, "I will sit a moment with you if you have no objection— I am a little weary. But not in his house."

I stood, rather stiffly. I had a hazel basket at my feet filled with potatoes for my own use, and I reached for the handle. Before I could touch it he had stepped in among the salads and his fingers brushed mine coldly, and then withdrew.

"Your poor hands," he said.

"It is only dirt, George. It will wash off."

He said roughly, "Leave it," and shifted his hat and portfolio and took the basket from me. "By God, I would rather die than see you scrabbling in the muck. If you were my wife...."

"Any further word on that subject and there will be no conversation. I compromise myself enough merely by standing here."

"Marriage has made you hard, Margaret. Hard and discourteous. But that is only to be expected when your taste runs to marrying whinstone."

469

I turned away. He took me by the arm and I felt his hand trembling.

"Margaret, don't use me ill. Seven miles I walked this day, just for the sight of your face, and I have not been well. Let me sit a little while and talk, and let bygones be bygones."

We sat, because he would not come into the coolness of the house, on a green-painted wooden bench Malcolm had made for me outside my kitchen door. In deference to the conventions of Highland hospitality I offered him whisky. He refused everything but water, which I drew for him from the well. He sat sipping it, holding the cup unsteadily, staring out over the garden.

"It has a pleasing aspect, although whether it will still please you in winter is doubtful."

"I shall still be here in the winter, though, come what may."

"You shouldn't say that." He set the cup down, spilling a little. "You don't know what may come, Margaret. No one knows." His face in profile was bony and drawn: he sat, perhaps deliberately, with the scars toward me. Presently he said, "I've given up the drink, do you know. I tell you now... it was the hardest thing I ever did, except to see you married to that—" His fingers closed convulsively on his knee. "No— don't go. I'll say no more of it. I gave it up for you."

I watched the bony fingers clasping one another, the gaunt, untidy limbs, the nodding head, jerking from time to time as if with an uncontrollable palsy. It seemed impossible that those restless fingers had ever touched me, in an intimacy I could no more contemplate now than if it had happened in another life.

He said, gazing out over the garden, "I came to thank you for giving Glen Sian your good opinion of me. It seems he will not turn me off this season."

"I am glad to know it."

"I took it very kindly that you should speak so well of me. You have no reason to love me— what I bring upon myself by my own folly is hardly your affair." He turned abruptly. "Maybe you did it for the sake of an old friendship. I dearly like to think so."

"You offered me intellectual friendship in a wasteland. I will always be grateful for that."

"I would to God it were not an intellectual friendship now. I never loved anything more than you, not even the bottle."

Pity, fatal pity, which he had always inspired in me, stirred, and I said, perhaps with more gentleness than I had intended, "I never knew you...."

"Had my weakness? Always. Always, Margaret. I came to it in joy in my youth and I returned to it in misery. It was all I wanted. I dose myself with other poisons. I drink things to make myself sick, to make me forget, anything to stop wanting it. But it comes in my dreams, like you, my dear love— you come to me too, when I sleep. And there's no end to it, no end— maybe the river. Who knows?"

I laid my hand on his knee. Gently he brushed it aside.

"No, don't do that. It reminds me too much of the only time you ever touched me. And I threw it all away, base, lecherous bastard that I was. I was never worthy... and the irony of it is— that that was all I wanted of you then. I never loved you. I only wanted that knowledge of you— carnal knowledge. I thought what a triumph, to have had your beauty—me, an ugly man. Who would ever think you could give yourself to me? And now I've paid for it, my dear, by loving you. The love struck me down like a curse, and it came too late. Too late to sanctify anything between us, too late to make you forgive me— too late for anything but this. I die for love of you."

We sat in silence: the sun had moved, and its warmth no longer touched the bench or the wall behind us. Above us, light no longer filled the room where Malcolm and I slept, and had loved, and would love again.

"I wish you had never come."

"I will not come again. I wanted only to tell you, in case there was no other opportunity. And to give you this."

His fingers were trembling on the ribbons of the portfolio, and the heavy paper quivered as he withdrew it.

"I could not forgive myself for my behaviour at the wedding. I beg you to accept this as a token of my goodwill. You need not tell him where it came from, or ever show it to him."

It was myself, in a strange, half-lit world of pencil and smudged charcoal, dressing alone on the morning of my wedding, in a faithful reproduction of the silk gown and the roses which had adorned it, and the heavy necklace with its antique gold links and polished, dark green ovals. My face, in the fantasy of his art, was veiled by my hair, an abstract portrait with downcast eyes: his subject might have been any woman. In his scholarly, elegant hand he had written the date of my marriage and the title of the portrait, *an bean-bainnse*. The bride.

I cannot remember what words came to me, if words came at all. He was fumbling in the portfolio.

"I could not help myself. There are two others. Forgive me."

The technique was the same in these: the unerring hand, the purity of line, the faces obscured in a wash of shadow, and yet familiar; the fall of silk from a naked shoulder, the bared breasts, the abandonment of the embrace. Lovers, in a candlelit world which should have remained theirs alone. The final portrait was of lovemaking; only afterwards I recognized its powerful tenderness. The woman's face in rapture was my own.

He took them gently from me, as though they were precious to him, and numbly I wondered that he could inflict such torment upon himself.

"Give them to me."

He gave them willingly enough, although he knew what I would do. I tore them, as I had torn his letter, into fragments.

He said, "It will do no good. There are more visions of the same in my head. And one should never destroy beauty— I intended them to be beautiful."

Their beauty was undeniable, their eroticism compelling and repulsive. What were they but poetry made visible, the haunting, illegible pornography hidden in the drawer, in the shadowed room and in the mind of the man who loved me, in that artist's world of shadows and in the light of day?

"And what do you intend to do with these... visions?"

"Live by them. Comfort myself with them. Love you through them, though I may never touch you. Don't you find them beautiful? Do you not see truth in them? Or don't you see that in his face, what I show to you?"

"If your purpose is blackmail, I will not answer for the consequences."

"I intended only to create beauty, and to love you. As for blackmail— look into my face and tell me if you think me fool enough to invite that hand's attentions again." Then he said, very softly, "I hoped you would take them as my wedding gift. You could have kept them secretly. There was only love in the giving. I mean you no harm."

He left me, with the fragments in my lap. Later I burned them, repressing the desire to reassemble them, these half-lit, voyeuristic visions of my marriage. Visions that had haunted his nights now haunted mine, and I woke, imagining some sound in the house, imagining that Malcolm had come home.

There was nothing, no wind, no sound, no shadow in the darkness, no living flesh, only emptiness, the empty night, the dying fire, and the memory of a dream of loss, unspeakably painful, unspeakably vivid, which refused to die, as dreams die, with the coming of the light.

Haunted by the empty rooms, the cold, dead, weighted air, I drew the house around myself, furnished it, and tried to convince myself that it was my home. My writing desk and chairs and a sofa arrived from Ardsian, shrouded in canvas against the rain and wheeled in a hand cart by two burly and inarticulate members of the household, who contemplated entering the factor's house with apprehension until it became obvious that I could not unload the furniture myself. They removed their shoes and walked softly in damp stockinged feet on the carpets I had laid, arranged the pieces and left a hessian bag full of discarded draperies from Charlotte on the floor. She did not come herself, and I realized that although I was expected to pass like a spirit between two worlds, my visits to Ardsian would never be reciprocated and my invitations would remain unheard.

One other voyeur needed no invitation, and took advantage of Malcolm's absence to manifest herself in my garden. Her arms and feet and a shapeless assortment of clothing, both men's and women's, were filthy, and she stank.

I said, with no obvious show of surprise, "Cò tu?" Who are you?

She said in a high precise voice, as though it should have some significance, "Mairi," and then, with an insolence that did not escape me, "Dè 'n diofar dhutsa?" What is it to you?

"It would be something to you if my husband were at home. He has a particular dislike of tinkers."

She laughed shrilly, still crouched among the rain-wet cabbages with her arms around her knees, and her answer was so rapid and idiomatic that it was incomprehensible. Very little in the musical flow of her speech was recognizable except Malcolm's name, and mine in the vocative tense: the rest were obscenities. Then she lurched to her feet; one naked leg was shrunken and looked incapable of supporting her, and my furious impulse to strike her was arrested by the realization that she was lame.

At the top of the stone steps she turned, still laughing, still cursing me, with the mane of filthy hair tumbling around a feral little face, then she raised her fingers obscenely and spat, and flung herself down the steps. By the time I reached the place where she had stood she was wading into the shallows of the lochan, with curlews exploding from the reeds around her: then their cries died away into the mist and there was nothing, only what might have been a child or a dream, a fragment of my fevered imagination. Only the knowledge that she had called Malcolm familiarly by name, and now, like him, eluded me.

She reappeared, not the grinning, insulting phantom in the garden where I expected her, but as a musky animal smell in the very house. I had locked the doors before leaving on horseback: when I returned an hour later the kitchen door was standing wide open. There was no possibility of Malcolm having come home, and housebreaking was unknown in Glen Sian. Nonetheless, there was property of value in the house as well as my money, and with blind courage and fury I hurled myself up the stairs.

She was standing with her back to me in the dimness of my room. The bed was strewn with my clothing although nothing of Malcolm's had been touched, the doors of my armoire were open, and she was gazing at her reflection in the mirror, holding my wedding gown against her filthy skin. She

473

wore nothing but a patched chemise, and she seemed to be fumbling with the many hooks of the gown. Her reflection was rapt with pleasure.

She must have heard me, and when she turned her mouth was a soundless O, perhaps of surprise, perhaps of fear. Some remnant of sanity made me throw away what I had brought, the stiletto from Malcolm's study, and I hit her, bodily and in the face, until she crumpled into an unresisting heap with the silk whispering over her. I wrenched it from her and sat with it cradled in my arms, weeping and cursing her: time seemed to have no meaning, and vaguely I wondered if it was possible to have killed her. She neither moved nor cringed, although her eyes were open, as though anticipating further violence: she was utterly still, lying on the floor where she had fallen. She did not look at me, and I made no attempt to touch her; the room was silent except for the sound of my breathing. Then gradually, with an odd animal grace, she drew herself together and came to her feet, seemed to stumble a little and stood motionless, the tangled hair hiding her face. Eventually she moved as though in a daze, finding her way with one outstretched hand. I heard the unhurried steps retreating, and then nothing.

I sat where I was, cradling my wedding gown, and tears of rage and shame and violation dropped on silk already despoiled by her fingers. And although she had gone, she remained with me, in her stillness and smallness the embodiment of the spirit of the cold, dead rooms, the passive, beaten child whose veiled eyes saw nothing but the violence of the world. Whose veiled eyes, although the child was dead, still watched the world without hope and without pain, and were the eyes of Malcolm.

On the night of Monday, the second of September, I woke paralyzed by fear, and by the certainty that a hand had passed close to my face. After a day of storm there was no sound but the wind that harrowed the night, and no light but an endless expanse of cloud illuminated by the hidden moon. The dead weight of fatigue overcame me, and I fell into oblivion once more.

I woke again, hours later. The eerie, oppressive ceiling of cloud had lifted and the night was a driven sea of moonlight: the moon, obscured no longer, poured over the bed and the chair beyond it. He slept there, fully clothed, the rough black hair spilling away into shadow, the moonlight bleaching his face.

I neither moved nor touched him: my touch would have awakened him. But I lay in the darkness watching him until night closed my eyes, and in that time, until the moon withdrew with the passing of the hour, nothing disturbed him, neither the intensity of its light nor the sound of the rising

474

wind. He slept as though exhausted or utterly at peace; and I slept also, and also at peace, as I had not slept since his departure.

I woke alone, in the hesitant greyness that presages dawn. The chair was empty, the stained baggage left neatly piled in the kitchen. The land, the oldest of his mistresses, had claimed him. It would always possess him before me.

We stood in my newly furnished sitting room. The sun, that rare spectacle, was setting, touching this west-facing window with copper.

He had been home for three days, and it was difficult to reconcile myself to his restless presence although I had hungered for it. I felt a certain shyness, a physical reserve, and he was uncommunicative and withdrawn. The journey had not been a pleasant one: the weather had been unremittingly foul, and what passed for roads in the Highlands as bad as he had expected, including the seventeen traverses of the Pass of Corrieyairack, which had been falling into disrepair in the thirty years since the army had built it. Nor had his business prospered; the stock offered for sale was unsatisfactory and the price of Cheviot rams exorbitant. Another journey might be necessary in the spring.

He did not seem to relish the prospect. In October he would be thirty-six years old; he felt infinitely older in spirit, and three years had passed since he had ridden those four hundred miles twice within the space of a few months. The road was harder than he remembered it, the journey remarkable only for its discomfort. Disdaining the lice and companionship of the inns, he had passed his nights on the ground, and all his clothing was soiled and smoky: he had lost weight, which with his height he could not afford, and acquired a harsh, rattling cough for which he refused all physic but whisky and hot water. Since his return, we had not made love.

In that time, also, he had given me his gifts: a gross of Madonna lily bulbs because I had spoken on some forgotten occasion of their scent in my childhood, a Lanarkshire nurseryman's catalogue, a bundle of novels haphazardly chosen by one who did not read for pleasure, a cut glass bottle of attar of roses. He had watched me intently as I opened them, as though he were unaccustomed to the act of giving and was uncertain that his gifts were acceptable.

He smoked and coughed, watching me with those ice-clear eyes.

I had been showing him the new writing desk, the two graceful mahogany chairs, the upholstered sofa, the crystal bowl on the unpainted mantel, incongruously elegant, and filled with the last Michaelmas daisies. If the effect was reminiscent of Ewen he made no comment. He merely glanced at the walls, remarked, "You want more pictures," and drew out the delicate chair at the desk. He waited for my assent.

I had prepared a fire, and knelt with the intention of lighting it. The westering sun threw his shadow across the wall and dyed the white plaster scarlet.

The clock in his study struck the half hour. The year's imperceptible decline into darkness seemed to take him by surprise.

"So soon," he said. "The summer is leaving us, Margaret."

He coughed and stared into the light, immersed in thoughts wherein the sun had no dominion. I left the struggling flame and knelt beside him, gazing with compassion into his face.

"There will be other summers."

"Will there? Will there, Margaret?" Then, "I would have given you the summer as a gift... I would have given you the sun."

What difference would that have made? The country of our spirits, the internal landscape, would still have been like this, a succession of shadow and fleeing light, ephemeral happiness, dying now as the light dies, as the year, as dreams die.

He got up abruptly, leaving me where I knelt. A weight of dead coldness possessed me. I followed him to the window, where he stood staring into the twilight.

"Malcolm... I know the barley is finished."

"To hell with the barley. We can live without it."

"Is there no possibility of saving it?"

"No. And I'll tell you something else. All Raasay is rotting in the ear."

The angry sun had vanished. Neither of us moved to light a candle.

"How do you know this?"

"I heard it in Badenoch from a Raasay man. I have no reason to doubt it."

"Have you told James?"

"I have that privilege tomorrow."

"Is there anything I can do?"

"You can go and tell him for me if you like. At least he won't ask you what you intend to do about it." He coughed shortly. "There's humour for you. Whatever I do will be the devil's work." Then, after a silence, "You made a bad bargain the day you married me."

"I don't think so."

"By Christ, I do."

The night was now wholly dark. Our reflections were insubstantial phantoms in the firelit glass. He seemed not to notice my hand on his arm.

"I never liked this room. I don't know why— if there was a reason I've forgotten it. I never cared for the house either... when I left it in the past it never mattered a damn to me if I came back or not. But this time I thought, Margaret will be there. Margaret will know what to do."

He paused, and we stood facing the darkness but not one another, and our faces fell away into the shadows of the night.

"You give life. You gave life to this house. You gave life to me when I was dead. It was all I could think of when I was away from you. A night with you to counsel me— a night with you to comfort me—"

He was silent: and in that silence, between our two shadows on the firelit glass, between his mouth and mine, between my tears and the desperate fury of the act of love, between the act and the fragmented dreams that followed, came the faint, insistent voice of the rain.

And between us fell the shadow. Between our limbs entwined in an act of increasing desperation, not of love but of survival, between our souls, imprisoned by sundering flesh and by more than flesh, between my mind, haunted by fearful imagination, and his, immersed in the cold recognition of a certainty. From me, who could offer him nothing but a counterfeit of calmness and confidence in the future, he sought reassurance and occasionally advice, but I was no farmer and no gambler, and his sense of isolation became more acute. He was adamant that the barley should be destroyed, to cleanse the soil and prevent infection in successive years, but even if he could have raised a flame in the sodden fields the tenants opposed any suggestion of burning, and he convened a series of meetings in the estate office in an attempt to persuade them. These, like discussions with James, invariably ended in savage argument: no agreement was reached, no contingency plans were decided upon: the barley was ploughed under, cut for fodder or harvested, although the grain was as bitter as gall. The oats remained unripe, and still uncut.

I lost my lover. The man who possessed me was himself possessed, by a knowledge and foreboding James dismissed as the chimeras of a morbid imagination. It was not imagination but an unendurable restlessness and fury that drove him from Ardsian to the fields, from the fields to An Reithe, where he passed two days and nights inspecting the sheep and interrogating the shepherds, sharing their crude accommodation: this investment remained sound, although the hope of financial stability for Glen Sian was rapidly diminishing. He walked the house at night, in the heavy darkness: sometimes he did this to reassure himself that there had been no frost, or, as the month progressed, that the rain, now drizzle, now an onslaught of sleet, had not turned to snow after midnight. By the low red flicker of the banked fire one night I woke and saw him standing at the window, staring sightlessly over the garden. He was naked, as he always slept, and his skin was as cold as stone. Although I spoke his name he did not answer, and although his eyes were open they were unwavering: he was asleep. In the morning he recalled nothing of the incident, and although he became visibly more remote and more driven, it did not recur.

My twenty-sixth birthday passed unremarked: no one appeared to remember. Afterwards, Malcolm left Glen Sian briefly to attend the Falkirk trysts. His absence, after the intensity of the past few weeks, came as a relief, and I passed the time, at his instruction, smoking and salting an immense quantity of fish and game. Toward the end of the month the physician who was to attend Charlotte arrived from Edinburgh, a grey man, grey hair, grey eyes, grey skin, grey manner. His name was Mackintosh, and I was entertained at Ardsian and introduced to him. He sat next to me at table and posed persistent and embarrassing questions about my past and my accent, which piqued his interest: and his fingernails and linen were unclean. I also renewed my acquaintance with Charlotte's parents, and those of her family who had accompanied Mackintosh on his foray into the wilderness, and suffered their attentions and enquiries concerning my marriage and my absent spouse. One of the younger women confessed to having cast an eye in his direction on a previous visit, although he had eluded her in an entirely characteristic manner: when Malcolm was disinterested in a woman his disinterest could be a thing of insulting coldness, and I wondered that she had not been more sensitive to it. I found myself calculating the cost of their clothing, and the meal over which James was presiding with conspicuous bonhomie, and Malcolm's opinion of it and of them was unspeakably clear in my mind.

I had not told him of George Cameron's visit: I never intended to do so, and fortunately it was not repeated. The girl demanded a separate explanation, and when this second absence of the year became known, she did not so much reappear as manifest herself in a profusion of small annoyances, breakages and a petty theft from my kitchen. On Malcolm's return my temper was raw, and we had a sharp altercation, which so many of our recent conversations seemed to have become. I found his disinterest in the subject of Mairi deeply unsatisfying, although past experience should have prepared me. She presented herself at the door the following day when I was alone, a degree cleaner in person and wearing her wild hair tied back with an old stocking. She had a creel of not particularly fresh fish as an offering, and a split lip.

"He has a heavy hand," she said, and swung away, leaving the fish on the doorstone.

I consigned her gift to the midden and confronted him that evening. He had been at Ardsian, and I thought that perhaps as he had not spent the day in the saddle he might be more inclined toward conversation. It seemed that this was not the case. We had a more than usually silent meal, and he went, as was becoming his habit, to his study, where he could sometimes be found at one o'clock in the morning. He was seated at the secretaire in the dimness, with only a single candle burning. There was a cut glass tumbler of whisky near his hand, as well as several volumes bound in black leather which I recognized from the estate office, and four or five heads of grain. The imperfect light dipped and fluttered, and he glanced up sharply at the disturbance. It was obvious that he did not welcome it, although I could not know why.

I felt there was scant necessity for a preamble. Whatever other matters oppressed him, he had never lost his unerring ability to read my thoughts, when he chose.

"The child came to me this afternoon, with what I assume was an apology."

He said, "That wee bitch," and returned to his papers. When it became apparent that this was the extent of his comments or opinion, or this conversation as far as he was concerned, I said, "What did you do to her?" and he looked up again, half turned from the secretaire, with the candlelight thrown over one eye. His gaze was terribly clear and unwinking, and as pitiless as a hawk's.

"I told her to bugger off. That was what you wanted, wasn't it?"

"Malcolm— you struck her."

"And what the hell did you do, with nothing less than a knife in your hand?"

"She told you that?"

"She tells me all her troubles. Now for Christ's sake, leave me alone."

"Are you on such intimate terms with her then?"

"She's familiar enough to me."

"My God. Do you stoop so low?"

He had turned away. He turned that stark, unwavering gaze on me again.

"What did you say?"

"I said nothing. Words fail me."

He threw the sheaf of papers aside and the movement set the candlelight whirling. So many shadows, and so little light: he cared nothing for the obscurity in which he worked, and it mattered nothing to him if he wrote or merely sat in complete darkness: nothing written would help him now, nothing left unwritten would signify.

He said in a soft voice, taking something in his fingers, something beyond the candlelight, a sere and mottled husk, "Do you see this, àlainna?" Àlainna: beautiful. Beautiful Margaret, he had called me in the night, the last time he had touched me with love. "Do you see what it is? This is a thousand deaths in my hand, and maybe yours and mine. And it matters not a drop of shit to me what you think or don't think tonight."

He pushed the mottled husks away, and the faint candlelight let them disappear. But not before they had allowed themselves to be identified: not a sample of the inferior bere, or the infected barley, but the life-blood of Scotland and the mainstay of Glen Sian's diet, the only crop that would survive this inhospitable climate and sustain us through the winter.

The oats were diseased. And the shadow between us was death.

We are all gathered here, in this field on the periphery of morning. It is Friday, the eighteenth of October, in the Highland book of days the least auspicious of the week for reaping. The sun has not yet risen, although the sky is streaked with promise: a fair day, after weeks of rain turning occasionally to bitter sleet, and for the first time in recent memory Glen Sian's peaks are visible, Saobhaidh, Riabhach, Creag na h'Iolaire, sombre against the wash of colour seeping from the east.

It is cold, October's keen, damp coldness, reminding the blood of winter, and it is the business of wresting this harvest from encroaching winter that we are about. The grain is wet, glistening with rain and flattened in great swathes by the ravages of weather. We will reap this field, and other fields, under whatever sun or rain may fall, from the moment the crop is visible until the last flaring of light, with scythe and sickle and stiffened hands, without rest, until the last sheaf is cut.

On every acre of oats in Glen Sian we are gathered, man and woman, farmer and cottar, manservant and housemaid, minister and minister's sister, factor and factor's wife. And at the rising of the sun, in every field, the man with most authority will cut the first handful of corn and raise the Iolach buana, the reaping salutation. Many have come to this meeting place wearing their Sabbath clothes to avoid giving offense to the god of the harvest. But the god of this harvest is the man who waits impatiently with the scythe in his hand and the glittering, smut-riddled grain soaking the leather of his boots, and his eyes assess only the angle of the light: and their finery and their deference to older spirits signify nothing to him.

Morning comes. October's mists hang upon the land: the tawny light pierces every eye, spreading fairness upon this field. He cuts the first handful of oats, scything it with a viciousness that will not be disguised, and in the first blinding rays of the sun he holds it high above his head, and passes it sunwise three times around his head, followed by thirty pairs of eyes.

I prayed that he would not mock this ritual, atheist though he was, and the rustling whispers stilled; and there was silence as he spoke, his beautiful voice carrying easily to every anxious, waiting ear.

"I will give thanks to the King of grace, for the growing crops of the ground.... Bless Thou Thyself my reaping, for the sake of Michael of the hosts, of Mary, the branch of grace, for the sake of Columba of the graves and tombs...."

In this field on the edge of morning, on the periphery of winter, the silence was powerful and profound. The Catholics among these reapers, and there were many, blessed themselves and reaped in the serenity of their devotion: their gods, gods of the dark Celtic underworld and gods of the Christian morning, would not fail to succour them now and in the hour of their deaths.

And I, troubled Anglican, who had not prayed since the morning of my wedding and was increasingly uncertain that my God had bestowed his blessing, I also prayed as I cut and stooked, following the scythe in a haze of fatigue, hour after hour until my hands bled, and my back ached, and that dark spirit drove these reapers on, furious, tireless, as though possessed of some inhuman strength.

Lord, have mercy upon us.... Christ, have mercy upon us....

Rain interrupted the harvest: hail and wind and sleet disrupted it. The Sundays of the twentieth and twenty-seventh of October delayed it, with every scythe in Glen Sian idle. To have forced labour in violation of the Sabbath would have incurred a universal displeasure, and even Malcolm did not attempt it, although he had no personal compunctions and was out of the house from ten o'clock in the morning until the darkness brought him home. I passed the afternoon sleeping, completely exhausted, and was not aware that he had returned until he came to the bedside. It was very dark: there was no light, either in the room or from the stairwell.

There was rain on the window: always, always in this cursed year, the sound of the rain. His clothing was wet, the cold hand on my face running with rain. He said very quietly, "Help me. I can't see," and my fingers scrabbled with panic, trying to strike a spark. His hand fumbled against mine and the tinderbox fell to the floor. The noise seemed to pierce the silence.

"No light, for Christ's sake. It will pass. Only let me lie beside you."

The distortion of his vision passed, and in its wake came migraine. He could not tolerate movement, speech or candlelight, the pressure of a cloth soaked in water or my tentative offer of alcohol: ordinary sound seemed magnified, and my conversation, conducted in whispers, was clearly unwelcome, although he seemed to want my presence.

Eventually, toward midnight, I drifted into a nightmarish sleep: sensing that my slightest movement on the bed caused him agony, I had retreated to the chair. An hour or so later I woke. He was vomiting.

When he could speak, he said, "You shame me. Go away."

But I did not leave him, and he seemed to surrender to me then, abandoning that obsessive dignity. And although tenderness had recently been mislaid between us, it was possible, in the face of that vulnerability, to give and receive an intense, yearning tenderness. As though this were not only one hour for ourselves in the vastness of Glen Sian's night, as though no fear could taint that night: as though, unafraid, we loved.

From half past six until eleven, by the light of the rising moon, with cut hands and clothing soaked to the armpits from the sodden grain, we harvested. White and black oats, the white greyish and inferior, the black so riddled with smut that the kernels crumbled into powder in the quern. The meal they produced was astringent and laxative, and, with potatoes, would provide the substance of Glen Sian's diet until the following summer.

There was not enough time, not enough labour. By the last week of October some seventy acres remained uncut.

All work ceased at twilight on the thirty-first, the eve of the Celtic feast of Samhain. Although the great red moon of preceding nights would have illuminated the fields, the reckless preferred games of divination, and the superstitious would not risk an encounter with the spirits of the dead on this fearful night. As though by some conspiracy known only to themselves, those few men and women still reaping near me drifted silently homeward, and by the cold afterglow of sunset I found myself alone in a sea of shadowed corn. Malcolm was not with me, nor did I know where, in Glen Sian's hundred square miles, he was: he could not or would not predict his movements, and it was now possible, in the course of this bitter harvest, to pass days and nights without seeing him.

The night was cold and haunted, not by the ghosts of the Celtic dead but by my sense of ghastly futility, by a deadly fatigue, by the exhaustion of my mind. The hand of the heiress had cut roses once, an heiress now cut by stubble; the knee bent to the earth in this primitive dance had once known a more graceful decline to the accompaniment of silk.

Hand-cold. The hands stiff and reddened in the garden, the walled garden of my childhood; the black frost killing all; the monochromatic colourlessness, the icy mud between my fingers: hand-cold, the gardener had described it, this was not work for the heiress. The crimson bricks against the grey winter sky, the unmoving scarlet. Dread, sexual dread, turning my blood to ice.

Tha father, lass.

Moon risen, casting my shadow before me on the rutted track. Hurrying now, leaving the darkened sea of grain to a living movement: a small cold wind from nowhere awakening the corn.

Memory and apprehension, born of exhaustion and imagination. The downward road: sharp cold air, autumn's melancholy always in my blood, and never more so than on this night. Strong moonlight... my shadow leading... the slow, heavy thudding of my heart.

Stubble here, a low haze of smoke, the acrid taste on the wind. The night darker, darker: sharp, sudden pinpoint of flame suspended in the distance, some defiance or celebration. Moving, the fire moves with me, travelling in the dark cloak of night: miles of darkness, my only companions these ghosts and the reapers' moon... this road, ever descending, leading nowhere....

I fell into a bottomless pit of sleep, still clothed, lying across the bed.

I woke at some unknown hour. The moon had passed its zenith, and Malcolm, strangely and fiercely elated, had come home.

He had touched nothing, drunk nothing: his intoxication was his triumph over the bitch, Glen Sian. A still night now, although bitterly cold; the cold was nothing, the work was nothing; he would cut the seventy acres himself, and leave the rest for the devil to glean.

He came to me as he had always come, darkness within darkness, a faceless lover, powerfully aroused, drawing me down into darkness. I was a prisoner of the darkness above me, darkness moved within me, spilling the hot flood of his semen into the mouth of my womb, possessing me so deeply that orgasm was neither of body nor spirit, and surpassed pleasure, and became death, an infinitesimal death of the senses. Again and again, and yet again, now drifting, giving me secret, intense joy, loving me as he had loved me in virginity, with exquisite fingers, now taking from me the pleasure he had taught me, which he adored and of which he was ashamed, spilling the sweet salt gift, the life gift, against my opened lips. And then he who had imprisoned was my prisoner, and I arched above him like a goddess, and wreathed him in the darkness of my hair, and watched orgasm transform his face.

There were no hours, there were no secrets. I was goddess and whore and lover, passionately beloved; he was darkness incarnate, god and devil who possessed me, and his possession of me was ecstasy.

We lost our souls in one another, and to a sleep as profound as death. And in that night and in that sleep, the devil, challenged, burned the oatfields not with fire but with ice, and had his harvest.

And in that night, and of that tumultuous darkness, I conceived Malcolm's child.

XIV

He blamed me for what had happened, as I would blame him, as though, had we not held one another in sexual thrall for that fragment of time, our lives would have remained unaltered.

I was not certain of my pregnancy until the middle of December, and by then it was impossible to approach him. Impossible to know if he suspected: perhaps. Under normal circumstances he who was so sensitive to the rhythms of my body would have marked any aberration, but these were not normal circumstances. His powerful sexuality was extinguished, and his attention concentrated upon Glen Sian's catastrophic harvest; and the monthly subterfuge became a pattern of deception, hiding from him first my desperation when the flow failed to appear, and then the malaise and fatigue that afflicted me within weeks of conception.

No child could have been conceived at a less auspicious moment, by a woman with fewer maternal instincts, of a man whose experience of paternity was more bitter or more grudging. Malcolm's illegitimate offspring had been as unwelcome as himself, and he had never regarded the prospect of issue of our marriage with other than resignation and resentment. I believed that the memory of his childhood had so scarred him that he thought himself incapable of paternal love. What had caused my own revulsion was less certain: perhaps the fear of entrapment which had always haunted me, the loss of myself to this unwanted child, the fear of the loss of Malcolm. In the darkness of those weeks, in the death of the year, with Glen Sian feeding on his life's blood, we seemed to live increasingly apart: we slept together but seldom touched, and the bonds between us seemed tenuous at best. He blamed me for the loss of the harvest, as though the land had betrayed him in the space of a night's inattention: if he had been aware of my condition he would have considered that a more insidious betrayal. Alone, I constituted a liability, yet one more responsibility in a multitude of crushing responsibilities. With child, I was the hostage to fortune he had always feared to give.

There was no immediate shortage of food. What grain could be saved was dried over kilns, and threshed and winnowed and ground, although the resulting meal was almost unpalatable. The barley was inedible, unfit even for brewing, the bere similarly affected. We had root vegetables, and potatoes stored in straw-lined pits across the estate, and cattle, the Highland economy's other staple, not for consumption but sale. At the Martinmas tryst the price of cattle had risen as the markets scented war; it would not fall for fifteen years. The sale yielded a little cash, and enabled Malcolm to appease the estate's more persistent creditors, but grain was unavailable for purchase. Crop failure was general throughout the Highlands.

After Martinmas heavy snowfalls closed the passes, sealing Glen Sian into the tomb of winter. There was no mail, nor news, nor offer of help: beyond the Highlands, the world was ignorant or indifferent. Years of scarcity were not uncommon here, and occured as regularly as one in three. The scale of this disaster would remain unknown, at least until the spring.

I refused to consider the possibility that I would not live until the spring.

The atmosphere in the house was funereal. When Malcolm was at home, which was seldom, he was not restless but preternaturally still, as though driven deep within himself, not in the grip of melancholia but in a raging silence, his mind hurling itself against inalienable facts, insoluable problems. He believed himself responsible for what had befallen Glen Sian; he had foreseen it and lacked the will to impose his foresight upon James and others: he believed, irrationally, as he had of Ewen's death, that he alone could have prevented it. He did not ask for counsel now, or reassurance; nor could he allow me the comfort of naïveté when I told him I found his behaviour, the monosyllabic curtness, the complete asexuality intolerable, and that for the sake of my sanity some normal relations must resume.

He had been sitting in his study for two or three hours. There were no candles; there was no heat. He had not moved except to refill the cut glass tumbler on the secretaire with whisky, which he drank increasingly. It had no effect upon him.

When I had finished what I realized was an hysterical diatribe, I wept, out of weakness and self-pity. He had always had a singular capacity for ignoring tears.

He said, "And where the hell have you been all these weeks, with your mind closed against me like an oyster? Christ, in all the world I have only one living soul to talk to, and where are you? Where are you, Margaret? And is that all you can say to me, that you find life intolerable?"

"I cannot bear the coldness of your manner."

He dragged back the heavy drapery, and light strained through the frost on the glass. My garden was a dead place beyond it, a wasteland of drifting snow, buried, frozen roots.

"There will come a time when you and I will be grateful for that. There will come a time when men and women will beg at your door, and steal from you, and try to strip your garden, or bleed your cattle, or take the oats from your horse's mouth. There may come a time when your horse or mine will die, or I will put them down. There may come a time when your father will fall ill, or your aunt, or yourself, or me— and God help us both if that day comes, because I would give you the very blood from my veins. So don't tell me what you find or don't find intolerable. Your life has been a dream, Margaret. Christ, we must have all been dreaming."

I tried to reach him, comfort him, insist upon my own reality, and strengthen my claim upon him when every hour of daylight seemed only for Glen Sian. *Do you not think I understand you? Do you not think me capable of understanding?*

And always, always the rejection, the icy withdrawal, or an unexpected ferocity which had become his only expression of the fears that haunted him.

"Jesus Christ, how many times do I have to say this? I have nothing to give these people. Do you understand?"

"I have money! Take it, for God's sake—"

"And what the hell would your money buy, or mine for that matter? Nothing, Margaret, nothing. There is nothing to buy."

"How shall we live then?"

"By my wits. And the grace of God, if you want to believe in it."

I was losing him... in body and spirit, he was turning away from me.

"Malcolm... I cannot bear this without your help."

"I have no help to give to anybody. I cannot even help myself."

"You must help me. I have no courage... I remember the last time. I was ill. I was... so afraid. Malcolm... I am so afraid now."

He said, with surprising gentleness, "What are you afraid of, Margaret?"

Of dying, of bearing your child... the summer of my life with you, such evanescent sweetness, is descending into hell.

"I have not the courage to watch my life... our life... falling away from us. We had so little time to be happy, Malcolm. So little time."

He said, "Life is the instrument by which we are hurt, and our lives are not our own. We are pawns of circumstance. You knew that when you married me. You knew there was no possibility of happiness."

Is it my fault? Will you never love me again? Do you not love me now?

In the last week of 1771 I drank this bitter cup down to the lees. My pregnancy was confirmed by a visit to Glen Mor and consultation with my aunt. My father was out in the parish, and knew nothing of the examination or the ensuing conversation. I was asked if the child was wanted, and if Malcolm knew. I told her that I could not lay this burden upon him at so inopportune a time; and although I was well aware that there was no love lost between Malcolm and my elders Deirdre spoke of him with unprecedented compassion, and I became sensible of that compassion extending itself to me, as though she knew the nature of my days and nights and the strangers we had become to one another.

Then she asked me if I were fully cognizant of the dangers of abortion. This was the darkest territory of my mind, into which we did not venture further. My immortal soul was not a subject for her judgment, nor accountable to Malcolm, who had never considered himself morally accountable to me. But my life and my sanity seemed a frail thread, and death was too nearly perceptible in the future to invoke it now.

Conception and birth and maternity remained unreal and unbelievable. I did not believe in the reality of the child, or the transmogrification of myself into the mother of a child. I never believed in its future, or my own in connection with it; I never sought to divine its sex or called it by any name. It remained unloved and unacknowledged by me, a subject of willful blindness, so perhaps I condemned it before birth to nonexistence, nonentity.

And with it all things I cherished, all love and all hope of love, passion and all hope of passion, safety and the hope of safety, were lost. It seemed that the very essence of myself as Margaret was falling into the void.

On Thursday January second, 1772, the moon was rising over silent snow, throwing a naked tracery of branches across the trodden courtyard: moonlight stained the fantastical patterns on casements sealed with ice. It might have been midnight: it was five in the afternoon, and the cold was so intense that flesh exposed to it was frost-bitten within minutes. The temperature had fallen below zero on the last night of the old year, and remained there as if the very mercury had frozen in the bore.

A single candle burned in the estate office. The room was deeply cold, and the ink had solidified in the standish. He sat smoking, drifting in a current of thought so removed from the present that he might have been sleeping: he who was always upright hunched like a great bird of prey in the chair, and the coldness of its wood could be felt through the doeskin of his breeches. Every day without some catastrophe, without the familiar, shattering cold, without news carried of illness or death, every day when there was still enough to eat was a victory, one day less in the year's imperceptible crawl toward spring. The unnatural orderliness of the table would remain until then, as though the normal business of administration had been suspended: the quill, the ledger, the perennially echoing strongbox had been superseded by these, the knife, the pistols, the sword, insurance of order in a different dimension, of justice where necessary, and of his own survival. He had never feared death and did not fear it now, by misadventure or starvation, but his life was a safeguard for other lives for which he held himself responsible, and murmurs of disaffection had already been heard: the sword alone would be a potent symbol of authority if rumour ignited into riot.

For the moment, there was silence: the killing cold had stifled the voices of dissent. There was no peace, but there was no violence either, only the mailed fist of winter tightening upon Glen Sian. Nor was there peace here, within the confines of this room; nor peace nor solace in his bed; nor peace in sleep, now gnawed with nightmare and pierced by shards of memory, senseless and alarming. Nor peace in solitude, in the wasteland of his mind, in the blinding white wasteland of the hills.

He was summoned to the morning room a little after half past five: the sealed square of paper had been pushed under the door. He swore and crumpled it, snuffed the candle and went out, fumbling with the key. The estate office was now kept locked, a precaution against intrusion or mischief.

It appeared, to his incredulous eyes, that he had been invited to a tea party. The silver spirit lamp was hissing on the table; the blue and gold Sèvres service that evoked such poignant memories had been replaced with a set of more modern design, cream-coloured and measled all over with rosebuds. A perfume of tea, disconcertingly like roses, mingled in the damp air with the bitter scent of coffee.

He waited to be acknowledged, fighting the desire to send the whole dainty, insulting arrangement crashing to the floor. Charlotte was wearing the favourite kingfisher-blue gown with its brilliant pattern of chrysanthemums, which could no longer be fastened and had been left open to reveal a voluminous white silk sacque. Her dishevelled hair was insecurely pinned with a pair of tortoiseshell combs. She wore no other ornament.

"Ah, Mr. Scott. I see you are amenable to conversation, if it does not take too much of your time."

Disarmed, he said rather stiffly, "I hope I find you well, madam."

"I have never felt better in my life. This business is much exaggerated. Please avail yourself of my fire— the rest of the house is abominably cold."

He went to it, not warming his hands but replenishing it for her with peat; he was intensely conscious of her eyes upon him. Her hand, also swollen and bare of jewellery, was hovering over the tray.

"You will take a dish of tea with me?"

"I would prefer coffee. I dislike tea, and never drink it."

Her brows rose delicately. She selected a miniscule cup, and the coffee smoked as she poured it.

"And do you also dislike sugar?"

"I prefer most things uncandied, including conversation."

She said, "I see that with you there is no possibility of dissembling. Sit down, Mr. Scott, and let us speak honestly to one another, though the truth may choke us both."

He sat rigidly opposite, the cup and saucer balanced on his aching knee, very aware of the absence of the sabre: considering it unsuitable for a lady's presence, he had left it on the marble console in the hallway. He focused his eyes and his fluid, ungovernable thoughts, haunted by the room and the perfume of the tea, and the ghosts of the child who was himself and the young man who had been Ewen; the ash-grey of Ewen's damaged escritoire; the silk upon the walls; the vanished summer, the vanished sun, the vanished innocence. He concentrated his mind upon her, above the clamour of ghosts.

"We find ourselves once again in this perilous situation, Mr. Scott."

"I am glad you have the intelligence to perceive it as such. I had thought that neither you nor your husband, nor any one else for that matter, had grasped its gravity."

"You do me an injustice. My thoughts are of little else."

"Then I suggest you unburden your mind. The responsibility is mine, not yours, and your husband will not thank you for it."

"Can anything be done?"

"What may be done will be done. I cannot provide supplements of corn as upon the last occasion. The people must make shift with what they have, potatoes and so forth."

She said, with an earnestness he found contemptible, "Mr. Scott, have you lived an entire winter upon potatoes?" and he leaned forward and put the cup of cold coffee gently on the table between them.

"Madam, I have eaten the stubs of tallow candles. I have eaten maggots and putrefying flesh. I have eaten nettles. I did not then have the luxury of potatoes. I pray you do not talk to me of hardship."

"I pray it does not come to that. I do pray, in all sincerity."

"I hope your prayers will be answered. It is not my desire that you nor any of you should suffer unnecessary distress. And the people have great resilience. I will do what I can for them."

She said, "You are very kind, far kinder than you think," and he uncrossed his long legs in a subtle prelude to departure.

"There is no place for kindness in my business. What famine does not carry off I intend to encourage to emigrate. There is a list of prospective candidates in my office, those I consider suitable for removal. The estate can bear their loss— they are mostly undesirables and persons of no consequence."

"I once called you an impertinent fellow, Mr. Scott. My opinion has not altered, but I cannot but be appreciative of your genius for administration."

"I merely consider it sound business practise. Perhaps we may discuss it in the future, with other projects which have fallen temporarily into abeyance."

She said, as though she had not heard, "I've a fancy to have this room rehung in the old colour. D' ye think our pockets will run to it?" and the dark blue walls seemed to oppress him further. "I have many plans for the future, although sometimes I think they have no hope of fruition."

He said nothing: a weight of coldness and deadness seemed to lie upon his tongue, a taste of cold earth and bitter coffee, and the easy lying reassurances refused to be spoken. In this seemingly inconsequential conversation he recognized valediction, and angrily, as he had rejected all Ewen's similar attempts, he rejected it, and refused to answer when she said good-bye.

He turned from me, increasingly remote, confronting whatever darkness dwelled within himself. I lived within my own silence, and if he noticed that I who had attempted to offer him comfort and hope had become withdrawn and pessimistic, he did not comment on it. We lived, two physical shells in occasional proximity, our souls estranged, obsessed with matters of which we did not speak: perhaps we could not speak of them. Where he went was unknown to me: what occupied him was seldom discussed. His stamina remained immense, and immobility infuriated him: he believed that to be visible was vital to the stability of the estate, and when the weather permitted he covered many miles on foot and on horseback, but the situation in Glen Sian had already begun to deteriorate. He did not speak of what he saw either to me or to James, but his sleep was haunted by nightmare, and he became adamant that I eat well, dosing me with bitter infusions against scurvy that induced nausea in his absence, and opening the first dusty bottles of claret, insisting I drink it for my blood. He supplied me with game when it could be found, and for the first time since our marriage he prepared meals for me, coarse, simple food, sometimes savoury, sometimes repulsive, all rendered poisonous by the catharsis of revulsion in me.

He persuaded me to eat, sometimes gently, sometimes less so. The effort of obliging him was too often a desperate act of will, and occasionally I imagined that he knew: at other times I was certain that he did not know. He asked me one evening if I were ill. I had lost weight to the point of gauntness and was frequently light-headed, although I concealed this from him. I attributed it to sleeplessness and melancholia, and he did not question me further. He did not appear to have noticed the cessation of my menstrual flow, and there had been no intercourse: my one attempt to initiate it had been rebuffed, and I had learned beyond forgetting how cruel is the message of rejection in a lover's back.

I was too much alone. In the brief afternoons when my domestic work had been accomplished I carried burning peat on a shovel into my sitting room and read or wrote by a meagre fire, reflections of suicidal despair or painstaking translations of Ewen's journals. His voice, his distinctive charm, his philosophy, his many doubts, his harsh self-criticism, even the sharply startling revelations of his sexual history comforted me: the distant past, unknown to me, the recent past I shared... myself, a phantom of unreality perceived through the eyes of love... a younger Malcolm, recognizably vital and acerbic even in the web of the past... James, by turns filial and obnoxious... webs of shadow, speaking ghosts, truths and revelations....

I never shared these journals. I never allowed him to find me seated at the desk, fire dead, house cold, light diminishing, with tears on my face, wandering in the past as though in some lost, sweet country, mourning with an exquisite grief all things lost, all love lost, ourselves, lost.

On the thirtieth of January Charlotte gave birth to twins, a son and a daughter, after twenty-seven hours of labour. The son, born fifteen minutes before his sister, lived until a little past midnight. The daughter, who was to be named Margaret Charlotte, survived the exigences of birth and the concerted attempts of the attendant physician to kill her with carelessness and uncleanliness.

My dear Charlotte, unable to pass the afterbirth, was cut, and bled massively. Her womb, Mackintosh told me, was as ripe as a pear, and he perforated it in the course of his curettage. He tried to staunch it by the insertion of rag tampons, but the haemorrhage was so profuse that blood was later found pooled beneath the bed and soaked into the floorboards.

She screamed only once, from behind the bed curtains during his ministrations. Through the rest of the night and in the faint staining of first light she was barely conscious, her pulse scarcely perceptible, her eyes half opened and fixed upon my face. She was dosed with hot wine and brandy and subjected to nightmarish torments, stone bottles of boiling water, steaming cloths on her breasts, and opium. She spoke lucidly to me at dawn, asking me to pray for her, and lapsed into silence. She turned then, knees drawn up to her face, and suffered one last convulsion: and, mercifully, she died.

XV

Her death haunts me still.

She was buried on February seventh, six years to the day after Ewen and in a grave beside his. The wind was southerly, and fog shrouded the graveyard. There were few mourners, perhaps because of the sheer strength necessary to walk the miles from the outlying townships, perhaps because James loathed the custom of funeral hospitality and had declined to offer it. There were also reports of typhus on the estate, and while the full impact of famine had yet to be felt supplies were dwindling, and social contact between neighbours was becoming suspicious and grudging.

I fainted at the funeral, and knowing Malcolm's hatred of public display I conducted myself with dignity when Gerard Mackintosh revived me with his vial of sal volatile: I did not call him an incompetent butcher before the small crowd of witnesses, although I had told Malcolm on the morning of her death. I even thanked him with due courtesy, and Malcolm supported me until we were out of sight of the mourners, after which he carried me. He did not speak to Mackintosh, or to James, but there was a brief exchange with my father, who had left a sickbed in Glen Mor to conduct the funeral. Later he came to the house; I heard the undercurrent of their voices in the kitchen, but no sense of their conversation was conveyed to me. When my father, limping very badly and accompanied by a silent Malcolm, laboured up the stairs, I lay with my back to the door and pretended sleep. Neither of them disturbed me, although my father lingered at the bedside as if he would speak or make some physical contact with me. Eventually he took something from his pocket and left it on the table, his breath wheezing and, as always, laden with spirits. He departed shortly afterward, and there were no further domestic sounds or movements. What remained of the afternoon vanished into the fog: what remained of my shocked sensibilities bled away into blessed darkness.

The wind veered, southerly no more. When I opened my eyes it was to candlelight, and a drifting whiteness beyond the window. Malcolm was sitting in the armchair by the bed, smoking, a glass of whisky on the floor beside him.

"There's a letter from your auntie on the table for you. Your father brought it."

"I could not bear to speak to him.... Do you understand?"

"I understand you. Give me credit for that at least." His hand reached precisely for the glass, as though he had sat with it beside me for hours. Then he said, "Walk in the shadows for a time if you must, Margaret. I've walked in them myself. But at the end of the day, remember me. The dead are dead. You and I are still alive."

"I feel half dead. I feel as though it would be better to be dead."

"I know all those feelings. You can die or you can live. In dying there's an end to pain, in living, none. Death seems infinitely preferable. The dead have no memories. Nor do the dead love. I still have that poor gift to offer you."

Tears, ceaseless tears.... who said that tears disturb the soul, so that it knows no rest? Who whispered of the bruised soul's passing, and the falling

492

snow that was God's displeasure visible? Whose are these cruel superstitions, rumours of the white wrath falling upon the souls of those I loved?

Do you believe it? You with your Celtic face and voice, you who speak and love and dream a language older than Christianity, you who live by rituals and incantations half repressed, half remembered, your mind always balanced between the primitive and the progressive with no sign of unease... do you believe in it? Do you believe that Ewen was a sinner? Was condemned by God because the snow fell on his soul in passage? Do you believe in purgatory? What were his sins? What were Charlotte's sins?

"There was never a soul so full of grace, and as for your friend, she was a Christian woman who did her duty and was loyal to her husband, and to you. The snow is only the snow, Margaret. God knows how you came by these terrible imaginings."

"I told you about Mackintosh. That was not imagination."

Beyond the haloed candleflames the eyes were ice-clear, watching me.

"I told you to say nothing more on that subject. I know what you think, and I believe you, but that will not bring her back. Let her go, Margaret." He came to his feet in one fluid, graceful movement and to the side of the bed. He sat, and our hands clasped with an intensity I had thought forever dead in us. "Will you eat if I bring it to you?"

"No... I want nothing."

He said, "Don't turn away— there's been too much of that," and I lay arrested in the motion that was my defense. "Is it so abhorrent to you, Margaret, this business of bearing a child?"

The world was very still, confined to a circle of candlelight. Beyond ourselves, nothing else existed: in this bed where passion had had its estate, there was no emotion.

"How long have you known?"

"Long enough to see the misery it causes you. And who can blame you? I don't."

Time passed, was suspended in the candlelit world. He lay against the pillows, my head in his lap. Very gently he unfastened my hair, and stroked it where it spilled across his thigh.

"So many nights I dreamed of this... I dreamed of loving you. Then I dream of you leaving me... I wake up with the horror. I think that would finish me."

If he thought I slept, exhausted by grief, if he felt my tears, he did not cease to stroke my hair. The room darkened; the hours of this bitter day passed into night. The candle was perceptibly lower: perhaps he, too, had slept.

"Tell me the truth. Is the worst still to come?"

"Oh, yes. The worst is not yet upon us."

"When will that be?"

"Spring, summer. When the land quickens. That will be the worst time." There was a silence, then he said, "Life, death… my only life is with you. My only death is without you."

In the night we loved, defying the inevitable, the invincible, the encroaching darkness; yet one more ounce of sweetness pressed, yet one final hour of immortality.

He sat with his back to the hard sky of February, the white peaks dazzling, the ice blinding on the naked branches, and falling when the wind stirred them to splinter in the courtyard.

It was Monday the seventeenth, and it was his habit to make himself available on Monday mornings in the estate office, although every other day of the week, including Sundays, he might be anywhere on the estate, fostering the local suspicion that, like God, he was omnipresent.

No one came: no one would come. The house was as dead and still at noon as it had been at dawn, as though it had never awakened from its sleep of death. He closed his eyes against the winter light and the shadows it cast over the unopened account books, the untouched whisky, the pistols on the table, like old friends whose proximity reassured him, and whose invitation was never withdrawn.

Sometimes, of late, Ewen's presence in this room had been almost palpable, as though he would see him if he raised his eyes suddenly, and without apprehension he examined the sensation and wondered if it were a portent of his death. It was strong now, not imagination but knowledge. He opened his eyes.

There was nothing, only the cold reflection of light on the steel of the pistols and the faint trace of his breath in the air. He snapped open his watch, read the time, snapped it shut with a curse. There were footsteps on the stair.

When they came in he was standing with his back to the room, his hands clasped beneath his coatskirts. He gave them a moment to assemble, aware of the heaviness of their breathing, and turned. There were seven men, all farmers from Glenkill township, all showing evidence of illness, the nature of which he immediately began to assess.

Beginning the ritual of conversation, he said, "Good morning. Welcome to you," and the spokesman, a small man with bulbous pale blue eyes and a head too big for his body, responded politely, "Good morning, A Mhaoir. God and Mary be with you."

He answered curtly, "And with you," and cut across the standard enquiries after his health and the condolences on the death of the ban-fhlath. "What brings you from Glenkill this morning?"

There was a movement among them, and the spokesman lifted a sack to the table, carefully avoiding the ledgers. It was stained with a seeping dampness and its smell was nauseating.

He stood without moving, his mind grappling with this new dimension of an unfolding hell.

"Are they yours, Ròis?"

"They are all ours, A Mhaoir. All Glenkill potatoes. In every pit it is the same, but they were whole and sound when we dug them."

One of the others, a thin man with black hair and a weak face, who ran one of the more notorious stills on the Glenkill farms, said, "In the name of God, what will we do? We have nothing but these— the oats are finished, and the wife is six months gone."

He said, not raising his eyes from the suppurating heap, "You have cattle?"

"Only the two, A Mhaoir. By the hand of Mary, how should I manage without them?"

"It seems to me, Peadair, that the hand of Mary is on your cattle, and the grace of Mary is sparing your lives. Go home and do what is necessary to feed your wife and bairns. And let none of you, not one man of you, eat potatoes in that condition, or suffer any of your family to eat them, or give them to your stock."

The spokesman, Ròis, came forward on broganed feet and reclaimed the sack. It had left a malodourous stain on the end of the table, which he attempted to remove with a fraying sleeve.

"What shall we do, A Mhaoir?"

"I will come to you in ten days' time, and tell you what potatoes may be spared from other stores in other townships. The murrain may not be general. I have seen no evidence of it so far among my own supply."

"Then God has favoured you. May He look so kindly upon all of us."

There was no insincerity in the remark, and he answered without sarcasm, only an ineffable weariness, "Go home, all of you, and do what you must. I will come to you in ten days' time. The blessing of God on you."

The stain and the stench remained in the office when they had departed. The afternoon sun, blinding on the rivers of ice on the casement, reached the lockplate of the pistol nearest his hand. The past was a distant country, hazed with light: he perceived it as golden although he knew that it had not been so, and a fragment of memory pierced him and was gone, irretrievable and unbearably painful. Time was a river bearing him, sometimes striving, sometimes helpless, toward an unknown destination. The prospect of the future was invisible: only the light on the lockplate was real.

And then there was no more light.

The month bled away into greyness, into fog, into days of sleet and unexpected snow. He covered a third of the estate and knew that further investigation was futile. The disease was ubiquitous, and no supply of potatoes was unaffected, including his own.

He sat in the estate office on the last day of the month, with the familiar accoutrements at hand: the whisky untouched, the candle trailing a stream of flame, the rain freezing on the casement behind him. The deep gloom of the afternoon was curiously soothing, and even the familiar enclosed scent of mildew that was the essence of this room seemed clean.

He lit the pipe and extinguished the candle: its light affronted the darkness and was offensive to his eyes. A rosary of horrors bound his mind, from which there was no escape: in darkness or in light it was endlessly repeated; its images, unlike the images of childhood, no benevolent insanity would expunge.

The open door... the waiting darkness. *The blessing of God on this place*, and the assaulting smell.

They are all dead here. They are all dead....

Death by disease, in the insanitary conditions that bred typhus; death by starvation, where the lice, vainly seeking warmth, clustered in the eyelids of the newly dead; death by suicide: the decapitated corpse in its wedding finery, the decomposing neck severed by the rope still dangling from the cross-beam, the eyeless head lying beneath the table, the almost illegible letter on the dresser singing the praises of the promised land, America. Eighteen families, farming sixty-eight acres, with an average of ten children each..... *This is a goodly land, where the ground gives three crops a year.....*

Hail to you, the peace of God on this place, and here, nothing stirs. These, untouched by decomposition, lie buried under the snows of eight weeks, unseen by their neighbours since the new year: the snow brushed from the face renders it recognizable. *God and Mary be with you here*, and here they lie withered and shrunk together, three in the bed in an advanced stage of decay, the householder in the byre. Here there were no cattle, and the dogs crept out timidly with swinging tails, into the open air, where he had shot them.

He drank now, his hand still steady. The room was darker, the hiss of the sleet uninsistent, time, the black river, unmeasured and unnoticed, bearing him away.

Aenghus, he said, Aenghus, come with me. Leave her and come with me, but there was no sight in the vacant, bulging eyes and he was no more visible than the ghost he imagined himself to be, a phantom drifting, detached, from door to door, discovering death, perhaps bearing it like a gift, a token of esteem.

Aenghus, leave your wife. She is dead. Come with me. Take my hand.

The eyes, sightless eyes, idiot's sunken eyes. This was the vicious, furious man, red-haired, red-limbed, heavy-fisted, who had cursed him as a child in the peathags. He had nothing but one of the dry oatcakes that sustained him on these rides, but the gibbering, gaping mouth refused it, and he could not lift him to his feet without unnecessary violence, which would have seemed an insult to the woman already dead.

Drifting: shivering now as though with ague, the barefoot, shuddering child wandering through the mist, eyes sightless with horror, mouth salivating with truths too unspeakable to be told. Dead or dying, drifting on a black river of death: further from the candlelit world of his nights in a house untouched as yet by pain, further from the peace which had been his resting place.

XVI

I owe my life to Malcolm. My sanity was not within his power to save.

Days and nights are obliterated from my recollection. Other memories have no basis in fact, because they happened only in the hell of my imagination: only Malcolm could have confirmed or denied their reality. The women in my garden, some shoeless in the snow, who held up their children for my pity while they plundered my vegetables; furtive sounds in the dead of night; the shadow that moved in the clear, bitter twilight, although he had told me to feed no one, succour no one: did he feed and succour this?

It is late winter, with no hope of spring. Nothing moves except to scavenge, nothing lives except to die.

James at Ardsian, in the neglected drawing room, toying with an ugly ring of Charlotte's and telling me of his intention to remarry; a dusty bottle of sack on the table and a bowl of candied ginger at which his fingers, with bitten nails, were picking delicately. He wore black and was dishevelled, and shivered repeatedly although he seemed not to notice that there was no fire. He did not appear to be aware of my condition and I did not enlighten him: he did not speak of Charlotte by name or mention his daughter, apart from remarking that she had jaundice. His evenings, he said, were passed agreeably with Gerard Mackintosh at cards or backgammon. It was a pity that the weather did not break; he found the confinement of winter depressing. He did not, after very obvious consideration, attempt to give me the ring: perhaps it had occured to him that it was worth something.

There is no rain, no blessed thawing, no bird, no thrush's song in the blue hour of evening, only the blinding cold at midday, the fresh snow, God's displeasure, falling constantly. The sun, as seldom seen in this winter of desolation as it was in the summer that spawned it, is a burning red that gives no heat, a lingering red at twilight. The days lengthen imperceptibly, but we do not sit on the doorstone now, nor on the green-painted bench: there is no seed and neither harrowing nor sowing: no resurrection of spring, no redemption, only death.

Malcolm... Malcolm... breaking his fast with hot water, telling me the minerals rendered it palatable; Malcolm forcing me to eat. Raw onions: they could not be cooked because cooking destroyed their goodness. Raw kale, raw cabbage, raw turnip. If he hunted successfully, the liver was reserved for me: he ate the contents of the stomach, and other organs, which I found unspeakable. Infusions of pine, so bitter that I came to believe he was dosing me with abortifacients: but the life within me remained tenacious, despite the vileness forced on me by that implacable stranger who was more than ever my demon and my tormentor. Nights when I hid my tears from him, knowing his hatred of weakness: nights when mind and body refused to continue this unequal struggle and I could not swallow what he fed me, or vomited after eating. Nights when he bathed me, a limb at a time, in basins of scented water, and held me in his arms in the candlelit, inviolate world of the bed, and sang to me, although he could not sing, he whose speaking voice was so beautiful. And when the candle died and the fire died, as though we slept in fear of death's loneliness, we woke entwined in one another's limbs, survivors of the night.

Days of hell, of imagined horrors, which he told me never happened; nights in which the shards of memory were pitiless and utterly clear. Days and nights when the body lived, and the soul was dying.

He forced life upon me, which I did not want. He stretched me out upon the rack of these days and nights, and made me suffer, and made me live. He believed he had averted the crisis he sensed was threatening me, and some of the savage tension that possessed him dissipated when he was with me. I accepted what he did for me; I behaved normally; I ate and drank, while he denied himself; I no longer protested. My mind closed against the unspeakable anguish of my life, and his love and its injuries could not touch me.

Typhus and smallpox were familiar killers. Now came scurvy, blindness and the dropsical condition called hunger-oedema, companions of malnutrition.

Twelve people died of raging dysentery in the outlying crofts of Glen Mor in one week, five in the space of the next. There would be no relief from this scourge until summer. Deirdre wrote to me in a fine, shaky script, in carefully oblique phrases: a letter delivered to the estate office which had been lying on the floor for several days as Malcolm went there less often. *It hath pleased my God to spare my life and yr Fathers, but the burthen upon him is great; on Tuesday there were seven dead unburied in this poor Place. One here who sends you blessings hath not suffred in his health.*

It ended with a plea for news of me, and although eventually I wrote to her praising Malcolm's efforts, and he promised to deliver it, I never believed that he did so. The passage of mere paper had become irrelevant to him.

The cattle began to die. Of exposure to the vicious cold, of excessive bleeding by ignorant farmers, who resorted to this traditional source of nourishment to sustain their families, of starvation, and finally of disease. The murrain spread rapidly until, by the end of the black winter of 1772, it had claimed more than a quarter of all Highland cattle.

I moved inevitably toward nervous collapse, tormented by my fear for Malcolm's health under the weight of responsibility he bore and the inhuman demands he made upon himself; by my own continuing illness; by my anxieties for Deirdre and my father, for whom a difficult and inarticulate love was only now struggling to be recognized; by an inconsolable grief for Charlotte.

Without warning the abyss opened, and my demons waited for me. Although fresh snow had fallen the savage cold had abated, and the evening was stained with an unspeakable beauty and clarity of light, the impossible promise of spring. Malcolm was deeply withdrawn but not insensitive to it or its poignancy: he sensed also the fragility of my spirit, and although he offered no facile hope or comfort, in his stillness he spoke to me.

The light was ebbing. My hand came to rest on his sleeve.

Light, and then afterlight. The silence held us in intimate communion. I did not want him to speak of the spring or the future or to offer me lies or reassurance: I did not know what I wanted of him. The ferocity of his will when it was imposed upon mine, by which he had forced me to live, was fearful; tenderness between us now was rare, an unaffordable luxury; sexuality seemed dead in us both. I withdrew my hand, not knowing what response I had expected from him, what response I would not have resented: perhaps the gesture was my cry for help, which by my own unpredictability I had warned him to ignore.

He went out later on foot, on business he did not specify, nor did he tell me what time he would return; when he had gone I found the pistols on the table, and the sword on the desk in the study. I wandered the house as the night and the cold deepened, and could not sleep without him. Finally

I pulled a heavy silk shawl around me and lay on the sofa in my sitting room. He was unarmed, or virtually so, and he had told me that opinion, already bitterly prejudiced against him, had been further poisoned by famine: my imagination inflicted terrors upon me as every hour struck and died. Eventually I must have slept: some sound or instinct woke me. I moved as though disembodied through the darkness of the kitchen; the door was open to the night, and a candle in a shuttered lantern stood on the floor. There was a drain in the pantry, which he had built himself, and a stone channel in the floor, and he was standing, naked but for his shirt and coat, sluicing bloody water down the drain; rivulets of blood were streaming from his thighs and groin, his feet were laced with bloody water. He looked up as though I had made some sound, and the steam rose like smoke from his skin and the sponge in his hand and the bucket on the floor. His shirt was soaked in blood and plastered to his skin; his face was spattered with blood.

He dropped the sponge into the bloodstained water.

"Bring me a drink, will you, Margaret."

I saw myself passing through the firelight, leaving the river of blood running through the sluice in my pantry floor; I saw the tunnel of darkness that led me to his study. Terrified that if I hesitated I would see that bloody spectre in the doorway, I groped for the glass and the decanter: my disembodied eye saw my hand splash spirit into the glass and pick it up, and nervelessly let it fall. It disappeared into the tide of darkness and coldness in which I drowned; I never knew if it shattered or merely rolled on the carpet, if he heard me or sensed what had happened, if he came after me. I was no longer the sick and suffering prisoner: I was bodiless: I was a screaming spirit in a rushing darkness: I was in a place of safety where he could not reach me.

The room smothered me; there was no light, only the stifling darkness, the dead coldness, the weight of insufferable pain. He came to the door but I had locked it against him, with the full force of my body. His voice spoke to me but I could not hear him; I made no sound. If I made no sound I would cease to exist and he could not find me, and he could not injure me. I was beyond screaming: I was beyond cold: I was beyond pain and beyond this life, beyond the protection reason would afford me: and in the void of terror, in the dead blackness of the night, the dead grey light of the moon, demons came. Cries and whispers, tormented, flickering faces, dreams or hallucinations, and then the moon was gone and the weight of terror in the room was unendurable, and the night was bitter, bitter, and the fall was endless.

Lying across the door, frail, nauseated, numbly chilled, hands and feet without sensation, in my womb the nightmare fluttering, the agitated incubus. Against my eyes candlelight, as though a candle were burning on the floor.

"Margaret, open the door." No threat, no honeyed reasoning. His voice was without emotion. "Margaret, listen to me. I know you can hear me."

Perhaps he heard something: perhaps the wounded, sobbing cries that haunted my night of dreams.

"Margaret, I have sat here since midnight. I will not sleep. If you want me to come in, tell me. I will not come in without your leave."

No touch on the door, no forcing of the lock. He knew it was not locked.

He left me alone, but I was not alone. The guttering candle bled light across the floorboard. He waited; he would wait forever, all the hours of this nightmare that remained.

I would never sleep again.

..... God knew what time it was. Not dawn. There were candles burning, no other light. I lay in bed. And he, not close, was watching me, with eyes whose expression was hidden from me, veiled by the shadows. Impossible to know the thoughts they concealed: his spirit always eluded me, his heart had never been mine.

No blood, no bloodied clothing now, only the rough, clean, soot black hair, the drawn, impassive face, a pale shirt soft with laundering. No neckcloth. This was not the clothing of the night before. The blood had been no hallucination.

Later I heard myself whispering, and he leaned forward as though he would have touched me. The motion, arrested, fell away into shadow, another infinitesimal tragedy.

So much blood. So much....

"Some of the men believe in sacrifice. I did it for them." Darkness, darkness... the horror of this: innate contempt and revulsion.

"It was the blood of a bullock, for Christ's sake, not mine."

Salt tears: they did not cleanse me. He had always been impervious to my tears.

"Drink this. It will do you good."

Something from his hand to my lips, a stain like blood drifting in the spirit, some opiate in the cognac. I said, "Malcolm, have you poisoned me?" and a sleep like death embraced me, and closed my eyes against his pain.

It might have been dawn or twilight: the light was an enigma, and no recognition of season or date remained to trouble me, then remembrance came, and the light was seeping away. Evening... rain was running on the glass. I could not recall why I should be grateful for the sound of rain.

The resumption of normality seemed of paramount importance.

He was sitting in the kitchen, in darkness: here the sound of the rain seemed louder, driving from the east. I sat without speaking on the seise, nor did he speak to me.

"It was not a dream."

He said nothing.

"I hoped it was. I hoped you would forgive me. You cannot know how dear you are to me."

He said, "No. That is something I will never know."

Silence. Rain hissing into the flames.

"A fear haunts me, Margaret, that what was on your lips has been a long time in your heart."

"You know the truth of that."

"There are no truths for me any more. I never thought I could feel pain again. Life holds many surprises, doesn't it, so many refinements on suffering." The fire was very low: he did not move to replenish it. Perhaps he was as grateful as I for the darkness between us. "You told me last night that you thought my death was imminent. If that is so, there are matters of which we must speak. I have a considerable sum on deposit in the Bank of Scotland. I also keep money in the house. I will show you where it is tomorrow. James has a copy of my will... Henderson in Glasgow acts for me. You are my sole beneficiary."

If by closing my eyes I could have obliterated all knowledge of the abyss that was opening, not for me but between us; if my every sense could die, neither should there be any more pain.

"If you should bear a son, I ask that you give him none of my names. My Christian names are all I legally possess. I prefer them to remain mine alone."

Silence now: he was darkness in the flickering darkness before me.

I said, "If I should die in childbirth, everything I have is yours."

"I don't want your money, Margaret. All I ever wanted was your love." He was silent; then he said, "Life carries us toward irrevocable things. The course of life is not reversible."

The past was a sweet, lost country....

"So it is. Maybe in death it will be given to us to return to it. And maybe in death it will be sweeter than it ever was in life."

Later in the night, in the black river of our lives, time carried us toward irrevocable things. A white-painted brick was thrown through the window of my sitting room; and uninsistently, the bleeding began again.

***

502

He kept the brick on the table in the estate office until he knew every stain of crotal, every paint flake, every fragment of mortar, then he took it in his pocket and fitted it into the wall of a byre that still stank of ammonia and manure, although the cattle lately kept here were now dead. It came away easily into his fingers, and he put it into his pocket again and took it to the door of the croft.

"Where's your son, Diar?"

There was death here too, in the fetid darkness, a terrible muteness of sorrow. The face hung before him against the yawning hole of the door, silvered by the rain, the pale eyes inflamed and encrusted, the mouse-coloured hair alive with vermin, and completely grey.

"I have only two sons living."

"My business is with Coinneach."

"He does not come here now." The door began to close. He thrust his boot against it, ignoring the outrage, the shrill burst from the shadows within, the stench of disease and derangement.

"Give this to him. And tell him if he brings another of these to my house there will be no hiding from me."

"Go to hell. We ask you for bread— you give us stones. Go to hell, you bastard."

The door closed. The brick lay where it had fallen, glistening in the rain. He returned home.

The second brick was left on the doorstone that night. Two nights later it was a veritable cairn of bricks and broken mortar. Then, at three o'clock one afternoon, when I was alone in the house, ten men came and asked to speak to Malcolm. I said that he was not at home. Politely they requested to be admitted, in order to wait for him. I repeated that he was not at home and the spokesman, with infinite courtesy, apologized for having disturbed me. I locked the door and within a few minutes only their footprints remained in the rotting snow.

He sat in his study, at the secretaire. There was a glass dish on the papers full of ash and shreds of tobacco: he was watching the smoke rise, disturbing the ash with the blade of the stiletto.

"I want their names."

"How can I give you names?"

"Then give me faces, and by Christ I'll put names to them."

I had not touched him since that night, the fatal beauty in the light, the unspeakable fall into darkness. I saw my hand, with the dispassion of the disembodied, fasten on his sleeve.

"You are *obsessed*." He stared at me, with those cold, burning eyes. "Leave it— what purpose does this serve? You say they hate you— leave it, for God's sake. No harm was done to me."

He said, "No one has insulted me to my face since I was fifteen years old. No man will abuse me and violate my home and intimidate my wife, no man will tell me to go to hell without I bring hell to him."

He did not, as I feared, leave me and go out, but he did not come to bed; and on the stroke of three o'clock that disembodied spirit which had become myself drifted silently into the webby circle of candlelight and watched him from the doorway of his study, covering yet another page with indecipherable script, his face in profile almost at peace, as though the work gave him satisfaction. He did not appear to hear me or to sense my presence: and later, even as the night was dying, he came to our room, although not to bed. He sat in the chair, smoking endlessly, watching the morning bleed into being; then he left me with no word of acknowledgment, although he knew I was awake. In the study there was no trace of the night's activity, no discarded, blotted papers, no books of record lying open. The quills, some stained, some fresh, were arranged in the tankard: the stiletto had been removed. How long I stood there I never knew, rearranging what had already been arranged, tidying the emptiness he had left, trying to read what the night had created, seeking him, always, in his presence as his absence; abandoned, in his silence.

The hope of spring was as false and futile as the hope of peace. Snow was falling on the morning of Saturday March fifteenth, an anniversary he hated; at first delicately, and then by the time he had reached the estate office with a white intensity that blotted out the light. He had slept little and eaten less: his body ached, his bowels were locked, his mouth filled with a lingering taste of iron as though some slow poison of uncleanliness were working in him; the rheumatism in his knee had been aggravated by savage activity and by the relentless cold. The immense physical stamina upon which he made such demands was failing him, and for the first time in his life there was an intimation of weakness, the body's punishment for the soul's driven abuse.

In the snow's hypnotic silence, memory came: this loathsome anniversary, twenty-one years in the past, the virgin boy's deflowerment, the aftermath in all its unspeakable sickness and secrecy.

He opened his eyes, and the white nothingness filled them: the snow fell endlessly. Some one had come into the room, although he had heard nothing.

He said, "What do you want?" and the voice behind him, which he seldom heard, said, "I would have a word with you, on a matter that concerns you."

The eyes and the voice had not altered with maturity, or the passing of years in France; the eyes were the eyes of a younger man, gazing out from the bloated mask of the servant. The face was still faintly freckled, despite its indoor pallor, the dark auburn hair, unwashed and tied with ribbon, was patched with white at the temples. In his youth he had thought Coll MacGregor tall: in the bloodless analysis of a second, as his mind dismissed a hundred reasons for this meeting, he saw that this was no longer so.

He said again, "What do you want?"

"Talk is running high against you, Scott."

"And what talk do you hear, boot-boy, living under your master's bed?"

"Men talk to whores, and over the heads of other men they perceive as eunuchs. Riot is upon you, Scott. Affray is upon you. There are those who would have your life."

"What do you want for these prophecies? Money?"

"You always had a gift for insult. Your wife was kind to me, when she was always in the bosom of her friend, my lady who is gone. Your wife spoke to me, and was pleasant to me, as ladies are pleasant to servants. Pleasantries are rare to me. I tell you for her sake."

"Who talks, MacGregor?"

"Young men. Men who would marry, if the factor permitted the marriage. Men who would work the land of their fathers, did the factor not forbid subdivision. Men whose wives have been polluted. Men whose virility has been mocked, here and at the doors of their homes. I am no enemy to you, Scott. Look to it."

"Coinneach Cameron?"

"Among others."

"Who does he run with?"

"Young men of his kidney."

"Torcall Gunn?"

"And his brother Raonull. Ruiseart and Uilleam their cousins, Gilchrist MacGregor, my cousin. Caillean and Daniel, his brothers. And others. They take your sheep, and talk of sodomy among your shepherds. They say you condone it."

"If these are lies, and I find them out—"

"There is no word of a lie in what I say. I tell you for your wife's sake only. You are nothing to me."

Silence; the soundless onslaught of the snow. The hazel eyes narrowed at it, gazing beyond his shoulder, the eyes of a hard youth disguised by the flaccid, indoor face.

He said, breaking their reverie, "When you've wiped your master's arse this morning you can send him to me. I have something for him to read."

The eyes rested on his face with an intense, bewildered injury: then the cruelty was accepted as a matter of course, as a language understood by both.

James sat buffing his nails. The snow had stopped, and the sky was suffused with sunset.

You ineffectual prick, he thought. Your cattle are dying, your people are dying, riot threatens you. Would you buff your nails at the seat of judgment?

James looked up, startling him, as though he had spoken aloud.

"I don't see what this has to do with me."

He turned from the window, where his breath had clouded the glass, obscuring the painful clarity of mountains and the illusion of beauty in the land.

"I am not yet capable of affixing your signature to documents of import. If I were, you would not hear from me from one end of the year to the other."

"Are these measures necessary?"

"They are necessary. Perhaps you would care to read it again."

"I require three days to consider it. It will cause great lamentation among the people."

"Are you deaf, man? Your people have been crying for months. What matter a few more tears?"

"My responsibility—"

"Your responsibility died at Culloden. How many years can you sustain failure? How many years can you live like this, asking for blood from stones?"

The buffer disappeared.

"And you propose to pay each of these five pounds upon removal? Where is the economy in that, or do you consider this an investment in the future?"

"If the bounty is from my purse and not yours I fail to see that it concerns you."

James said, "You know what people will call this. I call it a vendetta."

"I applaud your imagination."

"Malcolm, if my father knew—"

He said, "There is a sickness in your land, and it is not of my making. And it is not peculiar to Glen Sian. Seventy men left Glenmoriston last year to go to America. Five hundred went from Islay, and three hundred went from Skye. Glenmoriston never sees above four hundred a year for all his lands, and you have less than that. Your daughter is your hope of the future, man. What will you leave her? Your accounts are two years in arrears, your roof leaks, your cellar is empty, and your people are idle and consumptive. They dream of America, they feast on dreams. Let them go, and be damned with the rest of the agitators."

He turned again to the piercing clarity of light, the sky stained by torn clouds.

James said, "How is Margaret?"

"Margaret is with child, and unwell in body and spirit."

He was aware of James's shock, and then an honest attempt at kindness. "My dear fellow, I had no idea."

"That will be your epitaph," he said.

"Is there anything I can do for her?"

"Care for her in my absence. I must be in Inverness before April eighth to apply to the sheriff for the writs."

"It is not a foregone conclusion. I told you I require time."

"Bankruptcy limits your options. Sooner or later you will have no choice, and time is pressing me."

James came stiffly to his feet.

"I will take your papers, and give them careful consideration. In the meantime— I offer my congratulations."

He said, "Save them. They are not wanted."

He was alone, in the dead silence of the room. The sheaf of closely written pages had been taken and the table was bare except for the brick he kept on it, which had excited no comment, the pistols neatly arranged, the sword in its sheath lying the length of the table as though at a court martial. The iron taste of sickness filled his mouth. He had not eaten for some twenty-three hours.

In the lingering twilight of spring, the first thrush of the year was singing. He leaned his forehead against the cold glass and closed his eyes, and yielded to an anguished yearning for death's peace, and freedom; and its beauty broke his heart.

XVII

I was asked, years later, if I had known the nature of his business in Inverness, and why I could not have exerted my influence to dissuade him from it. If he had thought it advisable or necessary to tell me, he would have done so: if he had required my opinion he would have asked for it. If I had pressed him, he would have lied with facility to keep his purpose secret. He was not a man one questioned. He did not order my life or interfere with the running of my household or the disposition of my time or my money, and I did not presume to judge him in matters relating to Glen Sian. I believed his judgment sounder than mine, untempered though it was by humanity. And so, rationally, I did not know; but in my heart, I suspected.

He left me at the least hospitable time, apart from the dead of winter, that could have been chosen for travel in the Highlands. Continuous rain had melted the heavy snows and the rivers were in spate, the Sian itself was swollen and turbulent, upon the point of flooding; by Wade's road on a fresh horse Inverness could be reached in three days. But Wade's road had not been repaired for twenty years, and my gelding, which Malcolm took instead of his ailing stallion, was jaded and ill-fed. The journey might take five days or a week; the date of his return was uncertain. I remained alone, with Malcolm's stallion my responsibility and Malcolm's angry spirit my companion in a shadowed, whispering house.

Jesus, is it so much to ask that you do as I say?

Is that what you want me to do? Sit at James's table like a specimen and be examined by that misogynistic butcher? Perhaps you'd like him to attend me at the birth. That would soon rid you of me, wouldn't it?

I had not fully understood the state of his mind until then, until I saw the expression on his face: until I realized that what I had said, out of the bitterness of my soul, must remain unspeakable. I had not fully understood how savagely I could hurt him, how he blamed himself for my pregnancy and feared the possibility of my death.

And here, in this dark room, in the rainy shadow of an April afternoon, here too was pain, the memory of frustration, the taint of ignorance and fear poisoning our last attempt at lovemaking. I needed his comfort; I hungered for it; it seemed our only meeting place was here. I felt no desire for him, only a hollowness within, a terrible hopelessness and solitude, a bereavement. My only salvation was this, the assertion of life in his sex. I initiated it and he came to me as though from a great distance, his spirit deadened and weary: he entered me and his erection failed. I knew then that pregnancy repulsed him; he resented the unseen presence of the child in this most intimate communion, or he feared that he would injure me. Articulate though he was, and however explicit the language of our lovemaking, he withdrew from me into silence; too ignorant myself to reassure him, I lay in the darkness, abandoned. In the morning he left me; superstitiously, he would not allow me to watch his departure. The rain took him from me, and now spoke to me endlessly with his voice, and the whispers of other voices. I drifted through the days, and every sound I made was an affront to the silence of the rooms. I sat in his chair and wore his coat over my clothing and drank the claret he had left for me, I physicked his vicious, restless stallion; I slept at night with candles burning and a pistol on the bed beside me.

Nothing happened. James did not write to me or visit me or send any one from Ardsian with game for me, although later I learned that this had been requested, along with a groom for the stallion. Mairi let herself into the house one morning and left a hare propped up in a basin draining blood, and reappeared in the evening to cook it, pointing a carving knife at me and saying in a sharp, high voice and, startlingly, in English, "You... eat..." and then bringing a plate to the table and sitting down opposite me. She devoured her portion in utter silence, punctuated only once by a singularly sweet smile, which haunted me more than the presence or absence of any other thing in those days.

And then they came. I did not sleep unclothed when I was alone— I wore Malcolm's coat over the shirt and waistcoat and the riding skirt with the placket that would not fasten; and when I heard the stallion screaming I was on my feet with the gun in my hand as though I were running in a dream.

Memory fails, and the order of things shifts. I wore no shoes, but I was conscious of nothing, not the icy rain in my eyes, not the mud dragging at my ankles. My hands and my brain worked mechanically: I reloaded in the rain, in the darkness, with shaking hands, cursing myself; I pulled the trigger and the charge lit and fired. I heard some one shout, "Christ and Mary, is the bastard at home?" and then another voice, "It is the bitch. I saw him go."

And there was time to remember, to hear the voice in my mind, his voice, which spoke to me always: *aim for the groin if you want the stomach, aim at the stomach for the heart.*

And now, no time. All gone, thrown away, falling into the night, no time to lay his cherished guns carefully out of the rain, no time to find them in the firelight. The perpetrators had gone, their work done. The stables Malcolm had built, of stone; the roof was slate. Nothing would burn but the couples, already alight, and the grain and the straw stored there, and the horse, screaming for release, secured with a halter in his loose box so that I would have a measure of control over him, although Malcolm had never restrained him.

I threw his coat into the water at my feet and soaked it and wrenched at the door. The iron burned my hands: in another minute it would not have opened. There did not seem to be smoke, only an intense, airless heat intolerable to my eyes: my very lashes seemed scorched: I thought my hair would burst into flames. I threw the coat over my face and went in. My skirt was smouldering; fed by the inrush of air, fire bloomed above and around me. I felt the bolt on the wood and hit it with something, perhaps my hand, perhaps some implement I had carried in with me. He had torn the halter from the wall, the leather dangling, and even in extremity he could not relinquish his jealousy of me; he threw his quarters against me, slamming me into the stone wall, an old malevolent trick. I remember only beating him with the flat of my hands, screaming, "Get out, get out, get out," and then, in all that ghastly light, the pale spark of his shoe against the stone as he threw up his head and plunged forward into the night.

Rain fell all the hours of darkness that remained. It was raining at dawn, when the roof collapsed and the obscenity of destruction was laid bare. I was sitting in the kitchen, with my burned hands bound in soaking cloths and a constriction like death in my lungs: the rain, carrying the ash, was running in a black river on the eastern window. The smoke must have been visible for miles.

The pain had begun with the coming of day: it seemed inevitable that I should labour alone who had carried this child in isolation and loneliness. I propped myself on the stairs but I could not climb, and wrapped still in Malcolm's damp coat I gave myself to him. I called him again and again, until my voice broke and the jealous silence of the house smothered me, and the spirits of the cold dead rooms flickered out of the shadows and claimed me— things real and imagined, terror made flesh, until the afternoon. Then there was movement in the shadows, living sound in the endless drumming of the rain: a scarred, cadaverous face, a trembling man without the strength to lift me. And then, as though in my anguish I had summoned her, a limping phantom who crooned to me; and together they carried me to bed.

At some hour of the afternoon or evening, this unequal struggle ended. I lived. My child died.

My house was full of people, voices that would not be identified, fragments of conversation in a language that would not be understood.

I drifted, bodiless, on the ebbing river of my thoughts. Hours, days, darkness passing, blood and time draining away.

I had given it no name, no identity, no welcome, no love, no hope of existence, and the child of my flesh was gone. I had never held it, never heard it cry, never been told of its death. It had died unbaptised. Malcolm and I had no religion... I had lost mine because it would not serve me, his only gods were himself and me. But in the dark world of his spirit, the hidden soul that was Celtic, there was a superstitious devotion, a consciousness of gods. What provision was made in that other world for the souls of unbaptised children?

I wanted to ask him. I wanted to know by what name we should have called it, I wanted to reach for him, but I had no strength. He came and went, one of the shadows that crossed my mind, and when he came to stay he sat in the chair by the bed and stared at the wall, unseeing. I watched the shadow of the rain on his face, and when he turned to look at me his eyes were dark, expressionless. It was a face I did not recognize, a man I did not know. I had not lain with him in passion in this bed or conceived this child, which I had not loved as I had loved him.

I did not know him, and because I could not embrace him or speak to him I lost him there in that darkness. I wept, endlessly, effortlessly, the tears the only warmth in that cold room, and he leaned forward and dried them with his handkerchief, gently but in an oddly detached manner, as if we were unacquainted. We did not speak; we did not seem to exist in the same world. I felt that if it were possible to lift my hand and touch him, my fingers would encounter nothingness. So we did not discuss our lost child, not then, not, with one exception, ever again. It went to its grave without a name, and no one ever told me where it was buried.

And when they came to him and told him that his only legitimate issue had been a son, he covered his face with his hands and wept. And in his soundless, inconsolable grief and my inability to comfort him, the lost soul found its resting place, and dwelled forever between us.

He was there: he had come from outdoors, there was a cleanliness about him, the scent of April. Was there spring in this dying place?

His hands were cold; roughened hands stroking the hair from my cheek. Our son would have had his eyes, green eyes, and his bristling black lashes, and his mouth, and his beautiful hands, bringing coolness to a burning face, and tenderness to one unloved.

"Well, mo chiall, how are you this morning?"

"Better, I think."

"I've brought you something." Their fragrance was already filling the room.

"Oh... violets...." Wet with dew or rain; indescribable sweetness, an ecstasy. They grew at Ardsian in profusion, in the orchard and the wood. "Are they from James?"

A stillness came into his manner, and I knew that this was yet my gift, to be the only living being who could injure him. He said, very quietly, "No, they are from me."

As violets fade, these folded quickly and were removed. They were not replaced.

.... In the evening, the mist pressed against the leaded panes. In the night the rain began again, beating against the glass like hands, like running steps, like whispers.

511

What did you do with my child? Did you bury it? Did you give it a name? By what name did you call it?

What did you do with my son?

.... Another evening. He was punctilious in his visits. He had brought me the heavy silk shawl to wear, as he knew I was fond of it.

I said, "I want to be well again."

"You will be well," he said.

"I want to be out in the air. I want to be in my garden."

"It's cold today. You would not want to be out there now."

"If I die, will you marry again?"

"You are not going to die. I would never allow it."

Malcolm— do you love me— do you love me—

From the kitchen there was a smell of cooking: my aunt, who had stayed, preparing supper. He would bring something to me on a tray: I would eat very little: he would go. The evening was not yet night; the afterlight lingered in the sky.

"When you were away... there was a great unhappiness in this house. You may call it fanciful, but I was conscious of ghosts."

"Yes," he said. "Mine among them, and very nearly yours." There was a silence, then he said without expression, "This house was a hell to me once. You brought peace, but I have never known happiness, neither here nor anywhere else."

"And now... the peace has gone."

"If it has, you are not to blame."

"I... was sorry... I could not save your saddle."

"Christ, is that what you think of me?" Then, "I sometimes wonder what wrong I did you to be punished like this every day. Is it what I always said, that you could never forgive me? That you would turn it on me like a weapon? What was my sin, Margaret?"

Then there was pain, and he was shouting from the top of the stairs, my aunt's distant voice in answer. By that time the blood was a burning torrent staining the clean, scented sheets. Eventually some one brought candles to the room; he had not left me to bring them himself, and by their light I saw that he had sent for Doctor Gerard Mackintosh.

It was done in daylight, when the haemorrhage had ceased. Malcolm held me with implacable strength; Mackintosh inserted a ball of linen into my

512

mouth and his instruments into my vagina. Cautery closed one of the fistulae: the other was pared and sutured. Unconsciousness came as a blessing.

He confined my bowels and emptied my bladder and subjected me to mechanical douches: the danger of septicaemia receded; a lingering infection ensured that I would not conceive again. By the end of April Mackintosh ceded his care of me to my aunt: although he had tried to engage me in conversation, I had not spoken to him since the first of his tortures had been inflicted upon me, nor would I communicate with him through Malcolm. On his last visit, when he was alone with me, he made a business of closing his bag, relinquishing his responsibility, then he leaned forward and said loudly into my face, "If you were my wife you'd be away to a bedlam."

I said, "If I had the disposal of you, you would be charged with murder."

He left me.

In the evening I was still sitting in the same chair, which Malcolm had moved closer to the window so that the morning sun might fall across me when I sat there. I wore the heavy embroidered shawl and a nightgown. I had not been clothed since the night of the fire, and out of spite or ignorance Mackintosh had forbidden me to bathe. The squalor of my person reflected the disorder of my mind, and it seemed to me that he had spoken the truth.

The casement stood open; the air was soft, soft. My aunt had not yet come to close it against the night, which she considered harmful, although I always opened it again after she had gone. Malcolm did not share the room with me, and as I had not left it for nearly a month I did not know where he now slept, or, until he appeared beside me, if he were even in the house. The table where his pistols had always lain at night was bare, and the small accoutrements of his occupation had been removed, with much of his clothing. There was an implication of permanence in this, but it had become impossible to know if that was his intention.

Deirdre came then, with the nightly offering of a candle and a glass of claret, and a stone jug filled with wild cherry blossoms that shed a delicate perfume as she arranged them on Malcolm's table. Then she turned to close the casement and I took her hand, driven by a need to touch something that lived, something that would touch me. When my fingers groped for hers she took them, very gently, and clasped them as though to encourage me. Hers were cool and dry, with swollen joints, and I who had become obsessed with mortality realized that she was old ... my fierce, unyielding aunt who had never bowed to any force, neither famine nor invasion, would one day submit to death; and unless one or the other of us could reach farther than this she would die as she had lived, as unknown to me as any stranger.

"Sit and talk to me, Aunt."

She hesitated, seeming to consider her time and the wisdom of humouring me: to sit was idleness, to sit on a bed a desecration in her canon of housekeeping. Then she relented, leaving the casement unfastened and the candle unlit, and the twilight deepened, and we talked.

At first our conversation was inconsequential, and then, gradually, it acquired intensity and penetration. She spoke with that curious compassion of Malcolm's isolation and my duty, of the increasing hostility toward him and the necessity of my resuming my life beside him. The past was the past, she said, and the wounds of the past were undeniable, but they must be allowed to heal; otherwise life would destroy me.

I said, "You cannot possibly understand. You never bore a child, you were never sickened with guilt because it was not wanted, you were never subjected to such disgusting medical treatment as was forced upon me in this room. I have been violated, body and soul. You cannot know how I feel."

She said, "You do not know the meaning of violation. What was done to me was violation."

And she told me her experience, not probes and cautery and indignity, not the betrayal of a lover. The voice in the perfumed dimness spoke of rape over a period of hours, by an unknown number of men; of wounding with nails and teeth and fists and steel and booted feet; of savage and repeated assaults, one of which caused her to conceive. She spoke of aborting herself. She spoke then of the man she had loved, whom it had been her desire to join, and that, in the long aftermath of her life, nothing— nothing—had signified, because in body and in spirit she was dead, and with him.

The horror receded, but would never recede; the night, undisturbed now by her voice, held us. Then she rose and lit the candle, and the world was unchanged and irrevocably changed, illuminated by a knowledge so terrible that I wept, although she did not.

"Could there have been no marriage, no happiness for you?"

"There could be no marriage. He was married." Then she said, "We loved one another for one summer and one only, the summer before war. All Glen Sian was our marriage bed."

I said nothing, understanding. So well understood.

"Then he went away, and a year later he was dead. The English killed him, or maybe those who came with them. I buried him."

She left the candle burning and closed the casement, and paused there limned against the night: dignity and austerity and enigma incarnate: by her own revelations defined, yet ever elusive, withdrawn from the world, like Malcolm.

She did not turn from the window, or move.

"Who was the man you loved?"

She said, "He was George Cameron's father."

I heard the murmur of their voices later, Malcolm's voice and hers, and the sounds of domesticity in the kitchen: these two dark spirits who attended me, and professed no affection for one another. And it seemed that although there was still little warmth in these fragments of conversation, the fragments themselves were communication. She had always understood him: since childhood he had recognized her: their souls were ancient, fierce, unChristian; they were of a world together, of which I was not a part.

He did not come to me that night: he walked in the garden in the darkness. Later there was moonlight, which I had always loved, bleaching his pillow and the white blossom, arranged with an oriental simplicity on the table where his pistols should have lain, and shedding petals on an opened book left there. And the page, the fallen flower, the perfume, were reminiscent of some sorrow too elusive to be recalled.

When it became possible to behave as though very little had happened, we spoke of Inverness and the untimely interruption of his business there. I never questioned the powerful intuition that had brought him home to me; I knew only that he had left Inverness even as the fire was burning. His business had been delayed until Lammas. He did not specify its nature, or reveal anything other than a cold impatience.

At Whitsun I was visited by the Sheriff Clerk, who took a precognition from me in Malcolm's presence, concerning the events of the night of the fourth of April for submission to the Procurator Fiscal. Subsequently we learned that no charges of arson would be brought: there were no suspects, and my evidence could not be corroborated.

Malcolm accepted this quietly, merely folding the letter with an insignificant remark regarding Lammas, and continued to absent himself on Glen Sian's affairs. The land was immortal and he was its servant; it quickened although death had harrowed it, and demanded husbandry in its season. The dead who had lain entombed in the winter snows were discovered and interred, and their names were struck from the rent rolls: the rooftrees and cross-beams of their dwellings were confiscated and used in the rebuilding of our stables. Putrefying cattle were burned where they were found, to discourage those who would still have fed on the poisoned meat. The heather, too, was burned, and a pall like the day of judgment lay over the townships, until it was said that the smoke of Malcolm's burning would blacken the eye of heaven. The last potato pits in Glen Sian were opened, and the contents found to be rotting: the spring was still and warm, the air humid, and imbued with invisible sickness. The spores awaited only the spade to resume the cycle of destruction. But the people must till the land, and the people must be fed.

Supplies of peasemeal, potatoes and seed-oats were made available by the government in late May. For the Western Highlands these allowances were distributed at Fort Augustus by the army. Rioting ensued, and many arrests were made; several of the rioters were women. The cost of this relief was astronomical, and was to be borne by every landowner.

I pleaded with Malcolm not to leave me again, to send some one else to Fort Augustus. He merely laughed at me, as though he relished the prospect of confrontation, and three days later he brought twenty garrons over the Saddle in the company of hired drovers. There was no rioting in Glen Sian when these supplies were distributed, because it was done in the very courtyard of Ardsian, with an occasional flicker of the curtain which was James's gesture of support.

Time, the black river, carried us onward; the current of our lives resumed its course. What had passed was past, but nothing healed, and nothing was forgotten.

James and I had tea in the orchard: the everlasting revolution, once more bringing blossom and decay.

He would be thirty-one in August, and I twenty-seven in September. We had not seen one another since before my illness, and as we sat in the swaying shadows I noticed that since Charlotte's death the fairness of his hair had turned an equally fair, pure silver. Knowing his vanity I did not mention it, but, being James, he had no such compunctions, and he lacked the subtlety to disguise his shock at my deterioration.

"This is improvement, is it?"

"My mirror tells me so."

"Then thank God I didn't see you at your worst."

He sat gazing at my hand on his arm.

"Am I very altered?"

He said, "None of us is untouched by hell. Our humanity will not sustain it … although I can think of one or two not notably afflicted in that direction. I gather your spouse was less than pleased with the fiscal's investigation."

"He wanted justice. I don't blame him for his bitterness. I share it."

"You must understand something, Margaret. Very little of consequence happens here, and even less notice is taken of it elsewhere. It is your responsibility to ensure that that situation continues. If Malcolm is bent on justice he is perfectly capable of forcing the issue himself. I don't want that, and neither should you. God knows where it would lead." Then, "It would not be possible for you to identify any person in connection with that night."

"That was the opinion of the Sheriff Clerk."

"But if it happened that you could … I want your promise that you would come to me, and only me, with that information."

"I cannot be bound by some childish promise."

"I don't ask in a childish spirit. If you love him, protect him. My greatest fear is that one day he will overstep the mark."

Silence. Around us fragrance, stillness, a rain of tinted petals.

"How many years is it since we sat here, and you first warned me against Malcolm?"

He said, "Too many. And you never learn, any more than I do." The honeyed sweetness, the flickering light, the bridal rain of petals, his fingers delicately brushing mine as though by accident. "Everywhere the pattern repeats itself. I make the same mistakes, I dare to hope for the same impossibilities and invite the same rebuffs. Isn't this a little like you, Margaret? Don't you think we have a good deal in common?"

"What are you saying to me, James?"

"I think you know. I want to leave this place forever. I think you want that, too. Can you deny it? Can you tell me that after this past winter, something didn't die in you? Something of your soul, Margaret? Something of yourself? Maybe... something of your marriage? Can you tell me with honesty that another such winter wouldn't kill you, oh, perhaps not bodily ... not yet ... but in every other way? Is this what you imagine life to be? Cannot you imagine something else?"

"Life with you?"

"Life in France, in a kinder world. Sunlight, music, pleasure. Perhaps me, in time, if that was what you wanted. You know I always loved you, Margaret. Why do you think I was so jealous of my father? Think of it. Must life always be like this, so savage, so pitiless? I say it could be sweet. I want that sweetness for myself."

"And you would take me as I am, in this deplorable condition—"

"That will change, Margaret."

"Married to another man, upon whose compliance you seem to presume? You must be dreaming."

"I don't intend to force a confrontation with him. You could leave separately, and join me in France later."

"And be a mother to Charlotte's child?"

"She would have wanted no other."

"And share your bed? Would she have approved of that, too?"

"Charlotte was aware that I cherished a certain tenderness for you. She was not without experience of other men. I was ... not her favourite."

"... I wish this conversation could be unsaid."

"I don't. I regret none of it. Life gives us nothing but what we seize for ourselves. I can give you freedom, and perhaps happiness. If he can give you more, then, as you wish, this conversation will be forgotten. Except ... in the stillness of your heart, Margaret. I know life has made you contemplative, like me. You still may hear it then."

I was much alone, and in the stillness of my heart he never ceased to speak to me. And in my hours of contemplation he sowed doubt in me like a sickness, and everything I saw was poisoned, and everything I was, was diseased.

Upon my aunt's return to Glen Mor another guardian had appointed herself: Mairi, unobtrusively caring for my house and garden, which no longer interested me. By degrees, she extended that care to me.

She healed my body; my womb still wept a bloodied mucous, of which she relieved me, although she could not salve my spirit or the wounds inflicted by my own sexuality. I had conceived in ecstasy, and engendered only suffering and indelible fear and guilt. I was not fecund, I could not grieve, I could not heal, or contemplate a resumption of sexual relations ... as woman, as lover, my instincts were unnatural. As Margaret, I was not certain of my survival.

Nor could she heal herself. She was physically strong, although whip-thin and undeveloped, but her left leg was wasted and considerably shorter than the right, and she balanced increasingly on the ball of the left foot: she fell often, which provoked her to incoherent rage, and she found assistance intolerable. Her moods were volatile, sweetness, sarcasm, ineffable compassion emerging without warning: her intellect was starved but her soul, trembling between genius and insanity, was visionary and poetic. Where she loved, she was greatly gifted, with intuition and an abnormal sensitivity: gifted with vision, like Malcolm.

I knew her: her madness and her courage and her insufferable pride, the starvation of her every sense for comfort and affection, the loneliness and deprivation and mortification of her life. I gave her my gratitude and my pity: she craved love, which I could not offer. And she knew me, she knew my fears and my vulnerability and the painful disjointure of my relations with Malcolm; and she played upon me with subtle cruelty, with fantasies and with lies, and she poisoned where she had healed, and the poison she inflicted upon me festered, until I believed her.

She had no beauty, physical or spiritual, although beauty could pass like a shadow over her dark little vivid face: she could bring it without artifice to herself, as her crippled body assumed attitudes of grace. She had not his eyes: she would have been truly beautiful if she had had his eyes. She reminded me of no one: I denied the resemblance, as I denied her lies and her sexual fantasies, although in his absence I saw Malcolm in her face, and in her

518

absence she came between us like the ghost of my dead child, like the daughter I would never bear him, and I knew that she was his.

It came to me, not a thought, not a fear, but as an invitation, the voice in the stillness of my heart, in the moonless, colourless nights; and it spoke to me of freedom, not of loveless adultery but of easeful death. It was very real, this wish; its very reality was frightening: although death was alluring and promised peace, enough sanity remained to me to recognize that I had gone very far into the darkness in my contemplation of it.

And I could not free myself: nothing could help me, nothing. Malcolm had gone beyond me into some private obsession of his own; we encountered one another like strangers and conversed courteously and emptily ... with such emptiness. The days passed, the nights passed, the currents twisted and deepened, the surface of the black river of our lives was glassy and undisturbed. The intolerable noise of reconstruction ceased and the horses returned to the stables; the rain fell, the potatoes flourished without blight; the air was smothering. He came home in the dimness that passed for night; he left the house before dawn; he did not sleep with me, nor was there any attempt, nor, apparently, desire to resume sexual relations. He walked the night like a caged tiger, perhaps trying to forget me in the garden I had sowed and the house to which I had brought femininity. All around us the ravaged earth was restored, reborn, while within us the love was dying. And, God help us, neither of us seemed to care. In our hearts was nothing but a hard-learned apathy. In our hearts was nothing but nothing.

On that last night there was a moonrise, late enough to be visible in the brief darkness of high summer; neither he nor I was sleeping, and we sat on the green-painted bench in the garden together and watched it. He was smoking and withdrawn, although lately I had taken refuge in his silence: it did not intrude upon me or press me for intimacy.

It was darker, and the night was damp; the light of the rising moon illuminated our faces. He had washed my hair for me earlier, with a dispassionate kindness, and it brushed against his shoulder. Unexpectedly he touched it, and when I did not speak he did not remove his hand.

"Those lilies I gave you, will they bloom this summer?"

"No. Perhaps next year."

"That is a pity. I liked the name: it reminded me of you." He smoked: the night was still, the light cold and colourless. "I always thought of you that way ... and my body was always my gift to you, my act of adoration."

"Malcolm ... this is unChristian ... to speak of sex as godhead ..."

"I speak of us, and what you are to me. You were always my madonna, and when you took me in that silken mouth, I was a god."

He sought his communion in secret pleasures, in the lips, in the salt flower of the vulva and the silken mouth, and, aroused by the exquisite sensuality of his gifts, I offered invitation. But my spirit could not meet him, and my body was a damaged place, inhabited by ghosts and memories and the fear of injury and the dread of pregnancy, and my womb resisted him even as he entered me. He sensed it, and came convulsively and joylessly, as though intercourse were some savage struggle for his very life. It ended; everything ended. I closed my eyes against the unbearable nakedness of his pain.

XVIII

On Sunday the twenty-second of June, 1772, copies of this document, neatly tied with red ribbon and signed and dated by the Sheriff Clerk Depute of Inverness, were served upon those named.

SUMMONS OF REMOVAL
James Gordon Gunn Stirling of Glen Sian

vs

Diarmaid Cameron and Coinneach Cameron alias Kenneth Cameron, Torcall Gunn, Raonull Gunn of Carinish, Ruiseart alias Richard Gunn, William Gunn, Gilchrist MacGregor alias Stirling, Caillean MacGregor alias Stirling, Daniel MacGregor alias Stirling of Monnymore, Grizel Chisholm MacGregor alias Stirling, the name of MacGregor being outlawed.

Whereas it is humbly meant and shewn that James Gordon Gunn Stirling, Esq. of Glen Sian, Heritable Proprietor of the Land and other parts after mentioned, that by the Act of Sederunt of the Lords of Council and Session, dated the fourteenth of December, one thousand seven hundred and fifty-six, entitled, 'An Act Anent Removings', it is provided That Where a Tenant hath not obliged himself to remove without warning, in such case it shall be lawful to the Heritor or Setter of the Tack, either to use the Order prescribed by the Act of Parliament made in the year fifteen hundred and fifty-five entitled 'An Act Anent the Warning of Tenants', and thereupon pursue a warning of ejection, or to bring his Action of removing against the Tenant before the Judge Ordinary; and such action being called before the Judge Ordinary at least forty days before the term of Lammas, shall be held as equal to a Warning executed in the terms of the aforesaid Act; and the Judge shall therefore proceed to determine in the Removings in terms of the Act, in the same manner as if a Warning had been executed in terms of the aforesaid Act of Parliament.

That Diarmaid Cameron and Coinneach alias Kenneth Cameron, residing at Bearradh Farm, are Tenants, Subtenants or Possessors under the Pursuer of a Dwelling House and other premises and pertinents thereto attached at Bearradh, lying within in the parish of Glen Sian and Sheriffdom of Inverness, on a title of Possession which will expire as to the House, Gardens and Grass on the said Possession at and against the term of Lammas next, and as to the arable Land under Crop, at the Separating of the Crop from the ground, in the year one thousand seven hundred and seventy-two.

That Torcall Gunn and Raonull Gunn, residing at Carinish, are joint Tenants, Subtenants or Possessors under the Pursuer of a Dwelling House and other pertinents and premises thereto attached at Carinish, lying within the parish of Glen Sian and Sheriffdom of Inverness, on a Title of Possession which will expire at and against the term of Lammas next, in the year one thousand seven hundred and seventy-two.

That Ruiscart alias Richard Gunn, William Gunn, Gilchrist MacGregor alias Stirling, Caillean MacGregor alias Stirling, Daniel MacGregor alias Stirling and Grizel Chisholm MacGregor alias Stirling, residing at Monnymore, are joint Tenants, Subtenants or Possessors under the Pursuer of Dwelling Houses and other pertinents and premises thereto attached at Monnymore, lying within the Parish of Glen Sian and Sheriffdom of Inverness, on Titles of Possession which will expire at and against the term of Lammas next, in the year one thousand seven hundred and seventy-two.

That the Pursuer is desirous that the said Diarmaid Cameron, Coinneach alias Kenneth Cameron, Torcall Gunn, Raonull Gunn, Ruiseart alias Richard Gunn, William Gunn, Gilchrist MacGregor alias Stirling, Caillean MacGregor alias Stirling, Daniel MacGregor alias Stirling, and Grizel Chisholm MacGregor alias Stirling, shall remove from the said Possessions respectively occupied by them at the terms above mentioned, and to obtain a Decree of Removal against them accordingly in order that the Pursuer or others in his name may enter thereto and possess the same.

Therefore the said Defenders ought and should be declared and ordered by Decree and sentence of me or my Substitute,

I. To flit and remove themselves, Bairns, Family, Servants, subtenants, cottars and dependents, Cattle, Goods, and gear, forth and from possession of the said Subjects above described with the pertinents respectively occupied by them, as aforesaid, and to leave the same void, redd and patent, at the respective terms of removal above specified, that the Pursuer or others in his name may then enter thereto and peaceably possess, occupy and enjoy the same,

II. And in the event of their opposing this action to make payment to the Pursuer of the sum of Ten pounds Sterling, or such other sum as shall be modified at the Expenses of Process, besides the Expense of Extracting and Recording the Decree to follow thereon.

All in terms of the Act of Sederunt and the laws and daily practice of Scotland, used and observed in the like cases in all points as if alleged. My will is herefore, I command you that on sight hereof, ye pass and lawfully Summon, warn and charge the Said Defenders personally, or at their dwelling places, to appear before me or my Substitute, within the ordinary Court Place at Inverness upon the seventh day next after Court Day, to allege a reasonable cause to the contrary. With Certification According to Justice given under the hand of the Clerk of Court at Inverness, the twelfth day of June, Seventeen hundred and seventy-two years.

The document was entirely in English, and no Gaelic translation was available until a single handwritten copy was provided by George Cameron, cousin of the defender Diarmaid Cameron, and circulated among the affected households. Even then fewer than half of those whose leases had been terminated were able to read the summons of their own removal. An appearance by any of them to dispute the removals before the Sheriff Clerk at Inverness was out of the question. The legal process was intimidating, and no man whose rent was three years in arrears could afford the sum of ten pounds required as compensation for obstruction.

The writs, nailed to the doors of the dwellings while the inhabitants were sleeping, had been delivered in a manner both provocative and insulting, and there were allegations of cowardice against the man who had served them, and a growing conviction that the confrontation for which many hungered was almost upon them. On the afternoon of Friday, August first, at Bearradh farm, it came.

Although it was Lammas he had not been collecting rents; he did not specify what would occupy him, but he said that he would not return late. By half past seven, driven by apprehension, I rode to Ardsian.

The door of his office was open; in this sultry evening, in the greyness before storm, faint candlelight sliced the dark corridor and spilled at my feet. Their voices died as they became aware of my presence: James, immaculate in silken waistcoat, supporting on a chair a supine man whose face was obscured by bloodstained compresses; Gerard Mackintosh, recognizing me with a flash of annihilating disgust; and Malcolm, seated behind the table and the table littered with pistols, candles, papers, stained and discarded handkerchiefs and neckcloths. His unsheathed sword lay on the floor with much of his clothing: the stench of excrement was nauseating. The left side of his face seemed disfigured with ink, as though ink had been thrown at him. Briefly the eyes opened, and burned in the discolouration, then they closed. No one spoke to me.

"My God. What happened?"

They opened again, the left eye so swollen that the lid would barely lift.

"A little popular resistance, my dear. Morrison, I present my wife."

The supine man made a ghastly effort to sit upright.

"Madam, your servant."

They compelled him to lie back, still with the bloodied cloths across his face. James was blanched, as if the heat and stench were sickening him. Although his hands never left the injured man, Mackintosh said curtly, "As you are here, madam, the least you can do is persuade your husband to be examined."

Surprisingly, he consented, and stood impassively while Mackintosh probed and sponged him and passed the candleflame before his pupils: they spoke only once, when Malcolm removed his shirt. His left breast, like his face, was savagely bruised, and the nipple was bleeding. Mackintosh prodded it until he pushed his hand away.

"Look to Morrison. He needs you more than I."

"This was a blow that might have stopped your heart."

"It would want more than that."

He dressed again in the obscenely stained shirt, and Mackintosh and James assisted the unknown Morrison to his feet. He stood, supported by them, holding the bloody compress to his face, and I saw that he was or had been a handsome man, balding, in his fifties, with a fine, humorous mouth and cleft chin: his ruined clothing had been expensive, and on his right hand, which he extended, he wore a heavy gold signet ring.

"Good night, madam. I doubt we shall meet again."

I answered as though in some twisted nightmare, aware of nothing but the gallant flicker of courtesy in this inexplicable hell.

"Good night, sir. I am sorry for your injuries."

"It is the nature of my business, although not usually in so extreme a degree. Good night, Scott. I am grateful for your courage."

He was visibly weakening, and Mackintosh initiated the withdrawal. James followed without a word. Everything, it appeared, had been said, except to me.

We were alone, and it seemed we had never been so alone. The night was still, with thunder but no rain, and no wind to clear these hellish shadows of the stench of human faeces.

He had seated himself again behind the desk, with the ghastly paraphernalia of the day. He swept the papers aside and took a bottle and a glass from a drawer, and I watched with an unspeakable compassion as he attempted to pour a measure: his hands were trembling, and he cursed and put the bottle down, and sat with his elbows in the litter on the table and rested his face in his hands. Without speaking I poured it for him: he accepted it without expression, drank, and pushed the glass across the table toward me, and, in utter silence, we shared it. Then he pulled open another drawer and tossed a leather case onto the papers, fumbled with it, and removed a cheroot, which he cut and lit with difficulty. Blood had dried beneath the nails of his right hand.

"Morrison's," he said, although whether he meant the cigar or the blood I did not know, and he did not elaborate.

The smoke filled the candlelight. In the heavy rainless night there was no sound, only smothering silence.

"Who is Morrison?"

"He is a sheriff officer, sent from Inverness."

"Why?"

"To witness the legal eviction of undesirable tenants." He opened his eyes, and the effect of the blazing, bloodshot irises against the bruising was indescribable. "And if you entertain any doubt as to their undesirability, I think circumstances have proved it beyond question. Morrison was blinded—that was Siubhan Cameron's handiwork. Your friend Cameron was there, too, heaving bricks for all he was worth. By that time there were fifty, sixty people in the house and outside of it. I had piss thrown in my face. I had clods of shit thrown at me. I had a shower of burning peat thrown over the horse. I had bricks in my face and bricks in my gut and stones on the back of my head. They pulled Morrison down and the women beat him, with their fists and their feet and the iron spades they use to cook their bannock, and they held the poor bastard's face under water and tried to drown him. Diar Cameron was sitting on the doorstone with his coat over his head, rocking back and forth, and his bitch of a wife was screaming at him to stand up and fight like a man. I managed to come to where Morrison was and I stood over him with my sword in my hand, and I told them to disperse or by Christ one of them would die, and there would be soldiers in Glen Sian tomorrow. And when that bitch came near to me I threw her down on the ground and told her I would kill her, and she never moved from that time until I got Morrison into the saddle." The ash fell unnoticed from his hand to the floor. "Give me another drink, will you."

He drank it without speaking: silence seemed to be what he wanted. I sat opposite him, watching the restless activity of his hands, wondering if I would wake or dwell forever in this new region of hell.

Eventually he said, "I will have your friend Cameron taken up for mobbing and rioting, and that bitch for assault on Morrison, and Coinneach Cameron for what he did to you. And I will have the land from them, and any one else who offers me similar treatment."

"I wish to God you would stop calling him that."

He said with an odd little quizzical smile, made hideous by the bruising, "Is he not, Margaret? Was he never your friend? You were my friend once."

Whatever he could read in my eyes, in my thoughts, I kept them focused upon him.

"I will consider your judgment disordered by what happened to you today, and make allowances for that remark."

"Then it will not concern you if I have him arrested."

"Do what you like. You always do."

"No," he said, "Only sometimes. And of course, we must be grateful to him, as they told me he saved your life. Why would he come to my house in my absence if not out of tenderness for you, and some desire to spare you his cousin's attentions?"

"I daresay there are women in Glen Sian who cherish a certain warmth of feeling for you. You are not obliged to respond to it."

"Nor did I."

"Nor do I."

He leaned back, as though the effort of remaining upright were too much, and stared at the litter on the desk, flicking papers with his thumb. His left eye had swollen further, and was scarcely open.

I said, "What will happen now?"

"Oh, life will never be the same. They will never forget what they did, and I will never forget them. And when they come to stand before me in this room with their hands all around their bonnets, I will remember them, and there will be no peace from me ever again."

"Malcolm ... you cannot mean what you are saying."

He gazed at me through the smoke and the shadows.

"My dear, I do mean it. Bearradh was my Rubicon. Let them bear the consequences."

I thought, as will I.

"Malcolm, let me care for you. Come home."

He ground the cigar into the floorboard and rose, and some instinct made me move toward him even as he swore and caught the chairback. He had not yet regained the stone or so he had lost in the unspeakable months of hunger, but he was more than six feet tall and the sudden deadness of his weight was almost insupportable; then he pushed me away gently and stood alone, leaning against the table. A moment later he said, "the key," and I fumbled with revolted hands through the stinking garments on the floor for the key in the pocket of his bloodied waistcoat. Eventually he snuffed the candle and left the table and came out of the estate office with me, and I locked the door. I remember little of the ride back. I had never known the reliance I had placed upon his physical strength and his protection, and his condition alarmed me. The night was stifling, alive with lightning; both horses were agitated and difficult, and he would not relinquish the stallion to me.

Nor had the nightmare ended. He bathed in the lochan, in the lightning's reflection, and walked back naked through the garden and dressed in clean clothing, and sat for a time on the sofa in my room, drinking without complaint the bitter tea I had brewed for him, although I knew he disliked it: the fierce, erratic restlessness, the fury of reaction, had left him, and I thought it might be possible to persuade him to sleep. He gave me that travesty of a smile.

"If only that were true, my darling, that you wanted me in your bed. What a delightful encounter we would have, me nursing my aches and pains, and you all the wounds of your spirit."

I said, "I wonder that you carry a sword, when you can inflict so much damage merely by speaking."

In the hot, haunted night, there was no sound; only the stirring of a wind in the darkness, uneasy and unsettling.

He said, "I am going out. I have unfinished business," and the heat and stillness seemed to darken and collapse on me. I felt I was smothering.

"Malcolm ... for God's sake, don't go."

He turned from the door and said, very gently, "God the protector was never in this house. And I do nothing for his sake, or yours."

I did not know at what time he returned. I woke, after hours of waiting, to find him lying on the bed with his back to me, the last time I saw his splendid nakedness and the cruelty of the injuries inflicted upon him. He slept deeply, for Malcolm: the glass on the floor held a grainy residue of the opiate he had never allowed me to find, and he was very still, except once, when he attempted to turn, and some consciousness of his body's pain disturbed him. He did not move again.

He slept, from the time I saw him, another twelve hours, and while he slept a soft rain fell, and quenched the fires at Bearradh.

A slow haemorrhage had begun in the Highlands, which would not be staunched: the white-sailed ships had carried hundreds out of destitution, and beyond the reach of landlords and agents, into the golden-hued west, to an America burnished by the lies and letters and ideals of those who had preceded them. Among those who went now were Torcall and Raonull Gunn, unmarried men in their twenties, who abandoned their holding at Carinish and respectfully requested the five pounds' bounty that had been promised them. They were given it, and they took care that all should know where their destiny lay. They either prospered or died as emigrants: they were not seen again in Glen Sian.

Coinneach Cameron, Gilchrist MacGregor, Caillean MacGregor and Ruiseart Gunn were charged with riot, assault and battery and three other men with rioting and mobbing at Bearradh farm. No other charges were brought against Coinneach Cameron, although from a window at Ardsian I identified him as one of the arsonists who had visited our property. I was reminded severely by James, who stood beside me, that arson was a capital offense, and to be certain of my identification. At that point Coinneach Cameron, who was detained in the courtyard with others, recognized me and vanquished any lingering doubt in my mind by shouting at me in Gaelic, "Has no one burned your long hair yet, bitch?" Perhaps for reasons of policy, James affected not to understand either the sense or the sentiment of this, and Malcolm, thank God, was not present. George Cameron came under the fiscal's scrutiny at the suggestion that he had incited and participated in riot, but he was not immediately charged. Siubhan Cameron, wife of the defender Diarmaid Cameron of Bearradh, was questioned concerning her actions on the first of August, but no charges were brought following the disclosure of her pregnancy. Homeless but unwilling to quit the land before the harvest of crops to which, by custom, they were entitled, they lived in a tarpaulin shelter on open ground with the two children under five years of age who remained alive of their family of twelve.

The residents of Monnymore who had not been arrested, William Gunn, Daniel MacGregor and Grizel Chisholm MacGregor, the woman they shared as wife, remained in possession of their dwellings although their lease was void at Lammas. No attempt had yet been made to evict them, and they regarded this as a victory.

William Morrison returned to Inverness by gradual stages, accompanied to Fort Augustus by Malcolm and resting there for several days before resuming his journey. His wrist had been broken at Bearradh, and he had regained the sight in his right eye but only partial vision in the left; and in retrospect it seemed to me that the impairment of Malcolm's own vision, which was not yet apparent, dated also from the assault upon him. They would both give evidence for the prosecution at the Circuit Court in September.

In late August, the potato crop failed.

Depths of anger and of fear I had not known I possessed had been disturbed and were manifest in my dreams, and until the dreams faded in the hour after waking I was shocked by the fury of my own emotions. In this slow finale of my life in Scotland I had come full circle, and dreamed and raged and wept and woke with the same clenched fists and anguish of the early years.

That it was ending I had no doubt: the moment of conclusion was not yet here, but our days and nights were merely final movements. Glen Sian obsessed Malcolm utterly: he was seldom at home and where he slept was not known to me. I felt vulnerable, frightened, betrayed by his silence and his secrecy and his absence as my lover: that he should have abandoned me, made no effort to regain me or to find me in the dark place to which my spirit had retreated, was unbearable. He hurt me without touching me, without perhaps knowing that he did so, and I suffered savagely, and the coldness and rigidness that possessed me in his presence became the uncontrollable reflex of the wounded: pain for pain.

He was due to appear in Inverness on the morning of the fifteenth of September, my twenty-seventh birthday, at the Circuit Court: he did not invite me to accompany him or to sample the subtle charms of the town, which I had never seen. The night before his departure he returned early to the house and spent the evening in his study, perhaps in contemplation of his evidence. At one o'clock in the morning he was still there. The desk had been tidied, the glass dish emptied of ash, the papers concealed to his satisfaction. His watch was lying open on the desk, very audible in the stillness. He did not look up.

"Ah," he said, "my guardian angel, hovering as always in perfect silence."

"Are you coming to bed, or do you sleep on the floor? Or do you sleep at all?"

He said, "Margaret, it is very late, and I am tired. Go to bed, and I will see you in the morning."

"And you? Will you go to bed? Where do you sleep, Malcolm? With whom?"

He said very quietly, with his eyes upon something on the desk, "Margaret, I have had an evil day, and despite what you think I do not enjoy the prospect before me. Now leave me alone, for Christ's sake, and go to bed."

"Do you sleep with Grania, Malcolm?"

He looked up, and although I knew he lied, the pain was indescribable. "Sometimes."

"And Mairi. Do you sleep with Mairi?"

He had been reaching for his cut glass companion on the papers: it was half filled with whisky. The stillness in his hand and his face and his body were like the deadness of pain within me.

"You have slept with her in the past, haven't you? In the little rooms, she told me. Your tastes are quite catholic, aren't they? Whores, virgins and little girls... but not your wife. You only sleep with your wife when you want an alibi."

Even I sensed the effort, the control: he did not move, he did not come to his feet, he did not rise to the unspeakable. He sat in the stillness with the candlelight illuminating half his face; he did not reveal what was in his eyes. He said, "If ever a woman could shrivel a man's soul, and shrivel his prick, that woman is you."

I knocked the glass, his precious crystal, from the desk, and heard it shatter. He came to his feet, not with the grace of earlier years but stiffly, as though enduring an accumulation of pain with the stoicism of the child and the man.

He said, very softly, "You were born to break my heart," and, without touching, left me.

Eight days of autumnal warmth and solitude were given to me. There was no spiritual peace in this interlude. It was my valediction.

I rode to Bearradh, roofless and stinking, the charred heart open to the sky, the white stones which had decorated the doorstep scattered in the scorched and trampled grass. The pitiful relics dragged from the flames still stood ignored six weeks later in the sun and rain, symbols of futile hope and instinct: there was little use for wicker chairs and rugs and dressers and spinning wheels under a billowing tarpaulin, and no neighbour in Glen Sian would undertake either to store or to remove them.

Nothing, then, but the crumbling walls; nothing moved but the wind, and a curlew inscribing the desolation with a poignant, startled sweetness. Nothing here to salve my conscience. Malcolm had suffered, but not in this measure.

I rode on. Other days, other shadows, other desolations followed. I visited Glen Mor, and left Ewen's journals and mine wrapped in brown paper on my narrow bed, as though protecting them from some impending conflagration of my own. My aunt received me with a cool politeness. My father and George Cameron had walked together to Inverness, where MacNeil believed he could mediate or offer his services as a translator: all business of the court was conducted in English, no word of which was spoken or understood by any of the men on trial.

Revelation had severed her from me, as though she were ashamed of it, and conversation was difficult. She alluded vaguely to a failing in my father's health but would not be drawn on the subject, and gently closed her mind and the house against me. I behaved with reciprocal courtesy and left, as was expected of me.

And now I sought the shadow of myself, the small signatures of my presence and my past in the silence of Ardsian. I had avoided the house when James was in residence: he had presumed once too often on our conspiratorial intimacy, and the memories of Charlotte were still memories of vivid pain. But James had gone finally to Inverness after weeks of indecision, and one last act of renunciation and remembrance remained to me. I walked through the house in a vast inner silence: none of their voices spoke to me, no remembered sweetness came, only the unhealed savagery of absolute recollection. The morning room: the splintered wood, the broken brass, the empty crystal bowl, nothing here of the golden ghosts, only an old number of an Edinburgh newspaper discarded on the floor and a cup half filled with greyish coffee. The dark red room: the damp, close air, the motes of dust in the sunlight, the dark spirit in the night, myself, betrayed and violated. And now, Charlotte's rooms: nothing here but the dusty perfume of face powder, the dust on the surface of her dressing table, the door left open for the comings and goings of the white cat, who fed elsewhere and returned to keep this vigil in the centre of the wrinkled counterpane. The blue and lemon silk stripes of the chair in which I had sat and watched her die. I held the cat in my arms and sat there for a time, talking to it of nothing, but it was indifferent to me, intent only upon waiting for Charlotte.

I left the house, and left myself, my younger self, the vulnerable friend who grieved and waited and had never healed and could not release these dead spirits and allow them rest, or myself peace, and I walked in the garden among fallen and falling leaves. There were flowers enough for me, and I cut them and took them to their graves, and prayed for their spirits, and for Malcolm, whom I had failed and who had failed me. And the years and the pain and the grief and the obligation to love and to mourn and to suffer became a passing of shadows, and left me, and I was released. There was no more here for me.

I was in my garden on the evening of Sunday the twenty-first when Malcolm returned. I was not inclined to meet him in the house, or to leave the night: something melancholy and astringent in the dying year appealed to me. The mist on the water, the tawny light, fading even as I watched, the calm before the onslaught of winter, next week, next month, tomorrow: this autumn, like my resting place, was ephemeral, an illusion.

He came through the twilight toward me and I turned away before he reached me; we did not speak, but stood perhaps five feet apart, staring out over the lochan toward the east. There was no moon and the stars were faint: fog was lying on the lower ground and on Riabhach beyond. His boot had crushed some plant, and a bitter perfume rose between us; when he spoke his breath was visible.

"How are you, Margaret?"

"I am well enough, thank you."

"You seem better, stronger. Is that so?"

"I believe it is. I hope so."

He said after a pause, staring out over the water, "How strange that after all this time there should come a moment like this, when the one who always receives the kiss still desires it, and is hurt by its absence."

"You said some vile things to me. Don't expect me to forget them."

"I don't expect it. I know how long your memory is."

I turned only briefly, long enough to see his face, to know that he still possessed me. Whatever he was, he was still Malcolm, my lover, my god.

"What do you want of me?"

"No, Margaret, what do you want of me? You must know—you seem determined to injure me in every way possible to achieve it. Out of courtesy you might tell me what it is, while we can still talk to one another."

"One day, I will want the truth from you."

"You'll have more truth than you can stomach. Maybe that will content you. Christ knows I can do nothing else to please you."

It was darker, and perceptibly colder. Neither he nor I moved toward the light.

"I assume the court decided in your favour."

"Yes. Your friend Cameron will bruit the verdict about soon enough, I have no doubt."

"You must be satisfied. You have your victory, you have your land, you made your point, and James dances to your tune. What happens next?"

"James applies for twenty writs for Martinmas, then he buggers off to Edinburgh for the winter and leaves me in peace. The degree and the quality of the peace depend upon you, my darling."

I said, "You ask me what I want. I want freedom."

It was very silent. Very dark, and bitter cold. The crushed, medicinal fragrance rose sharply in the darkness. He had moved, although he was barely visible: insubstantial and unreal.

He said, "From me."

"Not necessarily."

"Then from what?"

"From this place, before it kills me or drives me mad."

His silence told me nothing, and I said nothing further to illuminate it: another word would be too much, a year of words would not suffice.

He said, "You must think it was pleasant for me."

"I don't know how it was for you, as you never told me. I know only that everything we loved is dying, and I can neither stop it nor feel any real regret at the process. I cannot reach you, Malcolm. I no longer know truth from shadows. I believe everything I fear."

"So I'm to be the monster of this piece, am I? The Borgia, the bastard, the whoremonger, and let us not forget, the incestuous corruptor of young innocents. That was what you thought, wasn't it, Margaret? Among your mementoes of a failed marriage, another unspeakable little sin."

"I hoped this would be civilized, but I see there is no point in discussing it."

"No, there is no point. If I thought death would end the disease in my blood called Margaret I would have killed us both last winter. But I was afraid of the afterlife— that I would be cursed eternally to love you as I love you now. That would be judgment enough even for you."

There was nowhere to go but out of the darkness. He followed a pace or two behind me; we did not look at one another in the light. We did not speak. There was nothing else to say.

***

Coinneach Cameron and Ruiseart Gunn were found guilty of riot, assault and battery and were sentenced to three years' transportation. They escaped easily from the Tolbooth in Inverness after less than four months of imprisonment. Coinneach Cameron did not return to Glen Sian. Ruiseart Gunn was rumoured to have been seen briefly at Monnymore, from which property his brother William had not yet been evicted, but was said to have travelled on. Gilchrist MacGregor was found guilty of mobbing and rioting and was fined forty pounds sterling and imprisoned for two months. Two other men were imprisoned for three months. The charges against Caillean MacGregor were found not proven, and he returned to farm at Monnymore and nurse a festering hatred of authority.

I was told some of this by George Cameron, who came to see me within a few days of his return from Inverness. Malcolm was, as always, absent: the harvest was in progress, and Malcolm's eyes and ears as personified by Mairi had not lately been inflicted upon me.

He was persuaded to come in. There seemed at first no purpose for his visit; it was clearly dangerous, and he was agitated and restless and had been drinking heavily. I offered him water, as I had on the previous occasion: he refused it and asked for whisky, and sat on the edge of the chair holding the glass as though subjecting himself to some exquisite torment of self-denial. Eventually he succumbed to it. His right knee continued to jerk uncontrollably as he sat: he did not seem to notice it.

He said, "You know he plans to take the school from me."

"I thought the school was at my father's disposal, and at the discretion of the elders."

"It goes beyond that. He has written to the session and told them my morals are corrupt. He supplied details of my ... past indiscretions. And ... other things. Margaret, I go to prostitutes. He knows. He told your father. He told your father what happened in Edinburgh. He has written of it to the session."

After a long time I said, "What has he written of, George," but he appeared not to hear.

He said, "It's only a matter of time before they call me. They can ruin me. Then there will be nothing left. I might as well be dead." He was weeping a little: he dragged a fraying cuff across his eyes. "I know you have scant regard for me as a teacher. The brats mock me... I drink too much... but I have nothing else. If he takes it from me I might as well be dead, or go on the roads peddling pictures ... I've done that before—after it happened— after I left Edinburgh."

"After what happened?"

"Hasn't the bastard told you? No tittle-tattle on your pillow? I'll tell you, then— you may as well hear it from me. I was your father's protegé. He sent me to Edinburgh, and I distinguished myself by studying theology and seducing the daughter of the advocate for whom I was clerking. She was— she was fourteen years old. Montgomery was a Freemason. Henderson in Glasgow was Glen Sian's solicitor, and Malcolm did business there for him and for the son when Glen Sian died. Henderson and Montgomery were acquainted. They spoke of me. Henderson and Montgomery are both Freemasons. You cannot imagine what that means. What they could do, and did. Henderson told Malcolm, and put the weapon in his hands. And now, if you can't help me, God knows what he can do to me."

As though from a great distance, I heard myself ask if Malcolm were a Freemason. He seemed visibly to shudder.

"No. God ... no. No ... I would know. I never heard anything of it. I would know. Your father is a Freemason. So am I." The restless knee quivered: his head was trembling, and his hands. Bony, ice-cold, the nails unkempt and unclean. He smelled faintly of sour linen, and the orris root powder with which he dusted his body. "I haven't told you the abomination. I was sick. I had the clap. She bore me a child, a son. They both died. They turned me away from the door ... there was a white wreath on the door, and they shut it in my face ... and Montgomery never spoke her name again. I would have married her if they had let me. I was ... not without honour in those days." Then he reached out convulsively and took my hand. "Margaret, as God is my witness, I was cured. When I touched you, I was clean."

Pity, that terrible crippling disease, distorted everything which had happened, and was happening still, and it was somehow possible to remove my hand with kindness, to be gentle. Perhaps even then I knew we would not meet again.

"My dear, I think you had better go. There is nothing to be gained from this."

He was crying uncontrollably, in a paroxysm of self-contempt which seemed also to embrace me.

"Jesus, do you think I came here just to ease my conscience? I came here to tell you what I've done to him. I have written letters myself. I have written an account of what happened at Bearradh, at my poor bloody cousin's farm. That day, and later that day. I have written an account of that bloody farce of a trial. Did you know William Morrison was a Freemason, too? And, by repute, the Sheriff Clerk? That Morrison gave him a sign in court? Did you know that was why no one had me charged, because it was made known to Morrison?"

"Justice is not so corruptible."

"Oh, Margaret, Margaret. Married to that Machiavellian bastard, and yet so naïve. I could pity you. I could— I could kill him."

"Please go."

He let me take the cup: he rose, and crossed the floor with his odd, trembling walk. He was very stooped, and wasted, almost consumptive. At the door he grasped my hand again and clung to it with inordinate strength.

"Margaret— Margaret, promise me something, on your holy honour. Give me your word you will never tell him about me. I walk in fear of him day and night. Promise me. Promise me."

I said nothing. He said with a strange dignity, "I understand. I will not trouble you again. God bless you."

I wept for him when he had gone, and for all former things.

An afternoon. A morning. A night. On my book of revelation the seals were broken, and the knowledge was terrible to me.

Malcolm was standing in our room with his back to me; he had always indulged in this ritual cleansing upon his return to the house, and lately after ironing his shirts I had laid them in his chest of drawers, perhaps in some stubborn attempt to deny that we no longer truly cohabited either in this room or in any other sense.

The coat he had left downstairs stank acridly of peat. I carried it up over my arm.

He had stripped to the waist: the shirt and the crushed neckcloth he had been wearing had been neatly folded and placed on the floor. The patient laundress would retrieve them, as she would air this garment until the affront of its smoke had been removed.

I said as much.

He said, without turning, "That is endemic in my business."

"You told me you were harvesting."

"I did, and I was. I was also within doors for a time."

"Was one of the doors Grania's?"

He took a clean shirt from the drawer.

"Yes. As a matter of fact, one of them was."

"Is that all you have to say?"

He put the shirt on and fastened the cuffs. Then he came toward me with that light step, so very light for a man of his height, and he took me very lightly by the shoulders, with no more than a suggestion of his strength.

"Sit down, Margaret."

"I have things to do."

"I said, sit down."

I sat. He sat also, in the wing chair where I would always see him when I closed my eyes and remembered this room.

"I have never justified anything to you. What I do, where I go, what is done in the course of my business. I do not intend to begin now."

"Your business is nothing to me, although God knows I find it repulsive. But if you insult me with adultery, I will not forgive it."

He said, "Yes, I did go to her croft. Yes, she did invite me to her bed, and yes, I accepted her invitation. It has been a long time, and Grania and I are old friends. Is that what you want to hear? Because I'll tell you that if it is. It would be a lie but you think me a liar, and you've made up your mind to condemn me no matter what I say."

I said nothing. I could not look at him, although I felt his eyes burning my face. He said, "You'll never have enough from me, will you? If I cut out my heart and gave it to you, it would not be enough. Not after Grania, not after An Reithe, nothing. You always want more. I hurt you, yes, not once and not twice, but more times than I can remember, and God knows I've regretted those times, but you never accept my regret. There always has to be more. Christ, I'm so much in your debt I'll never be free of guilt, and this last ... for this last, I'll be paying for the rest of my life."

He got up.

"Where are you going?"

"Out."

"You just came in."

"I am going out again. Somewhere I may be sure of a welcome." He began to knot his neckcloth in the glass; his reflected eyes did not rest for an instant on my face. "Instead of having accusations thrown at me, because my coat smells of the native air." He turned. "If I may trouble you for that?"

I let it fall to the floor.

"Take your coat and go to hell. I don't care if you never come back."

He smiled briefly.

"Oh, I will always come back, a gràdhach. It's my house."

He returned about five or six in the morning. The table was still laid for supper. I had sat in the kitchen all night by a fire now falling into ash; beyond the window, the day was opening with a blue, autumnal clarity.

He came in. If he was surprised to see me, he did not reveal it.

"You went to your whore." He said nothing. "And now you come back to me."

"Yes."

There was a knife on the table, a thing of good steel with a staghorn handle. I picked it up and threw it at him. Then I went out.

He followed me along the hall without any particular haste. I was at the bottom of the stairs. He took me by the shoulder and wrenched me round to face him. He was holding the knife.

He said in a soft, deadly voice, "Don't ever do this to me again."

"I wish it had been a bigger knife. And by the living God, if you go to that bitch again, it will be."

Something came into his eyes: not anger, not outrage, although I had used him outrageously: something poignant and indescribable, almost respect, almost tenderness.

"At least I can make you feel something for me. I thought that too was dead."

I said, "I have nothing to say to you," and, almost courteously, he removed his hand.

I walked all day on the hill, in the changing light, in the rain, in confrontation with my soul. He had released me, but he would never let me go.

Night, the good shepherd, drove me home.

The kitchen was dark, the candles unlit, the meal unprepared, a film of dust lay on the furniture, the clothing was unlaundered. The house was no longer mine, and its petty tyrannies were irrelevant.

I passed through the dark hall and at the foot of the stairs he came from his candlelit study and took me by the forearm. I did not resist; there was no point. This was inevitable.

There was a polished oak chair with arms in his study, beside the desk; I sat in it, and he knelt abruptly on the threadbare carpet and turned back the mud-spattered hem of my skirt to the knee and took the heel of my riding boot and began to remove it, something he sometimes did for me. I said, "Please don't touch me," and his eyes came up to my face and remained there for an intolerable time: then he gently released my foot, and physically and spiritually withdrew.

He said, "At daggers drawn, I see."

He sat. The usual glass was on the desk, nearly empty: he refilled it and pushed another toward me. I said, "I don't want it. I loathe your whisky," and he picked up the glass and set it down near me so forcibly that it spilled.

"It's good French brandy. Drink it."

I left it untouched and closed my eyes.

"Where the hell were you?"

"I was out."

536

"I was out too, and the object of some derision. Do you know why? Because I was looking for you, and people knew it, and said, that poor bastard's lost his wife. It must have been very amusing."

"I did not find it so."

"Nor did I, by Christ."

I opened my eyes.

"What did you expect me to do, after you came to me still damp from rutting with your whore?"

He reached out from where he sat and slapped me across the face. There was an absolute silence.

I said, "If you touch me again, I will kill you."

The leather case and the glass dish full of ash were on the desk. He took the half-smoked cheroot from the dish and lit it in the candleflame, and sat back in the chair, smoking, in profile to me. Then he said, "I am standing on the edge of a precipice, Margaret, and I am about to go over it and take you with me. In the name of God, stop it from happening."

"I have no power to stop anything, or to help you, or myself. It is as it is. Isn't that what you said to me once?"

"So now you cast up the past to me."

"I don't cast it up— it made us. It cannot be unmade. Neither can the things between us be forgotten, or forgiven."

He turned toward me.

"Is this what we've come to?"

"You led me to believe it was inevitable. You said there was no possibility of happiness."

"So much wisdom. And so much courage, all come down to nothing. What a waste."

We sat in silence. He smoked, staring with lidded eyes at nothing. I drank the brandy, and allowed it to take me out of my shivering, affronted body, out of the smoke and close confinement of this room dominated by his presence.

Eventually he said, "You never wanted the child, did you."

I thought, not this. Not now.

I must have said it, because he looked at me through the smoke with those cold, burning eyes.

"If not now, when? Shall we put it away and keep it for the future, some twenty or thirty years hence when I might visit you and say, 'remember the old days when we loved one another? How pathetic we were.' So tell me the truth, Margaret. You never wanted my son, did you?"

"No. Perhaps I knew even then that there was no future for him."

"The experience might have made a woman out of you."

"Would it have made a man out of you?"

He said, "Vile tongues, vile tempers. We would have made miserable excuses for parents," and poured another measure into his glass.

"I should like to go."

"I would prefer you to stay. We may never speak again, and there are certain matters to be discussed. I take it you intend to leave me. Where do you intend to go?"

"To England."

"I see. The prodigal returns. A certain arrogance, don't you think, in presuming you will be welcome."

"I have no choice. I am not welcome here."

"And if I said I would prevent you?"

"You know what you are capable of doing. I am not afraid of you."

The cigar had gone out. He lit it again and sat with it, resting his forehead in his left hand. His eyes were closed.

I said, "Do you love your whore?"

"I have nothing to say to you about Grania. I never have had, and I never will."

"Is she Mairi's mother?"

His eyes opened.

"Is she what?"

"I know she bore your other bastards. Did she farrow this one as well?"

"No."

"Then whose is she?" He said nothing, but his eyes never left my face. "I asked you a question once. You answered me. I want a different answer tonight. I want the truth."

"You will have what I choose to give you."

"Is she your daughter?"

"I don't know."

"How can you not know?"

"Her mother was a whore."

"Do you mean she was a prostitute?"

"In a manner of speaking. It was one of the trades she plied on the road. So you appreciate my problem, a gràdhach. She might have had a hundred fathers. I might have been one of them. Is there anything else you would like to know?"

Darkness, and waves of sound like the sea buffeting my ears. I was sick and exhausted and afraid that there would be no escape from this room: that he would torture me with this terrible gentleness until I died.

"How old is she?"

"Six years younger than you. I was fifteen when I fathered her, or not, as the case may be."

I no longer wanted to hear his voice, to share these shadows with him. I made some attempt to rise. He said, "No, I think you should stay. You've always quested after my soul. So sit down and feast your eyes upon it, and tell me if you like what you see."

I heard the clock striking: the number of strokes was unknown to me. Time, the black river, was endless. I was drowning. The voice was destroying me.

"Let us talk a little of my mother. Glen Sian seldom speaks of her, but I think Ewen told you some sanitary story of how she miscarried and died. That was not precisely true. Shall I tell you the truth of it?"

And he told me, whether I wanted to hear it or not. He told me how Margaret Campbell had died in my garden, and he spared me nothing. When I covered my ears with my hands he rose from the chair and removed them gently and repeated what I had tried to muffle, in the patient manner of the best teachers, and in the silence that followed, the screaming silence, the stark absoluteness of horror, the watch lying hidden against my skin chimed faintly, and he remarked, "Your watch is slow, Margaret. You must have it seen to." And then he drank the rest of his brandy and said, "Do you know what I thought at Bearradh, Margaret? I thought, this is how death comes. This is how I will die, like my mother, one against so many. And do you know what they were saying to me? They told me they would carve out the eyes from my face, because my eye was the evil eye, and they told me they would cut the heart from my body, to see if I had a heart. And one of them, who was Coinneach Cameron, told me he would cut off my head and put it on a stake and bring it to you. And I believed him, and I was not afraid. And do you know what I thought, Margaret? I thought, I must not die this way, because Margaret would see me. I must not let her see me that way. That was what I thought."

And then he began to tell me about Mhaire.

In the dead hour of night that followed, his voice was almost a whisper.

"So you see why I don't sleep with my daughter, although she has sometimes made it known that it would not be repugnant to her. She cannot be held responsible. She knows nothing, either of who she might be or the nature of the fire she plays with. And neither do you. This sordid little glimpse of my soul is nothing to the filth still lying there."

"Nothing you could say would surprise me."

"No?" There was a terrible pause. "Ewen was your lover, wasn't he?"

I said, "How dare you."

"Did you think he wasn't capable of it? That he could only love with his mind? I'll tell you something about Ewen. He loved women, and he loved men. He touched me once, when I was very young, but to me to be touched by any living hand was to die, was to be killed. And I screamed, although I made no sound. He never did it again, and we never spoke of it. I never told a living soul, and I hated him for it, although I loved him. And I never forgave him." There were tears in his eyes: he ignored them, as he had always been capable of ignoring pain. "It was James, wasn't it. Your lover before me."

"James was never my lover. I never loved him, or any man but you."

"Then who was it?"

"I gave my virginity to George Cameron."

He was still, so still, his right hand supporting his forehead, the clean linen fallen away from his wrist. The long scar of the razor was visible in the candlelight, and the hard, slow pulse beneath the skin.

He said, "You're a liar."

"Am I?"

The long, bristling lashes were lowered: his eyes, his soul, were hidden from me. He said, very softly, "You gave that poxy bastard what you denied me."

"You had abused and violated me. Nothing else remained to me."

He lifted his right hand to his eyes: the hand was shaking. "How could you? In my heart, when I came to you, I was innocent. If I could have been a virgin boy and given myself to you, I would have. And you gave that chancred whore what you denied me, who would have died for you. How could you, Margaret?"

"You forced me to."

He closed his eyes. Nothing moved but the candleflames, the light and shadow across his profile, the tears on his face: but they were already cold: with the heel of the scarred hand, not gently, he removed them, the tears for Ewen and for me. All these things were past.

"Well, Margaret, what shall we do with the dregs of the night? Shall we kiss and be friends, or should I go out and find your drunken cunt of a lover and cut his throat? Or should we merely go to sleep, you in my bed and I in your sitting room?" The burning eyes held mine, pitiless, although his lips were smiling. "Oh yes, another secret. You were obsessed with the desire to know. I sleep in your sitting room— at my age the floor loses its appeal. So I sleep on your sofa. The room has a perfume of you. It comforts me."

The light was dying: the darkness was everywhere. I stood: he remained in the shadows. With immense effort I walked to the door.

He said, "Why did you tell me?"

"I wanted to hurt you, as you have always hurt me."

The shadows opened and received me: the cold dead rooms waited for me, the ghosts, the whispers, the sorrows imprinted on the very air identified now, and silent. The house was dead, a dead shell around me: all things, all hope, all love, all passion, all grief, were dead in me.

I remember that place, and its evocative Gaelic name. It was by this name that Mairi identified it when she told me George Cameron was dead. It might have taken an hour to reach it. The light was strange, subdued, the river here tormented by rapids in its descent from the heights: eternally it is tormented, until it loses itself in the eternal sea.

His body had begun to decompose among the rocks where it had been found: in its removal from the icy water some of the bloated, dead-grey skin had been dislodged from the bones. His eyes were opened and hazed with white, the cadaverous face disfigured beyond recognition by purplish contusions. Death's transformation of him into corruption was uncompromising, and I looked for a long time upon its loathesomeness although I had been told that this was not for me to see, and then I allowed myself to be taken away.

We walked in silence, disappointing those who had come to watch. Malcolm offered his assistance as I mounted, and I disdained his hand. The language between us now was eloquent, and I heard the first dissident murmurs in the crowd as I left. He did not follow me.

I took only a change of clothing from the armoire, and a pistol, and my money. All else I left: in the hard country between myself and my destination no sentiment existed. These things were in a portmanteau at the bottom of the stairs when Malcolm came in.

It began then. He asked me where I was going and I told him. He said that he would not let me go, and I said that nothing he could do would prevent me. And then I turned my back on him and left him at the foot of the stairs.

He came up, with that light step, not quickly, and found me in our room. I had gone back to do something that seemed necessary and significant: it seemed more civilized to remove my wedding ring and leave it on a table than to dispose of it more forcibly, in a manner that might offend him. But the manner I had chosen was offensive in any case, and it did not now matter what I did: we had passed beyond civility, beyond reason. I struck him across the face with every ounce of strength I possessed, and my strength was enough to disconcert him, and he released me, and I ran half way down the dark stairs, where he found me. Twice I managed to free myself, with defenses he had once taught me; I smashed my elbows on his forearms, I bit him, I drove my nails into the flesh of his hands and clawed his face, trying to blind him. He dragged me with a terrible deliberation from stair to stair, and my life became only second upon second of tearing, biting resistance, and the shadows and the floorboards were my passage to hell, were marked in seconds and in inches, were a frieze of grotesque, abortive struggles; and finally, in the room, the injuries I had inflicted upon him caused that deadly embrace to falter, and I fell to the floor and clawed at his boot for the knife he carried, and attempted to stab him. He forced the knife from my hand and wrenched my arm behind my back, and in that resounding, pitiless silence, that void, I screamed; and, as though the sound were something he could not bear, he struck me, with intense violence. And we fought like animals, until I could no longer endure the fists and the teeth and the strangulation, and submitted, and he raped me savagely, on the floor, and then repeatedly on the bed. Not a man, not an enemy, not a human adversary, but hell incarnate, an instrument of ferocious sexual hatred, committing unspeakable acts of violation and punishment. What he raped was inanimate: he would have killed what resisted him. The bed was stained with semen and blood and urine, hair torn from his scalp and mine, blood from beneath my nails. The hands, iron, inhuman hands, lifted me and tore my limbs apart, and he penetrated me again, deliberately, unspeakably; the pain was unbearable.

I was cold, everything was cold, the night, his skin, his sex, his semen. He withdrew from the despised receptacle, myself, and left the bed. I crawled a little and lay still, my hair across my face; I was shivering. His shadow returned and stood over me; I felt eyes, and then the weight of his coat.

I hid from him in the darkness, behind my closed eyelids, and eventually my mind and body relented, and gave me freedom from him.

When I opened my eyes there was light in the room; he had lighted candles. He was sitting in the chair, smoking, his manner remote, austere. Only the bloody furrows left by my nails on his face were an aberration, an abnormality: only the iron taste of blood, and the semen, and the pain.

He watched me rise from the bed, and remove the remnants of my clothing. He said nothing. He watched me cleanse myself of him as deliberately as he had defiled me, saw that after I had washed him from my body I perfumed it, and dressed it for riding, and left every article of clothing he had touched or stained lying on the floor. He watched me remove the wedding ring and leave it on the table. It was five o'clock in the morning.

The portmanteau was at the foot of the stairs: I took it with me. He was on his feet now, following me through the house and out of doors, the light step pursuing me without haste. My horse was still saddled; I put my foot in the stirrup and eventually, after many attempts, mounted. He was standing near the opened gate: the presence in the night, the dark spirit, never at peace, never at rest, never loving but destroying. Life had taught him no lesson but this, to savage what it offered. I had loved him.

He seemed to be waiting for me, as he had always waited for me, as he would always wait for me in unguarded moments, in unconscious thought, in dreams, in the ambush of memory: in the colour of eyes, in an aquiline face, in a voice reminiscent of this country and this wasteland of years.

He seemed to be waiting for me, at the end of the night, at the end of everything. He did not look up as I passed him. I could not speak to him: I attempted it. I could not speak.

He said, "Go to hell."

I left him.

Interlude: Evesham 1772

I crossed Corrieyairack in a snowstorm, and on its vertiginous heights nearly lost my life. That was the last injury his country inflicted upon me.

The rest is silence: the memories are mine alone. I was not pursued, and I would have killed any one who had attempted to come between myself and Evesham.

As it was in the beginning: the soldier and the infant, the soldier and the child. Now the soldier and the woman sat in firelight in the library, and he smoked Havana cigars, the scent of which was hauntingly reminiscent of other nights, other silences and conversations, and we drank pale old cognac and talked, respecting the barriers with which we defended ourselves against one another.

"If you had known that I was here instead of Barbados, would you still have come?"

"I was encouraged to regard this house as my home. I hope I did not presume too far in returning to it as such."

"It is also your inheritance. That has never been revoked."

Another pause: no sound in the house: it was late. We were alone, and in the dimness the undercurrent of our former lives became an unspoken conversation underlying the restraint and conventionality of this.

"Is the marriage irrevocably ended?"

"Yes."

"You will not go back."

"No."

"Some men can be very persuasive."

"I will never be persuaded."

His face, in introspection, was as bony and enigmatic as ever. In the weeks of this leave, now drawing to a close, his skin had lost none of the darkness of ten years in the Caribbean. He was fifty-five years old, deeply lined, and gaunt: where his hair was not grey it had been burnished by the sun. His limp, almost imperceptible in my youth, was now pronounced. On his left hand he still wore the gold signet Catherine had given him.

He said, "I never ceased to consider you my responsibility, and my protection is still yours to command. If I can be of service to you in this matter, or any other, I expect you to tell me."

"The marriage is over. There is no need for vindictiveness, and there is nothing more to be said."

"Your parting was amicable, then?"

"You will forgive me if I say again that I do not wish to discuss it."

He had always laughed as though he were unused to humour, abruptly, as he did now.

"God, how you sound like me so many years ago. Maybe it is possible to inherit through proximity after all."

"The country disordered my character. I may recover from it. I doubt it."

"Why should you? I never did." Then, as though changing the subject, "You know that war is brewing in America."

"I heard something of it. I hoped it could be avoided."

"It will not be avoided. The radical factions want a blood-letting, the freetraders' fortunes are at stake, and the army injures too many quick sensibilities. If it comes before this commission is ended, I should feel obliged to remain with the regiment."

I said something noncommittal. My mind, ever haunted, ever sensitive, tried to divine his intention, and armour itself against this increasing intimacy.

"I told you once that soldiers live on borrowed time. I never believed it so implicitly as now."

I said nothing: in silence was my defense.

"I sense that life has wounded you, so much so that when we met I knew it was forbidden to embrace you. You rebuffed me without words."

"You see too much in me, and imagine the rest."

"I don't think so." Then, "I want you to touch me, as I direct you." I said nothing: my mind was a void. "This is not some crude invitation to my bed. I want to tell you something." Silence; no movement, either his or mine. "I assure you, I share your ordeal."

In the shadows, in this dream that had no beginning and no end, from which it seemed I had never woken, he removed his waistcoat and stood in his shirt, and my fingers touched him, trembling, the damp coldness of my palm against his spine ... and the million nerve ends of my flesh could not interpret the past as it was written on his skin, could not recognize the nature of its disfigurement, the massive corrugations which reason identified as scars.

He said, "That is Glen Sian's legacy. I was flogged there."

He moved away from me, put on his waistcoat and refilled his glass and mine. I was sitting on the footstool now, further from the fire's light, close enough for him to have touched me if he had wished to do so. His voice, the voice of my childhood protector, the voice in my anguished dreams, was dispassionate, precise.

"I believe in fate. I believe I was marked out for this ... my rank was incapable of defending me. I was delayed in Inverness with Colonel Bancroft and a company under the nominal command of a lieutenant named David Brevet ... Henry Francis David Brevet, who is now, I am given to understand, a member of Parliament. The battalions had preceded us to Fort Augustus. We were ordered to Invermoriston, from whence we conducted business in the neighbourhood, the nature of which I am certain it is not necessary for me to describe."

He was smoking again. The smoke and the firelight and the cold stillness of the room and the unfolding nightmare were part of another nightmare; the inevitability of the outrage committed against him became a memory of my own flesh, an indistinguishable violation.

"Bancroft was ill, his wound was unhealed, he was half mad with pain, and his perceptions were distorted by opium, and his obsession with me. It must also be said that I was unstable at the time. I was in pain, I drank too much, and hell was all around me. The nature of our situation rendered our association intolerable ... and, in the event, I displeased him. He struck me a blow across the face, and I attempted to kill him. Had it not been for the intervention of his minion, Brevet, and the company sergeant-major, I would have done so, and forfeited my life.

"I was confined, and in the morning I was taken out into the street. Brevet read some sort of charge, and I was seized up in the presence of the assembled company and flogged. I counted the strokes, and the drummers also kept count, and this was useful to me because, toward the end, I understood them to say that there had been two hundred and twenty-eight. It is not unusual to award private soldiers three hundred and fifty lashes at a time for trivial offenses."

Then he said, "If I had told you sooner, I might have wept with you. But the time for tears is long past, and mine have all been shed."

He drank, almost meditatively.

"Shall I pursue this, or have you heard enough?"

"Tell me ... the truth."

"The truth," he said. "What is the truth? Is the truth that we were all murderers? Is the truth that I was innocent? He struck me, I struck him, compounding the offense, he abused his rank and ordered pain and humiliation to be inflicted upon me— out of hatred, out of love, out of some perverse desire to subdue me, for some private gratification or as an example to the regiment— I told my truths at Fort Augustus and he told his, and because the men were in a state of mutiny upon our arrival a court of enquiry was convened. In view of the gravity of the offenses we were separately brought before a general, who I thank God was not Cumberland. No charges were laid against me. Bancroft's court of enquiry resulted in a regimental court martial, at which I was present. The principal witness was Brevet, who gave evidence against Bancroft. Two sergeants and four private soldiers also gave evidence, in my favour. Afterwards, Brevet too faced a court of enquiry and was dismissed the service, which was what he had always wanted. It would seem that time has dissipated the cloud under which he left it. Bancroft was found guilty and cashiered. Had it not been known to the president of the court that his father was an intimate of the King's, he would have been hanged. I daresay he would have preferred it."

Then he said, "And the sad dénouement is this, the life you and I have shared. My marriage died an unnatural death, my body is obscene, my vertebrae afford me constant pain, and my kidneys function at a fraction of their capacity. I may never sleep with a woman of my own class, and I have never had a mistress, with the exception of dear Jane, who forgave much. You have not forgotten Jane."

"No."

"I knew you had not. My wife remains faithful to a crippled, titled bastard whose perversities she enjoys more than mine: a man I cursed and feared and despised, who was my friend, remains faithful to me. At the end of life, in the love of other men, in all the brutality of lust and the sublimity of passion, he will always have been faithful to me."

"And you?"

"In all the years, I have never ceased to love you, and to hope that by my love there might be peace and reparation for us both. Is that not possible, Margaret?"

"If I could have loved you once, I would have done so. It is not possible now."

His voice revealed nothing, neither disillusion nor disappointment. The fire was long dead, and I could not see his face.

"The regiment is transferred to Halifax. Will you go there with me?"

"I cannot. I have nothing to offer you."

"As my daughter, my companion. My wife, if it pleases you. I have no other in the eyes of the regiment, and none either in the eyes of God."

"I cannot. I am damaged. You can never understand."

He said, "By my God, can I not," and as he had in the dream, the long nightmare we shared, touched me, took my hand in the invisible, cold, strong hand, and mine did not respond, but lay dead in his. "I told you this a long time ago. I am your servant, and I will serve you until I die. My life is yours. Do with it what you will."

Life offers a gift, not very often. One rejects it, and one comes to regret. Life is very short.

And in these cold shadows, the shadow of myself, the hollow, haunted self, I rejected him.

THE FACTOR

I

July eighth, 1773: two o'clock in the afternoon.

Because of the heat he did not work in the estate office but in the library, where the French windows stood open to admit an uncertain wind. The very atmosphere was overlaid with ghosts.

… May, a thrush singing, a shower of white blossom from the trees. *This is my young friend, Miss MacNeil*.... Eyes full of light, staring into the light, eyes which had never faltered when they had looked into his face; fierce, wounded, resolute: had looked into his soul.

... Fog, cold, autumnal dampness: passing ghosts, the ghost of Margaret.

And now this, all love's language spoken. Nothing left but this, enslavement to her spirit, nothing to love, nothing to hate, nothing to embrace, nothing to subdue, nothing to comfort or be comforted by, only this: the passion for the unattainable, the lost, the forever destroyed.

He raised his eyes. Nothing had disturbed him, and yet he had been disturbed. He left the desk and walked into the gallery. There was no one. He stood for a time leaning on the ornate wrought iron, the images of thirty years flickering into life. Childhood: hunger: rejection: abuse: the starvation for beauty, for affection, for safety; the ephemeral illusion of Ewen's world. The intolerable loss of innocence. The loss of hope. The loss of Margaret. The loss of everything.

He dismissed it and stood in the shadows, smoking, watching the arabesques of smoke dissipate in the currents of air from below. He might have been alone: the housemaids were working behind closed doors, in rooms that were seldom entered. The smoke drifted, and time, and the visions, the uninsistent voices of the past.

He walked back along the gallery, his footsteps echoing.

Nothing had changed in the library, but a cooler breeze was blowing from one end of the room to the other; a paper or two had settled on the floor.

He picked them up and set them under the bottle of brandy which had been his companion since the forenoon, removed his waistcoat, laying it on the chair where he had hung his coat. Perhaps half an hour passed, and once more he paused, the word in his racing, illegible script half formed. His eyes moved from sunlight to shadow, and to the doorway.

Nothing.

The time was seven minutes past three.

Perhaps five minutes later he heard the horses. The summery wind had momentarily died, and in the absence of its soughing rustle the hooves and the knocker and the unhurried footsteps approaching the stairs seemed unnaturally loud. He scrawled a memorandum across one of the letters and reached for another, the only sounds in the library now the ticking of his watch and the intermittent scratching of the quill. The footsteps reached the first floor and continued their approach around the gallery: the voices were an indistinguishable murmur.

The footsteps came to a halt.

Two men, unremarkably dressed, stood in the wide double doorway. He recognized neither of them, although the portents of a turbulent spring had warned him of this possibility.

He said without rising, "Good afternoon, gentlemen. May I be of service to you?"

Although he had phrased the question in Gaelic the response came, as he had known it would, in the precise English upon which Inverness prided itself.

"You are Malcolm Magnus Alasdair Scott?"

"I am."

"We are sheriff officers, sent to convey you to Inverness where a statement will be taken from you. You are under arrest."

"On what charge do you presume to arrest me?"

The elder of the two unfolded a pair of pocket spectacles, and from the inner recesses of his coat removed a closely written document. The charges were numerous, and it seemed that many minutes passed in the course of reading them.

"You are charged with wilful fire-raising, by wickedly and maliciously setting on fire and burning to ashes the premises, dwelling house, barns, kilns and property of the tenant Diarmaid Cameron of Bearradh farm, and appropriating and burning the movables of the said Diarmaid Cameron, on the second of August seventeen hundred and seventy-two... wickedly and maliciously setting on fire and burning to ashes the whole premises and properties of poor men of the township at Monnymore, Glenkill, Carn Dubh and Cnap na Stri, at the Martinmas term of November last, and offering diverse instances of oppression and real injury....

"...burning pastures common to the people... the appropriation of three pounds sterling belonging to the tenants Daniel MacGregor called Stirling and Grizel Chisholm, of Monnymore, which was secreted in the dwelling place of that property.

"You are charged with culpable homicide in the death of the said Grizel Chisholm on the twentieth of November seventeen hundred and seventy-two, with culpable homicide in the death of Iain William Chisholm of Monnymore on the fifth of December seventeen hundred and seventy-two... with culpable homicide in the death of Margaret Carr, on the seventh of December seventeen hundred and seventy-two. You are charged with murder in the death of Seoras Colla Cameron, on or about the fifteenth of October, seventeen hundred and seventy-two."

Silence, and the silken rustle of leaves.

"You will come with us, Mr. Scott."

"I will not quit this house until I have spoken with my employer."

"Mr. Stirling is from home."

"Then I will stay for him. In the meantime I will write to my solicitor." He sensed doubt, impatience, wariness. "I may do as much, I think, without your permission."

The younger man said, "Disarm, sir, slowly, if you please."

He slid the knife from his boot and laid it on the papers. The time was twenty-two minutes to four.

"Do you carry a firearm?"

They were placed on the far side of the desk. *Heylin, Cornhill...* the light on the lockplate an enticement and a mockery. Behind him the library dimmed, as if a great hand had extinguished the sun.

He wrested his mind from them, from the invitation of the guns, the dimness and uneasiness of impending storm, and wrote, *I am this afternoon charged with capital offenses and taken to Inverness. Attend me there immediately upon receipt of this.* The ominous stirring in the dark air heightened his nerves and theirs: one was staring at the sky as though apprehensive, and eager to be gone. He sealed the letter, drank the brandy that remained in the glass, crushed out the cigar.

"Give us assurance of your conduct, Mr. Scott, and there will be no need for these."

And, for an instant, when he saw the irons, his horror of confinement was uncontrolled.

He stood, and was aware of a new expectancy in their stance: they were armed, and for the first time he sensed a dutiful readiness to kill him. He moved toward the chair where he had hung his coat, conscious of the voice ordering him to stand still. His hand continued until it touched the light grey silk of his waistcoat.

He paused with his hand resting on it, and turned cold eyes on them.

550

"Have the goodness, gentlemen, to let me put on my coat."

And then James arrived, and there was a moment of bitter privacy.

"Is this your bloody hand against me?"

"Malcolm, by the Lord God, I swear not. Tell me what to do."

"Send this to Henderson, and take these. Open my desk in the house and bring me what you find there. My guns and my watch are on the table. Keep them for me."

And that ghost, elusive, intangible, nameless because he would not speak her name: superstitiously, as though she were dead.

"Shall I send to—"

"No. Leave me in peace, will you."

"Malcolm, for God's sake—"

"I have no god."

There was darkness and an absence of darkness, although there was no light: with the few coins on his person at the time of his arrest he had bought candles, and kept the rats at bay. During the nights he wrote, walked the cell, and composed his statement and his emotions, none of which he would release until Henderson had come. There was no message from Glen Sian: no money, and neither clean clothing nor the wherewithal to obtain fresh candles, tobacco, soap, clean water, nor the stiletto in his desk, nor his talisman, her ring.

The third week ended. The stench, the vermin, the town, the darkness, the isolation, the hostility of the gaolers, the furtive ghosts who came and went preyed upon his mind; his body had always been disdained, and he ignored its suffering and its humiliation. The heat was intense; the rain fell; Inverness's perfume of shit and tanneries and the sea invaded even this fastness of justice. The month ended: the phases of the moon moved in his blood and his absence from the land obsessed him. He withdrew to it in mind, immersed himself in Glen Sian in spirit as he had done in life, and in its constant, changing beauty and intransigence found peace. Came to it as a refuge and a homecoming, and was comforted, and slept.

On August eighteenth, as the town played host to the tinkers and peddlers and horsetraders of the Marymas fair, Henderson arrived from Glasgow, bringing with him letters and assurances from James, the stiletto in a parcel of shirts, a bottle of brandy, and the news that once more bail had been denied him.

***

Sometimes she spoke to him, in the endless uncounted hours, out of the black river of the night. Sometimes it seemed she was almost visible, and in that single manifestation would heal all torment. In seeing her, he believed he would die, and was emptied of all but the last passionate desire: vision, death, freedom.

Sometimes I pray for your safety.

He thought, pray for me now. And the cry from the heart's core which had echoed throughout his life, other betrayals, other desertions, greater and lesser bereavements. *Why did you leave me?*

The dream of a clean rain became the sound of rain in the street. In the rain was peace, quietus, redemption. *Let me be clean.*

O guardian of this night attend me, deliver me from the black sleep, let no nightmare sleep lie on me.... I shall not be slain, I shall not be wounded, I shall not be blinded, nor made naked, nor left bare. Christ will not forget me.

No seed of fairy hosts shall lift me, no earthly being shall destroy me.

In the heat of the last lingering day of August Henderson returned, with two other men: one, obviously appalled by the fetor of his surroundings, pressed a handkerchief to his nostrils. Henderson, with a warmth that was not assumed, shook hands, peering closely into his face.

"My dear Scott, how do you do?"

"I envy you the freedom of your peregrinations. I trust they were on my behalf."

"I apologize most humbly. We have applied to the High Court of Justiciary in Edinburgh for bail. This takes time." He appeared without actually doing so to summon the others to join them. "I present Sir Henry Hamilton, your advocate, and Mr. James Matheson, his junior."

Matheson, red-haired, pallid, and speaking through the handkerchief, mumbled and extended a limp hand. Hamilton was tall, heavy, wore a coarse horsehair wig, and spoke in an incisive, colourless voice.

"My dear sir, is there anything you immediately require?"

"A cup of coffee, and some tobacco."

Henderson, with the gentle courtesy that was one of his most attractive qualities, said, "I shall step over and see to it. Perhaps Mr. Matheson would care to accompany me, by your leave, Sir Henry."

The coffee was carried across from the principal inn, with two cups. Matheson did not reappear, and the solicitor was dismissed with an imperious wave of Hamilton's hand.

Advocate and accused sat, assessing one another.

"Is it not customary to be attended by your junior on these occasions?"

"This is an informal conversation. I seek to compose a portrait of you, merely for my own edification. There will be opportunities enough for Mr.

Matheson to join us." He examined the coffee cup with distaste: it was noticeably dirty. "I understand you are a native Gaelic-speaker. Would you prefer that this conversation be conducted in that language?"

"I would have taken you for a Glasgow man."

"Things are not always what they appear to be, is that not so, Mr. Scott?"

"And is a hopeless case not always without hope?"

The eyes, as colourless as the voice, examined him for an instant; then he withdrew a small leather pocketbook and spread it on the scarred table.

"You have a Socratic habit of answering a question with a question. Are you a lawyer?"

"I am a farmer and an administrator."

"How did you come to be here?"

"In the Highland manner. By a settling of old scores."

Hamilton was recording both questions and answers verbatim in what appeared to be shorthand.

"I have read your statement— now I seek the truth. I do not presume to judge you, but I will not undertake to defend you unless you answer to this indictment, privately, to me here. If you are guilty that is a matter for you and your conscience, and for me and mine. How do you answer to these charges?"

"I will answer you as I will answer in court. I am not guilty of any crime."

"Explain the circumstances of the first charge. Omit nothing."

The events of August first, 1772, were transmuted to several pages of symbols. The coffee was now cold in the cups.

"And William Morrison of Forres will corroborate your account?"

"I have written to him with that request."

Hamilton said, "Did you return by night to this disputed property, and set fire to it?"

"If that were the case, I must needs be indifferent to the fact that arson is a capital offense."

"Indifferent, brave, or foolhardy. Or driven by the desire to impose your will upon others." He paused. "I see you have courage, Mr. Scott. Have you that measure of courage? That supreme confidence?"

Their eyes met.

"I am not guilty."

Hamilton turned over the page.

"Where were you on the night of the first and second of August?"

"At home in my bed. I took a sleeping draught."

"Were you alone?"

"I was with my wife."

"Will your wife confirm this to me?"

"She is in England. And it was my understanding that spouses may not give evidence."

Hamilton said, with no perceptible interest, "When does she return?"

"She resides there."

"Husband and wife do not dwell together? Why is that?" There was silence. "And before you instruct me to mind my business, which I perceive is your desire, I will tell you that this is my business. You live separately. Why?"

"The marriage became untenable. The circumstances of our separation are too painful for me to disclose."

"Is Mr. Stirling of Glen Sian acquainted with your wife?"

"They are friends of long standing."

"And I may confirm these sad circumstances with him?"

He said coldly, "You are welcome to do so."

Another page.

"You shed light on many aspects of your present position, and not merely by what you say. I perceive you are a man of warm temper, and maybe of extreme principle. Is it possible that your principles, your dedication to improvement, were misconstrued by those who experienced the vigorous exercise of those principles?"

"Everything I have done was within the law, in the presence of others, and after the serving of legal notices of removal. When those notices were ignored and scorned, after the offering of violence to me and to those accompanying me, other measures were implemented. Those measures were not employed until due warning had been given, and several days of grace had passed. Every opportunity was given to those who were evicted to remove their goods and chattels before their dwellings were razed, and by that time those properties were legally in the possession of others. The 'pastures common to the people' were in fact open moor, which was burned to encourage new growth from the heather. This does not constitute an offense."

Hamilton consulted his watch, and passed a pristine handkerchief over his jowls.

"Explain the circumstances from which each charge of culpable homicide arose."

"I would have a cup of water first, unless you invite me to partake of something stronger."

"Alas, I am a son of the manse, and I pledged many years ago never to touch alcohol. A sad decision. I often regret it."

The water was warm and foul. Hamilton remarked, "They say there is typhus in this place."

"It does not matter."

"Speak to me of Grizel Chisholm."

"She was a joint tenant of Monnymore— she lived there with several men, with whom she had conjugal relations. All notices of removal were ignored— when the property was cleared and fired she climbed onto the roof and refused to leave it, although it was in flames. Eventually the roof fell in— she fell with it— the interior was alight— she was taken out by those present, myself among them— she was burned. It was my understanding that she was delivered of a child, and died."

"And the weather, was it sharp?"

"The weather does not signify. Her death was due to her own folly. She was told many times to get down."

"Who was Iain William Chisholm?"

"Her father. He was a tinker, a drunkard and a bigamist who lived there from time to time with the others. At one point fourteen of them occupied the house."

"Any one of whom might have appropriated the disputed money?"

"Even so."

"And the circumstances surrounding Iain Chisholm's death?"

"He was openly suffering from a cancer of the face. He died several days after his daughter, in the presence of his family. That was your culpable homicide."

"And Margaret Carr?"

"Margaret Carr was ninety-eight years old. I am weary of your questions."

"There are witnesses who say you cursed this woman."

"Do you think I'm Satan, that I curse people and they die? The world would be lighter of my enemies if I could say as much."

Hamilton said, "We will speak further of this matter. If I have fatigued you, I am sorry." And then after a pause, with inexorable calmness, "Are you guilty of murder?"

"No."

"And yet you were upon the worst of terms with the deceased. Indeed, some years previously you cut him with a razor, in the course of a dispute in a public house."

"The razor was his. The intent to injure was his."

"What was the reason for your animosity?"

"He was a drunkard and a profligate, and a source of filth and abuse. He fomented rumours— he was disruptive— he undermined my authority— at Bearradh he incited riot, and was to have been taken up for it. Henderson and Montgomery in Edinburgh will tell you."

"Were you aware that he wrote an explicit account of the events at Bearradh to the Evening Courant, an account of you which is particularly damning?"

"Am I to fear the dead hand of his vengeance?"

"No, unless he died by yours. Did you kill him?"

"No."

"It has been said that he was unswerving in his devotion to your wife."

"You do not need to question me, if others are so forthcoming."

For the first time Hamilton smiled.

"I told you, Mr. Scott, I seek only to compose a portrait of you, for my own entertainment. And in my portrait I see a jealous, thwarted lover. I see a man with a predisposition toward violence, which you do not successfully control even now. I see a man in the final days of desperation, confronting the disintegration of his marriage, and upon the point of losing what he prizes— his woman, his honour, perhaps the confidence of his employer, perhaps his employment itself. A man who is capable of killing to remove the attentions of an unwanted rival, to silence a source of irritation, to impose a fearsome strength of will upon others who would contemplate resistance. The law would not dispose of Seoras Cameron, the law would not stop his mouth. You are the law in Glen Sian, are you not, and you consider yourself beyond recrimination. You are the law that silenced him. You are capable of killing— you impress me with your capabilities."

"Do you prosecute or defend me?"

"Did you kill him?"

"No."

Hamilton snapped the covers of the book together and came to his feet. He did not offer his hand.

"You will be hearing from me. In the meantime, is there anything you want?"

"Remove me from this place, before I die."

"I will do what I can for you. I see that suicide is not beyond your capability either."

He turned, waiting for the door to be unlocked.

"I will defend you, and decry those witnesses who will speak against you. The end result may not be justice, but the game will be worth the candle."

The door shut. Bail was granted eight days later.

He did not contemplate the future: he exercised the ferocious will which had always served him, and conducted his affairs throughout the closing months of 1773 with discipline and efficiency. James had retreated to Edinburgh, where he had deposited his infant daughter with Charlotte's doting family; he wrote that he would return before the circuit court convened in Inverness in April. He continued to dispatch nervous, cheerful homilies in his childish hand until the passes to the south were closed, and his silence came as a relief. Hamilton, too, wrote with information and advice, often a dozen pages at a time, and paid a courier well to carry these increasingly unwelcome packets through the snow from Kyle of Lochalsh; he expected detailed replies and, grudgingly, was given them.

In January one of these contained an enclosure for Inglis MacNeil, whose favourable testimony Hamilton sought.

It was not a happy meeting, although the reasons for Margaret's departure had always been obscured. They stood in the parlour, the smoke of their breath drifting in the air: no hospitality was offered or expected. MacNeil broke the seal on the document and held it to the winter light: for an exhortation of Hamilton's it was uncharacteristically brief. Eventually he folded it and coughed loosely into a soiled handkerchief.

"I will not perjure myself on your behalf. You know my opinion of you."

"The request is from my advocate. It does not come from me."

"What do you expect of me?"

"Appease your conscience and send me to the grave. That would give you some satisfaction at the end of a disappointed life."

MacNeil said, "You are unworthy of the love my daughter bore you."

"I know." There was a virulent silence. "Now let me tell you what will happen if I am found guilty. My presence will be removed from the land, and the land will be sold. I have seen the correspondence; I have seen the documents. They await only Glen Sian's signature, and the land will lie open to the southern graziers. If I go, the people go. If I fall, Glen Sian falls. If I prosper, my hand is on the land, and my protection is over the land, and my will is the salvation of the people, and that will endure until I die."

MacNeil said nothing, staring at him with fierce eyes. He was rumoured to be suffering from dementia as well as physical infirmity.

"Write of your intention to my advocate, and have it carried to me. The courier stays for you."

MacNeil seemed to awaken from the torment of his visions.

"To me you are the embodiment of evil. But you are the devil I know, and my daughter failed in her duty toward you. I will speak on your behalf. And may God forgive me."

The rivers of ice turned to rivers of flame, burning in the midday sun on the window of the estate office, reflecting on the lockplates of the pistols lying near his hand. He conducted little business at Candlemas: he who had always been treated with deference was now shunned with the aversion shown the condemned or the terminally ill. Death seemed to lie upon him like a mantel of invisibility, and those who spoke to him were rare.

There were flickers of impending violence. On An Reithe rams and wethers were slaughtered, doused with inflammable oils and set alight, attacked by unknown dogs or driven over the precipices. By March there had been twenty such incidents, meticulously recorded in his journal, and on his instructions the shepherds were now armed.

In the weeks that remained to him, he was profoundly alone. Mairi came and went, pilfering clothing from the abandoned wardrobe, voicing opinions as radical and acerbic as his own and directing them where they would inflict the most damage.

"I miss the dominie, although he was a great man for the drink. He was a great man too for the talk."

"And what the hell talk did you have with him?"

"Ours was a social intercourse," and he laughed savagely. Displeased, she said, "I am not so uneducated as you may think. He wanted to draw me without my clothes, and he was not averse to paying for what he wanted besides the drawing."

He said only, "You unholy slut. The blood runs true in your veins," but she failed to arouse either suspicion or sexual jealousy; what she offered he rejected with revulsion, and, like the rest of the world, she withdrew and left him alone.

As the time for his departure approached, he went to Grania. There was no intercourse, only an hour's sparse conversation by the fire, the giving and receiving, with little comment, of money for her burial if the verdict should condemn him, no reminiscences of the past, no divination of the future, no touch of hand, no physical contact. Instead they spoke of commonplaces, of the weather, of the tenants who, because she was his mistress and a Macdonald of Keppoch, had always rejected her; they spoke, also, of her illness, with the stoicism innate in both. Then he finished the whisky she had given him and rose stiffly, the pain of the rheumatism in his knee aggravated by the dampness of the night.

"My blessing on you, if you will have it."

"And mine upon you always, Colm."

They did not say good-bye.

The river of time became a slow draining of hours on the night of the second of April. No vivid overlay of memories was here: the rooms were only the rooms, Margaret's possessions were only unnecessary, abandoned things. But her spirit lingered, and he willed her to him with intense desire, spilling his seed in the perfumed silk; and in the morning, with her ring and Ewen's

558

rosary on his person, he spoke the words of parting to her he had not spoken in life, and left the spirit in the silent darkness of the house, and locked the door.

He came into court at fifteen minutes past ten on Tuesday, April twelfth, 1774, emerging into a monochromatic dimness punctuated only by the scarlet robes and crimson crosses of the Lord Commissioner of Justiciary. Inverness was shrouded in salt mist. Rain, which would continue throughout the day, was pattering on the high windows.

The Advocate Depute began the lengthy procedure of reading the charges. In the stillness that followed the rain was clearly audible.

"Malcolm Magnus Alasdair Scott, you have heard the charges brought against you. How do you plead to your indictment?"

"Not guilty."

His voice was heard for the first and only time: by Scots law the accused was neither questioned nor cross-examined, nor would he speak again in his own defense. Nor would this court adjourn until its business was concluded.

There were no opening speeches. Sir David Macaulay Gore, for the Crown, summoned his first witness, Siubhan Cameron, who came demurely into court escorted by the macer. The sheriff substitute of Inverness-shire laboriously translated the oath into Gaelic, a process which would be repeated for almost every witness, making even the briefest question and response interminable.

"Will you identify the panel?"

"He is Scott, the factor."

"And you know him well."

"Yes, to my sorrow. I know him. He burned my house and persecuted my husband and son, and now my son is gone from me, and my husband is insane."

"Your dwelling house was at Bearradh farm, and you are the tenant of that place."

"We held the land since our marriage, many years ago, until he took it from us. It was his will that we should leave it, and when we refused he burned it, and drove us into the night, and myself in my shift with a child in my arms and another in my belly."

"And the circumstances of your removal... was violence offered to you?"

"He is a violent man. We knew this, we knew he was coming, so our friends gathered to preserve us from him— maybe ten or twelve came. It was not in our minds to provoke violence— it was he who brought the violence on himself and the other who was with him."

"You admit there was violence on the afternoon of the first of August at Bearradh."

"It was in our defense only."

"Were the terms of your notice of removal very clear to you?"

"No, we did not understand them. They were in English only."

"Did the factor not explain them to you, and make the consequences of ignoring the notice clear?"

"His explanation is the flat of his sword, and in his fist. Every one knows that."

"Did you suffer injury on the afternoon of the first of August?"

"Yes. I was hurt, and threatened by him. He said he would take my life."

"Why would he have threatened you in that manner?"

"His manhood was hurt. And it pleased him to throw me down, with child as I was, and to threaten me with his sword, and to do injury to my friends and my family. And when he was overwhelmed by our number he went away with the other, and came back alone that night, and burned my house to ashes." She produced a handkerchief and dabbed her eyes, although they remained dry. "And the sorrow of it is that I was left to bear my child under the sky."

Macaulay Gore said gently, "Do you assert without any doubt that this man fired your house?"

"It was always his intention to take the land from us. He coveted the land, the fruit of the corn and the profit from the malt, and he cursed us, so that our cattle died."

"Do you mean that by malediction he caused ill luck to fall upon you?"

"By the hand of Mary I saw him myself, walking three times against the sun around our house, maybe four or five months before the serving of the notice. There is ill fortune in his look. This is common knowledge."

Macaulay Gore said, "Seoras Colla Cameron was your husband's cousin, was he not?"

"It is true." She wept in earnest now. "He was a good, kind man, a gentle creature and a scholar. What crime was his that he should be killed by that fiend?"

"It is the purpose of this court to discover the truth, that you may rest and be comforted. I have no further questions to put to you."

Hamilton, who had not once raised his eyes from the blank pages arranged before him, lurched to his feet and addressed her in his metallic voice. His Gaelic was supple and precise, and she seemed discomfited by it.

560

"Is it true, madam, that you were closely questioned concerning your activities during the riot at Bearradh on the first of August 1772?"

"It is true."

"And would have been arrested for inciting to riot but for the compassion of the procurator fiscal upon the disclosure of your pregnancy?"

From the bench Lord Hesketh, Lord Commissioner of Justiciary, said, "This is not relevant to the charge, Sir Henry."

"My Lord, I will prove that it is. I will prove that this entire affecting testimony is a pack of lies, and that this woman was not only active in the incitement to riot but a veritable fury who was capable of inflicting, and did inflict, grievous injury upon the panel and upon a sheriff officer of this jurisdiction who accompanied him." To Siubhan, "Your husband was an associate of the factor's and received pay from him on several occasions. Is this not the truth?"

"It is the truth."

"And in time of hardship your husband and you benefited greatly from this association and the generosity of the factor toward those who worked for him. Yes?"

"I do not deny it."

"So you were not persecuted but favoured, more than the common run of tenant."

"At that time, yes, we were."

"And when that favour was withdrawn, because of your husband's and your son's hostility toward the panel, and because your son, Coinneach Cameron, was arrested, and indeed convicted of committing riot, assault and battery— you conceived a pernicious grudge against this man. Because your son was brought to justice by him, and in this court found guilty. Because your husband has lost his reason, through no fault of the panel. Is that not why you hate him, madam, and seek to injure him?" Silence. He produced an object from his pocket. "Do you know what this is, madam?"

She said faintly, "It is a corp creagh."

"For the benefit of the jury, it is a clay figure used in malediction, made by ill wishers in the image of the intended victim. You will observe, madam, that there are steel pins inserted into the body of this figure, into the eyes and into the groin. This object was found on the doorstep of the panel's house in January of this year. You, madam, are known for making these to satisfy the requests of your friends. You, madam, placed it there, or caused it to be placed there. It is you who curse this man, in a spirit of calculated vengeance, as on other occasions, by this method, you cursed a woman of the township of Glenkill who offended you. Do you deny that this is your handiwork?"

She glanced briefly toward the dock, and then away from it.

"I made it. It is a little thing, against the injury he did us."

She was followed by William Gunn and Daniel MacGregor, the partners of Grizel Chisholm. Gunn was chaotically abusive and would not be brought to order even by Macaulay Gore, who was obviously eager for his testimony: eventually he was expelled from the court. MacGregor, a weedy, balding man in his forties, was red-eyed and incoherent, saying only, through the interpreter, "He would be a very cruel man who would not mourn for her."

Hamilton, controlling his impatience, said, "Is it not true that the panel repeatedly requested your wife to descend from the roof, and even caused a ladder to be brought to assist her to do so?"

"If it was brought I did not see it. He wanted her to burn."

Hamilton said, "That is a lie. Indeed, so blatant a lie is it that the panel, who is a man of sensibility, attempted to climb on to the roof himself in order to compel your wife to descend, giving no thought to his own safety, but in order to offer her assistance as it was plain that she had become frightened by her situation. And that when the roof collapsed, the panel was among those who attempted to assist her, despite the flames. Is this not true?"

"It is not true. He was keeping the others from her so that she would die. I saw him—"

"You are a foul liar. Your wife was given what succour was possible in the presence of several witnesses, and it was only upon the commencement of her labour that the panel, out of decency, withdrew. You and the others of your household, with whom you shared the favours of this unfortunate woman, have now determined to pursue the panel because you blame him for her accidental death. A death, I may say, which, had you the courage of the panel, might have been prevented if any of you had offered her such ready assistance."

Macaulay Gore called Gilchrist MacGregor, late of Monnymore, skilfully coaxing from him the language of condemnation. Hamilton consulted his leather pocketbook throughout.

Eventually he rose and said, "Your testimony, sir, is constipated by rage, and the excreta of your lies stinks to heaven. You were charged with riot, assault and battery as the result of your participation in the events at Bearradh farm, and of those offenses you were found guilty, and were imprisoned. Is that not so?"

MacGregor said, with an obscene gesture that brought an interjection in English from Hesketh, "Yes— by his will, and I would do the same to him, the evil bastard."

Three hours had passed. The court did not adjourn for refreshment, but wine and cakes were placed at the elbow of the Lord Commissioner. Hamilton and his junior requested basins of smoking coffee; James Henderson, behind them in black, and wearing a fashionable wig, accepted wine. Sir David Macaulay Gore availed himself ostentatiously of water, and, following a murmured consultation between Hamilton and the Lord Commissioner, wine and biscuits were carried to the dock. An indefinite sun was attempting to penetrate the fog: the glare on the speckled glass was brief. The rain continued.

Caillean MacGregor spoke, and was discredited by the verdict of not proven which had left a stain on an already dubious reputation. The relations of Margaret Carr were summoned. They differed on the age of the deceased, the time of day at which the house was fired, the actual time of the factor's arrival, and the substance of what he said. Macaulay Gore, not lightly called the devil's advocate by Hamilton, evoked from their testimony the confusion and despair of the dispossessed, and throughout the process of translation expressions of sympathy were seen on the faces of the jury. These were not the unruly inhabitants of Monnymore, or the embittered harpy of Bearradh farm: these were staid, religious crofters, intimidated by the language and ceremony of the court and by Inverness itself, fumbling through painful recollection in Hamilton's pitiless quest for truth.

"There was wind, and it burned.... There were four, five men with him... they worked for him. He spoke to them in English— they were not of our people."

"If the panel spoke to these men in English, how can you say without a doubt that his words concerning your mother were, 'Damn the bitch, she has lived too long'? Do you yourself speak English?"

"No. I have no knowledge of that language."

"Then how do you know what he said?"

"It was told to me by a friend who was there, who spoke English, that that was what he said."

"It would surprise you then to hear the truth of what the panel said. 'Damn the bitch, she has lived too long when life brings her to this.' Those were his exact words. It is not a temperate comment, nor a courteous one, nor even a wise one, but it would seem to express, rather than malice, a degree of impatience and frustration at your failure to make preparations. You had several days' warning. Aware of your mother's infirmity as you were, why did you not spare her this ordeal when you knew that the factor was coming?"

"She was bed-ridden. I could not lift her myself. I was waiting for my husband to come."

"And the house was fired while she was still inside, in her bed?"

"Yes— God help her, she cried out, and never spoke again."

"Was the factor aware that she was inside the house when it was fired?"

"I do not know. I think so."

"Did he not ask you to account for all the members of your household, and to take your goods away?"

"I cannot remember. There were so many there— they were all burned out that day."

"How many properties were cleared on that occasion?"

"I cannot remember the number, but I would say there was twenty houses."

"Would it surprise you to know that only four properties were cleared that day, after legal notice of removal?"

"Yes, I would be surprised. The whole township was burning that day. They came and told me he was burning all of Cnap na Stri."

"Your mother suffered from a weakness of the heart, did she not?"

"Yes. That is so. But that was no reason for her to die. She was in good health otherwise."

"Why did you not have her gently conveyed to shelter elsewhere, when you knew that the day of your removal was approaching?"

"We did not believe it would happen to us. We prayed that we would be spared. We were driven away like dogs, with only the clothes on our backs. It is a cruel man who would do that to the people."

Hamilton summoned James Stirling of Glen Sian, and permitted himself a hint of cordiality.

"You have been an intimate acquaintance of the panel since your childhood, have you not?"

"Yes. He has managed my family's affairs for nearly twenty years."

"And you have absolute confidence in his ability to do so?"

"Yes."

"Do you sanction his policy of improvement?"

"We deemed improvement necessary for the repair of my finances, on the clear understanding that all such measures should be stopped if they proved harmful to the people."

"And by and large, he has observed this edict."

"I accede to his judgment. He is better equipped to determine the requirements of my estate than I."

"Is he your friend?"

"I regard him in that light."

"Have you ever observed in him a predisposition toward violence? Toward malicious cruelty?"

"He has neither of those qualities, nor would I tolerate them."

"But his language is malicious."

"He has a sharp temper … I have a spiteful temper myself. To my knowledge he bears no malice toward any of my tenants."

564

"So he is an able administrator, and your trusted confidant?"

"Yes."

"Were you acquainted with his wife?"

"I honoured and admired her." He paused, perhaps with more effect than he knew. "I would say more than that. I held her in such high regard that I asked her to marry me. She refused, as her affections were vested in my factor."

"And after the marriage of these honoured friends, did your sentiments toward her change?"

"No, they remained the same."

Hamilton passed a handkerchief lightly over his brow.

"And he did not upon any occasion evince jealousy, or hostility upon that issue?"

"On no occasion did he ever evince any such hostility toward me, in this or any other regard."

Hamilton consulted his watch, bowed slightly, and withdrew. Macaulay Gore said, "Your father, sir, was Ewen Stirling of Glen Sian, was he not?" and James, who had never entirely lost his expression of silken surprise, abruptly snapped shut his own watch, which he had been surreptitiously studying.

"Yes."

"Was he not that same Ewen Stirling who was arrested on suspicion of high treason after the late rebellion, and incarcerated in Edinburgh?"

"He was not charged, and he was released after a period of wrongful detention. My estates are not attainted, and my father's honour is unsmirched. I resent your cowardly insinuations."

Macaulay Gore apologized with graceful insincerity.

"Do you reside permanently upon your estate, Mr. Stirling?"

"I pass the winters in Edinburgh."

"Were you in residence at the time of violence at Bearradh farm in August two years past?"

"Yes."

"And are you fully cognizant of all that passed upon that occasion?"

"Of course."

"Do you permit your factor a free hand in the conduct of your affairs?"

"I have said that I rely upon his judgment. He has more knowledge of his business than I."

"To the extent that he may have implemented measures of improvement with such zeal that he was led to overstep the law in the execution of his duty?"

"He has behaved in every respect with perfect legality, and with my full knowledge and acquiescence."

"Are you upon the verge of bankruptcy?"

Hesketh, from the bench, said, "Sir David, this is irrelevant."

"My Lord, if you will permit me, it is highly relevant to the charges if, in seeking to repair his finances, Mr. Stirling has countenanced criminality."

Despite the dimness a flush became apparent, spreading to the roots of James's hair.

"I am not ignorant of the law, sir, and I must remind you that your business in this court is the pursuit of fact, not indulgence in insulting speculation."

Macaulay Gore said, "I thank you for your instruction," and bowed. There were no further questions.

The time was six minutes past seven in the evening. Muir Montgomery, James's solicitor, entered a courtroom in which there were increasing signs of restlessness. He was a stately man of sixty, hawk-nosed and arrogant: he and Henderson, close friends and fellow Freemasons, acknowledged one another with their eyes alone. Perhaps in deference to the occasion or previous criticism, he did not prominently display the masonic seals on his watch chain which were ordinarily visible. Hamilton lurched to his feet, elicited a respectful testimony as to the length of Montgomery's acquaintance with the accused, his cautious and temperate character and sensibility to the law, and withdrew. Macaulay Gore attacked with vigour: both Edinburgh men, he and Montgomery were bitter enemies.

"The deceased, Seoras Cameron, was known to you as a student under the name of George Cameron, was he not?"

Montgomery said coldly, "He held a position of no responsibility in my offices for a brief period of time."

"And subsequently incurred your wrath by his seduction of your daughter."

"Yes."

"And fathered her child."

"Yes."

"A bitter blow for any gentleman. To loathe such an ingrate would be natural."

"I am no hypocrite. I do not grieve for him."

"And yet it would seem that your fraternal association led you, initially, to afford this young man a rapturous welcome, and to admit him to the very bosom of your family."

"He betrayed the trust which had been placed in him."

"What manner of young man was he, that your affections were so engaged, and a lass of tender years should be so susceptible as to grant him the ultimate favour?"

"He was a vile profligate, addicted to drink and prostitutes. I will commit no perjury to burnish his memory."

At eight o'clock candles were brought into court, inflicting an unbearable assault upon the prisoner's senses, which were heightened by incipient migraine. The wine had reappeared at his elbow and he moistened his lips with it: the savage onslaught of pain began, and although the unwavering stare with which he had regarded every witness did not alter, his concentration on their evidence diminished, and he remembered only fragments of Inglis MacNeil's flagrant perjury and the testimony of William Morrison of Forres. Both witnesses resisted Macaulay Gore's attempts to discredit them, MacNeil by a fierce intransigence and Morrison by his sincerity and conviction. At twenty minutes past ten James Henderson, peering anxiously through the smoke, scribbled on a card, *How are you, my friend?* and sent it to the dock. He turned over the card, unmoved by this solicitude, and wrote with the stub of pencil which had accompanied it, *This is a hard chair, and does not improve with sitting*, and then, *I would sleep if I could.*

Henderson read it, seemed to give him some indecipherable message with his eyes, and pocketed the card. Hamilton was intent only upon his next witness, and his pink-lidded junior was attempting to stifle his yawns. Only Hesketh, on the bench, his bony face cadaverous by candlelight, was observing the proceedings with a predatory interest.

Dr. Gerard Mackintosh testified to the condition of the accused after the violence at Bearradh; it had been as unpleasant a case of traumatic shock as he had ever seen, and it was a tribute to his constitution that he had not sustained permanent injury, as had William Morrison. No, it was not possible that the injuries had been self-inflicted, or were the result of a conspiracy between the accused and Morrison. No, he did not believe it possible for the accused to have gone abroad in his condition and committed the alleged act of arson within the given time. No, he had not provided the opiate taken that night, but he had attended the household and provided opium in sufficient quantity on other occasions. He had not noticed a spirit of reckless vengeance in the accused that evening: on the contrary, he had been self-possessed, and had never been observed by Mackintosh in any derangement of temper. Yes, he had examined the deceased, Seoras Colla Cameron. It was not possible to conclude without dissection, which had not been carried out, whether the injuries had been sustained before or immediately after death: the corpse had been in an advanced stage of decomposition, and he had not considered further examination necessary. There had been gross evidence of consumption. Death had been caused, indisputably, by drowning. He had not discounted suicide.

At ten minutes past eleven the laborious process of translation was resumed. Roìs Grant, Peadair Mackinnon and Iain Ross spoke on the factor's behalf. He heard them indifferently, untouched by the sincerity of their testimony. Yes, he was a hard man; he did not encourage friendship, but he had provided grain during the months of famine and the grain had been the salvation of many people. Roìs Grant had witnessed the brawl in the public house. The factor had been attacked with a razor; the scar was still on his hand, where Macaulay Gore could see if it he wished. He would be a saintly man who would not respond to that measure of provocation. Macaulay Gore drifted through the smoke to within a few feet of the dock and hesitated, looking for the first time into the face of the accused. What he saw there did not encourage him, and he moved away.

James Ross, John Baird, Robert Smith, sometime shepherds, occasional employees of the factor. No, there had been no gratuitous violence in the removals, nor had the factor permitted cruelty or levity during the business of removal.

Again, unwillingly, he moistened his lips with wine, overcome by pain and nausea and the desire to urinate. Hamilton submitted letters of commendation from Mr. John Burrel, factor to the Earl of Arran, Vice-Admiral Sir Alexander Lockhart of Carstairs, Mr. Samuel Naismyth, secretary of the Wool Society, Sir William Armstrong of Dounie, Mr. John Robson, his factor, Mr. Hugh Elliott, breeder of Cheviot sheep. "A person of the strictest integrity... he bears a most respectable character...." "All improvements to be implemented with the greatest respect for the indigenous population...." "Incapable of being guilty of those charges brought against him, and upon trial they will be shewn to be unfounded."

The jury of fifteen, which included eight local landowners aware of the desirability of improvement and sensitive to legal precedent, listened attentively. Macaulay Gore's closing address, demanding verdicts of guilty upon all charges, lasted for half an hour, Hamilton's for twenty-five minutes. This was a gentleman, who had risen to his present position by his own admirable efforts, who had patiently borne the calumny of these accusations and the burden of proceedings of thirteen hours' duration, not with the appearance of guilt or fear but with the most perfect composure. Being possessed of the trust of his employer, why would he risk all by such flagrant and deliberate acts of lawlessness? Absurd, also, to suppose that despite his animosity towards the deceased, Seoras Colla Cameron, he would invite that same Seoras Cameron to meet him at some unspecified hour, at some unknown and deserted place, to deprive him of his life; absurd to suppose that the deceased would accept such an invitation; absurd even to entertain the supposition that murder had been committed. The jury had no alternative but to declare his innocence.

At one o'clock in the morning the Lord Commissioner of Justiciary instructed the jury to ignore the second, third and fourth charges, "which have failed", and directed them to concentrate their attention upon the first charge of wilful fire raising, the three charges of culpable homicide, and the charge of murder.

"If you are satisfied beyond any reasonable doubt, if you accept the evidence that the panel did, by means unknown and by the application of force, commit murder, it would be appropriate for you to convict. If the matter remains mysterious, wholly unexplained, and there is no ground upon which you may safely rest your verdict, then on that charge you should find him not guilty...."

When, after fifteen minutes, he ceased to speak and the jury retired, the sound of rain was still audible on the night-blackened glass. Hamilton was seated, gazing at his endless papers; his junior was biting his nails. James Henderson, behind them, sat with his head bent in deep introspection. James Stirling had returned to the courtroom, and, disfigured by distance and shadow, his face and silvered hair might have been Ewen's. The black river of rain ran on the glass, on a salt wind from the sea.

The ring was in his pocket; as the bell tinkled after sixteen minutes to signify the jury's return he closed his hand around it.

The chancellor rose.

"The jury find the first charge in the indictment not proven against the panel, by a majority; of the fifth, sixth and seventh charges, not guilty by a majority; and of the eighth charge, by a majority, not proven."

The skeletal face above the scarlet robes was also lost in distance, the eyes only dark sockets.

"Mr. Scott, it is my duty to dismiss you from the bar; and you have the satisfaction of knowing you are discharged by the opinion of the majority of the jury. I would enjoin you to remember that your guilt or innocence is unproven, and that the law is a two-edged sword, an instrument of chastisement no less than defense."

He left the court, the smoke, the voices, Hamilton and Macaulay Gore's reciprocal congratulations. The unjudicial night received him; the rain, at least, was clean.

II

July thirteenth, 1774. At some unknown hour of that hot week, between one of his visits and another, cancer had claimed his mistress, whom he found dead in the early morning. He dug her grave and buried her, with her rosary and the crucifix which had always been the silent witness to their intercourse. In the sunlit evening he burned her croft and possessions and the money he had given her, and sat in the bleached grass near the grave watching the flames. No nightfall came, only a drawing in of shadows, and smoke, and memory.

At half past two in the morning the roof fell in, and he left her and never returned to that place, nor spoke her name again.

He entered his house in the blue hour before dawn, and in the indistinction of his vision, dread and hope and elation seized him like an illness and he thought she was his hallucination made flesh: was Margaret, the precursor of his death.

She lay in his favoured position for sleep, left arm under her head, her callused feet arched as though in the steps of some arrested dance. Her face was buried in his pillow, and veiled in long black hair: what was visible of her profile was a cameo of his own.

As though she sensed his presence she woke, opening sleep-drenched eyes and arms and legs with a sinuous grace. Offering herself, her soul, her youth, her undoubted virginity, with a sweet, provocative smile, the shirt guilelessly disarranged to reveal one boyish nipple.

The bleakness in his eyes rejected her, and he was aware that she was weeping when she left him. He sat in the armchair by the bed, closing his mind against the assault of memory and the recognition of desire, and morning came, and the burning sun illuminated nothing.

Sunday, the twenty-fourth of July, 1774. The day had been hot, nearly eighty degrees, with a strong wind blowing from the south. Now, in the evening, it had veered and was easterly, bringing the promise of rain.

The road transversed steeply half a mile above Glen Sian. Across the glen the ephemeral masked the eternal, the shadow of cloud driven in from the sea obscuring the shadows of five mountains: on the horizon shafts of sunlight were still visible. Here he had walked with her with Ewen's spirit in his mind, still vividly recalled, and as real to him now as in the hour of vision.

The dimness increased: the scarlet horizon was veiled with coming rain. The wind died, the light vanished like a blown candle, the incense-like fragrance of the pollen that had risen like a cloud on the moor still clung with strange sweetness to his clothing. The harvest occupied his thoughts, the absolute necessity of rain, the change in the smell of the air... on his blind left side, a man had emerged from the dimness and was standing in the track with one hand raised. He was Gilchrist MacGregor, whose property of Monnymore had stood empty for sixteen months.

"What do you want, MacGregor?"

"To talk to you. Only that."

When the blow was first felt he did not comprehend that he had been stabbed, until the blood, with surprising slowness, began to drip from his thigh. He dragged his boot from the stirrup and dismounted and another blow struck him in the back, tearing his left shoulderblade and sliding on the bone: until he felt the wetness of the blood and the difficulty in drawing breath, it had seemed only the impact of a fist. He turned, seized with coughing and the terrible constriction of the pain, aware that the rivulet of blood was running into his boot; aware that from the blindness and imbalance on the left side of his body some other force had come, and he was on the ground, with the face he recognized above him and another face beyond, and the obscenities and the threats of Bearradh were repeated with a slow explicitness. They had said that they would carve the eyes from his face, because his eye was the evil eye, and the knife that would have pierced his brain hovered in the bloodied fist. He jerked his head aside and the deflected blade tore his forehead and scalp. They had said that they would castrate him. The blade, the same blade or another, the same attacker or another, pierced his groin, stabbed deeply and withdrew, and as he attempted to crawl, to lift his own insupportable weight, to shield his flooding groin, he saw the knife drive down through his outstretched hand, impaling it on the ground. Then the knife was hammered into the stony soil and the hand savagely stamped on: the veins dripped then, with a preternatural slowness. There was now no pain, only the consciousness of blood lost, a seeping coldness, the inability to breathe.

In the night there was movement: a wind in the darkness like the sound of distant water; a living blackness and immensity that came, attempting to rouse him from the earth; the smell of stallion, the strange, iron smell of blood. He lay with his right hand pressed to his groin and the sweet breath passed over his face, and the blackness lifted and was gone: the night erased the sound of hooves. The pain of the blade transfixing his hand came to dominate and offend him; the rain was running on the steel and the slow, spreading network of blood. He closed his eyes and pulled it out: was no more wounded, no more blinded, was freed.

They spoke of him but not to him, although he was conscious and capable of understanding fragments of conversation: he opened his eyes and saw that the rain was golden as it fell between himself and the light. His blood-soaked clothing was peeled away and he attempted to cover his exposed penis; the shadow identified as James moved between him and the lantern on the ground and restrained him once more. Coldness and nausea seeped through him: the clamp restricting the flow of blood from his leg exerted an intolerable pressure.

Aware of his consciousness, they did not now discuss the probability of his death.

Ardsian was mentioned: her spirit would not come to him there. He repeated, *mo thigh féin*, until his voice was audible, and when they tried to lay him on the couch in Margaret's sitting room he resisted, repeating, *an leabaidh*, with increasing agitation until they carried him to the bed. His blood defiled the cleanliness of the sheets even as their fragrance embraced him. He was an object now, tortured by crude ministrations and by the scalding rush of alcohol into his wounds. A fragment of sugar was held to his lips: he refused it, and the bitterness was disguised in a spoonful of brandy and forced between his teeth. The drug stimulated his labouring pulse. It did not release him from the terrible clarity of consciousness or relieve his savage struggle for breath, or confer peace.

In the quiet hour of evening when the hands had ceased to torment him, the shadows, the thoughts, the half dreams, the rage, he opened his eyes and saw James crouched on the floor beside him. He lay on the right side of the bed, on her pillows and the invisible impressions of her body; he had pleaded to be moved and had attempted to move himself from this defilement of her place, but his distress had gone unnoticed or was misunderstood. He closed his eyes, conscious only of thirst and the death-like coldness in his limbs, then the import of what James had been saying made itself known to him, and the uncontrollable agitation seized him once more, and he said, No— no— no, until the hand, with uncharacteristic compassion, calmed him, and James said, "You are very ill. You know what I mean. Do you want me to send for her?"

He said again, "No." And then, distinctly, "Let me die in peace."

Another hour of torment: infection raging in his blood: Gerard Mackintosh's decision to amputate his left hand. Something on the table: unlit candles, the water he craved constantly: he threw them, his mind flooded with obscenities that came fluently to his tongue. Shaken, Mackintosh retreated. He was left alone, calculating the effort necessary to reach the sabre hanging in its scabbard, the stiletto concealed in the drawer. He slid heavily to the floor and fainted. Mackintosh returned: three men were required to restrain him.

And in an hour of lingering twilight, a perfumed presence in the room. A consciousness, in the interlude between sickness and exhaustion, of a delicacy that was reminiscent of Margaret: the remembered fragrance, the many flowers, the exquisite peace which had emanated from her, with which she had healed him. And he knew that Margaret had come to him: if death had come with her it would be an incomparable sweetness: as she had always given comfort, so her perfume comforted now. When he woke it was dawn, when this room received its light. She was sitting in the armchair: he saw the long, soft sleeve of her shirt and the fold of the riding skirt falling from the knee: her name would not come to his lips, he was paralyzed by the ecstasy of her presence. She moved, and the dawn illuminated her face and the worship and apprehension there. Mairi. The perfume was the perfume of cut lilies.

He turned his face away and wept.

He read Mackintosh's notes, left lying in the room, tore them into pieces and threw them at him.

> The first wound entered the right outer thigh, resulting in a ragged tear of the Quadriceps, and did not penetrate as far as the Femur. The blood loss here was estimated at one to two pints, altho greater in the body. Regarding the second episode, the blade was inserted at an angle causing a reasonable amount of superficial skin and underlying tissue damage, the considerable density of the Scapula causing the blade to slide. The third wound, to the groin, which was incisional in character, has had serious consequences without severing the Femoral artery. Blood has extravasated into the Peritoneal cavitie and in the first episode into the fascia and muscles. The injury to the hand has caused much muscular and vascular damage, and Gangrene has necessitated the amputation of two fingers to the head of the metacarpal bone.

The limits of pain were these... the humiliation and impotence of the bed, the number of steps to the armchair and the exhausting efforts to reach it, the steps to other bitter landmarks, the chamberpot, the opened window, the fireplace. The armoire at the far end of the room, like the land beyond the window, was unattainable.

Beneath the granulating wound on the shoulderblade his lung had been scarred, although neither he nor Mackintosh alluded to its condition. In the deep wounds of the groin and thigh, tubes had been inserted and discharge drained into the heavy dressings: the tubes were withdrawn gradually as the wounds began to close. He could not bear the pressure of any garment until James provided him with a long dark blue cotton banyan, which he did not know had been made for Charlotte: he wore this during his excruciatingly slow progression from one resting place to another. On his left hand the severed nerves were evident in the bluish cast of the skin, the numbness, and the deformity of the nails: those fingers which had not been amputated had been confined in a splint when it was determined that they were not gangrenous.

As it had in the weeks of his imprisonment, his absence from the land obsessed him: the inabilities of his own intractable flesh imprisoned him, the invincible strength was damaged. He had relinquished the essence of himself, dignity, privacy, solitude. Only the bitter fury was Malcolm.

***

James found him seated in the armchair, the banyan discarded for more familiar clothing, although the breeches were unfastened at the knee and his feet were bare and thrust into low-heeled shoes. The horsehair sutures had been removed from his forehead, and where the scar ran into the scalp the hair had turned white at the roots. His face was gaunt and badly shaved, his eyes deeply sunken. At James's approach he tried to rise, and his right hand slid on the arm of the chair; all efforts to straighten the grossly misshapen fingers of the left had been abandoned, and the muscles had atrophied and were useless.

He regained his balance, disdaining the ebony walking stick that leaned against the chair.

James said, "My dear Malcolm, please be seated."

"I will have another chair brought for you."

"I assure you, the bed will serve me." It was covered with a clean white counterpane, and did not appear to have been occupied recently: the four pillows which had been necessary had been dispersed. "It pleases me to see you so well."

He said sarcastically, "Oh, yes. So well," and sat.

"For God's sake, man, you are born again, where another would have died. A little gratitude would not come amiss."

"I'll tell you when it comes upon me." There was a silence. "My watch has stopped. What is the time?"

"Twenty-five minutes past one."

"And the date?"

"Monday, the twelfth of September."

The silence was reflective, painful.

"God. So long."

James said, "Perhaps you take my point." Then, "My investigation into the attack on you has proved abortive, which will come as no surprise to you." He said nothing. "And yet you still insist that you did not know your assailants, that their faces were covered, and that you could not and cannot identify them."

"Yes."

"Why are you lying to me?"

He said, very softly, "Because vengeance is mine. It is not your business, and it is not the business of the fiscal. It is my business, and I will finish it."

"You are a bloody madman."

"On the contrary, under the circumstances, I consider myself remarkably sane."

A brief communion which had not existed for years passed between them.

"Malcolm, I beg of you. Do not pursue this."

He smiled, very faintly.

"You and Margaret... so tender of me, so full of loving fears."

James rose.

"As I so foolishly expected some epiphany to have overtaken you as the result of your illness, I see no further reason for delaying my journey. In your absence I appointed a ground officer, who is presently fulfilling your obligations. In due course he will answer to you, as you will answer to me. In the meantime, you will correspond fully and regularly with me, and conduct your personal affairs with civility and discretion." He waited for some response: there was none. "I trust I will hear of no further unpleasantness concerning you."

"I am not well, and I am not some headstrong young fool. On my honour, it will be nothing of consequence."

James paused with his hand on the door, his face strained and aging and hauntingly reminiscent of his father.

"You are the coldest friend and most violent enemy I have ever known. And if you think I take your word on anything, you are much mistaken."

The door closed: the living and the dead were gone. He was alone.

On the night of his thirty-ninth birthday he sat in the estate office, with the pistols and the candles and the whisky on the table, and Dr. Gerard Mackintosh seated opposite him. Although James had been absent six weeks, he did not frequent the rest of the house, or allow Mackintosh's examinations in any room but this.

His glass was empty and he refilled it, pushing the decanter toward Mackintosh, who declined.

"You drink too much, Scott."

"Mind your own bloody business."

"Your liver will suffer for it."

He smoked, and gave Mackintosh a faint, sarcastic smile.

Mackintosh said, "Your left eye is blind," as though anticipating an answer, and when there was none, "How long has that been the case?"

"I cannot say. The process was gradual."

"Does it inconvenience you greatly?"

"No. In many ways it has sharpened my perception. I see the direction of my life more clearly. For a time it was obscured."

"I hope for your sake that it leads you toward retirement, and felicity. I can do nothing more for you, and I wish you nothing less." He hesitated:

the night's rain was audible. "Farewell, Scott. I shall not see you tomorrow. I leave early for Edinburgh."

"I wish you good weather."

"I thank you for the sentiment. I know you do not reciprocate my admiration."

As he reached the door his name was spoken rather sharply, and he turned back towards the smoke and candlelight. His fee had been paid: he was uncertain what further service was required of him.

"You may give me the benefit of your opinion as a surgeon, before you go."

"I will gladly do so."

"Will I have the full use of my prick?"

"My dear Scott, that is not for me to say."

He said coldly, "Then I am sure you will find it of some scientific interest if I let you know."

When Mackintosh left, embarrassed, the silence was absolute, the dampness palpable. Pain was the companion of the days, pain and imperfect vision and incoordination and the inability to breathe: in the nights were pain and the deadness of his spirit and the dead impotence of his flesh, his only lovers dead or vanished or held in contempt.

He had not known that Mairi was in the house until she came to his bed: her movements were of no interest to him, as no aspect of her physical or spiritual existence, the inexplicable gift of healing or the bitter gift of prophecy, had ever concerned him.

He did not speak, and she knelt on the bed and took his unresisting hand and kissed the scarred, closed fingers. When he did not respond she kissed his mouth. Her hair was scented with attar of roses, the oil gone rancid in the glass: the essence of death, dead sweetness, dead love, irretrievable ecstasy. She was Margaret's ghost, and she offered Margaret's gift of sex, and the gift she offered was poisoned, and the arousal as repulsive as death.

He said into the darkness, "I am your father," and the delicate, erotic sweetness was withdrawn; it was withdrawn forever.

They quarrelled with a sour finality, like old lovers, and she was seen less often, removing from him her peculiar companionship, her devotion and her service. He sensed her intention to leave Glen Sian, an illiterate, destitute Gael, a cripple, a woman, a spiritual innocent, and made no attempt to dissuade her. His own ceaseless striving had wearied him. He knew, and was indifferent.

He sat in his study on the night of March twelfth, the pistols on the desk, the brandy in the glass, and the pages of a meandering letter from James discarded in the candlelight. He had received these as regularly as the weather permitted and answered none of them, aware that James regretted their last conversation and was making overtures of peace. In the current epistle he wrote that he had formed "a profitable alliance", and would return to Glen Sian in April with the widow he proposed to marry.

He had read no further; the prospect of their intrusion was unbearable.

He could not tolerate them, the frivolity and inconsequence of their world. Grief had conferred no spiritual night, bereavement no scars upon them; they moved in the light and were creatures of the light. They had no concept of the darkness of the abyss.

Memory came... he allowed it to come, in the candlelight, on the edge of the night. What had been dormant was now explicit: the demons of his sleep.

He was hidden in the dark rotting leaves, in the bosom of the earth, a mist with the taste of smoke and the sea condensing in droplets on his hair and on the hide and rough fabric of their clothing: hunting as though for prey, for sport, they had found him easily, and when they found him they returned him to the house, with a leather gauntlet stuffed into his mouth. Blinded by the shirt over his head, penetrated by the fingers of the man who had raped her and by the same knife, until his anus bled, then he was sodomized by one or by several, the glove inserted into his soundless mouth, his eyes opened and shrouded by whiteness. The slimy glove was withdrawn, the shirt removed: his screams remained silent: his eyes, although opened, saw nothing. He was lifted, forced to suck the instrument of violation, tasting the blood, the shit, the semen, the scalding acidity of urine: was played with, the point of the knife cutting his foreskin and scrotum, and raped again, until his bowels convulsed and emptied and his anguished body experienced the first of many seizures, and slid from torture into oblivion.

Drinking now. The sound of rain in this house of spirits seemed intensely loud... in this room where Murdoch had beaten the deadness that was animate, the living ghost of his son, unable, with his crude intelligence and cruder sexuality, either to suspect or comprehend the nature of his violation. Attempting by physical and sexual abuse to awaken the dead numbness, urging the sexless child to manhood by masturbation and copulation in his presence, and repulsed by the shuddering response of his son to the damp pudenda of his whores; calling him cunt, and vilifying him in the obscene language of his homophobia.

Perhaps he had anticipated the compulsion of desire, the guilty fellatio in the dressing room between valet and employer. And later, the trembling hand caressing his scrotum, the fingers, aromatic with semen, caressing his lips. The murmuring... a revulsion at the sound of his name would possess him to the end of his life, a revulsion for his body and for Ewen, whom he had loved, and had never forgiven.

Sex obsessed him, the act filth and degradation between the legs of the prostitute Mhaire and the anonymous whores who succeeded her. She had mocked the soiled gift of his virginity, his scarred genitals, his failure to achieve erection, and her vituperation had become Murdoch's language of obscene insinuation. His attempt to stop her mouth had become a vicious strangulation: the inexpressible shame and rage found its climax in rape. He had thought her dead when he left her.

Nothingness had followed: the void. Years of violence and lawlessness, the black river of time. The tide of night had ebbed, the rain was still running on the glass. No names, no faces remembered, only acts of violence or of sex. Of those he had killed, Margaret's lover had been the most despised.

Her spirit now eluded him, in absence as in life. The pornographic language of love was silent; the hallucinations of her lovemaking, the exquisite, erotic dreams, had become only fragmented recollections of his savage abuse of her. And the dreams and the visions and the nightmares and the memories were indivisible, and he was haunted by his inability to remember the extent of violation. He believed sometimes that he had committed sodomy: he was conscious only of having damaged her as irreparably as he had been damaged.

The night and the voices were still, the rain soft and without menace. He snuffed the candles lest his fall should overturn them, and in the darkness placed the barrel of the pistol against his temple, and pulled the trigger.

The charge misfired. Black rain still ran on the unseen glass: the long agony of his life was unfinished.

Interlude: Fairlight 1774

The night was damp, with a degree of frost; the wind was a gentle southwesterly. Overhead, the stars moved with the passage of time: stars, in these and other latitudes, were the chart by which the sailor had lived. As he watched, the full moon climbed out of the sea and lit the Strait of Dover. The sea itself was calm.

At half past one in the morning the sea was still empty, its eternal rhythm, the very pulse of his life, barely audible at the foot of the cliffs, and it seemed possible that there had been no betrayal, that he had misheard or misunderstood, and dawn would restore the precarious order of things.

Some played this dangerous game for a lifetime. Some played only once and lost, and were gibbeted in chains or hanged at Hastings or Dover. He had played, and savoured, and profited from his trade for eight years, in the dark of the moon and on the roughest nights, sometimes monthly, sometimes not, according to a complicated calendar. He had never been afraid, and the sea was his life. He was not naïve enough to suppose that it would not be his death.

Stark moonlight on the hands of his watch: six minutes to two. The wedding festivities he had left would be ended; the run, if any were foolhardy enough to land a cargo in these conditions, finished, the evidence vanished, the hooves passed unheard in the night; the silent ships tacking back to the safety of the shadow that was France, a slow business tonight against the floodstream, with a light wind on the quarter. Boulogne, Calais, Dunkerque: Rotterdam for good cheap gin, Flushing for tobacco. He had once brought silk worth fifteen thousand pounds on a private commission from Ostend: because the cartel in London had refused his request for a percentage of their profits, he had conducted this secret trade with astonishing success for more than five years. He had begun his defiance with the schooner *Luck of Rye*, which they had offered him as an insulting test of skill. He had stood her into Rye Bay on a Christmas morning in broad daylight and landed her entire cargo on the Broomhill sands, having first ascertained that his whist partners in the customs house at Rye were absent on service, on leave, or in the pews of the parish church of St. Mary the Virgin. The beach had been cleared within twenty minutes. Two half ankers of inferior brandy and a severe reprimand had been his reward. With characteristic insouciance, he had sent thirty yards of raw silk to the home of the only female member of the cartel, infuriating her powerful lover and affording himself great amusement.

Then they had given him *Amitié*, and, in time, *Felicia*, and whenever *Amitié* lay idle in Boulogne he absented himself on what was assumed by others to be business in London, and took her down Channel to intercept East Indiamen, who were sometimes eager to sell beyond the revenue's jurisdiction: fulfilling the commissions forwarded to him by his agent in the City, occasionally transporting goods and passengers, once disposing of a corpse at sea, once carrying monies from sources in Paris to colonials in London. The cartel expended its vast profits on debts, taxes, and speculative ventures: his were spent on bribery, wages, agents' fees, the purchase of contraband, gambling, leasehold property for two mistresses kept concurrently in Mayfair, and on property abroad. The cartel's suspicions had never been proved, although he had been summoned to explain certain discrepancies, and had successfully done so. He had also been told that he stank of the service, and the commission he had held was still cherished enough in memory to regard this as a deadly insult. The game continued, but the cards were marked: the house was dealing against him.

And in moments of reflection he knew that time and life were running out. He was not young: he had no wife, no child, no permanent home and no legitimate career. The future offered nothing but the prospect of risk, another run, another dark moon, until fate and age should overtake him, or the cartel killed him for his double dealing, or the organization, already two hundred strong, was infiltrated by spies. He was wealthy; he was tired, not of the sea but of the life; the end of his time was dimly perceptible. And tonight, the end had come.

At twelve minutes past two he saw them, steering northwest by north and close-hauled on the larboard tack. The revenue cutter *Wasp* out of Hastings had *Amitié* in tow. Of the brig's vast sail plan only the forecourse and jib were set, and the maintops'l prevented her yawing at the tow. Astern of her the other cutter, identifiable now in the lens and the moonlight as the *Harvester*, was acting as a sea-anchor to keep her on her course. She was damaged in hull and rigging and, by her sluggish progress, still fully laden; although her cargo was unknown to him, she was returning from Boulogne. He had refused command of her, and tonight had attended the wedding of friends in Hastings: the bridegroom commanded a revenue sloop in these waters and had always been a useful source of information. When his attendance at that wedding and the coincidence of *Amitié*'s betrayal became known the game, and his life, would be over.

They were making for Hastings, clearly visible in the pitiless light. The current on the sea, the shadows on the gorse, his bleached hand holding the telescope.... only silence, some night bird stirring or the prearranged signals of men, the terrible, hammering impulse in his blood to run, to escape these consequences. Only the faintest trace of his breathing in the cold night, and the sea's seductive whisper on the shingle.

Only silence, and then deafness and searing, unbearable light as *Amitié* exploded. What little remained broached to and drifted toward the beach: *Wasp*, too, was on fire, showered with blazing debris, her tarred rigging fiercely alight, her mainsail vanishing in a scarlet sheet of flame. *Harvester* was standing away: no boats were lowered, although small figures, burning like torches, were soundlessly quenching themselves in the sea.

He watched until the sea was empty, marking the time and the position of the stars as at the beginning and the close of all actions: the wind still southwesterly, freshening slightly, the tide, all tides, turning.

THE UNQUIET SHORE

I

I lived alone at Evesham from November of 1772 until the end of January, 1774.

I left it for only one reason. Catherine was found to have a cancerous tumour of the breast, and would not submit to its removal without me.

I went to London, displaced once more: a woman without a country, subsisting yet again on the charity of others. I remained, not a friend, not a daughter, not a rival, present during the excision of the breast because she would not let me go, although Harlesdon, her lover of so many years, did not attend, and confessed to me that he could not have endured it. Now all female horror was within my experience: my own suffering and my sisters' was written on my soul.

In the days immediately afterwards Harlesdon stayed with us, although they had never openly lived together. Despite his innumerable debaucheries and the youthful lovers who had displaced him he remained, in his way, faithful to Catherine, and his tenderness toward her was immense. I sensed that I intrigued him, as the unobtainable intrigues the sexual connaisseur, and perhaps in other circumstances he would have made some advance. Perhaps I misjudge him: I think not. I remained aware of his interest, and his desire for my friendship in the gravity of those days, but whatever physical or familial comfort he sought was not offered, and he responded like the Harlesdon of my childhood, with freezing politeness and disdain. And yet, I pitied him: he loved her. We were all bound by inexplicable obligation, he who was not her husband, she who was not his wife, I who was not her daughter, nor Achill's daughter, nor his lover. Life had not taught me forgiveness, nor given me comfort that I should comfort others: that I should respond to her now with compassion seemed impossible to me. I told myself that I had come to her for Achill's sake alone. I did not acknowledge a difficult, wounded, resentful love, which could only now at the close of her life admit of forgiveness, and regret.

The fourth of March was the first night she left the house. Harlesdon sought my assistance in dissuading her, but Catherine was Catherine, and eventually she was dressed, her grey hair disguised with false curls and powder, the great, ravaged beauty in her face repaired and accentuated with cosmetics. She walked from the bedroom supported by Harlesdon; his lameness had become very pronounced with age, and I took her from him and brought her down the stairs myself. She was heavily bandaged and could not raise her right arm, and several times she sank in a vast, shimmering cascade of silk to rest beside me on the stairs: we sat together, with Harlesdon leaning on his malacca swordstick, watching our descent with undisguised anguish. And as we sat, she put her hand in mine; said nothing, only the bony, delicate hand clinging to mine; then she turned her face toward me and kissed my cheek, for the first time since my childhood.

I remembered it, not the open door and the carriage lights on the pavement and the liveried servants waiting, but the perfume and the kiss, throughout the hours of the night that would come, and the nights that followed. She rose; Harlesdon took her arm and inclined his head to me; the door closed and shut out the smoky dampness of a night poised between winter and spring. I was alone.

I did not now sleep well, and seldom before one in the morning: I was drinking coffee and writing in my sitting room when I heard the sound. The underservants had retired, Catherine's abigail was drowsing in the dressing room, and until the carriage returned the grooms were disposed to gamble in the mews. I was very conscious of being the only one awake.

The sound had been breaking glass, not close. It did not come again. Eleven o'clock struck in the house, and a minute or two later from the church: as the strokes died away the silence was profound. Then there was another sound, or series of sounds, faint, rhythmic, unidentifiable, interludes of stillness during which the night was hostile and the silence crawled on my skin. There was a pistol in the centre drawer of the desk. I kept it there: it was mine. I slid the drawer open and its weight was comforting. I don't know why I put it down, perhaps because it seemed better to be in the darkness than taken in the trap of the light.

He was upon me before the wicks of the extinguished candles had stopped smoking. And I fought, as I had fought on that other occasion, and he twisted my arm until the pain was paralyzing. I kicked backward and my heel struck bone; the forearm tightened cruelly around my body and something cold came to rest beneath my ear. The hand that held the pistol to my neck, the left hand, was not trembling.

"Any sound from you above a whisper, and I will kill you. Do you understand?"

English, without accent; a cultured voice. Very level.

"Where is Catherine Mordaunt?"

"Out."

The right arm eased its suffocating hold; the steel did not move from my jaw. The right hand slid beneath my waistcoat, where it lingered briefly.

"And when will she be in?"

"I cannot say."

The hand lifted from my breast. The pistol was withdrawn from my neck and gently pressed into my ribs.

"Light a candle, and by Christ Jesus, touch nothing else."

He must have known that my fingers were incapable: he felt for the chair and pushed me into it, and groped in the darkness, finding the gun and the candles. He tried several times to strike a light, cursed, and succeeded: the wick caught and his shadowed face was visible, intent on the business of lighting it. He was a tall man, roughly dressed, not young, perhaps forty, forty-five: his hair was unkempt, its colour difficult to distinguish, more coppery than dark. His pupils were dilated, the eyes intensely blue, the mouth thin-lipped, a cruel mouth: the face was as elegant as the voice, but drawn, as though with fatigue or illness. He leaned against the desk with my papers behind him and my journal opened at the place where his footsteps had interrupted me: the sentence I had been writing would remain unfinished, the rhythmic sound had been his bloodied spurs.

"Is there money in this room?"

"A little."

"Where is it?"

"In there."

He rifled the drawer until he found it: forty guineas. The fingers of my left hand attempted to remove the diamond from my right.

"Leave it. I don't want your damned ring."

The blood was roaring in my ears. I closed my eyes against him, and the faintness abated. I heard him move a pace or two, the spurs' metallic sound accompanying every step.

"Is this yours?" My riding coat. "Put it on." I neither moved nor spoke. "Come, madam, you try my patience."

I said, "I am an heiress. If you abduct me, you will hang for it."

He was very close, and death was close with him.

"I have already committed five capital offenses tonight. One more will make no difference."

The coat fell into my lap. I put it on.

Midnight struck, followed later by the sweet chimes from the church. The street was wet; lights still burned at upper casements, carriage lamps were passing across the square. The night was cold: I was trembling. Horses waited, rank with sweat.

"Mount," he said.

I mounted, astride. For whom had this saddle been intended? Not for a woman: none of this could have been intended for a woman.

"Give me your hand."

It was a manacle, and the other was entangled and locked to the reins.

"Now let us test your horsemanship."

I said, "As God is my witness, I will make you regret this."

It was impossible to see his face in the dim lights of the street.

"Good. Now allow me to acquaint you with my position. I am an excellent shot, and I have nothing to lose except my life, which seems a very little thing. If you draw attention to either of us by your behaviour, I will not hesitate to silence you."

We did not speak again.

We left the city, by God knew what bridge or at what hour. Only on the river was there life, riding lights, moored and moving vessels, haloed in a fine drizzle that gave way to the faint, late-rising moon. And then, darkness except for the moon, empty fields, a hard, stony road, a rising incline, open country. If I was to die it would be here, and now. He would kill me here.

I never knew where it was or how long we had ridden. I knew only that the country was steep and desolate, the drizzle had soaked my clothing, the horse had a mouth like iron, and the bit was dripping foam. I could not remember checking it or dismounting, only that the steel on my wrist was holding me, and my bladder was screaming for release.

He had turned back and was swearing fluently, telling me to remount.

"Christ, will you not suffer me to piss?"

I was unchained and led to the ditch. He held the other manacle, and stood with his face averted. Neither he nor I moved.

"Do you enjoy this? My subjugation?"

He turned, and in that cold light his face was drained of colour.

He said, "I would not humiliate a lady," and dropped the manacle and walked away.

I voided everything, in revolting spasms, the manacle dangling obscenely from my wrist throughout.

When I reached the road he was standing with his back to me, rummaging in the saddlebag. I thought how easy it would be to kill him, had I the means, had I the strength.

"Drink this. It will do you good."

I rinsed my mouth with it and spat; it was a harsh brandy.

"Come, then." Touching me, not with sexual intent, but impelling me toward the horse as though he knew I could not walk of my own volition. "Come." The thing fastening my wrist to the rein, the living warmth of the horse beneath me, the terrible solitude of the night, the terrifying, inexplicable kindness. "Your courage does not go unnoticed."

Another hour, toward the setting of the moon, a place I now know was twenty-two miles from London. Before we rode into the innyard he unlocked the manacle from my wrist and concealed it in his pocket. Candlelight was still visible at one of the casements, and the ostler did not appear surprised by our arrival, although no post-chaises were waiting and there was no other sign of life. I had to be lifted from the saddle. I was given a basin of coffee, and my hands trembled so much that I spilled what I attempted to drink. I saw that he transferred the saddlebag from the horse he had been riding; he paid for the horses, and apologized gracefully for the weals left by his spurs. Before we departed he attempted to push a pair of leather gloves onto my hands. I resisted him in utter silence, a very small resistance, and pulled them off and dropped them on the littered stone of the courtyard. He retrieved them, and folded them without a word and put them in his pocket. He did not attempt to restrain me with the manacle again.

We rode east, into the flush of dawn, a vast chorus of birdsong accompanying us. The sun rose, pearled with fog, over ploughed fields, hedgerows, the tender greens of soft southern England, where spring came early and winter did not kill. It was March; it was morning; I was still alive; the sun gave an illusion of warmth, the light gave me signs to read, this unknown country opened itself like a map. We rode through Tunbridge Wells as a clock was striking six. Another change of horses, and here it seemed that, for the distance travelled, a disproportionate amount of money was paid. Here it appeared that they knew him, although no name was spoken, and here it was very obvious to me that the horse brought to him was his own.

Fifteen miles from Tunbridge Wells, fifty miles from London, on the Rye road at Hawkhurst, we dismounted in the stableyard of an inn whose name I do not remember. It was nine o'clock in the morning, and he had driven me harder over that comparatively short distance than at any other time. I was exhausted, and he, who had seemed throughout the night possessed of an intense nervous energy, had withdrawn into a deadly reticence. His face, that highly boned, patrician, unshaven face, was deeply lined, and strained: he was older than he had appeared in the uncertain lights and shadows of the night.

He held me briefly against the sweating horse, as though we were lovers seizing these last moments for private conversation.

"The danger for me here is very great. And, consequently, for you. You are my guardian angel. Protect me." They were coming now, false smiles, false greetings, to take the horses, to take his money: my money. "Do what I tell you, and trust me."

I said nothing. He released me and turned to receive them with a smile as insincere as theirs, and I wondered if any one in the chaos and noise of this Saturday morning remarked that I did not speak to him or respond to his proferred arm. The sheer normality of my surroundings deepened my personal nightmare. A display of mercurial charm secured a heavy-beamed room up a narrow stair: it smelled of beeswax and smoke and mildew, and the chill when the door was pushed open was overlaid with the ghosts of two hundred years.

He followed me in, as he had followed me up the stairs, with the same measured music of the spurs: he carried the saddlebag on his shoulder, as though he intended to remain for some time. The aproned girl who had conducted us here twitched the counterpane on the bed with a glance at my ringless left hand, and moved to open the casement.

"Leave it," he said.

I heard him deposit the leather bag on the floor; I had turned my back on him, as if by refusing to see him I could deny his reality. The girl murmured something, oddly nervous for one who worked daily among strangers.

He said, "Bring her ladyship hot water for washing, and coffee, and something dainty to tempt her to eat. And oblige me by locking the door when you finish. I would not want her wandering, in her condition."

She squeaked across the floorboards, having indulged her curiosity: the door closed with difficulty as though warped. I heard her descend with heavy feet: there were voices below, dogs barking, horses, a cock crowing.

He said, "Enjoy your breakfast. And don't frighten the girl. I told her you were mad."

I turned. His hand was on the iron latch, his head bent to avoid the beams. He was leaving me.

"You bastard."

He looked directly at me, his eyes intense, unwavering, affronted. Then he pushed open the door and closed it. The key turned in the lock.

There were two worn Jacobean chairs, one near a table: I sat in it, turning my face from the light. Time passed, and did not touch me: neither hunger nor fear possessed me. My watch would have stopped, and I had no desire to mark these hours in this alien place, on this ordinary Saturday, by the end of which I would be dead. Perhaps escape was possible, perhaps the leather saddlebag contained a weapon or weapons: perhaps it was better to anticipate death. Even suffering, even courage has its limits.

The girl returned, and there was a significant interval between her unlocking of the door and the carrying in of a tray balanced on her hip. I made no attempt to force past her. I knew where that would end.

She left the tray under its linen cover and, without approaching me, asked if I required anything else.

"I will give you this if you bring me writing materials, and put a letter on the first post-chaise for London."

My diamond disappeared into a cleavage of unripe breasts, and she secreted my three scrawled lines beneath her apron, snuffing the candle with which I had sealed them, lest I burn the place down in my keeper's absence.

Achievement and exultation made me reckless. I could not eat, I could not remain sitting in the chair, I would not expose myself to the vulnerability of the bed. The saddlebag still lay on the floor where he had left it. I opened it.

It contained powder and shot for the pistols he carried; there were no other weapons. The brandy, what remained of my money and other, more generous offerings, a bracelet with a broken clasp, a sapphire earring, a gold watch and fob, a chased silver card case bearing initials and a regimental crest. Nothing that suggested an identity to me, only a criminal occupation.

Pawned, one of these would return me to London. Or see me accused of robbery. I replaced them, and was seated before the steps were audible on the stairs.

His left arm came into the periphery of my vision and the hand placed first my ring and then the letter on the table. Some bodily scent accompanied the movement, which had not been present before, reminiscent and unbearably poignant, the fragrance of bay rum.

He was standing on the other side of the table, his hands clasped beneath his coatskirts, staring down into the courtyard. Eventually he said, "What happens now?" I said nothing. "The door is open. If you wish to run screaming of my iniquities into the taproom, you are at liberty to do so."

I closed my eyes. His voice was level, even pleasant. "However, it has always been a Hawkhurst habit to mind one's own business. People find it healthier. Do you take my meaning?"

He turned fully toward me. He had shaved, and the unkempt coppery hair had been combed and tied with a black riband. "Why did you write to Catherine Mordaunt?"

"I should have thought the reason was obvious."

Silence. Somewhere, in a normal world, the morning was progressing toward noon, and life held peace, order, small frustrations, smaller happinesses.

"Lady Anne Villiers is an habituée of that house. Sometimes she stops the night, with her lesbian lover, while daddy dandles his whore." Whatever he wanted to see in my face, I refused to reveal it to him. "But then, you ain't Lady Anne Villiers, are you."

"My letter was in your possession. You know damned well who I am."

Again that mocking, heartbreaking scent. He leaned closer and turned the letter over. The seal was unbroken.

He sat in the chair opposite me, leaning back, resting his elbows on the arms. On the smallest finger of his right hand he wore a heavy, dull gold signet ring. He looked comfortable and at ease, stretching his legs and then crossing them.

"Now. As you are not old Cripplegait's daughter, perhaps you would care to enlighten me." I did not answer. "You use silence like a weapon. I wonder if you can use it like a fan."

Then he said, "Is that your breakfast over there? Did you eat any of it?" I indicated nothing, neither yes nor no. "I think you should eat something."

He left the chair and carried the tray to the table, moving the letter and my ring to one side. By his movements and the sounds I knew he was lifting the cloth.

"Oh, very dainty. I think you should eat some of this."

Ordinary, domestic sounds, cutlery, a spoon against china. He had buttered a square of cold toast and sliced it into mouthfuls. When he saw that my eyes were open, he pushed the plate uninsistently toward me.

"This conserve is damson, a great favourite of mine. Damned difficult to find, you know. Their season is very brief." I was weeping. "Especially in a hot summer." Silence came; I heard him replace the spoon. "For God's sake eat, or will you reproach me with starvation?"

"I cannot eat. I am not clean...."

The water she had left me had cooled, like everything on the tray: I could not touch it, as I could not touch this, because to touch implied acceptance. He brought a linen towel soaked in the water, and, impossibly, terribly, held my face in one hand and washed me gently with the other, as one would wash a child's face. I wept soundlessly: he wiped the tears from my closed eyelids. The palm of his hand beneath my chin was cool and roughened, his face so close to mine that a scar was visible, running into the left eyebrow; his lashes were dark, the coppery hair patched with white at the temples. The lashes lifted, the piercing eyes stared into mine, then dropped, and he began with the same implacable gentleness to wash my hands. His touch was unbearable, and I resisted him. As if the resistance were expected, he paid it no attention, and dried my hands. My heart broke, and my spirit: my body was trembling as though in convulsion.

"Who are you? *Who are you?*"

"Only a King's officer, fallen on hard times."

He was too close, too close. He sensed it, and straightened, leaving the damp towel on the table.

589

"Sleep if you can. I shall return at three."

The floorboards creaked until he reached the door. He seemed to pause there, as if waiting for something.

I said into the silence, "My name is Margaret Scott. And you?"

He said, "You may call me St. James," and left. I heard the key turn, with very little sound.

Impossibly, I slept.

He woke me. The light had changed, the tray and the jug had been taken, and a cloak that smelled indefinably of the sea had been laid over me.

"My God, will you drive me to death?"

"I regret it, but time is short. Make haste, if you please."

His haste was inexplicable: he did not harry me on the road, and a clear twilight had fallen before we entered Rye. In the afterlight a thrush sang, and another I had never heard.

He said, "Nightingales. They always sing in the churchyard at this time of the evening."

"Do you know this place?"

"I lived here."

The street was steep, cobbled, narrow, the houses half-timbered, the night, after the day's elusive warmth, damp, as though the sea were close. Although lights were burning ahead, it was almost fully dark.

"If you are very fortunate," the little, characteristic pause, "some one will kill me within the next few minutes, and all this will be nothing more to you than the watch that ends the night." Another pause, almost as though he smiled. "Assuming the identity of Lady Anne Villiers would serve you well in that instance."

"Is that what you want?"

"You might find yourself popular. I am not, here, at the moment." I sensed the pressure of his knee, and the bay's eager response. "Come, my dear. Let us go and test the warmth of the reception."

The inn was medieval, well-lighted, noisy; the stableyard at the rear was quieter, although lanterns were burning. He whistled a curious little tune as he dismounted, and what seemed to be a cellar door opened, revealing utter darkness. I knew that he had drawn one of the pistols from within his coat.

"Is there lamb tonight?"

And the answer, so peculiar that it must have been in code.

"Nay. Chance'll give us bread."

"Come," he said to me. "Quickly."

I stepped in beside him, and smelled sweat, neither his nor mine, the rank sweat of fear.

"Sweet Jesus... they said you was dead."

"Everything they said of me was a lie." I heard the soft exhalation. "Give us some light, there's a good lad."

A wick floating in an oyster shell revealed us, and the boy. He was fair-haired, fair-skinned; his eyes might have been dark by nature or dilated by his absolute fear. He kept wringing his hands; I now know the meaning of the expression. The man, St. James, did not notice or appear to notice this agitation.

"Jesus Christ, I'm perishing for a drink. And you, madam?"

"No... thank you."

"A dish of tea for my lady, and a glass of something for me." The boy hesitated, and again the vivid charm manifested itself. "Put it on my account, Lemuel. I'll settle with you sometime."

He did not speak while we were alone, and in that faint light his face was hidden from me. The boy returned, not with tea but with a steaming tankard of what smelled like negus.

"This was a-doing. I stole it."

St. James gave it to me, and I cupped my hands around it, grateful for its heat.

"Never mind. I thank you for it."

The boy said, "Tis a sin to steal."

I thought he sounded very tired.

"Yes, by God, I know."

I drank, knowing that I should share it with him, incapable of such intimacy.

"Has any one been to my house, Lemuel?"

"Rummagers was there on Wednesday. I seen 'em."

"Is any one there now?"

Strangely, both the boy and I knew what he intended.

"Oh, Captain, you dasn't go there now—"

He said, "Yes, I think I will," and the boy's response was instant and passionate.

"Nay, I'll go— you allus let me before." The smile was swift and beautiful. "I'll *fly!*"

He must have gone up through the taproom, where I assumed he was a potboy. Silence came, and the cold confinement of the cellar was smothering.

"How long...."

"He is the fastest runner I have ever known. He used to carry messages for me, before he saw the light."

"Is he a Methodist?"

591

"Yes. He was touched by the hand of God when Wesley preached here three years ago. His mother took him to the meeting— I went along too, for a joke. I enjoyed it immensely."

"You were not converted."

"No. But the music was very stirring."

Time, and the silence, went on.

"Do you trust him?"

"His father was in my business, like all his family. He was always true to me. His mother was my housekeeper. Now she's dead too, poor bitch."

I left the tankard near the glim in the oyster shell; after a moment or two he reached for it. The boy slipped back into the cellar very soon afterward, giving only a nod.

He said, "Well, madam, let us take the air," but he did not immediately move. "Lemuel—" and I sensed the boy's painful adoration. "I am going away, and I shall not come back. What I leave in the house is yours, so take what you want while you can. And I will give you Chess." There was a small, wounded interruption; he cut across it sharply. "Now listen to me, boy. Look for him on the Fairlight road, after dawn. And remember me."

His hand came down on the glim and crushed it out, and we left in darkness and in silence. I did not see the boy's face again.

The street climbed, and the cobbles were punishing. The moon had not yet risen.

"Leave the horses."

The nightingales in the churchyard were silent: the night was as cold as death.

"Come with me."

A low wall, the church on our right, overhanging, half-timbered houses, faint lights behind leaded panes. As we had climbed, so now we descended; toward the end of the street he released my arm.

"This is Watchbell Street. I used to walk down there, looking out toward the harbour in the evenings." The bruising pressure of his hand returned. "This is my house."

No lights. A small courtyard, a ghostly cluster of narcissi whose perfume tormented me.

After the night's clean darkness the interior was dead and cold. I heard him moving some piece of furniture against the door as if to ensure against interruption.

"Come with me."

"Let me stay here. Please. Please. I promise you."

"I would rather not."

I felt stairs: in the darkness of sense and memory, they became a familiar hell. I resisted him, and felt the response to my resistance, the application of strength: I refused the compulsion of his hands, and then I fought them, and for the first time cried out. He pulled me down, half lying, half sitting on the stairs, the dry hard palm over my mouth, his breath against my face. I felt the heavy beating of his heart, and then the hand on my cheek, my hair.

"Enough. Enough... don't force me to hurt you. Enough. Yes? Enough." The hand over my mouth withdrew; the other, on my hair, remained. "Now show me that tiger's heart again."

I allowed myself to be lifted, handled, compelled to walk and to climb; the darkness at the top of the stairs had acquired definition, the first faint greyness of moonlight. He did not speak, save once to swear to himself, as though he could not find what he wanted and dared not risk lighting the candle by which he might have found it. Then there was silence: I thought he had assembled what he had come for, perhaps clothing or personal effects. I heard the closing of what might have been an armoire, a metallic sound I could not identify, and then the hiss of drawn steel.

He came to the bed, on the edge of which I sat, the naked blade in his hand.

"Come, madam. My vanity is satisfied."

I said, "I will go no further with you."

He came no closer.

"I do not accept your refusal, and I have no time for this."

"I have money. Take it. Do what you want, and leave me."

"Madam, my time is very short. Believe me, I will kill you where you sit."

"I beg of you... St. James. I beg of you."

He said, so softly that I could not recognize the emotion in his voice, "For Christ's sake, stand up and come to me."

Fate touched me, the hand of God. The irrevocable moment passed. I rose and went to him.

In my dreams sometimes, I am still at Fairlight, where I witnessed the murder of a riding officer. I could not have prevented it, could not have warned him, could not have comforted him. In the seconds before the final thrust, he called St. James by his Christian name.

I could not have said how long we had been there, how much time had passed, how much passed afterwards, how long the lantern burned on the clifftop before it was answered by a flash from the sea.

Whatever the signal meant to him, he was preparing for departure. I saw the hand with its bloodied nails extending itself to me.

"Come down to the beach."

The moon was setting, there was no sign of dawn. The air was turbulent with salt and surf, and bitter cold: the sea was angry, limitless, invisible: the light vanished as if imagined. The hand entered the lamplight and rested on my shoulder; the spilled blood on his clothing revolted and obsessed me.

"Come, my brave girl."

My mind resisted; my coward's body craved life, and obeyed him.

He left the lantern burning, and I saw it from the sea. Impossible to remember the descent, only the sensation of falling, the pain in my hands, the bite of salt in the wounds, the shingle underfoot, the hissing tide around my ankles; the boat, the roughness of the sea. No one spoke, and there was nothing of him but the pressure of his arm and thigh and the gunwale against my back in the darkness.

I could not climb from a boat in that swell, but I did climb: had I fallen I would have drowned within seconds. He said only, "When I tell you," and I obeyed him, as in all other things. If those who waited on deck were surprised by my sex they did not comment in any recognizable language: he spoke to them in a fluent patois.

I remained close to the place where I had boarded, fighting the sickness and the motion, the noise in the darkness, a hard rain driving into my face, except the rain was the white burst of spray. Some one pulled me to my feet, into shelter. Others were there. A voice said in comprehensible French, "Shall we put the little one over the side?" and there was general laughter.

He said in French, without a trace of accent or the former patois, "Madame dislikes the sea, my friend. A man is never fortunate in his mistress."

He was closer than the others, and perhaps the only one who understood me although they must have heard my voice.

"Are you French, you bastard?"and felt his hands on my shoulders. The sea and the living thing that rode it threw my body against his.

"No, madam, but I learned it in a hard school. I was a prisoner of war for nine months. And these are very dangerous men, who have interrupted their dangerous affairs at my request. Show a little gratitude, if not for your own sake, then for mine."

The night drained away, and a flat sunless light came over that violent, shallow sea. I know now that she was a schooner out of Brest, that he paid for his passage and the unexpected extra, myself, with pieces of jewellery; that the passage, even for an experienced sailor, had been considered rough, and that the wind was contrary, and we stood off the coast of France for hours before it veered and we clawed into harbour. We had been at sea four days. I was ill and exhausted and the last vestige of dignity had been stripped from me.

Even then, he did not release me.

I remember only the sleet, obscuring like a curtain, hissing into the dreaded, dark water: the certainty that my hands would not support my weight, would not prevent me from falling. Sleet in my hair; an uncontrollable trembling.

My mind will give me no memory of how I reached the barque's great cabin: it gives me only what came afterward. It was not warm, but spaciousness embraced me: dark leather, a touch of gold on white paint, a smell of cleanliness. I remember no one else, only St. James, removing the sword belt and laying the sword in its scabbard across the bench seat beneath the salt-smeared windows, laying the pistols on the table; the sleet passing away; the reflection of the water thrown across the deckhead, illuminating the aquiline face. He was lying back in one of the deep leather chairs: like myself, he was filthy. I thought he slept, but when the youth arrived he opened his eyes, although he made no attempt to rise.

Their conversation did not concern me, although I was conscious of their attention. Then the boy withdrew, having called him Captain, like the other boy in another country, another life.

He said, "There will be coffee presently. And then, God willing, some sleep."

I did not ask if my journey was finished, my usefulness as a hostage at an end. It was finished for me. The deck moved beneath my feet. He might have been watching me. I thought not.

It balanced perfectly in my hand, the waterborne reflection shimmering on the exquisite inlay, the bluing, the gilt on the touch hole. It was a weapon of exceptional quality: the cock moved easily, the flashpan was lined with fine gold to prevent corrosion, the trigger required only the slightest pressure.

He pried it from my fingers, without anger, without shock, with no discernible emotion, speaking words beyond my deafness, unable to contain his blood. He had been holding me with great strength: now, gently, he released me. The other pistol, for myself or him, remained on the table, my intention, life or death, even then obscured, even to myself, as it is now.

II

Others, strangers, took me away. I did not resist.

It was late winter, and Biscay's initiation of me was cruel. The swaying lantern in the cabin was unlit and the port was sealed, the side damp with condensation, and the deck fell away at an insane angle. She was leaning into the sea with a strong wind on the quarter, and under a heavy press of sail: she plunged into the darkness, throwing me from my feet, forcing from me sickness, obscenities and prayers, when I would have preferred to remain suspended in shocked insensibility.

No one came, throughout the hellish night. Only she spoke to me, in the language of her element, the sound of the racing sea, the squeal of blocks, the bells striking a system of time I could not comprehend. Only the ship: the living motion, the nausea and terror in the blackness. There were no amenities except an unkempt cot like a suspended coffin, and a bucket, which had spilled my vomit across the sloping deck. Impossible that mere timber and mere flesh should sustain this punishment. The sea would break her, and break my mind and spirit, and take us together to our grave.

There was a single, muffled bell, no more. When sounds followed I ignored them until it seemed that the door was opening: when light penetrated my darkness I hid.

He was young, perhaps twenty; the faint glow behind him revealed the fairness of his hair. His clothing was rough and soaked with rain or spray, his hands fumbled at mine and were icy. After the foulness of hours, the cleanliness of the air spilling into the cabin was unbearable, and I wept.

He tried to lift me, but I resisted him, and I could not stand against the motion. Contact with the salt-soaked coldness of his body was like death to me, and as though that living, female spirit knew, she plunged and I fell, free of him.

He left me then, although he did not close me into the darkness again. When he returned St. James was with him. He, whom I had believed dead, lived; the hand that touched my face was cold, but strong and alive.

He spoke over his shoulder, crouched near me.

"Who was responsible for this?"

"Mr. Vaillancourt, sir. He said you wasn't to be disturbed."

The same face: the eyes, shadowed and intense, staring into mine.

"My quarters. Help me, Mark."

He said nothing to me.

Together they held me upright and took me out into the light, against the unchanging angle of the deck and its heavy rise and fall. I had no sense of direction, no sense of anything. We reached the stern cabin, where I had left him in the stench of powder and burned cloth and blood: here, too, there was light, and spaciousness, and a greater vibration; the sounds of the ship were louder, the sound of the sea was less. And then his sleeping cabin, the cot in the restless light: the coverings had been disturbed, and it seemed more closely to resemble a coffin. The other man was compelling me to sit, attempting to unfasten my coat; the coat and my hair were fouled with vomit. I resisted the hands until they became one hand, St. James's left hand, resting on mine. He did not restrain me but I became quiet, and leaned forward, covering my face. I heard him ask for brandy. The other man brought it, then left us alone.

He offered it to me, and held the glass to my lips. He was cleanly dressed in a white shirt and pale breeches, and coatless despite the cold; he did not once use his right arm, or refer to the injury. He offered the brandy once more, and although he held the glass for me he did not attempt to touch me again.

Finally he said, "These are my private quarters. No matter what you may have seen, or what you think of me, you are safe here. Do you understand?"

The deck shuddered, lifted, fell: there were shouts, and what might have been running feet. He ignored them, watching me. The lantern overhead threw his face into relief, and then into shadow.

"Safe?"

"Yes."

"That word has no meaning for me."

Shadow, light, shadow again. He did not avert his eyes from my face.

"You told me you would make me regret that night. I do regret it." The angle of the deck increased a little, as though the wind had freshened: his body accepted the motion unconsciously. "I hope you may find some comfort here."

His hand rested then, only once, on the bulkhead as he turned to leave me.

"If you need me, call to me. I will not be far away."

There was clean water in his cabin: in time, I managed to use it. I left the clothing in which I had lived and slept for a week lying on the deck. The linen in the cot was clean, if damp, the pillow faintly scented with bay rum. The motion was heavy, the vibration stronger. In sickness and exhaustion, I slept.

In the night and in the grey filtering of dawn the great cabin remained unoccupied, the deep leather chairs bloomed with moisture. The spiralling lanterns were extinguished with morning, but he was never there.

When I emerged from his sleeping cabin it was neither night nor morning, but, by the strong light, late afternoon. He was sprawled on the bench seat beneath the opened stern windows, with a faded blue coat across his shoulders: his eyes were closed, his head turned as though he found the cold wind in his hair refreshing. His left hand balanced a cup on the seat; his right arm lay across his thigh.

He opened his eyes, and sat upright when he saw me, then he stood. He looked very drawn, as though he had not slept.

"You do my poor wardrobe honour, madam."

"I had nothing else to wear."

"Your clothing has been laundered. It will be returned, perhaps today, perhaps tomorrow." Then, "Will you take coffee with me?"

He assumed my acquiescence and moved to arrange it, stooping to avoid the beams. Over his shoulder he said, "I advise you not to look at the sea. Others may tell you to watch the horizon... I find that beneficial only in the open air."

I sat where he had been sitting with the salt wind in my hair, shivering in the damp shirt from the wardrobe, shoeless, my legs drawn up and naked in his breeches. The clouds were painted with a late, deep sun, the sky was hard, the sea shark-blue and serrated with white. The wake was dispersing in hissing foam across the miles between myself and England.

We drank coffee in a strange, dead silence, as though every question and answer and accusation had been exhausted, and emotion was now superfluous.

The light was changing: it seemed an eastern sky, neither winter nor spring. The shadows on the sea's face were deeper. Neither he nor I had moved. The coffee and the cups were cold.

"What will you do with me?"

"When we reach Jamaica I shall place you in the care of my friends, who are infinitely more respectable than I. You will return to England from there. I will, of course, pay for your passage, and anything else you require. In the meantime I offer you my protection, and my inadequate apology." Silence, in which the sounds of ship and sea were not intrusive. "I could not have left you at Fairlight. I chose not to leave you in France. I could not guarantee your safety."

"And you guarantee it now."

"In this ship my protection is absolute. You have my word upon it."

"You would have killed me in England."

"You would have killed me, or yourself. I recognized the extremity of your situation. Please accord me the same courtesy." A strange, strained little pause. "I have shown you the worst of my nature. It was never my intention."

So still: so dead a silence: so ineradicable by mere words the offenses and the terror.

"He called you by name."

"He was a friend of mine."

The drawn, angular profile revealed nothing, neither regret nor grief. He stood, bending to avoid the deckhead beams, and seemed to hesitate, but he did not speak again, and the language of his silence remained unknown.

***

In the night my demons came, repressed but unforgotten; there was no light and no escape. I tried to climb from the coffin's confinement and fell heavily. The bruised mind screamed long after the exhausted body had been subdued.

I remember him now: I still see it: I hear his voice. The sounds in the outer cabin, where the dropped quill spattered ink over the page, the scrape of the chair, the sudden opening of the door, and him, faceless and unrecognized, concealed by the shadows. Shaking me, embracing me, restraining me, none of these things.

"Who has hurt you? Tell me, tell me...."

I struck him with all my strength, my fists blind weapons against the violation of his touch. Screaming at him, "You... you... you..." until my arms were dead weights, and the black stain spreading through his sleeve was the blood of the opened wound. He had endured every blow in silence. He remained kneeling on the deck with me, as though we had struggled for hours, the sharpness of his breathing the only indication of pain. I had not once struck him with a feminine conscience: he had not once reciprocated as a man.

It was not possible to speak, to release grief, betrayal, terror. I had no more tears.

He said, "Why this? Why now?"

"Because... you took my life." Silence. Pity: compassion: no understanding. Perhaps he thought I was insane; perhaps I was. "So many years... I tried. So many years. Now my life is a bloody wound, and you expect me to forgive you. You expect me to forget—"

He said, after an infinite silence, "Come and have a drink with me. I need it. I think you need it, too."

The spirit in the glass assumed the angle of the deck; the single lantern threw its restless light. The faded blue coat swung gently from the back of the chair: it gave no warmth, even draped over my shoulders. The vibration was more marked, and he raised his head as though listening. The ship was trembling, the sound altered; the vibration increased, poised, and the level of the spirit changed, the brandy climbed the opposite curve of the glass. The trembling ceased.

"Changing tack," he said.

"Why do you drive so blindly through the night?"

"No sailor is blind at night on the sea, and not often on the land, either."

"Do you never sleep?"

"I slept between midnight and three. My habits are largely nocturnal, and I like to see the dawn come up."

He leaned against the desk. The blood was drying, stiffening.

"Your...."

"It's nothing. I've had far worse."

"Do you carry a surgeon?"

"I don't need a surgeon. All I need is a touch of the sun." He drained his glass: it slid gently, with the quill, on the polished leather, so far and no further. "I want you to eat something. You owe me that, at least."

I closed my eyes until it came. Perhaps those who served him were accustomed to his peculiarities, or loved him, and forgave him them. It was brought to the door on a tray some quarter of an hour later, and strangely, movingly, as he had before, he served me. The bread was very slightly stale, the wine a good claret.

"When you were a child—"

The discreet, disturbing service ceased. He was listening.

"Were you punished for using your left hand?"

"I was rarely punished, and certainly not for that. I had a happy childhood, and although I was aware of animosity between my parents they were reasonably affectionate toward me."

"Where?"

"Bombay. My father sold his soul to the East India Company. They paid him back with rubies and cholera. Eventually my mother left him. He remained in India until he died."

"And your mother?"

"She died in Florence many years ago, after a series of affairs, including one with my father's brother. From time to time she wrote to me, then I went to sea and her letters were lost." A slight smile: there was self-mockery in it. "Her darling boy never saw her again."

"How old were you?"

"I was ten when she left. My father volunteered me for service aboard a company ship before I was eleven. When I returned to Bombay I persuaded him to allow me to be sponsored as a midshipman, which was what I had always wanted." Reflection, introspection, passing quickly. "The navy was my only home, apart from the last years in Rye."

"And you threw it away."

"I had no choice. The war ended, there were no ships. I had been wounded— I was told that I had not recovered. And I had offended some one, so gravely that no matter how complete my recovery or how many ships became available, there would never be one for me. After eighteen months of poverty and humiliation I heard the unspoken message, and I left. It was the only course that remained to me."

"You could have returned to India."

"I found other employment. I enjoyed it."

600

The light between us had altered. The night was draining away.

".... You have no wife."

"No. I was never married." An odd stillness. "And you?"

"Yes."

"Are you widowed?"

"No."

He said, "My sins are compounded," and moved from the desk. I did not see his face. After a moment he brought me a clean linen napkin from the tray; I hardly saw it, was aware only of the essential kindness of the gesture.

"You should have had children."

"Yes, I would have liked that." Then he said, without emotion, "I have a son, who followed me into the Royal Navy. He is twenty-two years old. He does not bear my name." The faded blue coat, discarded gently by me, lay on the deck, and he leaned down for it; for a moment the practised, expressionless mask revealed pain. The blood was very distinct in the strengthening light.

"Would you care to come on deck?" And then the smile, faint, dismissive, slightly cynical. "Perhaps not... it can be cold at this hour. If you sit there, you will see the dawn."

I heard his voice later, and the muffled responses of the watchkeepers, a little, relieved laughter as though his presence reassured them. Perhaps, like me, he was alone when dawn came: perhaps, like me, he watched it, illuminating the limitless, bitter solitude of the sea.

Perhaps, like me, he believed in the irrevocable moment, when loneliness is ended.

She was the *Ladywynd*, a three-masted barque of six hundred tons, built in Toulon in 1772 to his specifications, and named as a gesture toward his property in Jamaica, although I did not then know of its existence, or believe implicitly in the truth of anything he told me.

She was the instrument of my passage, both temporal and spiritual; she was a microcosm, and the faces of her world, which was briefly mine, remain with me still. Mark David Ransom and Vaillancourt, whose Christian name I never knew, Hook, Fisher, Chatto the boatswain, Bloom the gunner, Brichot, Grieve, Chretien, Harris the messman, wounded into silence by the memories of his battles. He was sometimes found folding and refolding my clothes, and, once, holding a garment of mine to his face as though he imagined it perfumed; he never spoke, unless in response to a direct question from St. James.

The others were nameless, a crew of thirty men, some of whom watched me with lust or contempt, some of whom turned away from me, effacing themselves, unwilling to be examined or remembered. To them I was the enigma, the intruder, for whose sake they were disciplined, forbidden to swear or spit or strip or piss in the scuppers as I passed: some, if not all, must have speculated on the nature of my relationship with St. James. There was no question of insult or insinuation: he would not have tolerated it, as he did not long tolerate the festering animosity between Vaillancourt and myself. He would not humiliate a subordinate in the presence of the men, but it was generally known that he had required an apology from Vaillancourt for his treatment of me that first evening, and that Vaillancourt had refused.

Nothing in his past, which had been privileged, had prepared him for St. James's response, and I, who had hesitantly accepted the conversations, the impeccable manners, the illusion of the gentleman, was perfectly capable of understanding that accidents at sea were not uncommon, and that if the apology were not tendered at once Vaillancourt would not reach his destination. Vaillancourt apologized. Instinct warned me to accept it, and, sickened by the coercion, I withdrew.

I dined alone that night and retired early, although sleep eluded me, and I was very aware of St. James's voice and movements in the great cabin an hour or two later.

"Has Mrs. Scott turned in?" No answer from Harris, only a clatter of cutlery. "Speak up, man, I'm not a mind-reader." And then, after a brief interval, "There is *nothing* wrong with it. Just take it away."

Three bells struck; there had been no other sound. He was sitting in the place we both favoured, on the bench seat, when I opened the door. I passed through the great cabin to the quarter gallery privy without acknowledging him, although he rose when he saw me and remained standing, stooped, until I returned, then he sat again with the brandy he was drinking. His coat this evening was newer, unfaded, and for the first time since his injury he had put his right arm into the sleeve.

"You keep your distance, madam, both physically and in spirit. Do I shock you so much?"

"You have made an enemy of him."

"He's a child. I'm not frightened of children. And I will not suffer you to be abused, in word or deed, by any one."

"You told me he had killed in France, with an indiscretion even the French found impossible to ignore. Those were your words."

"We're all killers in this ship. The only languages we understand are violence and the sea."

He leaned back and closed his eyes: the coppery hair was dishevelled, the patches of white at the temples very apparent. The cold sun and wind had burned his face; his was skin that would rapidly tan, despite its fairness, but he did not look well.

I could not bring myself to call him by his name.

"Are you in pain?"

He gave me one of those smiles, which could be so cynical and so poignant.

"Pain is a sailor's lot, my dear. It will pass." The smile did not linger. "Perhaps you would take a glass of brandy with me?"

I accepted it, and did not drink. He did not sit with me but paced slowly, restlessly.

"I have made a grave error, madam, which I find surprising in myself. I have come to anticipate our meetings with a certain pleasure, and to resent the withdrawal of your company. I saw it in your face this afternoon. I was disturbed by it."

I said nothing. He had reached his desk: he left the glass there, where it slid gently, spilling a little. He remained there, touched by the swaying light and the procession of shadows.

"From time to time... in the past week, you have allowed me the privilege of... not knowledge, but speculation. Your guard is almost impenetrable... but, very occasionally, I have been sensible of the woman behind it. This afternoon the deadness came into your face again. I value our peculiar acquaintance, and I ask that you not retreat into a fear of me which is unfounded."

He turned his back and walked around the desk; the glass moved very slightly, and the deck, the world which encompassed us. Then he said, "There are some things for you on the table. If you don't want them, pitch them over the side."

Eight shirts, neatly folded, of heavy white silk.

"Surely these are yours."

"They were made for you."

"But the silk was for some one else."

"They are for you, and they were made for you. I regret that they are only shirts. I thought you wouldn't care to have underclothes sewn by a common seaman."

"You are very kind."

His eyes came sharply to my face, very cold, very blue, very guarded. Then he said, "Too many ghosts, too many memories. I don't want to be alone tonight. Come and walk with me."

There was no light on deck, nothing but the flickering flame at the compass box. The wind, which had been fresh, had backed and fallen, and the swell was heavy but unbroken; there was no sound but the sea, and the ship's passage across dark waters, then some one said, "Tis a fair night, Captain," and I sensed that he was staring up at the sails.

"Aye. It is."

Then, as though I was visible to those beyond the compass light, the same voice spoke to me, warning the others of my presence.

"Good evening, missus."

"Good evening, Mr. Ransom."

I saw now, by the light of many stars: the night was a myriad of stars, their beauty beyond words. I saw the bony, elegant face in the compass light, the casual glance at the card; then he returned to me.

"Look aft, and see the moonrise."

He left me alone to watch it: perhaps he sensed the effect it had upon me. He paced the weather side, in a private reverie that was disturbed by no one, until the moon had risen fully, and laid the path of its light across the water, and touched our faces and the great driver overhead, and threw my shadow across the bleached deck, and illuminated all heaven: we sailed in silence, in the immensity of the night. Then he returned, and stood, not close, in profile to me at the taffrail.

I said, "Do you fear the sea?"

"No. I've never been afraid of anything, not death, not dying, not the sea."

"Then you are blessed."

"I don't think so."

"Who is Vaillancourt?"

"He is titled, he is a former French naval officer, and his true name is not Vaillancourt. I am carrying him only as a favour to his father, who behaved with honour and humanity toward me and other prisoners of war in Toulon." The smile, fainter still by moonlight. "I was also well paid, which would not dissuade me from disposing of him if the situation required it."

Time passed: the light on the sea was almost blinding.

"Where is he bound?"

"I carry him only as far as Jamaica. He can proceed from there to hell with my blessing."

"I thought he was an associate of yours."

There was a short, I thought amused, silence.

"No, Mr. Vaillancourt never dabbled in such bourgeois pursuits. Although I believe he intends to peddle his sword to certain radical factions, whose dedication to equality may offend his sensibilities."

"You speak of America."

"She casts a long shadow. The wise man takes note of it."

"And you, do you take note of it?"

"War was my business for thirty years. Men may talk of peace, but there is no peace. And there will be no peace." Then he said, "There is a great melancholy in spring, don't you think. A great yearning for something. One feels very alone sometimes." I said nothing. "I never thought that I would miss England when I left— as I knew I would leave— perhaps not so precipitately, but inevitably. I think what disturbs me most is that you will return to England, and I will not. I will not see an English spring again."

"And all this will be nothing more to me than the watch that ends the night."

"How strange that you should remember that. I would rather you forgot."

He turned slightly, as though toward me, and no further.

"Did you live long in Rye?"

"Longer than anywhere. I went there from Haslar... one of my officers had a house. I became fond of it. I leased the house in Watchbell Street after I found employment." A touch of sarcasm. "I became fond of that, too, which is some measure of retribution."

"You could return."

"To what? There's nothing for me in England but the rope's end. There never was."

"Why did you do it, then?"

"It was better than being a broken-down hero, entertaining the customs with threadbare lies about the seige of Louisbourg— or how I took Quebec with Wolfe."

It was very still.

"Did you?"

"The paths of glory led him to the grave. Mine were less exalted. Yes. I was there, in *Lightning*. And at Havana, in *Bacchante*— and *Bacchante* was almost the end of me. I told you there were too many ghosts tonight."

"Did you know a ship called *Telemachus*?"

The moon was high and cold now; time had passed, and its passage was not remembered.

"I think I knew her. Who served in her?"

"A friend of mine."

"Then he was fortunate."

"He was killed."

"He was still fortunate." Then, "You ask me questions no one has ever asked. I never thought I could answer them, or would care to."

"Surely... there were women...."

"Yes, and some of them were good friends to me. But friendship dies, passion dies. Love is not immortal. That was a lesson I learned rather late in life. I would think you've learned it too, as your marriage was a failure."

"You presume."

"Do I?"

It was unanswerable; it seemed there were no more words.

The light was grey; my clothing was damp, my body ached. His voice seemed deeply fatigued.

"How long since I've seen any beauty in the night. I thank you for that, and for your company."

"My... questions have been intrusive. I apologize for them. Your past is your own affair."

"The past is a country to which no one returns, and the future is a risk, and a dream. I have the present. It's enough." Overhead, the great driver quivered, and dew fell from the canvas: the wind had changed: the night and its dark introspection were passing. The smile was as faint as ever, the enigma as compelling. " 'To be sure I lose the fruits of the earth, but then I am gathering the flowers of the Sea.' "

"Are they your words?"

"Boscawen's. He was my admiral at Louisbourg."

He did not speak to me again, or speak my name, nor I his, when I left him. I did not look back: I could not bear the consciousness of his eyes upon me. There were truths here I could not contemplate, not his, but my own.

On the morning of Tuesday March twenty-second we were many miles south of Bermuda, close-hauled against a strong southerly wind. The sea was blue-green, given an appearance of shallowness by unseen weed: the chart marked this illusion. There were more than four thousand fathoms beneath the keel. For a ship there was safety in the sea's abyss, no reefs, no shoals, no secrets: for me there were other, unimaginable depths, and I feared them. I feared St. James. I feared myself, and what the long starvation of my soul had made, and if I had not known that my acute sensitivity in his presence had become sexual awareness, the knowledge was given to me that morning; and, I think, was given to him.

We had shared the quarter gallery with delicacy and precision, and he had never occupied it when I required it; and at that hour he was invariably on deck, where he spent most of the day. But he was not on deck: the louvred door swung open to the lively motion, and I saw him, naked to the waist, disposing of the dressings which had covered his wound, and the wound itself, an angry, healing furrow across the right biceps. But it was not the wound, nor his naked skin, nor the slimness, almost slightness of his torso, but the scars... many savage scars, as though the body had been disembowelled. I might have spoken, or recoiled, or made some sound of revulsion or apology:

I remember only that his eyes held mine without embarrassment or reserve. I did not wonder that he did not fear death.

"Havana," he said.

For two years I had not wept for any one but myself, and now, for him, for a resurrected stranger and the stigmata of his pain, tears came. I turned away from the light, but not from him.

Perhaps he would have spoken again, or smiled and dismissed it, or me. I knew only that there was a muffled sound in the companionway, and then a voice calling to him. His shirt was lying on the deck; he leaned down for it, and the sharpness of his response might have been interpreted as the interruption of a greater intimacy than mere conversation.

"Yes?"

"Sail in sight, sir. Due south."

"I'll come up."

He said nothing more to me. It was half past nine in the morning.

They were all on deck when I went up, right forward, with telescopes trained on the horizon. Vaillancourt ignored me and ostentatiously shifted his position; Mark Ransom had the watch. St. James had withdrawn into the reticent vigilance I had observed in him in England: there was caution here, and deliberate assessment. Whatever communion I had imagined between us had passed, and was forgotten.

The tension was palpable. Men attempted with naked eyes to see what was only a flaw in the lens, perhaps friend, perhaps enemy; all normal activity had ceased. There was no sound but the crack of canvas, and, watching St. James, I saw the flicker of irritation although he did not lower the telescope.

"Let her fall off a point." The noise ceased. "This is not a holiday, gentlemen. Go about your business."

Men drifted away, dissociating themselves from their companions, assuming attitudes of disinterest. He closed the glass and rested it on his shoulder. "Mr. Ransom, the newcomer is a brig, one of ours. Show her our colours, and if she speaks acknowledge her. If not, let her pass."

He came aft: the others dispersed except Vaillancourt, who remained, a small figure in an ill-fitting coat, drenched in spray, staring into the south.

"Madam, if you have letters to write, I suggest you write them now."

I had known it would come, that this unreal solitude must be broken, the tenuous link between us severed by the intrusion of the world. I had not anticipated this disquiet at the severance.

I spoke his name, and was surprised by the repressive coldness of his manner.

"How long?"

He said, "In time to interfere with my noon sights," and left me.

The seven bells of half past eleven were carried away on the wind. I went up, and stood near him in silence: the guns were running with spray, the scarlet ensign was at the peak. I wondered if the essence of this moment had changed, the anticipation, the calculation, the excruciating slowness and inevitability of the bloody embrace.

He said, without turning, "You can see with what alacrity your courier approaches."

"I have no letters. I cannot write of the enormity of what has happened, to a woman who might be dead by now."

He did not look away from the brig's approach: she had altered course, and no telescope was necessary to see her black and buff hull, the commissioning pendant streaming stiffly forward with the southerly wind that drove her; but I sensed that his attention was diverted.

"And what interpretation must I put upon that remark?"

"She was dying when I left her." His profile remained immobile. "I assumed you were familiar with her condition, as it was clearly she whom you sought as a hostage that night."

"I wanted Harlesdon. I would have slit his throat. And it is not the time for a discussion of this subject." There were figures visible on the brig's deck, vivid white and faded blue; she was carrying all sail, and plunging heavily. "See how she remains to windward. The wise enemy always takes the wind gage, and attempts to hold it throughout every engagement." He snapped the telescope shut: the brig was shortening sail, taking in all but her forecourse and topsails. "It would seem that our martial young friend wishes to speak." And, raising his voice very slightly, "Mr. Ransom, return the compliment. Fore and main courses, I think."

When it came, the voice was young and distorted, projected through a speaking trumpet across the intervening water as she rolled sickeningly toward us. Her single line of gunports was awash, which I sensed amused him.

"What ship?"

"*Ladywynd*, out of Brest."

"We are His Majesty's ship *Teazer*. Where are you bound?"

"Bridgetown."

It was a lie, or perhaps he had lied to me. I said nothing. I saw the speaker now, a lieutenant, hatless, with a fair, English face; I saw them all, the laggards and the hardened, the felons, the pressed men, prisoners of the service and of the life they followed, condemned to the sea, knowing nothing but the sea. I saw their faces aboard the brig, and reflected in some peculiar, mirrored dimension in the men around me.

"What are you carrying?"

St. James, beside me, murmured, "You impertinent young bastard," then he raised the speaking trumpet again.

"Madeira, claret, a little silk— and building materials."

"You have no intention of entering Boston?" He made a dismissive gesture of his hand. "The port is closed as of June the first. Until the damned government compensates us for the tea." A short pause. "How many days out of Brest?"

"Fourteen."

"You made damned good time. There is ugly weather south southwest of you. Take heed of it."

"Thank you. I will watch my glass."

"I wish you a safe passage."

"And I wish you speedy promotion."

There was a very youthful grin: the faded blue arm came up in salute. He returned it.

I said, "How do you dare to say so within his captain's hearing?"

He said, "He is the captain."

He turned away. Mark David Ransom had been listening.

"Very well, Mr. Ransom, let us curtsey and leave the dance." There was corresponding activity aboard the brig: the boy in the sun-faded uniform was gesturing, anonymous figures were aloft. For a moment he watched them with a curious stillness in his eyes, then he said abruptly, "Come, sir, let her fly— I'll not be shown up by some unseasoned luff. Get the t'gallants on her."

The bitter wind drove me below. He remained where he was, and later moved to the taffrail to watch the brig beating northeast to the horizon, until she was a vision that passed into obscurity, and, like all her sisters, was lost to him.

The night was violent, and the dreams. I sought the light because I needed its comfort, and perhaps because I sensed St. James's presence, drawn to him out of my personal darkness, as though he were not danger but refuge.

The light seemed very faint, and the air was cold, damp, with a bitter scent of coffee. There was a chart open on the desk and his head was bent over it; the whirling light revealed the wetness of his hair. The deck plunged suddenly, and the sound of the rudder was erratic: he raised his eyes, in shadowed sockets, and watched me cross from handhold to handhold.

"What is happening?"

"A touch of weather. The glass is falling."

"By very much?"

"Yes. Considerably."

I had reached him; his chair, at least, was motionless.

"What will you do?"

"It depends. I could lie to, but that would be very unpleasant, particularly for you." The shadowed light flung itself over the chart and receded, then returned. "I shall probably come about. It's always safer to run with the wind."

"Tell me where we are."

His shadow fell with the light across the chart. We were the culmination of the pencilled lines and the neat calculations, in a sea beyond the measure of fathoms.

"Here. This is an approximation, taking into consideration our position at noon yesterday— or more or less at noon, as our sights were interrupted— and the wind, and the deviation of the current. I could tell you more precisely if I could see the stars."

I said, "Nothing is a mystery to you. All is known, all is calculated," and was conscious of his stillness, and a dissonant roaring beyond the timbers of this world, which was the fury of the sea.

He said, "That is a mystery to me, and an entity. It suffers us to pass, and sometimes it demands a sacrifice. Its behaviour is not predictable. And the winds change, and the position of the stars is not immutable— they alter with the seasons, and with latitude. Only the relationship between the sea and the sailor and the stars is eternal."

"Like the woman who stands under an infinite heaven, on land she believes she knows, and the land and heaven conspire to destroy her."

In the silence there was rain or hail or spray against the darkened glass: our ghostly reflections were there as they had been in other nights, other worlds, in the angry prelude to other storms, in an imitation of intimacy.

"Who are you, Margaret?"

"I am a lost soul. I have no resting place."

"Why didn't you write to your friend?"

"My only friends are dead."

He came around the desk, but no closer, as though he sensed that his use of my name had been violation enough.

"Is she your mother?"

For him, who had never even seen me smile, it must have seemed a travesty of bitterness. He would never understand why I laughed: a hundred hours of this spurious companionship would not suffice to explain it.

"When you return to England, will you go back to her? Or to the soldier?"

"If you knew him, you would know he was in Halifax. My place is not with him."

"I thought you were his mistress."

"He was my guardian."

"It sometimes goes by that name."

"I was never his mistress. I believed he was my father."

"Then he's a bloody fool."

"I don't wish to know your thoughts, or your speculations on my private life."

"Is that why you married?"

"I married for love."

"Yes, and love looks like death out of your eyes. You must think me insensitive as well as criminal."

She seemed to shudder, and the deck fell away. The furniture, shackled to ringbolts, did not move, but the shuttered lantern overhead strained out and swung wildly, and the crystal glasses in their case, although restrained, smashed against one another. The chart and quills and heavy silver standish slid from the desk. Had I not been seated, I would have fallen with her.

He said, "I'm going up. I'll come to you when I can."

"St. James—" He was already at the door, with the oilskin dripping over his arm. "Let me come on deck with you."

"I can't allow it."

I said, "Don't leave me. I'm afraid," and he paused there: the pitching shadows gave only a chiaroscuro impression of the windburned face and the tense, exhilarated smile.

"You? You have more courage than a soldier of the line."

When one is in terror the moments of truth are endless, and mine endured for hours, while death clawed the night and the sea sought her sacrifice. The lantern smoked and showered me with burning tallow, the skylight leaked and the drops were salt; in the darkness beyond the coaming the companionway streamed water, not rain but the sea. In her bowels the pumps began. She was running before it, under driver and jib and topgallants alone: further attempts to reef were defeated, and the heavy seas into which she smashed swept one man overboard and threw a helmsman from the wheel. The shock of her uncontrolled breach to the wind communicated itself even to me. And in the seconds before others threw their weight on the wheel, my life, all our lives, were ephemeral, balanced on the strength of a breaking wave, and in the hand of God. The night and the moment and the dark world that encompassed me hung, and seemed to hang, and his sword fell from its hooks on the bulkhead, and the chair at the desk slammed forward; and then, with her timbers almost a human protest, she lifted. The sword in its scabbard slid toward me, the crystal smashed in its case, and the unsecured drawers of the desk slid open and spilled their contents: bullets, sealing wax, cigars, a pocket pistol, a silver card case, letters and objects that could not be recognized, or reached or replaced while I was unable to stand.

There was no dawn, only a greyness straining through the salt-caked glass, the bells were heard again, the slide removed from the skylight although neither sky nor person was visible. There were shards of crystal on the soaking canvas, his sword lay where it had fallen, his letters were blurred and scattered, the detritus of an unknown past into which I desired no invitation. I imagined a lessening of the sea's fury: perhaps this was so. The wind was still violent, but her movements, although heavy, were stable: she was carrying more sail.

Deadened with the aftermath of fear, I could not have moved, but when the sound came I seemed bodiless, beyond the pain of bruised flesh and acute self-knowledge. It was Harris, mute, intractable and soaked to the skin, with a pot of coffee and a single cup.

"Cap'n sent un," he said, and left me.

I drank it, and later slept; there were sounds and voices, of the sea and the living ship, but they did not disturb me. And no nightmare tore my sleeping mind, and no dream.

Once more she turned her white, serene face to the south, with gilded eyes on a blinding horizon, and with her, child of the north that I was, I entered eternal summer.

We crossed the Tropic of Cancer on the thirty-first of March. Now, favoured by the northeast trades, we averaged two hundred and forty miles a day, through an unsurpassable sea. By day there were dolphins, by night phosphorescence, in which I took a childish pleasure; the noon sun burned, the darkness was sudden, lit by distant, soundless storms or the thousand unknown stars beyond the rigging. There was beauty and coolness at dawn, when I sometimes rose and walked with St. James, and respite from the curious eyes of others in the indigo shadows of the dusk. Degrees of intimacy existed now, as the degrees of latitude had diminished. I had not sought them, but I was utterly dependent upon him, even for dressings when I menstruated. I had nothing and no one but him.

His behaviour toward me remained irreproachable. He never failed to greet me with pleasure and solicitude, or to provide me with what comfort was possible, but he did not force his presence upon me, or intrude upon my privacy. There was no physical contact between us, not even the most casual touch, no shadow of innuendo in his conversation, and the absence of invitation, or apparent interest, in one who was both virile and isolated was very marked: so marked that I knew it was deliberate.

We lived together, we dined together, we passed the hours of the nights in conversations which have become precious in my memory, and a skein of time allotted to us unravelled and was lost, in the turn of a glass, in the streaming of the log, in the wake of a thousand sea miles.

It was evening: it was the first of April; we were east of the Caicos Islands, with the hundred fathoms of the Mouchoir Bank to leeward. He was smoking, in the darkness at the taffrail; he had seemed happy, and now was oddly subdued.

Eight bells struck. Twilight had long vanished, and the moon, nearing the full, had not yet risen. The cigar glowed and faded and he threw it into the sea.

"I intend to enter the Windward Passage tomorrow. I expect to make landfall on Sunday."

"Then it is finished."

"The watch that ends the night. Yes."

"And you are content."

"On the contrary, I find myself becoming extremely melancholy. I think of all my actions, this has the greatest finality. There is no return. I find that difficult to accept."

"There was no return from the first night you dealt in contraband. That was the end of your safety."

"My life has never been safe. What life is safe? Is yours?"

"If it were, I should not be here."

"It was written," he said. "I believe in fate. Do you?"

"I believe in the doctrine of predestination. My survival was preordained. There seems no other reason for it."

He said, "My dear," and paused, as though it had surprised even him. "I never meant you any harm."

"The harm was done. It was not by you." Darkness on the dark sea, no moonlight to reveal his face to me. "Will you never go back?"

"No. I shall never return."

"What will you do?"

"Oh, I shall become a grocery captain, plying my peaceful trade from here to America."

"And if your peace is broken? Will you seek a letter of marque?"

His hands were resting a few inches from mine on the taffrail, where the day's heat lingered.

"Not in this lady. I built her for speed, and for the trade, not as cannon fodder. And war is a young man's game. I am no longer young.... No, I shall observe the proceedings with interest, and perhaps gamble against the outcome. And what will you do?"

"I shall write, and remember."

"It would be inappropriate to request that... occasionally you might write to me."

"I think it would be unwise."

"I think I agree." And he laughed: I had not known that so charming a sound could seem so inimitably bitter. "Poor old Saint James, so many sins.... I shall become a leathery old man with white hair sailing a skiff among the islands, drinking rum and dreaming of old glories, and what never was, and was never written." The moon was rising: I could have seen his face, but there was privacy in the sea, and I sensed that he sought it also. "Does the soldier love you?" Voices murmured where the compass light burned, behind our backs, in another world. They did not intrude upon us, or upon the silence between us. "I thought so."

He had moved, turned; I saw the fine profile now faintly in the growing light, lifted to the sails overhead. If what he saw there displeased him, he did not speak.

"Where is she now, the woman you loved?"

"When last I heard she was in Antigua, where her husband was lieutenant-governor. And I never loved her. The self-immolation of love has never appealed to me."

"Was it merely cold seduction, then?"

"It was a mutual seduction. She was younger than I, and I, difficult though this may be to credit, was almost as virginal as she. She was a passenger in *Conquest*, my first frigate. She was my admiral's wife."

He paused. Perhaps memory was sweet, perhaps insidious, an enemy and an assault, as it was for me.

"I was a captain at twenty-six. I was posted in '51. My son was born the following year. The affair continued for seven years." Another pause; this time it was bitter. "My son was raised as another man's heir, my inamorata decided, eventually, that life on a post-captain's pay did not appeal, and the cuckolded spouse attained a position of power in Admiralty, from which it pleased him to destroy me. He could not harm her, either physically or financially, because she far outranked him, and he, how may we charitably put it, feared the frown of the great. The humble post-captain was easier meat."

The moon had risen, and its light touched what I could not... his face.

"I was very conscious of my disgrace. If I could have been dispatched to the ends of the earth it would have been done. Fortunately, the war came— and Louisbourg, and Quebec, and Martinique, and eventually Havana, and *Bacchante*. And *Bacchante*, which I was given for my sins, was almost as old as myself and had the disposition of a syphilitic whore. Still, she was a happy ship, God damn her."

He was silent, staring at the sea.

"I never knew how many died that day.... I remember holding a middy's hand... sitting, holding the hand, although I had been standing... and his head lay against my leg... and his lips were moving, although he had been decapitated. One of my officers was dismembered... I only knew him by his hair. His face had been peeled away like a mask... a thick, bloody mask. I tried to speak, and I found that my mouth and nostrils were clogged with shreds of human flesh. That was my holy communion, with the flesh and blood of my friends.... I was not aware then of what had happened to me... I had months afterwards in which to contemplate it. I used to wake up weeping, for myself and for them, because I held myself responsible. And then I came to understand that they were to be envied. After the ignominy of their deaths, they were at peace, and it was I who was condemned to a restless immortality."

He turned, the moonlight at his back.

"Cuba is out there, off the starboard bow. You won't see it, or that other damned place Haiti. But I shall always feel it in these waters, like a summoning of ghosts."

"We carry our ghosts with us, in our hearts."

"That's true. And when you go you'll be another, and what was unwritten in our lives will haunt me more than all the blood I ever shed. And you will be the sweetest of my ghosts."

So he said. So he was, to me.

At half past seven on the evening of Palm Sunday, April third, I set foot upon the coral sand of Jamaica, and, with him, entered paradise.

III

Like all my dreams, Jamaica is an illusion, a sanctuary only of ghosts, her peace precarious, her gracious prosperity built on blood and human sacrifice. All who come to this island are enslaved, the whites to the cane and the market and the obsessive pursuit of wealth, and the disease bred by a languorous heat, and the debauchery inherent in this narcotic dream... gambling, alcohol, the south American weed, the sensuality which pervades an incestuous plantocracy: sex with other men, other women, neglected wives, jaded husbands, virgin daughters, uninitiated sons; sex with the blacks whose blood and suffering are the foundation of all wealth, sucking from their forbidden flesh the essence of an enigmatic race and an inscrutable continent.

And the blacks, slaves to the cane and the seasons and the insect and the sun and the tortures inflicted upon them, raped bodily and in spirit, take refuge from slavery in madness, or prayer, or magic, or ambush, or poison, or armed rebellion, and are mutilated, branded, whipped and hanged. All are Jamaica's slaves: all are punished, and all perish. None are inviolate.

She punishes with the pitiless sun, the waiting jungle, the alligator, the knife in the night, the poisoned cup, the obliterating hurricane. She punishes with this excess of beauty, beauty and savagery, beauty and death: the rains wash these blue mountains, the orchids that creep and tangle, the butterfly that feeds on decay, this lushness that is almost obscenity; the negligible tides of this coral sea sweep her pristine beaches. Her beauty is constant, the flower that fades and is daily renascent, but life dangles by a thread; death is sudden and often inexplicable. She is a memory and an illusion, an implacable killer, an unhealable wound.

And yet... I loved, and was loved... and in my dreams, we never left her. I, too, am Jamaica's slave.

Noel Coventry was sixty-four when I met him, and in his swarthy, unhandsome face I would come to recognize forty years of sun and dissipation and malaria: there was also humour, and immense vivacity, and a burning intelligence. His lips were smiling, but his eyes, so dark that the pupils were not visible in the lamplight by which we met, assessed my face and body and heavy, salt-stained clothing, and St. James's inflections and silences, and finally the secrets or revelations in my own eyes, and then, as if approving or intrigued by what he saw, or sensed, or had been told, he said, "You are welcome in my house, madam."

In the hard habitation of body and spirit over the past dozen years I had divested myself of feminine grace, and I did not assume it now. I merely extended my hand to shake his, and perhaps the masculinity of the gesture offended him; he raised my hand to his lips. His palm was as hard as leather, although his touch was delicate. I withdrew my hand, and he the intimation of a magnetic sexuality, and he said, "You must make yourself entirely at home. My housekeeper will show you your rooms."

The title itself was a Jamaican euphemism. She was perhaps forty, a quadroon of French and Haitian blood like others at Ironshore; her lips were beautifully sculpted, pale, her eyes the greyish green I would see in others of mixed blood. He had bought her in Port au Prince, christened her Jamaica for the island of his obsession, and taken her to his bed. Twenty years later she was still the mistress of his household, although no longer his lover or his slave; he had freed her upon the birth of their daughter, Mazarine. All this the still perfection of her face concealed on that first evening: she was only a slender shadow behind him with a lamp uplifted, her black hair hidden by the slave's white headcloth, the rubies glowing in her ears evidence of Coventry's esteem or possession. She did not smile or welcome me: the perfect features remained perfectly blank, the eyes shuttered, the habit of the slave.

Disquieted, I turned towards St. James, and knew the subtleties of his face well enough to understand that he was telling me to go. Coventry said, "A word with you, Leslie," and he gave me a little, enigmatic smile.

The woman with her upheld lamp glided away, and moths like birds blundered softly out of the humid night; she brushed them from the ornamented glass with a slim hand etched against the flame. Neither he nor I had moved.

"Are you leaving me?"

I wondered if they had noticed the absence of Christian names between us, or affection, or touch, so many absences: he was offering me only the untranslatable language of his eyes, and the faint smile which did not reassure me, and separation seemed suddenly imminent.

"I have business to discuss. I shall see you within the hour."

The lamp and the slender back and the slave who had preceded her, ceremoniously carrying my meagre baggage, were crossing the wide, flagged terrace with no apparent intention of lingering. St. James, still standing with Coventry near the stone stairs, inclined his head very slightly to me, and in his eyes I read again the request for my compliance.

She was waiting for me. Wordlessly she conducted me up a splendid staircase: mahogany appeared promiscuously throughout the house, from the broad seats in jalousied windows to the exquisitely carved bedposts and furniture in the suite already appointed for my arrival. The girl who had borne my parcel of shirts and the toilet articles I had acquired from St. James placed them on the pale silk bedspread; the woman rebuked her sharply in patois, and they were removed. The slender fingers laid them out pitilessly on the red and cream striped silk cushions in the window seat: the jalousies were tightly fastened, and the candleflames did not waver.

"Where you t'ing, girl?" And then, when I did not understand, "You garment?"

"This is all I possess."

Her face registered disapproval.

"What you wear in bed?"

"I wear my skin."

617

"I never hear of any t'ing so unChristian in my life." She moved with a rustle of hidden silk, although her gown was modest, and an accompanying sharp, sweet perfume which seemed an emanation of her mystery: she was the first woman of colour I had ever met, and I was deeply conscious of her grace, her coolness, the cleanliness of her linen and the salt in my hair, and my overheated body in its broadcloth riding clothes. "I speak to Mr. Coventry about it. What the Captain t'ink of, he bring you here with no t'ing but the shift you stand up in?"

This was unanswerable, the conversation of equals, and it disconcerted me: slavery was instinctively distasteful to me, and I believed then that she was a slave, so I merely sat beside the shirts a sailor had sewn for me at the request of his captain, and from which I would not willingly be parted, and asked if it would be possible to have some coffee, and some hot water in which to bathe. She was directing the girl to remove the bedspread and unfasten the white netting on the canopy: she did none of these domestic tasks herself. She said abruptly, in the same soft accent, "You the Captain wife?"

"No. I am not his wife."

She took something from the table on which were arranged great sprays of scarlet blossom, and slipped it into the lock of what I sensed was an interconnecting door.

"You have a key. He have a key."

"I don't want a key, thank you."

"Then how you sleep with the Captain? How the Captain come and sleep with you?"

"I don't sleep with the Captain."

And she laughed.

"Then you crazy, girl. He good-looking man— he good man, too. I see in he face. He have eye only for you."

I was beginning to perspire, and my hands were trembling with a nervous, inexpressible anger. I was not accustomed to challenge, insinuation, femaleness. I wanted the cleanliness of the sea, the living ship, the familiar routine, the guarded asexuality which had become companionship: my life with St. James.

"Would you open the window for me, please? I should like some air."

"The mosquito come in."

"I don't care about the damned mosquitoes."

"You soon care. Sometime the mosquito kill."

There were jalousied doors; they opened easily to the fragrant night, and I stepped onto a broad verandah, which by daylight I would see ran around all four sides of the house. The night seemed intensely dark, cooled by the north-east trades; the stirring of wind brought the sound of the sea.

I was still there an hour later when St. James came to me. The candles were burning low in my room, the coffee cooling while I had waited for him. He merely appeared, walking through the darkness; he smelled of cigar smoke and brandy, and still wore his heavy, sun-faded coat, as if the night's heat did not disturb him.

He sat rather tentatively on the balustrade, and the candlelight did not reach his face.

"I trust you approve of your accommodation."

"You may inspect it, if you wish."

"I saw it this afternoon. I thought the rooms were ...very feminine."

"Suitable for your mistress?"

"I gather from your sarcasm that something has displeased you."

"That is the general opinion of my status."

"I can assure you that that is not the case. I have not compromised you in any way, nor have I spoken of you in a manner you would find offensive."

"What did you tell him?"

"The truth. He has been my friend for more than twenty years... he knew the nature of my business." He paused; he knew too much of me. "He is a gentleman, by birth and in spirit. And in my absence he will afford you the same measure of protection. You may find him a most agreeable companion, and rather more intelligent than me."

I saw him very faintly now, in the light from the terrace below: the little self-deprecating smile, the youthful negligence as he relaxed on the balustrade. I did not offer him coffee: I felt inexplicably betrayed.

"So you are going away."

"Yes, I shall be gone tomorrow. I must make myself known to the customs in Montego Bay, much as that goes against the grain, and then I sail for Santiago."

"Cuba."

"Yes."

"And Havana?"

"No."

"A summoning of ghosts."

He did not speak. The wind stirred the darkness between us.

"Take me with you."

He said, "I can't."

"No, you would rather I sit here and fan myself, and prink myself out with frivolous clothes."

He said nothing for a time, then, "You have no idea, have you." There was movement in the heavy darkness, the unknown fragrance in the night, the smell of his closeness: a terrible, stiff, unyielding moment when he said,

"I shall be back on Saturday," and after a pause, "Good-bye." I thought he would go, but he seemed to hesitate, and the silence was potent.

He said, in the darkness, "I wish you would call me Leslie. It is my Christian name."

"I know what your Christian name is. Your friend called you by it, just before you killed him."

He turned his back and walked away, and although I imagined his voice in the night that too was an illusion, a dream that died in the vivid sunrise. He was gone. The sea was empty.

Ironshore great house was only four years old, designed by Coventry from books requested of London architects, and the final version of successive buildings on that site. Cool, constant trade winds swept it, and from its elevated position it commanded a panoramic view of the north shore, with orchards and gardens and hills ascending steeply to the south. Ironshore, as he had wished, had become a social magnet, and he had achieved his lifelong desire to wield influence as far as Government House: some in Jamaica believed he would depose the incumbent, Sir Basil Keith, as governor one day.

Si monumentum requiris, circumspice, he told me, and he took a proprietary pleasure in showing me the labour of his love: the mason's marks on blocks of stone numbered in England and shipped to Jamaica as ballast, the massive folding doors of native mahogany and the splendid joinery in the dining room, the figured French silk on the walls of the drawing room, which faced east to avoid the full heat of the sun, and the great salon opening onto the broad terrace of the north façade, where the sea was visible beyond Ironshore's fields of restless cane. As had been the case with his other houses, he had built much of it himself, and interfered ceaselessly with every other aspect of its construction. There was evidence here of a private man's lonely pleasures: he conducted me to a music room, where a pianoforte stood closed against the humidity, and a billiard room, where every window framed the same eye-searing beauty of brilliant blossom and relentless light. On the walls of the music room were botanical paintings which, without preamble, he told me he had done himself. There were broadsheets and books of music here, he said; if I wished to play, I would be welcome. I said that I had not played for many years, and he smiled rather poignantly and said, "In England. Ah, England...."

We emerged from the shadows of the house to the breathtaking heat of the morning, and he said, "By your leave," and put on the broad-brimmed hat he was carrying, and then, "If I may say so, Mrs. Scott, you must learn to cover your head."

"The heat is welcome to me. I have known too much cold in my life."

He lifted his face to the sun: he seemed, always, to listen intently to me.

"And yet— sometimes— I miss it, you know. I miss the cold... I dream of it. A cold wind... a cold rain... and roses. English roses. I think I miss those most of all."

The sickness of the exile was in his face, and in the intonations of a voice from which forty years in the Caribbean had not erased the northern vowels.

"Do you like a garden, Mrs. Scott? Would you care to see mine? Botany is my passion... that and the study of human nature, which is far less attractive."

Diffidently, as though he had long lived without congenial company, then with more animation as he sensed that my interest was genuine, he led me deeper into Ironshore's gardens, into intense shade where the temperature dropped to a refreshing coolness, across swathes of closely trimmed lawn steeping in a savage sun. His garden could never be English, and much of what he cultivated was mysterious, the hybrid of the sinister and the flamboyantly beautiful which was the essence of Jamaica: strange, monstrous native orchids, the fragrant litter of fallen frangipani, the almond-scented, fatal oleander. He paused by these, which had been pruned to form a hedge; it was blooming profusely and its perfume was overpowering.

"All parts of this plant are deadly," he said. "I have known men die from eating meat cooked over oleander wood. In the Caribbean poisoning is an art, Mrs. Scott, practised by every slave with a finesse worthy of the Borgias."

"Are you not afraid?"

In the shadow of the broad-brimmed hat his eyes were infinitely calm.

"I enjoy danger. And I admire the tenacity of the human spirit in captivity, the passion for freedom. And I find their culture altogether fascinating, what I am privileged to know of it."

"Yet still you chain them, and strip them of their humanity."

"I was chained and stripped of mine. I survived it. So will they."

Strangely, I was not shocked; nor did he seem irritated, only, as always, attentive.

"Are you an abolitionist, madam?"

"I am merely an observer of human nature."

He laughed sharply.

"May I continue, in all my iniquity, or have you had enough of me?"

Another hour passed; we saw no one else, and there was no sound but the piercing cry of peacocks seeking the shade. He talked of ginger and indigo and Ironshore's sugar on my table in the mornings, and Ironshore's lime juice in Ironshore's rum in the evenings, and laid my hand on the smooth, silvery bark, like driftwood, of a tree whose small green berries were pimento; he spoke of the blue-flowered tree of life and the scarlet Easter lily, and the orchids we would see tomorrow, imported from Guatemala and Brazil and Venezuela and the Leeward Islands; he showed me the iridescent humming-bird drinking nectar from the throats of blossoms; he offered me sprays of frangipani, whose fragrance haunted me. He invited me to dine with him that evening; then he said that the sun was cruel to English skin, and would burn my scalp if we walked any further. It was now two o'clock, and the heat and the silence were intense.

There was movement at last, the woman, Jamaica's namesake, crossing the dry grass in the shelter of an opened parasol. She spoke to him without deference, in rapid, curiously accented French: I was conscious of tension and friendship between them, born of intimate acquaintance, then she turned, without any acknowledgment of me, and retraced her steps beneath the parasol. Coventry watched her with a certain wryness, as if some cherished, tarnished affection lay between them.

"I am informed by the queen of my household that I am a fool for subjecting you to this. She says that you will burn as black as a nigger. You will observe, as a student of human nature, that she herself never walks in the sun."

"And is she, too, a Borgia of poisoners?"

"No. She poisons, like all that is female, with the bitter distillations of her love."

He kept Spanish hours, he said, although he brought forward his evening meal to eight o'clock for my benefit. He had summoned the dressmaker from Montego Bay, but she was employed on another plantation until the middle of the week, so I could not dress, much to the woman Jamaica's disapproval: I merely bathed and wore a fresh silk shirt, which had been subjected to relentless laundering. He rose when I came in, and lifted my hand to his lips, although once more he withheld the kiss; he had been drinking the usual rum and lime juice and its smell was heavy on his breath, but he was as courteous and attentive as ever, and there were masses of golden orchids on the table, which he said he thought I might like. We dined in the silent company of the slaves who served, and from time to time, without interrupting his conversation, he glanced from one expressionless face to another; the silver-mounted butt of the pistol he had worn out of doors was visible in the wide cummerbund beneath his coat. The meal was exquisitely cooked and presented, and small by Jamaican standards: it suited my appetite, and apparently his. His chef was homosexual, a Haitian mulatto who had renamed himself Etienne Liberté upon his purchase and the freedom he had subsequently been granted at Ironshore; Etienne's cuisine, he said, with that odd, defiant smile, had never revealed Borgian proclivities.

The meal ended: he did not seem to want me to go. I sensed his intense loneliness and isolation, and confronted my own.

We drank coffee on the lower terrace, by the light of a hurricane lamp. Beyond the portico rain was falling, resurrecting the perfumes of the day.

He smoked, having offered me one of his thin Cuban cigars. Nothing he did or said surprised me, although I did not, this time, accept it.

I said, "You were an indentured servant."

The rustling of the rain seemed to please him; he sat listening to it.

"I was a bondslave for twelve years down Barbados way. I know the diabolical relationship between the cane and the enslaved, and I loathed it. Still, it fascinates me."

"The tenacity of the human spirit."

"The tenacity of hatred. Mine for those who injured me in the past, the Africans' for me. I allow them to keep their tribal identities— I find them interesting. Some of them hate one another almost as much as they hate me." He offered me cognac; I drank very little. Beyond the portico the rain seemed louder. "They are not all of one people, nor all of one religion. Now my valet, Estevan, is a Mandingo... and Mandingoes are Mohammedans. Although he was brought from Africa, he thinks when he was five or six years old, he can still quote the Koran. His holy day is Friday— he will not lift a finger on that day, not if he were threatened with death. My field slaves are Coromantees, including many Ashanti: Coromantees are ferocious bastards. There have been uprisings among the blacks three times in the past ten years, always led by Coromantees. They tend to commit suicide when taken prisoner, so their spirits can return to Africa... I hanged five men and one woman on Easter Monday in 1760, and set the heads on poles in the fields. There was no more rebellion at Ironshore." The rain drifted a little in the wind: the flame in the lamp fluttered. "Some day they will kill me." The lips smiled: the shadowed eyes saw other elements of night beyond my vision or comprehension. "And you, Mrs. Scott... what are you doing in this house of reprobates?"

"I should think St. James made that perfectly clear."

"But you were not too unwilling."

"I have no intention of offering my private affairs for your delectation as an observer of human nature."

He gave that quick, pleasant laugh, apparently greatly amused.

"I've never been told to go to hell so obliquely in my life. Touché." After the laughter there was silence: the compelling eyes had returned to me, the full force of the personality was unleashed. I sensed that most women were uneasy in his presence: for another woman there would be danger here. For me there was nothing. He was no longer smiling.

"I speak frankly to you, and you respond with equal frankness. I attempt to entertain myself by disconcerting you, and you give me no satisfaction. What fires tempered you, Mrs. Scott, that you humble me with your composure?"

"You have nothing to teach me of the tenacity of the spirit."

The rain had stopped. The night was alive with rushing water, and piercingly sweet: the essence of despoiled paradise.

He said, "Does St. James know?"

"He knows nothing of me, and I know nothing of him."

"He is worth knowing. I have never met a man of such exceptional charm... I drink of his presence as if it were the elixir of youth." His eyes were hooded, unreadable. "I have known him many years. He was a very young officer when we met... he was with friends at Fort Charles. He was very shy, and rather uncertain... he had not yet begun to reveal that quality one finds so intoxicating. He had prize money... I advised him to invest it. Rosewynd was for sale— he told you of Rosewynd?"

"Yes."

"I wanted it. I had hoped to marry the woman who owned it, but she went back to Haiti— it fell into disrepair— he bought it for a song. I've managed it for twenty-five years, for a percentage of the profits. I was content with the arrangement; so was he. He never intended to return."

"And now?"

"He may settle. I doubt it. He thrives upon instability. He is a passionate gambler... he gambles with his life. He was deeply unhappy for many years...."

"He told me."

"Did he, by God." It seemed significant to him. "He was ill... he was unemployed... he believed he was persecuted. He drank a good deal... his letters were melancholy, almost tragic. I kept them all... they are exquisitely painful reading. The trade... you know the trade I mean... revived him, restored him to life. He adored it... he was addicted to it... that addiction has never left him. I cannot believe that he would willingly give it up."

"Is that why you allowed him to land contraband last Sunday night?"

He said, still in the same pleasant voice, "Have any of my people told you this?"

"No one told me. I knew, before you knew yourself."

He said, "No, you're no ordinary jill, are you," and crushed out yet another cigar. "And what do you intend to do about it?"

"What you do is of no interest to me."

The rain was falling again, like soft steps; and became soft steps, and the familiar perfume. She had not seen me, of that I was certain: her voice was intimate.

"Eduardo, what you do?"

He rose abruptly; she did not come further into the light, seeing he was not alone.

With a little bow he left me, and on the edge of the light they spoke in the accented French.

"Estevan is with him. He has been out. He should not go out."

He said, "Give him something to make him sleep," and the rest was unintelligible.

The perfume, the secret sounds of silk, receded. He returned.

"One of my people is ill," he said.

"I am sorry to hear it."

He sat, as though there had been no interruption, offering me cognac. Every movement was casual, even the withdrawal of the silver-mounted pistol from the cummerbund beneath his coat. He laid it gently on the cane table between us, where the light played on it.

"You enjoyed our walk this afternoon, I hope. Perhaps you would care to do it again."

"Yes, thank you."

"Perhaps walk alone through my gardens, or up to my orchid house, or to the beach. I should like you to feel at liberty to do any of these things."

"Thank you. I shall."

"I should like you to carry this on your walks. You can shoot, I take it." Our eyes met: perhaps he knew. "I shall be very pleased if you would take it."

I took it; it was heavier than the beautifully balanced weapon in the stern cabin. He was watching me.

"I will kill any man, black or white, who attempts to harm a guest of mine."

"I shall not call upon your chivalry. I rode two hundred miles alone from Fort Augustus to Teesdale. Your garden cannot afford me any terrors I have not already known."

He leaned back in the cane chair, steepling his fingers, regarding me with blank, unwavering eyes. I left him, and lost my way, and stumbled through the rain into the silent house and to the safety of my rooms: exhausted as if by a struggle with some primordial force, shivering, although the night and the rain were as warm as blood.

***

The primeval receded with daylight; he imposed convention upon me instead, and observed how it stifled and irritated me. I spent a quarter of an hour with a stylish mulatto who told me what was fashionable in Paris, and recommended her most elaborate patterns and fabrics. I selected swatches at random, said, "This, this and this, simple gowns for evening. These, simpler gowns for day. These, riding habits, these, shirts. That is all I require," and walked away to shade my eyes and stare out at the burning sea. The woman Jamaica, who had been appointed by Coventry to oversee these sessions, was decorously embroidering white silk on white muslin in the coolest shadows of the room. The greenish eyes lifted.

"Why you don't dress like woman, girl? You want the Captain t'ink you a man?"

"I said this would suffice."

She was on her feet, flicking through the swatches.

"What you talk about? Where you negligée? Where you petticoat? Why you want these colour? These colour not for you." Then, to the dressmaker, "You make for madame these t'ing I write— you make pretty, Paris fashion. And you make this for evening, for fitting tomorrow. You measure she now— also for slipper. You cut this neckline, so."

I said, "What the devil are you doing?"

I shall never forget her eyes. They looked into my soul.

"What you afraid, girl? You have beauty. You show the Captain how you blessed."

"It is impractical and indecent, and I will not wear it."

It was a thin, textured silk, deep blue shot with iridescence, and she saw that my eyes lingered upon it: perhaps she knew the starvation of that soul.

To the dressmaker she said, "You make this simple, like the madame say," and to me, quite gently, "This the colour of the sea. The Captain like."

I was half-dressed, and I could not countenance the wearing of this gown. I had seen it during the fittings, and because it was incomplete it had not affected me, but now its graceful exposure was a flaying of the spirit: my secrets, my skin, my soul, were naked, and I could not bear revelation.

She had come herself to oversee these preparations, brushing aside the clumsy ministrations of the slave Philomel, who was watching her with dislike. The delicate ivory hand gestured: there was a thin silver bangle on the wrist.

"Va t'en."

We were alone. The cool hands rested, not intrusively, upon my shoulders where the gown, as yet unfastened, revealed the pallor of skin untouched by

626

the sun and the weeks at sea. I did not look into her reflected face, although I was aware of the closeness of her body and of its clinging perfume.

"He downstair, girl. He wait for you. Pick up you pretty skirt."

"I cannot."

A moth fell singed to the dressing table, to lie among the frangipani petals. I am that moth, burned beyond recognition, not a bruised heart hidden in veined and translucent nudity, not a trembling virgin: I am dead, my eyes are dead, my femaleness is dead. I died in the darkness on the stairs, on the floor, and with my back to blind heaven, in unspeakable acts of rape. Dead flesh and dead spirit crave only peace, not this anguished resurrection.

"You heavy thought for one so young."

"I am not young."

"You young to me, although maybe you old in pain." Silence: nothing, no movement, no sound. "The Captain first word to me today is, how is my lady? He don't say, fetch me drink. He say, how is she? Is she well? Is she happy? I say I never see happiness in you. And he smile go. You the only t'ing make he smile."

"Is he not well?"

"He fatigué. I t'ink he have unease in he body. But he thank me and he bow... he do me honour."

Her hands remained on my shoulders. Her voice was almost inaudible.

"When I live in Haiti my master call me Soie.... He violate me when I have ten year, until I bear he son. And I kill he son, because he son my brother. My master my father... he gentilhomme français. And when I kill he child, he sell me to he friend, and he sell me to friend... and he sell me comme prostituée. Mr. Coventry he buy me there, and bring me to Jamaica."

Softly, somewhere, time was striking, the hour of reckoning.

"One year pass, and he not touch me. He know I kill if he touch. Then, one night, it happen. Not sweet... but the sweetness come. Then I give he child, my Mazarine, and he give me liberty."

"Where is Mazarine?"

"He send to school in Charleston. They think she Creole child.... She beautiful, Mazarine. She beautiful comme vous." The silk slid over my shoulders, greenish blue, deeper blue. She was pleating my hair now, revealing the hidden curve of neck. "I stay with Mr. Coventry until he die."

I sat still in the heat, the silk my only adornment. Her reflected face bent closer to mine.

"The sweetness come," she said.

The folding mahogany doors of the salon were half opened; they were speaking, and did not hear the heavy rustle of silk.

I saw them now: Coventry in the usual pale linen suit and, in a conversational diagonal to him, the coppery hair and slim, half-turned back. They were both smoking. Coventry murmured something; the faded blue coat turned fully, and the blue eyes pierced me. He did not smile. He was more deeply tanned than ever: his neckcloth was clean but creased, his hair clean and confined by a black riband; the whiteness at the temples disturbed me unutterably, as though I saw him touched by mortality. Coventry was offering me compliments, praising the gown and the flesh it revealed; ravishing, ravishing, he said: did Leslie not agree?

"Yes," he said.

The minuet of conversation began. He was drinking brandy, not the invariably offered rum and lime juice; brandy was the only spirit I ever saw him drink. I was given the lady's glass of madeira, which I despised, and under some pretext Coventry withdrew.

I said, "You had a pleasant journey?"

"It was very ordinary. I trust I find you well?"

"Yes. I hope your return to Cuba was a happy one."

"I imagine it was as tolerable as your sessions with needle and thread." Then, "Shall we dispense with this? I'm not in the humour to entertain Noel, any more than you."

Convention, which so confines the rebel, was welcome to me now. Time passed; the courses were removed; I saw in his face the effort of the effortless, the uncertainty of his friendship with Coventry; I responded to it and to him, and read the language of his eyes, which said, talk to me, pretend with me. Help me. The wine and the plates were changed. There was blood on the beef that was served.

I was seated at Coventry's right hand, and Coventry was speaking of the natural habitat of the orchids on the table; there were lamps between myself and St. James. I saw the slave step forward and remove his plate. Coventry stopped in mid-discourse.

"You eat like a bloody peahen, man."

He said, "I have our Spanish friends to thank for that."

The talk of orchids ceased, and the coffee afterward seemed bitter. Coventry left us about ten o'clock with some perfunctory excuse, and did not return. We sat without speaking on the lower terrace, by the light of the hurricane lamp, with the braziers burning tobacco against mosquitoes. There was no moon and the wind was fitful. I imagined I heard the sea.

"You leave your ship on a lee shore tonight?"

"She's in Rosewynd Bay. There's a four-mile break in the reef— it's enough, in daylight." A little pause. "I shall be taking her into Montego Bay on Monday, if it concerns you."

"Which allows you rather more than your accustomed time to land your contraband."

He smoked, as if he had not heard, although he had turned slightly, his weight on his right hip, his right arm along the back of the cane chair.

"I think the less you comment on my affairs the better, for both our sakes."

"Why do you do it?"

"Profit. Habit. My criminal propensities."

"Is that all you care for? Money?"

"Yes." The heavy lids lifted. "I have nothing. I owe my people, I owe Coventry, I owe you— forty guineas, wasn't it. I have no asset but the ship beneath my feet. How do you think I should live?"

"You have two thousand acres of cane."

"Unripe, uncut, unsold. In the meantime I subsist on charity. I don't care for the taste of that, either." The wind, from the hills every night, subsided, and the darkness was stifling. "My conscience is not overly sensitive, but your remark last Sunday distressed me. It simply seemed to confirm my suspicion that I cannot escape what I am." Silence: beyond the portico lightning illuminated the clouds. "I hated Santiago. I dreamed of them all... the child's head in my lap, my poor luff with his bloody eye sockets... every night, without fail... every night. In the end, I didn't sleep. I wanted only to talk to you, as we did at sea. I wanted to say so many things... ridiculous, inconsequential things."

We were alone, and then not alone. A shadow moved against the lighted window; there was a smell of acrid sweat and apprehension, and the coffee and brandy on the table were replenished. It had taken him greatly by surprise, and he seemed restless afterwards, as though some quality in the darkness disturbed him.

"In England my house was my sanctuary. I closed the door on the perils of the night and thought, no one can touch me now. I shall never be able to say that here."

"It was untrue, even when you said it. There is no sanctuary."

"Perhaps not." There was silence. "You were the only woman who ever entered that room with me. Who graced my bed ...." Then, "Forgive me, I've had too much to drink."

In all my readings of his face this evening, the subtle language of his eyes, I had not recognized physical pain: another slow and difficult revelation, as all I had come to recognize was unacknowledged and denied.

He said, "It's nothing. Only sometimes ... tonight is one of those times. Cuba saying to me, come and die with the others."

I said, "We must go to bed."

He laughed, very softly.

"Come."

He looked up at me. The eyes were clear, very intense, the lips faintly smiling, and I saw what he must have been in his youth.

"Oh, I should like to. Very ... very much."

My hand was resting on his shoulder: perhaps he did not notice.

"St. James ...."

"Leave me here a little while. You've made me very happy tonight. I never thought to know such happiness again." He rose, and stood, very slightly stooped, as though in unconscious anticipation of the confines of a ship. "They say the sun dances for joy on Easter morning. I've never seen it. Perhaps if I weren't a bloody murderer, I might have done."

I left him there, learning this bitterest and subtlest of lessons: the fragrance and the poison were one; the beauty and the death were one; the sweetness came, and was suffering; the lover and the beloved die in one another.

IV

The hours are long when they are passed in meditation, and in solitude from darkness to darkness. There were no answers, there was no question, only a desperate turmoil, an incoherent struggle of instinct and memory, no enlightenment either in his presence or his absence; no knowledge, only that I was lost.

He sailed for Venezuela at the end of Easter week and was away for fifteen days. I had asked to accompany him: perhaps surprised by the request, or considering it naïve or provocative, he refused. So, denied whatever consummation the sea would have forced upon me, I walked on the shore, assaulted by the light at noon, and in the swiftly falling shadows of the evening. I walked in the garden, letting the sun beat oblivion into my eyes. Coventry was preoccupied and often absent, and although he disapproved of my behaviour he did not speak of safety or of danger to me; he told me only to stay away from the cane fields, and left me alone.

I slept: I had an endless capacity for sleep, as though in the aftermath of debilitating illness. And I walked again on the beach, haunted by the mystery and familiarity of this sea which had always been his life... as I had sought the essence of a man once loved in the hard land that possessed him, so now I sought revelation and comfort in a sea as unforgiving as that land.

I am a prisoner of reason, as much as a victim of memory. The wounds of the past are unhealable, the future impenetrable. There is no revelation. I am struggling against the irresistible. I am fighting for my life.

It will end, as it must end. Nothing will become of us: nothing will begin; nothing is written or unwritten; there is no fate, no inevitability.

I have not dreamed the forbidden dream.

I am not lost.

I remember the wind and the roaring of the reef, like the monotonous note of a shell held to the ear, indefinite and disquieting.

The sky was clear and paved with light, unknown, southern stars: the moon, near the full, had not yet risen. I walked in the garden, the wind pressing against me, almost chilly, and smelling of the sea; dry leaves, petals, the wrack of hot days, blown across heated stones; its strength, like the distant thunder of the reef, disturbed me. I walked along the porticoed lower terrace. One of the cane chairs had blown over. There were no lamps burning in the house.

I passed the music room. The moon was visible now, in a racing southern sky; the cloud remained on the horizon and moved on that periphery; the stars were undiminished. I walked south, into the moonlight.

They were sitting in the shadow of a lignum vitae, which Coventry had called the tree of life; the moon, quivering through the blown branches, gave no warning of their presence. Then a voice spoke from the confusion of light and darkness and said, "Why you come here, madame?" and, with a curious gentleness, "Tais-toi, busha. Bianca woman come," and for the first time I knew that he was not alone.

"What are you doing here, Estevan?"

"He no dormir. He spirit die. You go now, madame."

The wind blew, the tree of life rained living blossom; the moon fell across another face, disfigured by night's amputation. The skin was colourless in the moonlight. The mouth salivated; the black hand wiped it clean. The shadows obliterated what was real, and what imagined.

The voice murmured, "You go now."

I walked on, in rising wind: moonlight falling through the laths of an open roof, across the arrested flight, like hundreds of moths, of suspended orchids, some with a perfume like incense in the night, others tiny, noxious, hideous, their nectar overrun with stinging ants. Coventry had brought me here; it had seemed beautiful then. Coventry was here now.

He was seated where we had sat, the evening's immaculate coat discarded: the moon cast my shadow at his feet, but he did not acknowledge me. He was inhaling acrid smoke with immense concentration; the wind cleansed the air, and the moth-like orchids quivered.

"Sit down," he said.

There was a pistol similar to the one he had lent me on the bench beside him. I sensed his eyes upon me as I moved it.

He said, "No fear. Good. Very good," and drew on the burning cigarillo again. The act was slow, as though the smoke were narcotic. "Well, dear Margaret, what's the matter? Don't you like the wind?"

"I thought the sea was very rough."

"It will pass." His voice was calm, very detached: I saw only his profile, and the moonlit smoke. "It will pass. I know them ... I can smell them. There's no hurricane in that sea tonight." Then he turned his head; there were tears on his face, which his manner compelled me to ignore. "You don't sleep with St. James, do you?"

"Do your servants tell you everything?"

"They are not my servants, and it is a matter of honour to them to keep me in complete ignorance." He drew his right hand across his face with dispassion. "I have eyes. I have instinct. I know what passes between a woman and a man sitting at my table." He inhaled the smoke again: the shadows of hanging orchids spilled across the moonlight at our feet. "I think you should. I think you would find it richly satisfying. He was always a lover of women... not a libertine's fondness, but an empathy. I never had that exquisite gift of female trust.... Life has made me repellent in my own eyes, and in the eyes of lovers."

I rested my hand on his sleeve. He responded no more than he would have in a dream.

"Noel—"

He removed my hand very gently, held it for a second, and released it.

"There is nothing you can do for me ... even in friendship. When will you leave him?"

"Soon. I must go soon."

'Tell me when you wish to go, and I will arrange it for you. If you should wish to depart in his absence, I could arrange that also."

"I could not go without .... taking my leave of him."

His voice was remote; I was passing into the dream of the smoke.

"Partir, c'est mourir un peu. You will die more than a little. As I am dying now."

The moon was setting; there was no promise of morning. The air still seethed with the sound of distant surf. I could not sleep now: my hair was tainted with the smoke of the burning weed, my mind stained by the night. I opened the jalousied doors of my room and stepped out onto the verandah. The horizon was clearer, the indefinable blueness of the dawn unfolding. Gardens below, the imposition of an unnatural order upon secondary jungle, the sea of cane, the sea itself, the eternal enemy. And the sailor, home from the sea, although this would never be his home, nor mine.

He was sitting in the dimness outside his opened doors, at the table where we had dined on the night before his departure for Venezuela. The table, its cloth tugged by the wind, was laid as though for breakfast. He saw me seconds before I saw him: he was coatless, his shirt opened to the waist. I had become exceptionally sensitive to him, and it was apparent that he was attempting to conceal the scars on his body, casually fastening the shirt and resuming the neckcloth he had discarded even as I approached.

I said, "I am very glad to see you."

"And I you. Will you join me?"

"When did you come back?"

"Yesterday morning. The glass began to rise at about half past nine last night. I watched it until midnight, then I left. If it had fallen further I would have gone back out to sea."

"You shouldn't ride that road at night."

"As you are sometimes at pains to point out, night holds no perils for me." Then he said, "You look tired."

"I haven't slept. I found the atmosphere oppressive."

He poured coffee for me. There was fruit on the table, papaya, melon; also brioche.

"Have some of this. I cannot possibly eat it."

"St. James ... you are not ill?"

He considered, not the answer but its phrasing, for a moment.

"Havana disordered my bowels. I don't eat much— I can't. And I am certainly not ill."

The sun was lying across the lawns and the cane; the cane and the sea glittered. He was placing fragments of brioche on the balustrade for the small, brilliant birds which were always attendant upon this table. The woman Maica had admonished him for this, telling him that it attracted cockroaches; he had merely laughed, and said no child of India could be intimidated by a Caribbean cockroach, but he had become more circumspect in the practice.

The birds arrived and he sat watching them with pleasure, tossing occasional fragments. I spoke his name and was aware of his attention, although he did not respond, and asked if he had ever been conscious, as I had become conscious last night, of Coventry's homosexuality. I thought, again, that he considered his answer.

"If that is the case, I may truly say that it has never manifested itself in my presence. And I should like to know how it was communicated to you."

"He speaks of you in terms of intimacy ... as if he has an intimate knowledge. He said that you had always been a lover of women ... implying

633

that he was not, could not be. His mood was strange ... it was not offensive ... he was deeply depressed. He often speaks of you in that manner ... as though I know nothing of you. But then, that is the truth."

He asked me, quite gently, if I had been insulted.

"No. Neither by action nor implication."

"Then the rest is nothing to me. Absolutely nothing."

It was fully day. The vivid birds had taken flight; the strange intimacy of the dawn had passed, the stranger fears of the night had become this ordinary aftermath: the voices from the lawns as the litter of leaves and petals was swept were Africa's voices, rising not in song but an inexpressibly melancholy sound, the body enslaved and the soul in exile. No one returns from these dark shores, no one. All are homeless, all are enslaved.

He said, as if he were reading my thoughts, "Come up to Rosewynd with me this morning, and tell me if you think I can ever live there."

I could tell him without seeing it. He would never be happy there, as I would never be happy in any other place; neither of us, after this place and time, would ever know happiness again.

There are places that forbid the stranger; there are houses that embrace. Rosewynd was one of these. Half a century older than Ironshore, and more classically colonial, it had been neglected for twenty-five years and was riddled with rot and termites: the old black man who served as general factotum for the absent overseer solemnly pointed out damage from sun and hurricane and the annual forty inches of rain, but it was beautiful in its decay; its potential was great, and its atmosphere serene.

We walked through the rooms on the ground floor, the slave an omnipresent witness, then we retired to a broad verandah and were served glasses of lime juice and water; a trail of red ants appeared instantly and invaded the bowl of coarse brown sugar. The slave, calling us master and mistress, which discomfited us both, withdrew with a palmetto fan into the musty interior. We sat in the flickering light and shadow of a jacaranda tree, ostensibly waiting for the overseer, Langley, who never arrived, drinking the sweetened lime juice and listening to the birds, discussing the extent of the repairs necessary and the outlay of capital required. When conversation lapsed, it seemed less from constraint than a mutual desire to sit cradled in this silence: on this, the afternoon of Sunday, the first of May, I tasted peace as I had not known it in years. He was leaning back, coatless, his eyes closed; when he spoke again it was not of Jamaica or the present, or of England and the turbulent past, but of India and his childhood, the adored friend who had died of cholera during his year's absence in the Company ship, and of the ships and conflicts and islands and men of successive commissions, of his only other particular friend, a lieutenant slightly older than himself, who had been killed, not by enemy action but by accident.

"I was the youngest child... that was India. The others died, and there were none after me. I had no brothers... he was my brother. I loved him. I love him still, as he is in my memory." He was silent; in the sweetness of this place, it was the first touch of melancholy. "God knows what he would think of me now. I never imagined either of us old."

"You are hardly that."

He gave me the smile reserved for Margaret, the sweetness and the poignancy.

"No?"

The light changed; the sea, Rosewynd Bay, had altered a little with the passing of time, brushed by wind and current, like wrinkled silk. He stirred, not restlessly.

"And what of you? Your childhood was a happy one, I hope, spoiled beyond endurance by the soldier?"

"I was not conscious of being happy, although I suppose I was. There were no other children... I was very solitary."

"You still are. I think you are one of the most self-contained human beings I have ever met. How did you come to be Mordaunt's ward?"

"I am the child of a non-jurant minister... a Scot. I am a spoil of war." There was a silence: sixteen years of my life passed in memory, and I did not sense, I knew, that he understood. "He returned to the army, I returned to Scotland. I remained there until October of 1772."

"Where?"

I told him.

"Why did you leave?"

"My marriage ended," and I knew what he wanted to say, but he did not ask.

He said, eventually, "When you return to London I should like you to do me a service. I should like you to carry a letter to my banker at Coutts."

"I will do it, gladly."

"I have money there. I can't touch it and I can't return for it. I want you to have it."

"I don't—"

"I know you don't. This is something I want. Call it reparation... give it to the poor. I don't give a damn. But take it. Do this for me, Margaret. Remember me."

The shadow of the jacaranda had moved, the colours of the sea deepened; the lowering sun spilled across the table and my cheek, the coppery darkness of his hair, the graceful, peeling symmetry of the fanlight over the door. Our horses were brought; I was called mistress again; the absence of Langley, the busha, was apologized for; we were wished "bon dios" in a curious corruption of the Spanish; Rosewynd withdrew its gift of peace, although the intimacy it had conferred remained.

Coventry was entertaining that evening, he said: he had declined to attend, and would dine alone and walk on the beach. If I would join him, he would be happy. It was a little thing, and happiness is a rare commodity.

"That very much depends upon what you intend to serve me."

"Oh, I shall have a single prawn and a bottle of champagne. You will eat a cold lobster, and discourse knowledgeably throughout on the habitat of the Guatemalan epidendrum."

It was the first time we ever laughed together. Love heals, although the wounds are many. The sweetness comes.

He spoke that night of the associations of the past eight years, the hierarchy of the brotherhood and the six members of the cartel who governed it, and had, he believed, ordered his death. He named them for me: with the exception of the Earl of Harlesdon, he had met none of them. He spoke also of the brotherhood's suspicions, of disaffection and betrayal from within, of his own cautious preparations for withdrawal from what had become less a profitable gamble than a relentless progression towards the gallows. Then, having touched upon it, he dismissed it. The moon was full, and the voices of Coventry's guests occasionally audible from the opened windows and the terrace below; he seemed to crave the eternal, speaking silence of the sea, and we left the candlelight and the blundering moths and went down to the beach. I walked, carrying the flat morocco slippers which had been made for me, with the surf creaming around my ankles; he walked above the reach of the tide, and seemed happier, untouched by the shadows he had evoked.

Eventually we sat, I on the coat he had spread for me, he resting on his left elbow, watching the great expanse of stars: he seemed, although thoughtful, at peace. In time we spoke again, of the beauty of the night, the constellations and this almost tideless sea, and I lay back and closed my eyes, my head cradled by the sand, embraced by the scent of the night and the cloth, the sea's salt, the essence of him. I sensed his movement beside me, and perhaps his intention, and allowed the caress, the ineffable tenderness, the lips against my mouth and my naked breast, the exquisite sensuality of the suck and the kiss. Whatever this was for him, for me it was love's act: I loved him, although I feared him, and the intensity of his desire, and this slow dream of sex, of offering and receiving, was poisoned, poisoned irretrievably. Although the body remained languid it was dead, it was lifeless, and as though he sensed that the consent and the spirit had withdrawn he released me. He called my name once, sharply, as I walked away. I did not turn or listen to him, and found myself running, impeded by the sand: when the lights of Ironshore were visible I halted, leaning against one of Coventry's jacarandas, and waited for him. Finally he appeared: he, too, had been running. Neither of us spoke. Then he said, "You forgot these," and gave me the slippers, and left me on the edge of the garden and turned back toward the sea.

The moon was setting, its terrible potency diminished. I sat in the cane chair, tormented by the visions of the night, for many hours before I heard him return. He came out onto the verandah and stood staring over the gardens. He was smoking; he did not acknowledge me, although I knew he was aware of my presence. Time passed: the wind from the land had died, the wind from the sea had not yet come. It was almost dawn.

Eventually he said, "I thought you cared for me. I was mistaken."

His voice was without expression. Dead, so dead; not a ghost, not a demon, but living flesh, the passionate arousal, the cherished spirit, the wounded, desired body. Everything dead now, the mouth's caress, the ravishment of joy: what was written was now unwritten. There was no shame, there was no hope, there was only this, inarticulate emptiness.

He did not speak my name, or move.

"Why did you break with your husband?"

I could not tell him; I could tell no one. We never spoke of it. He never knew.

I said, "He raped me," and left him.

There was nothing now, only pain and uncertainty. He was courteous and withdrawn, and the polite insignificance of our conversations wounded me terribly. He was not a stranger, who had flowered in the warmth of our acquaintance, and shared his memories and observations; he was not a lover; he was not now a friend, because his companionship and his passion had been rejected with devastating finality. He was a man whose Christian name I had never dared to speak, except privately, when the syllables lingered on my tongue like a word in an unfamiliar language. I had never embraced him, I had never stroked his face, although, briefly, when he had kissed me, my fingers had caressed his hair. To touch him sexually was unthinkable; even to touch his cheek with tenderness was denied to me.

He behaved as if nothing had happened. Perhaps what he had offered had seemed insignificant to him, a moment's pleasure in a sensuous paradise. He was susceptible to women: he was no hedonist but neither was he ascetic, and his loneliness, both physical and spiritual, had been intense. This was not love... *the self-immolation of love has never appealed to me.* Nor would the pollution of rape, the violation of mind and spirit: this had repulsed him, this had been unspeakable; there was nothing to say, no question to be asked, no answer to be given.

I did not consider that it might haunt him, acquiring degrees of abhorrence and significance; I could not know the futility and impotence of his rage, because there was no vengeance that could be executed, no justice exacted for my sake, nothing to pursue, to kill but a ghost and a memory. Our intimacy had been as great as it was unnatural, the loss of him now most bitter when my soul's revelation of love for him was most clear, most painfully manifest.

The manipulation of other lives had always given Coventry pleasure, and we were puppets in the shadow play he now chose to direct. Ironshore was en fête: it was his sixty-fifth birthday, and the occasion not only of expensive indulgence but a certain self-congratulation. He had outlived his contemporaries, defying the sun, the disease, the endemic vice, the perils of the field and the nights, the black man's poison, the killing insect, the machete. The hungry soil of his island prison would wait a little longer for him.

St. James had gone downstairs: I envied him the charm and insouciance which would carry him through this ordeal. I could not dress and sat alone, appalled by the noise of arrivals, and music, and voices, a maelstrom of festivity into which I must descend, until Maica came to my room and reproved me. She had brought Philomel and two terrified slaves who laced me and tugged my bodice lower and repeatedly powdered my breasts, and attempted to affix to my hair the spray of virgin orchids sent up, with sardonic humour, by Coventry. I had no jewellery except my ring and earrings, and this was not considered enough; she offered me the pearls Coventry had given her when their child was born, and gently I refused them. Nor would I carry a fan; the language of the coquette was one I had never been able to speak. I was persuaded, in time, to accentuate the frozen features in the glass with cosmetics, and anoint myself with perfume. It was very late; the midnight supper would soon be served. She observed me critically. The gown, a thin silk of an intense deep green, was not approved of; it was not elaborate, the colour was too dark; my skin was too deeply tanned.

"You walk too much in that damn sun. You black like Guinea slave." She, who would be seen by no one, was elegance itself, the rubies glowing in her ears, the slave's headcloth abandoned tonight for a turban of black silk. "What the English lady say of you? What the gentlemen say?"

"They are nothing to me, these planters and colonials. I don't give a damn."

"Then take you God-damn-you downstair. Mr. Coventry, he waiting."

She opened the door for me, admitting the humid heat, the smoke of many candles, the cloying scent of frangipani; and it was very evident that Coventry was otherwise occupied. I did not see him but I heard his voice; his suite of rooms was not far from mine, and his companion was young and female. His door closed, and a frisson passed through the cool fingers on my wrist, although her face revealed nothing.

She spoke in pure French, not the argot she shared with him.

"He torments me, he torments himself. He is impotent."

She released my wrist.

"You go now and find the Captain. Many jackal prey here tonight."

I saw the girl later, and there were no revelations in her face; I saw Coventry; I did not see St. James, and when I did he was not alone. Coventry came and stood behind my shoulder, murmuring a compliment into my hair. He was a little, convivially drunk, impeccably dressed to the diamond in his stock, and he smelled of cigars and perspiration and female musk, which he had attempted to disguise with eau de cologne. There were acts of love in which, apparently, he still indulged with pleasure, and I sensed that this was not his first sexual adventure of the night.

"You give me joy, I hope, dear Margaret?"

"I wish you happiness. I wish it were within my power to confer."

"Then confer a kiss, and that will be my happiness."

I kissed him lightly on either cheek; his skin was bloomed with moisture. If he sensed the slight hesitation, he would justify it by his own secrets and proclivities, not mine.

He summoned sweet champagne for me: the tray was proffered in immaculately gloved hands. The black face beneath the horsehair wig was sweating as profusely as the goblets.

"Do you see that woman?"

"Yes." Then, sensing that something less curt was required, "Do you know her?"

"Oh, yes. And you should know her also. For many years she was 'darling Lizzie' to a gentleman of our acquaintance."

Another small, exquisite torment: he enjoyed them, but she was nothing more to me than a shadow who moved in a dream. I would soon be gone, and they would remain, these dwellers upon the volcano, these, wealthy and anachronistic, whom emancipation and uprising would obliterate, these women, preening in obsolete fashions, with jewels winking in unclean hair, these men, who had built an empire upon despised humanity, these soft-footed slaves: all this, the great windows open to the moon and the mosquito, the heavy fragrance of night-blooming flowers and the iodine smell of the sea, all this would not exist when I had gone, as a dream disturbs and dies, and cannot threaten, because it is not real.

She was taller than I; her unpowdered hair was dark auburn, her eyes grey, but not a grey like mine, her gown of pearl grey silk. She had never been beautiful, but she was radiant; the very pale skin seemed incandescent. It was not possible to know her age: the face was wilful, passionate, with a strong, fine mouth and high cheekbones, and she was alive, vibrantly alive and responsive, even as I was dead.

She was Lady Elizabeth Hamilton, wife of the lieutenant-governor of Antigua, and Coventry emphasized her title and presented me to her, so there should be no doubt that, by birth more than marriage, she outranked me. She tapped her fan against her cheek: the lace and iridescence of the mother of pearl guards complemented her skin and the pearls she wore to enhance it.

"So... you are lately come from England. I envy you. That, and other things."

"As you cannot know, madam, you cannot envy."

I imagined Coventry's enjoyment of this: card for card, stake for stake.

"We have a mutual acquaintance. I envy you his friendship."

And I knew beyond doubt who she was. The faithless inamorata of seven years, the inflicter of pain and disillusion.

She said, "If you should see him, and I should not, commend me to him."

"I am certain he will make himself known to you, madam."

"Oh, I think not... I think not. He is no moth. And I am no flame."

I found him upstairs on the broad verandah outside our rooms, smoking, and drinking brandy. There was heat lightning over the sea, and the perfume of the night seemed intense, the music a private concert, the voices and laughter inconsequential. The darkness here both salved and disturbed me, because I shared it with him.

He said, "Elizabeth is here."

"I have met her."

"I don't want to see her."

"That would be uncharitable, as she plainly wishes to see you."

He watched the lightning, smoking; the music died briefly, and I heard the sea.

"You don't care for parties, do you?"

"No. I have been too much alone not to feel like the ghost at the feast."

The music resumed, the composer recognized, the composition familiar, a minuet once danced and unforgotten: unbearable memory.

"St. James." He responded with the slightest movement of his head. "It is discourteous to keep her waiting."

He crushed the cigar out on the balustrade and walked away into the heavy darkness.

I did not wish to witness the reunion of old lovers, but he brought her to the terrace directly below my room, so their conversation should be known to me. She opened with skillful coquetry; he responded with beautiful manners; I recognized in it a mutual salute. Then she said, "Time has been your slave."

"And yours. The promise of beauty in the girl is more than fulfilled in the woman."

"Still so gallant.... Your life agrees with you."

He laughed. Perhaps she was aware of the bitterness in it.

"You should have remained in the navy. You would have been an admiral by now."

"I think not."

"I think so. A rear-admiral, at the very least."

"It was otherwise ordained." *It was written, even as this is written.* "How is your husband?"

"The same, alas."

"And what mischief are you doing here?"

"I am visiting— it is permitted occasionally. I return to Antigua within the month, the dreary duty to resume." There was a rustle of silk, a gesture made and perhaps not rejected. "Oh, my dear, you look so well— so much better than the last time."

"The last time was a lifetime ago. Another man... another world."

She said, "Fletcher is at Fort Charles. We shall meet in Spanish Town; he has agreed to show me the cathedral. Come with me. I have spoken of you to him... as a friend. He remembers you."

He said, with immense bitterness, "What, as your 'cousin'? Is that how you want us to meet?"

"You may meet him as a man, or as your son. He is worthy of you."

"Time has made you too generous in your memories of his father."

Again a silence. Perhaps she touched him, or he her; perhaps their isolation from one another was as intense and inviolate as mine.

At length she spoke again.

"You have land here? Noel mentioned it."

"An old investment, which proved prudent in the long view."

"Prudence is a new departure for you."

"One acquires it with age."

"Shall I tell you what I think? I think you never change. I think you merely bide your time, waiting for some indication of the political wind's direction."

"There are portents enough for those who care to read them."

"I read more than portents. I read what London writes, and what English Harbour answers. And I know you, Leslie— my God, how well. This is a whirlwind you cannot hope to reap."

"I thank you for your observations, Lizzie."

"They are given with a full heart. We are in a season of calamity. Remember what I have said."

"I shall."

"And me."

"I shall remember you always."

She did not say, *and love me*: the silence that followed was eloquent, the lightning over the sea stronger.

She said, "Do you think it will rain?"

"Almost certainly. Before dawn."

"I must call for my carriage. I was invited to stop the night.... I knew you were here.... Perhaps I hoped— too much." Words were spoken, which were not meant to be heard. "Please don't. I have none. I merely hoped— that was all."

There was no further conversation: I never saw her again, except in his eyes, in the injuries she had afforded him, and could still afford him, and in the obsessive imagination and hallucinations of the night. He was not seen again after one o'clock; I did not know he had gone to walk on the beach; I had not seen her departure and suspected that she was with him. Coventry took possession of me and exhibited me for more than an hour, relishing the elaborate foreplay of social intercourse and repeatedly requesting that I dance with him. Music was my passion, he said, he saw the memories like shadows on my face; why should passion be unfulfilled? I danced a set with him, the object of excruciating scrutiny, and retreated to my room: I knew then that I was ill, and my need for privacy was intense. It was four in the morning, still dark, and raining; the music haunted the delirium of the next hours.

I must, unconsciously, have called out to St. James; there was a door behind the door and both were locked, but they were opened from his side and my room was entered. Maica was summoned, and came alone; the house was quiet now, the guests departed or asleep, light rising from the sea. I heard him speak of malaria, fearfully: I heard her say that I was poisoned: whether by design or mischance, or by what substance, was never known.

Sickness possessed me like a demon, every thirty minutes for seven hours. My bowels opened; welts broke upon my skin, my eyelids, my ears, my labia, the soles of my feet, my lips.

She said, "Go away, man. You shame this girl."

He said, "I have seen her ill before," and then, "For God's sake, do something for her."

She said, "Minou... listen to me."

He gave me water, and I thanked him; the courtesy seemed to distress him. His face was drawn; he looked very old.

"Minou, I make you a little charm, somet'ing you wear against you heart. Somet'ing make you well."

It was only a sachet on a cord. He lifted me in his arms to receive it.

She said, "You good man, Santiago."

He held me still, and stroked my hair, I who had never spoken his name. And he caressed me with his voice, speaking of tomorrow or the day after that, when he should take me to the sea, and we would bathe together, we should walk naked in the sea, and there would be no more concealment, there would be no shame, and the sea would heal me and cleanse me, cleanse us both, and we would be baptised by the sea, and reborn together. All this, he would do with me.

"Minou... what you dream?"

Leslie, I said. Leslie.

"He sleep, child."

She bathed my body, brought it bitter liquid, gave me opium; the torment had not eased, although the violence of the spasms had abated. I did not know that he was sleeping within the sound of my voice. I did not speak his name again.

On the seventh day, he took me to the sea.

We spoke little: what was unspoken was understood. Our lives had altered, and this, feared and desired, was my committal, the absolute of my trust in him.

He walked naked into the sea and, eventually, I joined him: he had been swimming, strongly, unlike most sailors, granting me privacy. I stood with my back to him, my breasts hidden, my head bent; I was trembling, closing my eyes against the sea's brilliance, closing my senses against him. He spoke my name, and his hands, cooled by the sea, anointed me with the salt gift of its water, until my skin burned and glittered with the sun and the sea's reflections, and the ebb and flow of the water and the hands and the heat and the perfect silence, the sea's silence, were both sensuous and innocent: as naked as Adam, as naked as Eve, we stood in perfect communion, neither acknowledging the other. He kissed my shoulder, and the nape of my neck, sensing that this could be given, and this, to caress my breasts, although I could not yet turn toward him, and then, gently, irresistibly, he compelled me to turn, and he gave himself to me in that instant, the salt and the sun in his hair and on his skin, the beauty of his naked body and of the sex veiled by the sea, the sea the only world around us, embracing and baptising, the lucid sea caressing as he caressed, the sea in his eyes.

He loved me, kneeling, his head bowed; my fingers loosened the black riband and it drifted and was lost, and I caressed his hair; what was offered he took with intense passion, unspeaking, with hands and lips: throat, nipples, belly, the concavity of bones. He caressed my hair, my other hair, although he did not enter me with his fingers, as though he sensed that I could not give this, then, kneeling still, he embraced me, my hips, my buttocks, his mouth against my skin, and came, my name a litany on his lips; his semen drifted, and the sea cleansed him; when he raised his head his face was transfigured. And I kissed him, as I had kissed him, as I kiss him still, in dreams of passion, of that place and that hour, which haunt and give no comfort, kissed his mouth and his eyelids and the scars upon his face and the savage scars on his body, his hands and mouth and sex cool and salt as the sea, the burning heat of the sun on his skin. He did not watch me leave the sea; he swam a little, and then, naked, he walked from the water and dried his body with his shirt, and dressed, and sat beside me, the salt drying in his loosened hair and on his skin, his face in repose youthful and refreshed, his eyes narrowed against the light. Although there was little tide, time and current deepened the iridescence of the sea.

He said, "I shall always hold this memory most sacred, and most precious. I never thought such beauty was possible."

"I want to give myself to you... but I cannot."

"If I never knew anything more of you than what you have given me, it would be enough. It would be everything." There was a silence; I knew what he was going to say. "I am going to Spanish Town to meet my son. I don't want to, but I feel I must. I should be very happy if you went with me."

"I met your mistress. I don't want to see your son.... I don't want to be reminded of years I can never share." He said nothing, gazing at the sea, the white hair and the dishevelled copper drying in the sun, the white his mortality, the promise of severance, the irretrievable years. "The past is a lost, sweet country. We cannot return, we cannot relive."

"Your past is equally lost to me."

"I could never have given you a child."

"You are my child, and my sister, and my friend, and more than any of these, my lover. The past is your absence... you were not given to me. And if your past could be relived, or lived with me, I would give anything... anything. You cannot know. You cannot know, Margaret."

We remained until twilight, every hour evanescent, until they, too, day and evening, were lost, distilled, of the irretrievable sweetness of years.

V

There was little wind the morning of his departure for Kingston, from which he would ride the fourteen miles to Spanish Town. The weather was exceptionally hot, the sea dead calm under clouded skies. These conditions persisted for days, until a light rain fell, and the sea quickened as though prophesying storm; the mercury in Coventry's barometer dropped but there was no storm, only the smothering heat. Sleep was impossible. Coventry and I played cards on the terrace at midnight, the flame unwavering in the glass and thunder below the horizon. The weather oppressed him, and he attributed his unease to the barometric pressure, which he said affected the brain, but he was subdued and uncommunicative. Every inch it fell was an inch closer to hurricane, and he had cane to lose.

It fell further. The sea was flattened and swept with rain, the light grey, the days airless and intolerable. By night, on my dishevelled bed, I prayed for wind, not the great wind I feared, the serpent's coil of destruction sucking its power from the sea, but a resumption of the cooling trades, an end to this dead calm. I prayed for St. James, for his safety, for his happiness, for his quietness of mind, listening to the rain, imagining rain in Spanish Town, rain on the face of the sea.

The season of calamity was upon us: it would claim its victims. I listened to the rain, and remembered the baptism in the sea, my rebirth and his, and he seemed close to me in the living night; the sounds in the night were imagined or dreamed; the rain was only the rain.

It was a shadow on the mosquito netting draped around my bed, then the moon was obscured by cloud and the shadow became living flesh, not in the darkness of that moment but in the candlelight that would be shed in horror: the eyes opened and discoloured, their pupils grossly misshapen, the tumours and deformity of the face, from which part of the jaw had been amputated.

He was death animate, blinded, consumed by cancers, repeating the word *cunt, cunt,* endlessly so that I should comprehend it; and later, not then, as he strangled me, but afterwards, I understood. I remembered the word, and that I had understood it, although it had not been spoken in English but in the language of another country, by another man I had thought would kill me.

But he was dying and insane, and I was not myself to him, I was not Margaret: I was only female, past, present, remembered or unknown. I was only what he called me: I had no name. I was nothing. As he had no name to me, was nothing to me when I killed him.

He did not die immediately. He was kneeling, entangled in the bloody netting, when they came. I had locked the door, although he had forced the jalousies open; the order of things is unclear; I cannot remember. Coventry, his hairy nakedness hidden only by a shirt, his mistress with him, also half clothed, as though she still shared his bed; the Muslim Estevan, whose holy day this was, carrying a machete; other slaves, their blackness overwhelming, bearing weapons perhaps more fittingly turned upon the white master than the white slave dying on the floor.

Supporting, embracing, she took me from the bloodied bed, pried the stinking pistol from my fingers; my hand and arm and chemise were soaked with blood. He was still breathing, half tangled in the draperies, bleeding profusely from the wound, his eyes opened. As she passed, she pierced his outstretched hand with the heel of her slipper, and consciousness remained in his face; it reflected a momentary anguish. Coventry brushed by me, smelling of sweat and marijuana; he carried the other pistol, the mate, which I had removed from the seat in the orchid house. He was leaning down; he looked into the face and spoke, although his words were not audible, there was no sound, no sound, and then he placed the muzzle of the pistol against the head on the carpet and fired.

She took me away, from the smoke and the stench and the candlelight, into the darkness and coolness of another room I did not recognize, which was St. James's room. There was nothing of him here, no possessions, only the lingering scent of bay rum like an essence of himself, and his spirit, his ghost, came toward me in the darkness, and embraced me as I fainted.

He had only one name to Coventry and no past, as Coventry had no past to him; at the end of his life the past had become only the years they had shared. The rest was half remembered, the dream that dies upon waking, and in that dream his life became mine, a complex web of relationship and experience and time in its every dimension. My past, my present, my future were and always would be inextricably bound to him.

The only name he possessed was MacIain. That this was neither Christian nor surname was irrelevant to Coventry. It sufficed, for one who was enslaved; apparently he desired nothing else, and time withheld his other identity. To Coventry he was a savage, an irrational and unpredictable object of sexual desire, eventually submitting to Coventry's peccadilloes but never a willing or an ardent participant, neither welcoming nor resisting acts of humiliation and the occasional infliction of pain. Secrecy and irony heightened Coventry's pleasure: the submissive lover of the afternoons and the humid nights had risen to become his overseer, teaching himself to read and write the English he so despised, exacting labour from the blacks, who feared him, an inarticulate presence whom Coventry occasionally summoned from the shadows for the delectation of Jamaican society. When Coventry resorted to prostitutes of either sex, he confined his activities to Haiti; when he returned from Port au Prince with a quadroon mistress this relationship was conventional. He did not now compel his lovers to join him in copulation à trois, although he had required it of women in the past: neither the woman's spirit nor the man's could be broken or seduced, neither could be compelled to desire in one another that which he found addictive in them both, and in time he recognized that their hatred of one another was not merely sexual revulsion but jealousy.

Pleasure and a peculiar peace came from paternity and domesticity, and he was conscious of his own passage toward conformity and his gradual disengagement from the most durable and turbulent of his liaisons. Intercourse with MacIain was infrequent and unsatisfying. He attributed this to age and familiarity, and the enigma of the woman, her sex and her race, was more stimulating than the impenetrable mystery and hostility of the man; and when, in time, he desired to renew their relationship, the submission was a physical resistance which he did not then challenge.

He knew, now, why that had changed. The act of a second becomes the reaction: a thousand, thousand seconds linked him and his past and his lover to this hour, of the day before his lover died, and the seconds had become not separate but an indefinable whole. Time bears us all, unresisting, upon a tide of irrevocability.

He told me this himself when I returned to Jamaica, after Boston, when I was alone.

His lover was dying, in the final stages of tertiary syphilis, riddled with cancers of the testicle and brain and necrosis of the lower jaw, tibia and femur. With the approach of death he had been moved from the spartan quarters he had occupied as overseer to this wing of the house, and dosed ineffectually with quinine, opium, and a tincture of lignum vitae prepared by Maica, which Coventry suspected was poisoned.

Their intercourse had never been social; flesh was the language of their communication, and conversation, when his lover was conscious or rational, was almost inarticulate. The disfigurement of the face and body haunted him; he found these vigils a source of unrelenting pain.

His defense was the assumption of casualness, as though it was of no consequence: he sat by the bed and smoked yet another cigar and answered and asked the same questions.

What is this place? Why am I here?

One of the guest rooms... in one of the guest rooms, MacIain.

Is that what I am to you now? Your guest?

There was a silence, a faint sound of rain; the wind from the shore teasing the white nettings of the bed. The smoke drifted; the gaunt face on the pillow turned away very slightly, a little gesture of revulsion: the eyes remained closed. He seldom spoke now; his speech had become unintelligible, and his frustration and anger when he could not be understood was intense and often violent. On these occasions only, he was restrained.

The face, turned aside in its greying hair, seemed curiously at peace. Coventry took the mutilated right hand and felt the faint pressure of its response. Tentatively, he stroked the hair. He thought his name was spoken.

Of what was said to him he understood only the first word, *kill*, slurred almost beyond recognition; the rest was gibberish, and, disquieted by what he had heard, a request, a confession, a threat, he said, "Don't talk. Rest. We'll talk tomorrow."

He administered the drugs, still believing they were poison; his lover wept, fighting him, and slipped into unconsciousness.

Silence; all the silences, lived and remembered. The rain ceased, the wind fell light, the pattern of cloud and the colour of the sea altered imperceptibly.

He remembered the night and the act, and the day which had preceded them. They had quarrelled over the loa, the engraved copper disc he had seen half-hidden beneath his lover's shirt: there is a curse on my life, he had said, the blacks are making obeah against me. Coventry had called him a superstitious animal, a white nigger, torn the loa from his neck and gone to his supper party at Palmyra.

He had seduced a woman there, an army officer's wife, but the brevity of the encounter had not satisfied him: he returned to Ironshore at three in the morning. He found his lover, ignored for the years when heterosexuality had appealed, writing in his quarters, tracing childish letters and words in an unknown language. That there was some part of his past Coventry could not reach, some part of his life he would never possess, infuriated him, and he took the papers from the table and mocked the infantile writing, and tore them into fragments, and, aware at last of some emotion in the gaunt, closed face, he untied his stock.

"Take off your clothes," and, when he was not obeyed, "I said, take them off."

"Take them off yourself, you English bastard. They belong to you."

He tore the clothing from the body and the shreds of humanity from the soul, and invaded and claimed the flesh. He did not expect resistance and was excited by it; it had never been offered with such bitter intensity, he had never been rejected, and this was a physical and spiritual rejection; and by this act of rape he was aware of having unleashed inhumanity in himself and in his lover. In the night he whipped him, inflicting great pain, and woke alone. Syphilis, contracted from a Montego whore, manifested itself within three months. There was no further intercourse: the dying flesh achieved its freedom.

He had been Coventry's slave for twenty-seven years.

They were cutting cane at Ironshore, and further up in the hills, at Rosewynd and Palmyra and Cinnamon Hill, cutting in the beauty of the sunrise and the implacable white heat of noon; occasionally they cut by moonlight or torchlight, and burned the fields to rid the cane of the impeding blossoms and leaves; cutting in the fear of sun and hurricane, driven by the whip and the busha and the market, feeding the rollers and the fires, ten tons of cane for a ton of sugar, for Bristol and the London exchange. It was the slave's world, the driver's world, the melancholy song, the flash of the machete against two thousand acres of cane, the cloying stench of boiling sugar and distilling spirit in hair, on clothing and skin. I left it when I left Ironshore, for the coolness of the ferns in the valley and the deep red earth, and the decaying peace of Rosewynd great house.

I sat where I had sat with St. James on the wide verandah, in the flickering shadow of the jacaranda, and in the afternoon, Saturday afternoon, as Coventry was burying his lover at Ironshore, I watched the towering thunderheads rise from the sea until the light was blotted out. The onslaught of rain seemed white; the sea, Rosewynd Bay, the valley, vanished into mist; the rain fell for hours or minutes; time passed; the valley emerged like Eden, its beauty and fragrance unbearable; the old man, who had retreated into the open doorway, came on sinewy bare feet and removed the untouched lime juice and its attendant ants; the roaring of the rain rendered conversation unnecessary.

The sunset was coppery, Jamaica's peculiar redness, as if all the blood of her suffering was transmuted into light. With the advent of evening the old man brought me rum, as though he knew white women drank it in secret, as though he sensed my desire for self-obliteration: I did not want the rum any more than the lime juice, but there was a curious compassion in the gesture and in his wordless solicitude. In the twilight, perhaps grateful for the absence of the elusive Langley, who was in the fields, women emerged, gracefully carrying burdens upon their heads, pausing to speak in musical voices and in an unfamiliar language to the old man on the verandah, and then, becoming aware of my presence, startled into an obsequious withdrawal; their naked children, clinging to them, were fearful of my pallor, as though I were one of the undead. To them, whiteness was master and overseer: it did not wear a woman's face.

With the coming of night, a clouded, sighing night, the old man brought a lamp, which I indicated I did not want: he placed it on the wet planking at the top of the steps, where it attracted huge, soft moths and other, smaller insects. The night opened its heart: a thousand predators and victims stirred beyond the faint circle of light: the old man pointed to fireflies in the darkness, which I watched, and then ceased to notice. He did not expect Langley: I suspected that Langley did not exist, as I did not exist in this suspension of time and reality. In the night, he advanced a little closer, and asked me if the Captain was coming: I spoke for the first time in thirteen hours, saying that the Captain would not come, nobody was coming. He continued his patient attendance on me: at some time in the night, as though weary of standing, he asked my permission to sit. He did not attempt to touch me, or the rum, or the pistol on the table near my hand, which I had discharged into the body of Coventry's lover. I recall neither sleeping, although I must have slept in the chair, nor his first words, although his voice, Africa's voice, and the subject of his discourse remained with me always. He spoke of Africa, telling me his African name, which I remember although I cannot spell it; among slaves of other tribes he called himself Cudjoe, signifying that he had been born on a Monday. He had been taken by Arab slavers, and brought to Jamaica in a year he thought was 1720. He had not come then to Rosewynd, although he had known it when it was a younger house; he was a field slave then, he said; he did not use the pejorative 'nigger'. He had known them all, the hurricanes, the crop failures, the uprisings, the malaria and drunkenness and suicides of the masters, the malaria and suicides of the slaves: Seguin and Lydia Seguin and Coventry, and the splendour of Rosewynd in its prime, when Ironshore was an acre of struggling cane encroached upon by jungle. He said that Rosewynd was a place of ghosts, but when the Captain came to live there with me it would rise again: he did not relate the young, diffident naval officer who had purchased Rosewynd from Seguin's agent in 1747 to the man who had accompanied me upon my last visit, and I did not say that I would never live here with him, that time, binding and unbinding, would not allow it, that we would never be buried here together: I said nothing, felt nothing. All was written, all was ordained. He said that he knew the busha was dead: how he knew was uncertain, but he told me that Coventry had buried him, and would remain by his grave for nine days, and on the ninth night the busha's spirit would depart. He said that he was not a Christian, and believed in obeah, and practised it. *Minou, I make you a little charm....*

He said he would pray for me.

His voice was hoarseness, and then a whisper, and then nothingness. The night was dying, the dawn white with mist, the sea and the blue mountains pearled, silent. I was alone.

I prayed for myself, for my sanity, knowing that I who was capable of killing could, by a finger's touch, shatter this dawn with a final shot: I prayed for St. James, and for his peace in his meeting with the unknown son, far from the sea they both loved: I prayed for release from pain, from memory, from fear. The sun rose, as though upon the first morning of the world.

He did not speak to me immediately: he dismounted and came up the steps, out of the new sunlight into the shadows of the jacaranda, and drew out the other chair, and sat. After a few minutes, without undue haste, he slid the pistol across the dew-misted table away from me. Then he leaned back, as he had sat that afternoon, speaking of India and the past; his face was drawn, as though he had suffered greatly in the night. He had known that he would find me here and yet had feared, perhaps to find me, perhaps the irrevocability of his course: he loved me, and this, too, I saw in his face.

I returned to Ironshore with him. He took me to his room, which I had briefly occupied in the dying hours of Friday night: my suite of rooms had been stripped and sealed, the doors locked, the jalousies nailed shut. In all the time that remained to me at Ironshore they were never opened again; the rooms given to me now faced the sea, and it was the sea of which I was most conscious, the distant sighing of the reef, and the shuttered stillness of the house at noon.

He did not open the jalousies to the light, and the dimness and coolness of his room and the indefinable essence and scent of him, which had comforted me, embraced me: he undressed me with infinite tenderness, and loosened my hair, and caressed it; his face was still and intent; these revelations were beyond pleasure, and were worship. He caressed my feet, held them lightly in his hands, stroking the arches, kneeling, resting his head against me; I stroked the hair of the bent head and the hard bone of his cheek, and he held my hand to his lips. I did not resist him, or respond. He wanted my complete nakedness, the damp silk slid away; he lifted me and I lay naked on his bed, where his spirit had loved me and kept its vigil; he kissed the feet he held, and parted my thighs, and stroked my hair, and caressed the dampness and the silk of the vulva. I spoke to him, not from fear but reminiscence and uncertainty; he said, "No. This is what I want," and kissed me, the softness of his hair against my thigh; I spoke his name, and he entered me with his tongue and, exquisitely, with his fingers, giving this most delicate gift, and the vulva flowered and gave its sweetness to his tongue. I held his wrists, sailor's wrists, and he left me, undressing without haste, beauty in his nakedness and in his arousal against the burning light, the savage scars on his belly revealed, like his sex, without shame.

There was great beauty in his lovemaking: no ecstasy yet, only peace, a deep and passionate offering of self, even now anticipating rejection, even now both feared and desired. The invitation was mine: had I withdrawn he would not have insisted. He entered me with infinite patience, sensing the instinctive resistance, the anticipation of pain, moving within me with exquisite slowness, as though he would wait for me forever, beyond pain, beyond shame, beyond memory, until I should come to him, cradling me, lifting me, until his bones were mine, his flesh mine, his scars mine, in the eternal rhythm; I clasped him strongly, as with silken hands, embracing him, and he was not a ghost, not a memory, not a shadow, not the incarnation of the past, either in its terror or its sweetness, but himself and none other, not to be compared, not in the most infinitesimal second, but one greatly loved, who received and cherished my body and its scarred and injured spirit. I tasted myself on his lips, and my spirit and my womb embraced him, and I called him what he had been to me for many weeks, my love, my love, and felt the convulsive joy of his orgasm, and my womb received the sweet salt of his seed.

We slept in one another's arms, he within me: he did not leave me, nor now, nor ever. Beyond the little deaths of the senses, the darkness of the deadened spirit, he waits for me still.

VI

I may say that I alone am responsible for my life, that I am invulnerable, that the politics and the fates of nations cannot touch me. I may live in naïveté, and in bliss, ignoring the signs, the warnings. I may say, it is not written, and yet, it was written. No man is an island, and no woman; we are not inviolable; time bears us, irresistibly, upon its fatal tide.

The years have not diminished him, nor has death deified him: he is as he was. I loved him, as I love him still, to the exclusion of all else: a thousand words would not confine that love: though I wrote until my life's end no ink, nor heart's blood, will evoke him. My passion for him was absolute: for the man, who was my dear companion, for the spirit that opened to me and responded with its sweetness, for his body and his sexuality, which were my renascence. In him, I was reborn.

That we should remain together was without question. My life was with him: I did not contemplate leaving Jamaica without him. He was older than I, his health in some measure damaged, but life is precarious, and in this fever-ridden island it was not unlikely that I should precede him to the grave, or that we should die together: no woman could ask for sweeter consummation. I prayed for ten years, that we should have ten years together: it was not long, it was not eternity. For some, love cannot survive a season, or a year: he knew it, as I knew. Passion dies. Love is not immortal. He said this himself to me. Love is not stronger than death; it confers no immortality.

And yet, as I live, I prove him wrong. Yet, of itself, love is immortal.

His life was briefly mine: the time granted was not enough. I could have loved him for a century without surfeit of him: my greatest desire could never be fulfilled, to have known and cherished and protected him throughout every epoch in that life. The fair child burned by the fierce sun of Bombay, speaking fluent Hindustani to his ayah, the crowded, stinking kaleidoscope of the streets and the days, the cobra in the garden, the clacking birds, the peacocks, the smells of the harbour, the roar of the monsoon rain, the child passionately interested in them all, sketching in pastel, thinking, dreaming, talking to forbidden strangers... a sensitive, affectionate, sharply intelligent, compassionate child, the youngest and only survivor of seven, victims of cholera and typhoid. And later, to have loved him as a young man, the very young officer, the midshipman baptised in blood, the prisoner of war.

I was a prisoner of war from my twentieth to my twenty-first year, from February twenty-second to October fifteenth, 1743... before you were born. I was second lieutenant aboard the Tonnerre, a former French prize... she drove ashore that afternoon near Toulon... the squadron was defeated. My captain committed suicide... twenty-nine of us were taken prisoner... twenty-four of them died. We had nothing... no medicine, no letters, no razors... what little I had in my pockets was taken... it was not returned. The guards were ignorant, not brutal, but completely insensitive...men died of typhus... there was dysentery... consumption... we had worms... I had every kind of vermin... they refused to remove the dead.... I memorized the Articles of War. I wrote three plays, in my head... I taught navigation to one of the midshipmen... then he died. I became fluent in French.... I calculated once that I spent six thousand seven hundred and eighty-four hours occupied by those pursuits. I told you it was a hard school... it was a rock on which men's hearts were broken.

And yet you believe that, too, was written?

Oh, yes. I believe there is a purpose to everything, if only to have made me what I am. But after I was exchanged and went back to sea, the first enemy I killed I killed for them... for my friends, and myself.

He was mine, but what he had been would never be mine. Aged twenty-three, the commander of the sloop *Hazard*, wounded in the head and face at Cap Finisterre on the second of October 1747. I was two years old... and still, on the fine, tanned, creased skin beneath my lips and fingers, he bore the scars. Commander, two years later, of the brig *Vivid*; a post-captain at the age of twenty-nine. At Louisbourg in 1758, in command of one of eighteen frigates there; with Wolfe at Quebec in the annus mirabilis; war in the golden weather; at Martinique in 1762, in command of His Majesty's ship *Lightning*. Another woman's lover, old in adultery, the begetter of an illegitimate son... if he had been mine then, before the cruelty of wounds and illness and rejection had disordered that bright spirit. And then Havana, and Havana's aftermath. The older, embittered, suffering man, discarded by the woman and the service, drifting down toward oblivion and criminality... to have been with him then, to have prevented the inevitable.

What is your son's name?

James Fletcher Hamilton. It was as much of my name as she cared to give him.

Did he know, when you met him?

I don't know. I was introduced as an old friend of his mother's.... He can draw his own conclusions.

Did you care for him?

No. Not particularly.

Did you love her?

I became... attached to her. It was not enough.

Why did you allow it to happen?

I had no control over it... and, not for the first time, I bore the consequences of my impulse.

He had lived by violence, and been moulded by it, since his childhood, and that loss of innocence was irrevocable, yet he was, essentially, a gentle man, courteous, generous, humourous, honourable, a man to be loved, and admired, and emulated, as others had loved and admired him: the friends of his youth, of whom he spoke only to me; a generation of midshipmen upon whose malleable characters he had left his indelible impression; the girl, virgin seducing virgin aboard *Conquest*, rocked in the arms of the Caribbean.

He was not a secretive man, nor given to sensational disclosure. What I wished to know, he told me: he repressed what seemed explicit, or irrelevant, or potentially injurious. He did not speak of his long affair with Elizabeth Hamilton, or of the birth of their son: these revelations hurt me, and were deeply private, and he did not freely offer them. Nor did he illuminate the years and the debaucheries that followed, although I sensed that these liaisons had further disillusioned him. He spoke without regret or subterfuge of the drug that gambling had become to him, the vast sums won, the independent commissions undertaken to finance his losses. Before his initiation into the organization he had committed highway robbery several times: in later years, upon the instruction of others, he had carried out the execution of informers.

I did not judge him, or believe in judgment. In conversations, I lived his life; his experience became mine: I became him. If I could have become him utterly, inhabited his skin and his soul to the obliteration of myself, I would have been happy. I would have killed any who injured him. I would have died for him, would have given my life for his. In him, I came to life, I lived with an intensity learned from him, with his vividness. With him, the light died: in his death was mine.

A life is not relived in a week, or a month, or a succession of months. Memory is shadows, subtleties, nacred with significance, experience understood only on reflection, pain apprehended through the prism of maturity... pain relived is undiminished.

In conversations, in the aftermath of lovemaking, in candlelight, in the living silence of the nights at sea, at sunset on the beach while the sea spoke of eternity and the tide erased our footprints, in the shadows of Rosewynd's jacaranda, encouraged by him, I evoked the past, its ghosts, and the ghost of myself, that vanished, anguished Margaret. I told him things of which I had not, could not have spoken; I never spoke of them again; as his secrets lie within my heart, so mine were wounds upon his, and now are known to no one.

I spoke of my childhood, my perception that I was an encumbrance on a dying marriage, despised by Catherine and, in the early days of alcoholic depression, only tolerated by Mordaunt; I said that I had never been secure, never assured of my worth; I spoke of the incest, as I had perceived it, which had stained my adolescence, the awareness of unrequited desire, the revelation, with maturity and introspection, that the potential for requital had existed; I spoke of Scotland, the horror and the poignancy, the piercing glimpse of rapture, the love and the loved, now dead... that I had not wanted the child of my marriage, and by my hatred had condemned it to death... that I had tasted madness, and the fear of madness haunted me even now... that sometimes I had believed myself lesbian, because I had been incapable of contemplating sexual relations... that I alone was responsible for the last night in my marital home... many memories, but not the last... the unspeakable.

We had made love at Rosewynd, in the afternoon, on cushions on the floor of our room: the house was still, embracing us with its peace, the slaves absent or discreet, the contractors gone away. Under other circumstances I would have considered my abandon shameful, with another man, in another, less sensuous climate; but it was not another country, and he was not another man, and the love was a consecration of that hour and that place, and the lovemaking exquisite.

He had been silent, listening; the room smelled of new timber, fresh paint, mildew, the twenty-five years of neglect, the frangipani I had cut, of the cigarillo he had been smoking, and had taught me to smoke; his skin smelled of sex, and my perfume, and cleanliness.

"How can so beautiful a spirit inflict such cruelty on itself?"

"Perhaps I deserve it. Perhaps I am all those things."

"Let me tell you the truth, and I want you always to remember it. You are the most female of women... and I cannot tell you the pleasure and joy and comfort you give me."

I wept, although I would not willingly have despoiled that hour with my tears.

He said, "I love you. I shall love you until I die, and if the spirit is immortal I shall love you beyond death. That is the truth."

But although he said, remember me always, he leaves me by degrees, and fragments: his voice ceases to speak to me: I am as insubstantial as he: I am myself only a shadow among shadows: the Margaret he loved fades from existence, and is no more known to me.

He asked me to marry him in the early autumn of that year: he had just returned from La Guaira, running before the serpent's coil through the Lesser Antilles. I thought him preoccupied and depressed, and the proposal incomprehensible, and a source of exquisite pain.

We were sitting in the darkness: he had eaten nothing that evening, wanted nothing: we had not loved since his return: Havana's legacy was twisting in his bowels. I laid my hand on his, and his fingers embraced mine, although he did not look at me.

"Would you, if you could?"

"Yes."

"Then marry me. Who cares what we do here? Who in God's name would know?"

"I am happy as we are. Aren't you?"

He released me, and rested the heels of his hands against his cheekbones, his eyes closed: he said nothing. I rose and went to him, and held his head against my body; the burning vivacity had left him utterly; with pain, I sensed an unutterable weariness of spirit.

He said, "Dreams die. It was my dream... only once... to ask you."

He did not speak of marriage again: it was I who spoke of it, with an agonized tentativeness, and he who demurred, for reasons which were then unclear, and to which hindsight gives perfect clarity. On the fifteenth of September, my birthday, he gave me an emerald and diamond ring: I wear it still. With it, in my heart, I married him.

Write to Mordaunt, he said. Tell him you are alive. The letter would be forwarded if the regiment had been transferred.

I said that I could not. Too many reasons, too many miles, too much silence: I understood now how months and years could fall into the breach.

Even Eve in Eden was accountable, he said. Was it so impossible to speak of what had happened to us?

I, who wrote so fluently, attempted it for his sake: too much and too little. Words would not be summoned: they had greater power to injure than enlighten: these were blows I could not deal. To think me dead was, perhaps, kinder.

I told him I had sent it. It was the first time I had lied to him, and the knowledge poisoned many hours which would otherwise have been sweet. But I was not alone in deception.

In the late autumn of 1774 he was absent at sea, carrying produce from this verdant paradise to the barren islands of Aruba and Curaçao. Trade to the restive colonies of Massachusetts Bay, New Hampshire and Connecticut, importers of Jamaican rum, coffee, sugar and molasses, had become uncertain, if not hazardous: the port of Boston had been closed as of the first of June, and the Royal Navy enforced that blockade; and newspapers circulating among planters and politicians invariably found a repository in Coventry's billiard room, where they were read, by me at least, with the conviction of impending disaster. Recent numbers of the radical *Boston Gazette* and the more moderate *Evening Post* reported the convention of delegates from all colonies in Philadelphia; what was christened "the first continental congress" was in progress from the fifth of September until October twenty-sixth. The rhetoric arising from this conference of lawyers and administrators was inflammatory, and its purpose and existence seemed more to incite unrest than to conciliate. The isolation of Boston and its unregenerate citizens, destroyers of tons of East India Company tea in the now infamous acts of vandalism dubbed the Boston tea party, was an unremitting source of tension. The Quebec Act, recently passed to facilitate the government of Canada, extended its borders south and westward, from the fort at Detroit to Illinois, recognizing the validity of French civil law and allowing without persecution the practice of Roman Catholicism in France's conquered colony, by the stroke of a parliamentary pen wresting this vast, savage, fur-bearing territory from those who considered it their birthright, and affronting colonial traders and land speculators, prospective settlers, colonels of militia who feared incursion by an enemy, and the descendants of Protestant bigots. Incurably aggrieved, this congress passed, among other fatal resolutions, its Declaration of Rights and its retribution on behalf of Boston, a proposal to ban completely further participation in the slave trade and trade with Britain and Ireland, importation of East India tea from any source including Holland, the importation of wine from Madeira, and the importation of sugar, molasses, coffee, rum, indigo, tobacco or pimento from the British West Indies, as of the first of December.

Thomas Gage, general, and governor of the unhappy colony of Massachusetts Bay, wrote to his masters in London while pursuing his hopeless policies of non-confrontation, "If you think ten thousand men enough, send twenty; if a million is thought enough, give two; you will save both blood and treasury in the end." His was the soldier's thankless task, and his prescience was ignored. He was a voice crying in the wilderness. The torrent of eloquence from the throat of a young Virginia lawyer fell more favourably on the ear of Congress.

"I am not a Virginian, but an American."

The entity was born, the die was cast.

By Christmas of 1774 we were still living at Ironshore: the restoration of Rosewynd would require a year. The importation of building materials and furnishings from France and Italy was an excruciating process, the contractors slow, slave labour unreliable and sometimes unobtainable, white craftsmen, and there were few, in demand on every plantation, and their skills and time proportionately expensive. For months Rosewynd remained the gracious ruin it had been for a quarter of a century: repairs progressed, faltered and were resumed, barely keeping pace with the subtle, relentless damage inflicted by the climate.

The affairs of Rosewynd were my exclusive concern. I ordered and harangued and interviewed, on paper and in person, in the white heat of midday, and in dripping, malarial afternoons with the red earth splashed to my knees. The delays and the endless invention of lies to excuse them infuriated me, even as I became aware that our efforts to create a future from chaos and unconventionality were incapable of fulfillment. Our life was an illusion, a dream of transient sweetness. Eventually I would embrace the sweetness, cease to fear and anticipate the future, cease this defiant insistence: accept what was, and what would never be.

Jamaican society had not embraced me: it was corrupt and predatory and prejudiced, and I did not participate in its rituals or offer my private life to feed its remorseless appetite for scandal. We lived, unmarried; whether that fact was known did not concern me, or occasion me any shame.

Our relationship had not begun with subterfuge, nor was it conducted in secrecy, but we had never made a business of being lovers. Life had assaulted a demonstrative child and diminished my capacity for display, and St. James, although affectionate by nature, could withdraw into reserve: weeks passed before he held my hand in the presence of others, or walked with his arm around my shoulders, or kissed me openly on his return from sea.

I hated these separations, the anguished severance, the dread of every storm. When it was possible, when the port of call was not a hell-hole, when he desired my interpretation in Spanish, a language I had learned that year and one he loathed and refused to speak, when Rosewynd released me or Coventry assumed the burden of my duties, I accompanied him, and this, too, was discussed over the tea-tables of Trelawney parish; this too is immutable memory, indescribable joy.

There are days in the calendar which are fatal, which will kill; they remain unknown and recur yearly with innocence until imbued with that significance, after which they are hated. That day in January of 1775 was fair; the year had not yet dawned upon which it would destroy my life. I was walking an endless white beach with Coventry; the sea was restless, iridescent, the year, like the shimmering expanse before us, pristine, its potential unknown. There was little conversation, but the silence was not constrained: we had walked in this manner in St. James's absence for several months. Circumstance had divested us of pretense, and by its savage alchemy Coventry had become what I was to him, a companion in remembered horror, and an intimate in loneliness.

He was walking barefoot, his stockings in his pocket, stabbing at the ebb and flow around us with a malacca stick: he complained of pain and numbness in his legs. His feet, like the nakedness glimpsed that night, were hairy and unbeautiful; one of the toes had been crudely amputated, a fact of which, like most of his life, he had never spoken.

He said, "You understand now what I mean. Partir, c'est mourir un peu."

"Yes. I die every day I am not with him."

"And the sea, you love that, too? Or do you tolerate it, for his sake?"

"I fear it, when I am with him, and when I am not."

"I thought so. No woman could love that widowmaker." Silence: only the sea's voice, the reef, ephemeral and eternal. "You love him, and it gives me joy to see it. I would not have his happiness jeopardized, or yours." Again, silence: on that windy shore it seemed to encompass us. "I have never betrayed a man, or a woman, or a confidence, but I tell you this for his sake. You think him in Bermuda. Bermuda is a useful source of information. There is a keener market further north."

"The ports are closed."

"A closed port and an embargo are no obstacle to him."

No. Nor would they be.

"How long?"

"Since last autumn. There's no money in Aruba."

"Are others involved?"

"Yes. We all have rum and sugar to sell. He pays in gold. There are those who find that more satisfying than a letter of credit from a sugar factor in Bristol. It is not illegal.... yet."

Bermuda... twelve hundred miles away... a necklace of reefs, a dead volcano in a sargasso sea.

"He reserves another commodity for the future. The night you arrived he landed a thousand Charleville muskets: he acquired more last summer. He keeps them at the distillery. He inspects them from time to time but he has, as yet, made no arrangements for their disposal."

"Can they be moved without your knowledge?"

"No. The warehouse is secure. Access to it is solely through me. It would be impossible."

Cloud, hanging like smoke on the mountains to the south; shadows passing over my face; the eye, seared by so much beauty, accepting the dimness with gratitude. The sea darkened, the air seemed cool. Beyond this point was mangrove, sea grape, the shallow river, stained like blood with the deep red earth of the hills, the scuttling of land crabs, the rustling, whispering claws.

"When he attempts to move these muskets, will you tell me?"

"Yes."

Beyond the stones and the snakes and the deadly mosquito and the mangrove and the lurking alligators, beyond the broken shells which could never survive the reef, beyond the shimmering curtain of heat like a phantom between myself and the future, was Rosewynd Bay... his anchorage... and in the coolness of the mountains, Rosewynd, never to be mine.

"Thank you for this, Noel."

He leaned on the stick, unsmiling, the dark eyes impenetrable.

"Consider it reparation. It's little enough."

There were charts in that house; they were not St. James's, and the pencilled calculations were not his; perhaps they are there still, bearing the pinpoints of the brass dividers that pierced a fathomless sea. The Windward Passage... to Bermuda, thirty-two degrees fifteen minutes north latitude, sixty-four degrees, thirty-eight minutes west longitude... to a destination further north, between thirty-two and forty degrees, north north west, north by west, the points of a compass subject to variation, a westering course conceding to sea and wind and current... at an average speed of seven knots, a thousand, two thousand miles....

It was not illegal. It was trade. There was little peace, but there was no war, no severing, no crime; for him, there was little risk.

Eleven days. I could not have known, in the hours and the play of seaborne light across his charts, that I should calculate these possibilities now as he had taught me, staring at the deadness of configurations and soundings which were the living sea.

When he returned... not Bermuda's cold sun but the Atlantic in winter would be written on his face. And on my heart.

He arrived, unannounced as usual, in the early afternoon of Sunday, January twenty-ninth, when I was at Rosewynd. On my return, he was sitting on the terrace before his opened doors. The coolness of the shadow after the sun's assault seemed pleasant to me; we talked of inconsequential things, then, at a little past four, he told me he wanted to rest. I thought him tired and subdued, constrained perhaps by an intuition that I knew of his activities. I did not recognize the onset of recurrent malaria.

Darkness is swift and complete in those latitudes, as sudden as death. By nightfall he was acutely ill. The parasites in his blood consumed him; he was gripped by convulsions, his teeth clenched, his skin icy; I closed the jalousies at his request, and the candlelit hell we shared became stifling. In the night I stripped and lay naked against him, in some primitive, instinctive attempt to transfer my heat; he lay in a seeming peace, as though I had arrested the uncontrollable trembling.

I slept an hour; he became restless, the embrace disturbed him. I dressed and sat in the cane chair near the bed and heard the rain, the palms, the sea.

He said distinctly, "The enemy."

Perhaps he saw me: I thought not. The intensity of his vision was very frightening.

"There is no enemy here."

He closed his eyes.

In the blue hour before dawn he was burning: he was neither conscious nor asleep. Coventry was invariably alone at breakfast, taken every day on the terrace outside his suite: I walked around the house into the sunrise and found him there with the coffee, the cigar, the newspaper, the pistol his companion even now.

He came with me. It was the only time he revealed the nature of his affection: I would neither see nor sense it again: St. James never knew. It was revealed by nothing but the tenderness of his hands, but all things were heightened in that hour, and I sensed also, no, I knew, by his hands, that he had been a surgeon.

He spoke very softly: only the fingers of the left hand acknowledged him, and he looked up at me directly, measuring the pulse in the carotid artery.

I said, "For God's sake, help me."

Coventry withdrew, taking with him my absolute trust. Time passed; the morning opened, vivid, ephemeral; he had been burning for five hours; throughout the evening, the night and the morning he had drunk nothing, nor urinated. He opened his eyes, and said with such anguish that I thought he was dreaming, "What do you want with me, eh? Poor, sick, old bastard... what could you want from me?"

"I want you, Leslie."

His pulse was very fast, and faint: repeated attacks would kill him.

He said, "Margaret, bury me in England."

He did not speak again.

Midnight; and the morning of another day. Maica and I attempted to give him cinchona bark, cinchona ledgeriana, which had been sent from Cinnamon Hill and crushed to powder in claret: the only specific for malaria, it destroys the infective agent. Its smell and taste were revolting, and he refused it, saying that it sickened him.

She was sitting by the bed, her face, like Coventry's, impenetrable, the introspection of the slave: he was lying in my arms, sweating heavily, as he had shivered and burned and sweated at intervals, eight, fifteen, twenty-four hours: the silk sheets were transparent with his sweat.

Like Coventry, she used him with ineffable gentleness. He had drunk and vomited, and refused, for two days and nights.

She said, "You listen to me, man. You drink this or you die, and make this woman widow before she wife."

In illness, as in health, he was intensely sensitive. He drank, and the sweat running on his face did not deceive me. He wept, but we both pretended otherwise, and the pretense comforted him.

With recovery came depression: he who was always mercurial seemed reflective and subdued. Twice a week he visited the ship, lying off Gun Point Wharf with an anchor watch aboard, and the office he kept in the town, but he did not speak of returning to sea, and his activities between thirty-two and forty degrees north were not confided to me.

His spirit had been shaken, either by a perceived risk or an intimation of mortality. What he needed of me, I gave. I asked no questions.

Coventry kept a twenty-two foot skiff called *Eleuthera* in Rosewynd Bay; although we had been offered the use of her, she had never previously interested St. James. Perhaps he hungered for the sea. We took her out one morning in March and steered southwest, running down the trades, with Jamaica to larboard and a thousand fathoms beyond the reef.

He seemed very happy, bareheaded, barefoot, his salt-stained, seagoing shoes thrown into the sternsheets, the strong wind blowing his hair; he made fast his lines and came effortlessly aft to where I sat gripping the tiller. We sat for some time together in the silence and the spray, his hand over mine, the sun burning our backs, the tan sail thudding.

He said, into the silence, "I have been offered a commission. In Philadelphia, in January, and lately by letter."

The silence resumed, the spray bursting in the sunlight, our shadow passing, with the shadow of clouds, across the sea's face.

"I said I was too old... they said there were others like me. I said that, in my heart, I still held the King's commission... they said they knew of my seniority. I said I had forfeited it. They offered me a higher rank. I said that I would let them know." His hand moved, releasing mine. "Let me take her now."

I moved away. He sat in profile to me, the coppery hair blown over his face, his head lifted, his eyes on the sail.

"If you do this, everything we have... our lives, Rosewynd... everything, goes for nothing. For a cause you do not espouse— you don't espouse it, do you?"

He did not answer me. Although I knew him utterly, this I never knew.

"Could you divorce yourself from your country?"

"I already have."

"You spoke of returning. There's no return from a traitor's grave." Spray like rain on my face, stinging in my eyes: salt on my lips. "If England wants to crush this insurrection, she can smash America to atoms. No rabble could stand against that power. No one will resist."

He said, "Yes." He did not turn his face toward me; the tanned left hand eased the tiller, the canvas trembled and filled.

"St. James—"

"Yes."

"Listen to me."

"I am listening."

"I am a child of rebellion. I saw its aftermath, not immediately, but visited upon the next generation. Would you be prepared to risk that? For God's sake, you stood in the line of battle. Would you hazard your life against that?"

"It would never happen."

"How can it never happen when it's almost a certainty?"

"War is a chimera. The fear of war is profitable. Christ, I'd rather die in a broadside than of boredom shipping limes to Aruba."

"Or a thousand Charleville muskets from Brest to Montego Bay." He shifted slightly, the light across his face, his eyes upon me, the colour of the sea. "In your heart, you are a naval officer. In your heart, you never left it. How can you put guns into the hands of those who will kill your brother officers?"

"When a man dies, he dies because fate has decided it, not because the musket that killed him was of my supply."

She dipped, and lifted to the sky, leaning hard over, the water creaming down her side. Eleutheros... before her, on this tack, only a trio of windswept cays in the Serranilla Bank, and the coast of Nicaragua three hundred miles away.

He said, "I want to put diamonds around your neck. All I have is the ship and the sea. I don't know the land, and I hate slavery. If Noel offered for Rosewynd, I'd sell it."

Time passed, the sea here indigo and aquamarine, the land distant, mountainous, a fallen cloud in a necklace of surf. We drank watered wine heated by the sun, and ate crabmeat and bread; he quoted the *Odyssey*, grey-eyed Athena, and the west wind singing over wine-dark seas; I removed the man's hat of plaited palm I wore and threw it on the bottom boards, and took off my shirt, and sat naked in the sun.

He said, "You make it very difficult for me to apply myself to my seamanship."

Eventually he, too, removed his clothes, and lashed the tiller; in the heat of the sun we made love, awkwardly, passionately; I drank his essence, and tasted my wetness on his lips.

An hour: two hours.

He said, "Shall we come about?"

"Must we?"

"Perhaps a little further. With the best will in the world, I shan't have you back before nightfall."

"What does night matter to me, as long as we're together?"

I slept fitfully beneath a canvas, on the breast of the sea, but the motion was very lively and I returned to him, seated as though he had never moved, with his left hand on the tiller, the northeast trade still at his back, the sun, declining, in his eyes.

"Do you know where we are?"

"Of course. Take a glass and look over there."

So I saw Negril and its infinite beach, vanishing beyond the power of the lens, and ours were the only human eyes upon it; the sea was ours, and the beach as empty as Eden.

"I shall take you to that beach one day, and make love to you there, and lie with you all night beneath the stars."

We sailed through the great bath of westering light, and came about, the tiller down to larboard. *Eleuthera* swung into the wind, her light-drenched sail thundering, up on the larboard tack; at his shouted commands, I eased her tiller until she came closer to the wind; she leaned hard over, taking water across her bows. From forward he shouted, "Put your helm up," and we steered due east: the dashing spray over her bows lessened, the sail hardened; he made all fast and came aft to me, laughing, and took the tiller.

East into evening, toward the moon that laid its glittering track across the sea, as on other evenings under the dew-drenched, quivering driver, on the Atlantic, where I had learned to love him. East until morning.

"St. James."

He was gazing at an infinity of stars, their constellations a map to him, his face uplifted, abstracted, as though in the presence of mystery.

"When did you know that you loved me?"

"On nights like this, at sea." The shadow of the sail trembled faintly; the wind was very wet; it seemed cool, almost cold. "I wanted you.... I am only human, and you are very beautiful."

"I am not. I am very plain."

"Whoever told you that was a damned liar."

Time, and the stars' passage, phosphorescence on the sea.

"You were so afraid... and I wanted you so much. I dared not even touch you... and the more we spoke, the more I wanted... not the woman, not merely a woman, but... you. The soul, the spirit, the mind, the heart. I couldn't bear to contemplate leaving you. I thought... perhaps once, at Ironshore, before leaving... you might allow me. I never thought it would be as it was— for myself, least of all. One who so ardently avoided commitment finds himself astonished by love."

He slept an hour or two: his was the sailor's gift of instant sleep, instant wakefulness. I took the tiller, watched the stars, an infinitesimal mote of nothing, dust on the sea.

East into morning. He woke, seemingly refreshed: the chilly sleep and the watches of the night were natural to him. We ate a little; I tried to disentangle the sea's hands from my hair; as we had talked the sun down, like Heraclitus, so now we ran the moon into a dimness which was not yet dawn. We talked of India, of his childhood; for the first time, he gave his parents flesh.

"My mother was a Saumarez. It was considered very poor judgment on her part to have married him, and of course all the dire predictions about India came true. When my father came ashore he made a fortune, literally— which she was always very quick to remind him, and me, that he was very chary of distributing.... He was considered a handsome man, but dour... unaffectionate... disciplined. He had no vices, and she, poor bitch, had them all."

"What was she like?"

"She was thin... not particularly pretty, although she had great charm... her voice was beautiful. Her name was Charlotte. My father called her Letty, which she hated."

"My only friend was called Charlotte."

"My uncle called her Carissima— I overheard it. He was not her first lover, nor she his.... my childhood friend's name was David. I told you, didn't I."

"He died of cholera."

"Yes. Poor little bastard... he would never have made a soldier. He was a gentle soul."

There was silence. Some thought of which he did not speak had caused him great pain.

With gentleness, I recalled him from it.

"And your father's brother?"

"He was a damned rogue, and I adored him. He gave me a midshipman's dirk, that year of his affair with my mother, and told my father to send me to sea, as it was so obviously what I wanted.... He was always a great champion of me. Eventually, over a period of years, when my mother's infidelities became known, my father convinced himself that I was not his son. And so, when he died, he left his considerable estate to some one else. That news came to me some months after my release... it was not a happy year, after Toulon."

"And you had nothing?"

"Absolutely nothing. He was perfectly justified. My uncle was dead in the South Seas; my mother never cared to refute it. I would only have spent it foolishly... it was a bitter blow, all the same."

"Would you have left the sea?"

"No. I would never leave the sea... except, perhaps, for you."

Sunrise: the mother of pearl sky, the molten light on the sea. In the minutes after rising the sun's heat was palpable.

He gave me the telescope.

"Look there, and see the sailor's nightmare."

To starboard, the glassy surge of undertow, the smoke of spray in the sunlight. By day on the shore, it was unheard, by night a sullen thunder; here, standing well up to windward, the air quivered to its sound. It was the voice within the shell, the menace, the remorseless undernote, not of the sea but the reef.

"This is as close as I want to come to that. The undertow there would be as strong as a river— it would suck a ship onto that coral and smash out her heart within minutes, and the coral would tear the flesh from your bones. The sharks feed there, and the barracuda, and the barracuda is the more dangerous predator, because it will follow its prey into shallow water, even to the beach."

I gave him back the glass, imagining the salt of spray across my mouth.

"Stand away, for God's sake."

His fingers closed around the glass; the brass and the beaten wood of the tiller were bloomed with moisture. The sail steamed; the smoke and spray of the reef fell away into the tumult of the sea.

He said, "The reef is death, and each one of us crosses it alone."

"I would cross it with you, if you asked me to."

"Dear Margaret... dear child. I believe you would."

We came into Rosewynd Bay a day and a night after leaving it, not on the tide, not in a white dawn, but anonymously in late morning. No one saw us haul down the sail: no one watched us through a telescope from the seat beneath Rosewynd's jacaranda. Although sometimes I am there, watching the sail and the sea, like wrinkled silk in the beauty of the morning: I wait, in the coolness of Rosewynd's cloud, but I dream, and he never comes.

***

667

The steep, twisting streets of that harbour town spill, with garbage and brilliant shrubbery and weeds and rotting fish heads, down to the sea and the beach; the gaudy whores parade, the freed men and women of colour, the mulattoes poling bumboats in the harbour, hawking fruit and heavy rum, the naked children diving for coins, or begging, plucking at a silken sleeve or the tail of a crushed linen coat until sent sprawling into a gutter overflowing with Jamaica's plentiful rain; planters' wives perspiring under parasols carried by impassive slaves, men of business in sour, sweat-stained suits, their pallor in proportion to their arrogance. White cockroaches, the blacks call us... Creole, colonial, Englishwoman: we are all one to them, as faceless and contemptible as one race to another.

It smells, this town, rank offal in my memory: of sugar and complacency, of the sea's pungency and the tar and hemp and effluent which are the sea's business: of salt, and ships, and slavers, and sailors, and venereal whores. My excursions to the harbour are always regarded as an unnecessary evil by the slave Estevan, whose especial duty it is to escort me: Coventry trusts no one else. Estevan is six feet four inches tall, his head shaven, his age perhaps fifty. An indefatiguable horseman, he wears Islam like a garment: in his left ear there is a thick gold hoop, a mark of individuality encouraged by Coventry. Occasionally during the twelve mile ride we speak, sometimes in French, the language of his first, Creole master; he indicates beauty and hazards in the road with equal gravity, guards my person, conducts me to the harbour steps and instructs the boatman, and waits on the wharf an hour, perhaps two, for my return. Perhaps, in his eyes, I too am a whore, and my love and my lover sin and sinner. I think not. In his impenetrability there is humanity: he has loved, perhaps still loves, perhaps both master and slave.

The black man want me because I white, the white man because I black. I don't want no man now, Marguerite... not even Eduardo.

On Gun Point Wharf on the morning of Monday, the twenty-second of May, 1775, I bought St. James a shell, a king helmet, one of those that feed on sea urchins in these sandy shallows: I bought it as I had bought triton, murex, cowrie, conch, from the freed slave who daily displayed his wares, cleaned sponges, sea fans bleached with salt, shells on palmetto leaves, buckets of living scallops. The man, who had no age and no right forearm, (*...the shark take, mistress...*) stood beneath the lash of the sun with necklaces of shells on the stump, sometimes in the company of a golden-haired child with green eyes in negroid features, and took the coins from my hand and blessed me as he always did in the name of Christ his master, before Whose power all men would be humbled, and the child folded the clean shell into crushed brown paper and gave it to me without meeting my eyes. The transaction was viewed suspiciously by Estevan; the shell was worthless, and perhaps the seller, whose naked, knotted calves bore the corrugations of the whip, was contemptible in his poverty or his humility.

He asked me, in French, if I would wish him to take the shell. I said that I would carry it aboard with me, and he inclined his head as though this, too, had been expected, and summoned the boat for me.

I went out to the ship, silent, restless, riding at her anchor, the epitome of loneliness and desolation. Only Harris lived aboard, faithful to his captain's peculiarities; all the others whose lives I had briefly shared had scattered throughout the Caribbean, with the exception of Mark David Ransom, who occasionally reappeared.

I went below to the great cabin. Harris, having seen me aboard with the usual monosyllabic greeting, left me as he would leave us, alone.

St. James was standing, as was his habit over charts, reading the exceptionally fine print of a stained news sheet, the reflection of the water thrown across his face and quivering on the deckhead, the strong left hand lightly resting on the desk, against the slight swell under her keel.

"First blood," he said.

It was dated, *In Congress, at Watertown, April 30, 1775.*

> The barbarous Murders on our innocent Brethren on
> Wednesday the 19th Instant, has made it absolutely necessary
> that we immediately raise an Army to defend our Wives and
> our Children from the butchering Hands of an inhuman Soldiery,
> who, incensed at the Obstacles they met with in their bloody
> Progress, and enraged at being repulsed from the Field of Slaughter;
> will without the least doubt take the first Opportunity in their Power
> to ravage this devoted Country with Fire and Sword.... Our all is at
> Stake, Death and Devastation are the certain Consequences of Delay,
> every Moment is infinitely precious, an Hour lost may deluge your
> Country in Blood.

I stood with the shell in my hands and my life fell into a vortex; it died, with the first blood spilled on an April morning at Lexington and Concord. I cannot remember having given him the shell, although I found it later among his possessions. All I hear in it now is the moaning of a thousand years of coral, the voice of the reef, which is death.

Boston, "this cursed place" as it was called by its guardian, Lieutenant-General Thomas Gage, was of no strategic value except for its harbour, a treacherous anchorage guarded by a chain of shoals and islands. Its shallow inner roads, strewn with tidal marshes and mud flats, were almost unnavigable, and the harbour and its rivers were prone to freezing, subject to the Atlantic's winter fogs and at the mercy of its storms.

It was to this inhospitable bastion that an army of twelve thousand withdrew after the skirmishes at Lexington and Concord, entrenching itself in a classic dilemma: an army with its back to the sea can only be relieved from the sea. The surrounding countryside had allowed Gage little choice: its topography was as hostile as its populace to the deployment of regular troops, and colonial marksmen had perfected the art of ambush.

At the end of May, a month punctuated by alarms and excursions, three generals disembarked from His Majesty's Ship *Cerberus* and joined the beleaguered Gage in Boston, dispatched by a government rendered anxious by blood-letting and convinced that Gage's conciliatory policy now required an infusion of strength. Major-General the Honourable William Howe, younger brother of the admiral Richard, Lord Howe, was no stranger either to the country or its potential for peculiarly savage warfare: having seen action at Fontenoy and Culloden, he had fought with Braddock at the Monongahela and at Ticonderoga, where his eldest brother had been killed, and had served under Wolfe at Quebec. A Whig member of Parliament, his distaste for the commission now offered him was undisguised. The tenderness of Americans toward his brother's memory had prejudiced him in their favour, and he openly criticized the King's "invincible obstinacy" in the present inflammatory atmosphere.

With him, and at thirty-seven the youngest of the generals in Boston, Major-General Henry Clinton was, like Howe, no stranger to the country. The son of an admiral who had been the unhappy governor of New York, he had held a commission in that militia until quitting the colonies for mildly distinguished service as aide-de-camp to the venerable whoremaster Sir John Ligonier, and in Germany during the Seven Years' War. A widower, he was a peevish, difficult, lonely and introspective man, who described himself miserably as a shy bitch, although he would find solace in Boston in the person of his housekeeper, a sergeant's wife, who would remain his mistress until his death.

The third member of this triumvirate, so mocked in London broadsheets, was the handsome and flamboyant cavalry officer, "Gentleman Johnny" Burgoyne, at fifty-two the oldest and least experienced of *Cerberus*'s generals. He had been notorious for eloping with the daughter of the Earl of Derby and living with her in France on the proceeds of a sold commission until the outbreak of the Seven Years' War, upon which his father-in-law, in a timely display of magnanimity, forgave the errant couple, and Burgoyne's rise in rank, with the Earl's influence, was appropriately meteoric. Playwright, politician and dedicated libertine, chronically unfaithful to his wife although by all accounts devoted to her, he accepted the appointment in Boston as a temporary measure at the specific request of the King, and would use her death as an excuse to escape the trap of Boston and return to London. It merely deferred an ignominious American destiny.

As these three, and Gage, with no mandate but to assess the situation, entrenched themselves in Boston, and authorized forays and foraging raids, and proclaimed both martial law and an amnesty for all rebels except the incendiary Samuel Adams and John Hancock, in whose house Clinton lodged, an undisciplined force was gathering in the outlying districts, acquiring greater strength as the weeks progressed. It was an army that moved within a cloud of rank body odour, its uniforms ill-fitting or nonexistent and rotting unlaundered on the wearers' backs, an army so intoxicated by egalitarianism that it habitually refused to obey its officers, and so devoted to the consumption of rum that it was said no New Englander could fight or say his prayers with the benefit of a bottle a day. This rabble in arms, however, knew enough of strategy to seize the initiative from Gage, who, after weeks of impotent skirmishing, belatedly prepared to fortify one of the promontories overlooking Boston, Dorchester Heights to the south of the city. Boston's network of spies provided forewarning of Gage's plan before the proposed night of June the eighteenth. In the chilly dawn of Saturday, June seventeenth, Burgoyne himself observed that the rebels had thrown up impressive earthworks under cover of darkness on the heights above the houses on the Charlestown peninsula, to the north and separated from Boston by a half-mile channel. The earthworks were fired upon, with little effect, as few of the guns in the harbour could be so elevated. By early afternoon the tide, the lack of flat-bottomed boats, the mud flats and marshes of the Mystic River, which would have offered a safer if slower approach, and the pressure of time convinced Howe of the necessity of a frontal assault. As second-in-command at Boston, he took two thousand men across the channel in rowing boats and landed on the Charlestown peninsula. Outnumbered, with losses even as he moved his men from the beach, he advanced, under constant fire from marksmen in the deserted village of Charlestown, evacuated over a period of weeks because it was within range of the guns of warships in the harbour and the battery on Copp's Hill: from this vantage point Clinton and Burgoyne were observing the efforts of their superior. The deadly fire continued until Howe sent a message across by boat requesting the battery's participation, whereupon, with a dramatist's flair, Burgoyne recorded, "We threw in a parcel of shells, and the whole was instantly in flame; our battery afterwards kept up an incessant fire on the heights; it was seconded by a number of frigates, floating batteries, and one ship of the line." Although Clinton would later seize an advantage and cross the channel with marines in support of Howe, Burgoyne, like the citizens of Boston who were crowding onto rooftops, merely witnessed the spectacle of war.

> If we look to the height, Howe's corps ascending the hill in the face of entrenchments, and in a very disadvantageous ground, was much engaged; to the left the enemy pouring in fresh troops by the thousands, over the land; and in the arm of the sea our ships and floating batteries cannonading before them; straight before us a large and noble town in one great blaze— the church-steeples, being timber, were great pyramids of fire above the rest... the roar of canons, mortars, and musketry; the crash of churches, ships upon the stocks, and whole streets falling together, to fill the ear; the storm of redoubts, with the objects above described, to fill the eye; and the reflection that, perhaps, a defeat was a final loss to the British empire in America, to fill the mind; made the whole a picture, and a complication of horror and importance beyond any thing that ever came my lot to be witness to.

In the space of an afternoon, in June heat, until the shadows were lengthening across this rough, rising, unreconnoitered ground, impeded by stone walls, rail fences, brick kilns, barns and the earthworks thrown up by the Massachusetts and Connecticut regiments under the American colonel William Prescott, with reinforcements flooding across Charlestown Neck to the secondary entrenchments on the steeper Bunker Hill behind Breed's, which Prescott had favoured, Howe's forces advanced and were repulsed, and attacked, and were again repulsed. For the edification of a hostile audience on the rooftops of Boston, the dead and the dying and the wounded, the felons, the debauched, the callous and the innocent, the scarlet coats, the gilded gorgets and the homespun of amateurs fell and lay scattered in the rough grass, twitching, alive with flies, a litter of human flesh, blood, brains, shit, viscerae. The living fought on, sweating, blinded, enraged by desperation, choked by the smoke of burning Charlestown and the taste of the bitten cartridge. Howe's artillery, initially supplied with the wrong ammunition and slowed by the marshy ground before Breed's Hill, came at last into position, and poured a devastating fire on the defenders of the breastwork; the light infantry, one company reduced to a mere five men, attacked the redoubt, feinted, and attempted again and again, drawing fire from the Americans until the defenders were rifling the pouches and pockets of the dead for powder and shot; finally a combined assault of infantry and marines "tumbled over the dead to get at the living". The defenders, now without water or ammunition, broke and fled to Bunker Hill, where those waiting to reinforce them were caught up in a headlong rout.

Howe held the field, but if it was victory it was Pyrrhic in nature: one of those who had defended the redoubt "wished we could sell them another hill at the same price." On this half mile of slaughter lay four hundred American dead, and two hundred and twenty-six private soldiers and non-commissioned officers; many of the eight hundred and twenty-eight who were wounded subsequently died of gangrene. Sixty-three officers were wounded by the scrap iron the enemy had used for ammunition, which produced an uncommon suppuration, and twenty-seven were killed.

The stifling heat of Boston's summer tormented the wounded, and the army, and the now blooded Continental army, regrouping and preparing for a seige. An impudent colonel remarked to Clinton, "You may be lions, but you are lions confined to a den." On the third of July the keeper of the lions' den, the Virginian George Washington, arrived in Cambridge to command the Continental army: a planter, slave-owner and former surveyor, he had been Braddock's aide-de-camp during the savage Monongahela campaign.

Gage was relieved in September and recalled to England, where he was held responsible for the bloody and inconclusive battle on Breed's Hill. Instead of grasping the nettle he had always tried to circumvent it: he was thought unfit for higher command. Howe assumed the role of commander-in-chief, trapped in Boston by the advent of autumn and the chronic shortage of ships in a navy diminished by years of peace. The regiments to reinforce him were scattered throughout the West Indies, in Canada, in Ireland, in garrisons in Scotland and England, in Minorca and Gibraltar; the machinery of parliament, in providing the men and matériel of war, ground no more rapidly than the mill of God.

I woke from my dream of him to his lips on my breast: there seemed no reason for the single candle burning in the hour before dawn, except to afford me the beauty of his nakedness and the joy of losing myself in his eyes, veiling his body with my hair, rising above him into ecstasy, possessed and possessing him so deeply that he seemed to pierce the very mouth of my womb. He came with me, with passionate ardour, and again as I lay in his arms, my body and his yet one, my cheek against his, the veil of my hair across his face.

"My goddess," he said.

He remained within me, quiescent sweetness: I drifted between sleep and the small death of orgasm; he stroked my hair, languorously; conscious of my weight upon him, I raised myself.

He said, "Don't leave me."

"I will never leave you."

I lay beside him on his pillow, my hair mingled with his, my face against his shoulder, caressing the dampness of his skin and penis, caressing the massive scars.

He said, "My dear love. My dear, dear love," and, with great gentleness, "Sleep now, darling."

I woke as I had slept, on his pillow, my left hand where he had lain. The sheet, delicately stained with lovemaking, was cool, the bed empty.

Daylight did not always find us together. Although we loved and slept within the sound of the sea, in my bed, where malaria had tormented him, it was not unusual for him to wake early and walk abroad, or take coffee on the terrace before his opened doors, and read the aging newspapers at sunrise; but the jalousies were closed, the cushions undisturbed; the vivid birds had not been fed.

The formal clothing, much of it unworn, remained in the wardrobe: the faded, salt-stained coats and shoes and sextant had been taken, and the private, leather-bound log, which was never left aboard the ship. Nothing else, only the dead silence of an unoccupied room, a book he had been reading, the shells, on a window seat and on the escritoire. There was no letter. He was only a voice, remembered, and the living essence within me, a slow, hot welling as of blood, as the womb surrendered what it loved. And this bitter revelation, that I should be the last to know. Of all this household, the merest slave who had heard the gravel beneath the hooves had been more privileged than I.

I saw Coventry at eleven o'clock. It was his custom to return from the fields at that hour, drink coffee, and sleep until the killing heat of midday had passed.

We sat in his study, on the first floor: here the light also burned, piercing the closed jalousies.

"Do you know where he has gone?"

"I gave him a letter for Charleston. Whether he will take it himself is a matter of conjecture."

"And his cargo?"

"Beyond salt, which is in great demand in Charleston, that too is conjecture... and a matter for his conscience."

He had flavoured the coffee with rum and was drinking meditatively, the leather case of cigars lying open on the mahogany desk, although he did not touch them.

"And his other commodity? Does he carry that?"

"He has a warehouse in town. He removed some of his commodity to there several weeks ago."

"You said you would tell me."

He poured again, half coffee, half rum, the hairy hand pausing; he selected a cigar and cut and lit it with studied indifference. "I have known men die for a moment's inattention at sea. Their minds linger on domestic strife, on sex, on fond memories of home, on the whore in their beds or the virago waiting at the wharf. You could have said nothing, and done nothing, to prevent him, and whatever you would have said or done would only distract him from his purpose now."

"You knew this, even as you promised me."

"Yes."

"For his sake."

"Yes."

I closed my eyes, closed myself against him, and upon a terrible, prescient grief: unspeakable, unendurable.

He said, "His natural element is the sea, and he has no fear. He is an addict, and nothing is stronger than addiction. Not man, not woman, not love. He lives for his drug. The fault is not yours, and the power to change him is not yours. Accept it or leave him, while you can."

I opened my eyes: he was watching me, perhaps surprised or intrigued by my stillness: perhaps the agony was all too perceptible.

"War is all but declared. If he is taken—"

"I cannot imagine any circumstances under which he would allow that to happen. He is not an ordinary man. He was not born for an ordinary death."

In the afternoon and evening I was at Rosewynd; I remember nothing of what I did there, except the sea, the wind and the current, the reflection of the sky, evening deepening the waters, the stillness of a house whose heart had long since ceased to beat; the voice within the stillness of my heart, which said, you will neither live nor die here. It is only now that you live, and die.

In his absence I was half myself; in this small bereavement, I tasted a greater. My preference for solitude, my devotion to private pursuits, my relentlessness in conducting the business of Rosewynd, and my disinterest in the social round which so pleasantly diverted him disturbed Coventry, who assumed that mine was a curable loneliness, which the friendship of other women would assuage. Although his penetration of human nature was intense, his understanding of me was minimal: perhaps I was an enigma too peculiar even for him.

I dismissed Richard Langley, who had been overseer at Rosewynd for six years, on Sunday the sixteenth of July, when he refused, not for the first time, to carry out instructions which did not come directly from his employer. I was by now better versed in the affairs of this plantation than St. James, who took surprisingly little interest in it, and I had sought and received Coventry's advice on every aspect; and I had the measure of Langley, a failed Methodist who, when drunk, abused the slaves physically and sexually, and when sober pined for England and contemplated his damnation. On that particular

675

afternoon, when he said that he would work for the Captain or Mr. Coventry but not for a woman, I informed him of St. James's displeasure, and told him the reasons for his dismissal. He called me a nigger-loving bitch and spat at my feet; I threw the weathered conch I kept as an ornament on the top step after him and called him an arrogant white bastard; the shell broke on the damp red earth imprinted with his heels. There were no witnesses but, suitably embellished, the details were known by sunset in every quarter. He did not consider his dismissal final until it came from Coventry.

At my request, Coventry began the search for a replacement. At sixty-six he still carried out many of the duties of his new overseer, whom he considered inexperienced. The blacks feared him, perhaps because of the rumour that he practised obeah, perhaps because they knew intimately a cruelty which was never more than sensed by me.

His mistress was as reticent as I. I did not seek her friendship, nor she mine: it was an organic thing, a communion of femaleness, born subtly, with few words. She simply appeared, sometimes to sit in complete silence in the coolness after sunset, sometimes with a glass of lime juice, or fresh quills, or a lamp, or a message from Coventry, although never the words I wanted her to speak. Always the slave's headcloth, the rubies in her earlobes, the beautiful, unsmiling mouth, the beautiful composure of the hands. Hers was a tireless, invisible labour: in my presence, the only impression she gave was of inscrutable repose.

She said one night, in the aftermath of a flaming sunset, "Eduardo tell me he take my child from school if this war come to us. He say he go to Charleston and bring."

And I knew to whom the letter had been written.

"Will you go with him?"

"What you t'ink? Black woman walk with white man in Charleston when Christ come again. Not before."

"And when your child comes home?"

"She Mr. Coventry daughter. She not my child then."

"Do you write to her? Does she tell you how it is in Charleston?"

"No. She not my child for many year. She not want nigger maman."

Nothing, in this island of incomparable beauty, had ever expressed more of human suffering and ineradicable evil.

"Why you shock, Marguerite? Sugar money blanch my child, and she inherit this earth. Octaroon inherit only the white man bed."

"Have you ever said this to Coventry?"

"What he do? C'est vrai." Then, "Why you not make a bébé with the Captain, Marguerite?"

Darkness seeped between us, too much silence, too much truth.

"I cannot."

"Who tell you this?" And then, in French, "Some leech with dirty nails? What does man know of the womb? What does man know of woman?"

I said nothing. In the darkness between us was the sea.

She said, gently, "You want the Captain child?"

"It will not give him immortality."

The cool hand rested on my wrist.

"I know your heart bleed for that man, no more than he bleed for you. When you first come here, I see he sometime at night. I see he lonely... you know what I mean. Jamaica make man blood hot... maybe woman too. And he good man, Marguerite. He good man. I ask him one night, maybe he want somet'ing I can give, maybe somet'ing some girl can give."

"Please don't."

"You listen, girl. I tell you that man faithful to you, before he love you with he body, before he make bed with you. He look in my eye, and I t'ink yes, yes, maybe... but he don't want me. He want you. He tell me."

I said, with a terrible bitterness, "Are you such good friends?"

"Santiago and I good friends. Not lovers. We never lovers. One night, he say he lost, he body and soul belong to you. I say that slavery. He say, love is not slavery. Love liberates, even as it binds."

And he was with me in the darkness, an intonation in a stranger's voice, a manifestation of vivid spirit. And was gone; is gone, leaving me bereft.

Mine is the immutable slavery of the heart, his the freedom, mine the pain.

It was not the storm, merely an awesome suggestion of its power; it was passing at sea, a living malevolence in the rising note of the wind. The candles dipped and fluttered in their glass chimneys: even through closed windows and tightly fastened louvres the sounds in the night were audible... lashing palms, a table overturning, thunder, and the furious sea.

It was seven in the evening, and the iron storm shutters had been taken from storage; some of the house slaves had already moved valuables into the cellar. The others were waiting in a palpable terror and stillness, oppressed, as I was, by the sounds outside and the absence of instructions from Coventry. He was seated at the head of the table, drinking the customary rum and coffee, smoking and reading, or pretending to read, the Kingston newspaper. From time to time he consulted the barometer in his study. Neither he nor I had eaten.

I said, "Will it pass?"

"We shall know by midnight, one way or the other. We cannot hope to escape without damage."

Then he looked up, not without compassion, and crossed the carpet, already soaking beneath the shuttered casement, and returned to the table with a generous measure of cognac in a glass, left it near me, and resumed his seat and his pretense of reading.

"You told me they sometimes turn. Do you think this will turn, and come ashore?"

The haze of smoke was dissipated by the unseen draughts; my fingers were cold, nerveless. He looked up again, perhaps at some sound, perhaps to answer me, although no man could predict the passage of a hurricane, the time or the currents or the conditions under which it was born, the strength of its winds, the path of its destruction or the whirlwinds spawned on its periphery, or what would come or not come before its death: it was perceived as an almost human entity, but it was without malice, without pity, the most indiscriminate of killers.

There was a furtive tap on the door, and the slave Philip crossed the carpet on soundless feet. I observed Coventry's instant attentiveness, as always when approached by his slaves, as though of long habit he anticipated attack: his hand beneath the table had moved to the butt of the pistol.

"Horseman coming, master."

He said, "Then light his way."

I left the room, perhaps unnoticed by him. One of the doors on the north façade had been opened and rain was sweeping the terrace; impossible to know the strength or direction of the wind. A drenched slave in a tarpaulin coat was holding a glowing lamp against it, and then the light was extinguished. The house was full of shadows, fear, the insane voices in the wind, the litter of palm fronds blown across the floor, the smell and tumult of the sea.

I closed my door. Despite impending disaster my bed had been made ready, the fresh linen brought, the candles lighted, the frangipani in the vase; the rain was driving against the jalousies, the rich carpet here, as in the dining room, soaked, the draperies swaying in the draught. If sleep came this night, the sound of the sea would haunt it.

I sat at the dressing table with my back to the door, closing my eyes against the candlelit reflection of the room behind me: my hands were trembling: nothing came to me, no prayer for safety or an end to the suffering of the past thirty-one days.

His hands were cold, as cold as mine, as cold as death, and wet; no warmth in the body, in its soaking clothes, but an immense, living strength in the embrace. The cold skin against my face was wet with blown salt.

I said, "Will you go again?"

"Yes," he said.

"Then take me with you. I would rather die with you than live here without you."

He said nothing. There were no more words, except what was, and what is written.

I passed the night of my thirtieth birthday between Cape Fear and the edge of the Sargasso Sea, in uncharted depths, perhaps a thousand or two thousand fathoms. The prevailing wind was a fresh southwesterly, varying little and suggesting autumn with every degree of latitude: the land, some fifteen miles abeam, remained an unseen presence, ominously named, and increasingly sensed.

I had lost him, with the passage of sea miles between this pencilled calculation and the hot sun of Montego Bay. He had withdrawn from me into state of reticence and tension, in which there was not a little of the exhilaration of anticipated danger: it was implicit, and my unquestioning acceptance of it had been the condition under which I was allowed to join him.

There was little intimacy, and no sexual contact between us. With the proximity of the coast and the approach of his destination, the heightening of his nervous tension became acute: he was restless and stimulated; his body ached, its old injuries awakened by the cold, his bowels painfully disordered. Although he seemed to draw comfort from my presence, he questioned his judgment in having permitted it, calling it a sentimental weakness in which he should not have indulged. Hurt by this, I effaced myself, did not demand his time or reassurance, did not speak of the fear which, unlike him, was my constant companion.

He dined with me on Friday evening, the fifteenth of September: it was not a happy birthday. Harris served mutely and withdrew; the wine mounted the curve of crystal, assuming the angle of the deck, and mirrored her rise and fall on this tack, spilling from time to time. He drank a little, in a toast to me, and then no more.

He said, "I expect to make landfall on Sunday night."

"And then?"

"Two, three hours at the most. I shall be glad when it's over."

There were four or five cigarillos left in the Russian leather case he kept on the desk: he returned with it and lighted one; his fingers were trembling. I spoke his Christian name, which, of habit, I seldom used: he looked up sharply, as though wary of it.

"Is it always... like this, for you?"

"In action, always. I hate the prelude, and the aftermath."

Silence: the sound of the sea, the heavy rise and fall, the following wind driving her, like an arrow, toward that invisible coast.

"Must it always be this way?"

"For the present. This is all I know. It would be easier for me if you were at Ironshore... and very, very much more lonely. If I neglect you... you will understand, and not think too badly of me, I hope."

He seemed to be listening. Always, the voice of his other mistress took precedence over mine.

"Must you go?"

"Perhaps not. If they need me, some one will come." Then he said, "Perhaps you won't want this, but it would please me if you had it of me tonight. The earrings are at Ironshore... if we are separated for some reason."

It was an emerald and diamond pendant, carried carelessly in a box in his pocket; he seemed uncertain, diffident, watching the transparent emotions on my face; intensely sensitive as he was, and superstitious like all sailors, he must have known the significance he had given to this gift. I should never wear it without an association of fear.

"Perhaps this is not the time, but neither of us are children, and there may be no other opportunity. If..."

"Don't speak of it."

He smiled faintly.

"If. I should want you to do two things for me. The first would be according to your judgment."

Silence. The pendulum of the light, swinging across the dark wine, the diamonds in my palm, his face, hollowed by the procession of light and shadow, an aquiline mask.

"If we come under attack, you will destroy my private log. Throw it overboard, and my sword."

He must have sensed my eyes upon it, the worn leather of the scabbard, the fouled anchor in the pattern of the gilded hilt. For this blade he had returned to Rye. With it, I had seen him kill. Louisbourg... Quebec... Martinique... Havana... and I was to consign it to the dark ignominy of the sea.

He said, "It were better in the sea, if I were taken. I should not want to surrender it."

"And if that should happen?"

"At best, I would be imprisoned. At worst, I would lose everything."

"And what is my second duty toward you? That I should deny all knowledge of you?"

"Yes. You are not responsible for my folly, and you will not pay for my transgressions. I will say what I must to prevent that, and you will do the same."

"You ask me to tear out my heart."

"If I can tear out mine, so can you."

He left me soon afterwards, not like a lover: what he loved now was flying through a starlit sea, in the dark of the moon, driving at nine knots an hour on the same unvarying tack. The night was very cold between decks, and colder still in the wind, dampness dripping from every shroud, every straining sail. I heard the watchkeepers' voices in the darkness, and some one stamping his heels on the deck; nothing from St. James, not even the regular passage of his feet, although I thought I heard him cough. He came down before dawn, having instructed Mark Ransom to take in not a single reef, and slept briefly in one of the leather armchairs; the sharp clarity of the autumn sunrise woke him, and he returned on deck.

I walked there with him in the forenoon. It was possible to imagine warmth in the sun, although none in the wind or this dark, northern sea. He spoke little, only of the quality of the light, which was inimitably September; if we were observed or overheard by any of the watch it was not apparent to me. The same rigid discipline prevailed: he did not tolerate familiarity, or nudity, or obscenity of language or gesture.

"If any man so much as touches you," he said, "I will kill him."

We walked, his pace matching mine, the wind moulding my skirt against his thigh. I had thought I should outfit myself with masculine clothing in view of the unknown crew and the many uncertainties of this voyage, but he thought otherwise, believing that a woman's presence was a calming influence upon the men, rather than the reverse. His opinion of them as a company was not shared with me, although he said once, watching them, "They have no loyalty."

At eight bells of the afternoon watch I was again on deck: the declining sun seemed molten, although cold in the shadows to leeward. There was still no land in sight; Cape Hatteras lay ten miles to larboard. Ten miles, he had told me, was the usual limit of small vessels patrolling inshore, whose range of vision from the crosstrees, under lucid conditions, was some fourteen miles. If we were to be seen we would be seen, before sunset.

I went below. St. James was in the chartroom in the company of the second mate, Simon, a slow-spoken, enigmatic colonial who referred to me as "the lady", or "your wife, Captain", a misconception of which he had not been disabused. My ear lingered on the unfamiliar accent.

"You will note the presence of extreme shoaling at the mouth of the Delaware bay."

"I have noted it, thank you. You are a Baltimore man, I take it?"

"I have that distinction, sir." Then, "You know these waters well, Captain?"

"Not intimately, but I have had some experience, from Antigua to Halifax." A pause. "You were a master's mate, in...."

"*Atalanta*, sir. She paid off in Portsmouth in April of sixty-five. It took me three years to get home."

He said nothing: it was not a silence that lacked comment, but of consideration. There was something here of interest to him, although I could not know what it was. I heard the heavy rustle of charts.

"Very well. My compliments to Mr. Ransom, and would he lay her on the larboard tack. Steer north by west. I shall come up at dusk."

At sunset he shortened sail, taking in her royals and topgallants, so that the great pyramid of her canvas would not hold the last rays of the sun on an otherwise dark sea. He revealed nothing of the nature of his thoughts. When I saw him, briefly, during the endless night, we spoke only of commonplaces, nothing of love, or fear.

I saw America in the final flare of sunset, off Cape Henlopen in swiftly shoaling waters, on Sunday the seventeenth of September: the leadsman right forward in the chains, swinging, and chanting the message of the dripping line in the utter silence on deck.

"By the mark, thirteen...."

The smell of salt, tidal mud, the indefinable smell of the land, obscured by coming night.

"By the mark, ten...."

The boatswain, a Creole, right forward, poised to knock off her anchor. Mark David Ransom, aft, close enough for me to smell the salt and acrid sweat in his clothing. He was a Rye man, the third of generations of smugglers, and a committed Methodist; how conscience and heritage had been successfully reconciled was a matter between himself and his god. Perhaps he lived in the certainty of redemption: his composure, beside me, was intense.

The darkness was almost complete, except for the cloud of my breath.

"Deep... six."

St. James, on the windward side, said sharply, "Jesus Christ."

The flat, colonial voice, apparently unperturbed.

"Sandbar."

She did not strike. There were no lights on the shore, no other sounds.

"No bottom."

St. James said, "Thank God for that," and then, "Helm a-lee," and she came up slowly into the wind under topsail and jib, all else furled until this business should be completed.

"Let go."

Her anchor splashed into the darkness, in eleven fathoms of water: it was my signal to retire, and I obeyed it. I saw nothing of his transaction, and heard nothing more until her anchor came home, save the creak and splash of oars and the muffled thud of boats alongside: the rest was carried out in deafening silence, with, once, the heart-stopping crash of something falling on the deck above. I did not see him paid, although his payment was in gold; I did not see the transfer of cargo, by a tackle suspended from the yard, although the procedure had been described to me; I did not, in truth, know the nature of the commodity he carried, although I was later told that he had landed one hundred cases of Charleville muskets, packed in grease, five to a case, with bayonets of fluted steel sixteen inches long, and shot moulds, each musket weighing rather more than the eleven pounds two ounces of the antiquated Brown Bess. I did not know that he had also carried another, more volatile commodity, gunpowder, in such chronic demand that his purchasers had attempted to persuade him, unsuccessfully, to name his price for supplying more.

After some two hours I heard the capstan, and she came to life, heeling over as the canvas was set and sheeted home, turning her head from the perilous land to the darkness of the sea. The soldier's wind was against her now, but veering, the precursor of weather, and, lighter of her cargo, she fought it with characteristic truculence. Eventually... eventually, he came down, perhaps only to the privacy of the great cabin, and not to me.

He said very little, merely asked for my assistance in removing his sword, then he closed himself into the quarter gallery privy. I heard him coughing, and then a prolonged spasm of vomiting.

When he emerged he seemed composed; sat on the bench seat without reference to it or to the events of the evening, took without comment the brandy I had poured for him and drank it, holding my right hand with a pressure of emotion which was not otherwise evident.

It was perhaps two o'clock. Her bells were muffled, or silent.

Some time later, I disengaged my fingers and knelt on the deck, easing the salt-stained shoes from his feet; he said, not loudly, "Leave them," and then, "I am— not very clean." His feet in the soiled stockings were swollen, a condition to which he had never been subject.

I took them in my hands, my head against his knee, stroking them; he said nothing; time became nothing, only this, my small act of love.

He slept profoundly where he sat, his face, even in sleep, guarded and withdrawn, not the vivacious, passionate lover, the vivid spirit, but another man both older and younger; and this, the manifestation of an older life, which I had never known and never thought to know.

I brought a boatcloak and covered him, and myself, embracing him; and slept, not as he did, in the exhaustion of the aftermath, the epilogue of danger, but fitfully, disturbed by the rising sea and the spray on the blackened glass, the shallowness of his breathing and the heart's imagined pause; and the night was cold, September's forgotten cold, the dawn sunless, autumn's rain veiling the sea.

Time, binding and unbinding, takes what it has given.

He is nothing now, only this... incomparable sweetness remembered. No immortal hero, no vigilant spirit, no guardian, no partner in the exquisite sexual adventuring of the last, golden days... I hunger for his body still, which was my communion; nothing loves me, nothing comforts me; I confront only an unalterable truth, after which I ceased to live.

He is only this now: with him, in him alone I live. The rest is dust, and shadows.

How shall I speak of what he became to me, as the year was dying? How shall I say that I loved him more, and more deeply, and more subtly, with clearer eyes, in recognition of his faults, and of his crimes; how is it possible to love yet more, and desire more, that which is already loved utterly?

He was my soul; he was myself, my other self. I loved him for the man he was, and for the vulnerable child he had been, as vulnerable as my son would have been, or the child we would have made together; I loved him for the young man, war's paramour, and the youth that remained in his spirit, and his manner, and his ardour. I loved him as Leslie, in whose presence time was not, and yet time relentlessly devoured the hours, and the days, and nights, when I desired eternity. I stood before him as naked in spirit as in body; what had been defiled, he exalted; what was restored to me was for his pleasure and his joy, and for mine. In him was revelation, was my very life; in this, he was my god. His tenderness toward me was profound, our sexual happiness intense; familiarity conferred intimacy, gave richness to our experience of one another... in daylight, in candlelight, in fragrant nights, when the taste and the kiss and the ascent were heightened, were ecstasy. Without shame, with perfect candour, I talked to him, telling him what I felt, what I sensed, what I wanted, the exquisite experience of orgasm always an epiphany, a revelation... we spoke of secrets, dreams, fantasies, pornographic and delicate; he spoke without reticence of his experience of me, what pleased him, what he desired; sex, like perfume, permeates the memories of my days and nights with him, rises like fragrance from my diaries; sex and revelation. I had never spoken, or been spoken to, of the nature of sexuality; I had never thought to know again the abandon of self and reason, when the language of love is the whore's language, transformed; that I could say with intense yearning to this beloved man, *fuck me*, and that it should be his desire, and his response, and that in this there was nothing of obscenity, or fear, but only passion's self.

We loved, in darkness and in light, in the sun, and in erotic secrecy: the world was ours in all its sensuous richness. He was seldom absent. This was not a renunciation of the sea, but a respite, a consummation. His return was inevitable. That I should go with him was unquestioned, either by him or by me.

In this coral sea there are no seasons: a twelvemonth and a twelvemonth and a twelvemonth pass, distinguished only by subtle shadings of rain and blossom and harvest; the changing iridescence of the sea is eternal under the sun; the voice of the reef is immortal. If I had returned to Rosewynd I would have found it as I left it, poised for the life that never came, the jacaranda ever falling, ever renewed, the shadows where they had always lain at particular hours of the day; the dawns white, the sunsets the lucid heart of flame; the air sweet, and moist, the litter of petals where they always were, on the paths or in the foam of the waterfall.

All lost: all fallen into the irretrievable sweetness of years.

On the last day we passed together in Jamaica, we had gone to Rosewynd, and inspected the coffee trees and the pimento, and the rooms, a preponderance of green among the furnishings and carpets and wallpapers, a colour that gave repose. We sat on the verandah in the jacaranda's shadow and watched the clouded, blue mountains and the sea's dark blue horizon... if he left it with regret or premonition he did not reveal it to me, although he reined in by the waterfall, where, once, he had loved me; the poignancy of that memory was very clear in his eyes. Had he wished it, I would have acquiesced.

We walked on the beach that night, and sat in the warm sand; the moon was very late in rising, the wind calm, the sea quiet. We talked, and did not make love.

In the night, in my bed, he woke with an audible gasp: I was not asleep, although the words he spoke were not coherent. He was sitting on the edge of the bed, surrounded by the film of the netting, his eyes closed: I put my arms around him and we sat caught in the net like moths: he was trembling. He said only, "Oh, Christ... the things I saw," and nothing more. I brought him a measure of cognac, and his robe; his breathing had slowed, and he was staring at the carpet. I opened the jalousies and returned to him.

He said, "I should like to sit outside a moment."

We sat in the soft, moonless night; the palms and the cane were still, the sea muted, the stars suspended in an infinity of light.

He said, "I dreamed of Havana."

"I know."

"I saw my death. I saw what was done to me, and that I had died. I should have died... other men did, younger... children, some of them, some from trifling wounds. No one could ever tell me why I survived."

"It was God's will."

"Some one told me that. I never believed it. I never thought God concerned himself overmuch with my affairs."

Then he said, "I have loved you more than I believed possible... more than I thought I was capable of loving. I have never loved any one before... not as you and I love. I never thought myself worth loving... much."

"How can you say that?"

"Because I believed it was true. I have been... very lonely in my life, more lonely than I knew, at the time. I had friends, of whom I was fond, and they were killed. I loved David... not... in that manner... but... as one is always drawn to the hero of one's childhood.... I never thought he would go before me. There was no one else so dear to me as you."

What perfect mathematics are these, that pain is commensurate with love.

A long time later he said, "Shall I tell you what I dream sometimes? Love's dream... I think of it on waking. I think of us in London, in a house somewhere... our house. Waking late, making love for hours, as though there were no time... and then we walk, or ride together in the park, and in the evening we go to the opera. You wear something beautiful, and I am suitably self-effacing... we drink champagne, and I hold your hand, like this, and we are very, very happy."

The moon was rising from the sea. He watched it, and I his face.

He said, "What arrogance to suppose that we are God's only creation—that ours are the only eyes in the universe to marvel and observe."

The sky was now delicately brushed with cloud; the moon, on the edge of its vapour, cast first a halo and then a circle of iridescent light. As the cloud drifted and the moon wavered, strangely gauzy, lost in mist, the formation reminded me of snow, the rotting, textured snow of nights on the cusp of spring.

Eventually the cloud passed, the sky was infinite and clear, the palms unmoving, the sea faint and restless on the beach. One of the flowers from the branch where the bright birds came scavenging, in dying dropped on the terrace at my feet. There was an imperceptible suggestion of the dawn which would commit us to the sea.

He still held my hand, as in his lover's dream.

He said, "Thank you. I shall sleep now, a little," and then, "I have been very happy here with you."

It was Saturday, the twenty-third of December, and paradise was lost.

To reach a certain point on that chart, seventeen hundred miles from Montego Bay, had taken five days and fourteen hours in September, driven by a strong southwesterly. To make good that distance in December seas, in rainy squalls and, occasionally, the fog of the Carolina coast, which streamed in rags on the bitter wind, had taken seven days, twenty hours. We had not yet experienced a true, killing cold, but conditions were unpleasant: the air between decks was humid, almost fetid with condensation; clothing, bedding, the canvas deck covering, the very leather of the chairs in the great cabin, were perpetually damp; the only source of heat was the galley fire, and the transient warmth of its meals.

We had kept Christmas together quietly, clearing the Windward Passage, with little change in the ship's routine and nothing to distinguish the day from others in these latitudes, except for the benevolent mood among the men off watch, induced by the sun and an increased ration of rum. St. James and I gave no gifts to one another, except a brief, transcendent sweetness of lovemaking in the darkened cabin, on the bench seat, in utter silence, with a stain of sunset on the sea and the voices of the watchkeepers audible through the opened skylight. I imagined our limbs entwined like glass, transparent, living sculpture, the beauty of his body within me, the act and its climax wholly revealed and visible to me, its rhythmic embrace, the spasm of completeness, body and spirit in utter communion. This he had given to me, the knowledge of beauty in the act of love.

There was no more sweetness. The first of January was pitilessly cold, the light blinding; the breath smoked, the deck was slippery with ice; frost burned the fingers of those who worked swollen cordage through the stubborn blocks; the freezing sea, spilling into scuppers, burned their naked feet. Clothing, aired briefly in the galley, could not defend the chilled flesh, although Harris performed this small service faithfully for his captain, and sometimes for me.

I walked on deck in the forenoon, where I was not an encumbrance; it was preferable to the clamminess below and the men ignored my presence, cursing the weather in robust language until rebuked by Eyre, who had succeeded the colonial, Simon. St. James was particularly silent and uncompanionable until the noon sights were taken; there was a netting of frost on the sextant. Then he told me he was going below.

I remained for perhaps twenty minutes, and then went down also.

I found him in the great cabin, sitting on the damp canvas of the deck covering, his back against the bulwark where the timbers ran with condensation, his arms clasped around his legs: his head was resting on his knees.

"Pain," he said. "Such pain."

Aware of the cyclical nature of malaria, I had brought with me cinchona and tincture of opium; but this was not malaria and he refused the opiate, perhaps fearful of its effect upon an enflamed bowel. I had nothing else to give. I remained kneeling with him, in the cold; he did not move or speak again.

I stayed with him for perhaps an hour, then he rose in obvious anguish and closed himself into the quarter gallery. In the twenty minutes before he emerged I died, as every lover dies in the suffering of the beloved.

For the next two hours he left me at intervals and returned, crouching again against the bulwark, unable to relieve himself either by vomiting or evacuation: the pain increased, until he wept. I sat close, not touching him, shivering. The cold was intense.

"When we go back to Ironshore... will you see a surgeon?"

His tears could not have hurt me more if they had been acid.

"This is what surgeons did for me. Christ, they couldn't let me die in peace."

Time passed, in this terrible intimacy. The skylight was hazed with frost, the light on the sea inclining toward dusk. I no longer knew the twilight hours of winter: it might have been half past three.

Some one came to the door and spoke: Mark Ransom's voice.

He said, "Let him come in. He knows."

I seldom saw compassion between men; I saw it now in the windburned face, the clear English eyes. Winter and the sea clung to him. He crouched without effort near St. James.

"Strange sail on the larboard quarter, Captain. Eight miles, maybe."

"Alter course three points to starboard. Steer nor' nor' east."

"May be only curiosity, sir."

"Even so. No royals, no topsails. You perceive her from the sea, she views us from the land. Bear the difference in mind."

He left us. Evening came and shrouded us from any potential observer. We made a pretense of normality, and Harris served our meal; St. James and I went up, and walked a little, although he left me after speaking to the watchkeepers. I stood near the compass light, listening to the crack of canvas; the sea was black, the stars not the Caribbean's paving of light but the remembered, bitter pinpoints of January, flashing prismed colours.

I was aware of Mark Ransom's presence although I could not see his face, nor he mine. He said, close to me, "Why don't you enter into Christian marriage with the Captain?"

"I am not free to marry him."

"Then he should renounce you. Adultery is a sin in the eyes of the Lord, and Christ loves a sinner who repents."

"What was vouchsafed by God is not for you to judge."

We never spoke of it again. If the sin was mine, I have paid for it.

I remained with St. James throughout the night. I could do nothing for him. He lay on the deck on bedding from the cots, naked below the waist save, poignantly, for his shoes and stockings, and I massaged the cold, scarred flesh of his abdomen with a salve I kept for my hands; he would not allow me to speak of his condition to any one, so I could not summon Harris for coffee, nor would he take cognac or laudanum. The sea was very heavy; his body was rigid with anguish and tension, the anticipation of a summons. There was very little light; the night seemed savagely cold; the muffled bells marked our progress through hell.

At eight bells, four in the morning, he dressed and attempted to lie in the chair, went again to the quarter gallery, returned after half an hour and drank the cognac, spilling a little of it.

He said, "For God's sake, don't remember me like this. Remember me as your lover," and then, "Christ, I'm so ashamed."

Perhaps an hour later, he could no longer sit, and walked ceaselessly, bending his head beneath the beams, as though oblivious to the heavy rise and fall of the deck. A faint greyness was visible through the salt-encrusted glass. He left me again, and returned.

"Blood," he said.

At half past seven he drank a great quantity of undiluted purgative from the surgeon's chest he kept in the sleeping cabin. Its effects on him throughout that afternoon and the night that followed were so severe that I believed he was dying: it is possible that he thought the same. The night was unspeakable. I lived it with him, sometimes in an intimacy he would not otherwise have permitted, cherishing his body in its spasms of bloody diarrhoea: he did not now speak of shame. On the morning of the third, he slept for the first time in forty hours, in the leather chair: I slept on the damp bedding on the deck beside him, as though on the breast of the sea. When I woke in early afternoon, he was not there. I did not see that the tarpaulin coat had been taken, and searched frantically, foolishly, for him, opening the louvred doors of the sleeping cabin, the quarter galleries, the chartroom, encountering only Harris.

"Cap'n's on deck," he said.

I returned to the great cabin, and fell asleep in his chair.

The sound of the rudder woke me. The lantern overhead was burning; there was darkness on the sea, which might have been midnight, or evening, or early morning. He was seated at the desk as though he had been writing, the logbook opened, and the pocketbook in which he kept his pencilled observations and alterations of course, but the entry was unfinished, the final line undrawn. Beneath it he had written, *Thursday, January fourth*, and his hand was resting on the dim expanse of the page, as though its blankness were legible.

He said, "I shall not do this again... and it was very wrong of me to have expected you to endure it. My life has fallen into perspective. The night made some things very clear." Then, "I want to love you tonight. I don't think I can."

"There will be other nights."

"So I tell myself." Silence, the sea's silence and the ship's, an impenetrable silence between us. "Give me something of yours, for tomorrow."

He would accept only a handkerchief, nondescript but for its perfume. In the night he asked for my love, which I was as incapable of giving as he of receiving. There was little sweetness, only desperation and futility; the spirit and the exhausted flesh failed. I did not bear his beloved weight again: the words of a lifetime were never spoken.

I breakfasted at seven bells, half past seven. He came down and drank half a cup of coffee, standing, warming his hands around the cup, snow melting on the tarpaulin coat; he had been on deck since leaving me, at perhaps half past three. Pain remained in the lower right of his abdomen: he was, he said, otherwise well.

At eight the log was hove. She was making good nine knots, driven by a southwesterly wind, steering northwest, close-hauled on the larboard tack. The sea was heavy but moderating. After a night of sleet, the glass had risen and the temperature dropped; the cordage had swollen in the sheaves, the deck was icy, the glazed ratlines offering a perilous foothold for those required aloft.

At noon there were snow squalls, and the sea was obscured in a driving curtain of white, bitter, hard flakes cutting into eyes, the skin of the face, the ungloved hands of every man aboard, and the naked feet of topmen. The light was strange, opaque, the sextants useless: her position was calculated by dead reckoning alone. Now I knew his destination, although, on principle, he never mentioned it. We were some twenty miles off Newburyport, two hours away with, at best, four hours of daylight, and in these shoaling waters sometimes seventy and sometimes eighteen fathoms beneath the keel.

Perhaps an hour passed. Axes chopped the ice from her washports; her scuppers ran with the sea; the spray froze in fantastic patterns; my lips were

690

cracked and dried with salt. I wore the breeches I had had his tailor make, and two shirts, and a waistcoat and long riding coat, and was shrouded in a boat cloak, with a soft woollen shawl drawn over my head and shoulders: I was relatively warm, and had the advantage of gloves. My fingers, therefore, could more easily accommodate him when St. James asked for the time. It was nine minutes to two.

"My watch has stopped," he said, and returned to the weather side, leaving me in the comparative shelter of the companion near the wheel, although I would have preferred to have been with him. It was two o'clock precisely when the cry came from the masthead.

"Sail on the larboard quarter!"

There was a suggestion of light, before the darkness of the winter closed down; I saw how snow is grey like rain, like veils of rain on a clearing horizon, and then the light was lost again. The telescope came into my hands, although I do not remember him giving it to me, or how long either he or I had held it, only the silent miniature in the lens, a pyramid of tan sails emerging from the snow, no colours visible on this tack, her hull, throwing up an impressive spray from that sullen sea, shining black and buff. The glass was gently taken; the voices oddly detached. I did not hear his among them.

I reckon she's come around Cape Ann.

Well, she ain't no bloody invitation to the dance.

He said, "Alter course. Let her fall off three points. Steer north by west."

The voices ceased their speculative murmuring, and I heard Ransom shouting for hands to the braces; men ran, heaving, slipping, ice falling like shards of glass from shrouds, stays, canvas. St. James stood, immobile in the tarpaulin coat, the snow in his hair, leaning to the angle of the deck, his eyes not upon me or the oncoming vessel but on the sails. There were two men on the wheel, as always except in calm weather; they were both unfamiliar to me.

One said, "Steady she goes, sir, nor' by west."

I left the shelter of the companion again, felt for handholds. It was suddenly very necessary to be with him. He was gazing aft, the telescope resting on his shoulder, his face, although drawn, deeply composed: he seemed not to notice my presence, and I did not interrupt his thoughts.

The lookout called, "She makes more sail, sir!"

He observed it through the telescope, his breath a faint cloud whipped away by the wind.

"She's setting her t' gallants, sir!"

Ransom came up, and was standing in silence.

"Setting her royals, sir!"

691

The telescope did not waver, although its weight was considerable.

He said, "You young fool."

Ransom said, "Shall we follow suit?"

"No. Too visible."

She was lifting beneath us, smashing down in a cross current, answering to her helm with spirit, the wind right across her quarter. Spray cascaded over the beakhead; I imagined the gilded eyes and pure white face sheathed in the sea's salt ice.

"Time," he said to me, and waited patiently as I took off my glove and fumbled for my watch.

"Three— no, four minutes to three."

He looked at the sky.

"Come, darkness," he said.

The brig opened fire at approximately three, at extreme range, a single shot from her bowchaser, a thirty-two pounder; this signal to heave to was followed by another. The shots were barely visible, spouting spray like a dolphin, a deadly procession of waterspouts, well clear. A little snow was falling, twisting like sand across the deck. There was no jubilation around me, and no retaliation: every man was needed to work the ship; there was neither time nor leisure for loading or running out, only a deadly concentration on the next minute and the order it might bring. I prayed for darkness.

The brig altered course, to due north, it was thought, although it was impossible to determine her position precisely. By this alteration she would overreach us, and had revealed her full length and presented her broadside; she was clearly, now, a ship of war, and her colours were visible, the scarlet ensign almost black in the fading light. He stood watching her, removed from me and from this hour, with no emotion in his face, directing his full attention upon her, his mind alive with the possibilities of the immediate future and the visions of the past. Through his eyes, I saw his ghosts.

The second mate, Eyre, loitering by the wheel in a pretense of indifference, remarked, "He's cutting it fine," and then the tongues of fire flashed from the brig's side: a single shot found its mark. Spray rose from the sea and fell heavily across the deck; the impact was muffled, and there was no indication of damage. The carpenter, Vetch, was below inspecting the hold when St. James said, "Oh— Jesus Christ," and turned a little away, as though from the onslaught of the weather.

The brig had struck, intent on her pursuit and under full canvas, heedless or ignorant of the danger of shoals and sandbars, although the chart was littered with them. Her foremast had carried away, taking with it jib, yards, rigging, men: from a living thing of vengeful beauty she became a chaotic wreck, the seas bursting over her. Her mainmast fell with a distinct crack, like a careless shot. She had only minutes to live.

He had turned back and was staring at her, with no apparent pity. His arm, beneath my fingers, was trembling.

He said, "My blood is very thin these days," and then, "What a waste."

Mark Ransom came up, ignoring me or, perhaps, what he had heard.

"Shall we cast a boat adrift, or put a broadside into her?"

"Leave her to the sea." He turned his back on the wreck, I thought deliberately. "Stand by to come about. Put your helm down."

"Helm a-lee, sir!"

"Off tacks and sheets."

Forward, they were barefoot on the icy deck, letting go the headsail sheets to allow her to swing into the wind, all sails, topsails, jib, forecourse, driver, maincourse in confusion as she came round and further round, almost into the wind.

"Mains'l haul!"

Eyre, at the compass, was rasping his hands, muttering, "Come around, you bitch, come around—"

"Let go and haul!"

Ransom said, "South-east by east, sir. As close as she'll come."

She had crossed the wind's eye; the men at the braces had hauled her yards round. As the sails were sheeted home she came steady, leaning into the wind, on the starboard tack, her sails taut and bulging, shrouds vibrating, water pouring over her lee side, men grasping for handholds, falling, cursing, the topmen still aloft, shivering witnesses to the advent of the night. My teeth were chattering so violently that I could not speak.

He said, almost inaudibly, "And now, if it please my God, I will take you home."

Let her fly, lads— let her fly....

Reckoned we'd never see they Caribbee girls again.

Nor done I neither, by Jesus.

The rasping hands again, like roughened leather. Eyre, jocular, almost impudent with relief.

"I seen eternity a few times afore, but never that close, by Christ."

And his voice in the dimness, its elegance, now sought vainly in the speech of other men.

"Then you haven't lived."

Mark Ransom, near me at the binnacle, consulting the compass, was singing under his breath.

Who would true valour see, let him come hither... one here will constant be, come wind, come weather....

Let her fly, boys, let her fly....

There's no discouragement, shall make him once relent....

Some one shouted then, and he was silent: all was silent, save the vibration of the rigging, the sluicing of the sea, the heavy fall of spray. The sail, two or three miles away, to the northwest, was visible to the naked eye.

Eyre said, "She's a frigate," and a sigh seemed to pass through the men, not hauling, not working ship, but stilled; spectators, striving to hear the next words from their captain.

He was staring through the telescope across the starboard quarter, beyond the tumult of sea and spindrift which was the dying brig. He seemed to stand badly, as though the pain of the forenoon had worsened.

He said, "No. Sloop of war."

I was close to him; he gave the glass to me. The sloop was leaning steeply to larboard, pinned at that angle by the strength of the wind that drove her: she opened fire with her bowchasers as I watched. Had the range been closed the shot would have smashed into our stern, destroying all below.

He said, "Young," not urgently, and stepped away from me, walking a pace or two with the gunner, steadying him as he slipped in the dry, gathering snow.

The gunner left him, with a stiff-legged, delicate tread, like a man walking on ice; his mate detached himself from the others and followed him. There were no names called, no shouting, only a great economy of effort. The silence on deck was profound.

I renounced him then, whom I loved, and gave him again to the life which had made him; this was no hour for me, for love, or the expression of my fears; love and dread and the future were here renounced. My claim upon him was finished.

Two courses remained open to him. He could run to the northeast, which would present the full length of the ship as a target if the sloop luffed, or crowd on canvas and hope for darkness and the open sea. His mind, always mercurial, did not linger upon its decision.

"Get the t' gallants on her." And, perhaps at a mild question, "We have no bloody choice, man. She'll overhaul us otherwise."

The topmen were still aloft, clinging with stiffened fingers; the effect of the increased canvas was felt immediately. Vetch, the carpenter, loomed out of the shadows; they conferred.

He said, "Good," and then, unexpectedly, came to me, with little expression either in his face, in the absence of light which was not yet darkness, or in his voice.

"What time is it?"

"..... four... I think."

"Destroy the log and the muster book. When you leave me, walk slowly. When you go below, don't linger."

"And the sword?"

"Bring the sword to me."

I prayed in the great cabin, which was undamaged and in darkness; his pistols had been taken and I knew that he wore them; my gloved hands fumbled, removing his sword from the bulkhead. I prayed for courage, that if we should die it should be together, that he should not suffer, that I should not see him die, nor he me. I knew why I should not linger in this place, which had been our sanctuary: I knew, upon leaving it, that I should not see it again.

Harris met me in the cold darkness of the companionway. Beyond him I was aware of some one, perhaps Chatto, unlocking the arms chest. Overhead there were sounds which, as though borne in my blood, I recognized, although I could not have known them.

My strange, whispered confrontation with Harris continued, he asking me for the sword, in more words than he had ever spoken, and I refusing to give it to him. Finally he said, "I was his coxswain at the Havana. Let me do him the honour."

St. James was walking slowly up and down the weather side, a few paces in either direction; he had taken off the tarpaulin coat, which some one had tossed by the binnacle. Beyond him, the sloop was crossing our quarter. He showed no surprise at Harris's appearance on deck, and spoke to Ransom over his shoulder as he extended his arms for the sword belt.

"Alter course three points to larboard. Steer due east."

Movement through the final minutes of light; sails flapping in confusion, and Ransom's voice, far hoarser now than in the sweetness of his hymn.

"Another pull on the weather forebrace, there— now belay!"

There was an abrupt, fragmented exchange with Eyre, who seemed to express the opinion, unsolicited, that the cargo should be discarded, the colours identifying this ship as British bent on and run up.

St. James said, "There's no damned time for that," and then, "For Christ's sake, man, do you think I'm a magician? They want our blood. What does a flag signify to them?"

I heard Harris murmur, "... luffed..." and the sloop opened fire, a full broadside, each gun in succession as was customary in failing light, the flames hideously vivid, illuminating the drifting snow... the noise and shock of impact were unspeakable. The foremast fell, snapped where it was lashed to the top, foremast, topgallant mast, yards, men, over the starboard side. She slewed, wounded although not yet fatally, wreckage clinging to the bulwarks, her miles of rigging a killing net for those who were trapped on the forecastle

695

eath it. Some one was shouting for Hook to clear it, although Hook was dead; Chatto was stumbling forward with an axe, the sailor's futile instinct; the weight of wreckage had already crippled her; the next broadside would pass through her unprotected stern.

I heard St. James shouting, and the gunner's reply, saw the slow-match burning. Only four or five guns would bear, and Young fired them himself, the rearmost, closest to us, first, with savage recoil. There was now no order but insanity, obscenities of rage and defiance and encouragement... I was not among these men, I had no existence. In this, I knew the prelude and the aftermath... the substance of his life was in the sloop's response.

She fired, in succession, many guns, too many for me to remember, each gun inflicting a greater degree of devastation, each firing more precise, more distinctive, louder than her previous broadside, and I believe he knew by their very sound the nature of the charges before they shattered the stern, the boats, the taffrail, exploding in a whistling hail of grape, because some one, perhaps he himself, threw me face down, with an impact that injured me. I struggled to rise, winded, gasping: they were all dead around me at the wheel, Harris's disembodied arm twitching, steaming at the stump, his fingers clenched around my wrist, his entrails spattered, viscous fragments clinging to my hair and sleeve. I tried to stand, and was thrown bodily across the deck. Braces, scythed cleanly and released from enormous tension, became instruments of decapitation. Mark Ransom was near me now, close enough for me to recognize by the compass light, which still burned, illuminating hell. He was dying: by his voice and his clothing alone, I knew him.

There was no light then, only darkness, the sensation of falling snow, melting beneath my cheek, blood, viscerae, sea water. She was dying, we were all dying. There would be fire soon, or she would broach to and founder. I heard Mark Ransom say distinctly, "Jesus—Jesus." Pinioned to the deck, I could not see who held the faceless head, and then he came to me, and Mark Ransom died.

He was attempting to free me, free the hair torn from my scalp, which had been driven into the deck, and the means by which I was impaled; tears or blood were falling on my face from the darkness which was him; across my mouth the iron taste of blood. He was speaking to me but I could not answer, and other voices, cries, screams, terrible profanities, obscured the sound and the sense of his voice. My mind refused to identify the smells, spilled blood, torn intestines, excrement, the taste on my lips, the meaning of the hideous obscenities screamed at him by one who lay near me: I sensed that he left me and rose, with immense difficulty, as though he were wounded, although I could not know the nature of his injuries: there was a rasping intake of breath, and silence. Now Eyre, too, was dead.

He returned to me, and lifted my head onto the folds of the tarpaulin coat; the movement caused me intense pain, and I could not free myself to look fully into his face; the hot substance was falling faster, a steady stream; he sensed it and withdrew, and then wiped my face with something, perhaps the handkerchief I had given him. I called him my love, but he seemed unable to hear me: I felt him raise my hand and press it to his lips. Time passed; sensation had drained from my arm and I could not feel or respond to his fingers. It was intensely dark; there was no light. Some one came, staggering, and spoke to him, asking him what should be done; he kissed my hand once more, and left me. In his absence I seemed to sleep and surface again, brief, torn dreams, which distressed me: I woke alone among the dead, and drifted again. Perhaps twenty or twenty-five minutes passed before the sloop came alongside.

He was with me then, seeming to sit beside me on the splintered deck. At the sound and the impact he bent down to me, and caressed my face, and said, "Now we shall die together."

He did not speak again to me: I never heard his voice again. He fought in silence, only the blades, the sparks, his laboured breathing close to me, and a young voice gasping, "For Christ's sake— for Christ's sake—" I closed my eyes and took him with me, into my darkness, my sleep of peace, where he lives still.

Snow. Wood smoke. The sound of rain on the glass of an uncurtained window, a scarlet sleeve and a hideously scarred face, fragments of an opium dream. Boston was nothing more to me than these. A city besieged and under martial law, its civilian populace evacuated with nothing more than bedding and household effects, an army of twelve thousand trapped between the naked hills of winter and the freezing waters of the Mystic and the Charles, a rebel army of ten thousand encamped in the surrounding countryside. Both were decimated by sickness, deprivation and desertion. The lash, the army's panacea for insubordination, failed to dissuade the opportunists within its ranks from looting and organized theft: foodstuffs were limited and exorbitantly priced, dysentery rife. There was a critical shortage of fuel. Two-thirds of Boston's houses were of timber, and were demolished by order and burned.

My life was saved by an army surgeon with some experience of splinter wounds, who did not mistake for gangrene the blackened contusion of my flesh, and so did not immediately consider the amputation of my left arm. He was assisted in the grisly business of healing by a Quaker woman in whose house I was lodged, who twice daily changed the dressings, with their immense quantities of blood and bloodied serum and granulating skin, cleansed my

697

body of its menstrual flow, fed it, and conferred on it the prescribed doses of opiate, from which I prayed I would never wake.

Throughout January my life remained a tenuous thing. I suffered delirium, in the throes of which I might have spoken names which would otherwise have died with me, and lockjaw: I did not believe my recovery was the will of God. This torture, this death of body and mind, was too demonic to have been inflicted by His divine hand.

The snow gave way to icy rain, the precursor of a spring of war, and in the shadowed afternoons the distorted phantom of my drug-induced sleeps acquired reality, and became a senior officer, with a flat epaulette, gold fringed, on the shoulder nearest me: the broad cuff of his coat, laced discreetly with gold, was the dark blue of a royal regiment. His presence was not insistent, but I ignored it, and was indifferent to it. He remained an hour, and then left me.

There was very little in the room, apart from the bed with four turned posts, a fireplace, unlaid, a figured rug on the bare floorboards, and the straight-backed chair in which he sat, some twelve feet from me. On a subsequent afternoon, escorted by the woman Elizabeth, he moved the chair a few feet closer, and sat in the requisite silence for perhaps an hour. I was in great pain; the surgeon had that morning made multiple incisions in the muscles of my shoulder, to lessen the adhesive properties of the effused blood, and I did not respond to his presence.

The room darkened: there was rain on the glass. I though he sighed, and the rush seat of the chair creaked.

He said, "One cannot live in profile, even when ignored."

The chair had been moved, so that his face was visible: his head was bent as though he examined his hands, his legs crossed in an attitude of negligence. The left side of his face had been melted by fire, and the eye was blind.

He said, "Believe me, I share your disgust. This secondment was not of my choosing." Then he looked up, fully into my eyes: I averted mine and stared at the rain.

"I am required to put to you once more those questions which you have refused to answer, and to remind you that, should you maintain your silence, you may find yourself in contempt of court. That would have serious consequences for you."

"What more serious punishment could your court inflict upon me?"

He said nothing.

"Am I your prisoner?"

"We are all prisoners in this hellish place."

"Am I under arrest?"

"No. You are not a prisoner, and you are not under arrest."

"Then I have nothing to say to you."

"You do yourself no good by this intransigence. You cannot help one who, by his own activities, is already condemned."

He was still alive.

"Then I commend him to God. He is nothing to me."

Forgive me... God forgive me.

He said, after a silence, "Madam, if you have friends in Boston, let them be informed. Your position is precarious. If there are those who may persuade my superiors to look with clemency upon your case, I urge you to name them."

I moved my head, nothing else, and closed my eyes.

"Consider it carefully. There is very little time."

I coughed then, blood and matter; he brought the woman Elizabeth, and left me to contemplation of my ghosts; toward midnight the surgeon, Dalkeith, was called, with his gift of oblivion. I asked him to let me die, and in the darkness of successive days and nights I sought death, I yearned for it; I no longer prayed, either for myself or for St. James; his name was a wound upon my consciousness, inflicting unbearable pain.

All I should ever know of Boston was pain, and blood, and wounds; and the wet cobbles of a narrow street, seen at the end of February through the flawed glass of the window, to which I had walked. Rain falling; the acrid stench of wood smoke and wet ashes.

He came in unexpectedly and found me at the window; I did not leave it, and he did not sit while I was standing. The hour of interrogation was upon me once more, and in this murky absence of time I had not noticed, not prepared myself for the defense and the silence.

He said, "Have you given the matter of which we spoke your consideration?"

"Yes. I have considered it."

"Do you wish me to convey a message to any one?"

"No."

"Have you no connections? Here, or in Jamaica?"

"There is no one who cares for me, either here or there."

He said nothing, did not move. The street remained deserted, veiled with smoke.

He said, "Who are you?"

"I am no one... only a lost soul."

"Forgive me, madam, but I have not a metaphysical mind. I am attempting only to establish an identity, and to serve your cause, if I may."

"Your gallantry is misplaced."

"Nonetheless, I am an officer, and I hope that is an honourable estate."

"What is your regiment?"

"The Fourth... the King's Own. Do you know it?"

Yes. I knew it, and under what name it had fought, and who was its lieutenant-colonel at Culloden, and the name of one of its majors.

I said, "What regiments are in Boston?"

"I cannot tell you. I may say only what regiments are not."

"Is the Eighth here?"

"No."

"It was in Halifax."

"It is transferred. Do you know this country?"

"No."

"The Eighth departed Halifax for Quebec in November. I have had little news of it since then. Do you know some one in that regiment?"

".... The colonel."

"Bigoe Armstrong?"

"No."

"He succeeded Mordaunt in the autumn of seventy-four."

"Why?"

"He returned to England. You gave the impression that you knew him. You must have known that his wife had died."

So much rain... so much rain, like tears. How could a sky contain so many tears, a city so much grief?

He would have pursued it, pinioned it, dissected the truth, as I had been pinioned, and probed, and cauterized, for my corporeal good: the cough and the blood delivered me from any further questions.

On the night of Friday, the second of March, the rebel bombardment of Boston commenced, answered by mortars and cannons within the city. By Sunday night the continental army had occupied the disputed Dorchester heights, and every aspect of the city lay within the range of its guns. On that night the vibration of falling masonry could be felt throughout the house; fires burned in the timbered remains of those buildings not already pillaged, and dense smoke choked the empty streets: it was later known that the Americans had fired one hundred fifty-five round shot and thirteen mortars into Boston.

Toward midnight, it was decided that the residents of the house should take refuge in the cellar, and the Quaker carried a candle up to my room and compelled me to leave it. There were others in the cellar, a black woman, perhaps a slave, a young white girl who had been redeemed from prostitution, and two or three neighbours, with small children who screamed continually. The woman led me in by the right arm, through falling plaster dust.

I said, "I hope they pay you well for this," and she gazed at me with colourless eyes.

"I am a physician, and I gave thee refuge out of charity. 'Inasmuch as ye have done it unto one of the least of my brethren, ye have done it unto me'."

The bombardment continued, and the screams, and the palpable terror of those around me. I felt no fear; I felt nothing. After an hour I left the cellar and returned to the darkness upstairs, illuminated by moonlight and explosions. No one dissuaded or followed me.

On the afternoon of Monday, March fifth, there were troop movements through the streets and toward the wharves, and a line of transports deployed for the embarkation of a force to attack the rebel positions on the Dorchester Heights. By evening, the rain which had been falling increased to a violent storm; the gale would continue throughout the night, fouling anchors, causing several of the ships to run aground, and destroying Howe's final hope of retaining his grip upon Boston. The rebels were now entrenched in two hastily constructed forts on the heights, and no gun could be elevated to fire on their position; the harbour had been rendered unsafe for shipping. On March sixth, Howe conceded the inevitable, and announced that he would obey, at last, the orders received earlier in the year. The army and some thousand loyalist civilians would evacuate Boston.

On the night of the sixth, I was visited once more by my interrogator. Although he had left his card propped on the mantel in my room I had not read it, and his name remained unknown.

I heard the murmur of voices in the corridor, muffled by the icy hiss of rain, then he carried a candle into the darkness, where I stood by the window; I remember the sleet glistening on the coarse wool of his greatcoat, and the burned skin of his hand. I said nothing, and turned my back on him. His reflection in the darkened glass became more distinct: he had lighted the candles on the mantel.

He said, "Good evening, Mrs. Scott."

The bloodied, broken watch on the table, which I had not touched since it had been taken from my neck, might have revealed my Christian name. Only one in Boston could have told him my surname.

His reflection approached me. The scarred hand took my right hand gently, our first and only physical contact, and prised open my closed fingers; the other placed a heavy signet in my palm. Later, for many years, I would wear it, with his emeralds, on my left hand.

"I was asked to convey this to you."

"You saw him."

"Yes. Last night."

He said nothing else; did nothing; did not move.

"He spoke... of me."

"He confirmed certain suspicions of mine."

"Did you speak of me to him?"

"I told him you were among friends. It seemed to comfort him."

"Please allow me to see him."

"I cannot."

"Please. Please. I beg of you."

He said, "He is dead. He was hanged at eight o'clock this morning."

The first transports from Boston arrived in Halifax on the second of April. Tenacious winter had not yet abandoned that last great bastion of naval power in North America, and deprivation was not exclusive to Boston. Howe's army remained there throughout the spring, feeding off humiliation and the hope of an attack on New York.

Halifax and Antigua remained in close communication; slow convoys departed with regularity, and frigates and smaller vessels sailing independently, carrying despatches, observing the manoeuvres of their American counterparts, as thirsty for the blood of the privateer as any who had hunted us.

I sailed in one of these, a discreet arrangement which ended an embarrassing and insoluable problem: I carried papers that gave me the identity of a colonel's daughter, and fifty guineas loaned to me in Halifax by Henry Stanhope Smallpiece, which was repaid by a draft on the Bank of England. He was killed in September of that year, in Howe's costly victory at New York.

I reached Jamaica on the second of June. It would have been St. James's fifty-fourth birthday.

His clothing and possessions and the shells, and my clothes, were as we had left them; when I slept, it was with one of his coats in my arms, or on the bed; when I returned to England I would sometimes wear them, too fearful of losing what little remained of him to have them laundered, or discarded.

He had left a letter for me and a copy of his will at Ironshore... months passed before I opened or could bear to read either. He had bequeathed to me the assets on deposit at Coutts' bank in London, and Rosewynd. I never went to Rosewynd again.

For the rest, there is no *then*; there is no *afterwards*... only the unbearable grief, and his eternal absence, although he spoke to me, day and night; my mind was never free of his voice, nor would I have wanted so desolate a liberation.

I was ill: the sun healed the body and dried the wound, and stilled the asthmatic cough; the hair grew where it had been torn from my scalp, and was white; I was given solitude in which to grieve and die, or recover. Coventry followed me to the beach one night, and into the sea, where I was standing with his pistol in my hand; I asked him to do for me what he had done for his lover. I could not speak St. James's name, although he himself often said it; he told me that I insulted Leslie's spirit by my behaviour; I affronted his ghost, and then he left me, with the responsibility for my life or death in my hand. Even courage has its limits... the body lived, though the spirit died.

He drank with dedication, and smoked his South American weed: under the influence of both, in September, he gave me all the letters St. James had written to him in the course of their long friendship, and said that they were mine. Later that night, he said he would not offend the dead, whom he honoured, but he wanted to make love to me: he did not use those words. My last sanctuary was closed to me.

I left Ironshore at the end of that week, having sold Rosewynd to him for forty thousand pounds. It remained a beautiful corpse, upon which the sun and rain worked a relentless decay until October third, 1780, when it was destroyed by the most devastating hurricane in Jamaica's history.

I wrote, following the peace of 1783, to the president of Congress; in London and in Paris, between this revolution and the terror of another, I met the American ambassadors. My requests were courteously received; letters were exchanged, and I believed them sincere. No records remained of his trial or execution, or any others during those weeks; if they had existed they had been lost or destroyed; the disposition of a criminal's bones in quicklime signified nothing in the annals of a rebellious colony, or a new and blooded nation. He was not its hero, and his grave remains unknown.

Interlude: Evesham

There is no time now, there are no seasons; summer comes, and does not touch me; spring is devoured by winter. There are no memories of these years, because they are not lived. Time's only significance is my severance from him.

He would be fifty-five today... he would be fifty-six... time, passing, bears me from him, and across the bitter waste of years he lives; he is alive, vivid, laughing, tender, and passionately beloved. In the present, is only his death.

I have touched, and been touched, on only two occasions, always at the lover's hour, l'heure bleue, the hour of desolation. I am not the only one bereaved. Mordaunt also mourns, not Catherine, but the futility of his life, the remembered wasteland of his marriage, and the lesser failures, the disappointments and the losses, the great gift squandered, the draining away of time. Those who loved him are now dead; the greater, the unacceptable love, has been gently withdrawn, the lover dead and the memories immortal, what was, and never was, and was never written.

Now, in the blue hour, we seek our ghosts; we seek the dead, in the scarred flesh of another woman, and another man. There is no peace, there is no ecstasy. These die, and are gone forever; dreams die, love keeps its bitter immortality.

1790: THE SUNLIT ROCK

I

The child Margaret Charlotte entered Malcolm's life in the ninth decade of the eighteenth century. Britain remained embroiled in a bloody and protracted struggle with her American colonies, and was at war with France, Spain and Holland, who supported their independence. Taxes were high; there was agitation in Ireland and, as always, the fear of insurrection, and anti-Catholic rioting had convulsed London in early June of that year.

The child was eight years and seven months old in July of 1780, when she came into the estate office holding her father's hand, and wearing a short jacket the colour of old roses and a sprigged muslin gown. At James's bidding she sat obediently in the only other chair, and throughout the ensuing conversation her presence suggested itself only by the occasional thud of a slippered heel against the chair leg, a habit to which, in childhood, James himself had been prone.

Aware of the disapproval in the cold eyes across the table, James said only, "Behave yourself, Margaret," and the sound stopped.

"I hope this will not become a feature of our meetings."

"No, no. Assuredly not."

He examined the returns from the first tryst of the season. In a market fuelled by war, cattle had sold at Falkirk for an astonishing three pounds per head.

"I have never seen it higher than two."

"You will see it higher yet, until the peacemakers prick the bubble."

The child slid noiselessly out of the chair, leaving in it the doll she had been carrying, and was standing with her hands behind her back, examining something in the overflowing bookshelves. For one so young, there was a certain ostentation in this, as though she wanted to be noticed or rebuked. Malcolm ignored her, while remaining acutely aware of her movements, and James seemed oblivious.

James said, "Perhaps this shows the wisdom or otherwise of your dedication to the Linton. You may come to agree that I was justified in not committing myself until I—"

Something fell and rolled across the floorboards, a piece of veined quartz. The child turned with an expression of betrayal, and thrust her hands into her pockets.

He said nothing, controlling the profanity, and she retrieved the stone and put it into her father's outstretched hand. James said, not unkindly, "If you can't behave, go into the garden," and she went, without apology or any other sound.

The doll remained in the chair, forgotten by her and unnoticed by James when he left.

He had an inexplicable dislike of dolls. He had despised for its association with Margaret the old bisque doll she had abandoned, and had smashed its delicately painted face and burned the torso; and in the rainy dimness now some quality in the face of the child's doll disturbed him, and pierced him with some emotion, regret, grief, a desire for what would not be salvaged from the past, and what had never been. The rain, running on the open casement, obscured all minor sounds, the passage of feet in soiled kid slippers, the clamour of memory.

He raised his eyes, and looked into the face. A child's face of heartbreaking beauty, the eyes unwavering, dark blue, the mouth exquisitely shaped and small... impossibly small, and coloured like the doll's; the rose-coloured jacket had been removed, the muslin was patterned with roses. In the eyes, heavily lashed, unchildlike, he saw his demons: innocence which was not inviolate, not incorruptible. He held the eyes until they faltered, and then he bent his head again and wrote illegible, inconsequential words.

She said, "Are you doing lessons?"

"No. My lessons have all been learned."

She remained in the shadows, a presence as insistent and disquieting as the doll's. His dislike and distrust of children was profound: his own childhood was only another darkened dimension, an existence concurrent with this, into which he could pass without effort, sometimes involuntarily in nightmare or recollection of its horrors, and always with anguish at its betrayals and the savage death of innocence. This child and every other child, his own among them, was a pristine film upon which every impression was indelibly recorded. Upon the souls of his own children he had imprinted disdain, lovelessness and violence; and this now, himself, the burning eyes, the scars, the mutilated hand, the bottle, which he did not attempt to conceal, the loaded pistols with their invitation to death, which had not been forbidden to her, this too would be remembered, and written on her soul.

She said, "This is my doll, and I don't have to share her with any one. My mama said I should give her to Amelia, but I don't have to now." Then, "Amelia is dead, you know."

He looked up, the quill motionless in his hand. The eyes held him, dark in the shadows; in the eyes and the face nothing of Charlotte, or James.

"Yes. I know."

"Papa wept for days when she died. My mama wept, too. I didn't, very much. Do you think that was wicked of me?"

He said, "No."

"I didn't like Amelia very much. I didn't want her. Do you think that was why she died, because I didn't want her?"

"Death is impartial. Sometimes it takes what we love. Sometimes it merely takes. It has no discretion." She was gazing at him, listening intently, perhaps only to his voice and the accent that was not Edinburgh's. "Your sister died of measles. She would have died, whether you had loved her or not."

Silence; the sound of the rain; the dark, unchildlike eyes.

She said, "Why are people frightened of you?"

He said, "Why don't you ask them?"

She retreated noiselessly, on the kid-slippered feet. At the door she turned and said, "I'm not frightened of you," and went out, leaving it ajar.

On September third, 1783, after eighteen months of negotiations, the Treaty of Paris was signed, ending seven years of war. Some thirty thousand had emigrated from the Highlands between 1773 and 1775, encouraged by those who had preceded them, and published testimonials to a land once more offering its promise.

Throw off the Yoke of Bondage and the Shackles of Slavery, and Quit the land of Egypt for the land of Canaan. How can I say otherwise, when I never knew what actual freedom or the Spirit of Equality was, until I came to America.

In a world less primitive and less isolated than this, an industrial revolution was flowering, propelled by invention and discovery and expansion; the prosperity that would follow peace was manifesting itself in England. Here, the margin between survival and starvation remained as finely drawn as ever. The cycle of climatic catastrophe which would precipitate another, bloodier revolution before the decade's end spawned the reluctant spring and cold summer of 1782: in October, a crop which had been blasted by mildew was devastated by frost. Both cereals and potatoes were destroyed.

What relief was offered was belatedly organized by a government preoccupied with America, and dispatched and distributed too late to avert a famine general throughout Scotland. The winter of 1782 became this silent summer, wherein the starving and the dispossessed drifted toward death on the roads, or clamoured ceaselessly for succour or for pity. Dead and living,

707

they were merely the country of his mind made visible, and he felt neither compassion nor horror. He wrote to James, who was still in Edinburgh, "The people are in very poor case, and reduced to eating what herbs may be found in the barren fields. Do not bring your daughter to Glen Sian," and then, after a minute of almost physical pain, he amended it to "daughters".

Only death would still these visions, which did not come now in the guise of nightmare but were constant, uncontrollable. The voices of ghosts, the vision of the exquisite, child's face, the mouth too small to admit the instrument of violation, as his had been too small, the body's delicate sexlessness, not undefiled virginity but the state of being without sex, without provocation, without knowledge... beyond innocence, in a state of grace, as he had been without sex and without provocation.

Guard your children... guard them, in the absence of God.

The visions persisted, the rape of the child who was himself, the rape of the child who was not, the superimposition of her face over his, like the shattered face of the doll... the visions came and he did not resist them, or punish himself for them; his punishment for his survival was this, was enough.

God... God, deliver me.

The room had been stripped and painted and rehung with silk wallpaper, the couch relegated to the attics, the furnishings, in the modern style James affected, covered with hessian: it was and was not the dressing room where he had witnessed fellatio, these the rooms and yet not the rooms once inhabited by Ewen.

Malcolm... Malcolm, viens... and the fingers, delicately trembling, offering semen to his mouth, the taste of Ewen's semen on his lips.

Baise-moi.

The child, the soiled receptacle, the discarded garbage of himself, in this sanctuary, violated anew by one he had believed was an angel.

Baise-moi. Baise-moi.

The hand caressing his child's penis, anointing it with semen, the involuntary spasm of ecstasy and terror.

Baise-moi. Baise-moi. Baise-moi.

He had suffered another seizure in this summer of the dead, the brain's resistance, the body's fallibility, the visions and the voices and the unremitting pain.

The room, the ghosts, the emptiness of its space, blurred, and the tears were burning.

Do not let the people see you weep.

He thought nothing, felt nothing, regretted nothing. There was no fear, and no oblivion; no pain, neither the pain of the living or the dead, could violate him now.

He had turned war and catastrophe to his advantage, inducing young men to leave the land and join the Highland regiments recruiting north of the Tay at the height of the conflict with America. If their own poverty and the hope of employment and the impossibility of inheriting the barren familial acre did not persuade them to go, he resorted to the more compelling arguments of bribery and blackmail, requiring 'a son for the land'; no recruit, no renewal of lease. It was a crude equation, but effective in its time.

Famine and the fear of its recurrence, and the fruits of peace so seductively offered by the promised land, America, proved a powerful incentive to emigration. He selected those whom he considered suitable candidates, and cited the prosperity and potential of the new world, to which others had attested, and the Highland communities already established in Georgia and Virginia, the Carolinas, and in Pictou and Cape Breton. To the suggestible, he offered payment; for the recalcitrant and the undesirable there were subtler methods, although he had eschewed those acts of violence which had brought him to trial in 1774. He was no less feared for the legality of his actions, and no less hated for the barrenness of his heart. The contempt and the superstitious dread signified nothing to him. A hundred deaths by famine, a hundred emigrants, a decade of warrants and eviction and confrontations, the abolition of the ancient system of runrig and the redesignation of tenancies were nothing in the balance. The imposition of the turnip and the potato and the sowing of rye grass, all initially resisted and now in general cultivation, the annual raising of rents and the acquisition of those leases which had fallen vacant, the massive investment of his own capital in a flock of Lintons now numbering ten thousand, so that his profit alone as James's principal tenant fed the incubus of debt, the work of a lifetime, in the end, was nothing. The debts remained. The land was an anachronism, afflicted with an incurable malaise: the blood and the vision and the furious dedication had not been enough to cure it. The work of a lifetime was finishing, and yet it was unfinished. And it was not enough.

These were summers, but not as they had been lived before: there were no golden days, nor twilights, no music, no perfume. The golden hour had passed; the night, so desired, never came.

There was no peace, spiritual or physical. With the advent of summer the family returned for its annual sojourn at Ardsian, disturbing the silence of his days and the territory of his ghosts; the orchard and the gardens, where he sometimes walked and observed the turning of the seasons, were inhabited by women, the stepdaughters Caroline and Frances, prone to fits of giggles and blushing coyness when accidentally encountered, and the children, Eleanor, born in 1780, and the infant son upon whom James doted. That child would not survive beyond his second birthday, nor would the last issue of this marriage, another son, born in this spring of 1786.

He avoided them, possessed by a haunting sense of inevitability: that death, the death of the spirit, of innocence, was close; that she, like Ewen, would corrupt him. In the summer of 1786 she was fourteen years old, and the compulsion and the resistance and the loneliness were deepened by the sensation that she, Margaret's godchild, was Margaret in another guise, that this innocence and vulnerability, the still self-containment, the gravity of the eyes and the spirit, were Margaret's, and that he was the guardian of that innocence and could, without effort, end it.

The provocation and the challenge and the obsession of the summer almost physically sickened him: the fierce sexuality of other years, forced by solitude into quiescence, reawakened, and he was alone; the silk of the abandoned wedding gown was the silk of her vagina, a disembodied lover. There was no other mistress, no other whore, nothing but this, days without the sound of a human voice, and the silent, convulsive shudder in the darkness, intercourse with ghosts.

They had spoken but he had never touched her, nor she him. The fantasy and the dread of contact with her became the coolness of her hands, slightly damp and unperfumed, over his eyes in the estate office in the shadowed afternoon.

"Do you know who this is?"

He said, without moving, "A very silly young girl," and the hands were removed, leaving the impression of their dampness on his eyelids.

"I don't think you think so. Do you?"

They had not met since her arrival with her stepsisters from Edinburgh. The infant heir had died in January, and his brother in April, and he sensed dissension and fragmentation in the family, James and his daughter allied against Eleanor and hers. She, too, had been ill, of scarlet fever, and there was frailty and exhaustion in her face: the exquisiteness of the childish features had gone, the candour and gravity, and the knowledge in the eyes, had not diminished. The mouth, as beautiful as the child's, was unsmiling.

She said, "Do you?"

"No."

She seemed to have had enough; she moved restlessly to the door and loitered there, the shoulder half turned, the broad silk sash swaying, and then, like her, still.

He said, "What do you want?"

She closed the door, and remained there, the half turned shoulder filmed with the lace that veiled her breast.

"Kiss me. I want you to kiss me."

Baise-moi... baise-moi. Plus ça change....

"I don't want you to come again to my office and say these things to me."

"Why? Will you tell my father?"

"No. But you will."

"And what would he do to you? What could any one do to you?"

He spoke the name aloud which he did not consider hers: he had never before called her by it, and never would again.

"Margaret, go away. Don't begin something you don't know how to finish."

"I do know how to finish it. And I know how to begin it. And I think you want me to. Don't you."

He entered her, standing, against the table, penetrating her roughly, losing himself in the closed, dry fist of the vagina: she was only the instrument, not virgin, not human, not an entity. This was not a dominance of the flesh but of the spirit, and of death, and of the past, and of the blood in her veins and the living ghosts in her eyes.

He withdrew. There was no stain on the torn silk undergarment, neither blood nor semen. She was tearless, trembling, perhaps incapable of speech: perhaps she had expected only what she had offered, the delicate torment of inexperienced lips, the furtive, uncertain fingers.

He said, "I think you had better go."

Still without speaking, she slid the dishevelled silk from her thighs, over the black silk stockings, and stepped out of it and folded it, let the silk of the overskirt fall, with a subtle fragrance, to the floor. She seemed to be waiting for something, for some promise, or reassurance, or endearment. He said nothing, and she opened the door, and the sound of the silk receded and was lost in the darkening corridor.

The rain of hours had ceased, and the evening was drenched with perfume. He knew she had been cutting roses, and had come to walk beside him, still carrying them.

711

She said, "I saw you. I wanted to— I thought— that we should talk."

He did not slacken his pace for her, or turn his head.

"You must see that I regret nothing. And I should not want you to think I blamed you."

He said, "Don't walk on that side of me. My left eye is blind," and the step hesitated, and once more followed him.

"Why? Why should it be so?"

"Ask your father. I was about his business."

She had moved closer, on the right, not that radiant, provocative presence but something young, altogether younger, reflective and subdued. He thrust the mutilated left hand into his pocket and continued to walk, and to ignore her. Eventually he felt her fingers clasp his. It was a strange, affecting little gesture, less a lover's than a child's, and briefly he allowed it, and then withdrew his hand.

"It will not happen again."

"I wanted it. I was very unhappy. I thought you were unhappy, too. I told you, I do not regret it."

"Nor do I. But it will not be allowed to happen again."

They halted, by some unspoken accord. She did not turn her head, and the profile was thin and sickeningly youthful: it was not a woman's face but that of a girl of fifteen.

"Don't you understand? I want it to happen again. I *want* it."

He had never been moved by tears and was not now, nor by the immature beauty of that face, nor the unfulfilled promise of the body.

"I want it as it must be between men and women... not as it was. I know it must be.... more beautiful. I want to lie with you in your bed... and let you teach me.. and love you. I want you to love me."

"I have nothing to teach you, and nothing to give you."

She lifted drenched eyes to his, eyes, in the twilight, which at last were recognized, and he knew whom she resembled.

She said, "I cherish... a great warmth of feeling for you."

He did not touch the hair or the face: on such gestures, such hopes, she would live, and there was no hope.

"Give it to another more worthy. I am not for you."

Her face was very still and closed, as it had been in childhood.

She said, "They are right to call you dangerous," and walked away.

He met Eleanor Stirling near the house, perhaps intent on some agenda of her own, perhaps merely looking for her stepdaughter. It was not yet dark enough to avoid an encounter, and she called piercingly to him from the terrace, using his surname, to which he did not answer. Annoyed by this, she snapped her fingers.

"Scott! Scott, I say!"

He paused, with one foot on the stone step. She was a silhouette in his vision, obscured by the candlelight of the house.

He said, "Madam, if you want a dog, buy one," and withdrew his foot, and walked on.

II

In death the legends were magnified, and imbued with immortality.

On the morning of January thirtieth, 1788, in Rome, that architect of tragedy Charles Edward Stuart, the Young Pretender, died, having suffered a paralyzing stroke. A lecher and an alcoholic depressive, with whom conversation on the subject of his failed rebellion was forbidden because it threw him into such depths of melancholy, he had never returned to the country to which he had brought such disaster and misery. On the fifth of March, 1790, in Skye, Flora Macdonald died, as potent an icon of that dream-riddled epoch although she had passed part of the American revolution in Carolina, where her husband had raised a regiment of Macdonalds loyal not to blood or memory but to the Hanoverian king. She had never been reunited with the fugitive prince in whose escape she had played a part, but she joined him in Jacobite hagiology, yet another symptom of the land's lingering sickness of sorrow and nostalgia.

In France, the disease was a cancer of absolute power and corruption, endured for centuries by a restless, aggrieved, disaffected, unrepresented people, disadvantaged by treaties, and the importation of inexpensive foreign goods by a nation whose deficit stood at two hundred and fifty million livres, by unemployment, by the sullen geography of the land they attempted to farm, and by the natural and political cataclysms of 1788. James, at the Château Saint-Arnaud, wrote of the hailstorm of July thirteenth, which devastated the country from the Île-de-France as far south as Languedoc, destroying vines in the Loire, Alsace and Burgundy, ripping branches from elms and chestnuts, smashing windows, and killing birds and livestock in the fields. The harvest, of wheat in the Orléanais and the Beauce, fruit south of Paris and oranges and olives in the Midi, already severely damaged, could not survive a succession of thunderstorms and the weeks of drought that followed. Bread, from eight sous for a four-pound loaf in the summer of 1787, rose to twelve in the barren autumn of 1788, and to fifteen in February of 1789, when the Seine and the Loire were impassable with ice, and ice floes choked Le Havre, and snow fell from the Haut-Garonne to Provence. What little, inferior grain could be imported could not be distributed by river, or ground by mills frozen into immobility. The abrupt thaws of January brought not deliverance but flooding. The unemployed, the desperate and the lawless rioted in Paris, Rouen, Reims, Poitiers, Dijon and Versailles itself, and attacked bakeries and granaries from Picardy to Brittany: rioting became the endemic disease of Paris.

The recurrent violence, the spiralling unemployment, the price and the shortage of bread, the example of egalitarian America, and the pressure for constitutional reform by those enlightened liberals who had fought in that war of independence and claimed they had "brought back the seeds of liberty"... if a nation could be conceived of less visceral desires, what greater potential had this hunger and anger to spark revolution.

On Sunday July the twelfth, 1789, the Genevese director-general of finance, Jacques Necker, regarded by many reformers in France as the only potential saviour of the country and its people, was dismissed by Louis XVI and sent into exile. By Tuesday the fourteenth the rumour, if not the fact, of Necker's dismissal was known in Paris, and was used by fanatical agitators to ignite the inflammable. Rioting throughout the city became an organized quest for gunpowder, and led a mob estimated at fifty thousand strong to storm the fourteenth-century fortress and prison in the rue Saint-Antoine. What had begun as deliberate insurrection, with the waxen models of the heads of popular commanders carried on poles for inspiration, ended with the severed heads of the governor of the Bastille, the intendant of Paris, and the minister held responsible for a famine perceived as a plot against the citizens of France paraded on pikes through the streets, the mouth of the last, Foulon, crammed with grass and excrement to signify his crime. On the twenty-second of July Bertier de Sauvigny, Foulon's son-in-law, was also decapitated, and his heart torn from the palpitating corpse and offered as a deputation to the Marquis de Lafayette, commander of the National Guard and the people's darling, but nonetheless powerless to prevent this or any other execution of the mob's vengeance. At that time, the hero of America was in the process of drafting his declaration of the rights of man, with the collaboration of the American ambassador, Thomas Jefferson. The spectacle of human hearts and heads carried through the streets of Paris confirmed Jefferson's suspicion that here was not the democratic revolution of his experience, but the birth of bloody anarchy.

And then came la peur, a collective, obsessive fear, of roving armies of brigands, of conspiracy, of sabotage, of invasion by enemies, Britain, Austria or Spain, of the impending massacre of innocents or nobility, all unfounded rumours in a nation reeling under its own iconoclasm.

And there was still no bread. Drought had dried the rivers, and the mills were unable to produce flour for the volatile Paris market.

More significantly, attacks on châteaux began, in Picardy, Burgundy and Alsace. The Loire was restive, but remained quiet. The fear was ubiquitous.

Gifts to la patrie were solicited, as demonstration of patriotic fervour and the abnegation of the material: courtesans' jewellery, ancestral paintings, silver shoe buckles, objets d'art. All fed the bloody, newborn entity, the France of Liberty.

They sat in the estate office, with torn copies of Elysée Loustalot's *Révolutions de Paris* and Marat's *L'ami du Peuple* between them, and a tricolour cockade, incongruously vivid, in a bar of September light on the table where James had placed it.

"Un souvenir de Paris, or should I say, the latest fashion. Even the King accepted one, and has been seen to wear it," and then, tentatively, "Can you read that?"

He was conscious of the burning clarity of the eyes, raised from the Loustalot paper.

"Yes."

Tyrants, shudder and see how you and yours will be treated....

It closed along deep creases, as though it had been read repeatedly.

"Hearts torn out, heads on pikes— blood and liberty."

James coughed.

"I didn't think the children should be witness to such things."

He said, "No. They would never see them here," and thought perhaps the irony was not lost on James.

"Do you think there will be war?"

"I would think war is almost inevitable. However, we shall profit by it."

There was silence.

"Do you think... they may accomplish what they intend, without shedding innocent blood?"

What blood is innocent? Was mine?

He looked up.

"No."

The fair, aging face was more introspective than he had ever known, as though the turmoil in France had opened before James vistas and possibilities and culpabilities he had never contemplated.

"Do you think this is the end of the world, as we have known it? That there will be a great overturning of social order— even here— and that everything we hold dear will be taken from us?"

Everything I hold dear has been taken from me. What remains is nothing, only life.

He said, "It is insurrection in France, not the apocalypse."

The restive, haunted eyes lifted briefly.

"Perhaps it means nothing to you. You have nothing to lose."

He said, "That is true. I have nothing left to lose."

There was no sound in the house, only the wind, southwesterly, bringing salt rain from the Atlantic on a dark spring night. He was alone in contemplation of his ghosts, and of truths which had become manifest, and revelations which held no fear.

The darkness of the spirit tonight was physical: he no longer sat with candles, but like this, without light, listening to the wind's turbulence, the variations in direction and velocity. The intonation of the wind, after fifty-four years, was as familiar as the voice of a lover, the texture of the wind and the land and the sky, in every aspect, the texture of desolation, like the despised contours of his own flesh, in darkness and in light. There was no mystery, no enigma, neither in himself nor in the land, nor in this succession of storms and seasons: no mystery, only recognition, only knowledge.

He did not fear blindness, although he recognized its advent in a slow accrual of symptoms. Neither the body's fallibility nor its pain disquieted him. The conclusion of this life was known.

What remained unfinished would be finished; what was offered, he would take. There was no motive, no subtle vengeance, no quietus sought in young flesh naïvely tendered. There was only the dead loneliness of the spirit, and the wind in the wastes of the night.

She lay on his bed, trembling a little: the room was cold, shadowed with afternoon. She had undressed herself with nervous, impatient fingers, unaccustomed, without assistance, to the intricacies of tapes and laces. Her skin was veiled, translucent, scented with some perfume of iris and citrus, her hair, which he did not touch, already dishevelled on the pillow; skin and hair and ribboned underclothing were virginally clean.

The nakedness of the eyes, the fear, the desire, the innocence, was more compelling than the body.

"Are you going to hurt me?"

716

"No," he said.

"Kiss me."

He ignored her: small acts of tenderness and intimacy had not been known between them. These caresses were without desire, as though the lips and breasts and parted thighs were merely unfamiliar sculpture. He did not speak, nor she, although the skin and the spirit responded to him, learning sensuality.

He paused. The dark eyes were opened, drugged, languid... innocence despoiled.

She said, "Undress," and then, "Touch me. Kiss me."

He did not speak; the kiss was ungiven, the perfume stronger, from heated flesh, less innocent, the fair hair less a fallen angel's; the vagina was a hidden calyx, now liquid, now desiring. He withdrew his fingers and caressed her lips.

"Taste yourself."

And the drugged, soft rose of the lips opened, and sucked his fingertip, and then he withdrew it and resumed the slow violation of her, the ghost and the flesh and the innocence, until she was an instrument, neither mind nor spirit, and cried out, consumed by orgasm.

She slept then, briefly, with an abandoned sweetness, in his arms. The heavy hair lay against his mouth and he removed and caressed a strand, only once, with the fingers of his right hand, and tasted the perfume of sex, the essence of an unfamiliar cunt; so many women, so many ghosts, so many anonymous acts. In this was one last act of love, was reparation to Margaret.

At Whitsun, the ten families who retained a precarious foothold on the grassy floor of the Sian valley were issued with writs of removal and evicted. It was his intention to dismantle the ruins, and allow the urlar to be used as low wintering for sheep. In this, he fulfilled a prophecy of Glen Sian's obliteration, and dealt its last inhabitants the final, killing blow for which they had waited in fearful anticipation for nearly twenty years.

The dispossessed offered no resistance, and had no destination. They did not expect and were not given the customary compensation, nor was their embarkation planned or their passage paid to Pictou, like others who had preceded them: he had tired of gratuitous charity, and so they simply congregated, wraithlike and uncomplaining, twenty-three children and thirty-nine adults, where they were offered shelter in the churchyard at Glen Mor, from which the militant, alcoholic MacNeil refused to evict them. And there, in the sullen rain of June and the unseasonable cold, they remained, an intolerable burden on the resources of the village, a typhus epidemic in embryo.

He rode down in the rain one afternoon, partly to observe them and harass them with his presence, partly to provoke a confrontation with MacNeil, whose attacks upon him from the pulpit had become vitriolic. He dismounted near the manse, aware of the eyes regarding him from the churchyard, the calm, patient, insensate eyes of animals. Without spirit, without passion: like those who had preceded them, they could not resist the iron genius, progress.

O, brave Highland men.

Furtive movements, a fold of canvas falling across a face, a turning of backs, the withdrawal of a child into the shelter of a dripping tarpaulin; the only voices the whisper of the rain in the tangled grass on the graves.

He opened the gate and walked toward the church: the path was rank with weeds. The door opened easily: this, too, was habitation for the evicted, all women, who fell silent upon seeing him. He walked around the perimeters of the stone floor in the dimness. Here, too, rumour was not unfounded. They had scratched their names and histories on the small, flawed panes of glass, and the dates, *May 24, 1790, June 4th, 1790*, strange, pathetic little footnotes, not in a Gaelic which would pass with them but in English, as though with MacNeil's guidance.

Glen Sean peeple was here... the last pilgrims... wasteland... we are damned... God speed us faint of heart... honour to God above.

Even here, on the rain-speckled glass and in the silence of women, was condemnation.

He left it and walked out into the rain to the manse. The curtain was drawn briefly and fell again, and he saw or imagined MacNeil, although he did not come down in answer to the knock.

He stood for a minute or two with the rain running on his face, gazing up at the house, then he lifted his right hand to his eyes and cleared them, and the vision had passed, and the knowledge that their long antagonism had ended. The certainty persisted for twenty-four hours, until he was told that MacNeil had suffered a fatal stroke the previous evening.

He did not attend the funeral, and it was only after repeated assurances that the refugees in the churchyard were not Jacobins in waiting that James was persuaded to appear. Whether out of respect or superstition or a final desolation of spirit, after MacNeil's burial among them Glen Sian's last inhabitants dispersed, leaving only trampled muck and litter, and ineradicable engravings of despair.

He came across Saobhaidh from the southwest in the whiteness of the summer night in late June, cutting close to Glen Mor, perhaps intentionally seeking this encounter which circumstances had made difficult for him to force. He knew Deirdre walked here by the wall, and what ghosts summoned her, and she was sitting in that place where, as a child, he had sometimes seen her. He approached, and sat on the wall near her, his blind side deliberately toward her; she did not acknowledge him. The cold deepened, and the stillness, the lights of the village lay in a white scarf in the twilight, the narrow gorge of the river obscured by fog.

She said, after a time, "So the devil walks abroad." He said nothing. "This must be a triumph for you. Voice after voice in Glen Sian falls silent, until none will speak against you. And when you have silence where Glen Sian once spoke, what will you do then?"

"I will be deaf by then, old woman, and six feet under. Like you."

There was a silence, neither hostile nor companionable, then he said, "What will you do?"

"I will serve the incumbent. I will not leave this place."

"The living is not in my gift, but in Glen Sian's. He may desire you to leave."

"Then you may use me as you use the others, and evict me. My dead are here. I will not go."

Stars now, and the faint, earthy chill of the ground, the sweetness of cut hay, the unbearable, unspeakable sweetness and desire of the past, and the name and the presence between them.

"Have you no kin, apart from...."

"No. After sixty years, there are none who would know me where I was born." Then, "I will be writing to give her news of her father. It is right that she should know."

He said, staring into the obscurity of twilight, "And shall you speak of me? And of this conversation?"

"If you wished it spoken of, you would speak of it yourself."

Twice, in eighteen years, he had written to her. The letters had been returned unopened, the brief sentences unread, the anguished cry of her name unheard, disdained, held in contempt.

He said, "There must be a new minister, for the people's good. But you may die in Glen Sian with my blessing."

She said, still without moving or turning her face toward him, "What is a blessing from you but a curse from another man's lips? And when have you cared for the good of the people, when the people are nothing to you?"

He said, "Even as I was nothing to them, and nothing to any of you."

They lay in his dishevelled bed, in the aftermath of sex, and she talked with knowledge and reminiscence of France, and the Fête de la Fédération which had taken place on July fourteenth in Paris, a hundred and fifty thousand citizens gathered, noble and pauper alike, for an ecstasy of celebration a year after the fall of the Bastille. *Sing and weep tears of joy, for on this day France has been reborn.* He half listened, to her voice and to the rain, indifferent to both. The season had been unfavourable and the harvest seemed uncertain. He had abdicated his responsibility to the land, and for the first time in his life as factor the potential for disaster did not concern him.

The revolution of 1789 was finished, its ideals established bloodlessly; liberty and equality were enshrined; it was the dawn of a new millennium.

She paused.

"But then, you don't know Paris, or even France. Do you?" And then, as though his silence had spoken to her, "How well?"

"As well as I know you, and in much the same manner. The cunt first, the heart least of all."

She sat up, ignoring this, the language of their intercourse.

"When did you go there? What did you do?"

"I shed blood. And I was very young."

"Why did you come back? Do you love this place so much?"

"I don't love it."

"Then why do you strive for it?"

"Why do you do this?"

Silence; and rain.

She said, "I cannot resist the compulsion. I can't think of anything else."

The shadows deepened, the rain on the roof like the rhythm of the sea. He thought she slept, or was lost in introspection, or the planning of excuses for her absence. She spoke his surname: she had never, in all the years of their acquaintance, used his Christian name.

"Do you think I should marry for money?"

"You are Glen Sian's heir, and that responsibility alone should determine your decision."

"Then I think I must.... If my father should die, I should need your advice. And I should heed it, unlike him."

He said, "I am older than your father, and I am not immortal."

She laughed, at the intimation that he would not live forever, that he could be defined by the limitations of other men. His humanity was not what she desired: like himself, she held it in contempt.

They coupled with increasing intensity, with little tenderness, in an ever more insatiable craving for sensation. She desired intercourse even in Ardsian, in the dark red room which had been his, on her own bed in the mirror's reflection, on the floor of what had been Ewen's room, as though she would consume him utterly, and the territory of his ghosts. The outpouring of seed and self ceased to give him pleasure, and subterfuge, although to her erotic, did not appeal to him. He disengaged himself from the fervid dream of sex, and its sweetness, and the immortality it offered, and ended it. She returned to Edinburgh, in the bosom of an unsuspecting family, and wrote to him curtly in October with news of her impending marriage.

Now, in the house at the dying of the light, he arranged those icons to former gods which would not go with him now, the dried rose, the wedding ring, the rosary, on his desk where they would be found with those papers he allowed to remain. Others, and poetry, and the bridal gown with its stains of semen spilled in a profundity of grief, and other fetishes and detritus of his sexual life, he burned. The records in the estate office, for the consumption of others, had become terse, enigmatic: only in these last, private entries in his journal were there allusions to cancer and to blindness, only here, for my eyes alone, an implication of intent. There was no valediction, no regret, no fear.

He wrote nothing else.

He closed the door upon the house and the whispering dead at dawn on the thirty-first of October, the last great feast of the Celtic year, and his fifty-fifth birthday. The climb was punishing; the granite, the mountain's essence, tore both the maimed and the dextrous hand, and was found later in particles beneath the nails. The rock is black here, seamed with water, scoured by winds from the Atlantic, from Iceland, and from Spain. And now there is nothing in the sky but light, and a pair of eagles in suspension in the aching clarity of that air.

The first shot, into the bowels, shattered the spinal cord and the granite against which he rested; the injury was hideous. Yet still death refused him. In a final act of will he summoned it, and took it into his mouth like a lover. The brain died, the visions and the voices and the torment and the complexity destroyed within an infinitesimal second; the sound of the shot, in that infinity of light, lost in the vast silence of the land.

Made in the USA
Lexington, KY
16 March 2012